Confessors of the Name

Confessors of the Name

A NOVEL BY
GLADYS SCHMITT

L

THE DIAL PRESS   *Sch 56c*   NEW YORK, N.Y.

DESIGNED BY WILLIAM R. MEINHARDT
PRINTED IN THE UNITED STATES OF AMERICA

For Simon
whose guidance in concept
and advice in execution
made this—and all my
books—whatever they are.

Confessors
of the Name

Chapter 1

AN ENDLESS procession of clouds kept moving above the Imperial City that afternoon. White and luminous against the blue October sky and big enough to make the most imposing monuments look small, they passed across the sun and cast their racing bluish shadows down into the streets. Light came and went on the arches and the obelisks, the clumps of laurel and myrtle, the sacred oaks and the ancient sycamores. Thrown briefly into shadow, the faces of ten thousand statues—gods, emperors, public benefactors, deified speculators and consecrated prostitutes—stared at the empty avenues with remote and somber eyes.

Yet the wind that drove the great white masses east northeast moved only in the upper vault of the sky. No dust blew along the colonnades and porticoes; no breath of freshness moved in the narrow passageways between the tenements; from the balconies of the palaces even the filmiest of the varicolored awnings hung limp and still. Only in the topmost tier of the Flavian Amphitheater—the colossal roofless oval where fifty thousand Romans sat waiting for a trumpet blast—only in the highest and broadest sweep of seats, one hundred and sixty feet up from the ground, a few capricious gusts made themselves felt. Up there the wrappings on a lunch of dried fish and bread came loose and crackled; the ragged cloak of a shoemaker bellied out like a small sail; a bit of dirty papyrus was snatched out

3

of somebody's hand. Was snatched away and carried east northeast, over the white villas and the blue Adriatic, over the Dalmatian pasturelands and the grain and turnip fields of Moesia and Dacia, to the very limits of the Empire, where six Roman legions stood confronted by impenetrable forests, watching through a screen of dying foliage for the signal fires of the Goths.

The plebes in the upper third of the amphitheater were paying scant attention to the preliminary business going on in the arena below. The procession that skirted the edges of the sanded floor was like any other procession: there were the usual trumpeters, priests, magistrates, and sacrificial sheep. Last of all came the notables who were paying for the games—a dowager, a young man, and a young woman standing shoulder to shoulder in a white and silver chariot—their bodies muffled up in the voluminous folds of their white mourning garments, their faces at that distance blurred ovals with raisin-colored eyes. Here and there on the crowded benches—the benches were always crowded, everybody went to the games except the children, the Christians, the Stoics, and the slaves—here and there, somebody who had read the announcements all the way through mentioned the donors' name. The mother and her two children down there in the silver chariot were the last surviving members of the Herennii, a high patrician house that traced its lineage back to regal skeletons in Etruscan tombs. Their ancestors had sat in the Senate for more than three centuries; they drew their revenue from every corner of the Empire; and they lived a life of fabulous luxury in a huge palace of limestone and marble on the Palatine.

Funeral games, somebody said, hearing the wail of the trumpets. Memorial games, said somebody else. The old man—the old woman's husband —had gone up in smoke along with a ton of incense in the Forum two years ago. But when and how he had died was no concern of the plebes. It was enough that his heirs had seen fit to import four hundred gladiators from the best training school in Capua for the perpetuation of his glory and the gratification of his ghost.

These four hundred gladiators had been waiting for almost an hour in a subterranean chamber. Now, with a creaking of pulleys and a clanking of chains, they rose on a platform straight into the middle of the arena. Their visored helmets and jewelled weapons glinted in the sun as they lifted their heads and looked about them with light-dazed eyes. They had been gathered for this moment from all reaches of the Empire—barbarian prisoners of war, sons of Italian farmers whose property had been mortgaged away, unmanageable slaves whose owners had sold them to the trainers in disgust. Last night the donors had given them the usual pre-combat meal: they had been stuffed into stolidity or courage with clams and mussels, roast hare and partridge, cakes and wine. Now, a good third of them for the last time, they heard the surging, echoing salutes of the plebes in the upper tier; and they grinned up at those other hopeless ones whose lives they were about to brighten with steel, violence, crimson plumes, and blood.

4

The members of the equestrian class, seated in the middle section between the plebes and the senators, were less concerned with the spectacle than with the Herennii. Some of them stood up to watch the donors take their places in the first row of marble seats—rigid in the knowledge that thousands of eyes were fixed upon them, consciously erect and impressively tall—even the young woman, the smallest of the three, was given a good height by her coronet of dry, black, braided hair. Not one of these astute gentlemen, who made it their business to read the Acts of the Senate and the weekly bulletins from the imperial palace, could have been ignorant of the full name and history of the illustrious dead. Celestus Falconius Herennius—so they said to the sons who would inherit their banks and ships and factories—had proved to everybody's satisfaction that charm is the one indispensable asset in an age of violence. During the twenty years of his brilliant political career, eight emperors had had the purple snatched from their backs, had been murdered in their camps, murdered in the palaces, hacked, strangled, dragged through the streets, flung from the walls. Celestus Falconius Herennius had served them all, charmed them all, and survived them all. One emperor after another, from the chaste Alexander Severus to the voluptuous Balbinus, had enjoyed his company—his wit, his easy, ingenuous, informative chatter, his lively interest in hydraulic organs, Phrygian mystics, Parthian horses, ancient ancestral paintings, herb gardens, monkeys, and Aristotelian logic. Life was somewhat easier for him, of course, because the gods had given him a manly and attractive presence—a perennially youthful body, a candid and mobile face, a head of clustering black curls that had greyed only at the last. Consul under the younger Gordian, proconsul in Syria, prefect in Egypt, possessor of a staggering fortune and everybody's confidence, he had died two years ago at his table. Somebody had circulated the story that the hired mourners at his funeral had made up their own words to the processional chant: "On guard, down there, Pluto and Proserpine. Here comes Celestus Falconius Herennius. He lived to see eight emperors buried. He'll do as much for you, if you don't watch out."

His survivors were well worth watching. The luck of the son and daughter had by no means gone up in smoke with the remains of Celestus Falconius Herennius. Not two months ago, when three mutinous legions had thrust the purple upon their uncle Decius, an old general married these thirty-odd years to their mother's sister, the most undistinguished member of their entire family had become Emperor of All the Romans and Lord of the World. True, he had not yet given formal recognition to these elegant relatives of his, was not in the imperial box this afternoon, had not made his appearance at the palace on the Palatine. But his wife, the Empress Etruscilla, had laid all rumors of estrangement by seating herself in the front of the box under a ruffled purple parasol. A mild, plump, well-powdered woman, nervous with her new splendor, she turned her watery, short-sighted eyes toward the donors and offered them a gentle smile.

5

In returning the Empress's greeting, the widow of Celestus Falconius measured out her cordiality so carefully that it seemed inestimably precious. At their tables tonight the equestrians would describe for the edification of their wives and daughters the inimitable correctness of that smile, which barely changed the contours of the pale, closed lips, that almost imperceptible nod of the head. The daughter's smile was not correct—it was disquieting. Her brother's hand, coming down on her wrist, seemed to have roused her out of a heavy dream. She turned her body as if it were impossible for her to turn her head; only the red lips moved in the still whiteness of her face; and when she turned back to the arena, it was as if a statue had smiled. The young man rose from his seat, put the tips of his fingers to his lips, and blew his aunt the expected kiss. Seen from the back, he looked a little like Celestus Falconius, but none of the equestrians made the obvious remark that it might have been his father in the box down there. Something—a scholarly stoop of his bony shoulders, a certain jerky impulsiveness even in his gestures of gallantry—something made Favorinus Herennius unquestionably himself.

At the center of the arena the sheep had been slaughtered by the hooded priests—sheeps' blood and sheeps' entrails marred the level shining of the sand. The gladiators were marching in closed ranks to the imperial box, flourishing their gold-encrusted shields and jewelled swords. Just under the box they halted and shouted up in unison to the mild, plump woman that they who were about to die saluted her, and she made a flustered, ineffectual gesture with her large, soft hands. *She* was nobody to worry about, that much was plain, the equestrians said among themselves. The crabbed Pannonian, her husband, might give them some sleepless nights—he had an old-fashioned grudge against the luxury trades, and there was an incredible rumor making the rounds that he intended to tax the luxuries off the market by reviving some ancient republican office called the censorship. But the Empress, at least, was nobody they would have to reckon with: all her energies would be taken up in an anxious effort to fulfill the mere formalities of her new position.

The senators, sitting in a ring of marble benches directly behind the boxes, watched a gigantic German take a handful of swords at random from his comrades and walk with his burden toward the Herennii. Custom demanded that the donor examine the weapons: after all, he had paid a fortune for his spectacle, and good money had been thrown away on blunted blades before. The German was handsome—there were whistles and cheers for him in the upper tier—but the patricians kept their eyes on Favorinus Herennius, curious to see how a young man who had never outgrown his Stoic education would carry off this business of the swords. Like the rest of the dwindling group of Stoics, he abhorred the games, and whenever they were mentioned in his presence felt called upon to utter the same formula with a kind of quiet vehemence: How was it possible to get pleasure

6

out of watching other men's pain? How was anybody bettered by looking at a heap of bloody guts? No doubt, nothing could have dragged him to the amphitheater this afternoon except his dead father's claim on his filial piety; his protest was written clearly in his face. But there was something excessive about the solemnity with which he bowed to the German and extended his hand—a spare hand, darkened at the wrist by a tangle of hair, trembling a little, perhaps from tension, perhaps from self-consciousness. Did the hand remain poised above the blades, the patricians asked themselves, because he imagined that by this one gesture he made himself responsible for all the carnage that was to come? When he finally brought himself to feel along the edges of two of the swords, it was with an impulsive, almost violent gesture, at the risk of losing one of his fingers. "Yes, I see they're very sharp," he said, and sat down, turning to his sister and drawing the back of his hand across his lips.

The sister, Drusilla Herennia—she was scarcely taking the occasion in the proper spirit either, but not because she shared her brother's ridiculous convictions. If there was a skim-milk pallor over the perfect planes and curves of her face, if she sat like a mourning statue staring out at nothing, she had legitimate reasons: she could count herself one of the most miserably married women in Roman society. Nine years ago, on her sixteenth birthday, her parents had given her to a certain Eugenius, an ingratiating sophisticate of forty; and thereafter her unfortunate inability to adapt herself to a more or less usual state of affairs had turned her marriage into a calamity. For years she had made scenes with him over every new prostitute, every new flute-boy; and, while she remained totally absorbed in his inconsequential meanderings, he had squandered half of her fortune and all of his own. Only a month ago, she had left his house and come back to her family—currently, a Syrian woman was presiding in his atrium in her place. And the most fascinating and incredible part of the whole story was that she persisted in loving him. Her hope that he would come back to her—a hope which her frozen decorum would never have allowed her to betray to her patrician friends by a single word—was proclaimed to everybody in the senatorial circle by the fact that the donors' box contained an empty chair. True, she had tried to hide it under a white woolen cloak, a parasol, and a basket of roses. But she was deceiving nobody but herself; everybody knew that the chair was reserved for the amusing and incorrigible Eugenius.

Brother and sister could have taken an example from their mother, who sat on the young man's right, conspicuously attentive to the proceedings in the arena. Her head turned now to the left and now to the right, following first one group of gladiators and then another as they took their positions for the mock combat that always preceded the real struggle. Two hundred armed like Samnites were lining up against two hundred armed like Thracians. Today's fighting would be more than ordinarily bloody: if the

7

purpose of the spectacle was to nourish the dead man's spirit with blood, the ghost of Celestus Falconius Herennius should certainly be appeased by the end of this battle. Fifty flutes shrilled out the tune to which the gladiators would perform their dance-like fencing, and the music straightened her narrow back, stirred her thin fingers, seemed to set up a trembling in the silver ringlets that stood out around her head. These were her husband's memorial games; she expected others to respect them; and she herself, seen from the rear at any rate, was giving them her undivided attention.

A remarkable woman, her fellow patricians said. All the more so when one considered her worries. Nobody—she mentioned it only rarely, usually she merely spread her exquisite hands and sighed—nobody had ever been plagued with more exasperating children. This impossible marriage of her daughter's had produced no children, her son was not even looking for a wife, and all the vast holdings of the Herennii—the tenement houses in the City, the Italian and Sicilian villas, the African orchards, the farmlands in Phrygia and Bithynia—might very well pass into alien hands. Her son Favorinus—she would give him his due—had shown after his father's death a brief inclination to take some responsibility. But there had been so many quarrels between them over so many petty things—what rent to charge for a farm, how to manage a rebellious slave—that she had given up, she had seen that she must carry her burden alone if she wanted any peace. To tell the truth, he had never had the slightest sense of proportion. She and Celestus Falconius had turned him over to the Stoics, yes,—but the same highminded tutors had whipped hundreds of other young patricians into shape, and, so far as she knew, he was the only one to take to Stoicism as a drunkard takes to wine, to walk out of the lecture hall blind and deaf to the delights and duties of the world. He had turned his stubborn back on all the doors to prestige and power that his father had left open for his benefit, did not sit in the Senate, did not go to Court, had never sought a single office for himself. And if his fervor for Stoicism had begun to wane a little, it was only to make room for another obsession. For the last three years he had been spending most of his time with a certain Greek freedwoman named Charis—an impossible little person who filled her atrium with all the useless rubbish of the world—sculptors, philosophers, poets, mathematicians, and the pert, degenerate riff-raff of the pantomime.

And he certainly seemed to be going out of his way to prove his mother's case against him. He had not taken his seat among the Senators even when his own uncle had entered the Senate House to receive, at the hands of the Conscript Fathers, his purple cloak and rayed crown. Nor had he made any attempt to conceal his preference for his skinny little Greek. Almost any morning he could be seen with her in the antique shops of the Via Sacra, looking at musty pictures and chipped statues. Almost any afternoon one might run into the two of them in the Library of Trajan, taking endless

8

notes on a commentary that he meant to write on some deservedly obscure philosopher named Musonius.

As for the appalling mistake that the old lady and Celestus Falconius had made in choosing a husband for the daughter—nobody ever mentioned that. It was not the sort of mistake on which to exercise one's sense of humor; it was too precisely the sort of blunder one might make oneself. Among the suitors who had presented themselves, curled and perfumed with balsam and cinnamon, on reception evenings at the palace of the Herennii, there had been a young cousin with nothing to his name except a couple of turnip fields in Pannonia, with no recommendations except a blond, quiet, sickly sort of good looks and the sentimental claim that he and the girl had been playfellows years ago. He had been put, politely if somewhat firmly, into his proper place; and Quintus Decius, his father, visiting in his behalf, had been given to understand that such a connection was as much out of the question as the mating of a peacock and a pigeon. Perhaps the lady Sabina *had* elevated her eyebrows a little too much while her brother-in-law made his halting request. Perhaps the unfailing charm of Celestus Falconius *had*, during that difficult family interview, worn a bit thin. But how could they have known that the awkward, austere general would walk away from the battlefield of Verona with the Emperor's purple on his shoulders? Who would have guessed that the reticent cousin, possessor of a couple of turnip fields, would become sole heir to the rayed crown?

Down in the arena the fifty flutes fell silent and the dance-like fencing ceased. In the moment of stillness, while they waited for the somber tuba to tell them to take positions for the fight to the death, the gladiators looked up again, this time at the donors who had paid, and paid amply, for the forthcoming libation of blood. The young man rose to nod to the trumpeters, standing in clear view of those who were about to die. The Thracians, stationed directly in front of him, could see that his face was too long and thin, that there was a slight ripple in the bridge of his nose, that his grey eyes were small, strained, and expressionless. But the Samnites, waiting to the left of him, had a different view. His face, seen in profile, was sharply chiseled and faintly golden, like Nubian marble, except where the stubble showed blue-black on the set jaw and the pointed chin. His hair grew low on his forehead and broke at the top into dry black clusters and tendrils. His mouth was so cleanly demarcated that it seemed untouchable, yet it was an ardent mouth, with a full underlip.

He had been in the Flavian Amphitheater only once before, fourteen years ago, but when he stood up to give the signal to the trumpeters, something in the sudden, dizzying prospect of the rising tiers of faces brought back into his mind his first experience in this place. He had acquitted himself miserably that time, for a boy who had recently put on the toga of manhood. He had looked from the first row of the senatorial circle at a sliced belly with its guts coming out; he had raised his eyes from that horror to the terrace of faces—a terrace that had seemed to be slowly falling apart; he had heard two roars, the outward one and the one in his head; and he had crouched over and vomited seedy red persimmon juice onto a green parasol in the box below. Even now, as a man of twenty-seven, trained in all sorts of Stoic exercises for banishing unprofitable thoughts, he could not down the image of that green parasol splashed with red. The terrace of plebes, equestrians, and senators on the other side of the arena shimmered before his eyes and threatened to fall apart at any moment in a vertiginous sweep of shadow and sun.

"Why are you standing there like that?" his mother said. "Give the signal and sit down."

He waited deliberately for a few moments before he nodded to the trumpeters and took his seat. She was at him again—she was always at him when he was in his most vulnerable state. Whenever she caught him wrestling with an unanswerable question, reaching after a memory, brooding over a loss, she took exception to the expression on his face, she dragged his secret life out for everybody to see. He had made up his mind to endure these disgusting games of hers in silence; there had been other barbs at breakfast and on the way to the amphitheater, and he had let them pass. But his rage rose up with the taste of gall into his throat, so that he could not be silent anymore. "I hope you understand I'm here only because you forced me into it," he said. "So far as I can tell, I'll stay until this business is over. But don't flatter yourself that I'll be coming to your reception this evening—once I walk out of this slaughterhouse, I'll go where I please."

She did not compromise the dignity of her husband's memorial games by so much as turning her head. She sat precisely as she had been sitting for the last half hour—the slight patrician body bent forward, the sensitive hands, too thin for the innumerable rings, clasped in her lap, the sweet, attentive face gazing steadfastly down at the gladiators who were taking their places—the Thracians with their little round shields to the left, and the Samnites with their big oblong shields to the right—out on the shining sand. Almost everything about her—the wispy silver hair, the silvery veil, the mobile mouth—looked soft and kind. But he saw her hazel eyes shining hard through the general haze, as watchful and uncommunicative as a lizard's eyes.

"With whom is your dead father competing for your attention tonight?" she asked him, scarcely moving her lips. "When you're on your way out, when you're passing his bust in the atrium, be sure to mention to him where you're going. Tell him that you've got to spend at least part of the anniversary of his death with your prostitute, your Greek, your dirty little slave."

He did not need to answer for himself. His sister answered for him, resting her ripe chin on her curled hand, smiling with her painted mouth until the dimple showed in her cheek and the faint lines of perpetual weariness crinkled at the corners of her eyes. "Aren't you being a little loose with your language, Mother?" she said, and her voice was as softly malicious as her smile. "Charis has only one lover. If you call *her* a prostitute, what are you going to call your good friend Lollia Carina who never has less than three on her list?"

"I hope you've noticed that Lollia Carina is *not* among the people I asked in for tonight. When I chose my guests, I showed some judgment—which is more than I can say for you, my dear child."

"So far as I can remember, I didn't invite any prostitutes."

"So far as *I* can remember, you've saddled us for the evening with a pair of seedy Christians."

The dimple deepened. The tip of the young woman's tongue came out and moved slowly over her underlip. "But they're relatives, Mother," she said. "Poor relatives, of course, but you of all people ought to know that it's good policy to treat the seediest relatives with some consideration. A person can never tell how a cousin is going to turn out."

The young man smiled.

"And *you*," said the mother, without turning her head, speaking to him out of the side of her soft mouth, "what are *you* smiling about? None of us will have much reason to smile when the two of them go wandering around the atrium tonight—he with his beard and she in her shroud of a dress— Christians, blatant confessed Christians, on exhibit in my house on the anniversary of my husband's death. . . ."

He thought that they would abandon their ancient struggle for the moment—that other struggle had begun with such a crash and a shudder down below. The first rank of the Samnites and the first rank of the Thracians, rushing at each other, had collided in the middle of the arena, with a deafening crash of shield against shield, an ear-splitting ring of sword on sword. But his sister went on talking in the same throaty, taunting voice, as if she were completely unaware of what was going on out there on the sand. "Don't worry, Mother, *he* won't be there to find out that you have Christians in your house," she said.

"Who won't be there?"

"You know as well as I. Our uncle Decius, the stupid old Pannonian turnip farmer, the Emperor of All the Romans, the Lord of the World. You don't see him over in the imperial box this afternoon, and you're not going to see him at the palace tonight. He isn't on visiting terms with us, and I can scarcely say I blame him. If I were he, I'd have had my fill of the Herennii—"

The end of the sentence was drowned out by an angry howl from the spectators. Somebody had died in the arena, and died too soon; somebody had refused to put up a decent fight, had insolently gone off without rendering the proper service for his hire. Favorinus, looking over the marble barrier, saw the corpse not thirty feet away—a raw-boned farmer's son sprawled on his back beside his Thracian shield, his toes sticking out beyond the soles of his sandals. Strangely, the expected gorge did not come up at the sight of the Samnite sword standing in the hollow of his throat, the blood trickling from his ears and the corners of his eyes. There was nothing but the old inward ache, as if his heart had suddenly been left bare and vulnerable in his chest. Poor, beggared wretch, he thought, leaning against the barrier, what sort of world must it have been for him that he was willing to take leave of it so soon?

But he was giving way to a baseless and irrational emotion, his Stoic teachers would have said. They would have held that no real death had been inflicted here: the grievous death had happened long ago. The only valuable part of the man—the celestial flame-like essence breathed into him at his birth by the Nameless and Bodiless God—had been sputtering very low when he sold himself to the trainers, had smouldered always more dimly under heavy food and fleshly exercise, had gone out completely when he won his first victory at the cost of another man's blood. His death was nothing more than a deliverance from a life-in-death, and one ought to rejoice in it, if one had been foolish enough to let it disturb one's sober peace at all. And yet he could not look at the big, half-naked, awkward body, debased and soulless as it was, without thinking how the man had eaten mussels and apricots last night, how he had probably sat up late in noisy talk with his companions. Perhaps he had seen his father's mortgaged fields in his dreams, perhaps he had wakened wanting to taste home-water again—cold water drawn up from a country well. . . .

"Surely you're not going to be sick?" his mother said.

"No. Let me alone."

"Do you realize how many times a day you say that to me?" The look of long-suffering was on her face. "You've cut yourself off from me completely. You used to talk to me. Now I don't know what's going on inside your head any more than I know what's going on inside a stone."

Do you actually remember that I used to talk to you? he thought. What did I talk about—do you remember that? An insignificant tutor whom I was silly enough to love? A statue that I had found in a shabby shop? My inconvenient fight with the son of the distingushed Titus Pamphilius? He remembered how, as a child, he would come running to her, stopping breathless on the other side of the table in her little office. He had never dared to come round to touch her, because of the table and the clutter on the table—the account books, the money-bags, the bronze figurine of Mercury had always been between. He had talked and she had listened—she had a way of listening that suggested the most earnest concern, her bright brown eyes focused on the speaker, an endless stream of "No's" and "Yes's" and "Indeed's" purling from her lips. But soon enough he had fallen silent, seeing that one of her beautiful hands was holding the account book open to a certain page, and knowing that she was merely waiting—waiting to go back to her only realities. His finds, his loves, his struggles—he had been a fool to take them into her office. It was as if the fabled Harpy waited there to suck away their blood.

"What's the matter, darling?" his sister said absently, laying her thin hand on his knee.

He shrugged his shoulders. It would have been useless to try to tell her. If matters had been ill between him and Charis, she would have given him more sympathy than he could have used; but, obsessed as she was by her troubles with Eugenius, she found it impossible to believe that anybody could suffer from anything but love. The second and third ranks were rushing at each other over pools of blood, the corpses of the first rank were being trampled in the shifting battle—but for her it was all as remote as horror in an old wives' tale or death in a pantomime. Ever since she had seated herself in the marble chair she had been attentive only to the stir which might have meant that a new-comer had entered the senatorial circle, the voice that sounded a little like *his* voice, the shadow that might have been *his* shadow, falling from behind her across the white cloak and the African roses. "It must be half finished by now," she said in the same flat, tired tone, turning her head almost imperceptibly to see whether anybody was in the shadowy entrance way, waiting to come in.

"I wish you'd stop looking around like that, Drusilla," said her mother. "Surely you realize that you're making a spectacle of yourself."

The flush that came into the young woman's cheeks gave her a feverish look. Her brother laid his arm across the back of her chair and closed his hand around her shoulder, slight and pitiably cold under his fingertips. "You're the one who's making the spectacle," he said. "You were at her before breakfast, and you've been at her ever since. She's tired, she didn't sleep last night, give her a little peace."

"I'm tired myself—I'm tired of hearing how tired she is—I'm sick of her sleepless nights—I'm sick of the circles under her eyes. I'm tired of watching her mope around my house, waiting for that whoremonger of hers to come back. It's finished, I tell you, it's over and done with. He isn't coming back—it's time she started to think about something else."

What else? he wondered. The old lips were folded over some secret and gratifying knowledge; she was hatching some plan, and her satisfaction with it glinted in her pale eyes. But he had no chance to draw her out—there was a violent increase in the noise around him. Suddenly and all at once the wretches out there had grown weary of circumspection, weary of skill, weary of circling and parrying, weary unto death. And, to the delight of the plebes, equestrians, and senators—most of them were on their feet now howling like beasts—all the Thracians and Samnites had fallen upon each other, hacking and yelling, oblivious of everything except the compulsion to bring the terrible business to any sort of end. The clang of swords on shields rang above the multitudinous roaring of the onlookers. The sand was strewn with helmets and broken weapons; the piles of dead lay in great pools of blood. The pattern of the combat was completely shattered. There was nothing now but clanking chaos, separating here and there to reveal a scarlet plume, a hairy lifted arm, a red and furious face.

"Here was the perfect opportunity for him to come back if he really wanted to," the old lady said, raising her voice a little above the clanking and the cries. "A public affair, with everybody looking on, and no time for questions or reproofs—"

"He may come yet," said Drusilla. "He may wander in to see the end of it. Or he may come to the reception tonight."

"For all I care, he can stay away from the reception. If he doesn't come this afternoon, he needn't come at all."

Down there on the bloody sand, they were dying by the dozens. The horror was taking so many shapes that he could not keep up with it. He would follow one desperate figure breathlessly, as if the man's life depended upon him, until that figure went down with a cleft head, a lopped-off arm, a gashed belly, or a shattered breast, and then he would frantically fasten on another. Yet the two women went on talking across him, as though the three of them were conversing over fruit and wine in an upper chamber curtained in silk. The sly, malicious smile deepened the dimple in Drusilla's cheek, and at the sight of it he drew his hand back from her shoulder.

"Why, Mother?" she asked, almost in a whisper. "Why would you rather have him stay away tonight?"

The skin above the old woman's cheekbones, fine and dry and netted with delicate wrinkles, turned red.

"Is it by any chance that you'd like to have me sitting alone in your atrium this evening? Would you like to make it obvious that I'm a poor, deserted woman—one that ought to be divorced and would be glad enough to re-marry? Is it that Eugenius would be a serious inconvenience if our uncle Decius happened to walk in?"

"Why not?" The ring of daring in the old voice was strong enough to draw him, for an instant at least, away from the milling chaos. He looked at her hazel eyes and guessed what sort of reasoning was going on behind them: The Emperor's son—wasn't he still a shy and hopelessly sentimental boy? Hadn't he been prodding his wounds all these years, maintaining a ridiculous chastity, refusing to marry, wanting nobody else in Drusilla's place? There were no obstacles, really; divorce was easy and there were plenty of grounds for it—flute-boys, Syrians, a squandered fortune, and for the last ten months, not even an attempt to beget a child . . . The wife of Celestus Falconius who had asked the Emperor Gordian outright to give her husband the consulship, the lady Sabina Herennia who had bought six hundred acres of African orchard without seeing an inch of it, on the strength of the lemons and apricots alone—*she* was nobody to be deterred by timidity . . .

"Tell me why not," she said in a peremptory tone, tapping on the marble

14

barrier. "I'm willing to swallow a little of my pride. It's the least I can do, considering my mistake."

Drusilla took one of the roses—a big scarlet bloom shipped across the Mediterranean—and began to tear it, slowly and methodically, into bits. Her hands had grown too thin for beauty; every tendon, every bone showed through. "You make me laugh," she said. "Really, you take too much for granted. Well, it'll be amusing to see you making an ass of yourself."

"The Herennii can afford to stoop a little."

The young woman brushed the shreds of the scarlet petals from the skirt of her mourning robe with a swift, contemptuous hand. "Oh, stoop all you like, crawl around like a worm, it doesn't matter to me. But even if they'd have me now, which they wouldn't—I'm old, I'm used, I'm sick, maybe I'm barren, maybe it's no fault of his that we haven't had a child—even if they'd have me now, which they never would, believe me I'd refuse. I'll never divorce Eugenius. If I don't have him, I'll have nobody at all."

"You think you mean that at the moment, Drusilla. You think you won't divorce him, but let's wait a bit, let's wait and see. I can tell you this—you're not the sort to live single, not when one man—and an old, tired man at that—was able to stir up such an itching in your blood."

His sister put up her hand to hide the look of shame and suffering in her eyes. He turned toward his mother in anger, and at the same instant a spurt of blood from some severed artery, hurtling up under the barrier, made him start back in his seat. Rage at the blood, rage at the hateful old woman from whose body he had been unfortunate enough to be born, rage at the Samnites and Thracians that they should turn their fury on one another instead of on those who had brought them to this pass, rage at himself that he should have consented to witness this, rage at his eyes that were always drawn back to the horror, that would not stare at his feet or the sky but must always turn back, must see and see—fierce, un-Stoic, gratifying rage drove him out of his chair. "Listen," he said, "either you stop now and let her alone, or I walk out of this slaughterhouse and take her with me."

"No, sit down, darling," said Drusilla, reaching toward him, trying to touch his hand. "It's for Father—I can't come with you. I'll have to stay—don't leave me by myself."

It *is* for Father, isn't it? he thought, sinking back into the marble seat and resting his chin on his clenched hands. All these farmers' sons and prisoners of war and angry slaves went down for Father's ghost—which, since ghosts are supposed to be something less than their originals, must be a shoddy ghost indeed . . . Wry laughter started up into his throat, and he suppressed it with a shudder. The two women, conscious that his indecorous behavior had drawn hundreds of pairs of senatorial eyes upon them, had re-assumed their original air of frozen dignity; and he could not say which maddened him most, the skillful counterfeit of sorrow on his mother's face, or the honest grief, the sudden access of remorse at having forgotten Father, in his sister's eyes. It's two years today that he's dead and gone, my girl, he thought, and it's about time that you stopped deceiving yourself. When will you see that we were nothing but dolls to him—dolls to be dressed up and played with and exhibited in the houses of the great? When will you admit to yourself that he was only a fine, flamboyant imitation of a man, and that his love was only a fine, flamboyant imitation of love? Of course, you were his girl-child—you were a delicate and valuable toy—and he treated you with some care. But with me it was another matter—I was more durable, and he knew as much. I was the infuriating one, the stubborn one, the one that wouldn't be taken in. The spleen that he swallowed in the atriums of eight emperors—it used to boil up in him at the very sight of me. I was the one who got the goblet hurled in my face; I was the one that he locked in the cupboard for three hours. And when I refused to apologize, I was never sent to a tutor to be beaten—it gave him so much pleasure to thrash me with his own hands. . . .

"Just look who's come into the imperial box, Mother," said Drusilla.

A start of happy expectation set the silver ringlets trembling. She turned, she looked, and the most gracious version of her official smile was stillborn. It was only the Pontifex Maximus, head of the priestly associations of the Empire, come to pay his respects to the Empress Etruscilla. A lean, sickly man, still yellow from his last attack of jaundice, he bent awkwardly to peer under the purple parasol. The more womanly a woman happened to be, the more oppressed he was by her presence, and his stained and gloomy eyes seemed to be deploring the big, white, powdered breast.

"You think you're very clever, don't you, Drusilla?" the lady Sabina Herennia said. "It's unfortunate—isn't it?—that you weren't clever enough to keep a sticky little Syrian out of your husband's bed. *Both* my children are clever. I always say, when the estate runs to ruin for lack of decent management we can all sit down and console ourselves by reading your brother's remarkable little book on Musonius."

It was not worth an answer. He looked up at the sky, where the cumulus clouds had begun to pile upon each other. The wind was descending; some of the equestrians were rearranging their blowing togas and smoothing down their ruffled hair. In the senatorial circle, the betting had begun. The odds seemed to be on the Thracians, although, so far as he could see, there was nothing in the vast confusion to show which group would hold the field at the last. Not more than fifty of the four hundred who had come up on the platforms were still on their feet. They fought stolidly, without skill, with nothing but a dull, drugged endurance, thrusting at each other over piles of dead and wounded, losing their footing on the dark and slippery sand. A murmurous, discontented stillness had settled over the whole amphitheater. Everything hideous that could happen had already happened, and even the plebes had sunk into a gloomy irritability. Behind him people were saying that even the best men from Capua were a miserable crew; nobody ever got what he paid for anymore; seventy years ago, in the reign of Marcus Aurelius, it was not uncommon for half of them to be standing on their feet at this stage of the battle . . . He closed his eyes and thought how tomorrow it would be as if today had never been, how he and Charis could sit all day long if they liked in the rustling quiet of the Library of Trajan, taking notes on Musonius. He saw her as he had seen her a week ago, coming across the room with an armful of scrolls. She always came as softly as a bird, and yet everybody, even the most absorbed and withered of their fellow scholars, looked up to watch her pass. Not that she was beautiful. Her hair was thick and honey-colored, but noticeably coarse. Her eyes were big enough, but of that pale bluish grey which looks faded in the sun. Her face, with its prominent cheek-bones and generous mouth, was a little too spectacular for her slight body, and the body itself was so spare that the flawless white skin seemed tight over the bones. But there was a spontaneity about her, an ease and a buoyancy that brought all her incongruities into one compelling harmony. . . .

He started out of his dream because both his mother and his sister had shuddered against him. "Don't look, it's horrible," Drusilla said.

A single figure had detached itself from the dwindling chaos at the middle of the arena and was lurching toward the donors' box, asking for donors' mercy, holding up a shaking hand. It was impossible to tell whether this was an Italian or a barbarian prisoner of war. The face above the jewelled iron collar was so hacked and mutilated, so covered with blood and so twisted by agony that it was scarcely human. A great gash ran slantwise across it, from the left temple to the right jowl. The left eye dangled loose over the cheek on a pinkish string. A succession of sputtering sounds came out of the split mouth—half-formed words and animal cries.

He did not know what he was doing. He found himself leaning far out over the barrier, shouting "Mercy" in a hysterical voice and repeatedly thrusting out his hand, thumb upward, as if by this single act the horror could be arrested, undone. The thumb and the hideous thing beyond it veered so violently that he had to close his eyes, and when he opened them again he saw another figure emerging out of the melee—the gigantic blond German who had handed him the swords. He stopped behind the inhuman thing, and, towering above it, pushed back his visor and revealed a pair of furious, accusing eyes. "Put down your thumb," he said in guttural, barbarous Latin, and there was infinite loathing in his voice. "When it has gone as far as this, there's only one sort of mercy." And, without taking his eyes from the donor's eyes, he rendered it neatly—a dagger-thrust through the back—and walked away, leaving the corpse lying where it fell, with its mutilated face ground into the sand.

"You see, you might just as well have sat still," said the lady Sabina Herennia. "It was useless, absolutely useless, for you to take it upon yourself."

Charis, he thought, my thrush, my darling, see to it that your house is filled with lights and friends tonight. Burn me a brazierful of apple-wood to take the slaughterhouse smell away. Put a clean Greek elegy between me and the actuality of death. . . .

"Oh, that was horrible, horrible," Drusilla said.

She was weeping quietly into her handkerchief, and he almost hated her for weeping. That mangled wretch, out there—she was using him as an excuse. All her tears were really for Father, poor dead Father, and Eugenius, dear, lost Eugenius, and herself, her weak, desire-ridden self. And yet, even while he let his fury mount against her, he knew that he and he alone was the proper object of his hate and pain. It was he who had wearied of arguing with the old woman; it was he who had said, "Have your games then, do what you want, let me read, let me sleep." He had put the money-bags into the hands of the Capuan trainer, he had ordered the mussels and apricots, he had given the signals, he had felt the swords. And nowhere, not even in the house of the beloved, could he be delivered from the mutilated face. Nothing, not even her giving body lying against his, could take away the accusation that he had seen in the German's eyes.

"The trouble with both of you," said the mother, "is that you look too hard—"

Her sentence was broken by a shout from the arena. Some twenty Samnites were abandoning their chance at prize-money and their status as gladiators by throwing away their swords and shields. Silence—thick, sated silence—had settled over the tiers of seats. The scene in the arena, darkened now because a cluster of heavy clouds was passing across the sun—was without motion, like the tableau before a pantomime—the victors standing upright with their weapons in their hands, the vanquished on their knees among the wounded and the dead. And it seemed to him that this somber stillness was weighing palpably down upon him, that his body was being numbed by it so that he could scarcely move. . . .

"If you don't want those Samnites slaughtered, you'd better get up."

They were waiting for his signal of mercy, of course. He rose and thrust up his thumbs, not looking into the field, looking up instead at the curve of sky visible at the stony rim of the amphitheater—a sullen sky streaked with reddening clouds and dark with the portent of a night of rain. Those who had lost their bets had begun to lament their ill-luck; a many-stranded murmur rose from all three of the levels, growing and receding and growing again, like the muffled roaring of a distant sea. Drusilla's cold hand took him by the wrist and drew him down. "It's over, there's only the rewarding of the victors," she said.

There was a stir behind them in the donors' box, but this time the young woman did not turn her head. It was nobody—it was only two of the showiest Nubian slaves of the Herennii carrying in the bowls of coins that were to be given to those who had honorably survived the fight. There was music

18

then, fifty flutes playing a martial melody, and a spray of water that smelled of roses. Through the water, in and out among the piles of the dead and the dying, the victors came to the donors' box to claim their prizes. Some of them were cheered, some of them were hissed, and half a dozen of them, including the big German, were pelted with love-notes and bits of ribbon and flowers. They bore themselves vaingloriously, strutting and flexing their muscles and tossing back their long hair; but their faces, streaming with sweat and smudged with blood, looked dazed and shamed, and there was not one among them who could manage more than a dour nod when the bowls of coins were emptied over the barrier into their hands.

The public slaves were entering the arena to take away the dead when the three survivors of Celestus Falconius Herennius left the donors' box and started for the street. Out of consideration for their grief and respect for the illustrious ghost, the Empress Etruscilla waited a little before she moved toward the entrance-way, followed by the Vestal Virgins, the Pontifex Maximus, and the other lesser priests who had blessed the occasion with the required number of sacrificial sheep. Most of the corpses had been hauled out, and the new sand was being brought up in carts, when the senators rose and started toward the ramps, most of them in a hurry, since this was a reception evening—there was just enough time to bathe the sweat of the day's excitement away, to put on a fresh toga, and to fortify oneself for the next event with a pheasant wing and a goblet of wine. The equestrians lingered somewhat longer than their superiors; groups of them stood in the aisles while the sand was being strewn, discussing the rumor of the censorship. Dreadful, unbelievable, they said; a thing like that could ruin a man overnight. The public slaves had finished their task and the oval floor was one shining yellow surface by the time the plebes strolled down the ramp. They were in no great hurry. Their cramped quarters in the huge tenements would be hot even on so windy an evening as this; they had stuffed themselves with olives and dried fish at the games; why push and crowd to get home to a bowl of lentil soup, a piece of bacon, a loaf of bread?

When the last of the tired and desultory conversations had been carried into the street, the empty amphitheater was not still. Surging and receding, like the sound of the ocean in an abandoned shell, the rising wind rushed through the tremendous archways. It stirred the bits of papyrus and the rose petals left on the seats by the equestrians and senators; it shook the garlands of laurel that draped the imperial box; it made a long line of ripples in the sand. Steadily, always in the same direction, it kept blowing east northeast, over the splendid cities and the shining villas and the indolent turquoise bays, toward the uncharted country, the country of the Goths.

Chapter 2

DURING THE jolting chariot ride from the Flavian Amphitheater to the palace on the Palatine, Favorinus Herennius stood stiffly between his mother and sister, taking no part in their conversation and keeping his eyes closed against the light and the dust. He could not talk—it was all he could do to hold himself upright and keep a presentable face. The numbness that had weighed down on him toward the end of the games had congealed into an almost unbearable pain squeezing like an iron grip at the back of his head. It is nothing, it is only a headache, he kept telling himself. A bath will take it away, a little food will take it away. Before the first guest arrives at the palace, I will be well enough to set out for Charis's house. And for half an hour he tried to behave as though the pain did not exist: he forced himself to bathe even though the bright mosaics of fish and pleasure-boats in the bathroom shimmered before his eyes; he eased himself into a fresh dalmatica, picked at a breast of chicken served in parsley on a silver plate, drank a little cooled wine. If he could have done these things alone and in peace, without the assiduous services of two chattering slaves, the headache might have lessened. But to speak to them pleasantly, to make lively answers to their talk as if there were no pain, no vision of an eye dangling loose on a pink string—that was maddening, that was more than he could bear. "Don't shave me, I'll go unshaven," he said. "I'd rather use the time to rest." And, once they were out of the room, he lay down on his bed, pulled a cool pillow over his eyes, and fell almost immediately into a sound sleep.

He wakened to the rustle of the drawn window-drapes. A single lamp burned on the chest in one corner. The rest of the chamber—green curtains, greenish marble, white Babylonian rugs embroidered in yellow and green—faded into verdurous shadow. The pain was gone, there was no trace of it when he moved his head from side to side, and for the moment it seemed to him that he had suffered only from the pain, that, waking without it, he wakened in a state of utter blessedness. He had begun to stretch, he was on the point of smiling when the accumulated weight of the afternoon came down on him again—the big toes sticking out over the soles of the sandals, the split mouth making the incomprehensible sounds, the visor pushed back from the contemptuous and accusing eyes. What time is it? How long have I been sleeping here? How soon can I go to her? he thought, setting his feet on the floor. A fresh gust of wind turned one of the curtains back and showed him a stretch of evening sky crossed by the dark branches of a syca-more. And he knew that it was late, that his mother's guests would already be gathered in the atrium, that it would be at least an hour before he could make his escape. To take oneself away before the reception had begun was a minor discourtesy; but it would be unthinkably rude to be seen leaving the place without paying one's respects to an atriumful of guests.

He pulled back one of the curtains and stood at the window, looking out over the garden. Up here on the Palatine, the wind was stronger than it had been in the amphitheater; the dark clumps of yews and mulberries were in perpetual agitation; the flower stalks, cut back for the winter, trembled stiffly in the tidy round beds; only the marble was still. Under the even grey of the sky, the statues, the benches and the fountains took on a soft lustre. The big well-cover below his window, made of Carian marble and worked all over with a design of acanthus leaves, gleamed like mother-of-pearl.

"Well, look for it. At least you can look for it," said a desperate voice under the window. He knew it for the voice of Sylvanus the gardener, a very valuable slave. The fellow, a widower in his thirties, had supervised the town gardens of the Herennii for the past ten years. Last December he had furnished the Saturnalia table with figs grown under glass, his herb-garden had been the envy of two herb-fancying emperors, and his garlands were striking enough to have prompted Sylvia Reburra to try to buy him from the lady Sabina Herennia for twice his original price. "We'll have to hurry, it's beginning to get dark," he said, stepping out into view. "No—no—nothing as small as that—that's a piece of gravel. It's big, I tell you, big—about the size of my thumb." He strode around the well-cover, looking in all directions, stopping to kick at a stone in the clipped grass, shaking his head. He bore his spare body erectly, like a Roman, and was in fact Roman born; but the force of some Celtic ancestress asserted itself in the bleached yellow of his cropped hair and the dreamy mobility of his lips. "Not in the bushes," he said, "it wouldn't be in the bushes. Feel around in the roots of the marjoram over there, that's a good child."

Then he's talking to his daughter, Favorinus thought. And just then the girl's voice, the warm and reedy voice of a child of thirteen, came up from the marjoram patch near the well-cover. "Somebody is going to hear you if you don't take care," she said in the exquisitely pure Latin she had learned from Drusilla, whose personal slave she had been since the age of seven. "Anyway, you should have asked somebody to help you let it down. A person could hurt his insides letting it down by himself."

"Well, look now, everybody was busy. The old woman wanted the well covered, and she was perfectly right—anybody who doesn't know the garden could step right down into it in the dark. Besides, I've put the cover on by myself a hundred times—I don't know why it should suddenly slip out of my hands. Just find it—will you?—see, here's the place where the acanthus leaf cracked off. If we only had the leaf, we could stick it in again with a bit of glue, and nobody'd ever know the difference."

The girl came out of the marjoram patch, crossed the strip of lawn, and knelt beside the well-cover in the grass. Seen from the upper window, she looked like a statue carved in some happier and more innocent century: since she was only a little slave, nobody had bothered to starve her into modishness, nobody had plucked her eyebrows or twisted her hair into fantastic curls. But at the sight of the ingenuous body down there on the lawn, Favorinus experienced less pleasure than regret. She was growing into a woman now; the time for rumpling her hair and holding her up while she gathered the berries out of the mulberry tree—the time for all such free boisterousness was past. She shook her head, slowly, meditatively, and her soft brown hair swung like a sheep dog's ears on either side of her face. Her full throat and her round arms gleamed like the marble in the strange grey light. The white livery of the Herennii fell from her shoulders to her knees in simple folds—good wool and sheer enough to shadow forth the curve of a thigh, the tipped round of a breast.

"As big as that?" she asked, thrusting one blunt, childish finger into the gap left by the lost acanthus leaf. "Well, we should certainly be able to find it if it's as big as that." She straightened and focused her eyes, not on the lawn, but on the sky. "Oh, let us find it," she said, and went through some superstitious ritual that he had never seen before—she touched first her forehead, then her throat, then her left ear, then her right.

How far would a chip of marble fly? Favorinus asked himself. There was no glimmer of white between the two slaves and the statue of Venus. The lawn stretched in unbroken darkness from the pedestal to the bed of ghostly autumn narcissus, and from there to the fountain. Then, halfway between the fountain and the clump of laurel, he saw it, white and the size of a man's thumb, in the clipped grass. "Over there," he called from the window. "That's it, over by the laurel. Go ahead, Prisca, run and see."

Her fright was strong enough to bring her to her feet, but it did not last for long. "Oh, there's my lord Favorinus, he's been watching us all the time," she said, and smiled. He could not see her clearly in the waning light, but it was a smile that he remembered—she had given it to him freely since her infancy. Her freckled cheeks and her nose always underwent a tremulous change, and a small scar—the record of some childish fall—became a delightful indentation, a kind of dimple at the corner of her right eye. He recalled that her eyes were grey in shadow, but took on an amber warmth in the sun.

Her father had hurried off to bring back the chip of marble, leaving her to deal with the dilemma as best she could, and she stood astride the big well-cover now, her legs apart and her hands clasped behind her, like some sturdy sylvan guardian spirit of the well. "My lord and my master, if you tell my lady Sabina, we're certainly going to have trouble," she said, and her cheeks crinkled like thick cream. "You wouldn't tell?"

"Of course not. Why should I? But you'd better go and get yourself a glue-pot. You'll be in a pretty fix if your mistress comes out here with one of the guests and catches you gluing it in."

When she was gone, the sense of her warm, sane world went with her; and he was left alone to turn back upon himself again, to feel the remembered images crowding in. He turned quickly and opened the door onto the lighted hall, where the hum of conversation, muted and decorous, floated up to him from the atrium. Since this was a reception, seven tall Germans stood along the balustrade with wax torches in their hands, and the whole downward sweep was washed in yellow light. At the foot of the stairs he saw the new bust—green serpentine marble on a bronze pedestal. Then it arrived in time, he thought; then she hounded the sculptor into having it ready for tonight . . . That the Herennii should have set a likeness of the new Emperor in some conspicuous place was only to be expected—the news of the victory at Verona had prompted all the high houses in Rome to place orders for such busts. But the sprig of yew laid under the stern chin—there was presumptuousness in that: it proclaimed to all comers that Caius Messius Quintus Trajanus Decius was in mourning today for the late-lamented Celestus Falconius Herennius. . . .

At the foot of the stairway he stopped to examine the portrait—not, certainly, because it was worth any consideration in itself—it was the deplorable product of a hopelessly degraded art. He often wondered why that particular art had fallen into such decay; certainly the demand for it had never been as great; gods, emperors, senatorial dignitaries, gladiators, and charioteers were turned out by the thousands in the sculptors' yards, and each of them was more atrocious than the last. This bust, like all the others, had gone through the hands of several artisans. One had hacked out the head in the rough, another had been responsible for the streaks of hair, and still another had glued in an appropriate pair of glass eyes. The lady Sabina had, of course, engaged the services of the best corporation of sculptors in the City; but even they, working on a priceless piece of green serpentine, had been able to produce nothing but a crass and spurious mask of irascible dignity—angular jaw, thin mouth, sharp, jutting nose, and cold blue eyes. Does he really look like that? Could he have changed so much in these nine years? the young man asked himself. And he had an unreasonable conviction that his uncle had not changed in the least, that, if he should suddenly encounter him here in this hall, he would look exactly as he had looked in the old days, sitting in the stuffy little library in the house on the Esquiline.

That house—in his schooldays he had kept a journal to improve his Latin style, and his visits to that house had consumed more space in it than anything else. Still standing before the bronze pedestal, making a great show of being absorbed in the bust for the benefit of the glittering company beyond the archway to his right, feeling the cheeks and pushing the overweening yew-sprig a little further back under the chin, he remembered that house and the excessive names he had attached to it on the scrawled pages: "Yesterday Drusilla and I went up to The Temple to spend the afternoon with our cousin Herennius Decius . . ." "It must be a week now since I have had permission to go there, and I am confused and lonely . . ." "The house of my uncle Decius is the lodestar of my soul . . ." An unspeakably drab little place, his mother used to remark when he came back from it. The best a person could say for it was that it was clean—what did he find there that fascinated him so much? And usually he had nothing very interesting to report: he had watched the tadpoles nibbling at the water-lilies in the rectangular pool in the atrium, he had talked about his tutor to his aunt while she sat at her spinning. He had lain on the floor for an hour, two hours, while his pale cousin fanned the face of the sleeping Drusilla with a palm-leaf fan. And yet this quiet atmosphere was always charged with the possibility of a miracle. Suddenly, after long silence, the gentle cousin would turn and reveal to him, in such trustful and affectionate terms as he had never heard before, his innermost yearnings, his wildest dreams. His sister Drusilla, who bore herself with the rigidity of a Vestal Virgin at home, would be seized here with veritable ecstasies of merriment—she would fly around the table, flapping her arms, pretending to be a seagull in the bay at Capri; she would run into the kitchen and out again, transformed into a Bacchante, with a cluster of dried raisins hanging from her lips. Even his aunt Etruscilla would stop, in a matter-of-fact account of the months she had spent with her husband in a Dacian army camp, to conjure up a watchfire in an April night or the sounding of a trumpet in the frosty dark.

And in the shadowy little library with the curtains drawn against the glaring light of summer, behind the table heaped with official documents, was the stern presence that was the Genius of the place. Sometimes he came and sat among them—Caius Messius Quintus Trajanus Decius. Sometimes, in a flat voice that meant that the matter was too good to be marred by oratory, he read them a heroic page from Livy; and three times—each of them had been noted in the journal—his eyes, at once peremptory and tender, had been lifted from the scroll, had sought and held his nephew's eyes. Sometimes one received a frightening summons to the library: "I'm sorry, young man, to have to point out to you again that hounds are to be kept in the yard, not in the atrium. Since it was you who brought in the hound that made the mess, you'll get a basin and clean it up yourself." But always, at the moment when the discipline was handed out, the papers on the table —the payrolls of the Eastern legions, the maps showing the movements of armies, the correspondence of prefects and generals—were pushed aside. There was no barrier then, no hand fidgeting after some more significant task. The table between them was bare, and the hard, just judgments were delivered face to face.

He turned from the glassy, somber stare of the portrait bust and looked into the atrium. Congregated in the vast expanses of the reception hall were some eighty human beings, dwarfed by the yellow marble columns and the gilded ceiling—a great domed ceiling open at the top to a starless night. For the next three hours their asinine remarks would reverberate from vaults and niches; they would pose and preen themselves against pedestals of statues and busts, they would pursue each other over a hundred and fifty feet of patterned marble floor or avoid each other by making swift flanking movements in and out of the long colonnades. Pounds of the best beeswax were being consumed to light the place. Two or three old yews had been sacrificed to provide the garlands and festoons. And all this, he thought, all those bees laboring, all those twigs putting forth their leaves, all those Grecian quarries yielding up their stone, all those Chinese worms spinning out their silk—for what?

He straightened, assumed the proper smile, and moved from one to another of the little groups scattered about the atrium, stopping to place the required kiss of greeting on a powdered cheek, to lay his hand on a shoulder draped with silk, to ask such questions as would show an interest without involving him in protracted conversations. Near the statue of the weeping Niobe on the right of the atrium he joined a little company gathered around an imposing woman with a flair for dramatic narration. She was giving, probably for the fiftieth time, a circumstantial account of the murder of the Emperor Philip—her nephew, a tribune, had been in the camp at Verona at the time and had seen it all with his own eyes. Ugh, she said, a dreadful business—merely to think of it made your blood run cold—two soldiers had come up behind the poor wretch with a butcher's cleaver and cut his head right down the middle, straight through the skull, down to the teeth . . . "Which way?" asked a curled young consular, who was lolling

25

against Niobe's sandals and holding the links of his heavy gold collar away from his delicate neck. "Sidewise or crosswise?" The lady gave him a pained and withering look. Her nephew hadn't found it necessary to be that specific, but if the consular was really as interested as all that, she would ask him the next time she saw him, she said.

It was plain that he could not remain in this particular group without inhibiting the conversation. The murder of Philip the Arabian and the fascinating series of intrigues and acts of violence that had accompanied it were scarcely a subject for discussion in the presence of the nephew of the man who had profited most by that split head. Having complimented the histrionic lady on her amber earrings, he wandered off again, trying to imagine how it had been with his uncle Decius when the assassins had carried Philip's head into his quarters in Verona. What had he done with it? Looked at it to make certain it was the proper one? Held it like a bowl or a melon between his hands? Probably not, nobody would expect him to touch it. Probably they had laid it, neatly wrapped in a towel, on the floor at his feet. . . .

"You know you're curious to see him"—so his mother had said two months ago when Decius, victor in the civil war that had culminated in the battle of Verona and as indubitably the Emperor as the assassination of his predecessor and the will of a dictatorial army could make him, had announced that he would receive at least the symbols of his power from the hands of his peers, the senators. "Back in the old days, when he was nobody, everything he did was perfect in your eyes. Now that he has the purple, I suppose you're accusing him of all sorts of atrocities." What atrocities? There had been none that he actually knew of; and yet he had a disquieting sense that equivocal and evil forces underlay his uncle's rise to power. The world said that the Emperor Decius had come to the purple with cleaner hands than anybody since Marcus Aurelius, that he had been forced into the bloody and fratricidal battle of Verona, that the assassins had moved without his orders when they butchered Philip and strangled Philip's only son. But the world would have said as much for any reigning emperor, and he did not know. . . .

He sensed that his face had taken on the look his mother was always complaining about—immobile and preoccupied, the mouth slightly open, the eyes unseeing and expressionless. Smile, move about, talk to somebody, he told himself. . . . He joined the beautiful Maesia Publia and tried to assume a suitable look of amazement while she went on about the miracles of the Egyptian goddess Isis: she had alienated her husband by turning half her fortune over to the temple priests, and as her domestic situation deteriorated her claims for her sloe-eyed patroness grew more and more extravagant—tonight she was telling anybody who would listen about a doomed ship that had been drawn past the reefs by the sound of celestial cymbals and bells. He nodded his head in a mechanical show of concern while a melancholy equestrian, a dealer in oil of balsam, rambled on about the rumor of the censorship: the price of balsam oil was already prohibitive; with a luxury tax on it, it would not sell at all; he had ordered a supply of it from Ephesus three months ago, and could not cancel; by the time the shipment came into the port of Ostia, it would probably be a total loss. . . .

Like everybody else, he looked up at the sound of a carriage on the paving stones. But it was nobody—it was not even Eugenius, for whom Drusilla had been waiting outside the better part of an hour—it was only his cousin Paulina and her husband Probus, who glanced up uneasily as they passed under the yew-draped lintel, since they were Christians and the yew was sacred to Proserpine. He smiled because his mother was addressing a challenging question to one of the senators; she was plainly creating a tactical diversion to cover the entrance of the two unwanted guests, believing that, if she could only talk loud and fast enough, nobody would notice that their Christian scruples kept them from burning incense at the family shrine, a cupboard housing images of the ancestors of the Herennii, opened on such ceremonial occasions as this so that the spirits could take part in the ritual feast.

The thin young woman who had just entered the atrium was distinguished for nothing except a remarkable unwillingness to be parted from her husband. She made no effort to edge into the varicolored, jewelled crowd but stood on the margin of it, hanging on his arm and giving him a look of troubled solicitude. The husband was the taller of the two by three or four inches; his coppery head showed a little above her silky pale-brown one. She wore a dalmatica of white linen, girdled under her small breasts and pleated into an intricate series of tucks from her feet to her chin. Her face was oval, thin-skinned, and unrouged. Her lips were full and tender, but so pale that nobody would have looked at them twice, and her forehead was round and clear, like the forehead of a child.

I ought to go over and put them at their ease, he told himself. But his efforts to get on with them in the past had always ended feebly—the young wife was singularly quiet and withdrawn in his presence, and the husband had twice argued with him, stubbornly and none too learnedly, once over the meaning of a passage in Plato and once over the scansion of a chorus from Aeschylus. There was an uncomfortable quality about Probus. One wondered why he was not handsome; he had so many of the attributes of masculine good looks—the tall, lean figure, the narrow face, the coppery beard and curls. But something marred him—it was difficult to discover what—loose-jointedness, an awkward stance, a stoop that made him seem to be discrediting himself. And the sense of a nameless insufficiency that hung about him was not lessened by his wife's unquiet, seeking eyes.

"Come and have a bite with me," said a full-bosomed matron, in society for the first time after a confinement and eager to enjoy herself.

"I can't—not at the moment. There are two lost sheep over there—cousins

27

of ours—do you see? Drusilla ought to be looking after them. I'm going out to find her now," he said.

The broad square of marble paving blocks before the entrance, and the two flights of stairs that led up to it from the garden were illuminated only by the glow from the atrium; but the avenue of sycamores, leading straight out to the highway half a mile away, was marked at regular intervals by twin points of flame; fifty slaves crowned with yew-garlands stood under the ancient trees with tall pitch torches in their hands. The flames, turned this way and that in the unsteady wind, picked out a slave's bare shoulder, a pedestal overgrown with dark vine, the bow-arm of a marble Diana stretched white against the black foliage of a mulberry tree.

"Drusilla," he said in a whisper, sensing rather than seeing that she was there.

"Yes?" She was sitting at the top of the left-hand flight of stairs, her thin back sloping, her hands clasped around her knees. She had loaded herself with jewels in the hope that *he* would come. In the muted glow from the atrium, her brother saw the glitter of gold and emeralds and sardonyx on her wrists, around her neck, in the dry black coronet of hair.

"Paulina and Probus are here," he said.

"I know. I spoke to them on their way in."

"But they're wandering around the atrium by themselves. I thought that you—"

"Somebody will look after them eventually," she said.

"Who is there to look after them?"

"Oh, I don't know—somebody . . ." She turned and glanced at him furtively. "Eugenius hasn't come," she said.

He bit his underlip and stifled an exasperated sigh. Really, darling, he thought, I can see that for myself. If Eugenius had arrived, you'd scarcely be out here like Dido on the beach at Carthage. . . .

"Couldn't *you* look after them for a while, Favorinus?"

"That's not the point."

"What *is* the point?"

"Suppose our uncle Decius should come after all—would you want him to find you out here, playing exactly the role that Mother has picked out for you?" he said.

She unclasped her hands and straightened. "I'm not playing any role. That's the reason I embarrass you—because I behave precisely like myself."

"Don't be ridiculous."

"Oh, but I *am* ridiculous—that's the role that was assigned to me—" She started, laughed, and caught and kissed his hand. "Surely you don't want me walking around in the atrium in this frame of mind. Go in and look after poor Paulina. I'll come—honestly—by and by I'll come."

By the fountain in the middle of the atrium, an excited patrician lady was talking straight into Probus's beard, emphasizing her points by tapping

28

him on the chest. Near a window in the shadowy colonnade, Paulina was in grave converse with the melancholy equestrian. Perhaps it was because he was thinking of Charis' face that Paulina's countenance, seen against the uncurtained window, seemed so colorless and tired. Whenever people wanted to compliment this Christian and undistinguished member of the high house of the Herennii, they commented on how well she bore her twenty-nine years; but now, at this advanced hour and in the dim light that seeped into the colonnade, even her youthfulness was disquieting: her figure, slight under the tucked dalmatica, and her face, hollow-cheeked and with shadows under the eyes, gave her the aspect of a prematurely aging child. She and the gloomy equestrian fell silent at his approach, and he was disconcerted and pained to find that his hospitable gesture was really an intrusion.

The equestrian was the first to break the uncomfortable silence. "This lady and I were talking about the city of Ephesus," he said. "She tells me its history goes back to the beginnings of the world. I didn't know that, though I've stopped there several times—I have a brother-in-law there—"

"I changed ships at Ephesus once on the way to Egypt, but I don't believe I spent more than four hours there," Favorinus said. It seemed to him that he had unintentionally disparaged the residence of the equestrian's brother-in-law, and he hurried on. "Not, of course, that I wouldn't have enjoyed staying. The place is full of wonders, as everybody knows. The port, the markets, the gardens—" He broke off when he noticed that his cousin was not listening but was gazing out of the window with a detached and solemn look on her face. "Then, there's the Temple of Diana, and that remarkable statue—" why he should want to say it, he did not know, but he felt a certain vengeful pleasure in saying it—"you know the one I mean—it always seemed a little obscene to me—the Diana with the many breasts."

"The inns do a very profitable business," said the equestrian. "All through the year, people come to see the wonders—"

Paulina's voice broke in. It was a warm and intimate voice, more womanly than her presence. She was resting her cheek against the window frame, and she spoke into the night. "There are more wonders in Ephesus than you know," she said.

"I didn't know you had ever been there, cousin." The whole relationship between them and him had somehow been reversed. He had meant to talk to them a little for courtesy's sake, and plainly it was they who were tolerating his company. He, the patrician, had been crude enough to mention the statue to his shy and reserved cousin, and it was the equestrian who had graciously covered up his blunder. He felt distinctly like a fool.

"Oh, no, I've never been there." She was not looking at him. Her eyes were fixed on the clouds, diffusely silvered by a hidden moon. "I've never been anywhere, really. Only, if I were to go anywhere, I think I'd go to Ephesus."

"Why Ephesus? I can't imagine why the port or the market would interest you." He felt again that he was belittling the equestrian's commercial activities, but he was annoyed and did not care. "You'd be fascinated with the Temple, of course, but you'd never allow yourself to be seen there—"

"The port," she said, and it seemed to him now that she was studiously avoiding his glance. "I'd like to see the port above anything else on earth, except, perhaps, the grave."

The equestrian stared at his gold ring and turned it round and round on his finger. Favorinus moved a step closer, laid his hand very lightly on her cold arm, and asked, "What grave?"

"The grave of somebody whose name I don't think you would know. They say he lived a hundred years and didn't really die at the last. They say he will lie there, fragrant and incorruptible, in a kind of peaceful sleep until the day when the Son of Man comes down again from heaven. They say the earth above his head is never quiet—whoever looks closely can see it rise and fall with the coming and going of his breath. I wish I could see that grave in Ephesus—"

"One of your saints is buried there?" asked the equestrian, trying to treat the awkward situation as though the young woman were addicted to some such fashionable superstition as the cult of Adonis.

"Yes. The youngest of the apostles, the one that leaned on the Master's breast."

"I don't suppose my brother-in-law would be acquainted with the grave. But, if the lady likes, when I write him again I'll ask him to send me a handful of sand from the port."

"I would be very grateful."

"But why the port?" asked Favorinus. He had taken his hand away because the inertia of her arm had convinced him that she did not notice it; but he was still determined to force a glance from her wide-set eyes.

She straightened and turned toward him then, but with so impersonal a look that it was scarcely more than no look at all. "The condemned Confessors—all the Confessors out of Asia sailed from that port on their way to Rome," she said. "Those who were to die in the arena—those who were to be burned at the stake or broken on the rack or given to the beasts—it was on those docks that they turned to look for the last time at their native lands. Two hundred years ago a certain Paul of Tarsus stood there, at the end of a good race. Ignatius stood there, too, an old man on his way to be ground by the teeth of the beasts—like wheat, he said, like wheat for the bread of the Lord. Nobody knows how many have come in chains to the port of Ephesus for the Name's sake. They are legion, and the waves that wash the docks there must be crimson with the blood from their fettered feet." She was looking at him differently now. It was as if her eyes, like the eyes of the German in the arena, were calling him to account, making him guilty of the crimson stain in the Ephesian waves. Then her eyelids came down and her head turned slowly aside. "Ephesus is certainly a city of wonders," she said, "even without the Diana of the many breasts."

The equestrian cleared his throat. "Then perhaps the lady would like to have a splinter from the docks. I'll tell my brother-in-law. I'm sure he'll be happy to oblige you."

"You're very kind. My husband will be grateful, too." Her eyes, suddenly troubled, searched the stretches of the atrium. "Where *is* my husband? Do either of you see him?" she said.

Her question hung unanswered. Everybody had suddenly fallen silent. Beyond the door, the garden was agitated with light and sound. Carriage wheels rumbled and came to a stop on the avenue of sycamores; there were martial footsteps on the marble stairs; the leaves of the laurel and the mulberries were visible now in a reddish glow. The lady Sabina hurried to the door and waited there, her pale, victorious face, her fluttering veils, and her silver hair lighted up by the blaze outside. On the square of marble paving blocks two imperial slaves were setting down a cauldron of fire—the fire that always went before the Emperor through the City, the fire that would announce that the Lord of the World, omnipotent on earth as the fiery sun was omnipotent in heaven, was honoring the house of the Herennii with his presence tonight. Behind the cauldron-bearers came the lictors with the ax and fasces, and after them came other slaves with torches—gleaming Aethiopians anointed with oil and attar of roses. And after all these there was a moment of waiting in which nothing could be seen but the lighted boughs.

The young man stepped farther back into the shadow of the colonnade. He was alone; at the first flourish of imperial pageantry his companions had left him, probably in the mistaken notion that they were not exalted enough to be with him on so high an occasion. If they only knew, he thought, how tawdry he found it. He had never watched the entrance of an emperor without feeling an almost uncontrollable impulse to desecrate the hush by shouting some obscenity. And tonight it would be his uncle Decius who would walk into the prepared silence, his stern and decent person made cheap and ridiculous by a purple cloak and a rayed crown.

He bowed with the others and came up slowly before he permitted his eyes to focus on the figure that stood against the lighted foliage. And strangely, unbelievably, at the sight of that figure he was profoundly moved. The crown, the flowing cloak, the golden orb held stiffly against the firelit leaves—they did not debase the presence in the doorway—the presence exalted them instead, the austere vitality of the presence flowed into them and gave them authenticity and power. With the spare and undramatic gestures of a soldier disarming after exercise, the Emperor took off his cloak and crown and handed them to one of his Aethiopians. And the young man felt a tightening in his throat at this undeserved sign that for the time being Decius was neither god nor emperor, but a senator among senators, a kinsman come to a kinswoman's house to pay his respects to the dead.

It was to the dead that he first addressed himself, standing before the ancestors in the rigid, old-fashioned attitude of worship, his thick neck bent, his hands crossed on his chest. Such piety as his was scarcely fashionable anymore; it was an outlander's fervor for his adopted country's deserted gods. The others had murmured their formulas as if they were ashamed of them; he uttered his in a rough, unmuted voice: "Taste our wine in the dark country tonight, Celestus Falconius." And he stood there silent for a few moments before he turned, his face still stiff with antique reverence, and addressed himself to his hostess and to Drusilla, who had managed to enter unnoticed among the few court dignitaries who had followed him in.

And I, too, should go to the door and greet him, Favorinus told himself. And yet he could bring himself to do no more than step out of the dim colonnade and lean against the garlanded pedestal of the statue of Hercules. Over the subdued hum of conversation that had arisen when the Emperor had divested himself of the trappings of his power, he could hear the deep voice making gracious excuses for the late arrival: he had meant to be here much earlier, but certain dispatches had come in from the northern frontier; it was far too late for the lady Sabina to present her visitors to him in a formal line; the guests should simply stay wherever they were, and he would wander about and have a word with as many of them as he could. . . .

And now that he was moving slowly up the hushed and orderly atrium, pausing at each group of visitors, now that he appeared crownless and in a simple toga—exactly like the togas he had worn to supper in the house on the Esquiline, except for the broad purple stripe at the hem and across the chest—his nephew saw that certain marked changes had taken place in him in the last nine years. The fringe of hair at his temples, light brown in the old days, was completely white; his eyes seemed paler, perhaps because his skin had been weathered in the long campaign; his mouth was grimmer, more tightly set. His ascent to power must have aged and hardened him: he had dealt with demoralized and mutinous legions, he had ridden in the forefront of fratricidal battles; he had gambled at terrible odds on the bank of the Danube with the Gothic chieftain Kniva. What occasion, the young man asked himself, would he have had in the parleys and the councils and the driving marches and the battles to remember me? If I am anything to him after these nine years, what could I be but the one on whom he wasted his readings from Livy, the one who never troubled himself to take his father's seat in the Senate House, the one who sits dreaming and conversing while others strive to steady the pillars of a collapsing world?

Was he deceiving himself, or did the chill blue eyes actually keep flashing in his direction? When he turned from the last of those who waited to be greeted, a little group standing close to Favorinus, the Emperor, with his thin lips folded against each other, seemed to be smiling in spite of himself. "And Favorinus? How is it with Favorinus?" he said.

"I'm very well, my uncle." He blushed because his excitement had betrayed him into undue familiarity. "It was kind of you to come, I never expected it. That is—you do us more honor than we deserve, my master and my lord."

The Emperor's hand, sunburnt and crossed with hard blue veins, took him by the elbow and drew him in the direction of the door. "Is it warm in here, or am I still sweating over the dispatches from Dacia? Could we walk around outside? Do you think anybody would be offended if we stepped out for a breath of air?"

The company fell back to let them pass. Certain faces impinged upon his consciousness: Paulina and Probus together again near the fountain, his mother in an anxious flutter, Drusilla looking on with bitterness and contempt . . . Beyond the door, the wind was catching at the flames in the cauldron, making such long, gold tongues lash out that they had to take a wide detour to keep out of range of the fire.

Which of them chose to leave the brilliantly lighted avenue of sycamores and skirt the darkest wing of the house, Favorinus did not know. They walked in silence past the bed of autumn narcissus, past the statue of Venus, past a patch of marjoram that exuded a pungent fragrance in the damp air, over the marble well-cover where Prisca had stood—at the thought of Charis waiting, the young man was afraid to conjecture how long ago. The upper windows of that wing, the windows of the bedchambers, were lighted only faintly by single lamps. A voice, throaty and warm, came to them out of Drusilla's room. Prisca was singing while she puffed up the pillows and turned back the coverlet. She was singing some slow and solemn song that he could not place: the words seemed strange—he could have sworn that he caught the phrase "O Lamb of God."

It was not his place to break the quiet. The presence that walked with him—he knew it in the darkness only by the flutter of the toga and the somewhat labored breath—moved at a slow and regular pace. He is tired, he thought, I should take him to a place where we can sit down together. And he began to move diagonally across the lawn in the direction of a kind of summer shelter—a broken circle of marble benches surrounded by four pillars and topped with an awning—set up for lovers, so far away from the house that the noise of the atrium reached it only as a muted fall and swell.

But when they came to the chosen spot, he was disproportionately disturbed to find that the awning was gone. Sylvanus had had it taken down for a washing, and the bare tops of the pillars, vaguely discernible against the lighted sky, gave him a sense of exposure so disquieting that he turned and was about to move on.

33

"This will do very well," the Emperor said, letting himself down onto one of the benches.

"But they've taken away the awning."

"It won't rain. It's been threatening like this all day."

A solitary cricket emphasized the silence that hung between them. For no reason that he could tell, he had suddenly thought again of the cleft head. It was with them, it was with them as much as if somebody had laid it in front of them on the grass; and it seemed to him that his whole chest was being shaken by the pounding of his heart.

The Emperor shifted on the bench and exhaled in a long sigh. "At least there's no necessity for me to start off with an account of myself," he said, and there was mirthless laughter under his voice. "Unfortunately, all my doings are public property. What I do and why I do it, everybody knows— or thinks he knows."

The pale eyes, visible now because he was growing used to the dark, were staring somberly at the grass. In the old days, he had been convinced that they could spy out secret things—the suppressed defiance, the little deceits, the voluptuous visions: and now he had to struggle against a childish conviction that they had seen his vision of the split head.

"For instance, what happened at Verona. There must be twenty current versions of that. I know them all."

He had been silent too long. He wet his lips with the tip of his tongue and took a deep breath. "It's true that I lead a rather circumscribed life, but everybody I have ever heard express himself on that matter has shown an absolute confidence in my lord and my master," he said.

"And you?"

"I?" He glanced up at the bare capitals of the pillars, and his sense of exposure was intensified. "My uncle's dealings with me were always just, even in the smallest things. And if others who never knew him believe—if others are utterly convinced—then why should I—?"

"Sometime I'll tell you my own version of that story."

"I would be grateful for your confidence, my master and my lord."

"And I'd be grateful if you could manage to address me without my string of titles. Don't you want to sit down? No, over here beside me. There's no point in our shouting at each other across ten feet."

Once or twice they had sat in the shabby dining room, side by side like that, in earnest, halting talk, covering the hard silences by eating fruit out of one of the battered dishes. The scent of the man was the same—wool and soap and a trace of sweat—never any balsam, never any cinnamon. Philip the Arabian had had a passion for oils, had moved about in a cloud of attar of roses. . . .

"I left your cousin Herennius up in Dacia, in command of six legions."

"Yes, I know."

"They're dogs, those legionaries, poor sick dogs, I tell you. When I got them they were running wild. I was the one that had to beat them into a decent state. For months I beat them, and now they're tame. He has an easier time of it than I would have thought. They love him—" There was a ring of pride in that, and the darkness was uneasy with the old affront that begot the boastfulness. "One word from him, and they'd walk off the side of a cliff—" 968261

"He's well then—my cousin Herennius?"

"Well enough, according to his last letter."

"He was a good friend to me, the first friend I had, the only one for a good many years—"

The old, weathered hand reached for him through the dark and came down, heavy and stiff, on his knee. "And you, Favorinus? What have you been doing with yourself these last nine years?"

What have I been doing? he thought glancing up at the open sky, constantly changing in the fitful light. Nothing, my uncle, nothing to justify any hopes you might have had for me in the house on the Esquiline. I was a Stoic, a good Stoic for a while. I am still a Stoic of sorts, I suppose. I have what you would call a dabbler's interest in the arts—I found an ivory statue by the ancient master Nesiotes in an antique shop on the Via Sacra, and Charis and I have figured out between us what music the Greeks must have used with the lyrics of Anacreon. I have learned what it is to talk freely from the heart, with good companions. I have found myself a beloved, and I have written about half of a commentary on Musonius . . . The wind was making a rustling sound in the mulberry trees. The single cricket was complaining again in the grass. "I? Very little, really. If I told my uncle what I had been doing, he would conclude—and probably rightly —that I haven't been doing anything at all."

"They tell me you never go to the Senate."

"I went to the Senate once—a few weeks after I came of age—to take my seat. I went once, but I never went back—"

"Would you care to tell me why?"

Why? Because I failed to inherit my father's marvelous capacity for adapting himself. I couldn't conceive of flattering a tyrant to soothe his conscience; I couldn't vote "Yes," when no decent man could have kept himself from shouting "No"; I couldn't leap out of my seat and recommend five rounds of applause for a piece of legislation that I didn't understand . . . "Because I loathed the Senate. Long before I went, I knew I would loathe it. I knew by my father's talk that it was nothing but a travesty," he said.

"Nevertheless, I have to deal with it. Irresponsible and hypocritical as it is, it's still the Senate of the Republic and the Roman People—it's still the only body that has managed to survive two and a half centuries of tyranny."

A body, he thought, a dead body tricked out in ancient magnificence and furnished with strings and wires so that it could be made to move and smile. An obscene corpse that has been speaking for two hundred and fifty years with the voice of one imperial ventriloquist after another. . . .

"I mean to revive and restore the Senate," said Decius, suddenly getting up and turning in the direction of the lighted windows of the palace. "I don't know how—but somehow I'll have to revive it. I'm depending on a few good men—a few good men and the help of the gods."

He was walking swiftly out of the circle of marble benches, and the young man followed him, past the statue of Venus, over the dark lawn, under the creaking boughs. Revive the Senate—an hour ago he would have turned his face aside and smiled a one-sided smile; but now he suspended judgment, now he did not know. The vital force that had transmuted the orb and the cloak and the crown into authentic symbols of a living power— how would it fare when it asserted itself under the grimy ceiling of the age-old Senate house, commanding the Senate to bestir itself, to rise from the dead?

They walked in silence as far as the marjoram patch. Perhaps, thought Favorinus, they would walk in silence as far as the door of the palace; and he could not tell whether the prospect of such a conclusion filled him with relief or with regret.

"I see your herbs are flourishing."

"Yes. On the other side of the house there's a new bed of thyme—"

They had stopped, they were standing face to face. The hand was on his arm, he could see the icy flash of the pale blue eyes. "Listen, Favorinus. It wasn't entirely to pay my respects to your father's ghost that I came up here tonight. Such respects as I have to pay to your father's ghost would scarcely have been worth the journey up the Palatine. . . ."

"I know."

"I came to ask a favor. Come to the Senate. I want you in the Senate—"

"In the Senate? But why, my master and my lord?"

The presence, irate and imperial now, turned on its heel and crossed diagonally toward the avenue of sycamores. He hurried behind it with his heart knocking crazily in his chest; he pursued it until it emerged in the yellow light of the torches; and there it turned, and was no longer a presence, was his uncle Decius, smothering a blaze of righteous anger, taking account of the frailties of the young, and wanting above all things to be reasonable and just.

"Come to the Senate tomorrow because I ask it. That ought to be reason enough."

But tomorrow—he and Charis had made so much of tomorrow—the unhurried breakfast, the morning walk with their good friend Antisthenes, the afternoon at the Library of Trajan . . . He strove to discipline his face, knowing that it was visible now in the yellow light.

"But, since you ask for other reasons, come because my son Herennius is with the legions in Dacia—because I have certain good men to support me in the Senate, but nobody of my own flesh and blood. Or come because one piece of graciousness deserves another. *I* came to the house of the Herennii tonight."

He felt himself flush for his own shameful tardiness and for all that had passed between the Herennii and the Decii. He tried to conjure eagerness into his own face, but knew that his eyes were expressionless, that his smile was a forced smile. "It never occurred to me that you would want me there—I never thought that you would—"

"Well, now you know." The hard arm thrust itself through his and drew him up the flight of marble stairs. "I want you there tomorrow, at the early session. I'm making a speech, and I want you to hear it."

The only words he could summon up were as forced as the smile. "Certainly, my uncle. I'm very eager to hear it. I'll be sure to be there at sunrise," he said.

Chapter 3

THE STICK of apple-wood in the brazier had burned straight through the middle. Falling into pieces on the glowing ash with a soft clinking and sighing, it startled Charis out of her sleep. While the last of it was being consumed, parts of the elegant little chamber were picked out of the dark—the ivory Apollo in the niche, the cythera resting against the curved ebony chair, the gilded plaster fruit along the molding. Then the blaze died down and there was blackness everywhere except in the red ellipse of the brazier.

What time is it? she asked herself, sitting up on the couch. I've been asleep and that stupid slave has been asleep, and the fire is almost out, and nothing will be in order when he comes.

But everything was in order, of course; long before she had allowed herself to fall asleep, she had called in the slave and the two of them had worked for an hour, ridding the room of every trace of confusion left by the guests. The quill brought out for the old poet Berosus—while he was reading his *Sorrows of Psyche* to the company, a change had occurred to him and he had wanted to note it down at once—the quill and the ink had been returned to the cabinet. The raisin seeds left on the arm of the chair by the exquisite little male dancer Memphius had been removed, and the floor had been brushed clean of the mud which the painter Antisthenes had brought in from his sketching trip on the Aventine. Even the heavy scent of Orbiana Festina's perfume had been carried off by the damp currents from the open window; she sensed a salt-sea fragrance in the draught instead. Nothing in the room could possibly be amiss, nothing but the dent that her head had made in the cushion, and the scroll that had slipped from her hand as she was falling asleep. And yet she was uneasy, she could not be at peace until she could see everything clearly again. "Herodian," she called, three times and sharply at last, because the slave was snoring in the adjoining room. "Come in here and look after the lights."

He came into the room in his own good time—the fat, yellowish Levantine boy, with a lamp and a vessel of oil in his hands. His eyes, always small in his doughy face, were mere glinting slits when he had just been wakened. "All the lamps?" he said.

"Naturally. And put another stick of apple-wood on the fire."

He gave her a sheepish grin and went slowly, heavily about the business of replenishing and kindling the lamps. It was hard to tell how simple-minded he actually was—he moved like an overgrown infant and was forever biting at his thumbnail and slobbering over his chin, yet he showed himself cunning enough for his own purposes. She turned her back on him, rolled up the scroll, and puffed out the pillows. The air from the window actually smelled of wet grass; the salt-sea fragrance she had mistaken it for, she suddenly realized, had come out of her dream.

The couch and the wall behind it were lighted by increasing stages of brightness until the last lamp was kindled; but she waited to turn until the room was emptied of his exasperating presence and could give her an instant of utter gratification. Oh, it had been a sad and heavy dream, in spite of the glare of sunlight that had lain across it. How long would she have to wait for him? When would he come?

"Do you want anything more, my lady?"

"Yes. Put the melon back in the cold water. I thought I saw a fly in there—see if you can kill it."

He might put the melon in the water, but he would never catch the fly, dull lump of cheese that he was. Orbiana had told her a dozen times to sell him, but Orbiana had been born of a rich equestrian house, and had never known what it was like to be . . . He was gone, but she sat gazing at the wall, seeing the blinding line of waves again, parted now by the prow of a ship in the shape of a nymph—a wooden sea-nymph with barnacles in her gilded hair and a shining salt-deposit on her breasts.

There was a clatter of silver in the dining room. He had collided with the table, he would knock the blossoms from the stalks of autumn narcissus, he would spot the cloth with wine. "Oh, let it alone and go to bed," she said, and turned on a room that was chaste, perfect, irreproachable.

Irreproachable, beautiful—and yet there was no serenity in her enjoyment of it. Nothing—not his repeated assurances, not the liberal amounts of money his steward paid her every month, not the fact that the lease for this two-floor apartment in one of the finest buildings in the City was in her name—nothing could rid her of a persistent sense of impermanence. It was too costly: there was a fortune here in antiques alone, the white Babylonian rugs with the green and yellow birds and flowers would have paid three years' rent in a tenement, the money that had gone for a crystal vase would have bought a strapping slave. He had sensed her uneasiness, he had found far-fetched pretexts for repeating that everything here was hers as long as she lived, he had even insisted that the establishment was actually very modest: "You know, darling, I'd have set up something more elaborate if I could, but I have very little property of my own—only the two Phrygian farms and the almond orchard in Sicily—all the rest was left unconditionally in my mother's hands." Yet she had never learned to live in peace with this splendor; it was hers by his graciousness and by Fortune's; nothing but the clothes and jewels left to her by Marcellinus were her own.

He had tried to prove to her that it was he who had profited by the exchange, that she had given him in return for his negligible expenditures the sort of life he had yearned for in his loneliness. He had said once, laughing, before his friends, that no woman had ever brought a man a more extraordinary dowry—who else could have graced a household with such a crowd of artists and scholars and wits and women rich in experience? She often remembered that little speech; and, this evening, listening to the rare talk, she had thought only of how much he would have enjoyed himself if he had been here . . . When will he come? she asked herself again. When will he come and take away the memory of the sea and the ship with the wooden Nereid on the prow?

Now that the room was in order, her anxiety settled upon her person: Were there wrinkles in the back of her yellow dalmatica? Were the strands of pearls around her neck lapping over each other? Had her hair, curled and piled carefully on top of her head to give her height, been pushed over to a ridiculous angle while she slept? Covertly, keeping her eyes on the door lest he should enter at the wrong moment after all this waiting, she felt under the couch and drew out the mirror, a square of polished silver with a frame of silver shells. He was annoyed whenever he caught her taking these swift, uneasy glances at herself. "What do you think it matters to me," he had asked her, "if one of your hairpins is out of place?" The mirror revealed less imperfection than her anxiety had led her to suppose: the face that swam on the silvery surface was too spare to grow puffy in sleep; the brow was smooth, the eyes were alert and wide, the rouge was still sharp and neat on the lips. She scraped away a sliver of dried skin from the corner of her nose; she wet her fingertip and improved the line of a plucked brow. "I tell you, Charis, if you never did anything about yourself from morning to night, nobody would ever know the difference." But she knew better. She knew that any imperfection would destroy the whole precarious design, hat even the slightest flaw could turn the clear white cheeks into the cheeks of a starved child, could transform the big, attentive eyes into the terrified eyes of a slave—

And now she remembered. In spite of herself, she remembered the dream, and so clearly, so shatteringly that she was hard put to it to suppress a cry. The ship with the gilded Nereid on its prow—that was the ship that had carried her across the Aegean twenty years ago, from the island of Cos to the island of Delos where they had sold her as a slave. How was it that all those details should rise up in her sleep again after all those years—the barnacle-crowned hair and the salt-encrusted breasts? And more, more—the rebellious boy who had spited everybody by jumping overboard, chains and all, the overpowering sweetness of the cargo of honey that they had taken on at Cos along with the slaves. Everything, everything, the block, and the hands reaching up to prod her legs, and the chains around her ankles, and the red chalk crosses on her feet, and the voice of the auctioneer shouting that the patrician Marcellinus had purchased the slave Charis out of Cos, a female and in her tenth year, at the price of two thousand denarii. . . .

She would not think of it. She slid the mirror back under the couch and started up at once because the stillness had been broken by a whimpering, chattering cry. Cyrillus, her pet monkey, had been sleeping under the couch, and the mirror had touched him. Frightened out of his sleep, he was grieving like a sickly child.

"Come, Cyrillus, come, Sweet, come up here and sit by me," she said, sinking back on the pillows and snapping her fingers. The unhappy creature, shaking all over, leaped up on the couch and clung to her bare arm with his cold, small, hairless hands. She stroked him, repressing the shudder that always came when she first touched him. Why her lover should have chosen such a gift for her, she did not know. The presence of the little beast—his rueful and unseemly antics in these beautiful and decorous rooms—was somehow inharmonious, was almost an intrusion. He was too close to aching humanity to give her any pleasure; even when he was at his most cheerful, she was always waiting for the next spasm of grief or fright. Now she felt, slowly and apprehensively, down the frail bones of his spine. The fleas had been at him all summer, and even though she had powdered him faithfully every day, there were still two patches of pitiful bare hide.

"You're very late, my lord," said the voice of the City night watchman, close to the open window.

It was the awaited voice, but more lively than she would have expected at this hour of the night, that said, "Yes, very late. A quiet watch to you."

She put the monkey down on one of the Babylonian rugs, smoothed the cushions again, took up the lamp, and went to the door to let him in. His eyes shone and his cheeks looked flushed in the concentrated brightness. In their first months, the excitement in his face would have made her ask herself the one intolerable question: What woman has he been with—what patrician matron, what virginal daughter of a high house did his mother bring out in her war against me tonight? But the years had taught her that he could be thrown into this state by almost anything—an outrageous political comment, a new edition of an old poet, an instance of human suffering, a quaint conversation with a child. The kiss that he gave her was as honest and as ardent as she could wish. She went to the carved ebony chair and seated herself, leaving the couch for him, since he was bound to be tired as soon as the breathless excitement had passed.

"I'm sorry to be so late," he said, lying down and immediately sitting up again, seeking her forgiveness with his intent and luminous eyes. "Do you know, for the first time in nine years, I saw him tonight—"

It might have been anybody—an old tutor, a schoolmate returned on leave from the Persian or Gothic front.

"After all that wretched business he came up to the palace—"

"Who, darling?"

"My uncle Decius."

"The Emperor?"

"Yes, the Emperor."

She could not prevent herself from fetching up an exasperated sigh. The old Pannonian general who had taken so strong a hold on her lover's heart that once or twice he had actually named him aloud in his sleep, the narrow-minded champion of all the dour virtues of a lost century—she had always counted him out of the battalion that Chance had drawn up against her; the Herennii had, through their ill-judged pride, forever driven him away—her lover had told her so. And now he was marching against her—not merely a Roman, but the Lord of All the Romans, as much a Graecophobe as those conquerors who had crushed the flower of Greek civilization under their heavy heels centuries ago. "But you always said he would never come back," she said.

"It's the last thing I would ever have thought of. Imagine his walking into our atrium when there were eighty people in it—"

The atrium of the Herennii—she had never seen it. The eighty guests assembled there—if they ever mentioned her at all, they called her Favorinus Herennius's skinny little Greek courtesan. While she had sat waiting for him with nobody for company but a wretched monkey and an idiotic slave, their self-esteem had been flattered by the imperial presence—and *he*, for all his protestations of indifference to such things, had basked in that presence with the rest—

"Imagine his making a public gesture of reconciliation like that after all that we—"

"Yes, it *is* amazing. Really, the man must be something of a fool."

He gave her a sharp look. His hand, thin and tendinous, closed over his knee. Watch, watch, she told herself. Watch your lips, see that they don't fall open like the lips of a scolded child. Watch your eyes, keep them alert and blank, don't look at him like a frightened slave—

"I'd hardly call him a fool—"

"No?"

"Not by any means. He had his good reasons for coming, you can be sure of that. It certainly wasn't to honor my father's ghost—what honor he could pay my father's ghost wasn't worth the journey up the Palatine—he said so himself. I'm not exactly sure why he came, but I think—" He paused, and a slow and thoughtful smile grew at the corners of his mouth. "I think he came for me."

Came for you? What do you mean—he came for you? Did he descend on you with all the self-righteousness of an ancient Cato, did he take you by the scruff of the neck and try to pull you out of the morass that you have been floundering in with me and our friends for the last three years? "What do you mean—he came for you? What did he want?" she said.

"He wants me to take my father's seat in the Senate."

But if that was the sum of it, if all the Lord of the World required of him was his attendance at the Senate now and then, she had lost her temper too quickly. She was not afraid of the Senate—he had been there before. Now, for a month or two, to please his uncle, he might sit through a few of the dreaming sessions, answer the roll-call, vote, make an empty speech, drowse through the day's business like all the rest. And then one morning he would see the futility of it again. She would wake him and tell him, "You're expected at the Senate," and, after calling the Senate all the names he was in the habit of calling it, he would give her a kiss and go back to sleep. . . .

She looked at him ruefully, half smiling, but he did not return the smile. His eyes were fixed on his knees, and the tip of his tongue was moving slowly between his lips—a sign of concern and hesitation—he always wet his lips before he said anything that might give her pain. "The fact is, Charis—" He lay down on the couch and laid his forearm across his eyes. "The fact is, I have to go to the Senate tomorrow. He asked me to come because he's making a speech, and I said I would. I could scarcely refuse him after he'd put himself into such a vulnerable position by coming to the palace tonight."

She was on the point of laughing; it was so slight a desertion, and he had announced it with so much consideration and regret. The morning walk with Antisthenes, the afternoon in the Library of Trajan—a man to whom the separate details of their life together meant so much would hardly be won away from that life even by a lecture from the Lord of the World. She stood up and walked soundlessly toward him across the Babylonian rug, disregarding Cyrillus, who caught the hem of her dalmatica as she passed. His eyes were still covered, he was not conscious that she stood above him, and she allowed herself an attenuated moment of looking down at him—at the long legs and the hipbone thrusting sharply against the white cloth,

43

at the spare arch of the ribs, at the veined forearm and the tired mouth below it and the thick black hair above it, curling against the white pillows like the tendrils of a vine. . . .

And suddenly, quite unreasonably, only because of the abominable dream, she remembered the patrician Marcellinus who had bought her in Delos. The patrician Marcellinus, she thought, was beautiful in his own dry, elegant way when he stretched out on a couch like that with his forearm over his eyes. His fingers were long, too, and there were white half-moons at the base of his fingernails, and his skin was delicate and white. But he sickened, he withered, his hands lay on the coverlet like the talons of a bird, and now he was dead . . . She was glad that her lover could not see her. Tears, useless and unbecoming tears, were standing in her eyes. What is the matter with me? she asked herself. I am at peace with him, and he is at peace with me, and I have only to accept the ripeness of the hour . . . She bent down and kissed him on the mouth. He had taken no wine tonight— his breath was fresh with the smell of milk and butter and fruit—an innocent breath, like a child's.

Without stirring on the couch, he gave her a brief and automatic kiss. "Decius intends to restore the Senate," he said.

"Does he?" She returned to the ebony chair. She would not trouble herself to tell him what he already knew: Others before Decius had thought they could check the rampant power of the army by giving the Senate the dignity and power that had resided in it in the past. Others had put their hopes in the Conscript Fathers, and one of them had been left a headless trunk on the floor of the imperial palace, and another had died in battle, and another had opened his veins behind the lines, and two more had been murdered by the furious Praetorian Guards—their bodies had been dragged for hours through the City streets . . . "Isn't that a drastic move—restoring the Senate?" she said.

"What do you want him to do? Let the Senate sit and rot? Any move he makes is certain to be dangerous."

Then why move? she thought, feeling the polished rounds of fruit on the carved frame of the cythera. Why disturb the precariously maintained world in which at least a few could still taste the exquisite pleasures of a gracious life? It was a question she would never have dared to voice in his presence, and she realized with a small shock that she had voiced it in his absence— she had said it to the company gathered in this room tonight. And they had assented: the little male dancer Memphius had brought his exquisite hands together in soundless applause; the painter Antisthenes had given her a wise and disillusioned smile; the beautiful Orbiana had repeated the question, giving the word "pleasure" her own inimitable intonation; and the old poet Berosus had nodded his round and venerable head. What did they ask of the new Emperor? Not that he revive the Senate—that would unleash the jealous fury of the army against him. Not that he succor and restore the decaying provinces—that would call for such taxes as nobody would be willing to pay into the imperial treasury. Not that he would march out against the incalculable swarms of Goths hidden in the forest-lands at the borders of the world—that was a task for a god. Let him follow the accidentally salutary methods of his blessedly sleepy predecessor. Let him hold back black chaos as long as he could. "Has he anything else in mind? What else, besides restoring the Senate?"

"I don't know, he didn't tell me. Maybe later, when he has more reason for taking me into his confidence—"

Fear took hold on her, and she grasped at the cythera—a blurred discord rose from the strings. He took his arm away from his face at last and propped himself on his elbow. "What's the matter, darling?" he asked, seeking her eyes.

"Nothing." Only that it's a fearful thing to carry about—the Emperor's confidence. Only that sons, brothers, cousins, nephews have always come down with a falling Lord of the World. In my country, even in the days of the tyrants, when a man incurred the rage of the people, he went his way and lived out his life in some hospitable town on the other side of the water, and those that were closest to him blushed a little, grieved a little, and forgot the whole matter by and by. But your countrymen can never settle anything except by blood. In Rome, a cousin's second cousin must be murdered before the successor can sleep in peace. Even a child—they strangled Philip's seven-year-old child.

Whatever he had seen in her eyes, he had decided to disregard. "Look at Cyrillus. You scared poor Cyrillus with the cythera," he said.

"I suppose I did. Well, let him alone. He'll go back to sleep."

He let his arm hang down over the couch and made mournful coaxing sounds and tapped on the floor until the little creature crept across the rug, leaped up beside him, and hid its worried face in the white folds of cloth at his chest. "Poor Cyrillus. What's the matter, Cyrillus?" The spare hand stroked the flea-bitten back, slowly, with a moody and sorrowful tenderness, and she was suddenly stricken with unreasonable jealousy. Comfort me, too, she thought. Comfort me for the hours that I waited here alone, for the evil dream that wakened me, for the slow and ugly death of the patrician Marcellinus, for my exile in a crass and brutal country, for all the remembrances and all the forebodings that only serve to multiply the aching intensity of my love. . . .

The silence hung heavy between them. "It was a miserable day, I'm glad to see the end of it," he said at last.

Then end it well, she thought, leaving the chair and coming to him again. She stood beside him and drew his head over against her hip. Her hand passed through the warm black tendrils, over the hollow temple, down the cheek . . . Make a good end of it for both of us, love. . . .

"The games were horrible." He looked shocked, as though he had had

45

no intention of saying it, as though it had come out in spite of himself.

"I can imagine."

"No, you can't." He shook his head and pulled away from her, so suddenly that the little creature jumped off the couch, scampered across the floor, and cowered beside the cythera, chattering and curling up his hairless fists. "I thought I could imagine it beforehand, I thought I was prepared for it, but I wasn't. I saw a thing that I'll never get out of my mind—I'll be seeing it until I go to my grave—"

Then see it and bear it as best you can, she thought, stepping back a little and staring at the sane and perfect ivory Apollo in the niche on the opposite wall. Bear it as I bear the remembrance of dragging my fetters up and down the deck. . . .

"One of the gladiators ran up to the box and asked for mercy. He was so mutilated that his face was scarcely human. His eye was hanging out on a thread."

Why in the name of the gods do you do it? she thought. Why do you always have to spoil our peace? We know the world is black and terrible— your conquering countrymen helped to make it so. But we have built a boat together, so sound, so close, so filled with light that we need never know what waves we roll and pitch upon. Then why must you forever be reaching out into the dark and the tempest? Why must you pull in bloated fish and dead men's hair and show them to me?

"I did a crazy thing, I gave the mercy signal. It was too late, of course, he was too far gone, they made an end of him right under our eyes—"

"Try not to think about it. You'll feel better tomorrow, after you've had some sleep."

"Charis—" He was touching her now, he had laid his hand on her girdle. But the gesture was light and tentative and asked for something other than love.

"What, darling?"

"I can't get rid of the feeling that I'm responsible."

"Responsible for what?" She saw that he wanted her on the couch beside him, and she seated herself rigidly, knowing beforehand that, if he asked for consolation, she would not have it to give.

"For the games, for the slaughter, for all of it. I'm responsible for all of it," he said.

"Nobody's responsible for anything," she said in a weary and exasperated voice. To discuss the thing would be useless—such discussions had ended in a stalemate a hundred times before. The two of them—she had good reason to know it now—had utterly irreconcilable concepts of the world. He had been deluded beyond all changing by the Stoic lie: he insisted on believing, in spite of the evidence of his senses, that some sane, just Force, however obscure, however briefly revealed, made itself manifest among men. But she knew better—she had seen too much to imagine that anything divine could create or concern Itself with such senseless chaos—one was tossed into the confusion at one point and hurled out of it at another, and in the interim one behaved as decently as possible, with a reasonable amount of courage and grace.

"So you say, and yet I feel responsible. I was the one that paid the trainer."

Ridiculous, ridiculous! Who is responsible for the brandmark on my thigh? Who made me a slave? The dealer who waited for the boat on the island of Delos? The agent who bought me from my parents in Cos? My parents who had nine others and thought that it was better to feed nine at the cost of one than to let ten starve to death? Your just and reasonable Force who puts such an itching into a man's loins that every ten months he must get him another brat, another millstone around his neck? The sour soil that refuses to feed the swarm of wretches that breed on it? "You were the one who paid the trainer—that's preposterous! You could just as well say the trainer was to blame because he taught the man his filthy trade. And why stop with the trainer? Go back, keep going back, compile a history of any one of those dead gladiators, spend the next ten years finding out why he happened to be a gladiator in the first place, and see what you get for your pains. Likely as not, in the end, you'll have to fasten the responsibility on his grandfather's blighted onion patch."

She stopped and knew that she should have stopped sooner. Talk—searching midnight talk with friends, hard-driving talk with the merchants in the shops, pert and elusive talk with the inept members of the conquering race—talk was the only field of action left to her and her fellow-countrymen. And too many times of late she had been carried away on the bounding crests of her sentences, she had obscured his meanings and forgotten his needs in the irresponsible flourishes of her own eloquence. She did not dare to look at him. She made a forced and feeble gesture with her hands. "Let's leave it alone, let's go and have a piece of melon," she said.

"No, wait." His hand caught hers and closed upon it, and she could not tell whether it was his intention to master her at last in this old and exasperating argument or some compelling urgency that made his grip so strong. "Those deaths in the arena this afternoon—in your opinion, nobody was to blame for them, they were simply manifestations of general chaos, blind chance—"

"Can't we leave it alone?"

"In a moment. You would say then that everything is a manifestation of blind chance—the bad and the good—those deaths and our being here together—you may be right—it may be so."

His grasp was so tight that she could scarcely keep herself from wincing. He could never have held her so in anger—she knew now that he was driven by an inward pain.

"And yet I tell you, Charis, if the world is as you think it is, I don't want it, I reject it, I would rather be a heap of senseless ashes than live my life in such a world."

She winced, and he loosed his hold on her fingers. He was utterly remote from her now, was staring straight before him, his mouth parted, his eyes expressionless.

"When I was small—oh, eight or nine," he said in a flat voice, "we studied the myths—our teacher told us the accepted version of the creation of the world. Chaos was there first, he said, black Chaos moving over the face of the earth, and he explained Chaos to us as best he could—reasonless confusion, blind chance, no pattern to anything, everything happening by accident in the dark, meaningless birth, meaningless death. None of the others took the thing to heart, but for some insane reason I was obsessed with it for months—I couldn't laugh, I couldn't play, I woke up in the middle of the night, screaming because I was convinced that Chaos was back again. I invented the most horrible images—maybe to torture myself—I imagined the City turned upside-down at the bottom of the sea, I imagined perpetual night with the stars raining out of the sky, I saw my little sister acting like a prostitute, winking and pointing to her secret parts. When I heard the rumble of a carriage at night, I would run to the window to see that it was a carriage, not the sea washing up onto the land. You see—" He laughed a humorless laugh and gave her a brief, sidewise, shamefaced look. "You see, I have a kind of inborn abhorrence of Chaos. If it came again, if I thought it was here now—even a more subtle Chaos, a Chaos of the spirit, without the drowned cities and the careening stars—then I would simply leave the world to Chaos, I couldn't tolerate the world."

She offered no answer, since the only possible answer was an unthinkably cruel one. She sat rigidly beside him, trying to keep the utter weariness out of her face. Everything—the kisses that she had wanted beyond all reason half an hour ago, the room itself, the food waiting on the dining room table —everything had lost its savor for her now.

"Charis—"

If there was yearning in that, she did not want to hear it. A while since, she thought, when I came and stood and waited for you to reach up for me, I could have loved you. And maybe an hour from now I will love you again, after we've eaten a little and laughed a little and talked of other things. But don't ask too much of me, don't thrust me out into creeping darkness and try to have me under the falling stars. . . .

"Listen, Charis—"

"What, darling?" She was ashamed of the false patience in her voice, she was ashamed of her cool, uncharitable face.

"Oh, nothing, nothing," he said, turning and looking at her with strained and desperate eyes. "Nothing, you're right, we'll leave it alone."

And before he could embrace her, she had eluded his embrace, she had stood up and moved away, she was standing in the middle of the Babylonian rug and saying, in spite of herself, "I have a melon out in the dining room—a melon and some wine."

For an instant he looked appalled. Then, seeing her confusion, seeing her hand fly to her lips, he did something she had seen him do before in painful or embarrassing situations—he indulged in a burst of senseless merriment.

"Come, Cyrillus—come, you pampered little brat, have some melon with us if you're in the mood for it," he said, coaxing the creature in the direction of the green drapery.

"But it's late, the wine is probably warm by now, and I—"

"And you're plainly so tired from waiting up for me, poor thing, that you can hardly hold up your head."

The stupid Levantine had replenished only one of the lamps in the dining room. The single flame cast a sickly glow over the linen cloth, over the four banquet couches and the yellow curtains and the white pilasters crowned with sheaves of gilded wheat. The fly, probably sluggish with feasting, was crawling on one of the napkins, and he made much of getting rid of it, struck at it, chased it through the window into the night. Her lover stretched himself on one of the couches and she sat down on another, filling her plate with the unwanted and discredited food—a thin slice of melon, a pat of butter, a rusk of bread—watching his antics with the monkey and trying to smile. Even in her heavy-heartedness she was worried for the room —he had given Cyrillus a piece of melon rind, and now the little beast would run all over the place with it, would leave the sticky imprint of his paws on the linen, let the juice drip on the rug, smear the cover of the dining couch . . . Why do I concern myself with these trifles at such a time? she thought, grieving over the forced and tired brightness in his face. He smiled at her, propped himself on his elbow, and patted the side of his couch. "Come over and sit down, won't you? I'm not going to ask you to stretch out. Poor little thing, you're so tired, the moment you lie down I'm sure you'll fall asleep."

She sat beside him, balancing her plate on her knees. The ache in her chest was such that she could have turned and flung herself against him and wept. But that is for wives, not mistresses, she thought. Sobbing fits in the middle of the night are for the spoiled daughters of high houses, not for freed slaves. "Did you have a pleasant evening?" she said.

"About as tiresome as usual, until the Emperor came."

"Then Orbiana was wrong. She treated me with such tender consideration when you didn't arrive that I'm sure she thought you'd found yourself a fascinating girl."

He laughed and shook his head. "The only woman I talked to for any length of time, so far as I can remember, was my high-minded cousin Paulina. She and I had the most titillating conversation you can imagine—all about some Christian saint who's buried in Ephesus. It seems he's been

49

breathing in his grave for all of two centuries. There are those who have seen him do it—the ground moves up and down over his head."

He was performing an old ritual. Always, when he came to her from that alien house on the Palatine, he came prepared to lay a victim on the altar of their love. Somebody—the mother, the sister, some illustrious guest who had given distinction to the occasion, some woman famous for her wit or beauty —somebody had to be sacrificed to show that his loyalties to her were his only loyalties, that he had no other ties, no other home.

"They have the most childish legends, the Christians," she said. Usually he chose his victims among those secure in their charm or their dignity; it seemed strange to her that he had taken the sacrificial knife to his inoffensive and insignificant cousin tonight . . . Cyrillus had jumped down from the table with a piece of rind. She would not notice, she would go on talking this aimless talk until the melon and the bread and the wine had been consumed, until the break had been healed and some semblance of peace had settled on the room and he had found an occasion to take her hand.

"Yes, childish legends seem to be making the rounds," he said. "Maesia Publia was telling a story about Isis tonight—she went on to everybody about how Isis kept a certain ship off the reefs. I think it was in the Aegean. She—Isis, I mean, not Maesia—led the navigator away from the rocks with a convenient little orchestra of cymbals and bells."

In the Aegean . . . I crossed the Aegean once, from Cos to Delos, with a cargo of honey and fifty shackled slaves. Say it was some just and reasonable Force that put me on that ship, say anything you like and I will agree, so long as there is peace and confidence again between us, so long as you take my face in your hands and draw my head down on your chest. And if I do not come to you in joy and ardor, as I might have come an hour ago, I will come at least in kindness, with a chastened heart. I will heal you of your evil dream, and you will heal me of mine, and both of us will sleep. . . .

"What fools women are to let themselves be taken in by the priests of these cults—"

"All women are fools, darling, including myself."

"Are you a fool? I never noticed. I always thought—" He stopped and raised himself on his elbow and looked into her eyes. And in an instant the mask of feverish gaiety had fallen away, the eyes were steady and shining, the lips had folded against each other and were making a tentative kiss.

She leaned forward, she was on the point of setting her mouth against his when she heard the scratching at the back of the couch. She tried to disregard it, she tried to keep her eyes serene, but when the cold, damp, hairless little hands padded at the nape of her neck, her whole face went wild. "Don't, don't!" she said at the top of her voice. "Get down, you hateful little creature. Get down and let me alone."

Her plate had slipped from her knees. What she saw on the white rug at her feet—a rind, a crust, and a shuddering, whimpering beast—seemed to her as irreparable and as desolate as a heap of ruins. The words she had uttered in her fright still clanged in her ears. A hateful little creature—she had called Cyrillus a hateful little creature. And Cyrillus was his gift to her, and he loved Cyrillus: "He looked so miserable in the shop, darling, that I couldn't resist him," he had said when he brought him to the house. "He'll settle down in a day or so. Coddle him a little, he needs to be loved."

"He frightened me. I'm sorry. I'm terribly sorry," she said.

Without returning her glance, he knelt on the rug and picked up the clutter. His head was close to her knee, and she touched his hair, weeping, but he did not lift his face.

"Listen, Favorinus—"

"He *is* an annoying little animal. Shall I give him to my sister?"

"No, oh, no, I want him, I love him, it was only that he frightened me out of my wits."

"I'll put him on the couch in the other room."

"Leave him here, darling. Leave him here, he's all right."

"I have to go in there anyway to put out the lamps." He rose, set the plate on the table without looking at her, lifted the monkey by the scruff of the neck, and disappeared through the moss-green drapery. "Cover up the melon or the flies will come in," he said from the other room. "It's late, it must be almost morning. Both of us had better go to sleep."

Chapter 4

HE CAME to the Senate-house late that morning—late and tired and raw from having so little time to cast off the heaviness of his sleep and the warmth of his bed. For some moments he stood just inside the entrance, shivering; the place was cold and uncongenial; the air seemed danker and more penetrating than the fresher chill of the streets. It was half an hour past sunrise, the proceedings were well under way, and he could not bring himself to go down the long aisle to the row of consular benches at the front of the hall. He sank instead into the first empty seat he could find in the rear of the house, sustaining as well as he could the curious glances of his neighbors—Syrians, Arabians, Cappadocians, Cilicians—all new-comers to the Senate, oriental landowners who had bought their rank at a good price from one or another of the eastern adventurers who had snatched and lost the rayed crown.

To hide among the cultivated sycophants on the rear benches would never have occurred to him last night. Last night he had taken for granted that he would arrive on time, would give serious consideration to whatever was being discussed, would even stand up and offer some comment—since he was coming at Decius's request, he could scarcely do less. Yet such behavior seemed impossible, even preposterous to him now. He could only stare at the yellow flame that burned at the front of the hall on the altar before the statue of Victory. He could only try to control his yawning and his shivering and wonder why he had promised to come at all.

It was a dismal place, more dismal than he had allowed himself to remember. The whole interior, poorly lighted and filled with the smoke of the City, was as depressing as the closed chamber of a mausoleum. A long, wan shaft of sunlight, coming in from a high window behind him, encompassed the sacrificial flame and made it ghostly and insubstantial. There was a smell of dampness and stale incense; the blank faces looked as if they had just been exhumed; and even the Emperor, seated in the center of the consular row, was utterly devoid of the presence and power he had had last night. Seen from the back, he was only an old Pannonian general in an ill-draped toga, the decently clipped fringe of greying hair at the nape of his neck pressed in and made a little ridiculous by the crown.

From a spot to the right of the altar of Victory, Valerian, the Dean of the Senate, was addressing the Conscript Fathers, had probably been holding forth for the last half hour on the miserable condition of the military roads in Dacia, Moesia, and Thessaly. And who but an idiot would have crawled out of a comfortable bed, half-dead for sleep, to listen to Valerian? A pink, ponderous, well-scrubbed old man, he had survived a series of civil wars and assassinations, not by means of the charm of a Celestus Falconius, but by an uninvolved and imperturbable calm that made it possible for him to float above all calamities in a safe and roseate cloud of Olympian benevolence. Nobody had ever seen him ruffled; nobody had ever heard him raise his voice. At the moment he was speaking of collapsing bridges and crumbling watchtowers, yes; but that did not interfere in the least with his reassuring gestures or his bland, philanthropic smile. Perhaps the situation might be called grave, he said, but far be it from any of the Conscript Fathers to give way to pessimism. Several committees had already been appointed; construction would begin within a month or two; the sum involved would be tremendous, of course, but no Italians would be taxed, a special levy on the provinces involved would completely cover the cost . . . Stroking the round of white hair that lay like a wreath on his reverend brow, he went on to other matters—an arsenal in Apulum that ought to be enlarged, a string of new storehouses that must be built to hold the Danubian army's grain . . . Somebody had opened the door to clear the stale air, and a draught struck across the young man's shoulders. He shivered and thought how she would be waking now, with all of last night's wretchedness heavy on her heart. And I could have saved her that, he told himself, I could have spared her a conscience-ridden day if I had been there to kiss her out of her sleep. . . .

The plump and heavy-lidded Cappadocian in the seat beside him complained in a whisper about the open door. Only the most timorous newcomer would have bothered to whisper. By now, almost everybody was conversing—the murmur inside was louder than the noises from the busy morning street. Two Syrians across the aisle were going on quite unrestrainedly in their soft, sibilant Latin about certain of the dignitaries in the front row.

"There they are sitting together," one of them said to another.

"Decius's clever ones—the brains of the new regime."

About these "clever ones" Favorinus felt a certain curiosity; two months ago they had been raised to power by the strength of their wits alone; nobody had ever heard their names before. He bent forward, but through the lines of cropped heads and wool-draped shoulders he could see only a gesticulating hand, a shrewd profile, a bent, bald head. The other faction, the conservatives, who sat on the other side of the house, offering up an ostentatious show of attention to their leader Valerian did not interest him in the least. The jaundiced Pontifex Maximus, the suave Urban Prefect, the aristocratic and bored Secretary of the Imperial Treasury—he knew them all, he could see them in his mother's atrium on almost any reception night.

It was useless for him to have come, useless and stupid; the Emperor would never catch sight of him back here among the orientals; he sank back and closed his eyes and saw, for no reason, a vision of the library of Marcellinus's house on a Spring evening—plum blossoms in the vases, the guests sprawling at ease on the couches, and the slave with the white cheeks and the honey-colored hair standing against the white marble wall with a scroll in her hands, reading choruses from Aeschylus in her pure Attic Greek, reading until his loneliness was turned into longing and stirred on his lips. And sometimes, at the end of a strophe, she would look up at him, always with puzzled eyes. It was as if she asked him, "Why should you be sad? You are a free man—what cause have you for pain?"

"Here comes the vote," said his heavy-lidded Cappadocian neighbor. "The Dean of the Senate is calling for the vote."

"What are we supposed to be voting for?"

"A provincial tax, your Illustriousness. A tax to cover the new army installations in Moesia, Dacia, and Thessaly. I'll vote yes—everybody will."

He resented the implied advice. "I know nothing about the matter," he said curtly. "I don't intend to vote at all."

There was a stir around him, a pretense of significant activity while the meaningless vote was being taken. The Conscript Fathers rose one after the other and uttered the expected "Yes." The Urban Prefect conferred with Valerian and Valerian conferred with the Emperor; the "clever ones" rose and talked among themselves, accompanying their talk with gestures too lively and emphatic to be altogether patrician; the recorders went up and down the aisles with their quills and their papyri, nodding and shouting at each other. He shut out the senseless confusion and thought of her again, poignantly, as if he had never possessed her, as if she had never given him anything but a questioning look to brood upon. Friend's slave, friend's woman, the mistress of a thoroughly estimable man who was dying of a painful disease with the utmost patience and dignity—back in the house of

54

Marcellinus that Spring she was precisely the one woman no decent Stoic would have allowed himself to touch. He had not touched her, even when the emaciated hand could no longer reach out and brush her cheek. He had not indulged in whisperings and significant looks, even when the tormented eyes could no longer see. And strangely—very strangely in a world where decency was synonymous with weakness—on the day the will was read he had been paid for his decency. At the foot of the document, scrawled in so unsteady a hand that the procurator had to squint to make it out, there had been a note, written in sane mind and properly authorized: "To Favorinus Herennius, all the Greek works in my library, together with the slave Charis, whom I bought in Delos and educated with as much care as though she had been my own child."

And now they were checking the votes, with a shameful hypocrisy, since everyone knew that nobody would have dared to depart from the prearranged unanimous affirmative. "Carus Ammianus, yes," said the voice of the chief recorder. "Aemilius Anulio, yes. Lucius Domitius Aurelianus, yes." Yes, yes, yes, and the unleavened faces grew duller still with the singsong rhythm of it, and the ancient Victory who had watched the hard and honorable debates of free men for centuries—how could they bear to look her in the face? "Persius Didius, yes. Fortunatus Dolicho, yes." Slaves, he thought, all slaves. He saw it again in the shaken script of the dying Marcellinus—"the slave Charis"—and remembered how his heart had protested against it even in his gratefulness. No man can own another; master and slave are equal in the sight of the Nameless and Bodiless God; to show desire for an enslaved woman is to commit rape upon her, since she cannot refuse her master—so his Stoic teachers had said. But even without them he would have known it. How could he own another being, a being that was alive and unfathomable, a bearer of winged thoughts, a dreamer of mysterious dreams? He had freed her—to everybody's vast amusement, before he had touched her, he had set her free. "Ennius Rubico, yes. Horatius Rusticus, yes." Freedom had found a refuge in her house and his; nobody came there with a prearranged affirmative; he was the inheritor of all the liberal, untrammeled spirits who had once been Marcellinus's guests. "Claudius Vibianus, yes." Slaves, all slaves, with the brand-mark burned into their brains. "Romulus Virgilius—pardon me, you did not vote. Urbanus Vitruvius, yes." Yes, yes, yes indeed. . . .

The stillness that settled on the house at the end of the roll-call was broken by a stirring and a murmuring near the front of the hall—one of the "clever ones" in the first row had thrust up a lean protesting hand.

"Ummidius Pessinus, the new Secretary of Petitions," said the sleepy Cappadocian, more to himself than to his uncommunicative neighbor. "Valerian won't like that. Valerian won't care for that at all."

"Why not?"

"Because, your Illustriousness, the new Secretary of Petitions invariably comes out with all sorts of radical suggestions. Believe it or not—" there was a malicious gleam below the heavy eyelids—"he's said outright that the provincials have been taxed enough. He thinks it's about time more of the revenue was pulled out of Italy."

A brisk exchange was going on in the front of the house. It seemed that the Secretary of Petitions had just returned from the province of Egypt and wished to say a few words to the Conscript Fathers—there were certain pressing matters that ought to be brought to their attention. The Pontifex Maximus asked if it couldn't wait until tomorrow. Valerian thought it might very well wait until tomorrow. No, not tomorrow, today, said Ummidius Pessinus; if the permission of the Dean of the Senate was not forthcoming, he must appeal to the Emperor . . . "Give the floor to Ummidius Pessinus." It was the long remembered voice, the deep, rough voice that had addressed the ancestors with conviction in the atrium of the Herennii last night; and it had the power this morning to give authenticity to the occasion, to dispel recollections and dreams . . . The new Secretary of Petitions had risen and was advancing to the front of the hall without waiting for Valerian's benevolent nod. If there was a trace of aggressiveness in his bearing, he had his reasons: since his appointment to office, everybody had seen fit to remember what had been forgotten for a generation: his grandfather had been born a slave. Turning in front of the altar of Victory, he was waiting for the coughing and the shifting to subside. His person was spare and his face was keen, with a long sharp nose, and a peak of black hair grew down into the middle of his sloping brow. He squeezed a big handkerchief between his hands and looked out on the assembly with dark and surprisingly gentle eyes.

Far be it from him, he said, to drag out the proceedings any longer than necessary. An extra half-hour added to the session was, of course, a great hardship—by noon the Conscript Fathers usually complained that they were dying of starvation. Starvation was an uncomfortable business—nobody liked to starve—not even the Egyptian peasants. *Their* natural if inconvenient distaste for doing eighteen hours of labor on a diet fit for a new-hatched bird had led them to take certain measures which the Senate should know about. With everybody's indulgence, then, he would recount for them a few instances of rebellion that he had seen with his own eyes in the province of Egypt—keeping his report as brief as possible, since he knew how eager they were to get to their eels done in fish sauce. . . .

There was a calculated pause in which even the hostile senators nodded to each other in reluctant approval of the man's brilliance. Whatever one thought of his opinions, one had to admire his eloquence and wit. He was telling of a brief and harried journey across the olive groves of Egypt—How much of the world, Conscript Fathers, had been soothed and nourished for generations by the oil and the fruit? And what of the Egyptian olive groves now? A sorry sight, a very sorry sight. A man could travel for ten miles without encountering another human being; the noblest trees were eaten by armies of ants and strangled by wild vines. The skins that had held the oil lay rotting in heaps under tattered awnings; the limestone basins that had caught the precious drops were cracked or broken—hiding-places for field mice, nesting-places for doves. As for the peasants—all those stolid, patient, child-bearing, mouse-catching, vine-fighting peasants—one looked for them in vain. Five times they had sent their delegations to say to this august assembly that, after they had paid this tax and that tax and the other tax, they had nothing left—nothing—not the wherewithal to buy a loincloth or a jar of salve or a midwife's services or a piece of bacon. Five times they came, and five times we told them it was a just complaint, we would see to it in good time. But the good time was briefer than we thought, Conscript Fathers. The field-mouse and the locust have inherited one-fifth of the olive-land in Egypt. The peasants, unfortunately, are gone. . . .

They were all bending forward, listening. Over their sloping shoulders, Favorinus caught a glimpse of his uncle's back, erect under the graceless folds of the toga, the head high, the nape red below the fringe of hair. The face, he thought, must be as I saw it once some fifteen years ago—red with righteous anger because the steward had pilfered the tip that belonged to the garden slave—the mouth tight, an icy blaze in the pale eyes.

They were not all dead, Ummidius Pessinus was saying. Unfortunately for the magistrates and the centurions who had to keep order in Egypt, the peasants had some life in them still and were making serious trouble in the throes of their last agonies. He had seen hundreds of them, for instance, lying on their faces in the Temple of Horus. They had thrown down their spades, they had no strength left; since their Roman masters had refused to help them, they were submitting the whole matter to the judgment of their god. Incalculable numbers of them had become bandits—he himself had been warned that it was dangerous to travel with less than thirty armed men. If anybody thought he was exaggerating the extent of their misery, he could offer proof—he had noted down a few of the questions that they left with their gods at the rural oracles. He whipped out a little scroll from the folds of linen around his chest and read in a quick, flat, passionless voice: "Will they take my house from me because I cannot pay my taxes?" "When the child is born, shall I expose it?" "Shall I go to the ibis-rock and join the bandits?" "Would it be better to sell my sister or to strangle her?" "When the tax-collectors come, shall I run away or kill myself?"

He paused and squeezed his handkerchief. His eyes stared at the back rows, and it seemed to Favorinus that they had focused on his face. And somehow he could not bear to be looked at. The naked and despairing questions of the Egyptian peasants, flung out in that dry tone, had struck him with an unmanning force; he knew that his mouth was hanging open and that his eyes were expressionless. In his embarrassment he stared down at his knees and saw a series of strange images—a stone basin with a crack across the bottom of it, a stretch of red earth divided by a jagged gap, a crack around the orb of the world. . . .

"A few moments more," said the Secretary of Petitions, "and I'll leave you all in peace. Before I came home, I stopped at the resort town of Canobus in upper Egypt—an amazing city, beautiful, luxurious—if you'll excuse a vulgar expression, I'll call it what the Roman residents call it—the vulva of the world. There was a certain magistrate visiting there, and he did me the honor to invite me to supper. We took the evening meal—some thirty of us—on a little fleet of pleasure boats on the canal. There were Alexandrine dancing-girls to perform for us on the banks; our heads were continually being pelted with roses; our conversation, such as it was, was drowned out by fifty flutes. Seven oxen were slaughtered for that feast—seven oxen, and I have seen the children of the poor claw at each other's faces over a piece of rotten bacon in a garbage heap. The carcasses of the oxen were sheer waste, of course—we Romans have no taste for beef—my host was interested only in the hearts. The Egyptian peasants may be dying of starvation, but we, Conscript Fathers—we must have our ox-hearts—seven of them—stuffed with mussels and simmered in wine."

There was a burst of clapping. Everybody applauded the brilliant style, the telling images, the surprising and witty turns of the sentences—everybody but Favorinus Herennius, who sat staring rather stupidly at the floor, with his hands crossed on his knees. I must not speak of this to her, he told himself. If I make myself responsible for the questions they ask at the Egyptian oracles on the grounds that I have eaten figs grown under glass, fish out of season, rolls in the shape of butterflies—if I say to her that the meat we throw to one of our hounds would fill the hollow bellies of two or three who lie in the Temple of Horus, then the old argument will begin again and tonight there will be no love and tomorrow there will be no peace . . . Once in his student days he had tried to strip himself of everything except the stark necessities. He had cleared his room of the statues and pillows and embroidered hangings; he had worn no gold or purple but the marks of his patrician rank; he had refused to eat at his mother's table; he had nourished himself on Stoic fare—bread, honey, water-and-wine. But, after three or four months of such rigid discipline, he had abandoned the project—not because, as his mother said, he had begun to appreciate meat and cushions, only because it had seemed to him that he was morbidly preoccupied with the state of his own spirit, only because he had suspected his ecstasy of being a spurious ecstasy. And if I were to do it again, he thought, if I were to do it again because hundreds of thousands have nothing to eat, it would still be a meaningless exercise whose only purpose was to sooth my conscience. If I were to live on roots and water and walk the streets in a loincloth made of sacking, the peasants of Egypt would still go unfed. . . .

Something strange was happening to the applause. It had died down to a few desultory bursts of clapping, and now it was rising again in calculated, thunderous waves. The Cappadocian nudged him gently and nodded toward the consular bench. "Our lord and our master is going to address us," he said.

The Emperor Decius had risen from his seat in the middle of the front row and was laying aside his purple cloak and his rayed crown. Part of the applause was in recognition of this gesture of respect to the august assembly: unlike his eastern predecessors, who had sat in all their imperial trappings on a kind of throne beside the altar of Victory, he always stood before them in his toga—"A Roman among Romans, a Senator addressing his peers," somebody said. But the assumption of antique republican equality was only a gesture, nothing more; and his nephew, watching from the back of the Senate-house, knew as much. They all leaned forward too eagerly as he took his place before the ghostly flame; the peremptory bearing of the military commander was too evident under the ill-draped folds of white and purple woolen; the red mark of the crown, a stern reminder, still burned too plainly on his bald brow. "Conscript Fathers—" It was the same archaic formula that Ummidius Pessinus had used with such devastating irony, but it came out of Decius's mouth like a rap across the knuckles. It was as if he had shouted at them, "Remember what your name means and what you are here for." And, hurled out into the midst of the clapping, it was not an altogether auspicious beginning. The scions of the high houses in the front of the hall looked startled and offended; the Gauls and Spaniards who occupied the middle section stared dubiously down at their own laps; and the outlanders in the back, whose departed patrons had worn the purple with more flourish, cast each other small secretive glances, tight little smiles.

Those smiles, those glances—they stirred up too many painful remembrances—the young man shifted in his seat and covered his eyes. So, in the old days when the Decii still visited the atrium of the Herennii, he had seen his mother and father smirking at each other, amused over the fact that the old general had misnamed the vintage or started to serve himself, forgetting the slave that stood behind his couch. Have I changed so little as that? he asked himself. Do I still feel it with the helplessness of a child—the old affront, the pity and the rage that the lion should be worried by a pack of dogs, the desperate and useless allegiance? But I am no longer a child, I need not hold my peace—why have I hidden myself? How can I permit him to think that I gave him a false promise? Why am I not in the consular row, showing him at least one pair of honest and encouraging eyes?

"Conscript Fathers, you have heard bad news this morning. You have heard alarming news about the peasant population of Egypt and even more alarming news about the condition of our military installations on the northern frontier. As a matter of fact, for months and even years to come you will be hearing bad news. I came to the purple in an unpropitious hour—Goths to the north, Persians to the east, poverty in the south, mutiny in the west. I have nothing to offer you but repeated reminders of your adversities."

59

He knew the style and the source of it. The spare vocabulary, the straightforward, old-fashioned march of the sentences came straight out of Livy—that same Livy who had been read aloud in a stern and passionless voice in the house on the Esquiline. And it bored them, it even piqued them —it was as if he had asked them all to supper and served them sour home-made wine and beans and black bread. Even his chief adherents were hard put to it to keep their faces in order. In the little group of conservatives there were several frozen smiles, and one of the "clever ones" could not re-frain from turning all the way round in his seat to see whether the in-difference could be as vast as he feared it must be.

"Unfortunately for the peasants of Egypt, we must look to first things first. *Their* desperate business must be postponed for yet another month—we will consider it in detail at a later session. Meanwhile, we must ponder it, we must strive to find a way—all of us—this is every senator's responsibility. Today we have agreed—lightly, I am afraid, and after a very brief period of consideration—to lay yet another tax on the northern provinces, to demand yet another sacrifice of the hard-pressed people of Dacia, Moesia, and Thes-saly. . . ."

Their faces were blank again; their shoulders were sagging, it was so wearisome, it was so disheartening, they had heard it all so many times be-fore. It was late, they were hungry, they had fancied half an hour ago that they were finished with the Moesians, Dacians, and Thessalonians, and now the old man had wound himself up—if he finished in half an hour, they could congratulate themselves. Since it was the Lord of the World who ad-dressed them, they did not dare to pass the time in conversation. But they were almost ostentatious in their inattention: they shifted in their seats, pared their nails, yawned, sighed.

Almost imperceptibly, but certainly not without intent—since nothing chance or casual could come out of that stern mouth in that iron voice—the direction of the speech had changed. He had pointed out in fairly short order that a very hard measure had just been enacted here: during the com-ing winter, Dacians, Moesians, and Thessalonians would pay for it, not with the sale of emeralds or villas but by consuming less bacon, fewer loaves of bread. With increasing emphasis—the veins on his neck and fore-head were painfully visible now—he was dwelling on another sort of in-justice that was being perpetrated against the civil population all along the northern frontier.

It was the legionaries, he said—and a few of the dreamers started up at the explosive way in which he flung out the word—it was their own Roman legionaries who were ruining these provincials. Taxes, even the most op-pressive taxes, had this to be said in their favor: a man had time to save for them; they were imposed without brutality or malice by the impersonal hand of the law. But the depredations of the legionaries were arbitrary and capricious—a farmer whose year's living depended on his barley field might waken one morning to find that his whole crop had been confiscated by the Tribune of Supplies. Horses were stolen out of the stables; visiting officers moved into the houses of decent citizens, insulting and even assaulting their hosts; slaves were borrowed and never returned; provincial virgins were dealt with like prostitutes under their fathers' eyes. And all these crimes were carried out with unbelievable arrogance. It had come to such a pass that the northern provincials might very well ask themselves who made the worse masters—the legionaries or the Goths.

An old story, a burdensome story, and all of them found it hard to hear it with patience, thrown out as it was in its nakedness, without even the trappings of eloquence. For almost a century now the legions had been ravaging the border provinces. What else could be expected? How else could they be fed? The only alternative would be such unthinkable innovations as only the "clever ones" would be crazy enough to consider—a complete change in the system of supply, governmental expenditure on an unprecedented scale to keep the Danubian army furnished with cloaks and horses, grain and onions, wine and meat. What was the point of mentioning the trouble if you could not mend it? How could it be mended without imposing backbreaking taxes on Italy—even on Rome itself? And who would think of taxing himself, his relatives, his friends, his senatorial peers so that some farmer near Carnuntum could reap his barley crop in peace?

Who but the Emperor Decius? thought Favorinus Herennius, flushed, breathless, leaning far forward, unwilling to miss one of the stiff and angry gestures, one flash of the icy eyes. Into the shocked silence that had settled over the Senate house, he was hurling one unbelievable pronouncement after another: Henceforth the Imperial Treasury would assume the burden of supplying the legions, henceforth the people of Dacia, Moesia, and Thessaly would, in return for the oppressive taxes that had been put upon them so casually this day, possess the poor remnants of their belongings in peace. He was speaking of Italian indifference and Roman self-indulgence. He was speaking in terms that conjured up the frightening possibility of a censorship. He was shouting at these exquisite patricians, these cultivated Gauls and Spaniards, these dreamy orientals as he might have shouted at a demoralized cohort from the rostrum of a camp. And the spectacle was exhilarating, magnificent.

If he had not been carried off by his emotion, it was hard to say how long he might have held them all amazed and powerless. But under the pressure of his excitement—his nephew realized it with a sudden sinking of the heart—he was departing from his staid and measured style, his old-fashioned eloquence was falling apart. The language of the camp, harsh and realistic to the point of brutality, was breaking through. A weakness, a palpable weakness in an assembly of skilled rhetoricians—and they seized upon it and recovered themselves. Their eyebrows went up at the traces of his northern dialect; they smirked at the cacophonous word, the rural simile; they rocked back and forth with the rhythm—as persistent and monotonous as an Aethiopian drum. There was no need to reckon with his message. Whenever it was mentioned, they could discredit it by quoting some choice phrase from the barracks, some metaphor that smelled of Pannonian turnips and hay.

Dogs, hounds at the lion's throat, and nobody to help him. Ummidius Pessinus was wringing his handkerchief; the Secretary of the Imperial Treasury was examining his thumbnail; the Pontifex Maximus was making signals of despair at Valerian. Not that Valerian saw him. Nothing—not the brutal sentences themselves, not the signs of nerveless consternation in the front row—had been able to penetrate his roseate aura of benevolent optimism. And the idiot might have been able to save the situation if only he had kept his wits about him. He could be on his feet before the Emperor sat down, he could propose a vote of agreement on the whole substance of the speech, he could restate that substance in such florid, tricked-up terms that nobody would be able to recall one unfortunate phrase of the regrettable original. . . .

The regrettable original was plunging toward its end. The Emperor Decius was finishing off his speech as objectionably as any of them could have hoped, and the Senate was bracing itself for the customary five rounds of applause. Would nobody stand up? Not the Secretary of Petitions? Not the Pontifex Maximus? Not the Dean of the Senate? Then, he thought, I myself. . . .

But, once he was out of his seat, once he was standing at the back of the house with all their curious faces turned in his direction, it seemed to him that he had committed himself to do the impossible, that he would have to sit down again, in spite of the flash of recognition and gratefulness that came to him from the pale and icy eyes. It was not only his usual morbid shyness in the face of any public display; it was actual shame over the crass and tawdry thing he was about to do. To take the decent iron of Decius's speech and dabble it with a thin wash of gilt, to plaster it all over with green and purple glass stones . . . "Conscript Fathers," he said, and his voice faltered. Decius signaled Valerian, and Valerian gave the speaker the entire house with a broad gesture and a patronizing nod. "His nephew—the old man's nephew," somebody said. "Celestus Falconius's son—the last of the Herennii."

And suddenly his voice was coming out of him as smooth and mellow as honey sliding out of a jar. In exotic similes and far-fetched allegories, with complicated clausal harmonies and amazing terminal flourishes, in all the glittering trappings of fashionable oratory, he was repeating, to his own surprise, everything that Decius had said. Something—perhaps their startled attention, perhaps the discovery of an unsuspected power in himself—was beginning to dissolve the embarrassment and the pain. He was even taking a certain equivocal pleasure in it now: his voice was growing stronger and more ingratiating by the moment, his gestures were at once more graceful and more vigorous; the game was going to his advantage—every throw of the dice was better than the last . . . How long it took him to accomplish the stratagem, he did not know—longer, certainly, than he had intended—the exquisite and elaborate structure of the sentences took possession of him, bore him on and on. When he rounded off the final period, there was a moment in which they saw what sort of trick had been played upon them, a moment of silence in which their exasperation with his maneuver struggled with their admiration for his eloquence. Then the connoisseurs of rhetoric among them led a general burst of applause, and he bowed and seated himself, flushed with exhilaration. "Magnificent, your Illustriousness," said his Cappadocian neighbor. And suddenly a revulsion of feeling—against himself, against his speech, against the whole cheap exhibition—overwhelmed him, so that he almost laughed in the man's face.

While the remaining business dragged to its dreary conclusion, he made a conscious effort to take hold of himself. His knees were shaking, and two runnels of sweat had started from his armpits and were trickling down his sides. His head ached, and he was vaguely sick at the stomach, probably because he had taken nothing for breakfast but a handful of dried fruit. Her slave will make me a dish of eggs and asparagus, he thought. She'll sit at the table and talk with me while I eat, and I'll tell her how I got up and—But it suddenly occurred to him that his insane exploit on the floor of the Senate was the last thing in the world that the two of them could talk about in peace. It would be better to go first to the baths, he told himself, starting toward the entrance and responding mechanically to congratulatory murmurs and smiles. Half an hour of swimming in the cold pool would wash away the sweat, would put the necessary division between this strange and unaccountable experience and the usual concerns of their life together. It was early, it was only an hour past noon, and he would wait to go to her until he could talk about the banquet she was going to give next week, the reading that was to take place tomorrow at Berosus's house, the picture Antisthenes had sold to Orbiana, Memphius's role in the next pantomime. . . .

But as he stepped out of the dark building into the blinding post-meridian sun, somebody plucked at his toga. A black Aethiopian hand, rubbed to a high polish with oil of roses, held respectfully but firmly onto the fold of cloth. "I have a message for the lord Favorinus Herennius from the Emperor of All the Romans—"

"From Decius?"

"Yes, my lord and my master. There is a litter waiting for you at the back of the Senate-house—"

"But I have no need of a litter, I'm only going a little distance, as far as the baths—"

"No . . ." The thick lips curved in the sly and triumphant smile which slaves could seldom suppress when it was made evident to them that even free men are not always free. "The lord Favorinus cannot go to the baths at the moment. The Emperor his uncle expects him at the palace. The lord Favorinus is to come with me to my master, to eat the noonday meal at the imperial table."

"Are you certain?"

"Oh, yes, quite certain," the Aethiopian said.

Chapter 5

THE EMPEROR Decius dismissed his train in the garden and hurried alone up the marble stairs. On certain days– and this was one of them—the pressure of the crowd seemed intolerable; neither the arrows of the Goths nor the missiles flung by the war-engines of Philip the Arabian had ever harassed him like the mute requests and conflicting demands in his followers' eyes. Even when the door was shut on the crowd that had come with him from the Senate, their silent clamoring pursued him. And I must put it out of my mind, he thought. In a quarter of an hour, I must know what is to pass between him and me. . . .

The imperial slaves knew what sort of humor their master was in. His two blond body-servants, twin sons of an Alemannic chieftain, held out the basin of scented water and the towel without a word or a smile; and his steward, an emaciated Syrian eunuch, silently tasted and silently handed him his goblet of chilled wine. At prescribed intervals, near the gigantic green columns, the Aethiopian bodyguards stood half-naked and motionless, like black leopards under tropical trees. The Emperor Philip had remodelled this atrium according to his own lights—all the decorous protests of seven Roman architects had not been strong enough to argue him out of his dream of an oasis carved in stone. The granite broke into thick foliage at the tops of the columns, the walls were lined with sand-colored marble, the gilt on the ceiling shone like a desert sun. Under this colonnade the Empress Severa, hearing of the murder at Verona, had rent the stillness with the cry of a cockatoo. Over to this bench they had carried the body of the little Arab princeling—home at last from the camp of the Praetorian Guards —home, with his head dangling and his tongue hanging out—

He would not think of that. He handed the goblet back to the eunuch and thought instead of the old, salutary formula: Good out of evil, order out of chaos, peace out of blood. . . .

"Is there any other way in which I can serve my lord and my master?"

"You know we're to have a guest at the noonday meal?"

"Yes, your nephew, the lord Favorinus Herennius. I took him up to the library."

"Very well, keep him up there for a quarter of an hour," he said, "and then send him down here to me."

"Down here, my lord and my master?"

He followed the steward's shocked glance along the vast reaches of the atrium, and for the first time he noticed that the furniture had been carried out. Greek statues, hydraulic organs, carved chairs inlaid with ivory, cushions and drapes, tables of citronwood and couches of cedarwood—everything but a couple of marble benches was gone. Tomorrow in the Forum the auctioneer would offer them all to the highest bidder—the platter from which the Emperor Philip and the Empress Severa had eaten their fish, the bolster on which the little Caesar Julius Philippus had slept—these and all the trappings of oriental tyranny, the three hundred slaves, the ten tame deer, the fifty peacocks, the brace of tiger cubs. In the Forum tomorrow they would see that the Emperor had launched his austerities in his own house, would hear the bawling voice of the auctioneer proclaiming that every denarius was earmarked for the Imperial Treasury.

"Perhaps my lord and my master and his guest would be more comfortable up in the library—"

"No." He was not ashamed of this honorable bareness—let the young man see the room stripped down to the walls. "Here, as I said, in a quarter of an hour."

He turned on his heel and began to pace the length of the atrium, past one after another of the black bodies stationed against the stony palms. Ask him outright. Say, "Henceforth forestall the kind of spectacle I made of myself this morning. Write all my speeches for me, trick out my thoughts in the gimcracks that will make them more acceptable to fools." To anybody else, he could have made such a request with no hesitation. But this young man was different; nothing but the exigency of this morning's situation could have driven him to such a tawdry performance. Nor was it possible to wish him more pliable. Turning at the end of the colonnade, he had a vision of the two childish faces—his son's and his nephew's—looking at him across the dining room table in the little house on the Esquiline. His son

Herennius—mild, easily persuaded—the brow smooth under the soft fall of blond hair, the blue eyes respectful and credulous, the pure mouth always quiet, always at peace. And the other one—forever restless and passionately seeking—sighting behind every duty another more stringent duty, behind every truth a still more imperative truth, never able to rest on any moral authority, never able to quell the rebellion within.

One of them was where the gods, his country, and his father expected him to be—in Dacia, in the bleak autumnal northland, strengthening the Danubian line against the inroads of the Goths. The other was in Rome, doing only the gods knew what—writing some useless book, making love to a Greek freedwoman, talking the fine-spun nonsense of the Stoics with poets and philosophers and such. Yet the thought of the son making his dangerous journeys of inspection along the Danube roused only the tenderness one feels for what is close, familiar, predictable. And that other one among the scrolls up there in the library—to think of him was to feel again the old excitement before the unfolding mystery.

Put it to him outright . . . He turned at the end of the atrium and began to pace back again under the shadowy, tropical colonnade. But how shall I begin? he asked himself. How did Philip the Arabian begin with me when he and I walked up and down this same green colonnade four years ago? He remembered the dark arm thrust through his, the persistent scent of sandalwood on the eastern robes, the sleepy sidelong glance, the lazy voice issuing from the sensuous lips: "Let me make you my Urban Prefect, Decius. My City Guard is out of hand again. Half of them are arrogant Italians—they say they'll not put up with a Syrian Prefect any more. You have everything that's needed—a genius for enforcing discipline, a good white northern face, a very respectable name." But that sort of beginning, he thought, would never serve with Favorinus Herennius; he would only waste time disparaging his own abilities. . . .

"Considering the present crisis at home and abroad . . ." He was not actually thinking. He was staring down at the floor at his feet—one vast mosaic of a desert hunting scene—lions and jackals in their death-agonies or in futile flight. Philip the Arabian had always taken an excessive and somewhat vulgar pride in showing off this mosaic to his visitors: "Here, Decius, look over here. Three cubes of red in the lion's neck and one on the ground—blood, you know, that's blood." There had been blood at Verona—fratricidal blood on the battlefield, a growing splotch of blood on the towel that held the cleft head. And the little Arab prince who used to trail after his father in purple shoes, yawning at his father's enthusiasms and blushing at his father's vulgarity—blood had trickled from his nose and lips. The imperial slaves still tried to outdo each other describing how his corpse had looked when the Guardsman had carried him in—the rope still around his neck, his tongue hanging purple out of his mouth, his eyes popping out of his head. . . .

"The illustrious Favorinus Herennius," said the resigned voice of the steward.

So soon? Decius asked himself, stepping out into the middle of the atrium and watching the young man approach through alternating bands of shadow and sun. The diffident bearing, the rueful look showed plainly that he was still uneasy over the morning's exploit. Well, praise him, praise him, the Emperor thought, holding out his arms to indicate that the kiss of greeting would be welcome. Praise him for his performance and ask him outright . . . For the first time in nine years, he held the young man in his arms, and the sparely-fleshed shoulder-blades under his hands called up so many recollections that he had to control his face.

"Until you stood up at the back of the Senate house, I thought you hadn't come."

It was not at all what he had intended to say. He drew off, took his nephew firmly by the elbow, and led him toward one of the marble benches placed against the sand-colored wall in the shadow of the colonnade.

"I'll have to admit that I came late to the session, my uncle. Yesterday, between the games and—anyway, yesterday was a maddening day. It must have been close to morning before I fell asleep."

"No matter, no matter." He sat down on the bench and tapped the veined yellow marble to show Favorinus that he might seat himself. "You came, and you made a magnificent showing—"

"Did I?" The eyes—grey, luminous, searching—looked him straight in the face.

"There was something to be done, and you did it." He lowered his glance, he stared at the reddish vein branching over the stone.

"Yes, I suppose so. And yet it seemed to me afterward that I had done it at some cost—not to myself—I mean to the decency and honesty of what you said."

"That's immaterial."

"Is it?"

"I think so. Look, I have certain things to say to them, and their acceptance of those things is essential to the well-being of the State. Under the circumstances, what form those things are cast in makes no difference. My only concern is to have them put in a way that'll make them acceptable. And that takes schooling—art—a natural gift for language." What was the use of temporizing? "After your performance this morning, it occurred to me that you, yourself—"

"I?"

For an instant they looked at each other, and he knew that he had spoken too soon. Fear, incredulity, utter rejection were all in the young man's glance. "Yes, you. Why shouldn't it be you?"

"But I have no gift for politics. My uncle knows me—my whole nature is utterly unsuited to it."

68

"Why? Were you born incurably lazy?"

It had been intended as a jest, but he answered it in pained gravity. "No, I think I work well enough. I've even been known to work diligently, provided I work alone."

"Well, what else does a person need besides a reasonable amount of application and intelligence?"

"But there *is* something else. The gentlemen up in the front row with you this morning—they have it, but I don't and never will. Surely you know what I mean, my uncle." The eyes sought his again and got no answer. "It's a—how can I describe it?—a kind of plausibility—"

It was an ungracious word, a cruel word, and it struck fire in him. "Plausibility" implied duplicity, and his exasperation was such that he quite lost track of what the young man was saying. Completely unaware of the affront that he had given, he was going on about his incapacity for hiding his feelings, for expressing himself in carefully chosen terms, for making the necessary compromises. Stoic drivel, the Emperor thought, the sort of cant that the philosophers hand down from their airy thrones above the world. Carry it into life, carry it into battle, carry it into the Senate, and see what becomes of it—

"Am I to take it that you're more pure-minded than anybody who was sitting in the front row this morning?" he said.

"Not pure-minded." The cheek under the dark stubble turned red. "Probably only squeamish. Say I have a weak spirit in the sense that some men have weak stomachs. Say I vomit up what anybody else could digest. Those games that we gave for my father yesterday, for instance—they literally made me sick. I feel responsible for every one of the dead."

The truth behind the truth, the duty beyond the duty—the years had not changed him, he was pursuing the always-receding boundaries still. And it would do no good to shout at him; one could only tone down one's voice, one could only hold the fleeting spirit static long enough to explain. "But you're confusing yourself, Favorinus, if you think those dead gladiators are a matter for your private conscience. Write it up to the conscience of the State."

"I'm sorry, I don't understand, it seems to me—"

"Wait, wait, let me explain. In times like this, a man must have a double conscience—a private one and a public one—otherwise he'll go out of his head. The world as it is and the very state of being human—I've learned that they're tolerable only if we keep our private and public consciences apart. Your games, for instance—if you lay them on your private conscience, they'll naturally be more than you can bear. But if you step away from them, if you try to see them from the point of view of the State, they're something else. For Rome, for Romans as a whole, those games, brutal and hideous as they seem, are all for the best. For eight hundred years they've been putting iron into our blood—they've taught the plebes to respect the gods and the ancestors—generations of future legionaries have watched them and bet on them and walked away from them with a high contempt for death. No, the games that you gave for your father are no concern of your private conscience, any more than the dead that I left on the field at Verona are any concern of mine. Whatever's done for the State and adds up to the well-being of the State is on nobody's conscience. You're tormenting yourself unnecessarily."

There was a long and disquieting silence. He looked up and saw that the thin jaw was set in an obstinate line, that the grey eyes, drained of all expression, were staring at a moted shaft of sun.

"Isn't that so, Favorinus?" It was a general's voice, commanding the assent of a centurion.

"The Stoics say otherwise. According to the Stoics, every member of the State is personally responsible for all the acts of the State," he said.

"The Stoics!" Try as he would, he could not keep the scorn and impatience out of his voice. "Lucky for Rome, then, that it wasn't a Stoic who led the superior forces at Verona—wasn't it, my boy? If I had been a Stoic, if I had listened to my private conscience, the hundred and twenty millions who live in the Empire would be in a pretty pass today—"

"That much is perfectly true, my master and my lord."

It was lip service, nothing more—the remote grey gaze was still fixed on the dusty sunlight. A nameless restlessness was upon the Emperor now, he could not sit quiet any longer, he rose and walked back and forth in front of the bench, passing and re-passing the expressionless eyes. "Philip the Arabian—may he walk in peace with the gods forever!—Philip the Arabian was my lord and my master, my patron and my friend," he said. And, having said so much, he was driven to say the rest—all of it, without sparing himself. "I rose to power because he loved me as one outlander loves another. I ate at his table, I gave his wife and his son the kiss of greeting. When the burdens of the Empire were too much for him, he used to put his clammy hand on my arm—it was as if he drew a kind of strength out of my body—he trusted me with an unshakable trust."

The young man on the bench made a strange gesture, an opening and lifting of the hands. Pity, the Emperor thought, let him keep his pity. The just man is duly cleansed of the blood of his sacrificial victims by the just gods. "Did you ever see him during those last months when he was going to pieces? No, of course not, you never went to the Senate, you were busy with other matters, you were discussing the condition of your soul with your learned friends. But I saw him—all day long and half the night I saw him—I tell you, Favorinus, I could smell the sweat of his terror in my sleep. Everything went wrong, the gods were against him—threats from the Persians, riots and famines, trouble with the Carpi, raids on the northern cities by the Goths. And when he was told that the Illyrian legions had mutinied and chosen another Emperor, he came into the Senate house like a sleepwalker—he unclasped the purple and let it fall behind him—he actually took off his crown—"

"I know that, my uncle. Occupied as I was with matters you would consider trivial, I knew, like everybody else in Rome, that he had lost hold on himself and was utterly unfit to reign."

"So my public conscience told me. My public conscience prompted me to let him throw away his crown and go back to the tents of his fathers to live out the rest of his life in peace. But my private conscience interfered: Save the crown for your patron, insure the purple for your friend and his son and his son's son—that was what my private conscience said. And I listened to my private conscience—fool that I was, I listened. I stood up in the Senate and told him to take heart—the pretender to the purple was a phantom and would melt away like a phantom—in a week or two, the legionaries would do away with him themselves. And when it happened as I said it would, he was convinced that the gods had given me omniscience, and nothing would serve but that I should go posthaste to Illyria and restore his favor with the northern provincials, and strike the terror of his name into the mutineers—"

The spare patrician hand reached out, stopped him in his pacing. "I assure you," the young man said, meeting his look steadily, "I believe what everybody else in the Empire believes, even my uncle's most inveterate enemies. I know that my lord and my master came into power with far cleaner hands than any of his predecessors who reached for the purple—"

"Reached for the purple?" It was a harsh phrase, an intolerable phrase, more wounding than "plausibility." "Understand, once and for all time, that I never reached for the purple. The purple was thrust upon me by two Illyrian legions at the point of the sword. They were starved, ravening dogs, those legionaries. They had killed their phantom, they were through with Philip, and they settled on me. In the middle of the night they dragged me out of my tent and told me to take my choice: I could march back with them against the greasy Arab or they would send him my head in a basket and choose somebody else in my place. Your friends the Stoics, of course, would automatically have chosen an honorable death. But your Stoics have nothing to worry about except their precious virtue. It was different with me—I had to think of the shambles I would leave behind. If I had given my honorable head to be honorably chopped off with an ax, twenty weak pretenders would have risen in twenty camps, there would have been a dozen battles, some fifty thousand would have died. Believe what you like, it was for the sake of the Empire that I accepted the purple. It was for the sake of the Empire that I marched back with them and took up arms against him at Verona. It was for the sake of the Empire that the four thousand left on that battlefield met their deaths. If they murdered him in his camp because they were afraid I would let him go, that was not my doing. If the Praetorians strangled his son, that was not my doing, either—I would have saved him if I could. Whatever I did was done for the good of the State, and the State has profited by it. If the State is at peace, I am at peace."

And yet, as he began to pace back and forth again, it seemed to him that the young man must be thinking: Why have you told it all from beginning to end, why are you at such great pains to justify yourself? Now that his own voice had ceased to resound in the colonnade, the whole atrium seemed oppressively still. The Aethiopians—he had forgotten the Aethiopians—had transformed their faces into black masks of imperviousness, and the door-keeper stood like a figure in stone with his face toward the door.

"If I am willing to chalk up all that to the conscience of the State," he said, suddenly seeing where the whole harangue had led and wondering how he had lost sight of its purpose, "if I can live with myself after all that passed between me and the Arabian, then you'll admit it's difficult for me to see how the writing of a few speeches in a questionable style would be more than you could bear. Are you really afraid you might sully your soul?"

"Yes—call it that, if you like. My soul—my paltry soul."

"I'm to understand then that you mean to keep clear of the whole mess? Let the world go where it will—is that it?—so long as you and your soul are at peace."

The young man flushed and looked down at the bench. Slowly, deliberately, like a child trying to avoid the eye of a chiding pedagogue, he ran the tip of his finger along the edge of it. "I haven't seen my position quite like that," he said at last. "But I suppose it's a fairly accurate statement."

"Listen, Favorinus," he said, sitting down on the bench and laying his hand over his nephew's wandering fingers. "You deceive yourself if you think for an instant that you or anybody else will be able to keep clear of the thing that hangs over our heads. This is a vast Empire—the world has never seen the like of it before, and the chaos would be terrible beyond conception. Imagine how it would be with twenty pretenders to the purple in arms against each other—the windows of every house boarded up against arrows, no crops because nobody goes into the fields, the rivers crowded with floating corpses. Great wars and little wars would cross and collide with each other—the citizens would murder the magistrates, the legionaries would ravage one place after another—the roads would be impassible because of the bandits. One after another the provinces would fall away— Armenia and Mesopotamia to the Persians—Thessaly, Moesia, Dacia to the Goths. Africa—if we lost Africa, the gods themselves couldn't succor the City. Three months without the African corn-ships and we eat our dogs and cats—three more months, and we die. The calamity would be such that it would be better not to survive it. If the Empire falls apart, there'll be such chaos as there hasn't been since the beginning of the world—"

He stopped because the hand under his was clutching the edge of the bench. The times have made augurs of all of us, he thought. All of us have seen the ominous spots on the liver of the world—everybody is afraid. . . .

"If it's as you say, my uncle, then isn't it beyond all mending?"

"No, not by any means." He had gone too far, and to undo the damage he assumed a soldierly heartiness. "I've staked my life—literally, Favorinus—on the conviction that much can be done."

"What, my lord and my master?"

"Turn Romans back into Romans. Make us what we were in the ancient days, when a mere handful of us inherited the best of the world. Reform our manners. Revive the antique virtues—the patriotism and the piety. Cleanse the City, restore the provinces, discipline the legionaries, teach the Conscript Fathers to make the laws again, reawaken in everybody—plebes, equestrians, patricians—a readiness for self-sacrifice. Much can be done, everything can be done with the help of the gods."

"May the gods be on hand to help you, my uncle. If you're to accomplish such things as that, you'll certainly need the help of the gods."

It was impious, it was even a little impudent, but he let it pass. "There are still a few antique Romans among us, Favorinus," he said.

"Excuse me, my uncle, I would like to believe you. But those fifty thousand howling like animals in the amphitheater yesterday—is there one in a hundred of them capable of devotion?"

"Capable of devotion? Look at them and you'll see that they're wallowing in devotion. Give them a single conviction, give them the ravings of a Phrygian mystic or a crucified Jew and they'll do anything—starve themselves, maim themselves, crawl up and down the temple steps to please Isis, die by the score in the arena at Lyons for Jesus's sake. They're sick, I tell you, with unspent devotion. The ones that are drained of every trace of hope—they're precisely the ones who can give themselves over to a new belief. Ask the priests of Isis how many are willing to pay out their last denarius to buy flowers for the temple. Ask the priests of Mithras how many clamor to hand over their fortunes so that their filthiness can be washed away in a bath of bull's blood. Ask a Christian bishop what sort of soul-starved wretches creep to the basilicas and the cemeteries to nourish their emptiness on the body and blood of the crucified Jew. Those priests, those bishops, those crazy mystics—they're wise, Favorinus, they're a great deal wiser than we have been these last two hundred years. Their ranks are swollen because they offer belief to the unbelieving. And we've offered nothing—only skepticism and contempt—contempt for themselves, contempt for the State, contempt for the gods—"

He paused, knowing that, for the first time, he had caught up the elusive, fleeting spirit and was bearing it with him. The eyes were bright, almost feverish in their attentiveness. So in the old days, stirred by the heroic tales of Livy . . . His hand was too heavy on his nephew's fingers. He lightened the pressure and hurried on.

"I am a pious man," he said, and his voice shook because it had been years since he had spoken from the hidden core of his being. "I am a pious man, and I'll tell you—even though I know that you're tainted with the general skepticism—I have an unshakable conviction that I was not sent without purpose into this world. I believe I was chosen by the gods to carry the old, tried faith back to the unbelievers. If I am to have the purple for as much as five years, I will bring good out of evil, order out of chaos, peace out of blood."

"How? How, my lord and my master?"

"My remedies will be harsh ones. The canker that eats us can't be purged away. I mean to cut it out at the core."

"Yes, certainly, but how, my uncle?"

He had not meant to name his remedy. The idea of the censorship had come into his mind for the first time after the battle of Verona, and for weeks he had kept it as a kind of holy secret, had mentioned it only to the two advisers closest to his heart—Ummidius Pessinus and Valerian. Yet, since the rumor of it had somehow leaked out, the young man might take his silence to mean bad faith or limited trust.

"What you heard in the Senate this morning—that was nothing, those were stop-gap measures," he said. "Reform in Egypt, reform in Moesia and Dacia, reform in the legions—that's not enough. Rome itself is the source of the whole disease. The provincials starve and the legionaries march in tattered shoes—but we have our Alexandrine dancing-girls, our fish-sauces, our pantomimes. Well, we shan't be having them much longer. Nobody'll have them—not even the Metelli and the Glabrii. I'll lay such taxes on luxuries that those who have any concern for their fortunes will be glad to eat boiled pork out of pottery dishes. Maybe it'll take time, maybe it'll be a year or more before they resign themselves to the fact that they'll have to live like Romans. But they'll learn, they'll learn eventually, and in the meantime we'll have the taxes and the fines—more Egyptians will be pulled back to their fields with the promise of decent wages for their labor, more legionaries will be fed. In a word, Favorinus, I intend to revive an old republican office. We're going to have a censor—a magistrate to limit our expenditures and examine our morals. The first thing I'll ask of you is a new version of the speech I mean to make to the Conscript Fathers, asking them to give us a censorship—"

And now he fell silent because he sensed that the fleeting spirit had seceded. His high and holy dream was not enough. "A censorship?" said Favorinus after attenuated silence. And it was as if he had said, "Is that all you have to offer?"

"A real censorship, if it was rigorously administered—" His voice was unsteady. He was more wounded than affronted, and he straightened and withdrew his hand.

"Excuse me, my uncle—as I said a while ago, in the field of politics I'm

74

abysmally ignorant. But won't the intelligent people, the enlightened people, find the idea of a censorship—well, somewhat ridiculous? Won't they connect it with the worst part of our past, with all the narrowness and bigotry of Cato? A public office to pry into our private lives, to tell us what to eat and what to wear and how to conduct ourselves—in a society as complicated and various as ours, isn't it unthinkable—"

"Unthinkable?" He rose in anger, pulling the young man up by the arm. "You find the censorship unthinkable? Let me tell you, there are things more unthinkable than the censorship. It may seem unthinkable to you that I should force these dogs to live like men again, that I should revive the ancient disciplines, that I should raise up the gods and restore the antique piety. But *I* can't afford to find these things unthinkable—what I find unthinkable are their alternatives. That we should occupy ourselves with Greek poetry while the provinces fall away, that we should sit primping and tasting mushrooms and almonds while the barbarians gather on our frontier, that the chieftains of the Goths should eventually sit in the Senate house, that Jupiter and Vesta should leave their temples to a crucified Jew, that cities should be turned into shards and ashes, that wild horses should graze in the forums of Aquincum and Marcianopolis, that everything we built, everything we cherished should be wiped from the face of the earth—no, these are what I find unthinkable, these are what I must prevent, even if the effort involves my death."

A general's hands, laid on the person of an offending centurion—he loosed his hold, he looked into the grey eyes. There was nothing in them but the vacant stare that had always meant the flight of the elusive spirit toward the ever-receding boundaries . . . But, as he was about to turn away with a shrug, the young man's hand went out and touched him on the wrist.

"I'll write that speech on the censorship for my lord and my master."

"Why? Because I am the Emperor?"

"No, no, I . . . Say that I'll write it because I've been answered."

"Answered, perhaps, but scarcely satisfied."

"Satisfied?" A ghostly smile came and went out like a glimmer of uncertain sunlight. "Maybe I'm the sort that'll never be satisfied."

"Then why—"

"I don't know. For no reason and for a number of reasons. Because, if my uncle is willing to risk his life on this business, then I should certainly be willing to give it a few hours. Because, if a moment ago it didn't seem to me a workable solution, I know of no better solution. Because I trust my uncle—no, not only with a blind fondness—whatever you told me to do in the old days always turned out for the best."

It was enough—it would have to be enough, at least for the time being. Near the door at the other end of the atrium stood the melancholy eunuch, his face distressed over the length of the interview, and meat burning to a crisp. The Emperor laid his arm around his nephew's shoulders and led him out of the colonnade. "It seems we are required to go and eat," he said, stepping over one of the lions—three cubes of red on the neck and one on the ground. . . .

"Will you give me notes for the speech, my uncle?"

"Pages of them. You can have them after we've eaten." His hand rested again on the sparely-fleshed shoulder blade, and whatever anger was still within him could not direct itself any longer against Favorinus Herennius. What more could I expect of him, he asked himself, considering the sort of company I left him in these last nine years? Stoics, Greeks, freedwomen, artists—all of them so self-indulgent that the spirit of the great Cato strikes them as ridiculous.

"When will you want the finished manuscript?"

"Three weeks, four weeks, there's not that much hurry, I'll give you plenty of time."

Each of the thirty Aethiopians bowed and touched his forehead to the floor as they passed. The sickly steward at the door bowed and lifted a countenance filled with long-suffering. "I trust that my lord and my master will forgive us, inasmuch as we were given to understand that the imperial conference would be over within an hour. In spite of every effort on the part of the supervisor of the kitchen, the saddle of hare was so badly burned that it is scarcely fit to be eaten," he said.

Chapter 6

THE DACIAN city of Apulum—never beautiful, always new and raw and smelling of hemp and wax and salted fish brought in from the Euxine for the army—was uglier than ever in the somber November dusk. Not that it had been niggardly in its attempts to make itself presentable. Bales and barrels had been hauled in out of the main street; soldiers had polished their shields and corselets, and the slatternly wives of soldiers had washed their faces and combed their hair. Around the public square bleak and adorned only with three shoddy statues, a little crowd had gathered. The citizens of Apulum were waiting for their darling, Herennius Decius, heir to the purple and commander-in-chief of the northern legions. Not an hour since, a blast of the trumpet had told them that his boats had come to shore, back home from their regular tour of the Danubian frontier.

If he did not come with pomp, they were too close to poverty and taxes and the Gothic watchfires in the nearby forests to blame him for that. His train consisted of a tribune, a pair of centurions, and the twenty men of his personal guard, all of them unsteady on their feet after twelve days of rocking and pitching in a boat, all of them haggard, with wind-burned cheeks and bloodshot eyes. He walked among them, distinguished from the rest of them only by his scarlet general's cloak; but at the sight of that cloak a loud cheer went up in the square and was repeated, far off, by the legionaries who lived in the barracks on the other side of the town. The women among the watchers found him as comely as ever: the fair head, unhelmeted, was sheathed in silky, undulating hair; the slight body maintained, with evident and touching effort, the martial attitude. But two of his orderlies, looking into the square from an upper window in the one fine house in the city, cast significant glances at each other when he stopped in the light of the open door. The marsh-fever was probably at him again; his lips were tight and bluish, and there were dark circles under his eyes.

If they had ventured to say so to the young general, he would have cut them off short. He was by no means ready to conclude that his cold and his weariness were due to a return of the affliction that had troubled him since his fifteenth year. The damp beds on the boat, the tiring interviews with harried officers in the neighboring camps, the constant, eye-straining scrutiny of the horizon for the Gothic watchfires—these were enough to account for the aches in his bones and the pain in his head. The comforts of this excellent house, freely given over to him by the leading citizen of Apulum, would restore him within a couple of hours. He waved to the crowd, attempting to show them a cheerful face—there was nothing for them to worry about, nothing as yet—and passed under the lintel, shielding his eyes against a sudden flood of light. The atrium and the two big rooms that opened onto either side of it, a library without scrolls and a banquet hall without banquet fare, were much too bright for his tired eyes.

The same harassed look he had been seeing on the faces of the officers in the camps—he saw it now on the face of the rheumatic old orderly, all crippled with the rawness of the weather, who limped into the atrium and took his cloak and sword. "The general will have to hurry if he means to wash and dress. The Governor of Moesia is coming to join him at the evening meal," he said.

"Trebonianus Gallus?"

"Yes, he came into town a little before noon with a guard of thirty men. I signed an order to feed his guard at the barracks tonight. I hope I did the right thing about the Governor himself—"

He rubbed his burning eyelids. Trebonianus Gallus was the last man on earth he wanted to see in his present state of dullness and weariness.

"I'm sorry if I did wrong. I didn't know what else to do."

He laid his hand on the orderly's knobby hand and produced an unconvincing smile. "You were right, of course. What else could you say?" He felt a chill, an undeniably familiar sort of chill, beginning in the lower part of his back and radiating upward toward his shoulder blades and downward to his knees. "How much time do I have to dress?" he said.

"Not very much." The rheumy blue eyes of the old Pannonian regarded him with understanding and pity. "Put on a warm tunic, my lord and my master. A man bred in Italy could catch his death in weather like this."

With the orderly close behind him, he passed through the banquet hall—

two isolated places had been set at one end of the gigantic table—and entered a little chamber that served as an office. Here, because this cubicle of a room could be brought to a dry Italian heat by a pair of braziers, he spent most of his time. There was a table under the window, heaped with scrolls accumulated in his twelve-day absence. His clothes—a scarlet woolen tunic, long white leg-bands, and soft purple boots with crimson lacings— were laid out on an ebony chair. In the mingled light of the braziers and the lamps, the pictures on the wall showed clearly: a series of paintings on the tale of Daphne, tawdry in conception and muddy in execution. But the naked nymph fled her pursuer through groves of Italian poplars and cy- presses; swans floated on the blue southern inlets; the scenes were divided by the fluted pillars of his homeland; and he had come, in his homesickness, to love the wretched daubs in spite of their vulgarity.

Bred in Italy, irrevocably drawn to Italy, he thought, stripping off the clothes that had taken on the smell of the sweat of his anxiety. He lay face down on the bearskin coverlet while the old orderly knelt on the floor beside him and rubbed the warmed and fragrant oil into his neck, into his shoul- ders, into the spot at the small of his back that seemed to be the core of the cold. Italy, he told himself, was a little private garden, clipped and smoothed and rounded into deceptive amiability. Torn out of Italy and flung down in Dacia, a man was certain to find he had based his life on some thoroughly fallacious notions about the nature of the world and the intentions of the gods. Huge malevolent mountain ranges, waters that churned over jagged rock, stretches of marshland veiled in treacherous green, leaves dying in an agony of red and yellow, mists that rose round the boat like ghosts of reproachful ancestors, a wind that tore like a howling monster through a wilderness of trees—the very sight of such a place transformed just Jupiter and indolent Juno and warm-hearted Vesta into childish illusions. Journey- ing up and down the Danube in the November gusts, one knew a total exile, an all-embracing loss. Not the homeland only, but bright Olympus with it, was gone. . . .

He turned on his back, shivering at the shock of air on flesh warmed by the fur. Recollections of the journey kept returning to him. The people one saw on those tours of inspection! It was as if a new breed, something evil and not quite human, had sprung into existence on the Roman side of the Danubian frontier. In the deep gorges between one bald height and another, chained gangs of state prisoners with brute faces and shaven heads set the rocks ringing with the clink of their picks. By night, the red bonfires on the banks revealed such faces as one sees in fever dreams: bandits, de- serters, diseased women driven out of the camps, beggars with running eyes. One ate and slept only at the army stations; the inns of Dacia were in the worst possible repute. If you were fortunate enough to get out of one of them with your blood in your body and your wallet at your side, it was more than likely you would sicken on tainted meat. There was a story—and after this trip he was half-disposed to believe it—that many a traveler in Dacia had unknowingly eaten the flesh of a murdered man in his stew. . . .

"If the general would like to get into his tunic—"

"Yes, of course." He started out of his dream and sat up on the side of the couch while the folds of good dry woolen fell over his body, while the leg-bands were wound around his aching calves and the purple boots were pulled onto his feet.

The old man, finished with his ministrations, stood in the middle of the room, with the basin of oil in his gnarled hands and a painful, irrepressible curiosity in his face. "Was there anything unusual this trip, my lord and my master?" he asked in a timorous voice. "Anything new—"

"No," he said, shaking his head and smiling, "nothing new about the Goths."

The Goths, he thought, going across the room to stand in front of one of the braziers now that he was alone, was there something the matter with him that he did not share the universal dread of the Goths? In comparison with the renegades and wretches who had drifted from the camp towns into the hinterland, the barbarians seemed to him like incorrigible children, making their capricious sallies out of the clumps of willows along the banks, yelling at the tops of their lungs like boys let out of school, assailing the passing convoys with pebbles and arrows in much the same spirit as urchins pelted the City Guard. And almost every one he had ever laid eyes on had been cleanly, innocently handsome—tall, with blue eyes and flowing yellow hair, broad in the shoulders and narrow in the hips. "White demons," his lieutenants called them, but he had always found them less fearful, less demoralizing to the spirit than the trees and rocks themselves. The Goths— they were the enemy, and it might be that he took them too lightly; but if the contemptuous amusement he regarded them with was the source of his courage he could hardly wish himself different.

During the last tour of inspection, he had been made uneasy only by the absence of the enemy; in the entire journey there had not been one yell, one arrow, one stone. There was a rumor—he had heard it from the tribune at the watchtower on the bend of the river—that old Berig, king over three of the six tribes of barbarians, was dead. In a way, the rumor had already been substantiated: if the Goths were holding one of their seven-day funerals in their sacred grove, they would have no time for mischief-making along the banks. All of them, signaled in by the watchfires, would have gathered under the oracular trees, to beat their shields with their spears in the rhythm of the funeral chant, to listen to the ravings of their priests and prophetesses, to stamp and wail and throw their rings and necklaces into the pyre. . . .

It was hard to tell who would succeed old Berig, provided he had actually died. Trebonianus Gallus would certainly want to talk of that, would come to the table with all the pertinent questions: Who were the heirs-presumptive? Had any of them ever parleyed with the Romans? Were they well-disposed or belligerent? Was there any possibility that a new king would bring about a new alignment among the several tribes? Such questions, he had to admit, were of crucial importance. Four or five tribes, acting in unison, could prove a serious threat to the frontier. But he was fairly sure that there were three nephews in line for Berig's crown, none of them warlike, none of them distinguished, all of them less to be reckoned with than the redoubtable Kniva, a kind of Gothic plebe who had, by sheer tactical genius, made himself chieftain of their host. There might be time to check the matter, but it would be necessary to make a draughty journey upstairs to the room where the old correspondence was kept, and somehow he could not bring himself to leave the warmth of the brazier.

The clear red of the burning charcoal lighted up a murky section of the mural, a miserably painted facade of a Roman palace topped with a gilded dome; and he was vaguely troubled because it seemed to him that this section of the painting had played a malevolent part in his last attack of fever—yes, he had identified it with the palace of the Herennii. Those flights of marble stairs, those umbral colonnades and vaulted ceilings—they had seemed tremendous and inimical to him in his childhood, and the old conviction of hostile immensity had come again in his fever-dream. All the knowing and scornful ones, glittering with jewels and sleek with Chinese silk, all the unquestionably accepted and illustrious ones, among whom he had always felt himself a lesser kind of man, not even allied to them, closer to their slaves—it had been a reception evening in his nightmare, and all of them had been there . . . A reception evening in the palace of the Herennii, and he come home from Dacia, as he was always thinking of coming home, in a scarlet cloak, in purple shoes, commander-in-chief of the northern legions, son of the Lord of the World. He had waited on the threshold for the moment when the chattering assembly on the other side of the portal would turn in wonderment and see that the occasion was being graced with the presence of the heir to the rayed crown, had waited for the advancing shapes and the outstretched hands and the little pleased cries. But the only one to turn was an old witch of a woman in a serpentine silken dalmatica, who said in a hissing whisper, "Isn't he the son of the old Pannonian? What on earth does he imagine he's doing in purple shoes?"

Ridiculous, he thought, spreading his hands over the red embers. If I were to go home on leave and visit the palace of the Herennii, they would send their showiest Nubians to escort me up the avenue, there would be hundreds of wax lights in the atrium and laurel over the door. Drusilla would hurry forward in a rustle of white silk, as she used to hurry forward to greet Philip the Arabian, to offer me a cousinly kiss . . . And suddenly the unbearable thought was with him again—that face, which seemed to him as remote and unapproachable as the bloom of a water-lily, had been kissed by the lecher they had flung her to when she was scarcely out of her childhood; that body, the thought of which filled him with such holy awe that he would not permit the image of it to move closer than the margins of his consciousness, had been desecrated by that revolting jackal. And to her these were not things to be endured; these things she cherished above everything else; beside his embraces, everything else faded into insignificance—

The blast of the trumpet roused him. Trebonianus Gallus was being greeted in the square, and he was appalled at how little prepared he was to receive his guest. Gallus had come to the Dacian headquarters to call on him once before; it was a long journey from the neighboring province of Moesia to Apulum, and he would have been grateful for the gesture if he had not suspected that there was, in this show of courtesy, at least as much political expediency as personal friendliness. And the friendliness itself was questionable; it had a way of slipping over into something akin to forwardness. It was this boisterous familiarity that made him want to retreat when Gallus came into the room, bringing with him the dead leaf smell of the autumn night and striding up to give his host a resounding kiss. The ruddy tinge of the Governor's knobby face had been heightened by the cold; the wind had blown his black forelock to one side of his brow. He stepped back a little and tilted his chin at Herennius. He was short and made up for that lack by constantly moving about, scratching his temples and rubbing his cheeks and twisting his face into uncalled-for pouts and frowns and smiles.

"How's your health this time, my dear fellow?" he asked, putting his arm around Herennius's waist and making straight for the banquet hall. "I must say, you look a little green to me."

"It's nothing. I just got off the boat, that's all. I'm perfectly all right."

At the entrance to the banquet hall they almost collided with the rheumatic old orderly, who was bringing in a platter of sliced lamb. "Lamb," said the Governor of Moesia, sniffing at it. "I hope they've put pepper and garlic on it. Most people have no idea how lamb should be cooked."

"That's what you said the last time you were here." It was necessary to stand up to the man. To accept his easy-going incivilities without some show of spirit was to put oneself into the role of a child. And yet even the mildest retort always seemed much more antagonistic than the jibe it parried. Herennius had the conviction that he had been unnecessarily rude. "I think you'll find enough seasoning on it this time," he said, motioning his guest to the couch at the head of the table and seating himself just around the corner, at the Governor's left.

In spite of the iron brazier placed three feet behind the couch occupied by the host, in spite of the candelabra filled with transparent beeswax lights, the banquet hall seemed utterly cheerless, far too vast for two to dine in, lost in shadows in the corners, alive with draughts. The food that the orderly placed on the table—thick slices of lamb, lentils in a dark brown broth, a round loaf cut in four, slabs of greasy bacon, and a cruet of wine with the dampness of the cellar still upon it—all struck Herennius as singularly unfit to be put into the mouth. He suppressed a shiver and stretched himself on the dining couch with his back to the blazing charcoal, letting the heat strike full upon the area of chill. The orderly had taken himself off, and there was no further excuse for silence. "I had a very quiet trip up the river this time," he said.

"Well, what did you expect?" The dark eyes goggled at him; the small underlip thrust itself out. "They wouldn't have much time for pestering you —would they, my dear fellow?—considering that they had old Berig's funeral on their hands."

That was a certainty then. That was a certainty, and Gallus's spies were more dependable than his, unless, of course, some news to confirm the rumor was in one of the scrolls in that miserable confusion back in the office. He should have looked, he should have spent the little span of time between his return and the arrival of his guest in an attempt to find out what had been going on during the last twelve days, and he sensed that his conviction of his own insufficiency had not escaped the notice of the Governor. "We both of us had quiet trips, my dear boy. I hope you enjoyed yours as much as I enjoyed mine. They'll be the last for some time."

"Why?" Seized by a sudden chill, he had said it in a shaking whisper; the symptoms of his sickness and the signs of mortal terror—unfortunately they were one and the same. And yet a man could scarcely say, "Excuse me, your excellency, I'm not shuddering with terror—I'm shuddering because there's a purely physical area of cold at the small of my back. If I happen to be white in the face it's because there's such a pressure on my bladder that soon I'll have to excuse myself."

"Don't you know why?" The Governor felt the chipped brim of his goblet with one hand and gave his host a fatherly pat on the knee with the other. "But let's wait a bit for that," he said, jerking his chin toward the entrance, where the orderly had just reappeared with another hot loaf and a dish of preserved plums. "I had a long wait for you, you know, and I haven't had anything I could call a decent meal for days."

"I'm sorry. I couldn't help that. It was dusk before we got back."

"Oh, I managed to amuse myself. I spent a couple of hours at old Falconilla's house up there behind the baths. I can't say much for the place— it's steamy and the girls are the worse for wear—but they'll certainly do anything you can pay them for."

He hoped he would be spared the details of the sordid performance; he was having enough trouble keeping the greasy lamb on his stomach. Once, once only, he had gone to Falconilla's. Four dark rooms, decorated with grimy pillows and draperies, and everything—the wine, the covers, the women—smelling like dirty, damp clothes never hung out in the sun.

"He's gone now," he said, when the footsteps of the departing orderly had ceased to sound in the hall. "Let's get back to this business of Berig, if you don't mind—"

"Oh, but I do. It's a nasty business, a depressing business, and I'd like to enjoy my meal in peace. You know, this is very decent wine, much better than the stuff you had when I was here before."

Was he postponing his news to make it seem more impressive, or was he actually trying to frighten his host? "A nasty business, a depressing business —" the vagueness of the terms seemed deliberate, intended to make one feel that something ominous was taking place in that impenetrable wilderness of trees and stones. But the Governor would find it hard to upset him over the Goths; he knew them for what they were; he was not to be intimidated by hints and rumors. The small talk that the caprice or the malice of his guest required—the gossip of the barracks and the town, the news about the officers he had encountered at the stations along the frontier—he produced such talk in spite of the pressure on his bladder and the growing area of cold. The tribune Severinus had a gambling debt of three thousand denarii. A Syrian trader had come from Tomi to complain that nine legionaries had appropriated everything in his bazaar. It was a good five weeks since the tribune Tatianus had gone on a military errand to Sarmitzegetusa, and still there was no word of him. Either he had joined the brigands or deserted to the Goths. . . .

I am doing a very creditable job of it, he thought, stuffing my mouth with this disgusting food as though I were eating with an appetite, telling him about Aurulenus's horse and Sentius's wife, and showing not the slightest curiosity about his nasty, depressing business—

"You know, I've been thinking, my dear boy, that one of the two of us had better get in touch with your father, now that this affair of the Gothic succession is settled—"

His knife fell out of his hand and clattered against his plate. Probably somewhere in the heap of scrolls in the office. . . . He straightened and wiped a spot of splattered gravy from the front of his tunic. "Then it's been settled?" he said.

"That's right, you wouldn't have known about it. The whole thing came to a head down in my territory, so there's no reason for you to think there's anything the matter with your spies." He leaned back a little and cocked his head, and his dark eyes were suddenly filled with candor and benignity. "I wanted to tell you first, of course. I wanted you to know the whole affair inside out before anybody in Rome got wind of it. Now, don't upset yourself unnecessarily. It may not be as bad as it looks. Don't you want a little more wine?"

He shook his head vigorously and laid his hand over the top of his goblet. "What difference does it make who succeeds?" he said. "Of those three nephews of old Berig's—"

84

"Two nephews, my dear fellow."

"Two—three—what's the difference? So far as I've been able to learn, none of them is particularly popular, none of them could get the allegiance of more than three tribes at best."

"The nephews?" said Gallus, ostentatiously occupying himself with a dish of preserved plums. "Those nephews are dead issues, so to speak. Nobody in old Berig's family is going to reign. The barbarians are hot for war—you can take that much for granted. Before the old man was buried, before I set out for Apulum—you see, I wanted to make sure, I didn't want to throw you into a panic over nothing—before I started up the river, Kniva was crowned king of the whole lot of them. He's got the allegiance of all six tribes of the Goths."

"Kniva?" He knew that he had gone white as linen. The pressure on his bladder had suddenly become intolerable.

"Yes, Kniva. I saw him once at a parley, and let me tell you, my dear boy, he may wear a deerskin cloak and carry a mace, but he's no simple-minded barbarian, not that one. One of those cool, thin faces—you know the sort—smooth and absolutely immobile—no life except in the eyes. Beautiful and evil—"

"A Goth, like any other Goth!" Yet even as he said it he knew that from this time forth, he would look for it always among the other yellow-haired, blue-eyed ones—the beautiful, evil face.

"You won't think so once you've parleyed with him. And now that they've crowned him—"

He sat up and pushed his greasy plate to one side. "But how can you be sure they've crowned him?" he said. "After all, why would they take a commoner, with old Berig's nephews still—"

"Why would they take a commoner? Really, I can't say, they haven't troubled themselves to discuss the matter with me, you know. But if you're not convinced of the accuracy of my findings, you can always come back with me to Moesia and leaf through the reports yourself." He bit off half of a plum, and gave his host a hurt and affronted look.

"Believe me," said Herennius, "I hadn't the slightest intention of questioning the efficiency of your spies, I only wanted to ask—" He broke off and got up, clutching the corner of the table. "But we'll speak of it in a moment. I'm sorry, you'll have to excuse me, I'll be back in no time at all—"

The draughts in the corridor were icy against his feverish body. He could not suppress the shuddering any longer, and two orderlies and a centurion gave him quick, pitying glances as he passed. Somebody had lighted a lamp in the bathroom. It was an ugly room, bitterly cold, and crass with green marble and gilt; but the single flame reflected in the polished stone was cheerful, made a kind of haven of the place. Ah, he thought, relieving himself and shivering freely now, everything will be better after this . . . But the unmanning pressure on his bladder, once it was removed, only made way for all the other miseries. It will never be better, he told himself, making his way back through the draughty corridor to the door of the banquet hall. First there will be two days of chill, and then there will be an indefinite number of days of fever, and when the fever and the delirium are past—what will I come back to then? Kniva, testing the vulnerable spots all along the precarious frontier. Kniva, with the allegiance of all six tribes of the Goths. . . .

"Are you sure you're all right?" said the Governor, bouncing into a sitting position. "You do look green. Maybe you'd better go to bed."

He shook his head, sat down on the edge of the couch, and permitted himself a long draught of wine. "I think I was making an apology when I had to walk out," he said. "It wasn't, of course, that I meant to raise any question about the efficiency of your spies. It's only that the business is a little difficult to take on all at once. If it's really Kniva, with all six of the tribes, it's hard to imagine what's likely to happen along the frontier—"

"Hard to imagine? Not at all, my dear boy. Pandemonium will break loose in your section first—the new forts in my district'll hold them off a while. Ten to one, they'll make straight for Carnuntum or Apulum—just wait and see. Not that they'll necessarily get there, there's no point distressing yourself about that as yet, your garrisons are considerably stronger than you think. There's not a legionary in your army that can't be depended on to work miracles for you. That boyish charm of yours has gotten under their hides—no, I really mean it, they absolutely dote on you, you know. I'd stake a fortune on it that you could hold your present position until spring, provided you had plenty of supplies and ten or twelve thousand men out of Thrace."

"But how in the name of the gods could I ever get ten or twelve thousand men out of Thrace? That's mad—that's impossible—" He stopped, ashamed of the anguish and the urgency in his voice, knowing that the dark, protruding eyes on the other side of the table were seeing him as a whey-faced coward, unworthy of the scarlet tunic on his back, ridiculous in the role of heir to the rayed crown.

"Oh, come, now, it's not as bad as all that." The knobby, ruddy countenance expressed insulting sympathy; the steady, capable hand took up the cruet and filled both goblets to the brim. "Don't tell me your father wouldn't see to that. Suppose you could tell him how things stood—suppose you were to see him face to face—"

Face to face . . . For an instant it was as if he were a child again, magically secure in that austere and imperturbable presence. "Where would I see him face to face?" he said.

"Why, in Rome, of course. You'd have to write and ask for leave to go. You'd have to explain that developments here are such that you two had better sit down and think things out together. You'd have to—"

He did not hear the rest. Rapt, breathless—and doubtlessly ridiculous to the goggling eyes on the other side of the wine cruet—he saw a vision of the City in the purplish mist of an autumn evening: columns and triumphal arches dark against the sunset, porticoes and pediments gold behind clumps of laurel and oleander. Such sounds as he had not heard for months in the wilderness broke upon him: flute-song, laughter of women coming through a lighted window, chant of the priests of Isis moving with garlands across a square. In the garden of the Herennii he saw her scattering grain, and the doves going up—white and grey and purple wings going up past her remote, still face . . . "How could I go home? Almighty Jupiter, how could I go home?" he said.

In the few moments of silence that followed the rash question, he looked at the Governor, seeking some reason that would still the stern voice of honor in him and send him southward with a guiltless heart. But no such thing was forthcoming; there was only cool, deliberate waiting. He reached for his goblet and drank again; and the wine, sour and raw in his throat, stung him back into the actual world. "I could scarcely walk out of here at a time like this," he said at last. "Simply because I know my father would let me come if I wished, I wouldn't ask him to let me come for all the world."

"That's exactly what I thought you were going to say, my dear fellow," said Gallus, bouncing into a sitting position and giving him a pat on the hand. "I never imagined for a moment you'd consider leaving your post. And yet somebody'll have to go down, somebody'll have to make that trip. And a miserable trip it is—almost a month on the water—with winter coming on."

"I could send my sub-prefect. He's perfectly trustworthy—"

"Like that tribune—what's his name?—the one that started out for Sarmitzegetusa and hasn't been heard from since? Oh, no, I wouldn't do that if I were you. Besides, whoever goes down there ought to know the situation inside out. Much as I hate to travel, I suppose I'd better go down and present the case myself."

Loathing for the knobby, spotted face, loathing and the sudden taste of bile in his mouth made him clutch the edge of the table until his knuckles turned white. Dog—slippery, scheming dog—you used me for your own ends, he thought. Because you wanted to go to Rome, because you wanted to curry favor with the Emperor, you've been leading me this way and that all evening, taking me for what I am—a simple-minded child. . . .

"Don't worry, my dear boy, I'll get your Thracians for you. All you have to do is write your father and see that I'm invited to come down—but do it as soon as you can. I'll see to everything. It'll be better that way, much better. I can use terms that your modesty would never allow you to use yourself. Much as I hate the idea of making a trip like that in winter—"

He shoved his goblet halfway across the table and looked straight into the Governor's face. "Don't complain about the trip to me," he said. "You're itching to go down to Rome and see my father. That's what you had in mind from the start."

"Itching to go down to Rome? Am I really?" For a moment he looked startled. Then he bent forward, propped his elbows on the table, and rested his chin in his hands. "Yes, I suppose I am, now that you say so." He smiled and gazed at his host with sleepy and affectionate eyes. "You see through everything, don't you? You're wasting your talents, you ought to be in the civil government. It'll be to your advantage to have me go down, of course. But I'll have to admit I want to go down for reasons of my own."

"Am I to have the courtesy of being told the reasons?"

"They're obvious, they're perfectly obvious, my dear boy. I want to make an impression on your father—I'd like him to have me in mind when he thinks about promotions. I'm old, Herennius, I'm getting on toward fifty. I'd like a governor's post in some civilized place—say Syria or Egypt. Do you blame me? You shouldn't, really. If you were my age, you wouldn't want to spend another five years in a hole like this."

He was grasping at a straw of hope, and he knew it, but he could not hold his tongue. "You don't by any chance want to go down there so badly that you've been making matters sound worse than they are?"

"Worse than they are?" He rose from the couch with the spontaneous indignation of the double-dealer who is blameless for once. "You don't imagine for a moment—do you?—that I'd lie about a thing like this. Every detail I've given you this evening has been confirmed by my spies. No doubt your fellows got wind of it while you were on the river. When you get around to looking at your dispatches, you'll see."

"Yes," he said lamely, rising to indicate that the nightmare meal was over. "Yes, I probably will."

"What sort of person do you take me for, my dear boy?" The swarthy arm embraced him; the knobby fingers sank into his shoulders and gave him a little affectionate shaking. "I'd scarcely take any pleasure in scaring you out of your wits—now, would I?—especially when I'm scared out of my wits myself."

"I'll write to my father."

"Will you, really? Soon?"

"Immediately. Tonight."

One could be almost rude to him now, one could reject his invitation to an hour of gambling, one could hurry him through the atrium and guide him straight to the door. Now that he had accomplished his purpose, nothing else mattered; it was even obvious that he was happy to be given leisure for gloating. If it were only possible, now that the door was shut behind him, to lie down on the bearskin rug, to call for blankets and crocks of hot water, to shudder in peace . . . But there were the scrolls on the table in the little office, there were the messages of warning to be sent to the sub-prefects and tribunes along the river, there was the letter, the long and difficult letter home, that must carry no hint of sickness or incapacity or fright. . . .

The orderly walked up behind him in the windy corridor. "May I get you a bowl of hot milk and a couple of blankets?" he said. "It's going to be a bitter night."

"Not yet—not yet—I can't go to bed." His jaw was shaking so violently now that he could scarcely make the words intelligible. "An hour—maybe less—I have a letter to write. Get me my sub-prefect. I've got to dictate to my sub-prefect, now, while I can still talk. Hurry. I'm sick, I'm terribly sick," he said.

Chapter 7

By THE end of November, Favorinus Herennius was no longer making a point of his ineptitude for a political career. He had stopped telling his friends at the house of Charis that he had been drawn into the new regime against his better judgment, that his prose style had been so twisted out of shape by the everlasting speech-writing that he could not compose a decent letter any more, that the people with whom he was forced to associate either bored him or drove him to distraction. Now, when one of his earlier remarks was quoted back at him with understandable malice in the elegant little sitting room, he held his tongue and produced a shamefaced smile. If the crowd of them was irked with him, it was no great wonder—he was always sending a last minute excuse because of a summons to the imperial palace, he could never stay to the end of a reading or an argument because he had to appear, like every good member of a pious government, at the altar of the Capitoline Jupiter every morning at dawn.

But they were mistaken if they imagined that these enforced absences caused him no pain. He was always thinking of them, and with a strange poignancy. His desire to be with them was the same urgent yearning he had felt in the days when he had waited for an invitation to Marcellinus's house that first spring. When he and Ummidius Pessinus sat plotting policy in some deserted office after dusk, when he stood in the reception line to greet he Persian ambassador, when he made wearisome conversation with the aging ladies in the Empress's chambers, the thought of them was like a bruise on his heart. The occasion that he was missing at the moment—all the more precious because probably it was not a particularly brilliant occasion, her face—all the more woundingly dear because it was not an unquestionably beautiful face—would drive him to some window to stare at the melancholy night. And he was never consoled by the thought that he could see them all tomorrow. It was as if his last hurried parting with them had been a final farewell; it was as if the happiness that Marcellinus and destiny had given to him had dropped like a crystal vase from his careless hands; it was as if he would never hold the exquisite, unshattered shape of it again in this world.

And yet, except for these sudden and incomprehensible attacks of longing and regret, he was more at peace with himself than he had ever been before. He had always been a poor sleeper, he had come to take it for granted that he would spend a good part of every night staring dry-eyed into the dark; and now a few moments after his head touched the pillow he slept. In the past, too, even the best of the past, he had alternated between one feverish extreme and the other: either he had been filled with an exhilaration so intense that it could not spend itself, or he had been restless, tormented, searching insistently for some nameless balm in *her,* in their companions, in himself. The searching had ceased, at least for the time being. And, if the ecstasy had also departed, something else had come in its place—something that he had never experienced before—an easy buoyancy, a casual cheerfulness.

He would not have believed it possible, but he found himself happy because he could move among his new associates without being expected to reckon with the secret places of their hearts. The demanding intimacies, the naked confidences, the intense effort at deep communication which had been for him, up to this time, the only alternatives to utter loneliness, were not required here, would probably have been out of place. Even the strong personal bond between him and the Emperor Decius manifested itself only in a brief look or a random touch. And one was less conscious of the absence of the high, seeking flights than of a deliverance from the depressing conviction of inadequacy that came on those occasions when the spirit, for all one's prodding, simply refused to rise. In the offices, in the Emperor's dining room, at the altar of the Capitoline Jupiter and at the entrance of the Senate house a man never had to ask himself, "Am I really rising to this?" The problems, the duties, the arguments, the endless stream of rumor and information—one simply plunged in and was carried along. A burdensome hour broken by embarrassing silences was an impossibility; there was always far too little time for everything that ought to be said.

He and his recent acquaintances were bound less to each other than to the world they had in common; and it was amazing how much exhilaration could be generated by the confusions and dilemmas of that world. They were the elite, the possessors of desperate or preposterous knowledge that nobody else shared; the news that left the rest of Rome gaping was an old tale to them. Their mutual knowledge was the bond that made them linger late in the corridors talking to each other, or led them to each other's houses where the conversation might last through half the night. Up to the present at least, Favorinus Herennius had managed to detach himself as soon as current business was attended to, but he had begun to feel some regret when he refused to stop with Ummidius Pessinus at a wine shop or declined an invitation to take the evening meal at the house of the bald little monkey-faced Secretary of Petitions.

Early in his apprenticeship he had come to understand that there was no reason for him to associate with the conservative members of the government. Valerian, the jaundiced Pontifex Maximus, the suave Urban Prefect, the bored Secretary of the Imperial Treasury—the Emperor had more or less plainly removed them from the main stream of activity; they were assigned such tasks as the arrangement of public festivals, the revival of ancient rites, the reconstruction of shrines that had fallen into decay. All the really crucial matters—the censorship, the efforts to restore the provinces, the strengthening and disciplining of the legions—were in the hands of the "clever ones"; and he was one of the "clever ones"; in the street, in the Senate, in his mother's atrium he was constantly being pointed out as such. He who had always gone unattended after a late breakfast to some private destination now set out for the altar of Jupiter on the Capitoline half an hour before dawn, followed by a train of clients—threadbare patricians, impoverished equestrians, aggressive plebes who offered him their useless services in return for a morning meal and whatever he might choose to do about bringing their grievances to the attention of the Lord of the World. The visitors at his mother's receptions addressed him with a marked respect and the lady Sabina Herennia herself was forever urging him to bring his new companions home, was willing to overlook the fact that the bald little Secretary of the Privy Purse was a Jew and that the Secretary of Petitions was descended from a slave. "When," she kept asking him, "are we going to entertain some of *your* guests?"

One afternoon toward the end of November—so hot that it seemed as if summer had come again—he gratified that wish of hers more or less by chance. At the imperial levee in the morning Ummidius Pessinus had tentatively indicated his eagerness to see the first draft of the speech on the censorship. His curiosity was understandable, since most of the "clever ones" were convinced that the Emperor Decius intended to appoint him censor, and Favorinus had urged him to come and read the thing—provided he would excuse the scrawl and the corrections—about an hour after the noonday meal in the palace of the Herennii. The prospect of the visit had set the entire household into anxious activity: the library on the second floor was dusted from top to bottom, the best slaves were summoned into the atrium, a silver tray of peeled oranges and roast partridge was sent upstairs, and some bitter words passed between the steward and the mistress of the house because there was no snow to cool the wine. Any casual pleasure that Favorinus might have taken in the visit was spoiled by the confusion it had produced and by the aching realization that, if the painter Antisthenes or the old poet Berosus had come to pay respects, his mother would have served them lamb and warm wine with the worst possible grace. He was a little embarrassed, too, by the sight of Ummidius Pessinus in an intensely blue and none-too-tastefully designed dalmatica—he had seen him only in the equestrian toga before. Still, once they were alone together in the sunny library, with the speech and the tray and the wine on the long table between them, the customary awareness of common experience returned. Within less than half an hour excitement was high, the usual rivulet of sweat was running from the dark peak of hair in the middle of Pessinus's brow, and the two of them had lost their self-consciousness and were absorbed in the matter of the censorship.

"I certainly hope," said the Secretary of Petitions, looking up from the tenth of some forty pages of closely written manuscript, "that you're going to play up to the plebes more than you have so far."

He was startled, so startled that he avoided the kind dark eyes and stared instead at the marble bust of Virgil on the window sill. The Emperor had made no mention of the plebes when he had handed over the notes for the speech, and he himself had written the first draft as if the plebes did not exist, concluding that this particular measure, like any other, would stand or fall on the enthusiasm that could be stirred up for it among the equestrians and the senators. "I never thought of that," he said.

"But Almighty Jupiter," said Pessinus, squeezing his damp handkerchief, "you have to appeal to the plebes. In fact, there isn't much point in appealing to anybody else."

That was a frightening concept, and so new to him that he could not take in all its implications. He helped himself to one of the peeled oranges and broke it into sections, permitting himself to think only that some of the more complicated sentences in the manuscript might have to be written over again, that some of the more elaborate metaphors might have to be sacrificed.

"Here, for instance," said Pessinus, turning back to the second sheet and pointing to a long and intricate paragraph. "You're aiming this at the equestrians, and that's a mistake. So far as I can see, you might as well forget the equestrians."

"But I've slanted most of the speech at them on the grounds that they'll be harder to convince than anybody else—"

"You'd be hard to convince, too, if the measure was going to close up your jewelry shop or ruin your income from the incense trade. No, you'll never convince them. From their standpoint they have perfectly sound reasons for hating the censorship. Count them out. I did long ago. Take it for granted that they might as well be ignored—they're lost."

He stared at the manuscript and told himself that he had actually known as much from the beginning. The sight of the splotched and cross-hatched page held down by Pessinus's finger evoked the mood in which it had been written—a mood of exasperation and discouragement. A little ashamed to have his self-deception exposed, he detached the pulpy strings from his slice of orange with an air of philosophic imperturbability. "Very well," he said at last, "let's count out the equestrians. Let's say they'll resist the measure as openly as they dare. Even so, we're not thrown back on the plebes alone. We still have the support of the senators. Nobody's going to cut off the source of *their* income."

"The senators?" The Secretary of Petitions rose and started across the marble floor, turning up the edge of the scarlet Babylonian carpet. "What senators do you mean?" he said, wheeling round. "The Glabrii, who entertained eighty at a seven-course banquet last night? The Marcelli, who just bought a troupe of Alexandrine dancers? Your friends the Metelli, with their twelve villas and their two hundred and fifty slaves? Maybe you'll not cut off their means, but you're certainly going to turn their way of living upside-down. Everybody's not a Stoic like yourself. How many senators do you imagine are going to stand up and cheer for a measure like this?"

His mouth was filled with orange for the moment, and he could only shrug his shoulders.

"Not more than a tenth of them," said Pessinus, coming back to the table with his intensely blue dalmatica floating behind him. "And that tenth will be the riff-raff, the ones beneath the notice of the rest. The ones who lost their fortunes and haven't the wherewithal for luxuries, a few high-minded Stoics, a few Christians, six or seven Jews—that's the sort of support you'll get among the senators. We'd be mad, of course, to point that out to the Lord of the World. But you and I and the rest of us who have to deal with this thing—we'd better know the facts of the case. Play for the plebes, Favorinus, slant the speech at the plebes, get the support of the plebes at any cost. For all the help you'll get from anybody else, you might as well write off your censorship as a travesty—which it may very well turn out to be, for all I know."

The crushed mass of the orange was tasteless on his palate. He swallowed and looked up at the sweating face above him, and saw that there was desperation in the gentle eyes. And, even though his mouth was empty now, he could muster up no arguments against that desperation—he could only wonder how he had managed to deceive himself. "Am I to take it then that you think the censorship might as well be written off?" he said.

"Written off? No, not by any means. It can't be written off—not so long as Decius reigns. He's obsessed with it, he's made a vow to Vesta to see it established, he considers it the cornerstone of his domestic policy. It's a ma idea, a preposterous idea—I told him so when he mentioned it to me. And yet there's something dramatic about it, a sense of urgency, a daring that might stir people up—even the plebes, if we present it to them in the proper terms."

"Then somebody else ought to be writing this speech. There's nobody in Rome who knows the plebes less than I."

"Fortunately or unfortunately, I know them," said the Secretary of Petitions, seating himself before the scrawled sheets and taking a quill in one hand and a leg of partridge in the other. "Two generations back, you know, the Pessini were slaves."

It was the first time that any private matter had been referred to between them, and the host made a nervous, disparaging movement with his hands. But Ummidius Pessinus did not see it; he was absorbed in the speech—he was reading the close writing and gnawing at the partridge leg with equal avidity. "Do you mind," he asked without looking up, "if I make notations in the margin—little things that might appeal to the plebes—just here and there in places where you could easily slip them in?"

"Not in the least. In fact, I'd be grateful."

But that, too, went unnoticed; the Secretary of Petitions was lost in that complete concentration for which he was famous in the imperial offices—he laid the greasy bone on the polished top of the table and was following the lines of script with his fingertip. One could sit quietly watching him—he was likely to finish in less than half an hour; but in such silence one was bound to face certain distressing considerations, to tally up the actual number of senators who would lend their support to the censorship, to wonder how the plebes could be hauled out of their two hundred years of political apathy into the middle of the fight. And he could not face such matters at the moment. He felt suddenly debilitated, oppressed by the unseasonable heat, discouraged by the prospect of having to write the speech a second time—so warm and weary and heavy of heart that he knew he must either walk about in some other place or distract the reader by making useless complaints and objections.

He excused himself in an unheard whisper and, closing the door behind him, stepped out onto the little gallery which looked over the length of the atrium. That spot more than any other in the palace gave him a sense of the vastness of the place: the gilded vaults sprang up some fifteen feet above him, and the marble paving of the reception hall lay a good twenty feet below. He did not look down at once, because the heat in the library had made him dizzy. He cooled his arms on the marble balustrade and let his eyes follow the fine sweep of the ribbing of the vaults, up to the wreathed oval that opened on the sky. How many men, he thought, did it take to gild those arches? My great-great-great-grandfather—where did he find his laborers? Did he hire plebes or use his own slaves? How is it that the time I have spent talking to plebes in the twenty-seven years of my life could not be reckoned up to more than a few hours? If my father had made the tenements over to me, if I had offered to help my mother administer the tenements in spite of our quarrelling, I could have known more plebes—I could have stood for an hour or so every month, listening to their grievances in those dark and filthy halls . . . Those corridors, whose stench remained in his nostrils even though he had not breathed it for more than ten years, those almost lightless rooms, those garbage-cluttered stairways—they came unasked now into his thoughts while he stood looking out over the yellow marble, the wreaths, the cupids, and the gold. Think of that another time, he told himself. Think now of something to say to Pessinus, something trenchant, something brilliant—otherwise he may take you for an utter fool. . . .

But he was given no leisure for further thinking. At the far end of the atrium, two slaves swung back the heavy door, revealing the sun-drenched garden and a single figure standing in the entrance—his sister's husband, the long-absent Eugenius. The steward of the house, splendid in white livery for the Secretary of Petitions, rushed out from under the gallery to receive this second guest, and, seeing who he was, stopped short at the fountain in confusion.

"Who was it that you wished to see, your Illustriousness?" the steward said.

The visitor advanced to the middle of the atrium with a consummately casual air. He took off his light woolen cloak and handed it to the steward. He might have been coming back from a visit to the kennels or a chat with the gardener about the condition of the lawn. "Somebody ought to draw the curtains. It's abominably hot in here," he said.

"Whom did you wish to see?" the steward asked again, in an unsteady voice.

"The lady Drusilla, of course. Ask her if she'll be good enough to step out here and have a word with her husband."

Common decency—so the unseen watcher on the gallery told himself—required him either to go back into the library at once or to make his presence known to the guest. But his curiosity as to the reason for the sudden visit was strong, his urge to see how his sister would conduct herself was stronger still, and he could not bring himself to move. He crouched over the balustrade, resting his forearms on the cool marble and propping his chin on his crossed hands, and let his eyes follow the figure that was moving about, obviously at ease, in the splendid empty hall below.

Whenever he saw Eugenius again after an interval, he was surprised to find how much more prepossessing the man was than he had remembered. All the disagreeable things about his person—his stoop, his baldness, the loose and faded skin on his cheeks, the dark pouches under his eyes—were more obtrusive in remembrance than in actuality. In one's memory he was an exhausted old lecher, with more audacity than his position warranted; but when he walked onto the scene again he had a provocative and indefin able charm—distinguished if a little faded, frank and original if a little forward, so unaffected that one's distasteful recollection of him seemed intentionally malicious. With such perfect grace as a person seldom saw anywhere but at the pantomime, he strolled around the atrium, examined the statues, took sidewise glances at himself in the polished columns, held his thin, ringed hand under the splashing spray of the fountain. The white silk dalmatica, heavily embroidered in yellow and salmon color from the chin to the toes, would have made another man seem effeminate; but, hanging in intricately arranged folds around his thin and active figure, it suggested only a delightful fancifulness. His face was so good-tempered as to make his known vices seem almost harmless. The eyes were grey and lively, the nose was sharp and aristocratic, and there was a kind of knowing softness about the pursed lips.

The steward came out from under the gallery again to announce that the lady Drusilla was with a friend in the garden and would detach herself and come to him as soon as she could. That's a lie, thought Favorinus, and blushed because he felt that Eugenius must know it for a lie, must know, as he knew, that she had fled upstairs to her bedroom, was changing her dress, was trying to paint the whiteness of her consternation out of her face, was looking wildly about for the proper jewels, the proper flowers.

"Very well," said her husband, "go back and tell her to take her time. I'm in no great hurry, I have nothing else to do." And he seated himself out of sight, on a bench under the colonnade, not too far from the door. What he was doing there became plain after a while. He must have been pulling goose-feathers out of one of the cushions and blowing them about. Two of them, borne out on his breath, danced around for a little in the brilliant sunlight and settled near the pedestal of the bust of Celestus Falconius.

Some time passed before she made her appearance at the main entrance, by what back stairways and devious garden paths her brother could guess. The bunch of autumn narcissus in her hand could have convinced nobody that she had been strolling; the scarlet silk in which she had arrayed herself was too unwrinkled; not one hair in the dry black coronet had worked itself out of place; and, as she passed through a slant of sunlight, the emeralds blazed green at her throat and in her hair.

"So here you are at last, Drusilla," said the amiable voice from under the colonnade.

She stopped and turned. Her profile, seen against the green garden, was expressionless and white, except for the round spot of rouge over the cheek bone. "Don't complain about the time you spent waiting for me," she said. "It's a great wonder I came at all."

"I don't want to force myself on you." He emerged and stood near the bust of Celestus Falconius, facing her, with some five feet of shining marble between. "If you don't want to see me, I can always take myself off—"

She clenched her fist around the flowers, and her knuckles showed white.

"What are you doing here?" she said. "It's three months since you've shown your face. What do you want, you dog?"

He propped one elbow on the pedestal, leaned his temple against his open hand, and gave vent to a profound sigh. "Look, darling, I haven't the slightest hope of justifying myself to you. If you and your family get any satisfaction out of calling me a dog, I won't try to convince you I'm anything else. Let's say I'm a dirty dog, and shameless enough to ask you to do me a favor—"

"You're wasting your time. You've had all the favors you'll ever get from me."

He did not answer. He sagged against the pedestal in an exquisite display of wounded dignity.

"Go ask your Syrian to do you a favor," she said in a voice so shrill that Pessinus could have heard it behind the closed door.

"I can't, darling. I've sent her away. She isn't with me any more."

"What's the matter? Was she too expensive?"

"No, wearisome, simply wearisome. You always took her much too seriously."

There was a moment of silence in which her face was transfigured with a wild and irrepressible joy. Her hands trembled, and two of the narcissus blooms slipped out of them and hung—theatrical and ridiculous—head-down in the scarlet folds of silk. "What do you want of me?" she said.

"Well, since you're utterly convinced of my grossness—" He could not expose his wounded spirit by looking her straight in the face; he fixed his eyes instead on Celestus Falconius's chin. "Since you're convinced of my grossness, I'll be as gross as possible. If I tried to tell you how much you mean to me, Drusilla, you'd only conclude that I was covering up my real purposes, so I'll confine myself to the crass and urgent. I came—" He turned spread his arms at his sides, and gave her a frank and pleading look. "I came to ask for a little money," he said.

"Money?" It was a terrible thing to hear, a hurt animal's cry.

"Not very much money—"

"What for? To pay off your filthy Syrian?"

"No, not at all. I'll say this much for her—she went very quietly, she behaved better than most patricians. The money I need has nothing to do with her. In fact, it's for a gambling debt I've owed these last six weeks to Aelius Varius. Not very much—some five thousand sesterces."

A staggering sum to ask even of one of the Herennii—a sum that would have bought a farm in the Campagna or a modest villa near Capri. "Five thousand sesterces? Where in the name of all the gods do you think I could lay my hands on five thousand sesterces?"

It was an involving question—a simple "No," would have been enough Her brother knew that she could not help herself, that at any cost to her own self-respect she must draw out this interview. She had taken two o

98

three steps forward, she was breathing fast through parted lips, and her eyes were fixed with a sickening avidity on the long-absent face. As for the sprightly visitor—he was happy not to have been cut off short. With the care and restraint of one who did not dare to prolong his touch, he was picking the flowers from her skirt and putting them courteously back into her hands. And all the while he was suggesting possible methods of raising five thousand sesterces: Those orchards of hers in Dalmatia, those winter places she had rented last year—didn't she still control the revenue? *He* hadn't seen any of it for months—that much he knew. . . .

"I have nothing to do with it, I can't bother with it, I've been sick, I've left it all in my mother's hands." The tone was shrill and hysterical. She was plainly driven half out of her senses by his touch.

"Were you sick, darling?" He bent forward, all solicitude, put the tip of his finger under her chin, lifted her face to the light, and studied it with concern and tenderness. "Nobody told me that. You're better now, I trust. You look well—as beautiful as ever—" He bent forward and gave her a light and considerate kiss on the lips.

"Let me alone!"

"I'm sorry. That's the way with me—I'm always asking for too much."

"You're asking for too much if you're asking for five thousand sesterces."

"Three thousand?" He seemed to be enjoying his own audacity, and the whimsical, little-boy smile on his face implied that he thought she would enjoy it too. "I'm in a dreadful dilemma. To tell the truth, Aelius Varius threatens to have me beaten to a pulp if I don't pay off by tomorrow night."

"I haven't got it. I couldn't let you have it even if I wanted to—"

"I *could* go off somewhere until you raised it. How long do you think it would take you? Two months? Three months?" he said.

To the surprise and gratification of the watcher on the gallery she made one final and terrible effort: she straightened, turned her back on her husband, and walked rigidly in the direction of the door. For an instant he stood behind her, pursing his mouth and scratching his bald temple. Then, taking on an air of intense agitation, he started after her, caught up with her, twined his arms around her from the back, and, making confused and murmurous sounds, pressed kisses on her nape, her shoulders, her hair. What he said—and he said a great deal in a hurry—was broken and blurred by the kisses and the sighs. But her brother could gather the import of it: if *she* deserted him, then he was indeed deserted; if *she* had no mercy on him, then nobody would have any mercy; he was in disgrace, he could not continue to live in Rome, there was nothing left for him to do but to go away and lose himself.

And slowly—it was sickening to see, it was as if the dream of Chaos had come again and he had seen her naked—slowly she unbent, she let her head lean forward, she stood passive under his embrace. The flowers dropped from her slack hands and lay scattered on the floor around her. "Don't go. I couldn't bear it. The City would be unbearable if you were gone," she said.

"What else is there for me to do, love?"

"It's a great deal of money—it would take me three months to get it. I can't raise more than a thousand a month—not without mother's finding out."

He pressed his loose and sagging cheek against her neck. "There's my darling, there's my good girl."

She turned to him then. Her face flamed up, like the face of a mad Bacchante, and she turned and claimed the reward for her three thousand sesterces—the long embrace. He clasped her—with all the vigor roused up in him by his triumph, he clasped and held her. Her head rested on his shoulder, and he smiled and rubbed his cheek against the coronet of dry black hair, utterly pleased with himself.

"But I'll have to go somewhere until you send me the money," he said at last. "I could always go to Tivoli, of course. My sister's there for the winter season, she couldn't refuse me, she'd have to give me meals and a roof over my head. You can see, darling, how much I hate to ask her. If I hadn't lost my luck, I'd have gone to Rhodes—"

"Oh, go where you want," she said, pulling herself out of his arms. And passionately, as if she took some fierce enjoyment out of her servitude, she tore the emeralds from her arms, her ears, her hair. "Here, take this, and this, and this," she said putting them in his hands. "Now you can go to Rhodes and get yourself all the flute-boys and whores you want. Have I overlooked anything? Never mind, that ought to be enough."

For an instant she stood, disheveled and ridiculous, in the circle of scattered flowers. Then she turned and ran, with her scarlet silk billowing behind her, past the columns, past the gilded pedestals, through the open door. Her braid had come loose when she tore the wreath of emeralds from it. That black braid—he had not seen it flapping behind her for years—and it called up so wounding a recollection of the little girl running through the house on the Esquiline that he crouched down behind the balustrade and hid his face in his hands.

Let me go back to the library, he thought. As soon as that old male prostitute in the salmon-colored dalmatica has finished putting his spoils in his purse and taken himself off, I can go back to the decent quiet of the library—to the window open on a blessedly empty expanse of blue, to the absorbed reader, as passionless and undemanding as the marble bust on the window sill. Let him write a hundred notes on the margins of the speech, let him call for a change in every paragraph—changes enough to deliver me from the obligation to see a human face or hear a human voice. If I am in the library working at the speech, she will not dare to come to me this evening and lay her head on my knees, she cannot claim the luxury of re-enacting her shameful scene for me, I will not have to blush for the flattering lies she will tell herself. . . .

The inimitable Eugenius rearranged the folds of embroidered silk around his hips, smoothed the meager hair behind his ears, made a grimace at Celestus Falconius, and walked at his leisure toward the door. At the entrance he began to whistle an Alexandrine street-song, but, apparently on more serious consideration, abandoned it in the middle of a phrase. Favorinus sighed, stood up, and opened the library door on silence and a flood of sun.

"Just one more moment," said the Secretary of Petitions without looking up. "I'm on the next to the last page."

"No need to hurry." He sat down on the other side of the long table and looked at the finished sheets which Pessinus had laid to one side. There were scores of notes, in the margins and on the backs of the sheets; whole new pages would have to be added in order to build up the appeal to the plebes; fresh metaphors and new transitions were called for now, and some of the most carefully polished paragraphs would plainly be lost. And yet the task of rehabilitating the speech alone up here in the library seemed so congenial to him that, for the moment at least, he could not even regret the necessity of cancelling two engagements he had made with Charis—an evening at the house of the old poet Berosus and an afternoon at the pantomime. He ate a sliver of partridge, poured himself a gobletful of the fine Cretan vintage, took up a quill, and rewrote the opening paragraph on the back of the first page.

"You're in a very amiable humor, considering what you've got in front of you," Pessinus said. "I was afraid you'd want to throw it at me when you saw what a mess I'd made of it."

Favorinus filled another goblet for the Secretary of Petitions. "No, really, there's no mess at all. It looks to me as if you've outlined everything that's needed—I can just proceed on your suggestions." He felt a sudden and incomprehensible surge of affection for his visitor—he stopped himself on the point of reaching across the table and touching his hand.

"Maybe before you write the whole thing over again, you ought to consult somebody else."

"But who else is there to consult?" It was a simple question, uttered with only the slightest indication of emotion; yet it implied that the Secretary of Petitions, so far as Favorinus Herennius was concerned, was the outstanding mind of the new regime and would, without the slightest doubt, be appointed censor by the Emperor.

There was a moment of silence in which both of them, a little embarrassed, looked at the blue window and drained off their wine. Then Pessinus pushed aside his empty goblet, wiped his fingers on his damp handkerchief, and sighed. "If I were you," he said, "I'd have a word about the speech with Valerian."

"Valerian? That hippopotamus? What for?"

The Secretary of Petitions smiled, and the depth of his confidence in his host was manifested by the fact that he made no attempt to put his face in order. "Whatever you think of the Dean of the Senate," he said, still smiling, "we've got to remember that nobody, except perhaps yourself, carries quite so much weight with the Emperor—figuratively, I mean."

"I don't believe it. Look what sort of thing Decius hands over to him— processions, rituals, all the religious nonsense—"

Pessinus picked up a partridge wing and looked at it with grave and melancholy eyes. "The religious nonsense—" he said, "maybe it's ridiculous to you and me. But don't deceive yourself. Nothing is more important to the Lord of the World."

The Emperor's old-fashioned piety had made itself obvious enough in these first six weeks of Favorinus's service with the new regime. But he had never seen it as a source of imperial action or an influence on imperial policy, had told himself that it was a pleasantly archaic piece of quaintness, existing separate from everything else in some closed corner of his uncle's mind. That it could amount to more than this was a disquieting possibility, so disquieting that he dismissed the whole subject until he could give it more exhaustive thought. "What could he see in that big pompous idiot?" he said.

"Don't you know?"

"Knowing my uncle, no—"

"That big pompous idiot—that hippopotamus," said Ummidius Pessinus, chewing unhappily on the resistant partridge wing, "has the same value for your uncle as the ancient iron pots in the Temple of Vesta, or the fragments of the Old City Wall. He comes from a family that flourished in the days of the Republic. He's a living survival of the blessed times that were and ought to be again. His name—haven't you noticed how your uncle likes to say it?—his name itself is a magical thing. For centuries the Valerii have been Roman aristocrats. The Valerii were censors and consuls and augurs and Vestal Virgins in the days when the Pessini were slaves."

"But why would my uncle attach any importance to such senseless distinctions?" His protest was the more ardent because he knew that his visitor's assertion was true. "Look at his advisors—sons of freedmen, sons of provincials—one of them is even a Jew. After all, my uncle could hardly be called a Roman aristocrat. He's a Pannonian farmer himself."

"Yes," said Pessinus, laying the bony wing back on the silver platter. "That's exactly why he takes Valerian and the Old Wall and the iron pots so much to heart."

It was a penetrating analysis; it showed an insight into the more obscure places of the human heart that he would sooner have expected of himself than of the political realist on the other side of the table. He turned his head and stared blankly at the marble face of Virgil, and wondered what sort of blind spot he had been carrying about with him. "How could I miss a thing like that?" he said.

The gentle eyes begged him not to disparage himself. "Any patrician would miss it. I would have missed it myself, I assure you, if I had been born one of the Herennii. Patricians like your people take their aristocracy for granted the way the rest of us take the air we breathe—patricians like your people can see Valerian for what he is and can laugh in his face. But Valerian—believe me, my dear fellow—Valerian, with all the glory of his status shining like a nimbus around him, will never be a laughing matter to a Pannonian."

No reply was expected. The Secretary of Petitions was gathering the manuscript into an orderly heap.

"Must you go so soon?"

"I'm afraid so. The wine and the partridge were excellent—I've eaten so much I won't be able to take another bite tonight." He rose and walked round to the end of the table. "You'll talk to the Dean of the Senate then?" he said.

"About the speech? Not until I'm further along with it." The realization that his visitor was about to leave filled him with uneasiness. The thought of suspending work on the manuscript until such time as he could arrange a conference with Valerian was almost intolerable to him. If he had leisure, even an hour's leisure, his conscience would compel him to go to his sister's bedroom, to listen to her twisted version of the episode in the atrium, to offer consolation. "I couldn't wait. I'd lose my first energy if I waited. I mean to have a good part of it written before I go to bed tonight."

"Then show him the second draft of it." He picked up his crumpled handkerchief, thrust it into the belt of his violently blue dalmatica, and started toward the door. "Show him the second draft—it'll flatter him, and a person ought to flatter him now and then. I'm afraid he's more influential than most of us allow ourselves to think."

He did not accompany his visitor to the entrance, partly because he knew he would be embarrassed escorting him through the ostentatious splendor of the atrium, and partly because he was afraid there might be a sound of weeping in the upper corridor. He clapped his hands and summoned two slaves—the one to lead the Secretary of Petitions downstairs, the other to clear the library table—and, while the polished wood was being rubbed clean of the orange juice and the partridge grease, he stood by, restless and irritable at the delay. Then, having told the departing slave to inform his mother that he was too busy to make an appearance at the evening meal, he took up the pages and began to develop the suggestions in Pessinus's notes. One idea generated another, more phrases than he could set down came crowding in on him, and he did not leave the long table again until the middle of that night.

Chapter 8

"Now it's begun to bleed again," said Favorinus, banging the silver mirror down on the carved chest and holding a corner of the linen towel against his chin. "I might as well resign myself to missing the morning sacrifice. Because of your carelessness, I'll never get to the Temple."

The tall Aethiopian body-slave stood on the other side of the bedchamber with a lamp in his hand. The single flame, pale against the pulsing grey light of the window, brought out the gleam on the ebony planes of his face; his moist eyes stared over his master's shoulder with stubborn imperviousness. "If my lord and my master had not pulled off the clot—" he said.

"Pulled off the clot!" He looked at it on the towel—the ugly, blackish thing. "Am I supposed to present myself in public with a clot the size of a pea on my chin? If you'd watched what you were doing when you were shaving me—"

"I was watching what I was doing, my lord and my master."

"You're out of humor this morning, aren't you? You've been out of humor for quite some time—ever since I put you to the trouble of waiting on me four or five mornings a week, ever since I've been inconsiderate enough to sleep in my own house and require the services of my own body-slave."

Only the eyes moved in the bony, impassive face—they rolled in the direction of the open door to let him know that his strident voice might

waken his mother, his sister, scores of slaves. He turned away, a little embarrassed, and looked at his chin again in the mirror; it had occurred to him
that he had never shouted at any of the slaves in the palace before. The
habit of shouting was one he had acquired in the imperial offices. There,
surrounded by constant confusion and urgency, one shouted to make certain
that the really pressing thing was done; one shouted, without looking up
from one's papyri, at any one of a crowd of nameless, faceless government
slaves. But the Aethiopian who stood behind him had a name and a face:
this was Baubio, who puffed up his pillows, draped his toga, rubbed the
weariness out of his bones with powerful, gentle hands. To shout at Baubio
was to strike a blow on a mute, living heart. . . .

"Well, it makes no difference," he said. "Jupiter can manage without my
grain of incense for once." And yet, now that he had said it in so many
words, he was uneasy. Several of the "clever ones" had told him—not that
he believed it for a moment—that the Emperor kept spies among the priests
at the Temple of Jupiter and knew before breakfast who had missed the
morning sacrifice. He dropped the towel onto the chest and started for the
threshold, stopping long enough to lay his hand on the bare black shoulder.
'I'll sleep here again tonight, and probably tomorrow night."

The full lips trembled. The big, pained eyes refused to meet his own.
"My lord and my master is very much mistaken if he thinks I count on the
nights when he sleeps in another house."

Even if he had not seen the lamp reflected in the polished grey stone of the
hall, even if it had not been the slave Prisca sitting between the lamp and
the little pile of jewelry on a bench before his sister's door, the pregnant
stillness of the sleeping palace would have made him ashamed of himself.
The bench before Drusilla's door was beyond the top of the stair and, he
could have gone down without acknowledging the child's presence: her
hair had fallen forward, hiding her face, and she was presenting a lively
show of preoccupation, rubbing vigorously with the polishing cloth at one
of Drusilla's rings. Yet he felt so strong a compulsion to find out whether
she had heard him rage at Baubio that he strolled up to the bench and stood
before her. "May the gods walk with Prisca all through this day," he said.

The usual answer did not follow. He could have counted ten before she
raised her head, before her milky, freckled cheeks emerged into the lamplight from the two soft wings of her hair. Have I frightened her with all
that shouting? he asked himself. But there was no hint of fright in her face.
Her cheeks crinkled, the scar at the corner of her right eye deepened into
the familiar dimple, and the corners of her lips were indented by the remembered smile. For some incomprehensible child's reason, she had simply
chosen to omit the formal greeting. "My lady and my mistress is still asleep,"
she said in a whisper, "and that's a very good thing, I can tell you. She lay
awake crying half the night."

He was moved to nothing but impatience by the vision that the little slave had conjured up for him—the white face puffy with the endless weep ing, the string of pearls, Eugenius's last gift, clutched in the thin hand. I am raw, I am very raw and irritable, he thought. That's because it's more than ten days since I have soothed and renewed myself with my love . . The child's big eyes were fixed upon him. "It's a wonder I didn't waken her shouting at Baubio," he said.

"Baubio cut you on the chin, didn't he?" She laid the cloth and the ring in her lap, and leaned forward, propping her elbows on her knees and her face in her hands. There was an obvious struggle between solicitude and amusement in her crinkling face. "I suppose he cut you like that because he's afraid of you," she went on in a solemn and thoughtful voice. "You'd better get somebody else to shave you tomorrow. Tomorrow he'll be so fright ened of you he might cut off your head."

"I'm always in a bad temper when I get up these days," he said. "I used to wake up late and lie in bed—I'd wait for half an hour to collect myself, I'd sit for another half hour at breakfast, planning my day. And now, as soon as I've opened my eyes, everything I'm supposed to do comes rushing in."

"Oh, I know." She nodded energetically and began to rub another ring. "It's very sad, having the whole day filled up with things. And even if it isn't completely filled up, even if you can save an hour or two for yourself, that's spoiled, too, because you count on it too much."

How did she come by that sad piece of wisdom? he asked himself. He remembered how, coming home from an evening at the theater last week, he had seen her alone in the torchlit garden, solemnly and joylessly tossing a ball at a hoop tied to a mulberry tree—he had thought vaguely then that she should have been in bed. And I had a disheartening time of it that evening, too, he thought. We had nothing to say to each other, Charis and I, nothing but stupid complaints about the stupidity of the comedy. . . .

The blunt, childish fingers took up still another ring. Now there were only two of them left to be polished—a cameo with the head of Venus on it and a fine big onyx engraved with the figure of Hercules. They were such rings as would have pleased a child more than the emeralds and diamonds, and he wondered whether she had reserved them, as one reserves the plump est raisins on the cluster, for the last. "Is that why you're starting to work so early—so that you can have a little time for yourself this evening?" he said.

"Oh, no, I couldn't sleep."

"Why not?"

"Because, as I said—" her grave eyes chided him gently, asked him how he could have forgotten so soon, "as I said, my lady and my mistress cried all night. When my lady is crying, I can't go to sleep."

How is it with me then that I can sleep? he thought. She is my sister, and these seven nights, ever since she tore the emeralds out of her hair and ran from the atrium, I have heard her weeping on my way to bed, and her weeping has interfered no more with my rest than the whimpering of a dog

in the kennel at night. Yet this little slave to whom she is only a mistress—
and a hard mistress, too, in her exigency—sits tense in a dark room, listening
to that whimpering, so distressed that she cannot sleep.

"Well, she's asleep now, isn't she?" he asked in a faintly querulous voice.
"Since you were up all night, why don't you go and get a pillow and sleep
out here until she wakes up—which probably won't be until noon?"

"But I'm not at all tired, I wouldn't sleep. When she's finished crying,
when she turns over on her side and closes her eyes—I wish I could tell you—
it's the most wonderful thing in the world. It seems to me then as if I had a
new heart in my body, as if everything on earth were new, as if I had never
seen the sun coming up before. Oh, I wouldn't miss it, not for anything.
The palace is so quiet—everybody sleeping but you and Baubio. Everybody
but you and Baubio—how can I tell you what I mean?—all folded up in
God's peace. And it's so beautiful here in the hall with the windows getting
lighter and lighter like louder and louder music, and I sit here and polish
the rings and sing to myself in a whisper, and everybody is asleep and
nothing is the matter, and any minute now the birds will begin, and—" she
stopped, out of breath, and spread her stubby fingers in the light—"and how
on earth could a person go to sleep?"

For an instant he saw what he imagined she must be seeing—the world
and the palace folded in the peace of God. But what sort of wisdom am I
attributing to her? he thought. She is still half a child, a girl who tosses a
ball through a hoop in the empty garden, and I am endowing her with
concepts that belong only to the most profound followers of the Nameless
and Bodiless God . . . "But you must get on with your polishing, and I
must go to the imperial palace, to the Emperor's levee," he said. "I'm late
already—too late to get to the Capitoline in time to give Jupiter his grain of
incense—not that I think he particularly wants it—" He stopped, wondering
why he should feel impelled to show the child his contempt for the old gods.

She reached down mechanically for the last two of the rings—the onyx
and the cameo—and then snatched back her hand as if she had been on the
point of touching a hot brazier. The gesture was puzzling enough to hold
him there a little longer, even though the flame of the lamp was almost lost
in daylight now and the first shrill chorus of birds had begun. He bent and
took up the cameo with the Venus-head. "I think this is the prettiest one,
don't you?" he said, holding it out to her. "Is that why you were saving it
for last?"

She made a fluttering movement, like a sparrow caught in a net. Then,
as suddenly as she had started up, she settled down again. Slowly, deliberately, looking at him all the while with her big clear eyes, she wrapped her
fingers in the polishing cloth and took the ring from him in a swathed hand.
"I can't touch it. I'm forbidden to touch it," she said.

"Oh, come now, it isn't as precious as all that."

"But that's not the reason. I'm forbidden to touch it because there's an image of a daemon on it. If my hand is made evil by the daemon—" she took a deep breath— "then I can't reach up at the altar and take the bread and the wine—the body and the blood of Jesus, my Lord."

But what have I ever done for her that she should trust me with such a secret? he thought. I have given her cheap little dolls and trinkets; I helped her find a chip of marble from our well-cover; and once when the old Greek, the slave's physician, had to dig a thorn out of her foot, I held her on my lap and stroked her hair. How loveless and colorless her life must be if such casual kindnesses are enough to make her confess to me what is still a crime according to the letter of the law, and what would be cause in my mother's eyes for a beating with leather thongs or even exile to one of our dreary, isolated farms in Bithynia or Sicily . . . He felt the need of offering some acknowledgment of her trust, and yet he was incapable of meeting the unwavering candor of her eyes. "Really? Is that the way it is?" he said at last. And both the words and the voice sounded so fatuous that he blushed.

"Yes, that's the way it is. And I have a time of it, I can tell you. There are daemons all over the place. My lady's things are full of daemons. Every time I dress her, I come across a daemon—on the rings, on the embroidery, on the comb, everywhere." She looked him up and down, and smiled with satisfaction. "You don't seem to have any daemons on your clothes this morning," she said. "Well, you'll be late if you stay here any longer. Farewell, my master. May the Lord Jesus walk with you and cause His countenance to shine upon you and give you peace."

From the head of the stairway he looked in the direction of his mother's bedchamber, and was relieved to see that the door was still closed. Sometimes she would step into the corridor with her lively ringlets hanging about her shoulders and give him a conspiratorial look, as if the two of them were sharing the secrets of the morning together; she would lift her dry mouth for a kiss. This silent greeting was one of her ways of showing him that she was satisfied with his present behavior. There were other equally disquieting ways—she boasted to her guests of his connection with the Emperor, she magnified the extent of his official duties, she made it plain that he need feel no responsibility for the lands and tenements anymore. And her sudden friendliness, embarrassing in itself because he could make no honest return for it, was troubling also in its implications. He knew how elated she was that he had fewer and fewer evenings to spend with "the filthy Greek"; he was sure that she was appraising the persons and the fortunes of the patrician girls who came to visit her with their mothers on mid-week afternoons. Sometimes he was so uneasy that he picked a quarrel with her on the principle that to be on cordial terms with the beloved's enemy was to be disloyal to the beloved.

At the foot of the stairs he heard the deep hum of masculine voices coming from the dining room. His clients—he had forgotten his clients—as often as once a week he was amazed to find the little crowd of official petitioners waiting in their best togas to escort him through the streets. His delay on the upper floor had given them time to linger over the morning meal set out for them at the expense of the Herennii; they told him, like pleased children, that the steward had brought on an extra course to help them while away the time—a fine cheese with onion rings and a second round of hot bread. His mother had been surprisingly gracious about feeding them; her only complaint was that he did not use them to his best advantage: they could have been sent on errands, they could have stood by when he bathed at the public baths to help him dry and anoint himself. But how, he asked himself, coming out onto the dewy lawn and starting toward his litter, how can I send a threadbare equestrian or a consumptive scholar on an errand? How can I ask a shattered, vague-eyed offshoot of the Flavian line to render me the menial services of a slave?

They followed the litter, as they followed it every morning now, down the long avenue of sycamores. At the end of the avenue, the gardener Sylvanus was mowing the weeds with a sickle, and he straightened and smiled at his lord and his master. He also, thought Favorinus. The greeting that comes naturally into his head is something like, "May the Lord Jesus cause His countenance to shine upon you," and, since he cannot say that, he stares and says nothing at all . . . Lying back against the goosefeather pillow of the litter, he tried to recapture the hushed exaltation that had been upon him in the upper corridor. But the magic was gone; the being who had sung the praises of the newborn day to him was only the gardener's thirteen-year-old daughter; he could see nothing but a freckled, crinkling face and a pair of stubby hands. . . .

As soon as the litter turned into the street, he drew the curtains. At this hour of the day the City was at its ugliest. The streets were filled with a jostling and ill-tempered crowd—peddlers with stinking buckets of fish and mussels, schoolboys tagging after pedagogues with smoking lamps, pasty-faced civil servants on their way to the government offices with oily packages of noonday food, the last of the night's revelers sitting dejectedly against the columns or sprawled beside the urinals in drunken sleep. In other years, before the raw unloveliness of winter had come upon the City, he had escaped to some warmer, cleaner, more salubrious place. He and Charis had talked of spending the winter in Alexandria this year, but he had forgotten it, and she had not mentioned it. How many such hopes he had raised and omitted to fulfill of late, he did not know. But he felt an ache of remorse, and all the rest of the way to the imperial palace, he kept looking between the curtains of the litter at the peddlers in the street, hoping to find somebody with a basket of autumn narcissi or the remnants of a last shipment of African roses. For once he would make use of one of his clients and send him off to Charis's house with a present of flowers and a message of extravagant devotion. But it was useless, the season had advanced too far; the Campanian gardens were lying fallow now, and even the most enterprising of the speculators would not risk a perishable cargo to the first autumnal blasts. Myrtle there was, and ivy, and laurel freshly cut; but nowhere on the Palatine—and he was almost superstitiously distressed to find it so—could he catch sight of a single flower.

His disquiet was not lessened by his passage through the bloomless imperial gardens and the dim, dismantled atrium. He could never quite make up his mind whether the number of senators and equestrians gathered in the gaudy granite gloom was actually smaller than it had been in Philip's day or only seemed so because the clutter of furniture and ornament was gone. His clients would help to swell the crowd a little—he led them to a conspicuously empty place at the end of the right-hand colonnade and told them he would be grateful if they stayed there for at least an hour. His own status was such that he never had to waste his time in desultory talk in this outer chamber; the sickly Syrian eunuch caught his eye at once and signalled him as usual toward the less splendid and more intimate rooms at the back of the palace. At the door of the dining room where the chosen ones waited to give the Emperor the traditional morning greeting, he turned and looked back over the vast reaches of the atrium. The crowd *was* small; the new regime, with its program of reform and austerity, had certainly not captured the general imagination. But that was nothing to fret about; the Emperor himself had expected that. "A few good men," he had said. "A few good men and the help of the gods."

The "few good men"—some thirty of them, all talking, all gesticulating—were crowded into the little dining room; and his heart was lightened by the very sight of the place. All the old-fashioned simplicity, all the lovable quirks and crotchets of the present ruler, had been established here; of all the oriental frippery that had been here in Philip's day, only one purely official object remained—a curtain that had hung for decades between this room and the Emperor's sleeping chamber, a great white fall of Egyptian linen, luminous with sunlight and embroidered all over with palm leaves of purple and gold. The outer furnishings could have belonged to nobody but the Emperor Decius. The massive, battered table had plainly been sent down from an old country house; the fruit and bread were set out in pottery dishes; the cloth was fine red linen, but had been washed so many times that the corners were badly frayed. There were a dozen dining couches and half a dozen chairs, but most of the guests were on their feet. That always happened at the Emperor's levees: since there were never enough seats for everybody, the young men would not take their places until the older ones had asserted their claims, and the older ones were too engrossed in the noisy conversation to seat themselves.

Valerian was one of the few exceptions. He sat in benign and vacuous placidity on a couch some five feet in front of the curtain; his bald brow and ruddy countenance glowed against the gold and purple palm leaves; his plump hands lay pink and limp on his big, parted knees. Catching sight of him from the entrance, Favorinus was almost glad to see him looking so stupid; it seemed preposterous now that Ummidius Pessinus—who was making himself as pleasant as possible to the yellowish Pontifex Maximus—should ever have imagined *that* one in the role of censor.

He went to the battered table and helped himself to a rusk, an apple, and an ancient goblet of home-made wine. Munching on his apple, he looked about the sunny room at the clever, alert faces; and it struck him that no comparable area on earth held as much congregated intelligence as this dining room. To the right of him an illustrious advocate was explaining how all behindhand business in the urban courts could be cleared away at once to make way for the censorship cases. To his left, the bald, monkey-faced Secretary of the Privy Purse was outlining a plan for government subsidies to revive the olive industry in Egypt. On the other side of the table an ageing general, drawing a plan of the northern frontier on the cloth with his fingernail, was showing a visiting dignitary from Phrygia just what sections of the line were most vulnerable to the Goths. Any one of the half-dozen groups would have been happy to make room for Favorinus: invitations were coming at him from every side, nods and beckoning looks and smiles. If he continued to stand solitary near the bowl of apples, it was only because he knew that it was late and that in a moment a body-slave would thrust the curtain apart and initiate the more formal part of the Emperor's levee by summoning one of the visitors to enter the imperial bedroom, approach the exalted person, and drape the toga of the Emperor of All the Romans and the Lord of the World.

Favorinus had been given that signal honor twice—once at the very beginning of his political career when he had been called in and supplied with additional notes on the censorship, and once some ten days ago when the Emperor had asked him whether he would be willing to play host during the Saturnalia feast to a certain Trebonianus Gallus, Governor of Moesia, who was on his way to the City with a military report on the Gothic frontier. Others had been summoned two or three times each—the Pontifex Maximus, the Secretary of the Privy Purse, the Urban Prefect; but, for the most part, the Emperor extended the morning invitation either to Ummidius Pessinus or to Valerian. Favorinus had never given much thought to this traditional and purely official honor; yet now—probably because of his recent conversation with the Secretary of Petitions—it occurred to him that the Dean of the Senate had been summoned into the imperial presence a number of times in succession. The realization was so disturbing to him that he dropped the napkin on which he was wiping his hands, walked over to the little Secretary of the Privy Purse, and took him by his small and bony arm. "How do you like that for self-assurance?" he said, jerking his head in the direction of the big rosy mound of a man seated before the curtain. "He's taken to sitting over there now so that he won't have too far to walk when his name is called. How many times in succession is it now—three, four—that the Emperor has invited him in?"

"Five, I think," said the Secretary of the Privy Purse, his bright eyes blinking beneath his domed brow. "Five, but I wouldn't let that worry me if I were you. Something's got to be done to appease him. After all, he hasn't been given one significant assignment in the last two months. It's all the better for us—isn't it?—if Decius hands the formal honors out to him and saves the actual authority for Ummidius—"

He and everybody else in the dining room fell silent because the embroidered linen had been parted by the dark shoulders and shaven head of an Aethiopian slave. "Favorinus Herennius," said the throaty voice, "will pass into the imperial bedchamber and drape the toga of the Emperor of All the Romans and the Lord of the World."

He flushed with pleasure—any of the thirty of them would have been elated—but he knew that his spirits had begun to soar even before the slave had called his name. How persistently the thought of Valerian had nagged at him of late he had apparently never dared to admit to himself. Now, moving lightly toward the sun-drenched curtain, he had a buoyant feeling that, if *that* was well, then everything was well, that the house of the Decii would reign for a century over a decent, peaceable world. . . .

And, once he had passed to the other side of the luminous curtain, he was not the less high-hearted to see the head of that house for what he was—a stern old soldier, still in his tunic, sitting stiffly on the edge of his bed. That the world's hope should manifest itself in this ageing, leathery body, that the bedchamber of the saviour of the Empire should be like any old general's bedchamber, that he should lay his imperial togas in a big clumsy chest and lie at night under a coverlet with raveled fringes—it was enough to blur a man's sight with grateful tears.

It was to be a private interview—the Aethiopian drew the curtain close and departed. The formal kiss of greeting, aimed at the imperial hand, was waved away, and the closely-shaven, soap-scented cheek was raised to receive the family greeting instead. "May Jupiter sustain you through the day," he said, and seated himself on the threadbare coverlet, freely and gladly seeking the ice-blue eyes.

"And you also."

The voice was cordial, but the look was only a brief sidewise glance. There was an indefinable uneasiness in Decius's bearing toward him this morning—not displeasure, only a certain shyness, a new reticence. Etiquette required that, once the greetings had been exchanged, the Emperor should introduce the subject of the short conversation. But he remained silent, with his weathered hands closed over his bare knees. He remained uncomfortably silent for so long that Favorinus felt compelled to break the hush himself.

"Is my Aunt Etruscilla well? I haven't seen her for a week or more," he said.

"Very well—reasonably well, I suppose. Of course, she worries—"

He waited for a disquietingly long time to hear what it was that she worried about.

"In the last two or three weeks she's taken to worrying unduly about Herennius—"

The name came out of him hard, with a wrench. How he had blundered into saying it, the young man could not tell. He knew only that he ought to take hold of the conversation and lead it in some other direction; his uncle's face was red under the sunburn, and the stillness was throbbing like a physical wound with the old disgrace, the old pain.

"Maybe it's a good thing the Governor of Moesia is coming down," he said. "He'll probably be able to reassure her. Of course, it's only natural that she should worry. As the general was saying to our Phrygian visitor this morning, one learns to expect the unexpected of the Goths."

The Goths and their unpredictable nature were met with stubborn disregard. Decius turned and looked at him for an instant, and there was a glint of reproach in the pale glance. "My son Herennius," he said, plainly implying that, in spite of any attempts to the contrary, this morning's talk would remain with his son Herennius—"that was a strange letter he wrote to me—the one about Gallus."

"I hope he's in good health—"

"No, he's not in good health. I suspect he has the marsh fever. He's had it, you know, ever since he was fifteen." The voice was harsh, and Favorinus could have sworn he detected a bitter implication: There's another one of his weaknesses—ill health, marsh fever—go and tell that one, too, to the Herennii.

"My father had the marsh fever." His courteous motive was too obvious; he wet his lower lip with the tip of his tongue and hurried on. "He had it for six years, if I remember right, and then he took the cure at Epidaurus, and when he came back it was gone."

"It's plain from the letter that he's unhappy, too. . . ."

The unmentionable cause of that unhappiness took shape before him—the white face with the painted mouth, the emaciated hands tearing the emeralds out of the disheveled hair. The recollection moved him strangely, more than he had been moved by the actuality. He felt exposed and graceless. He could only stare down at his own feet.

"Unhappy when he has every reason to be more than satisfied with himself." The voice was assertive, almost boastful with wounded pride. "Those six legions that I left with him—they adore him. And they're a hard-bitten lot, I can tell you. He's the only reason they don't fall apart."

"I know that, my uncle."

The Emperor did nothing to dispel the tense quiet—Favorinus was left to deal with it as well as he could. And he was too baffled, too unsure of the underlying motives at work to speak of his cousin as he remembered him from the days in the house on the Esquiline, to speak freely or warmly from the heart. He praised the young general in the only phrases that he could grasp at—the conventional terms which the court was accustomed to praise him in. And he would have had a conviction of utter insufficiency even if his uncle had not stood up in the middle of a sentence and walked to the heavy chest and come back to the bed with a crumpled toga in his hands.

"Here," said the Emperor, thrusting the toga at him. "It's late, I'd better put it on, we're wasting time."

He was unnerved enough to be awkward in a skill of which he was a recognized master. Twice he gathered the long end of the first fold and tried to fasten it at the shoulder, and twice it slipped out of his hands. He flushed and moved round to the back, thinking he might work more aptly out of range of the ice-blue eyes; but even there he could produce nothing but a series of wrinkled, unsymmetrical folds.

"I see you're having your troubles."

"I seem to be unusually awkward this morning."

"If you're awkward, it's nobody's fault but mine. I upset you. Take your time."

There was another silence, a charged silence. The muscles in the sunburnt arms tightened, and the tendons in the creased neck showed tense through the sparse ring of white hair. Then the head turned and the pale eyes flashed straight into his for an instant. "Your sister Drusilla—you never mention her," said the Emperor, turning round again. "How is she these days?"

Blind instinct led him. He let his hand fall upon the hard brown shoulder. "My sister Drusilla is no better off than my cousin Herennius," he said.

"I've been told as much by a number of people." There was no gratified malice in the quiet tone—there was nothing but kindness and regret. "It's a pity, I'm sorry to hear it. We were always fond of Drusilla, my wife and I."

Fond of Drusilla . . . He remembered with a pang how in the years before her marriage everybody had been fond of Drusilla—not the Decii alone, but everybody of any importance—the elegant patricians who courted her and the eager girls who were charmed to have her for a friend, the old senators who wanted only to renew their tired spirits with an evening of staring at beauty, and the withered dowagers who relived in her their own departed dreams. "Where is your sister this evening? We're all so fond of Drusilla." How long it was since he had been greeted like that at the entrance of an atrium. Her partisans, all her golden, fluttering, laughing partisans were gone. And he himself—it was months since he had thought of her with anything except annoyance and bafflement. Nobody was fond of Drusilla anymore except a pair of Christian cousins and a thirteen-year-old slave. . . .

"We haven't changed. We're still fond of Drusilla."

His heart stood still and then knocked crazily. Instinct was pointing for him again, was showing him the preposterous possibility that the lady Sabina had not dreamed her audacious dream in vain. But that was unthinkable, he rejected the thought and held his tongue. He came round to the front, keeping his head bent down, and took up the length of linen that had resisted him at the start.

Then suddenly the hard, veined arm went out, put his hand away, pushed him aside. "Almighty Jupiter, how much does a man have to say to you before he gets an answer?" Patches of red showed on the weathered cheeks. The lips folded hard against each other, but they trembled nevertheless.

"I don't understand—"

"What don't you understand? That I should concern myself with your sister Drusilla after all that went on because of her between the Decii and the Herennii? That I should be willing to compromise my dignity? Listen, I have a great deal of dignity, more than I ever wanted. I have dignity to throw away, and I'll throw away a little of it if I like for Herennius's sake. Pick up the toga—it's dragging on the floor. My son is obsessed with your sister—that much even a fool could understand. We were mistaken, Etruscilla and I—we let him think from his childhood that he could have her. We were seriously mistaken, and I'm willing to pay a certain amount of my dignity—whatever that is—to wipe out my mistake." He took the length of linen out of his nephew's hands, reached behind him for a brooch that lay on the coverlet, thrust the pin into a bulge of linen at his shoulder, and fastened it himself. "That letter was the most miserable thing I ever read," he said in a quiet voice. "I wanted to ask you—will she cling to that wretch of hers forever? Isn't there anything hopeful that I could write to Herennius?"

He saw her again, all her proud rigidity crumpling as her husband came up behind her. He saw her again, turning to claim the bought embrace, and he could find no word.

"A good, decent boy," said Decius. "Handsome enough, too, and gentle—he'd never give her an hour of grief. Back in the house on the Esquiline, I could have sworn she loved him. Who's to say she wouldn't love him again if she had the chance? And now there are other things to take into consideration—I won't live forever, she'd be an empress, and her children—she might want children, most women do—her son would be heir to the rayed crown—"

"We don't deserve it." He gave himself over to the inner impulse, and clasped the muscular forearm and let his blushing face come down on his uncle's shoulder. "Whatever comes of it, let me say from the beginning that we don't deserve it," he said.

"Whatever comes of it?" The Emperor took him by the elbows and held him a little apart, but kindly, looking into his face with grave and questioning eyes. "You have your doubts about what'll come of it? Well, I don't wonder. How deep this business of Eugenius went with her everybody knows, and you'd know better than anybody else. If she had been less honorable, less single-minded, she'd have suffered less. She'd have gone like the rest of them and taken her pleasures where she could. And we wouldn't have wanted that, my wife and I and Herennius. Only, since it's obvious now that her husband won't be coming back, couldn't she divorce him, couldn't she—Fix this brooch, will you? I've put it in all wrong. Couldn't somebody ask her—not her mother, I don't want your mother to hear a word of this until the Herennii have an unequivocal 'Yes' to say to the Decii. You can see why, I'm sure. It's still dragging on the floor—up a little on the left side—that'll do well enough, it's never exactly right. How about you, Favorinus? Couldn't you talk to Drusilla yourself?"

"I'm afraid she'd consider me too partial an advocate. And I can't claim to have her confidence—it isn't the way it used to be with her and me anymore."

"No? I wouldn't know, of course. It's years since I've seen the two of you together. Somebody else then, some woman, some friend of hers. Somebody trustworthy, who wouldn't spread the story all over the City. We can't afford another rejection, as I said."

Some friend of hers . . . He thought again of the golden crowd that had fluttered around her in her better years—all of them gone. Somebody trustworthy . . . Of all the women who visited his mother's atrium, he could not think of one who would not whisper such a fascinating secret to at least one confidant. Then suddenly he saw his cousin Paulina standing at the window in the shadow of the colonnade, lost in the vision of a saint's grave. The pale, tired face—there was something incorruptible about the wan cheeks and the solemn eyes . . . "I know a woman who would be perfectly dependable, perfectly honest—"

"Whatever you think. I leave it to you. I don't even want to know her name."

Favorinus stood a little longer, ostensibly making a final survey of the toga, but actually prolonging this moment of complete understanding and confidence. Certain unsayable sentences ran through his mind: I love you as the saviour of the world and the genius of my childhood. I love your stern, honorable face and your crumpled toga and your raveled coverlet. However this business prospers, let it do no harm to the hard-won faith between you and me. . . .

"You'll look to it soon then, Favorinus?"

"Very soon, my master and my lord."

"When you have news, come and tell me." He laid his hand on the bright, embroidered folds of the linen, and there was an expectant murmur from the little crowd outside. As the curtain swung back, Favorinus tried to imagine his sister Drusilla in a scarlet wedding veil with her arm through the arm of his cousin Herennius. But, try as he would, he could not conjure up the desired image. Suddenly depleted, actually shaken, he scarcely took note of the congratulatory smiles of his colleagues, but went straight to the table and drained off two cupfuls of the sour home-made wine.

Chapter 9

THREE DAYS went by before Favorinus Herennius could bring himself to visit his cousin Paulina. The thought of asking her for her assistance—an idea that had seemed perfectly natural to him in the stress of his conversation with the Emperor—seemed utterly preposterous to him now. To go to her house on the Aventine, which he had not visited for years, to request an interview with a woman to whom he had never talked in private, to say to her, "I would like you to help me convince my sister that she should marry the heir to the purple"—each step in the procedure seemed more unimaginable than the last. Even so, he would probably have set about his task more promptly if it had not been for the weather. Heat and an unwholesome haze hung over the City; it might have been the middle of June, such crowds were loitering in the porticoes and colonnades. Even on the third day, after a drowsy midday meal with the Urban Prefect, he did not order his litter-bearers to take him to the Aventine directly; he told them to carry him to the Baths of Caracalla instead. A swim in one of the indoor pools, ice-cold and fresh from the aqueduct, would clear his head, would drive away the heaviness, the sense of oppression, the tendency to sigh.

He stepped out of his litter at the edge of the vast park that surrounded the Baths—one could make much better time on foot, since the grounds were almost impassable with the goings and comings of the bathed and the unbathed—and made his way up the lawn to the main entrance. The grounds were always crowded with out-of-town visitors exclaiming over the impressive facade and the gigantic portico, gaping while their Roman relatives informed them that the place covered thirty-six acres, that there were sixteen hundred marble seats inside, that you could find more statues, more paintings, more ornamental columns under this roof than under any other roof in the world. By long habit Favorinus had come to exclude from his awareness these architectural feats of sheer mass and number, and he looked neither left nor right while he walked through three ornate chambers to the only room he meant to use. He left his clothes in one of the marble cubicles that opened on the pool, stepped onto the broad band of mosaic that surrounded the water, and stood for several moments staring straight before him. Scores of pale bodies darted about in the greenish water; reflections of marble Nereids and bronze dolphins wavered on the surface; and at the top of the vaulted ceiling, seen through an oval opening, there was a patch of seasonless, hyacinthine sky.

He swam the length of the pool and back again, avoiding four little boys who were squealing and dousing each other, passing an emaciated old man who was floating on his back and staring at the oval of sky above him with a toothless, sweet, meditative smile. He had intended to set out again at once, but, by the time he reached his starting point, he found himself so breathless that he knew he could not take the length again without a rest. Panting, he took hold of the marble ledging and pulled himself out of the water; and, with his legs dangling over the side, he sat for some moments waiting for his heart to subside and watching the dim image of himself waver in the greenness below. I will have to swim more often, I am growing slack, he thought, and stood up to plunge in again. But, before he could leap, the water in front of him parted, and he found himself looking down into the face of his friend, the painter Antisthenes.

It was a remarkable face, keen and bony and distinctly masculine, in spite of the fact that its distinguished possessor had, for the last two years, been in complete bondage to the little male dancer Memphius. Self-contained and faintly scornful, it maintained its dignity even though the water was trickling over it, dripping from the sleek brown beard and plastering down the sparse brown hair.

"What are you doing here?" said Favorinus. "The last I heard, you were going to Tibur."

"I didn't. Like you, I've been detained here by a Higher Duty." He smiled a close-lipped smile and climbed up onto the strip of mosaic, shaking himself. In his nakedness he looked awkward and vulnerable—his shanks were too long, his shoulders sloped, and there was a marked concavity to the line of his hairy chest. But the wise, narrow head with its hollow cheeks and its disparaging mouth seemed to take no cognizance of the inadequate body. He seated himself on the edge of the pool with as much poise as though his insufficiencies had been wrapped away in one of his splendid dalmaticas. "I'm delighted to see that the imperial government allots you the time to take a bath," he said.

It was the first time any of the little crowd that gathered at Charis's house had seen fit to make a direct reference to his present activities. The tone was half disdainful, half affectionate, and he was dubious enough as to the real intent to stifle the retort that leaped into his mind. "What kept you in the City in such foul weather?" he asked, pulling a long trail of cold green water toward him with his feet.

"Heliocrates of Alexandria. You wouldn't have heard about him, locked up as you are in Decius's palace. He's a visiting Sophist. He held forth in the east basilica this morning to something one might reasonably call a multitude."

"How did he strike you?"

"How did he strike me? Like all the rest of the charlatans—another tricked-up cheat with the signs of the zodiac embroidered all over him in gold. He offered to hold forth on any subject proposed by the audience, the more trivial the better—a palace built on a pinhead is more to be wondered at than one built on a mountain, that's what he says. Several subjects were suggested, but he turned them down as too serious. It was a friend of your mother's, Anconia Metella, who took the prize for triviality by suggesting dust. And he really carried it off in interminable sentences—half an hour praising dust and another half abusing it, simply to impress us with his versatility."

"Why did you stay?"

"Why does a man stop to stare at a dead dog in the street? It's the fascination of the abominable. I stayed to disgust myself—" He broke off because one of the public slaves had come up behind them to offer them towels. Springing up, he snatched the two folded squares of linen from the fellow, tossed one of them at Favorinus, and began to rub his own body violently, as if he hated it, with the other. "And you should have seen the purses the women handed him," he said. "Several thousand denarii at least. And all the while the few real philosophers left in this rotting Empire have five or six pupils apiece. They walk the streets in rags and are the butt of everybody's wit."

The decline of philosophy and the arts, the decay of taste and manners—these had been the subject of much searching talk between the two of them, but he did not have the heart for it now. He sat motionless on the edge of the pool with his folded towel on his knees, and managed to produce nothing better than an unconvincing sigh.

"Of course, you wouldn't be worried about such trifles anymore," said the voice behind him, breathless with rubbing. "You're busy with more significant things. What are you doing at the moment? Formulating a new ritual for the purification of the City? I hear there's to be a really colossal religious festival, and all of us are to be duly purified. What branch of the government have you been assigned to? Are you an incense-distributor for the Pontifex Maximus or a garland-collector for Valerian?"

He was furious to have been identified with the sanctimonious supporters of the new piety and retorted that he was not concerned with religious activities but was writing the Emperor's forthcoming speech on the censorship.

"The censorship? Is that what you're up to? Well, they know your value, at any rate, they've put you right into the field of action, I can see. The life of action ought to agree with you. I always said, the life of action is the best escape."

"If it had been an escape for me, I could have run to it long ago. There's been a seat waiting in the Senate for me these last five years. I have nothing to escape from—"

"No, of course not. None of us have anything to escape from. Nothing but such minor things as the drivel of Heliocrates of Alexandria. It's a fine, healthy world we're living in, my dear fellow—"

"There's more the matter with it than a charlatan philosopher."

"Undoubtedly, undoubtedly. And you're working in the significant areas, of course."

"Dull as it may seem to you, it's just possible that a man is better employed trying to get the Egyptian peasants fed than mourning over the decline of philosophy and the arts—" He paused because he sensed rather than heard a sharp intake of breath behind him. "Some of us have to move," he said. "Some of us have to make a gesture, even a useless gesture—"

"Oh, I wouldn't think of suggesting that any of the gestures of your imperial uncle could be called useless. I'm sure they're all to the point, every last one of them, from the prospected purification of the City to the institution of the censorship. For all I know, he may work miracles. After all, miracles have been worked before. Wasn't it Augustus that found Rome a city of brick and left it a city of marble? So there's no telling what Caius Messius Quintus Trajanus Decius may do. He's inherited an Empire full of swine, to be sure, but it's just possible he'll turn them all into men."

"You can afford to take it lightly. You're not starving. You don't happen to live in Marcianopolis within reach of the Goths."

"But I don't take it lightly. In fact, I'm so depressed that I'll have to get back into the water. That's a pity, too, because just when the Empire is being committed to a program of austerity, I've used up one of the government's towels to no purpose at all. I don't suppose we'll be seeing you this week. But you'll be getting around to us one of these days, and we're properly humble in our degenerate futility, we'll appreciate any crusts and bones of your time that you can spare." The voice faltered; the old affection asserted itself, breaking through the mockery. He laid his hand lightly on Favorinus's shoulder, plunged into the green water, and was gone.

The argument had left the young man shaken; he was scarcely aware of what he was doing while he went back to his marble cubicle and dried himself; after he had put on his toga he was still so wet that the woolen clung unpleasantly to his body. Outside he found the air still dank, still oppressive; and when he finally reached the massive silver litter he knew that he could never bring himself to enter it—idiots that they were, they had not troubled themselves to take it out of the sun. Well, he could always walk; she lived only a little way from the Baths, on a by-street whose name he could not remember, somewhere near the top of the Aventine. He did not reprimand his slaves; he was too weary to complain; he merely told them to go back to the palace and started up the hill alone.

Even though the afternoon was far spent, he could not bring himself to hurry. His walk up the slope was desultory and devious, partly because he still hung back from the encounter with his cousin, and partly because this section of the City was strangely congenial to his remote and dreaming state—the shabby houses all shuttered against the heat, the stoops and door-yards empty, the drab streets still. The Aventine had always seemed to him to have only a nominal connection with the rest of the City, singularly lacking as it was in monuments and palaces, crowded with dull family houses and with the seldom-visited shrines of unpopular gods. This after-noon, dust-colored and smoke-colored under a pale sky strewn with racks of coral cloud, it was more than ever like a town in itself, a town set apart and forgotten. Even its most noteworthy landmarks scarcely stood out—he almost passed the Temple of Jupiter Libertas without seeing it—most of its gardens had been sold during the reign of Severus, and the ancient side-walls were crowded in by three-story houses of ugly tavertine. And the shrine of Bona Dea was even less noticeable: its bronze plaque was hidden by a veil of vine, and he would have missed it completely if his attention had not been drawn to two of the sacred snakes that had escaped from their cages and were sunning themselves on the leaf-cluttered steps of the stair. Meeting nobody, seeing no face at any window, no form on any threshold or balcony, he wandered through half a dozen streets and found himself on a steep byway which he had never come upon before. Here the houses were very poor and sparsely set; the paving stones were farther and farther apart, with clumps of vegetation growing between: rank flowering weeds and coarse wild grass. Looking up, he saw nothing but sky before him, and heard the slow, gurgling sound of the river below. He knew then that he had reached the edge of the Aventine plateau—a stretch of clay and weeds jutting out over the barren Murcia Valley—so high and still, so houseless and unpeopled that he felt as if he were standing at the very margin of the world.

He walked to the edge and looked down at a desolate expanse—the sparsely-vegetated Murcia Valley, the muddy Tiber, a crescent-shaped har-bor washing in at the foot of the Aventine. And on the shore of that harbor was a gigantic accumulation of marble—green marble from Africa, yellow

and purple veined marble from Asia, honey-colored marble from Greece—
columns and lintels, paving blocks and pediments, all crowded together in
awesome confusion. For a moment it seemed to him that he was looking
down on the ruins of some ancient capital. Then he realized that these were
the Old Marble Yards—they were not even guarded now—the imperial
government had not withdrawn a single load of stone from them in the last
fifty years. Augustus, the first of them, he thought, found a city of brick and
left it a city of marble. And others after him—Nero, Domitian, Trajan,
Hadrian, Severus, Caracalla—drunk on the vision of an invincible Empire
and an expanding City, flung up mile upon mile of marble walls . . . But
fifty years and more had come and gone since any emperor had called for
marble. These tremendous fluted columns, these blocks whose corners had
begun to lose their pristine sharpness, these huge pedestals fashioned for the
bronze and gold feet of heroes and gods—Decius would not use them, the
son of Decius would not use them, it was impossible to think of a time when
they would be used. . . .

A breath of rank, decaying vegetation came up to him from the Murcia
Valley. He closed his eyes and inhaled it; he was drawn effortlessly, irresistibly toward the thought of annihilation—as effortlessly and irresistibly
as he had been drawn to the seductive dreams that had intruded upon the
peace of his Stoic youth. What am I doing here? Why should I be wandering
about in this forsaken and unwholesome place? he asked himself. It was
late; if he did not go at once to his cousin's house, he might very well be
told that she was seated at table. He got his bearings at once—it was a
matter of walking down the main street, turning off at the second corner,
and stopping three doors to the right. He set out at a determined stride,
but found almost at once that he could not hurry. The heat of the afternoon
lay like a weight upon him, and his heart was laboring weakly, unevenly
in his chest.

When he reached his destination, he almost gave in to a superstitious
fear that the evil genius of the Old Marble Yards was pursuing him, simply
because the house of Probus and Paulina—a decent two-story building
covered with white plaster—happened to stand next door to a sculptor's
yard crowded with unfinished statues and sarcophagi. Actually there was
nothing remarkable in the coincidence. In recent years a good many sculptors had found it profitable to move to the Aventine; any enterprising fellow
could help himself to a share of the vast, unguarded pile in the harbor; some
of the slabs in the garden had probably been filched from the imperial store.
He was so preoccupied with these conjectures that he continued to stand
at the entrance, unable to recall whether he had knocked; and he was on
the point of knocking again when the steward opened the door—an ancient
and emaciated man with a reverend beard, his person as light and dry as a
kernel of grain. His bearing was so solemn and devotional that the young
man half expected him to say, "May the Lord Jesus cause His countenance

to shine upon you." But he merely omitted the greeting and motioned the guest into the small vestibule, only dimly lighted from one high window and divided from the inner chamber by a curtain of heavy undyed cloth. "And how shall I announce the honored guest?" he said.

"Favorinus Herennius, a cousin of the lady Paulina." Since the steward had spoken softly, he announced himself in a whisper.

"Will the honored guest seat himself? There's an iron bench just behind your Illustriousness. We ought to light the lamp out here day and night—it's really very dark. I'll tell the mistress of the house you're here. I'm sure she'll be with you soon."

As the old man parted the curtain to pass into the adjoining chamber, Favorinus caught a glimpse of young girls—some twenty adolescents, all dressed in white, all sitting on the floor in one straight line, and all bending diligently over a single length of white cloth. Once the curtain had fallen again, he could not be sure that the image had not been an illusion—it was a strange sight and the more like a dream-image because there was no noise to accompany it: no titter, no conversation, no sound at all. He put down an impulse to push the curtain a little aside, and applied himself to a survey of his surroundings; but even when his eyes had grown accustomed to the dark there was nothing to look at, nothing but the iron bench and the hanging lamp on a heavy chain. There were no murals on the walls, and the greater part of the mosaic at his feet had been covered with a heavy coating of blue paint. They have painted out some plump and rosy Ceres there, he thought; they have covered up her round arms and her opulent breasts. How literal-minded and bigoted these Christians are, slapping blue paint over a harmless piece of art. . . .

Yet when she came to him through the opening in the curtain, revealing for a moment the room beyond—the length of white cloth, the late-afternoon sunlight, and the bent young heads—he could feel no annoyance with her her manner was so spontaneously cordial. Her thin face was animated by a cheerfulness that almost overcame her natural sobriety. The silence in the other room had not been an austere silence then; they had not been stitching at a shroud in there—he wondered why the thought of a shroud should have occurred to him at all. Possibly they had been making a robe for their bishop or an altar cloth for one of their high festivals. Whatever they had been about, felicitous thoughts had been humming through their silence like bees; her cheeks were colored by a faint glow, and there was a lively light in her brown eyes.

"And how is it with my cousin?" he asked, standing up and feeling the weight of the heat again, a strange tremulousness and the need to sigh.

"Well, very well. But you must excuse me. We've been tearing cloth, and I'm covered with lint." Her thin, cool hand lay briefly in his and then began to pluck at the bits of fuzz that were sticking to her severe white dalmatica her long, slight neck, and her silky hair.

"Would it be indecently curious of me to ask what you're making in there? I saw it for an instant through the curtain. Is it a ceremonial robe? An altar cloth?"

She laughed and shook her head. "Oh, no, it's hard to tell whether we're ever going to find time for that sort of thing. There's too much else to do. The linen you saw in there—we're dividing it today. Each of the girls will take a piece of it home, and in a week or so they'll all be back with tunics for the poor."

"The poor of your association?" he asked, not out of curiosity, only because he felt called upon to indicate a polite interest. But he saw at once that the question had been unfortunate. Her straight pale-brown eyebrows drew together, and she shook her head.

"Oh, no, all the poor. Hundreds of pagan families, too. You mustn't believe our enemies; there's scarcely a tenement in Rome where we don't visit half a dozen pagan families."

He told himself that he had no reason to blush; there were scores of tenements in the City and hundreds of Christian visitors making their rounds with packages of clothes and baskets of bread; there was scarcely the remotest possibility that she had ever found her way into one of the buildings that belonged to the Herennii. And yet he was as uneasy as though she had actually witnessed some of the things the steward of the City property had reported to his mother: the children playing in their own excrement in the hallways, the old paralytic whose index finger had been gnawed away by the rats, the abandoned infant found in a heap of cabbage leaves in the rear court—a filthy lump of flesh, the steward had called it, still red with its mother's blood.

"Clothes enough to cover their nakedness," she was saying. "Oil and bread and a piece of bacon now and then, the barest necessities—" She stopped suddenly, and he knew that his mouth had parted, that he was staring at her with blank eyes. "I won't ask after your people up at the palace," she said. "Drusilla stopped to visit me yesterday, and I have all the family gossip. But Charis—how is she?"

He was touched by the fact that she had asked after Charis exactly as she would have inquired after a legal wife or a betrothed. Nobody but Drusilla ever asked after Charis; the matrons indicated their disapproval by a studied silence, and the young unmarried women ignored the whole subject of mistresses in order to maintain the fiction of their own innocence. "She's in Tibur at the moment—I haven't seen her in six or seven days," he said, suddenly remorseful that he should have taken as a matter of course a period of separation that would have seemed intolerably long before.

"Probus and I rented a villa in Tibur the first summer after we were married. It was so quiet there after the noise of the City that you could actually hear the stillness, especially at night. I used to get up and stand at the window and listen to the crickets. There were pines in the garden—no lights anywhere—absolute darkness and the chirping of the crickets and the smell of the pines—"

He flushed for his gross omission of one of the elementary amenities. That uncomfortable husband of hers, from whose bed she had risen in Tibur to drink in the silence and the scent of the pines—he should have asked after him at the very beginning. "How is Probus progressing with his epic?" he said.

And that, he knew immediately, was another unfortunate question. The unexhibited epic on which Probus had been working for an indefinite number of years was a family joke with the Herennii. She herself, well-educated as she had been in the best Stoic schools, doubtless realized the absurdity of the task her husband had set for himself. Who but Probus would take it into his head to recount the wanderings of some Christ-ridden missionary named Barnabas in the style and meter of the *Aeneid*?

"Oh, he's getting on. In fact, at the moment he's upstairs in the library, working on his new version of the second book."

Her voice was casual, but the pained and defensive look on her face unnerved him completely; he could not have felt more ashamed of himself if he had asked an unhappy mother whether her crippled daughter was to dance at the Saturnalia feast this year. "He certainly deserves credit for keeping at it in this heat," he said, feeling that he was only making matters worse, and wondering for the first time and quite incongruously why she and Probus had never had a child.

"May I take you up to see him? He likes an interruption now and then—"

But it was late, and the family would soon be called to dinner. He could see himself leaving the place, his question still unasked, his official business transformed into a graciously pointless visit to a pair of insignificant relatives on the Aventine. "If you don't mind," he said, touching her cool elbow, "I'd like to have a word with you first. There's a certain matter—"

She walked to the iron bench, turned around, and spread the skirt of her tucked dalmatica, to show him that she would sit down, completely at his disposal; and he had begun to search for the proper opening phrase before he remembered the wordless company on the other side of the curtain. "Not here, Paulina. In some other part of the house, where we won't be overheard," he said.

"Not here?"

"No, you see, it's a matter of state—"

"A matter of state?"

The look of alarm in her eyes—he had seen such a look in the big clear eyes of the slave Prisca, when he had tried to make her take Drusilla's daemon-tainted ring from his hand. A matter of state . . . The only matter of state that she could imagine his bringing to her was the news that Decius was about to begin a persecution. She actually thought that he, Favorinus Herennius, was capable of risking the hard-won confidence between him and his uncle by coming to warn her of the danger. Her faith in him was preposterous; and yet, as he looked at the unmasked and grateful face suddenly lifted to his, he was profoundly moved.

"Nothing important, nothing in the least important," he said. "It's a family matter, really, except that the Emperor happens to be concerned with it. The only reason for keeping it secret is that it's the sort of thing everybody would gossip about. If there's a room in this industrious household where nobody's sewing or writing, perhaps we could talk in private for a little, you and I—"

She sighed, and he could see that her thin hands were groping behind her; she had stepped around the end of the iron bench and was supporting herself against the wall. "No, I'm very sorry," she said in a breathless and hastening voice, "they're all over the house—Probus and the girls and the slaves—there's no empty room at all. But we could go over to the sculptor's yard next door, if you wouldn't mind walking about. There's nobody at home over there, his place is closed up, he's gone to Tivoli to do a shrine."

He nodded, and she opened the front door and went before him into the humid and oppressive air. She led him down a narrow alley along the side of her house; tufts of grass were growing between the paving stone. There was an iron gate between her property and the sculptor's yard, and the fact that she unlatched it with a practised hand set him wondering whether she came here often, and why she would wish to wander about in the dreary clutter, over the sickly grass and the packers' sawdust and sand. She made no attempt to bring him to the point of his visit. Probably because she wanted to show him that she was not in a hurry, that no obligation in the house on the other side of the wall was in her thoughts, she walked slowly and aimlessly beside him, stepping over the hands and feet of stone deities and dignitaries, holding the folds of her dalmatica close to her body in order to avoid contact with the "daemons" on the sarcophagi, commenting on how unfortunate it was that the sculptor hadn't asked one of the neighbors to water the plants on his balcony—nothing could save the oleander now . . . She was more shy with him than she had been in the vestibule, perhaps because she knew that he had seen her groundless fright and her uncalled-for gratefulness. A warm wind had come up and was blowing steadily across the yard, loosening a strand of her hair and whipping it against her cheek and brow. He had a sense of sidewise glances sent through the silky strands—nervous glances that fixed themselves sometimes on the ground, sometimes on the vacant windows of the empty house, but only seldom on his face.

Still out of breath, he began to look about for a place where they could sit, but the memorial stones and sarcophagi were all unacceptable; each had its daemon—its Cupid, its Psyche, its singing Orpheus, its death-conquering Hercules. The only possible place was a rough-hewn block of blackish granite whose flat top would barely accommodate two, and he was reluctant to force contact upon her, remembering how markedly she had rejected his touch. Well, one of us at least can sit, he thought, and stopped at the granite block and dusted it off with a fold of his toga. "Sit down, Paulina. I want to ask you for a favor," he said.

"A favor? I can't imagine what sort of favor I could do for you." Seated on the block of granite, with her hands folded in her lap and her face immobile and attentive, she looked like a figure carved on the lid of a sarcophagus. "Don't you want to sit down? There's room enough for both of us." The voice seemed all the more warm and womanly, issuing out of a form that held itself as if it were a thing of stone.

In order to avoid contact with her person, he seated himself on a corner of the granite slab, with one haunch on the stone and the other leg stretched out to support his weight. And now that he was committed to begin, he found himself almost incapable of making a beginning. The conviction that his errand was preposterous was somehow strengthened by the strangeness of his surroundings—the strewn, unfinished statues under the pale sky with its trails of coral cloud. There was nothing for him to grasp, nothing for him to toy with—he wanted a scroll or a pen or a goblet of wine in his hand. The fullness in his chest interfered with the flow of his sentences; they came out of him so breathlessly, with so many uncalled-for pauses in between, that a look of childish worry puckered her face. And, try as he would, he could not come directly to the point. He said a good deal that was obvious about the miseries of his sister's marriage, a good deal that seemed exaggerated and maudlin about the childhood connection between Drusilla and Herennius, a good deal that struck him as boastful about his desire to remain in good standing with the Lord of the World. But none of these circuitous advances made the broaching of the subject any the easier for him, and when he actually arrived at it his statement was as flat as a demonstration in geometry. "What I've been trying to make clear is that she's in an intolerable situation," he said, taking a deep breath. "Her marriage is a failure and nothing can mend it. Herennius has set his heart on her, and I can't see how we can refuse Herennius. If anybody could convince her, you could convince her. I—and the Emperor, of course—would be more than grateful if you could talk her into a sensible attitude. Couldn't you make her see that it's about time she divorced Eugenius?"

She had been staring straight in front of her, but now she turned her head and gave him a frightened look. "You mustn't ask me to do that, I couldn't do that. Much as I would like to oblige you, I could never do that," she said.

It was all that he could do to keep the patrician anger out of his face. Nobody had said an outright "No" to him since his childhood; nobody ever said an uncompromising "No" to one of the Herennii. And yet she was holding to her refusal with a scared but unwavering glance. "Would you be good enough," he asked, "to tell me why?"

"Because I am a Christian. With us, no marriage can ever be broken. With us, marriages are made once and forever, for this world, and for the world to come."

Once and forever, Paulina? he thought, turning his face aside to hide a sudden flicker of amusement and staring with forced gravity across the clutter of stone gods and heroes, roseate now in the oblique light of the declining sun. It was a wretched enough bargain you made for this world; must you cling to it also in the world to come? That loose-jointed maker of embarrassing epics they married you to—how will it be with you if you go hanging onto his arm through all eternity? Glancing up at the sky, he imagined the two of them floating arm in arm through a rack of pink clouds, with the same air of anxious solicitude that had marked them out from all the others in his mother's atrium. Then suddenly, for no reason he could name, the image that he had invoked in derision seemed to him infinitely pathetic, so that he was unable to suppress a sigh.

"I'm sorry, I'm terribly sorry, Favorinus. We've always been utterly useless to the rest of the family, and I was so happy when I thought there was something we could do. . . ."

Her humility quenched the patrician anger in him. I should make some gracious remark and go now, I should say that her kindness to Drusilla is favor enough, he told himself. And yet, though the light on sand and stone and grass was the red light of sunset, though the slaves in her kitchen must have put the evening loaves in the oven long ago, he could not bring himself to rise and take his leave. Easing out of his strained position to take his half of the block of granite, he found that his upper arm was resting against hers, that his knee was touching her knee. Her rigidity made him acutely, almost painfully aware of the contact, and he would have edged away at once if he had not been afraid she would suspect him of hostility. "I know very little—nothing, really—about Christianity," he said, not knowing what else to say, wanting only to dispel the uncomfortable silence. "Like you, I was trained in Stoic schools, and any Divine Intelligence that I can conceive of would either be completely unconcerned with my sister's wretchedness or utterly appalled to see a human being in such a state."

"But I am neither appalled nor unconcerned," she said, earnestly and without the faintest tinge of pride. "What she feels, I think I feel with her, at least in a certain measure—and you must feel it too, since you're so much closer to her than I. And if you and I can grieve for her, imperfect in love and understanding as we are, then imagine how much love and understanding there is for her to take—if she would only take it—out of the hands of God."

"She has no use for God. She wants Eugenius." He had said it in annoyance, partly because she had put him on the defensive by crediting him with more tenderness than he could honestly claim, and partly because of her remote bearing: she sat erect and motionless, with her hands lying upward and crossed and open in her lap. She was staring down at her own wrists, and he fell to staring at them too—white, thin, crossed with bluish veins. No bigger, he thought, than the wrists of a child.

"She wants Eugenius, and you give her Herennius." There was no malice in the serene exposure of his illogical position; she did not even permit herself to smile. "You give her Herennius, and if you press her hard enough she may even take him. I needn't tell you how tired she is—you know. But her years with Herennius will be a sleepwalker's journey, and everything that passes between them will be as insubstantial as a dream, and when she wakes—and she may wake—she will hate herself and any of us who have helped her betray her only reality. This has nothing to do with Christian doctrine. This much I would have known in the pagan shadow, before the clear shining of my Redeemer revealed the mysteries to me. And you know it also—in your heart you know it—" She turned and gave him, through a strand of blown hair, a bright and fugitive glance.

If he was unwilling to break off the conversation and depart, he was equally unwilling to carry it on in so charged and intimate a manner. "But I don't understand how you can apply Christian doctrine to somebody who isn't a Christian," he said in a tone that sounded artificial after her quiet earnestness. "The other mystery gods—Isis and Mithras, for instance—they never trouble themselves with anybody who isn't a member of the cult. Why should your Deity concern Himself with Drusilla at all?"

She smiled, and the smile made a subtle change in the contours of her wan cheek. "Our Lord concerns Himself with everything that lives," she said. "Whatever breathes and understands issued from Him in the beginning and can come to Him again on the Last Day, ransomed in His blood. His concern has no limits, and His pity is boundless. If a sparrow falls, if a beggar is turned away without bread, if an Aethopian slave who worships a black pebble is put in chains—He sees and weeps. The extent and the perfection of the Son's loving kindness passes our mortal comprehension but this much at least we know: He so loved us, He so pitied us that He freely vested His invulnerable and eternal Essence in our corruptibility He could have remained immortal, bodiless, ungrieving, with the Father forever. Instead, He descended into our flesh and died our death."

He nodded—how could one even attempt to grapple with such self sufficient fanaticism? He nodded, and knew that he had assumed precisely the air of indulgent forbearance as the equestrian who had offered to see that she received a handful of Ephesian sand.

But what had been acceptable in the equestrian was plainly not acceptable in him. She sat even more erectly now, she interlaced her thin fingers, she turned her head aside so that he could no longer see her face. "But I keep forgetting that you're a Stoic," she said after protracted silence. "The Stoics I know, find it particularly offensive to hear the words 'God' and 'flesh' in the same breath."

"No, really, I . . ." He stopped, knowing that he had never found the flesh degrading to the spirit; to this doctrine of the Stoics he had never been able to give the full assent of his heart. Once, three or four years ago, not long after his first visit to the house of Marcellinus—once, three or four years ago, on just such a wan and seasonless evening as this, he had sat near a window in the Library of Trajan, reading the teachings of the Stoic Epictetus: Renounce the world and the bonds of the world; forswear all human love as futile and perishable; say to yourself whenever you kiss a child, "Remember, tomorrow this child may be dead." And suddenly he had found himself unable to read any further—pushing the scroll halfway across the table, he rose and walked to the window and looked down into the teeming street. The sun, red and large in the autumnal haze, was going down behind the crowded pediments, lighting up the stones of the ancient buildings, the dusty foliage of the laurel, the faces of the hurrying crowd on the pavement below. And not one of that crowd had seemed to him to be moving vainly and without purpose. On what urgent errand is each of them going, to what mysterious trysts and solemn convocations are they hastening through moted shafts of light? he asked himself, leaning far out over the marble window sill. It had been with him then as if he were witnessing some high and holy festival—it was as if he were seeing the whole race of man moving swiftly from birth to death, carrying in their mortal bodies the inestimably precious capacity for love and sorrow and delight. "How beautiful!" he had said aloud, careless of those who sat reading in the dusky room behind him, forced to relieve his swollen heart of the sudden accession of wonder and tenderness. How beautiful the innumerable feet, hurrying always toward the tomb! How regal the white and vulnerable bodies netted over with purple veins. How miraculous the scarlet blood, the imperial crimson of the perishable heart. . . .

The warm and womanly voice broke in upon the recollection. She had taken his vague negative for the usual Stoic formula of self-disparagement: 'I'm not a Stoic, I only try to be a Stoic, I only hope to be worthy of the name before I leave the world." She was saying, shyly and yet with complete candor, that she was hardly a perfect Christian, either. Faith she had, or thought she had, and some degree of diligence. But in the attainment of Christian serenity she had been very lagging—her Bishop Fabian had told her so. Works—teaching the novices, visiting the poor, comforting the sick—works were the recognized way to peace. But, though she had applied herself to these works of charity and faith she was by no means the possessor of inward quietude, she still had a restless and demanding heart.

The turbulent, insatiable wanting—perhaps there had been a time when she would have exchanged it for the aerial, empty blueness of the Stoic peace. But not for years now, not since she had known Charis, not since she had seen the vision of the hastening multitude and known what high restlessness sent them seeking. "I have a demanding heart myself. I suppose I'll count myself dead when I lose it," he said.

She put her hair out of her eyes and looked at him gravely. There was a certain primness about her now—the air of the pedagogue—and it seemed so quaint, so out of keeping with her slightness that he had to suppress a smile. "Oh, but it's one thing," she said, "to melt away into the nothingness of some Divine Intelligence, and quite another—believe me, I have tried them both—to lay one's tired head on the knees of the compassionate Son of God."

"But I'm not as tired as all that."

She disregarded the flippancy and focused a long, appraising glance on his face. "No, not yet, I don't suppose you are," she said, turning aside and picking a piece of lint from the tucked cloth around her breast.

"But you think a time will come when I will be tired—"

"Probably. So many of us are. As the Last Day draws on, there are more and more of us who feel the weariness. The earth itself is tired, every year it yields less and less. The winds are lighter and the waters are sluggish and the virtue is passing out of the sun."

He closed his eyes and heard the slow gurgling of the Tiber at the foot of the Aventine plateau. He saw the columns and the pediments and paving stones strewn against the weedy green of the Murcia valley, and smelled again the sweet, rank fragrance of decay. "We tell ourselves such things to excuse our own insufficiencies," he said. "The weaknesses that we can't bear to admit in ourselves—we blame them on the sun. The sun will last, and the earth will last, and the Empire will last—unless, of course, we all sit by and wait for the Last Day, and let it slip out of our hands."

She did not answer. Her eyes were fixed on some apocalyptic vision, and her lips were folded over some secret and unshakable conviction of her own.

"And if I should ever find myself infected with that sort of despair," he said, loudly and belligerently into the stillness, "I can't imagine myself running to some Divine Comforter. I'd go back—" A sudden strong and aching loyalty to Charis broke his voice. "I'd go back and take what there is to take—and there's a great deal to take, I can tell you, even out of a tired world."

"Is there so much to take? I found that there was little enough," she said.

"Little enough? How much can a human being want? Before I was flung headlong into other things, I found that I could be reasonably satisfied with philosophy and poetry and art. Perhaps I sound hopelessly naïve, but I still put some value on friends. And I certainly—" he paused, seeing a vision of her standing in pine-breathing darkness at an open window, but the old, affronted loyalties drove him on—"I certainly put some value on love," he said, flinging the word across the desolate clutter of the sculptor's yard. "No, I haven't yet quite finished with love."

She started—he could feel her cool arm go tense against his through the folds of cloth. For an instant there was pain and confusion in her face; then she composed herself and raised her eyes to an upper window in the house on the other side of the stone wall. She is thinking of *him*, he thought, she is lifting up her heart to him there in the library where he wears himself away on a new version of the second book of his saint's *Aeneid*. . . .

When she turned back to him, her whole face was transformed and made beautiful by a slow and paradoxical smile, at once innocent and infinitely wise. "It's a common mistake among those who are not Christians," she said, "to conclude that we have set our minds against love. How could that be, when the Lord so loved us that He died for us, when He charged us, as He loved us, even so should we love one another? We are all friends and more than friends—we gather around the same table and eat the same bread in perfect communion—'sister' and 'brother' we call each other, and not as a matter of form—we are all of one family, all the children of God. Since He Himself is love, He rejoices in the love that is between us. He rejoices in strong friendships and in a sound marriage—"

He flushed to find himself glancing at the upper window. "And what is a sound marriage according to your lights?" he said.

"According to my lights?" She turned upon him the bright, impersonal glance of a teacher who has begun to forget the pupil in an enthusiastic surge of pure pedagogy. "But I haven't any lights of my own, you know. None of us have. Whatever we see, we see in the light of the Lord. And to him we are as children—still childish and rooted in the flesh—held fast in the flesh until the time of His return and our deliverance. And, because we are flesh and burdened with all sorts of longings and frailties, He has given us marriage, out of His pity, to sustain us in our mortality. So we come to marriage with a kind of awe, since we know we take it as an indulgence, a gift out of His hand. And, simply because it is His gift, we could never use it as the others do, merely as a satisfaction of the flesh or as a means of gathering more land or power to ourselves—"

She stopped short and went white in the face, realizing that she had reproved him. Then suddenly she made the first giving gesture that she had ever made toward his person—she laid her hand lightly on his knee. "What I mean," she said, "is that a sound marriage, according to our beliefs, is one that is maintained for no other purpose than to fulfill the intentions of the Lord. We take from His hand our one chaste cup, so that we can be delivered forever from the temptation to drink tainted wine. We comfort each other in our loneliness; we are alone, you know, we are exiles, we have no City on earth, our only citizenship is in the Kingdom of God, which is still to come. We nourish and sustain each other, working side by side with the Lord's yoke upon our shoulders—and it isn't always a light yoke: there are the sick to be healed and the poor to be fed, there are the catechumens to be taught and the treatises to be written, we visit the exiles and ransom the prisoners and comfort the slaves. It's hard to tell you—you can't imagine how tired we are at the end of the day and how blessed it is for two of us to share an hour of mutual peace. And then, too, husband and wife sustain each other in their terror, because, even in a fortunate reign, even when a philosopher like Marcus Aurelius is wearing the rayed crown, we're never really safe, we always have reason to be terrified, as you must surely know—"

The recollection of her groundless fear and her uncalled-for gratefulness was suddenly between them, clouding her bright look. She took her hand from his knee and pinned a loose strand of her hair into place. "How can I make you see what sort of love is between us?" she said, lifting her eyes again to the window of that upper chamber where he who had tasted the one chaste cup with her struggled in the oppressive heat to make his halting music for the Lord. "How can I make you see what it is to share with one yoke-fellow, one dear companion, all that must be suffered before the fulfillment of the covenant and the coming of the Kingdom of God? There are mornings when I am afraid to smooth away the hollow left in the pillow by his head. There are mornings when I say to myself: He's gone and will never come back again—they'll take him to the Urban Prefect, they'll send him to the mines in Dacia, he'll be thrown to the beasts, he'll be given to the fire. And when he comes home again—ah, God, how can I tell you what it is to see him come home again? Every return is a miracle, a kind of resurrection from death. No, you mustn't think us loveless, you mustn't believe for a moment that the Lord Jesus has locked up our hearts. But the love that is between us is a new kind of love, such a love as has never been in the world before, and I can't describe it, I could never make you understand—"

But I understand too well, I understand better than you do, he thought, feeling utterly remote from her now, staring at her thin, crossed hands. Whatever you feel when you hang on his arm in my mother's atrium, whatever comes surging up in you when you hear him at the door, whatever is between the two of you when you make your hollows in the pillows by night —all that is pity, nothing but pity, and what has pity to do with love? Compassion born out of fear—that is all that comes to you from the hands of your crucified God.

"I'm afraid I've burdened you with a great deal of talk," she said. It was as if she had sensed his thoughts and withdrawn herself completely from him now. And he was made acutely conscious of the extent of their intimacy by the sudden breaking off of it: it was as if a delicate and intricate web between them had been ripped apart.

"No, not in the least. I'm afraid I've kept you from your evening meal. I always talk too much."

"Not to me. You know, before today, I've scarcely had more than a word with you. I'm glad we had this little time together. I hope you'll come again.'

For some moments they continued to sit motionless, their upper arms still resting against each other. Then, at the same instant, both of them sighed

"I'm very sorry I couldn't be of service to you," she said, standing up and pulling her sleeve-bands over her wrists.

The marriage, he thought, I forgot about the marriage. What can I say to Decius? Who else is there to go to? Nobody, I'll go to nobody, the whole affair is unthinkable. If Drusilla is to be asked at all, I'll ask her myself—

"If there's ever any other way in which I could be useful to you—"

He stood up and nodded to her with curt formality. He felt a disproportionate regret that their encounter should be closing in a series of courteous banalities; it was like having a haunting piece of music, heard vaguely at a distance, prove itself to be a tawdry popular tune as the players turned the corner of the street. "If there's ever anything else, you can be sure I'll come. You've been very kind."

"Would you like to come upstairs and say a word to Probus?"

That was a jarring note. He shook his head. "No, I'm afraid it's very late, much later than I thought. The next time, when I come again—"

What had been between them was so thoroughly destroyed by this time that he scarcely thought how he might have wounded her feelings; he only noted that she walked stiffly before him through the iron gateway, and that when she said good-bye she did not offer him her hand. As he walked alone along the front of the house, he was startled by a burst of girls' laughter, a veritable spray of laughter from the first floor windows. And it annoyed him, it puzzled him, he thought of nothing else all the way down to the foot of the Aventine. How can they laugh, what do they have to laugh about, with their exile and their terror and their loneliness and their Cross and their one chaste, bitter cup? he asked himself, kicking a loose pebble along the street. How can they laugh, with the strength gone from the earth and the virtue gone from the sun and the Last Day drawing on and nothing left to them but pity, sickly pity, and their weeping, tormented God?

Chapter 10

THERE WERE times—and this was decidedly one of them—when Charis wished she had never laid eyes on Orbiana Festina. If the crowd of Saturnalia shoppers that jammed the Via Sacra that fine December morning had forced her into sudden proximity with any of her friends, even the gallant Antisthenes or the mild old Berosus, she would have considered it a burden. She was tired, she was harried, she was exasperated with the outrageous prices one had to pay for Saturnalia gifts this year. Besides, there was only an hour left before she was to meet *him* in the perfumer's shop, and his speech on the censorship, which he had left with her three days ago, was still unread. Any eyes demanding recognition out of the packed anonymity of the crowd would have encroached on the miserable fragment of time left to her for eating the noonday meal in a cook-shop and racing through the scrawled and blotted pages of his manuscript. But that particular pair of eyes, pale grey and lightless, staring out of dazed blankness into a kind of avidity—Orbiana Festina—really, it was almost more than she could bear.

"But how wonderful!" said Orbiana, smiling an automatic smile that had nothing to do with the stare. "I was just saying to myself this morning that I probably wouldn't be seeing you until the end of the week, and here we are!"

The crowd slowed a little as it passed them. Nobody could give Orbiana a cursory glance—people always looked long at her with thoughtful faces, would have looked long even if the lithe and subtle body had not been set off by yards of green Chinese silk, even if the face—the hard, round forehead, the full eyelids, the cheeks that looked as if they had been carved out of some pale and highly-polished wood—had not been made still more coldly arresting by the two big emeralds that hung from her ears and cast a greenish light along the jaw as far as the pointed chin. The slaves came up behind them—Orbiana's two blond Britons and her own fat, stupid Levantine; and the five of them blocked the street, and the Levantine stood there like an idiot baby with a leather sack of Saturnalia presents ready to spill on the pavement beside him, and the accursed speech—she was all the sorrier for it because she hated it so much—was being crumpled somewhere in the sack, and she could think of nothing to say, could only throw up her hands in a gesture intended to indicate that she was rushed, tired, ready to go out of her head.

"What you need is something to eat," said Orbiana, making a darting, abortive gesture toward a loose strand of Charis's hair.

She drew back involuntarily—she had never learned not to draw back from Orbiana's disturbing touch.

"There's an excellent cook-shop not ten doors down from here. Come on, darling, let me buy you something nice—a bit of chicken or some beautiful clams. I'm sure we can sit down in there. I just passed the place and there isn't any line."

Let me buy you something nice . . . Let me send my Nubians to serve your banquet . . . Borrow my villa any time you want it . . . Don't think of getting an advocate, my father'll settle it out of court for you . . . It was almost impossible to imagine the little coterie functioning without Orbiana. It was she who provided the rare wines and the exotic dishes that made brilliant occasions of Berosus's readings; it was she who found pupils for the philosopher Cleander and patrons for the painter Antisthenes. Her fabulous generosity to the dancer Memphius had carried him straight into the circle that met at Marcellinus's house; she had seen him performing with a cheap troupe of street mimes one night and had made him, in a matter of months, the pride of the Roman stage; and that was generosity pure and simple, since there was nothing any woman could ever get out of *him,* as everybody said . . . A dish of beautiful clams, a month's entertainment in Naples, a priceless bracelet—she offered them all in the same casual, tired voice; and the acceptance never softened the two lines of weariness that ran from the corners of her nose to the corners of her lips, never took the abstracted look out of her eyes.

"But I'm meeting Favorinus in less than an hour, and I have a million things to do."

"Are you eating with him?"

There was no hope of carrying off a lie—the eyes had suddenly become shrewdly attentive. "No," she said.

"Well, you do have to eat, don't you?"

"Yes, I suppose I do. But while I'm eating I'll have to read a speech of his—"

"A speech of his?" The wide, painted mouth curled a little at the corners. It was there again and would have to be appeased—the contempt for him and his patrician manners and his single beloved and his political high-mindedness. "I should have read it days ago. I tried, but it annoyed me so much that I couldn't finish it—" Her bitterness had broken through, she had said too much. "Roman oratory bores me. Still, I'll have to get through the thing before he comes—"

"In a cook-shop? Oh, really, now, darling—" The long, tapering fingers, heavy with rings, gave her an infuriating pinch on the cheek. "You don't think for a moment you'll be able to make anything out of a speech in a cook-shop jammed with Saturnalia shoppers. Come along, I'll buy you some beautiful clams and a cup of old Cretan." She turned and gave a fistful of denarii, uncounted, to one of her slaves. "Go somewhere and eat and take that Levantine idiot with you, and see that you buy him the same meal as you buy yourselves," she said.

"But I have to read a speech, I tell you."

"Well, read it, read it. I won't mind just sitting and watching you." To feel the cold stare invading her person while she tried to fix her attention on the scrawled pages, to sit wary and rigid, wondering what part of her body was under observation now—that was unthinkable, that would be too much. "I can't concentrate when anybody looks at me," she said, ruefully watching the leather bag bumping along the street behind her Levantine. "We'll talk—come on—we'll have some clams and talk."

But Orbiana Festina did not seem to take the slightest pleasure in her victory. Listless again, dazed again, she walked past the showy shops and through the milling crowd, intent upon some secret and exhausting preoccupation of her own. Now and then her lips would narrow in a closed smile at some passer-by—man, woman, child, it made no difference. And for the first time Charis noticed that those who evoked the smile were not distinguished by any particular charm or comeliness, but by the same dazed preoccupation that was visible in Orbiana's own eyes.

The silence remained unbroken while they pushed their way into the crowded cook-shop, while they waited in line for their clams, while they seated themselves with their plates in their laps against a moist wall that gave off the odor of an endless succession of fish stews. She sat very close to Charis—their shoulders, their arms, their hips were actually pressed together. But that was the only contact—her face was more wooden, more remote than ever in the watery, undersea light that came through the bluish awning dividing the shop from the sunny street. Whatever attempts Charis made at conversation went unanswered, scarcely seemed to be heard. When she said that the shops were loaded with the most horrible pottery out of Gaul this year—hideously red and ornamented all over with bulging wrestlers and charioteers—she got a slow half-turn of the head and an inappropriate sigh. When she launched into a criticism of Berosus's last group of lyrics, she stopped in the middle of a sentence because the round forehead was furrowed with a frown that obviously had nothing to do with the subject under discussion.

Oh, well, she thought, dipping up the clam juice with a rusk of bread, it's useless, she's going into *that* state again, she'll be disappearing again one of these days . . . And suddenly, in the cheerful clatter of the shop, in the good-natured bustle of the Saturnalia season, it seemed to her appalling that she should be sitting arm to arm and hip to hip with a woman who disappeared for days on end into the filthiest and most sinister corners of the City, into the dens and brothels of the Suburra—Memphius swore that he had seen her in the Suburra twice. The suave unconcern with which the members of the little circle were in the habit of accepting such behavior was counterfeit, of course; when the pale eyes took on the dazed, drained look, Charis knew that she was not the only one who felt the cold shock of horror along the spine; all of them, even the degenerate Memphius and the subtle Antisthenes, were appalled. She never took herself off at once; there was always a week or so when her spirit, gone out on some unspeakable adventure, left her person behind to wander about in its customary haunts, automatically talking and walking and eating, constantly staring, forcing them all to watch a spectacle of terrifying dehumanization. Once she was safely away, it was as if they had been miraculously delivered from physical danger; they were as merry as sailors after a trip across the Euxine; they smothered each other in unequivocal caresses.

"Let me buy you a plum pastry, dearest."

"I'm not very hungry—" She bit her lip, remembering that it was best to be compliant when Orbiana was about to disappear. Since she was bound to come back—exhausted, chastened, languidly affectionate, like a cat walking in after a furious night—since she would turn up again after six or seven days of wandering, the members of the little circle always saw to it that she took her leave in an atmosphere of peace. "I'm not very hungry, but I'd love a plum pastry," Charis said.

"If you don't want it, don't eat it by any means. You don't have to stuff yourself to please me, you know."

Any answer might be the wrong one. She brushed a crumb from the skirt of her pale blue dalmatica and sighed.

"What are you sighing about? You're always sighing."

"Nothing. I don't know. I suppose I'm tired."

"That's all a person ever hears out of you anymore. Morning, noon, and night, you're always tired." The voice, usually soft and smooth, was as rough as wet fur. The face, turned suddenly around in the watery light, was frighteningly vital, avid in the eyes, tight in the lips. "What do you do to make yourself as tired as all that? Don't you ever sleep? Do you lie awake crying over him like a twelve-year-old?"

"Scarcely." The air of cool detachment was hard to achieve. Until the present moment—she would avoid this cook-shop forever now, the smell of fish-stew would nauseate her to the end of her days—until the present moment it had never occurred to her that the breach between herself and her lover was wide enough to be obvious to anybody else. "There's nothing to cry about. Favorinus and I are on excellent terms, if that's what you mean." Such excellent terms, she thought, straightening her hunched shoulders, that we see each other once in ten or twelve days. Such excellent terms that my house is filled with the gifts he sends because he cannot come. Such excellent terms that we have arranged between us not to spend the feast of the Saturnalia alone together as we did in other years. I must give a banquet, we must drink and shout ourselves into noisy insensibility lest, seeing each other face to face, we should remember other Saturnalias and measure our loss. . . .

One tapering finger came down and pressed hard into the flesh above her knee. "Look, darling, if you want my opinion, you're being an idiot about the whole thing."

"Am I?" The question was addressed not to Orbiana Festina but to that deaf, blind Chaos in the face of which one tried always to bear oneself with a reasonable amount of dignity and grace.

"You certainly are. If you actually want him—not that I see why anybody would want him, he's a Stoic prig, he's inanely chaste, he probably makes love like a farmer boy, but there's no accounting for tastes, it's his much-touted good looks that make him so valuable, I suppose—although I must say there are times when he seems downright ugly to me, with that hawk nose and those pinched-in cheeks and those gaping eyes—but if you've set your heart on him, if you can't get on without him, then isn't it sheer insanity to stand around in that dignified pose, watching him drift off to somebody else? Show him you have a life of your own, show him you don't have to depend on him, make him jealous—"

The finger was no longer poking into her flesh. The whole hand, hard and ugly in spite of its whiteness, crude and primitive in spite of its rings, was curving round her thigh in a tentative caress. She stiffened and pressed her knees together. She would not have it—even in exchange for innumerable favors, even to insure a peaceful disappearance, it was more than a person could be expected to bear. Deftly, neatly, as one might pick a caterpillar off one's clothes and lay it on top of a hedge, she picked up Orbiana's hand and laid it in Orbiana's lap, among the folds of Chinese silk. "I haven't the slightest cause—or inclination—to make him jealous," she said.

Always unpredictable when she was going into one of her states, Orbiana

Festina had taken no offense. The hand lay limp and purposeless; the stare was directed somewhere else, seemed to be focused on the cheek of a girl who was asking for mussels at the counter—a flabby, yellow-white cheek filmed over with a blackish downiness. "Yes, make him jealous," she said again, but she seemed scarcely aware of what she was saying.

Make him jealous . . . But even if her desperation should ever lead her to such measures, she could think of nobody with whom she could hope to arouse his jealousy. The philosopher Cleander was a plump, inconsequential little man with a compulsive need to talk and a crippling inability to act. As for Antisthenes and Memphius, both of them were effeminate, capable of brief and superficial connections taken up in boredom or made necessary by self-interest; but actually they were involved only with each other. A masculine man, she thought, another Roman, another patrician. If I were to do that with anybody, it would have to be somebody of his class, somebody whom I would have to address as "your Illustriousness" until we got into bed. . . .

"I take it you don't want a plum pastry." There was a dull glow of humor in that. Henceforth, in their conversations, Orbiana would see to it that plum pastry stood for certain obscenities.

"No, I don't suppose I do."

"Neither do I, to tell the truth." She rose and started for the entrance. "The pastry around here is a bit too high class for my taste. Look, there's that Levantine of yours, sucking his thumb again. Make him wipe his face, he's slobbered all over his chin. I'll see you at your Saturnalia banquet then, darling. Let me send you some of my Nubians and Britons. How many have you invited to the feast? Twenty? I'll send you seven, seven ought to be enough." The farewell kiss was no more moist and clinging than usual. Preoccupied again, staring again, she snapped her fingers at her waiting Britons and lost herself in the crowd that jammed the sunny street.

But now that her disturbing companion had taken herself off, now that she could proceed to the perfumer's shop with nobody to sidle against her, she did not feel the expected relief. She was certain she was late: her sense of time had been suspended in the undersea dusk of the cook-shop, and the desultory conversations and protracted silences might well have consumed more than an hour. The thought of the unread speech recurred to her, and her heart stood still and then began to beat in a broken, crazy rhythm. And the crowd itself—the shoulders and the elbows and the swinging buttocks—seemed to be consciously, maliciously blocking her way. Three more doors to pass, she thought. The flute-maker's, the linen-draper's, the seller of fruit and flowers—he's probably waiting in front of the awning now, I could probably see him from here if that hideous hag in front of me hadn't perched three yellow plumes on top of her head . . . But when the plumes made a sudden turn into the linen-draper's, she could not see him; and, when she stepped across the threshold of the scent-shop, she was disproportionately upset to find he was not there.

She took a seat on the long customers' bench near the entrance and signaled the Levantine to put the leather sack under the bench and take up as little room as possible on the floor. The mingled odors of the perfumes—violet, cassia, cinnamon, rose, and balsam—pleasant at first, soon began to be oppressive. The shop was crowded with patrician matrons, all walking past her with preoccupied faces, all annoyed because they had to make a detour around her fat slave. She wanted only to be inconspicuous, but the proprietor, a thin and melancholy Greek who had served her regularly in the past, kept nodding and smiling and waving his fine hands at her to indicate that she was as welcome here as any patrician or equestrian, that he enjoyed her company and valued her trade. In order to avoid his eyes, she stared at the shelves behind him, but the sight of the ill-shaped and grossly ornate vials disgusted her—everything was cheap, everything was ugly this year. She became aware of a maddening, familiar sound: her Levantine was biting his thumbnail again. "Everybody's looking at you. Can't you keep your hand out of your mouth for a moment?" she said.

The boy wiped his wet nail on the skirt of his tunic and gave her an inane and shamefaced smile. "I'm very sorry, my lady and my mistress. It's just that there's one little rough place that keeps bothering me."

"Wait until you get home and can take a knife to it." Two matrons on the other side of the shop were discussing her—she was sure of it by their furtive glances and the ostentatious way they fingered the vials on the upper shelf. Are the two of you regular visitors at the atrium of the Herennii? she thought. Do you have marriageable daughters you would like to have him consider? Are you asking each other what a man like him can see in a common courtesan like me—not young anymore, too thin, with coarse hair and knobby collar bones?

The proprietor, having sold a fortune in balsam to a senator's wife, darted back to the customers' bench to make a public demonstration of his attentiveness. She liked the man—she had always liked him; he never addressed her except in the language of their mutual homeland; and the sight of him always reminded her that there had been certain lovely and unwounding things in the far past: the nimble goats skirting the white rocks of Chios, the scent of beechwood burning, the smell of a handful of roasted chickpeas. He deserved something, too, for his unflagging courtesy, and she leaned forward, her chin in her hands, and gave him a warm smile. "As one Greek to another, how is your Saturnalia business this year?" she said.

He shrugged and smiled back at her. "Always the same story, my dear lady. A little less business every year. Last year the oils went well but the powdered scents fell off. This year neither one of them has done too much. And look at my shelves—look what I've piled up. I'm in for a bad time of it,

I can tell you, if we have a censorship. Everybody says we can expect one in the next few days."

His voice trailed off and he waited, clasping and unclasping his exquisite fingers, for the bit of authentic court gossip which she, the mistress of the Emperor's nephew, might pass on to him, as one Greek to another; but at the mention of the censorship she could only think of the unread speech and stare at the entrance way and listen to the irregular beating of her own heart.

"Could I ask for a little service?" said an equestrian beauty, rapping on the counter with her rings.

"Certainly, certainly," said the proprietor, edging off. "You'll excuse me, won't you, my lady? Anyway . . ." his voice was mournful; his chance for inside information about the censorship was gone—"anyway, here comes my lord Favorinus." It was so, he had come, he was standing on the threshold, offering her a wide, apologetic gesture, a conscience-stricken face, a rueful smile.

Her sensations at the sight of him were so contradictory that she could not even nod at him, much less get up from the customers' bench and hold out her hand. If she was justly angry with him for having written such a piece of trash, she was contrite because she had not forced herself to read it through. If she was exasperated that he had come so late, she was infinitely relieved that he had come at last. Rigid, with her chin still supported on her trembling fists, she watched him cross the shop and stop in front of the bench. "I'm terribly sorry," he said in a breathless voice. But she could give him nothing but cold silence; she was afraid to talk; she was certain that her voice would break.

"I said I was terribly sorry." He was flushed, his eyes were shining, his breath was coming hard and fast.

She had meant to say that it made no difference. She found herself asking a question instead. "What were you doing all that time?" she said, and heard her heart knock crazily again. Only a legal wife could afford such a question. She had never asked it before, never in all their three years.

"I was talking to my sister."

"In that case—" she could not stop herself, it was as if some daemon had possessed her—"in that case, it seems to me you might have cut the morning chat a little short. Since you're living over there now, you can see her any time you like, and it's seldom enough that you make an appointment with me—"

"It was scarcely a morning chat that she and I were having." He had drawn himself up, affronted that she had chosen to disregard the obvious signs of trouble in his face. "I was certain I could get to you on time—I thought the whole business, important as it was, could be settled in half an hour. I was trying to argue her into doing something that would have done her an incalculable amount of good. Of course, I should have known her better than that—she'll never do anything about her life—all she wants is a chance to lament over her miseries—she wouldn't give them up for the world. And she certainly went on about them at great length this morning—"

In spite of his wounded feelings, he was offering the usual sacrifice; he was knifing Drusilla on the altar of their love. And yet there was something equivocal about the wording of his explanation. Candid he was not. He had proceeded secretly and deviously; he had seen to it that she got no hint as to what he and his sister had been talking about. "Once you've settled your family problems, you don't have much time left for Saturnalia shopping, do you?" she said.

"There's time enough, if we hurry." He took her by the hand and pulled her up. He laid his arm around her waist and drew her over to the counter, where the air reeked of rose and cinnamon. "I hope you made yourself comfortable while you were waiting—"

It was a tender overture, but the daemon in her would not let the irony pass. "Oh, I suppose I was comfortable enough," she said, leaning on the counter and playing with one of the miniature ivory boxes filled with powdered scent. "The proprietor was very attentive. And so were the ladies, for that matter. I've drawn as much comment as the four-eyed toad on exhibit at the Baths of Caracalla—"

He flushed and caught his underlip between his teeth. His jaw was covered with dark stubble; he had not had time for shaving—that much was plain. His hand, thin, warm, pliant, with the tangle of dark hair at the wrist, came down over her hand and the little scent box.

His hand—she rejected the sensation of weakness that came over her at the sight of it and the feel of it. He thinks he need only touch me to make me melt away, she thought; and the thought goaded her on. "If I had known I was going to have to wait," she said, "I'd at least have put on something a little less conspicuous. To sit on the customers' bench for half an hour—" she paused because she did not actually know how long she had been sitting there—"to sit on the customers' bench, all tricked out in a sky-blue dalmatica—"

He withdrew his fingers. "Why did you sit?" he asked in a clearly audible and peremptory voice. "Why didn't you shop? You could have saved your time, and mine, by buying a few things yourself."

Her embarrassment that he should take such a tone with her in the presence of some ten ladies of his own class was wounding enough, but it was negligible in comparison with another and more private pain. This Saturnalia shopping—they had made so much of it in other years, they had depended on each other's tastes, they had rejoiced together over happy finds—this Saturnalia shopping was nothing but a tedious duty to him now. "Very well," she said in a shaking whisper, "let's save as much of your precious time as we can." She straightened her shoulders and beckoned to the proprietor. "May we have some service?" Her voice came out of her strained and strident, and two of the other shoppers turned round to see. "All of a sudden it seems we're in a desperate hurry. Four three-ounce measures of powdered balsam in cedarwood boxes. Five glass vials of oil—two with cassia, two with violet, one with rose. No, don't bother to show us the vials, we're in a terrible hurry. Besides—" All the old Saturnalia recollections, the lovely green bottle they had found here last year, the gracious conversations they had had with the proprietor—all the old recollections had to be discredited, even abused. "Besides, to tell the truth, I never saw anything quite as ugly as the vials you're showing this year. Yellow, red, blue—whatever you have—one of them is as dreadful as the other."

"I'm afraid they're *not* as attractive as last year's designs," said the melancholy Greek, utterly relinquishing his identity and their bond as fellow-countrymen, offering her an obsequious tradesman's smile. It took him a long time to make up their parcel: his fine hands were awkward with the papyrus and the string. "They're the best we could find," he said, darting in front of them to clear the entrance way. "We do what we can."

In the bright street, in the jostling crowd, on their way to the leather-shop, they were briefly separated from each other. Somebody wedged between them, and she had to go on ahead of him for several paces, with the Levantine tagging behind. She knew, of course, that he would join her in a few moments—if she looked back over her shoulder, she could see his lean, flushed cheek and his black curls. But she was assailed by a wild mournfulness nevertheless: it was as if he would never know that her remorse was greater than her anger; it was as if he might turn at some corner and be irretrievably lost. When he came up with her at the entrance of the leather-shop she knew that he had been experiencing something of the same ache and the same loneliness—his eyes were distressed with searching, and he took a hard hold on her hand. "Why did you have to hurt the poor man's feelings? He's always been very fond of you," he said.

"I'm sorry if I hurt his feelings." She could say no more because her throat was tight. She could not look him in the face because the stinging tears were standing in her eyes.

"You've waited for me before. I can't see why such a little thing should upset you so much."

"It's not a little thing—you ought to be able to see that it's not a little thing. It makes me feel like a common whore."

He drew her into the little empty space under the flapping sign of the leather-merchant. He stood in front of her, in view of all the passers-by, looking gravely into her face and holding both her hands. He said—and he did not lower his voice—that their three years together should have set her mind at peace; that no patrician matron had a more single-minded husband than she had in him; that, save for her, he was really alone; that she was the only human being to whom he had shown his secret heart—his sole beloved and his only friend . . . If she had a sudden intuitive conviction that he was

145

speaking so earnestly because he was striving to convince himself, she thrust it away. If it occurred to her that what he was uttering here in the windy street was so sorrowfully impassioned because it was an elegy spoken over the dead body of their love, she put that thought aside. And when he had finished, she looked up at him nakedly, unreservedly, letting him see the remorse in her eyes and the tears on her cheeks. "It was Orbiana, I was upset over Orbiana. She insisted on eating with me, and she's going into one of her states again. She's impossible, she says the most upsetting things—"

"What did she say, darling?"

"Nothing—it doesn't matter—not since you've talked to me. All I need is a little time to talk to you now and then. I'll not be troublesome anymore," she said.

The front of the leather-shop was a kind of porch, open during most of the year, but closed off from the street in the brief winter season by two heavy cowhide curtains hung on metal rings. The smell of the trade was there; they had always enjoyed it together; and, stepping through the gap between the curtains, she was careful to smile and draw the usual deep, appreciative breath. They wandered about inside, hand in hand, letting the process of healing go on in silence, examining the chair pillows with the fringed edges, fingering the soft belts that hung on a pole in a row, picking up the tooled sandals and the wonderfully pliant shoes. It was he who broke the quiet. "Look," he said, holding up a rawhide cushion. "This is just the size to take on a sketching trip. Let's buy it for Antisthenes."

So he had stood in other years, holding up some happy find for her to see, all the strain, all the worry gone out of his thin face, his eyes bright with childish, uncomplicated happiness. So he would stand next year and for many years to come—he had not changed, it was only his unwelcome duties that had set the two of them a little apart. She said that the pillow was the most beautiful pillow she had ever seen, the perfect thing for Antisthenes. She told the shop-owner's son that he should look after the other customers first; most of the things they wanted they could find for themselves. And within half an hour of high-hearted searching they had made a surprising number of discoveries—white ankle-shoes for Orbiana, a calfskin pouch for Berosus, a fine leather case big enough to hold four scrolls for the philosopher Cleander, a pair of showy yellow sandals with long green thongs for Memphius. They called in the fat Levantine, who had been gaping at the crowds in the street, and loaded him down with presents. When the sack was full, they hung Berosus's pouch around his neck and balanced Antisthenes' pillow on top of his head. And while they stood laughing at him—the sight of him was ludicrous enough to force two or three of the patrician matrons to smile in spite of themselves—while they were laughing and leaning against each other's shoulders, it came into her mind that all the gifts they had purchased today were for the friends they had in common. She had run out of the perfumer's shop without giving him a chance to buy any presents of his own; and here, too, she had not asked him once about his private Saturnalia list.

"Excuse me a minute, darling, I'm not quite finished looking," she said, and left him at the counter, stacking up a heap of denarii. In her tremulous happiness, in her gratefulness to him for his forgiveness, she had set her heart on finding something splendid, something that he could give to his mother or his sister, or even to—

And suddenly she saw precisely the thing, there at the bottom of a heap of cushions—a magnificent bolster dyed in gorgeous purples and bluish greens. She dragged it out of the pile of inferior pillows. It was flawless, it was springy, it was stuffed with the downiest of goose-feathers; it was such a rare and costly bolster as anybody would be delighted to receive—yes, even the Lord of the World. The bolster was so heavy that she had to carry it over to him in both her arms, as if it were a baby. "Look at this one, darling. Isn't it beautiful?" she said. "I thought you might want to buy it. I thought you might want to give it to the Emperor."

"To Decius?" He hesitated—he was holding her off, he was playing for time. "It's a very handsome bolster, but I wonder if it isn't a bit too gay for Decius. I'll have to find something a little less flamboyant for him, I'm afraid."

Less flamboyant? She felt the flush sweeping into her cheeks, the tears standing in her eyes. It's *I* that am flamboyant, she thought—a bedizened Greek courtesan, a freed slave betrayed by a groundless fit of happiness into losing all poise, all distinction—a vulgar and ridiculous woman running about a leather-shop in a sky-blue dalmatica, clasping a hatefully gaudy bolster to my breast and calling him "darling" in the presence of a dozen senatorial matrons, any one of whom may be his mother's close friend—

"Still, it *is* an unusually fine bolster, and it's a pity to miss such a chance. Suppose we buy it for Orbiana—"

"We have a present for Orbiana." Oh, no, she thought, you can't set it right with your money. You can't put your hand into your pouch and have this sort of pain removed for a certain number of denarii—

"It's going to be a problem to find a present for the Emperor. I'd like to get him something fine, of course, but it's hard to know what—he has such simple tastes—"

His tastes! she thought, walking across the shop and letting the bolster roll out of her arms onto the pile. He has no taste, as everybody knows. His atrium looks like an abandoned barracks. He doesn't know how to drape his toga. The food on his table isn't fit for dogs. "Shall we go?" she asked, strolling back to him. She had intended the question to be airy, but it came out curt and cold. He stood staring at her, saying nothing, and the daemon lashed out again at the sight of his expressionless eyes. "Unless you want something else here, I could do with a little air. I've always hated the smell of this place. It makes me sick."

She deliberately pushed on ahead of him through the crowd, moving against the closely packed arms and backs with a senseless fierceness, as if she were in the middle of a battle. An ageing senator turned and gave her a dignified, reproving look; a plebeian woman cursed her; a handsome Nubian slave pertly quoted a maxim at her: "The more hurry, the less speed." And suddenly it seemed imperative that she get clear of the bodies that were pressing against her—her heart had gone wild again, she was going to faint, they would trample her to death. She made a wrenching turn to the left and darted into the entrance of a dancing master's establishment. There was nobody to see her in the dark little archway, and she rested her head against the stone wall and pressed her hand to her side.

A cheap, sinuous Alexandrine melody, played on the flute, came through the windows of the second floor. Somebody—some soft, heavy-footed patrician girl, she thought maliciously—was doing miserably up there. "No, not like that. Try it again, if you please," said a tired male voice, trying to temper disgust with politeness for the sake of the fee. Three times the melody was played again, three times the unhappy voice deplored the result, before Favorinus appeared. His face had taken on a mask of cool, imperturbable dignity. He was walking at a normal pace—no member of a senatorial family would permit himself to run after his courtesan on a public street—and looking about for her in a casual manner.

"Aren't you feeling well?" he asked without concern, glancing down at her hand pressed against her side.

"I'm perfectly well."

"You don't look it."

"I said I was perfectly well." Her voice, shouting above the flute, was hard and high.

He stepped up into the little archway and stood beside her, not looking at her, looking down at his sandals. "Very well, then. Let's have it out, since you're determined to have it out," he said. "Let's say that you're angry—or suffering. The moment I walked into the scent-shop, I knew you'd made up your mind to suffer. Now, exactly what is it that you're suffering about?"

"Nothing. Let me alone."

"I have a right to know what crimes are being attributed to me. What have I done to you? How, precisely, have I hurt you? By keeping you waiting for less than half an hour? Dastardly as that was, I think I've made sufficient apologies. Or was it the business of the bolster? Did I hurt your feelings over that? I'm sorry if I hurt your feelings. I, of course, have no feelings myself. Nothing hurts me—not the hateful way you behaved to our friend the Greek proprietor, not even the fact that you haven't so much as mentioned the speech I left with you three days ago—"

"That piece of trashy Roman oratory!" She had actually shouted it in her fury. A child turned in the passing crowd, dragging on his father's hand and looked at her in amazement and fright. "Roman oratory—small, bigoted mean as mean and bigoted as Cato himself—I couldn't imagine your writing it. Roman oratory—out of you—and we read the Greeks together, you were the one who was supposed to love the funeral oration of Pericles—" She had to stop because her heart was pounding in her throat. The music had begun again, thick and sweet as syrup of dates. She looked at him now, she saw the shocked, open mouth, the muscle twitching in the hollow of his cheek, and the eyelids coming down over the humiliated eyes. "Surely," she said, and her voice was a travesty of sweet reasonableness, "surely you knew how I would feel about it. Surely you couldn't have imagined for a moment that I—"

"That will be enough."

"You asked me."

"So I did. Now I know better. So long as I live, I'll never ask you again."

Never again . . . So long as I live . . . If blind fortune was hurling the two of them apart, what vestige of her reason still remained told her that she ought to bear it in silence and with dignity. But there was the known and inestimably beloved face, white and sharply beautiful against the dark stone of the archway. There was the music, unnerving and disintegrating, letting the tide of self-pity sweep over her heart. "It wasn't the speech," she said in a whisper. "You did what you could with the speech, I know. You made it what it had to be. It wasn't the speech, it was only that back there in the leather-shop I felt—" she paused, because the words sounded tawdry in her own ears, the words were as cheaply moving as the notes of the flute— "it came into my head that you didn't love me anymore."

"God Everlasting!" He was shouting, and the passers by turned to look at his furious face, incongruous above the insignia of his class, the splendid gold collar and the purple stripe across his chest. "Am I supposed to spend the rest of my life proving to you that I love you? When will you be satisfied? Tell me—will you?—tell me in so many words—what do you want out of me?"

"Nothing, nothing—"

"I freed you before I touched you. I haven't married, I haven't looked at another woman. I've flown in everybody's face because of you—everybody considers me a renegade—my class, my family, my friends—"

"I know, I know—"

"Whenever I have a few miserable hours to call my own, I run to your house. I've run to your house twenty times when I had to force myself to come, when all I wanted to do was fling myself down somewhere and go to sleep. What more can I do? Do you want me to murder my mother? Would you like me to set fire to the imperial palace? Shall I walk up to the Emperor and spit in his face?"

"Oh, please," she said, raising her shaking hand to her lips. Romans—a whole streetful of Romans—were witnessing this. Scores of eyes, inimical and knowing and gratified, were watching the fine patrician gentleman reading the law to his Greek courtesan.

"Are you worried about what they think of us?" he shouted. "You didn't seem worried in the scent shop when it was you who were giving the lectures and I who was making the apologies."

The music on the second floor had ceased. She could not see the upper window from where she stood, but she had a conviction that a patrician virgin was leaning over the sill, listening. She conjured up the face—soft, rounded, without one line of bitter knowledge to mar its freshness, the young lips parted in a triumphant smile. "Stop it!" she said in a hissing whisper. "Nobody can abuse me in the street. I'm not a whore."

"I'll stop when I'm finished."

He, too—was he like all the rest of them? Did he find nothing more exhilarating than the sport of giving a public lesson to a slave? "Oh, but you stopped me before I was finished. That speech of yours—" she said, knowing exactly where he was vulnerable, "that speech of yours—you couldn't afford to let me finish what I wanted to say about it, could you? You knew perfectly well what a piece of trash it was yourself. But that's not the worst thing about it—" She stopped only to savor her power; he was staring, appalled and fascinated, into her face. "The worst thing about it is its utter futility. Think of the weeks you spent on it—all those weeks—and it's useless, ridiculous and useless. These pigs—" she made a wide fierce gesture at the packed ranks of his fellow-countrymen moving slowly along the pavement— "look at those pigs—do you believe for a moment that you're going to turn them into men with a speech and a law and a few half-hearted fines? You and your crazy old Pannonian—what are you trying to do—imitate Hercules? This rotten Empire is filthier than any Augean stables. This dung you're shoveling has been heaping up for centuries—work at it all your life, and it'll be higher than ever after you're dead. Anybody but an incurable Stoic child with his mother's milk still in his mouth would see that it's a waste of time."

She stopped and looked around her at a nightmare world. The white faces, passing blurred along the boundaries of her distorted vision, were as ghastly as a chorus of masked Furies. A little closer, the Levantine stood, with his fat thumb moving slowly up toward his waxy face. And close, so close that she could feel his breath on her cheek, was her lover, red patches of rage on his forehead, on his quivering cheek, on his stubbled jaw.

"A waste of time?" he said in a voice shaking with controlled fury. "You never waste any time, do you? You're a shining example of a life well-spent. You go to the art shops, you play the flute, you read your sacred Greeks, you rush out of one lecture and into another—that's the impression you like to give, and some people are foolish enough to be taken in by the noble picture you paint of yourself. But the fact is, you never spend more than two or three hours a day on those exalted pursuits of yours—they're minor diversions with you at best. I'll tell you what your real business is—I know, I've lain in bed and watched you with your mirror—your real business is the ritual you perform on your body. Three-fourths of the day you're too busy even for kissing—you're bathing yourself, you're anointing yourself, you're dressing yourself. Your hair, the condition of your skin, the exercises you ought to take to narrow your hips and enlarge your breasts—how you look, how you smell, who said you were pretty—those are the only things you really care about. Not that I'm suggesting you change your interests—you're a free woman, you can use your time exactly as you choose. But please extend the same courtesy to me. Don't be too affronted if the new curl on top of your head doesn't completely absorb my energies. Don't consider me a dog if, in the middle of a two-hour discussion about what jewelry you ought to buy, my mind wanders off to such minor matters as how to feed the legionaries and what to do about the Goths."

She saw herself as he had seen her too many times, sitting on a low bench in their bedchamber, naked, thin, and unbeautiful, rubbing oil into her neck, her arms, her breasts. That she had allowed him to know her anxious concern for her small charms and the remnants of her youth, that he should have taken her anxiety for self-love, that she should have revealed all her flaws to him in the mistaken assurance that he loved them and pitied them . . . There was no more anger in her. There was nothing left but pain. She set one dusty sandal out of the shadow of the archway. "If you're quite finished, I think I'll go home," she said.

"Wait, Charis—" It was uttered so flatly, so despondently that she could not keep herself from looking at him. He also was bled of anger. His face was as unbeautiful as Orbiana Festina could have wished—pinched, exhausted, almost old. "Let me find you a litter—"

"No, thank you just the same."

She started out of the archway again, but he grasped her by the forearm and held her back. "When will I see you again, Charis?"

"Tomorrow, if you like." For an instant she allowed herself to dream that even this breach might be healed, that tomorrow evening they might kindle an apple-wood fire and sit on the couch, with Cyrillus racing back and forth across their knees. Then he winced and bit his lip and sighed.

"I'll have to stay at home tomorrow to receive a guest," he said in a toneless voice. "The Emperor asked me days ago if I'd entertain Trebonianus Gallus, the Governor of Moesia. He's come down to talk to Decius about the defense of the northern frontier. Day after tomorrow—by then I ought to be able to hand him over to somebody else for a few hours—"

"Any time you like. I'm your freedwoman, as you reminded me a while ago." She was too weary to feel any malice, but the sour words came out of her automatically now. "You freed me before you touched me—that's what you said. Well, you did, that's true enough, and I'm grateful and completely at your disposal, any time at all."

"Please let me find you a litter."

"No, I can find one perfectly well myself."

He turned away, and then turned back again to give her a long kiss on the mouth, within sight of the crowd, within sight of the imaginary virgin leaning on the sill at the dancing-master's window; but she could not shape her lips to return his kiss. Sentimental, she thought, Roman and sentimental, an evasion of the unbearable actuality, like the crimson roses that they scatter on feast-days over the corruption in their family tombs . . . For a little while she watched him moving with the crowd. Then she lost sight of him because she was distracted by a loathsome clicking sound, the sound of the Levantine biting his fingernail. He was standing under the dancing-master's sign, with the leather sack of presents beside him, Berosus's pouch still hanging around his neck, his thumb in his mouth, and saliva on his chin. "Slave! Pig!" she screamed at the top of her lungs. "How many times have I told you? How many times have I—" And she flew at him, as though she herself had never been a slave-child journeying from Chios to Delos. She flew at him and struck him twice, hard, with the flat of her hand across his stupid face.

Chapter 11

IT WAS a time of harassing duties, it was a time of mounting tensions, it was a time of growing apprehensions. In a word, it was no time at all to entertain a guest.

During the week that preceded the Saturnalia it seemed to Favorinus that any one of the "clever ones", chosen at random, would have been in a better position than he to discharge the obligations of a host. Not that the others were in an even-tempered state, by any means. No censor had been chosen as yet, and everybody was feeling the tightening stresses; their conversations were high-pitched and harried; the partisans of Valerian kept eyeing Ummidius Pessinus, and the partisans of Ummidius Pessinus kept eyeing Valerian. Every word that came out of the Emperor's mouth was examined for a possible clue as to which way his favor was veering; and, once he became aware of their scrutiny, his whole manner underwent a perceptible change. They could get nothing out of him anymore but the small talk for which he was so eminently ill-suited; and the morning receptions took on a strained loquacity, a rigid cheerfulness.

Why he had chosen to expose them all to this period of waiting, why he had not named the censor the day he launched the censorship, none of them could tell. The new measure had been presented to the Senate a week before the first day of the Saturnalia feast—the whole matter had been settled, somewhat anti-climactically, in less than an hour. With all the proper inflections, with no trace whatever of Pannonian dialect, Decius had read his nephew's elegant and ornate oration to a crowded house; and, so far as Favorinus could see, nobody had fallen asleep. The Conscript Fathers had furnished five rounds of applause for the brilliant rhetoric, had unanimously voted in favor of the measure, and then, in fairly large numbers, had unobtrusively departed for their villas by the sea. The mass desertion failed to ruffle the "clever ones"; it was to be expected and they were fully prepared for it—so, at least, they said. They could count themselves fortunate that a tenth of the august members of the senate had reconciled themselves to sitting out the winter in Rome. It would not be easy to keep an exemplary household, to justify the censorship to the frantic equestrians, to refuse to use one's influence in court for friends and relatives who had incurred ruinous fines by buying luxuries.

No, there was not one of them that week before the Saturnalia who had the unfailing verve necessary for taking Trebonianus Gallus to the places he insisted on visiting. Any one of the "clever ones", nagged as they were by public worries, would have resented his unflagging determination to enjoy himself. But Favorinus Herennius had private exigencies to add to the public ones. He was more harassed, more apprehensive—or so it seemed to him—than any of the rest.

Nobody else, for example, had to cope with the business of Drusilla. Nobody else had to walk into the morning receptions wondering whether he would be summoned behind the embroidered curtain and forced to admit that the Herennii had said another "No" to the Decii. The dread of that inevitable interview became an obsession with him. Every morning he went to the imperial palace in a cold sweat; every noon he walked out again with a sense of blessed reprieve. The bright air of confidence between him and the Emperor was clouded; Decius never approached the massive breakfast table when *he* was near it; and, whenever they talked, they talked haltingly and avoided each other's eyes.

As for Charis, he had not seen her—he would probably not see her again until they met in a shouting, drunken crowd at the Saturnalia banquet that they had been foolish enough to plan together. The tentative appointment he had made with her in the dark little archway on the Via Sacra had never materialized because of the demands that Trebonianus Gallus made upon him; and she, justifiably wounded, had sent back his wrinkled manuscript by a slave, together with a curt little note stating that she would be out of the City for several days. It was only from a chance encounter with the philosopher Cleander that he learned they would be visiting Berosus at his villa in Tibur.

No, he was in no mood to entertain a visiting dignitary. Any guest would have been a burden, and this particular guest had a superlative talent for making himself obnoxious. He reported to the steward that he had seen ants in his bathroom; he complained about the draught in his bedroom and disparaged the cook; he appraised and pinched and patted every presentable female slave. The daughter of the house, in no frame of mind for his banter since her quarrel with her brother, was harassed by his ceaseless conversation and affronted by his gallantries. When she was not pointedly absenting herself from the table, she made a crisis of the evening meal by taking exception to every word the visitor said. And even the lady Sabina—determined as she was to promote her son's political career and flattered as she was to be playing hostess to an imperial guest—even the lady Sabina could not refrain from wincing now and then behind her silvery veils and asking later how it was possible that the Governor, born a patrician and raised in the best society, could be capable of such monstrous vulgarity.

Vulgar he was, without any question; and yet his crassness was less disturbing to the exhausted Favorinus than his limitless energy. There was no place where he could escape that bawling voice: it roused him out of his brief and unquiet sleep, it shouted through the door above the noise of the water splashing into his bath, it hailed him from the hall outside the office of the Secretary of Petitions, and every time he heard it, he started as though he had been slapped in the face. Every half hour it issued some positive statement; there was no domain where the Governor was not an expert. He knew how the plebes would take the censorship—"They'll hate it worse than the equestrians, wait and see;" whether the currency was going to be devalued again—"Two more measures of copper to the denarius, I had it from the most dependable source, my dear boy;" what colors were unbecoming—"You're too pale for that green thing you had on last night, Drusilla;" what food the Herennii should serve their Saturnalia visitors—"After all, you're not entertaining schoolgirls. These people won't be satisfied with that sort of fluff."

For the first six days of his visit, Favorinus refrained from taking exceptions to any of the Governor's remarks; but on the morning of the Saturnalia, furious because Gallus was certain—he had had it on the best authority—that the matter of the censor would be settled before noon and that Valerian would be the man, he gave vent to his ill-humor by entering into a lengthy and ridiculous contention over a certain statue in the imperial gardens, a Roman Venus, about two centuries old, which he had passed almost every morning in the past four months, and which he had seen, as he stated with some heat on his way out of the palace, at least as often as he had seen the Emperor. The Governor insisted that the Venus was not Roman but Corinthian; he asserted, in fact, that the trademark of a famous Corinthian foundry was to be seen on the pedestal. All the way to the imperial palace, they continued the argument, calling back and forth from litter to litter—the garlanded merrymakers stopped to stare after them in the street. And, by the time they reached the Emperor's gardens, their rancor had grown to such proportions that they actually got out of their litters and went on foot to see the Venus, so that the point could be settled before the Emperor's levee. The trademark was not there, of course. Nothing that even resembled a trademark was to be found on the fluted pedestal, old bronze mottled over with a greenish patina.

"I can't see very clearly in this light, can you?" said Trebonianus Gallus.

"Of course I can see. If there was anything to see, you could see it. It's a good hour past dawn."

"The Emperor has fine weather for his little affair." He lifted his eyes from the pedestal to the streaks of coral cloud above the vine-covered arches and the little domed shrines set white in the deep green of the laurels and yews.

"So there isn't any trademark?"

"No. To tell the truth, I'm beginning to think I confused it with some other statue." The lively protruding eyes turned from the sky to the lawns, dew-drenched and emerald green in the clear December light. They were peopled with hundreds of statues and thousands of plebes—public servants and artisans and idle dependents on the dole who came once a year on the morning of the Saturnalia, to pay their respects to the Lord of the World.

"Then you'll admit that it isn't Corinthian?"

"Not at all, anybody can see that it's Corinthian."

"Would you mind telling me how?" He wondered if he was pursuing the subject to distract his own attention from more disquieting things. The procession of upper-class Romans that was moving toward the palace was depressingly small—most of the equestrians had stayed away to indicate their bitterness, and the number of striped senatorial togas on the broad white pavement was discouragingly small.

"How? Isn't that a bit hard to say in so many words? One sees a Corinthian piece and one knows by instinct. Take those fingers, for instance—no over here, on the right hand—"

"I don't see anything remarkable about those fingers. Charis has a little Roman Apollo over at her house with fingers much the same."

"Maybe so, maybe so. Anyhow, this evening we'll have a chance to see Didn't you say we were going to finish up the Saturnalia over there tonight?

Unfortunately he had said it, but at a time when he still believed that he and she would make up their differences before they were forced to recline beside each other at a banquet table, with some twenty of their friends and acquaintances looking on. And how do I know, he thought, what he's likely to do if I take him over there tonight . . . He shook the dew off the hem of his toga and cleared his throat. "Are you sure you still want to go over there I don't think you'll find it particularly exciting," he said.

"Of course I want to. *You're* going, aren't you?" The full, petulant under lip was thrust out in a faintly malicious smile. "Let's move along and present ourselves to your exalted uncle. I hate to stand in one place like this

"In a moment. There was something I meant to look into while I'm here—"

"What do you want to look into?"

None of your business, he thought, exasperated with the Governor and in a rage at himself. He had meant to do his looking about surreptitiously, and now he had aroused Gallus's curiosity. Down in this part of the imperial gardens, there were only the plebes, and he would never have wanted anybody but Ummidius Pessinus to know that he was giving the plebes a moment's consideration. The credit of the new regime was not really so low that any account had to be taken of these wretches in coarse brown woolen who would not dare to enter the atrium and take their share of the Emperor's Saturnalia bounty until their betters were gone. As for the pile of little Saturnalia presents that they were leaving for their master and their Lord—whether it was high or low was of no great significance. The Secretary of Petitions was the only one who believed that things had come to such a pass that one had to take the plebes seriously. Nobody else believed it—he took no stock in it himself. And yet he wished that he might wander about a little. "Why don't you go on up to the palace? I'll join you in the atrium, at the far end to the right," he said.

"Oh, no, I'll stay by you. I'd just as soon walk around and hear what the plebes are saying as listen to the nonsense a person gets in official circles these days. We can take a look at the pile of gifts if you want to. Not that I think it means much. All of you down here in the City are confused—every little detail looks important to you. All this reform—the censorship and all the rest of it—will be gone and forgotten when the real issue comes up—"

"And what, in your expert opinion, is the real issue?"

"The real issue? Ask any Dacian peasant—any thick-headed peasant whose turnip field happens to face the forests on the other side of the frontier. The hordes in the forest—they're the real issue. The Goths, my dear fellow, the Goths."

They walked on in silence then, down the lawn toward the shrine of Fortune, visible now at the foot of the slope. All of white marble, tinged with the glow of early sunlight, seeming scarcely more substantial than the cluster of clouds above it, the little chapel stood pale against the intense blueness of the morning sky. As the green swell of the lawns fell away, he could see the columns and the human beings milling around them—a grey and brown mass, not too impressive in size, yet large enough to preclude outright disgrace. The pile of gifts—small silver spoons and carved boxes, trussed hares and dressed poultry, bouquets of parsley and sticks of cinnamon, all piled in one heterogeneous heap—the pile of gifts was gratifyingly high, considering that this Saturnalia feast came at the end of a year of poverty and civil strife.

They wandered over to see the presents first. The Governor of Moesia stood for a long time, pursing his mouth and looking down at them, with his hands on his hips and his legs apart. "Fair," he said at last, "only fair, if you ask my opinion. Or will they bring up more stuff later? How long does it usually go on?"

"They keep coming all day." He said it flatly—the quarrelsomeness had gone out of him at the sight of the presents. They were such pathetic, ridiculously inappropriate gifts—a pair of scarlet sandals, no doubt from some cobbler, a length of homespun linen embroidered with the message "For my lady and my mistress, the most beautiful and virtuous Empress Etruscilla," a hideous yellow glass goblet, a curling-iron, a scrawny singing bird in a battered cage. And every now and then new hands thrust themselves into the area of his vision to lay new objects on the toppling pile—the raw, grimy, unbeautiful hands of the poor.

"What's your uncle supposed to do with this rubbish?"

"How should I know? It's his first Saturnalia."

Why must he call it rubbish just when a crippled old woman and a sallow, unlovely girl were coming up behind him, clutching little bags of herbs in their fists? Why must they creep and sidle and hold their clothes against their bodies, as if a governor's cloak and a senator's toga would be contaminated by contact with plebeian cloth?

"That's right, it is his first Saturnalia," Trebonianus Gallus said. "Well, let's hope he has better luck than some of his predecessors, let's hope it won't be his last. If you want to hear what these people are saying—that's what you do want, isn't it?—let's go into that little chapel down there. We can walk right past them if we go up the steps and into the shrine."

As they approached the twenty or thirty loiterers who stood in groups of fours and fives on the chapel steps, Favorinus knew suddenly and with amazement that he had never walked into a gathering of plebes before. And the pity that had almost unmanned him near the pile of gifts was transformed into something close to apprehension when he saw them in the uncharitable brilliance of the clear winter morning—cropped heads, thick necks, vacant faces and sullen faces, empty eyes and dogged eyes. There were no women in the crowd—perhaps it was their absence that made the group on the stairs look so hostile and grim. Their stolid bodies blocked the way; and whether they were refusing to move from inertia or from resentment, he could not tell.

"Shove them, just shove them a little, my dear fellow," said Gallus, exasperatingly close to him and nudging him in the side.

But any shoving that was done was done by the plebes. As if by a prearranged plan they closed in on the fine senator in his striped toga and the little Governor in his scarlet cloak and edged them backward up the shallow steps; they were not content until the two patricians were jammed back against a column. Then, all at once, the pressure lessened. They had had their sport for the morning and were satisfied; all but two of them went back down the stairs. Of the two, the one who stood on the first step from the top—it was plain that he was a tanner from the sickening stench of the unscraped hide that he exuded—was almost grotesquely gaunt. His dark, oily skin was stretched tight over his bones, and his eyes were feverishly bright in the hollows between his jutting cheekbones and his beetling brows. He was talking—it was obvious that he had been talking for some time—into the face of a meek, scrubbed, elderly idler, probably one of the thousands who lived on the dole. But his roving eyes indicated that he had lost all interest in his inconsequential listener: he was talking now for the benefit of the two patricians.

"Beef!" he said, slavering in his fury. "That's what they're handing out to us up at the palace this Saturnalia—beef and bread and sour home-made wine. Well, you can drag yourself up to eat that pig-swill if you want to. It's not for me, I won't expose myself to the insult, it's beneath my dignity as a Roman citizen. I ate twice at the Saturnalia table of Philip the Arabian. Arab dog that he was, he knew how to feed a citizen. There was everything you could ask for—clams and mussels, hares and pheasants, cakes that looked like crowns and rolls in the shape of butterflies. No, they can't make me eat and they can't make me scramble for their lottery tickets, either. I've read the list of prizes, and you'll not see me risking my neck for a length of wool or a pair of scrawny sheep. I remember the day when a man could hope to win a cow or a horse or a good-looking slave girl. But that was before the old Pannonian dressed himself up in the purple—that was before the old turnip-farmer made a barn of the imperial palace—that was before the old miser got the notion that Roman citizens could be fed like slaves."

He stopped and stared up at Favorinus, waiting for an answer. But there was no answer, there was only utter bafflement at the spectacle of this alien, incomprehensible mentality: the mind of the tanner was as strange to him as the minds of the Chinese traders who brought their silk to the margins of the Empire, and laughed when there was nothing to laugh at, and took offense when there was no discourtesy. To consider the homely fare on the imperial table an insult, to take the Emperor's stern adherence to the old Republican ways for miserliness . . . He guessed of a sudden what monstrous misconceptions had been growing for centuries in the hovels and the tenements, and he was afraid.

"I tell you," said the tanner, pointing his finger into his companion's pink and flustered face, "I tell you that a dog under Philip's table would have done better." He jerked his head backward and glared at the two intruders. "A dog under Philip's table, I said."

"Wait a moment, listen—" It was feeble, it was groping, he had not the slightest notion what arguments he meant to introduce with it. He knew only that if he kept silent any longer he would be guilty of gross disloyalty to the austere old general who had given authenticity to the purple and the orb and the rayed crown. And his uncle seemed dearer than ever to him now, partly because his greatness was vulnerable to their ignorance, partly because there had been no smile, no touch, no proof of the old intimacy these many days . . . "Listen," he said again, braving out the fact that he felt foolish and exposed, braving out the look of amusement in the Governor's eyes and the dull hostility in the faces that turned to stare at him from the steps and the lawn.

"To whom am I about to have the honor of listening?" It was said in a mincing falsetto voice and couched in a heavy-handed imitation of the involved rhetoric of patrician oratory.

"What difference does it make who I am?" he said at the top of his voice. "Whoever I am, it takes more than the absence of crown-cakes and mussels to provoke me into a public denunciation of my master and my lord. Only a fool could take him for a miser. It wasn't miserliness that stripped the imperial atrium. A miser hoards everything. The Emperor put everything into the public treasury. He never kept a single denarius for himself."

"Oh, come, now, my dear fellow. This is ridiculous. Let's go up to the palace. What do you want to stand around and argue with these ignorant people for?"

An uncanny glint came into the eyes of the tanner. He leaned forward, and the stench that came from his oily tunic was almost stifling. "That's right, don't waste any time, hurry up to the palace," he said in a sneering singsong. "Hurry up to the palace and get your dish of lamprey in fish sauce. Everybody knows there'll be two Saturnalia tables up there—one for the dirty plebes, and one for the dainty eaters like yourselves."

"Whoever told you that was a liar! All of us'll be eating from the same dishes today, including our master and our lord."

"Well, now," said the elderly recipient of the dole in a peacemaker's voice, laying his hand, white with idleness, on the tanner's dark and scrawny arm, "that puts another face on it, doesn't it? If everybody, even the Emperor, is going to eat from the same dishes, then nobody ought to feel put upon—"

"Keep your hands to yourself, you old idiot!" All the stored venom that he had to deal out in small doses to the two patricians came flying into the face of the mild nonentity. "Can't you see they're making a fool of you? Can't you see it's an insult to a citizen to give him a chunk of beef and a draught of green wine?"

"A chunk of beef and a draught of green wine," said Favorinus, trying to think what his uncle would have said, unable to depend, in this vast, benighted confusion, on any reasoning of his own—"a chunk of beef and a draught of green wine were what Cato and Scipio Africanus ate in better days than ours. They thanked the gods for it. They served it on feast days to their most distinguished guests. This Empire was built without benefit of raisin wine and mussels. It was a handful of farmers—simple, corn-fed farmers—who conquered the Carthaginians and inherited the world. And we've come to a pretty pass—haven't we, my friend?—if the food that was luxury to our ancestors is pig-swill to you and me?"

Even while he was speaking, what he said struck him as specious and crassly patriotic. The simplicity that would have been convincing in Decius seemed artificial in him; he had a momentary vision of Charis and Antisthenes exchanging a disparaging smile. And he was surprised that so shallow an argument should give the tanner pause and set several of the others, nearby and on the lower steps, to nodding their heads. "The illustrious senator has got something there," said the voice of an unseen listener from below. "My wife's father was a schoolmaster in Massilia in his younger days, and he tells me that the elder Cato, the one who was the censor. . . ."

Trebonianus Gallus laid a fatherly arm around his host's shoulders. "Come along, let's let well enough alone," he said. "If we don't move on, we'll miss the levee."

Favorinus looked about him. The tanner was staring down at his own feet, the elderly idler had disappeared into the shadowy interior of the shrine, and most of the others were either listening to the son-in-law of the Massilian schoolmaster or wandering off to see what new items had been added to the pile of gifts on the grass. To leave now was to concede to the Governor and depart without decisive victory. And yet to stay—if one were to judge by the look of furious brooding on the tanner's oily face—was to invite another public tirade against the Emperor. "Whatever you like," he said, and walked past the tanner and on down the stairs.

But they had not taken ten steps in the direction of the palace when the tanner started in again behind them. "Wait a moment, your Eminence! Don't retreat so fast, your Illustriousness!" he shouted across the lawn. "All that talk about Scipio Africanus—you can't take us in with that, we're not such idiots as you think we are. Our lord and our master—the crazy Pannonian—if he wants to pretend he's one of the old heroes, that's his affair. This whole reform of his—his censorship and all the rest of it—nobody asked us anything about it. It doesn't mean a thing to us if it works out, and if it doesn't we can't be any worse off than we are. We plebes are just like dogs now: we take whatever our betters toss at us. If you're talking about Cato and Scipio Africanus—they got something with their beef and green wine, they got offices, they got estates. What do we get? Games, lotteries, a few banquets on feast-days—that's all we plebes get out of your glorious Roman Empire. And we won't let him cheat us out of that. Tell him so—you seem to be a friend of his—go up to his levee and tell him so! Tell him we want our Saturnalia cakes and mussels. Once a year—once in every rotten year—we want our cupful of ten-year-old wine!"

It was impossible to turn and shout an answer at this distance, with crowds of grinning plebes looking on. And yet he found it very difficult to assume the customary patrician remoteness, to continue toward the palace with a straight back and a high head. To walk on as if the tanner's naked confession of his degradation had never been made was to deny his humanity, to agree that he was the animal he had called himself. What did he eat the whole year round that he should turn frantic because he was robbed of

Saturnalia dainties? Porridge and lentils, fat Lucanian bacon and black bread? How would a palate accustomed to that sort of fare react to fresh mussels? Possibly, Favorinus told himself, the result would be a sharp ecstasy, as poignant as anything I have ever experienced in the act of love . . . And the other plebes, tens of thousands of them all over the city —had all of them wakened this morning with such yearnings in their bowels, such visions of meat and white bread and exotic wines? How many mothers, expecting to carry fabulous morsels home to their children, would walk into the narrow rooms of the tenements tonight with nothing but bits of tough beef and rusks of bread?

"What are you chewing your lip about?" asked Trebonianus Gallus.

"Nothing. It's a habit of mine. And, furthermore, there's nothing more irritating than having somebody point that sort of habit out."

"You're in a very touchy mood, my dear fellow, and to save my life I can't see why. You should have known how the plebes were going to take the thing. Didn't I tell you so myself three or four days ago?"

"I wouldn't leap to any conclusions about their attitude. One crazy tanner scarcely represents the whole class."

And yet, all the way across the bright lawn, he was troubled by a sense of imponderable forces moving behind the drab walls of the tenements, forces so alien and complex that even as experienced a mind as that of Ummidius Pessinus must struggle to understand them and might very well struggle in vain. By the time they had reached the top of the stairs that led to the palace, he was breathless and his heart was beating at a rapid and erratic pace.

Nor was there anything in the sight of the imperial atrium to quiet his apprehension. He deceived neither himself nor Gallus by saying that the place looked empty for lack of furniture: the senators and equestrians who were there to pay their respects to the Emperor were undeniably few. The Saturnalia tables, flanking the lines of the columns, had scarcely been touched, either because there was nothing tempting about the food or because the appetites of the morning callers had been driven away by anxiety. Anxious they were—they stood about in small, uncommunicative groups, craning their necks every now and then to get a glimpse of the little private dining room, which was crowded as usual with the intimates of the new regime. And actually, thought Favorinus, exchanging lively Saturnalia greetings with every group that he passed, bowing with forced cordiality to the sickly eunuch who motioned him and his guest into the dining room with the usual unhappy air, actually the supporters of Ummidius Pessinus had no cause for nervousness. One glimpse of the crowd around the massive table made it impossible for him to imagine these captious, uncompromising intellects under the authority of anyone but their admitted superior, the Secretary of Petitions.

Trebonianus Gallus attached himself at once to the jaundiced Pontifex Maximus and the bored Secretary of the Imperial Treasury—the former had some correspondence he wanted the Governor to drop off for him on the way back to Moesia. Glad to be rid of him, Favorinus went to the table and heaped his plate with the Saturnalia fare, partly to show that the menu was entirely satisfactory to him, and partly because the business of eating gave him an excuse for avoiding conversation. The talk was as lively as ever, but strangely pointless and bodiless. Nobody in the dining room was making so much as an oblique reference to the forthcoming appointment. Some of them were complaining about the uselessness of their Saturnalia gifts, some of them were telling stories about the doings of their children, but most of them kept turning their heads covertly in the direction of the embroidered curtain, almost blindingly bright in the clear winter sun.

Not too far from the curtain, staring blankly at it like everybody else, Favorinus collided with the little monkey-faced Secretary of the Privy Purse. He should have offered an apology—he had actually knocked a rusk of bread out of the small, frail hands—but he found himself asking a question instead. "Has the Emperor called anybody in as yet?"

"Why, yes," said the bald little Jew, looking up with bright, startled eyes and grinding his knuckle into his furrowed, simian brow. "You came in late, didn't you? Hasn't anybody told you? He and Valerian—they've been talking in there for almost an hour."

Two drops of sweat raced down his sides—and that was ridiculous. It augured nothing but good—the fact that Decius had called in Valerian. Valerian would have been summoned to a private interview precisely because he was *not* going to be censor—and it was exasperating that the Secretary of the Privy Purse had not been able to see as much for himself. Behind the luminous folds embroidered with palm-leaves, the Emperor was doubtless explaining, consoling, offering beforehand the balm necessary to ease the affronted self-esteem. An unenviable task, thought Favorinus, wishing that everybody would fall silent, that some revealing fragment of a sentence would come from behind the folds of sunlit cloth. An unenviable task, to convince the self-assured ass that he must step down before a rival that he considered an upstart, the grandson of a slave. . . .

"Where *is* our candidate?" he asked, handing his plate, with most of the food still on it, to a passing Aethiopian.

The Secretary of the Privy Purse jerked his domed and gleaming head in the direction of the table. Behind a bowl of apples stood Ummidius Pessinus, alone and smiling a fixed smile, his handkerchief a wilted rag between his hands. And suddenly Favorinus felt such a wave of affection for that rare and utterly unpretentious creature, for his nervousness, his precarious good manners, his gentle eyes—that his throat went tight and he could not look the Secretary of the Privy Purse in the face. "Excuse me, I have to see him," he said, and started back toward the table to tell his good friend that he was suffering needlessly, that there was no cause for consternation, that in a moment now, in a moment—

He stopped in his tracks because the customary hush had descended on the dining room. The curtain was being drawn aside, the Aethiopian was stepping back, and the two figures—the soft, ponderous one and the hard, soldierly one—were issuing out of the imperial bedchamber, their arms clasped, their fingers intertwined. There was no trace of wounded sensibility in the placid countenance of the Dean of the Senate; the folds of flesh around his mouth were creased by the usual vague, foolish, philanthropic smile. And the Emperor—Favorinus could not force his eyes to focus on the face of the Emperor. That face had undergone an unbelievable transformation—there was in that face such a look as he had never seen before, an almost womanish, full-hearted look, a softening of the stern lips, a melting of the ice-blue eyes.

"Our Lord and our Master, Caius Messius Quintus Trajanus Decius," said the Aethiopian, using the full array of titles, since this was the Saturnalia and a weighty occasion. "Emperor of All the Romans. Preserver and Restorer of the World." The last of these epithets was new and had never been uttered before, though Favorinus had seen it embossed around his uncle's profile on the new denarius—two more measures of copper to the coin, the whole currency had been devalued again—and he had to struggle with an almost uncontrollable impulse to burst out laughing: Couldn't the Preserver and Restorer of the World have found a better place to put the magniloquent motto than on a debased denarius? His uncle's face—was it transformed like that when he discussed with the jaundiced Pontifex Maximus the mysteries of Bona Dea late into the night, when he entered the Temple of Vesta and approached the hearth and stood brooding above the sacred fire. . . .

Nobody in the room was looking at anybody else. All of them were standing precisely as they had stood when the curtain had swept back and revealed the disquieting pair—four or five of them still held their filled plates in their hands. A sick silence held them all; somebody should have broken it with applause, but it remained and seemed to grow, like a rising wave of nausea, until it was shattered by the Emperor's voice saying, "Happy Valerian!"

"Happy Valerian!" he said again, after clearing his throat; and his nephew knew that nobody had labored with him over this speech, that he had written it alone, in a melting ecstasy, seeing visions of the ancestors and the Old Wall, modelling every sentence after the old-fashioned style of the tellers of heroic tales. "Happy in the general approbation of the Senate and the Roman People. Accept the censorship, and judge our manners. Select those who deserve to remain among the Conscript Fathers. Restore the equestrian class to its ancient splendor; improve the revenue, yet moderate the public burdens; and accurately examine the wealth, the power, and the resources of the Roman Empire. Whatever decisions your wisdom leads you to make shall obtain the force of law. The palace, the ministers of justice, the great offices of the Empire shall be from this time under your tribunal. None are exempted, save only the consuls, the Pontifex Maximus, and—so long as she preserves her chastity—the eldest of the Vestal Virgins. Even these few, who need not dread the severity, will anxiously solicit the esteem of the man who will henceforth administer the Roman censorship."

Surely I'm not going to vomit, thought Favorinus, seeing a vision of a green parasol splashed with seedy red. A drink of water, what I need is a drink of water, that'll stop this heaving in my stomach . . . A thunderous noise was breaking all around him. The habit of sycophancy, nurtured by tyrants for centuries, had asserted itself even in the "clever ones". They were clapping, all of them were offering five rounds of applause for the Censor Valerian, even Ummidius Pessinus—he stood with his handkerchief on the floor before him, beating his hands together more furiously than the rest.

There was a fountain—he was sure he remembered a fountain—just outside the door. He turned and started for it, and was stopped by the little Governor, who stood grinning up at him, head cocked and arms akimbo. "Happy Valerian!" said Gallus, making a grimace. "I'm glad Valerian's so happy. Nobody else here seems to be."

"Let me alone—"

"Oh, come, now, where's your sense of humor? If you mean to be a politician, you can't afford to take every little setback as if it were a calamity."

He hated the man. He could have driven his fist straight into the man's revolting face. He walked past him without another word and went to the fountain, where he vented his fury and disgust by striking his fist against a bronze dolphin. But the pain of the split skin did not help, and the water did not help, and, leaning against the fountain and nursing his hand, he felt as if the marble floor were rocking and dividing under his feet. A crack in the earth, he thought, a crack running around the orb of the world . . . And, if two equestrians, acquaintances of his mother, had not come up to wish him a joyous feast-day and a prosperous year, he could not have controlled himself, he would probably have wept.

Chapter 12

HE NEVER drank much on the Saturnalia. For years he had held off to the point of rudeness all the tipsy and aggressively hospitable hosts who had tried to fill his goblet with their own hands. The pre-arranged national flight from all standards of human dignity and decency, the drunkenness and the debauchery—it was enough to make him sick with revulsion. By day he made the required rounds of Saturnalia visits in a raw state that verged on testiness. And by night, walking the avenues sulphurously bright with the lanterns of the revellers, exposed to bold, demanding eyes and subject to the touch of unrestrained hands, he felt as though he was abroad in a world gone mad, a world that was inviting black Chaos to come crashing in.

He never drank much on the Saturnalia. Yet on that first Saturnalia of the reign of Caius Messius Quintus Trajanus Decius, Restorer and Preserver of the World, when Valerian was named censor and two more measures of base metal were added to the denarius, he was drunk before noon. There was a split in the skin of his hand, and a crack in one of the columns of the imperial atrium, and another crack running round the orb of the world. And he drank as the patrician Marcellinus had drunk in the last weeks before his death, to numb his jangling nerves, to dull the pain.

That he should have felt the need of such an anodyne all morning was no great wonder, considering certain fatuous and exalted statements that his uncle kept making about the ancient family of the Valerii adding luster to the censorship and the censorship adding luster to the ancient family of the Valerii. Many of the "clever ones" plainly needed the same remedy; at the levee and at the little reception given later in the chambers of the Empress Etruscilla, everybody drank too much. And if he drank a little more than the others, he had his private reasons. Any personal exchange with the Emperor or with his suddenly remote and impervious wife was made so impossible that he could no longer deceive himself—both the Decii were waiting in the stern attitudes of ancient dignitaries for their answer from the Herennii. The imperial chambers and everybody in them grew more intolerable by the hour. There was no place to sit, no place to stand, nobody to talk to. There was only the table and the wine.

He told himself—and Trebonianus Gallus and the Secretary of the Privy Purse—that he would stop drinking as soon as he got out of the abominable place, as soon as he was delivered from the sight of the weathered hand clinging to the fat pink arm and the ice-blue eyes melting before the big, inane face. He told himself there would be no need to drink at the Saturnalia tables of relatives and friends of the family; yet everywhere he stopped another cause for drinking presented itself. He drank old Cretan at his grandaunt's because the withered cheek she presented for his kiss was so revoltingly smeared with powder and paint. He drank yellow Cyprian at the palace of the Metelli because the master of the house was showing such shameless attentions to his prospective son-in-law. He drank Syrian raisin, syrupy and uncongenial as it was, in the atrium of Flavius Labeo because the wife of his host, having passed her fortieth birthday last week, kept insisting to everybody that life, real life, had passed her by.

Well, then, he thought, I will be forced to do that disgusting thing when I get home: I will put a feather down my throat and all of it will come up together—Syrian, Cyprian, and old Cretan, the salt of my sorrow and the bile of my loathing and the mussels I ate at the house of the Glabrii because I had nothing to do with my hanging hands . . . And he did the disgusting thing—he had a great deal of trouble dissuading the ubiquitous Governor of Moesia from coming in to assist him—and walked about his own house for more than an hour thereafter, emptied, chastened, so lightheaded that he seemed to be floating through a dream. But here there was more cause for drinking than anywhere else except the imperial dining room. One drank to find courage for sending a slave to Charis with the message that she should prepare for an additional guest. One drank again because the slave, returning, had no word of love, could report only that the lady had said she and her house were completely at the service of her master and her lord. One drank because the presents were so tawdry, and the talk was so vacuous, and the gamblers were so avid, kneeling under the colonnade of the atrium in the red light of late afternoon, and the lovers were so utterly devoid of passion, exchanging their deliberate caresses in the purplish light of the dusk on the stairs.

It would have been wise to resort to the feather again—Trebonianus Gallus suggested it with malice, and one of the Alexandrine dancing girls suggested it with kindness; while the slaves bore in the wax tapers, he held the poor, bony, henna-haired thing on his knee because all the seats in the atrium were taken and she was plainly as exhausted and addled as himself. "Get it up. I've got it up three times so far today, and every time I did it I felt better," she said. But he was too depleted, he could not summon up the determination to inflict this violence upon himself. He would live out the evening as best he could; he was not actually sick anymore, it was only that things looked a little strange; wine always brought a pinkish tinge into the whites of his eyes, and today it had actually blurred his sight. When he stepped out of the palace, on the arm of the Governor of Moesia, he could have sworn that the whole garden was immersed in mist. The lanterns borne before the coming and departing visitors looked like swollen moons, and it seemed to him that one golden conflagration was burning up and down the avenue of sycamores.

Perhaps it was this distortion of his vision that gave an unlooked-for aspect to the carnival streets. The lanterns and their reflections in the marble walls and pavements, the revellers with their parted lips and loosened hair, the varicolored garments and the trampled garlands under his feet— he saw them all blurred and radiant, as if through tears. And it was peculiar—he tried without success to explain to Gallus—it was peculiar that a chance physical symptom should beget an emotional state: simply because his eyes were watering from the wine, his heart dilated and everything he saw seemed sorrowful and beautiful enough to make him want to weep. The drunken merrymakers who had seemed obscene and hideous to him in other years—they were as pathetic and blameless to him now as moths going giddily round and round in the nights of late summer, before the coming of the frost. What doom is hanging over them? he asked himself. How would they look to the eye of God, if the eye of God could see? And he saw the City, a frail foam of marble churned white against emptiness, and the delicate, mothy beings flitting back and forth in the whiteness, the glimmering of their lanterns as innocent and transitory as the glimmering of fireflies.

"You're walking into a ditch," said the Governor of Moesia.

"Am I? That's because I'm blind in the eyes and blind in the spirit."

"What are you talking about?"

He did not trouble to answer. A thin young matron, heavy-lidded and dreamy-eyed with too much wine, emerged out of the crowd, glided past him, returned, twined her slight arms around his neck, and raised her face to his. He drew his lips gently and considerately across her parted lips, and, though he had never seen her before, it seemed to him that the essence of his youth was on her mouth, that, in kissing her, he was bidding the better part of his days farewell.

"Not bad in the face," said Gallus, looking after her. "But much too thin in the thighs."

He envisioned her thighs, and Charis's thighs, and a pair of thighs that stood for the thighs of all womankind—white, netted over with blue and mortal veins, tapering down toward the knee in a fragile and pathetic line. Some of these women whose bodies brushed against his had breasts that ached with a long day of kissing. Some of them were pouring out their crimson sacrifice, and some of them cradled under the soft silk of their clothes and the soft skin of their bellies the seed that would come into the world as a bloody child. Women—it was far too long since he had lain with a woman. And for months now he had done the act of passion without ardor, he had accomplished the mystery without any sense of its holiness, without offering up his heart.

"One thing I'll say for your sister Drusilla—she certainly has a good figure."

He saw her as a woman giving herself to Eugenius. It was a loathsome image, and he turned his fury against the crass creature who had evoked it. "My sister Drusilla," he said, steadying himself against the bronze-winged feet of a Mercury, "my sister Drusilla is nobody to discuss in the street."

"Don't excite yourself, my dear boy. If she didn't want anybody to notice, she'd have her dalmaticas made thicker. But her looks won't last long, not if she keeps dragging herself around the house like some she-dog with the summer fever, ready to snap at anything."

"Can't you realize she simply doesn't like you?" he said, starting down the street at a fast pace, with his guest puffing up behind.

"Of course she doesn't like me. She doesn't like anything. Obviously, there's something the matter with the girl—"

He stopped again, stepped out of the stream of merrymakers and into a gutter filled with damp leaves and old papyrus, and struck himself in the middle of the brow. This ass had furnished, quite by chance, something that could be said behind the embroidered curtain when the Herennii were forced to say their say to the Decii. "Of course, she's sick," he said. "She'll have to go away somewhere—to Epidaurus, I suppose—she'll have to go to Epidaurus and rest." He saw her standing against a column at the Temple of Aesculapius the Healer at Epidaurus. She was dressed fantastically in a scarlet dalmatica with tattered sleeves and hem. There was a crazy garland set awry on her head. Her hands were cupped to hold wan weeds and shells and dead creatures of the sea, and her feet were caked with yellow sand. . . .

"You're incoherent, my dear fellow, I hope you realize. Maybe we'll take a feather to you when we get to Charis's place. Incidentally, it's suddenly dawned on me that you haven't the slightest idea how to get there—"

"You lie," he said, pointing his finger straight into Gallus's face. "It's true, I haven't seen her for two weeks and more. It's true, we parted from each other in the Via Sacra in bitterness. But I found her in the house of Marcellinus, who was my soul's friend, and she warmed me in my coldness and opened her door to me in my loneliness, and we built a house together against a long dark night, and even you, compounded of base elements as you are, ought to realize that there are things a person never forgets."

All the rest of the way he kept saying to himself in a manner he knew to be maudlin, "There is the street. That is the house. That is the door." But, once the door was opened, he could not think, "This is the room." It was not the stupid Levantine, it was one of Orbiana Festina's tall blond Britons who let them in. There were no lights, no welcoming voices—the guests had already withdrawn to the banquet table in the adjoining room—and he was admonished into a sober state by the darkness and the emptiness. What he could see of the place in the glow of the single brazier had an alien and ravaged look: that chaste and seemly order which Charis was forever striving to impose upon it was gone. The small tables were cluttered with earrings and bracelets and crystal goblets marked with the stains of painted lips. There were scarves of Egyptian linen on the backs of the chairs; discarded garlands lay on the couch; the rugs had been shoved out of place, and there was spilled wine on the floor.

"It looks as if they've been having a gay time in here," said the Governor of Moesia, tossing his scarlet cloak over the extended arm of a marble Apollo.

Very gay, he thought, following the blond Briton toward the curtain, whose weave showed plain in the yellow glow from the dining room. So gay that she has called her guests to table without waiting for me. So gay, perhaps, that she has not reserved my place beside her on the dining couch—maybe I will find her lying against somebody else. . . .

But when the curtain was pushed aside he forgot to look for her—it was uncanny, it was as if Thessalian witches had been at work, he actually asked himself whether he could have blundered into the wrong place. The statues, the clusters of golden wheat on the pilasters, the vases and medallions that he and she had bought together were all hidden in great dark arcs of Saturnalia greens. The table had taken on an abnormal shape: he stared at it for some moments, alarmed that his drunkenness had doubled its size, before he realized that it was actually two tables: an old one had been brought in from the kitchen, and both had been covered with an enormous white and green cloth. As for the dining couches—they gave him a giddy sense of time and space gone awry; they were strangely familiar, but they did not belong in the room—it was as if they had been transported by magic out of another time and place into this. But how stupid of me, he thought, I know she has only four couches, she told me she was going to borrow six more from Orbiana. . . .

His feeling of unreality was heightened because nobody had noticed as yet that he and the Governor had entered the dining room. They were all listening—some twenty of them—to a falsetto performance of an Alexandrine street song. Preoccupied at first by the strangeness of the room and the unfamiliarity of the people—half of them were such casual acquaintances that he could scarcely remember their names—he had noticed the sound at first only as a pain in his head. Now he saw that the singer was Memphius. Slender, blond, as sleek as a white rabbit, his chest and arms still pink from the depilatory, the little dancer was standing on the couch that he shared with Antisthenes, piping out the cheap tune and the salacious words in a grossly female voice. He had shed his dalmatica—it lay in a lobster-colored heap on the couch at his feet—and every now and then he lifted the skirt of his blue tunic, stuffed it into his mouth, and made the coy, wriggling motions of an eight-year-old girl.

If I had been here, Favorinus thought, she would never have permitted the banquet to get so far out of hand. She would have seen to it that nobody began to undress, she would have vetoed the filthy song . . . He caught sight of her on the far side of the table, on a couch next to the one occupied by Memphius and Antisthenes. She was blessedly uncompanioned but utterly unlike herself: her face was rosy with too much drinking, her lips were childishly apart, her decent rose-colored dalmatica was crushed, and her myrtle garland was pushed far back from her brow. She was the first to see him, and she raised herself on her elbow and gave him a half-defiant, half-apologetic look. There were other greetings then; there were introductions loud enough to drown out the shrill conclusion to the song; and Orbiana Festina, alone and lolling in a shining sheath of intricately tucked white silk on the couch directly in front of him, muttered something under her breath. She was in one of her states again, obviously; nobody had chosen to share a couch with her, even though she was unquestionably the most beautiful woman at the table. Or had Charis, in a petulant fit over the long absence and the late arrival, deliberately reserved her to spoil the evening for the uninvited and unwelcome patrician?

He started back a step because a Nubian, bearing a silver tray with a great scaly fish on it, passed between him and the lithe white figure on the couch.

"Aren't we going to recline?" Trebonianus Gallus said.

"Yes, of course—" He started round the corner of the table for Charis's couch, but there was so little space between the backs of the couches and the wall that he was afraid he would pull down one of the festoons.

"Wait a moment, wait a moment, my dear fellow—she's for me."

"That's Charis."

"Is it, though? Is that Charis, really? You don't mind—do you, Charis? —if I come over and join you. I'm leaving for the hinterlands early tomorrow, and you'll indulge an old soldier on his last night in town—won't you, you little Psyche, you veritable rose?"

She smiled—he could see her smiling through a great fan of laurel and the flames of three wax lights on the table. She was flushed, not with the fatuous compliments, he told himself—she would see the vulgar windbag for what he was in no time at all. If he was irritated, it was not because he was jealous; it was only because the Governor's brashness had consigned him to Orbiana Festina for an intolerable number of hours.

An uneasy silence had settled over his end of the table. The guests in other parts of the room were noisy enough—Antisthenes was telling Memphius that he reeked of cheap perfume, a monumental sculptress was explaining in a deep voice how to cast a statue in bronze, and a drunken little female stranger, probably from the pantomime, was squealing because somebody had dropped a cold plum down her back. To the right of the couch on which Orbiana lay was the old poet Berosus and his young Syrian mistress. To the left of it was an inane equestrian matron who had bored him on two other occasions, and the philosopher Cleander, who was far gone in wine. None of them said anything, and it was some time before he realized that *he* had caused the silence, that they had probably been reasonably merry before he came and stood behind Orbiana's couch, showing plainly that he was depressed by the prospect of their company.

"Don't be afraid, I won't hurt you," said Orbiana.

"Excuse me, I'm a little confused—"

"Don't be too sorry for yourself," she said, moving no part of her face except her painted lips. "After all, *I'm* going to have to put up with *you*—the more's the pity, considering what I might have been doing with my time tonight."

He let himself down beside her, seeing to it that a good strip of the couch divided them from each other. Their mutual hostility had always been there, but for three years they had covered it up with banter, with a conscientious exchange of small favors, with elaborate courtesies. Now, like a snake's head rising out of a tangle of grass, it had darted at him straight—so startling that he did not even wonder what unnameable thing, in what filthy hole in the Suburra, she might have been doing tonight.

"There's a lively couple to your right—entertain yourself with them," she said, lifting her pointed chin in the direction of Berosus and his Syrian.

Now that he had lain down, the blur of the wine was in his eyes again. The head of the old poet—round and topped with a sleek cap of straight silver hair—seemed to be swimming at him out of a mist, the low brow divided by a neat forelock, the eyes small and kind and dark, the mouth tremulous and thin. Every now and then the head jerked with palsy. A withered hand came up toward the mouth, carrying a piece of fish on a shovel of bread; but the bread fell from the shaking hand onto the silver plate, and the fish splashed into the goblet of wine. Then another hand—

the sunburned hand of the Syrian girl—bore a napkin into the range of his blurred vision and wiped a fragment of fish from the quivering chin.

The Syrian, the poor Syrian—he strove with his unsteady eyes until he got one clear, sharp sight of her: the slender, rigid body, the black hair falling in big coarse waves from the dark cheeks and forehead, the face one of those bony Semitic faces that seem to be keeping a precarious truce between passion and chastity. It was the first time he had seen her, but he knew that between her and Charis there was a bond, although there had never been any mention of it: both of them had been bought in the market at Delos, both of them had brandmarks on the thigh—oh, hard, raised scar touched in the dark by accident—sad, raw discovery cutting across the rising arc of love. And how could she allow the Governor of Moesia to pinch her ear like that? It was a sickening sight, the little white lobe in the stubby fingers, and he drank deep against it and turned to stare into the eyes of the Syrian—black, lustrelessly black, the black of charred wood on a dead fire.

"Are you looking at my girl, Favorinus?" said the old poet in a quavering voice. "We can talk about her all we want to, so long as we confine ourselves to Latin. Greek she knows, and Syrian, of course, but not a word of Latin, and perhaps it's better so. Look at her as much as you please—I like it—I get a kind of glow around the heart when I see she's admired. She's a virgin, you know—I found her filthy and in rags, they sold her to me for a song, nobody ever guessed how beautiful she was, nobody but I. Do you know, every three or four days I dress her up like the Queen of Babylon in transparent linen. I kiss her forehead, I kiss her chin, I kiss her belly and her feet, and then I send her off to bed. The gods are a cruel lot—any old man'll tell you that. I can forgive them everything else, but not these last, disgraceful, ineffectual fires. Tell me—does she look happy? No, of course not, how could she be happy? But she'll be well provided for when I'm finished, she'll have my house in Tibur and rent from three little farms. Meanwhile, it's surprising, but she doesn't seem to dislike me—"

She had understood the last sentence. She dropped her napkin into her lap and laid her brown young hand over her master's white and wrinkled one. Rigidly, like some goddess in a pantomime, she nodded and uttered a few words in Greek, but they were lost in a sudden surge of noise. Memphius was saying something snide. Cleander was saying something belligerent. A nameless female guest was saying something stupid—her elegant companion, a Greek physician, yawned in her face. Trebonianus Gallus was saying something clever in a very loud voice. He finished it off with a flourish of his gross and knobby hand, and everybody at his end of the table laughed, and Charis laughed longer than the rest.

"Really," said Orbiana Festina, pillowing her head on her wrist, so that her dark armpit showed through the slit in her sleeve—troublingly redolent of a mixture of sweat and cassia perfume, "really, the old man is enough to drive a person crazy. It's the same thing at every banquet—all he needs is three drinks, and he's disgustingly sorry for himself. Do him a service, will you? Lean over and kiss her in a couple of places he forgot to mention. She needs it—anybody can see that. A few more months of him, and she'll be out of her head."

He pursed his lips, cast a meaningful glance in the direction of Berosus, and shook his head. He had intended the warning to be subtle, but it was deplorably obvious, and he was relieved that another Nubian, darting in to set his portion of the fish before him, came between him and the small, kind eyes.

"Don't try to quiet me down," said Orbiana in an appallingly loud voice. "If he's so sensitive, let him stop making a public spectacle of himself. The fact is, you don't care a fig about his feelings. It's your precious Stoic purity you're concerned about."

And quite inappropriately—she was certainly in one of her states, what she did had no connection whatever with what she said—quite incongruously and suddenly she turned over on her side, so that her drawn-up knees were against his thighs and her warm and winy breath was in his face. Since to pull away from her would have been to provoke another outburst, there was nothing for him to do but lie there rigid, until another Nubian, leaning over the top of the dining-couch, offered them mussels and parsley, and gave him an excuse to pull himself up and offer his plate to the slave.

He was startled—they were all startled—by a pounding on the table. The philosopher Cleander—round and pudgy, the insufficiency of his chin hidden in his square black beard—was banging on the table with his little white fists. To his left his ageing and flat-chested companion was falling into a frowsy sleep. Across the bleared fans of laurel and the swollen flames of the wax lights, he was lecturing the painter Antisthenes. "Nobody," he was shouting contentiously, "not Socrates, not Zeno, not Seneca—nobody has ever equalled the divine insight of Pythagoras. Everything there was to give, he gave to his disciples in Crotona seven centuries ago. Women are rotten, boys are rotten, politics is rotten, friendship is in decay—the gods themselves are falling to pieces, the smell of decomposition infects even the upper air to the third circle of the spheres. Nothing endures but mathematics and music. Contemplate, calculate, listen to music, attain to the harmony of the heavens—that's what Pythagoras said."

"What is he saying?" asked the Syrian in Greek.

"Nothing," said Berosus. "Or wait, maybe I can explain. He's saying, in a word, that philosophy is the salvation of the world."

A wave of dull weariness had swept over Favorinus; he let his heavy eyelids droop and saw a strange conglomeration of images. Sometime he would ask Antisthenes to make a painting of those images—he would even suggest the palette to be used—pale hyacinthine blues and exquisite pinks and creamy whites above, and muddy browns and greens and greys below

The top of the painting would be blue, and there would be almost nothing in it—a flute and a cythera, and above the instruments a mathematical equation painted in pink, and above the equation, in white, a single star. Horizontally, across the middle of the painting, there would be a bar of bluish black—and under the bar, in semi-darkness themselves and looking up into utter dark, a great multitude. Berosus would be there, with a smouldering fagot in his vitals, and the Syrian dressed like the queen of Babylon, and Drusilla tearing the emeralds out of her disheveled hair. The tanner would be there, pointing to rolls in the shape of butterflies. A bloody infant would be there, wrapped in rotting cabbage leaves, and Ummidius Pessinus would be weeping into his crumpled handkerchief, and the Secretary of the Privy Purse would be holding a debased denarius in his little monkey-paw hand. There would be slaves uncountable and plebes innumerable, and a gladiator with his left eye hanging over his cheek on a pink string. Across the feet of the multitude, scrawled in red, would be the title: *Philosophy Is the Salvation of the World*. . . .

"Nothing but escape," said the nasal and incisive voice of Antisthenes. Hadn't he said the same thing earlier this evening? No, in a damp green place—yes, beside the cool pool in the Baths of Caracalla, with the water running from the point of his beard, he had called the life of action an escape. "But if you must run away, can't you find something better to run to than that drivel? Pythagoras—"

"I won't sit here and listen to you call the wisdom of the divine Pythagoras drivel. Pythagoras of Crotona is the one pure spring, the fountainhead—"

"Pythagoras of Crotona is the fountainhead of a lot of disgusting nonsense. Did you eat any beans today, my dear fellow? If you did, your spirit is in danger of immediate dissolution, according to your source of all wisdom, your one pure spring. Contemplate, calculate, don't eat any beans, never leave the mark of a cooking pot in the ashes of a fire, be sure to get the imprint of your body out of the bedclothes—that's the wisdom of Pythagoras, the superstitious old fool."

The argument would never be finished, that much was plain. Cleander was noisily weeping, was crouched over the table with his fists stuck into his eyes. The silver trays were darting round again, this time heaped with fatty slices of suckling pig. Who wanted it? Who, already clogged with the day's smoked eel, butter cakes, almond paste, stewed plums in cinnamon, could want anything except— "More wine!" Two of Orbiana's borrowed Britons assured him that he would have it in a moment. The mistress—the mistress of the slaves, not the mistress of the house: the mistress of the house was lying with her head on the shoulder of the Governor of Moesia, O bedraggled Psyche, O wilted rose!—the mistress of the slaves inquired contemptuously whether he didn't think he'd had enough. "Not nearly enough!" said a wild voice that seemed to be coming from the ceiling. Not nearly enough, and especially now, since they had brought in the pig's head, since the pig's head was giving him a foolish, philanthropic smile, and the palmy curtain was parting, and the two of them were issuing forth, arm in arm, the hard veined hand in the fat pink hand. Oh, melting eyes in the face of the World's Restorer and Preserver—womanish, full-hearted smile, softening the stern, just mouth—how could you do it? How could you take the earth's last decent hope and present it to a suckling pig?

"Excuse me, if my lord will move his elbow just a little, I'll pour him more wine."

He drank it, he drank it so fast that the wormwood taste of it caught in his throat, and Berosus got up and beat him over the back with a powerless fist, and the Syrian offered him a napkin and a rusk of bread, and Orbiana kicked at his haunches with her bare foot. He could see that Charis had sat up and was looking at him with solicitude—across the guttering lights he could make out the moist brow, the flushed cheeks, the big, grey, shining eyes. "Poor thing, poor sweet, you *are* concerned for me," he thought, and felt boundlessly tender, profoundly virtuous, deeply moved—so close to tears that he could not wait for his goblet to be refilled but had to help himself to Orbiana's.

"Here, now, save some of that for me," she said.

"Do you want it? Take it." He turned, meaning to put it to her lips, but all his motions were out of control. The rim of the goblet knocked against her shining teeth. A trickle of wine ran over her pointed chin. With his fingers—his napkin was on the floor with the garlands and dalmaticas that the company had been shedding for the last half hour—he pursued the purplish trickle down her neck, over her collar bones, between her breasts. She lay perfectly still during his explorations, and this corpse-like stillness made the experience almost devoid of pleasure: it was only out of a harsh and driving curiosity that he cupped his hand over the hard breast and pressed the rough nipple with his palm.

When he sat up again, it seemed to him that the room was peopled by a host of furies, there was so much movement, so much noise. Some of the guests had changed their places: the Greek physican was handling the little actress; the boring equestrian lady had wakened up and was trying her luck with a long-faced, saturnine poet named Statilius; the ponderous sculptress was sitting sidewise on the edge of her couch, holding an effeminate young wastrel, an acquaintance of Antisthenes and Memphius, on her knees. High-pitched words were flying in all directions, and, agitated and multitudinous, like a flock of varicolored birds, strange words, Syrian words, were issuing out of the mouth of Berosus's mistress. She was sitting with her elbows on the spotted cloth and her chin on her fists, talking, talking, talking—not to anybody, only to relieve some terrible burden of her heart. What was she mourning? The blossoming red-thorn bushes of her native wilderness? The sour wine and the white cheese and the lamb turn ing on the spit and the tribal music under the desert stars? "Oh, no, no more pork for me," the Greek physician was saying. "The very thought of pork is enough to make me vomit."

"But what am I to do with all this food then?" Charis said.

"Throw it out the window!" It was his own voice—sullen, hateful—and he had reason for hatefulness. Wasn't the old windbag gnawing on her shoulder? Wasn't her dalmatica pulled down so far that you could see the rise of her breast? Take all the food and throw it out the window—was he thinking it or saying it?—no, don't throw it out the window, put it in a cart and wheel it up to the imperial palace and give it to the Lord of the World. Tell the Restorer and Preserver to carry it to the tenements and leave it on the dirty doorsills, so that they can find it tomorrow—all the plebes who came to his Saturnalia table with yearning in their bowels and got nothing but precepts from Cato the Censor and tough beef and workaday bread.

Two greenish eyes flashed a warning at him over a fallen vase of laurel. "You're drunk. Control yourself," said Antisthenes.

"This is a rotten banquet—"

"You're drunk, I said. Take hold of yourself."

"Oh, come now, darling, he's not so very drunk." It was the voice that had read from the Greek Anthology in the house of Marcellinus, his soul's friend. Bird-like, conciliatory, tender, it rose above the shouting in the room and the roaring in his head. "He's not a bit more drunk than anybody else. It *is* a bad banquet, it's going all to pieces. Isn't there something we can do? Let's see. Who wants music? No, wait a moment, there are two poets at the table. Who wants poetry?"

"I," said the Greek physician, "want only one thing at the moment."

"Well, get it from somebody who can afford a six months' retirement," said the little actress. "*I* can't."

Charis had moved out of the brown arms of the Governor of Moesia. She was sitting erect now, adjusting the neckline of her rose-colored dalmatica with one hand and clinking a knife against the rim of her goblet with the other. She was going to impose order upon this banquet. Her determination to impose order upon it was plain in the lines of her face, blithe and forceful and slightly objectionable—though why he should find her objectionable he did not know, since her everlasting desire to impose order doubtless arose from a wish to make this world less painful for his sake. But maybe it wasn't for his sake. Maybe she only wanted to demonstrate what a cultivated woman she was, what a brilliant crowd of followers she had, so that the compendium of base elements would be properly impressed.

"The poet Statilius," she was saying—and gratified murmurs arose from all the ignorant who had never heard his name before—"the poet Statilius, a well-known—"

"A well-known shoveler of dung." Why he had said it, he did not know.

177

He had no quarrel with Statilius. In fact, he rather liked the fellow—there was a tonic bitterness in his talk. He had a sad, equine face—a long, unhappy nose, a pair of loose, discouraged lips. His poetry was worthless, of course, but now and again for years he had listened to the stuff with indulgence. Everybody, including the author, was looking at him appalled, and yet he could scarcely explain that he had intended no insult to Statilius, had simply been offended by the affectation in her voice, the complacent look on her face.

"The poet Statilius," she said again, and swayed a little—something ought to be done, she was drunk, and there was no telling what the old lecher might try to get out of her—"the poet Statilius, author of *Alcestis in Hades* and other distinguished works, will read the beginning of his new poem, *The Guard Describes Antigone's Attempt to Bury Polyneices.*"

"Oh, no!" It wasn't the affectation—he had resigned himself to that, but he simply could not bear to hear a desecration of that stark and piteous scene in Sophocles. Why must they draw their subjects from the Greek tragedians? Weren't there plenty of other topics at hand? Why not *The Secretary of the Privy Purse Mourns the Debased Denarius* or *Ummidius Pessinus Explains the Insoluble Tax Dilemma to a Delegation of Egyptians?* Why not *A Provincial Virgin is Raped by a Roman Legionary* or *A Tanner Makes a Request for Ten-Year-Old Wine?* He was actually on the point of suggesting one, but was admonished into silence by another kick from Orbiana's bare foot. Sitting up then, he propped his elbows on the table and fixed his eyes respectfully, contritely on the sad, equine face of Statilius.

"*The Guard Describes Antigone's Attempt to Bury Polyneices,*" said the author in a twanging baritone. "It's supposed to have a flute accompaniment, but you'll have to imagine the flute."

"Charis could play the flute for you." He thought nobody would suspect his real motive, that all of them would take it for a felicitous suggestion. But everybody smirked, everybody knew that he was pained when she lay down again beside Trebonianus Gallus, cheek to cheek, thigh to thigh.

"Charis is otherwise engaged—hadn't you noticed?"

It was a mild enough thrust, considering that he had called the man a shoveler of dung. It was a mild enough thrust, but it cut him to the heart.

"As I was saying, *The Guard Describes,* et cetera, et cetera, et cetera." He waited until the Syrian had stopped talking to herself, until Memphius had stopped giggling and had made his face a mask of attentiveness. Then, scratching his ear with the little finger of his right hand, he began:

> "Creon majestical! Vile guardsman that I am,
> I come with mouth wasp-stuffed to sting thy regal ear.
> Hear—and be stung—what thing transpired atop the crest
> Of that unfortunate crag where Polyneices' flesh
> Provides, dissolved by sun, feasts sumptuous for the flies."

Oh, but it was hideous poetry—stale, twisted, pretentious. How could he have listened to it all this time without realizing that it was an insult to humanity? Berosus's lyrics—were they as bad as that? Possibly, possibly—to save his life he couldn't remember a single genuine line. They had always taken their creations so seriously, the members of the little company, and all of them were probably as horrible as this; there was no telling what he would think if he looked with an uncharitable eye at the famous Thetis murals of Antisthenes, or, for that matter, at his own discourse on Musonius.

> "Having, with quavering bowels, pondered thy menaces
> That whosoe'er approached the putrefying mass
> With rites funereal would straightway hurl himself
> Into the ultimate grasp of executioners,
> And us, should we be proved neglectful, to the same—"

He groaned, and her foot was at him again, but this time it did not withdraw. It burrowed its way under his haunches, and that roused up a fire in his guts, an urgency that was close to pain. Pain, and a baffled, double fury—fury against the foot and against the twanging voice, impervious, droning on and on. . . .

> "Having so pondered long, and having climbed the hill
> In liver-whitening fear, foot-tortured by the stones;
> Having removed ourselves out of the noisome stench
> Which inconsiderate gusts bore upward from the corpse,
> We, sweating, sat—"

"We, sweating, sat! Oh, God, that's terrible!" Antisthenes was glaring at him. But Antisthenes, even if he was ignorant of the obscene foot, ought to have sense enough to see that the mere process of following such a malformed sentence through its hideous writhings was a kind of agony. And, after all that grotesque twisting and turning, to see it fall flat on its flabby predicate—"We, sweating, sat!"—

"It seems," said Statilius, "that an exception is taken to 'We, sweating, sat.' Shall we let the whole thing rest?"

"That won't be necessary," said Orbiana, pulling her foot away. "Lie down, stop being a baby and behave yourself."

She pulled him backward. The ceiling was covered with little coins of yellowish brightness, debased denarii dancing with the guttering wax lights. Then the Syrian, her face earnest and beautiful with pity, leaned over him and blotted them out by laying her thin, cool hand across his eyes.

> "We, sweating, sat. We sat, until in skyey blue
> Awoke the whirlwind's whorl, ten blasts, writhing as one,
> Veiling the leaves with dust, filling our maws with dust.
> Dust everywhere, dust, dust—O omnipresent dust!"

"Dung everywhere, dung, dung—O omnipresent dung," he said in an exhausted whisper, raising his face to the cool fingers of the Syrian—light touch on his eyelids, his temple, his brow.

"And when the plague of dust dissolved and sight returned,
Whom did that sight behold? That sight beheld the maid."

"Beautiful and tormented one, seal up your eyes," the Syrian said.

Seal up your eyes, retreat into the final citadel of darkness, there is no profit in protesting—why protest? If he asserts in his unspeakably malformed lines that Antigone ran to her brother's corpse howling like a wounded lioness, let it pass. You know—and men will know again when the tides of the centuries have washed the accumulated ordure from the face of the earth—that she came as he said she came, the sublime Sophocles. Softly she came, and nobody saw her, nobody knew she was near the corpse until she cried aloud with the sharp cry of a bird in her bitterness, even as a bird who finds her bed stripped of its nestlings—so Antigone came; and the Greek lines—clean, limpid, liberal—poured from the living heart of the dead poet, for the laving of the spirit, for the cooling of fever and the easing of pain. . . .

"Marjoram, hyssop, thyme, and sundry other herbs
She brought wherewith to hide the lump of rotting flesh—"

He had not meant to listen, but the Syrian had taken her dry and gentle hand away, and his ears had been opened with his eyes, and, having heard it, he was bound out of respect for the still-gushing heart of the dead Sophocles to take exception to it, to sit up, to point his finger straight into Statilius's face. "She did not!" he said in an accusing voice. "She brought nothing of the kind. Thirsty dust—that's what Sophocles said she brought. Not marjoram, not hyssop, not any other assorted dung therewith Dust—two handfuls of thirsty dust!"

"Oh, well," said Statilius, scratching his ear and sitting down beside the foolish equestrian matron, "I don't know why I ever started to read the thing at all. The fact is, now that I come to think about it, I don't know why I wrote it in the first place."

"Yes, that would be something to know. Why *did* you write it?" It seemed to him a significant, even a crucial question. He leaned forward and looked at the long nose and the loose lips candidly, earnestly.

"Will you have the decency to keep your mouth shut?" It was Antisthenes he had risen from his couch on the other side of the wax lights; and the glare of the clustering flames before him gave a wraithlike quality to his spare and angry face. "Maybe you're too drunk to realize it, but you've been intolerable this evening. Somebody should have taken you home and locked you up in your bedroom, where you could have done your suffering without disturbing anybody else—"

"Am I suffering?"

"Are you suffering? Excruciatingly, my dear fellow—agonizingly, and in the worst possible taste. And don't think that everybody at the table doesn't know why. Your pottery god fell flat on his face this morning—didn't he? It's a pity Decius isn't Hercules, it's a pity he isn't going to save the world. But you're the only one who's shocked at the revelation—you're the only one that thought he would. We're used to the world as it is, we learned to live with it long ago. So beat your head against a wall in private. Nobody wants to watch you—keep your agonies to yourself."

It was frightening, it was unbelievable, like a jumping pain in a tooth, and perhaps if he disregarded it utterly it would pass. "I don't know what you're talking about," he said. "What has that got to do with Statilius? I was asking him about his poem. I was asking him why he wrote it, what purpose he expected it to serve—"

"Do you want to know why he wrote it?" The wraithlike face came forward, and the furious greenish eyes flashed into his. "I'll tell you why he wrote it: to get from one day to the next, to keep from falling into a state of despair, from giving way to utter loathing or mortal terror. That's purpose enough, isn't it? What do you expect him to do—write like Sophocles?"

A rhetorical question—even in his drunkenness he knew it for a rhetorical question; and yet he took it up, he held to it at the risk of making a fool of himself. The talk was plunging wildly into limitless darkness—tame it, turn it into a harmless literary discussion, focus the candid, earnest look on Antisthenes. "There's another interesting question: Why *doesn't* he write like Sophocles?" he said.

"Because he lives in Rome in the first year of the reign of your uncle Decius. Because he's sitting on top of a garbage heap—an Empire that's falling to pieces, a world that's rotting away. Because, unless he's blind and deaf and out of his mind, he can't consider his own or anybody else's life anything but one long piece of futility. Because he's questioned everything and found everything utterly devoid of meaning. That's why he doesn't write like Sophocles."

"But Sophocles," said the mild voice of Berosus, "also questioned everything—"

"Not everything, not everything. Many things, yes—the state, the heroes, the gods—but not the condition of being human, not human life itself. That he never questioned, that he always saw as significant—the effort and the failure, the possession and the loss, the pleasure and the pain. With that faith he could take the full impact of life on his naked soul. And the people he lived with, the people he wrote for—for generations they were partakers in the same faith, for generations they came, seventeen thousand of them at a time, to the Theater of Dionysus to celebrate the dignity of Man—"

He did not listen. He stared past the spare face, past the dark fan of laurel, and saw them—the citizens of Athens, seventeen thousand of them at a time, gathering in the Theater of Dionysus in the charged light of a sacred morning to hear what new wonder their brother Sophocles was about to reveal concerning the awesome and unquestionably meaningful doings of Man. While the green hills behind them were still tinged with the earliest sunlight, they settled themselves with decorous dispatch on the night-cooled marble benches, and the air above them came to life with their hushed and reverent speech. Then that sound also lessened, and the Chorus came, chaste celebrants, and stood around the altar of Dionysus, and there was silence, living silence, vibrant with the beating of seventeen thousand hearts. A crystal chalice of silence, held up against hyacinthine blueness, to the greater glory of Man . . . His thoughts were attenuated, he felt himself drawn into that chalice, further and further into silence . . . until it was smashed by a howl, shattered into a thousand bits. All of them were on their feet in the Flavian Amphitheater—senators, equestrians, plebes, demanding higher piles of corpses on the bloody sand—and the slaughter-house smell came up and choked him, and the thing that was no longer human came running at him, the eye dangling over the cheek on a pink string—

"And we," said the enormous sculptress, arranging the head and arms of the sleeping wastrel as if she were making a corpse seemly for burial, "we don't take the full impact of life on our naked spirits? Is that what you mean?"

"Take it? How could we?" said the ghostly mouth on the other side of the wax lights. "How could anybody, even that one over there"— he flipped a contemptuous hand in the direction of Favorinus—"take on everything we've seen in this century—Goths, tyrants, revolutions, piles of corpses, the ruin of the arts, the sickening vulgarity? He's like anybody else—he'll not survive it, not with a living spirit. A living spirit is a very perishable thing. Beat it down with one violence after another and it collapses. One way or another, it's done for, it's gone. Oh, it has some choice, it can choose the manner of its going. It can, for instance, stand up with one fine last burst of courage—it can stand up and reject the whole loathsome mess and make a decent end of itself. Or it can, like that one and his uncle with him, waste itself away in a bustle of futile business, distract itself from the thought of the unspeakable total by dealing with the details, work itself into a shadow semblance of human vitality over a mutinous legion or a bridge in Dacia or the censorship. But all of us don't have such a remarkable talent for self-deception. Some of us—like Statilius, who amuses himself by twisting Latin—some of us simply hide what we know and entertain ourselves with our little pleasures as best we can. If I don't torture anything, if I have the Greek habit of precision and clarity, that doesn't mean there is any more life—real life—in what I paint than there is in what you heard tonight. I've covered some eighty walls in my day with overblown goddesses and flabby gods—eighty walls, and I tell you, all of them put together aren't worth as much as one little living figure painted on an Attic vase. I know what I'm doing—I know what trash it is, of course—I've told myself a thousand times, 'Paint from the spirit—nobody can be as barren as all that—once, once before you die, create a living thing.' But what's left of the spirit—here, now—in the reign of your illustrious uncle who proposes to restore and preserve this rotten world? Hope? High purpose? Valor? They're gone— anybody but a benighted child who's satisfied with painted toys knows that they're irretrievably gone. One thing's left, love is left—it dies hardest, it dies last. A morbid tenderness for another poor wretch who wanders around in the same nightmare, a sick passion for a corrupt body—that's with me still, that I can paint, that'll be with me until I'm in my grave. But look at it, look at it—" He turned and collided with the table so violently that all the flames shook. He took the dancer Memphius by the throat, his thumb under the beardless chin, and dragged him forward into the yellow glare. "Here's all I can really paint," he said. "Over and over, until I'm deathly sick of it, this face—this faithless, rotten, beautiful, cold face—"

They gasped, all of them, even Orbiana—he was strangling the little wretch. The actress began to squeal, rhythmically, hysterically, like a pig with a knife in its throat. His delicate hands were flapping, his tongue was out, his eyeballs were rolled up before the thin fingers released him. "Really, now, that's going a bit too far," said Memphius, rubbing his neck and giggling. Cleander rose and stumbled away from the table, his face noble with Pythagorean disgust.

"I must say," said the foolish equestrian lady, "that everything that's been said at this table tonight has been beautifully expressed—simply beautifully expressed."

I must wet my throat a little and make some sort of answer, Favorinus thought, helping himself to the remainder of Berosus's wine. But no answer was expected. There was a crash, but it was not the roof of a temple caving in, not the gate of a city smashed by catapulted stones. It was only that one of Orbiana's slaves, unaccustomed to the cramped quarters in the kitchen, had dropped a tray of sweets, which made not the slightest difference, since nobody wanted anything more: the very sight of the ravaged table had begun to be intolerable to most of them—they were moving out of the room by twos and threes, making their way to the garden or the little outer room or the carnival-cluttered street. Memphius was still there, nursing his neck with one hand and smoothing down his hair with the other, but Antisthenes had left, pressing both hands against his temples, hard, as if he thought his head would split in two. Split head, split knuckles, cracked column in the atrium of the imperial palace . . . On the other side of the room, the Governor of Moesia was dropping grapes into Charis's mouth—My bird, he's feeding my bird!—cracked world, cracked heart—

Is it my doing? he asked himself. Is she drunk enough, child enough to imagine that the old yearning dream can be evoked again, that, playing whore to the Governor of Moesia, she will be to me what she was on that evening clouded with plum blossoms when I was loving and innocent, when I left the house and walked the empty streets and told myself nobly, nobly, that she was with Marcellinus, a prince among patricians, a sage among scholars, dying and dear to me, my soul's friend? He turned his back on her and on all such questions. He turned his back and rested his shoulders and his elbows on the edge of the table. It seemed to him then that he was hanging by the elbows from the edge of the table, dragged at by the inexorable pull of death, the earth's perpetual invitation to the grave.

He caught himself on the point of falling forward; and, opening his eyes, he saw Orbiana Festina's face. It was still, utterly still, and for an instant he thought she was asleep. Then certain changes came about, certain slow and subtle shifts in the lineless, polished planes of brow and cheek and mouth; and he knew with an awesome flash of insight that she was not asleep, that the dreams behind her closed eyelids were waking dreams, that she had withdrawn from the world to accomplish in the dark chambers of her brain those unspeakable rites which she would have performed in actuality if she had not come to Charis's house tonight.

He watched, and knew that Memphius watched him watching. He leaned forward and watched the trembling of the eyelids, the narrowing and widening of the nostrils, the smile—daemoniac, inhuman—deepening the corners of her lips. The obscenities that absorbed and tormented her—he conjured them up in all their monstrousness, and his vitals took fire.

She raised her chin a little and looked at him through slits below her eyelids. "Oh, if you could see yourself!" she said.

Shameless, unfaltering stare, loose mouth giving her back a he-daemon answer to her she-daemon smile—he exulted that she should see them. Crude hand groping in the white silk, and she completely passive—the body unresponsive under his harsh investigations, the eyes and mouth contemptuous, letting him know there must be more than that and other than that, something extreme enough to match the crazy carnival that he had intruded himself upon. Then help me, help me, he thought, and the primordial hand came languidly up and made a slow, hard exploration under his tongue—and helped him, released all the words that he had never said—words whispered into his ear twenty years ago by a demented old hag of a slave, words malodorous with the stench of public urinals, words scrawled on the door of brothels, greased over with the sweat of the callers' hands. A long, convulsive shudder ran through her body. "Say it again, you rotten little Stoic. Say it again," she said.

He said it, he thrust it with a destroying kiss into her mouth. With his mouth, with his teeth, he put the imprint of it on every part of her that could be reached, until, suddenly static, she held him off, she looked into his face long and with a strange, detached solemnity. The room was still, there was nobody left but Memphius; there was no sound now but Memphius's hurrying breath. With the charged gravity of a priestess who summons the elect to the sacrifice, she took his face in her hands and whispered, "Come."

Come to the world's-end Saturnalia. Come away from the ravaged table, past the scraping leaves of the laurel, over the coupling bodies of the actress and the Greek physician, to a place where the ultimate rites can be accomplished in isolation—rites so extreme and shameful that even in this company they must be done alone. Not the sitting room, with the wastrel and the foolish equestrian lady on the couch and Cleander stretched out like a corpse, with vomit on his beard, in the middle of the floor. Not the garden, either—somebody here, pacing between the trees and the fountain —Antisthenes pacing like a madman back and forth in the thin light of the setting moon, with his split head held between his hands. Upstairs, then, to the bath—but somebody else is here before us—heavy breathing, unintelligible words, thud of a body pressed against the closed door. The bedchamber, then—yes, even the bedchamber, with her combs and jewels strewn about in the light of the single lamp, with the bench where she sat naked night after night, chatting and rubbing oil into her thin shoulders. Only put out the light—stop the wild striving of body against body long enough to—"Put out the light—"

"What's the matter? Are you afraid to see what you're doing?"

See it then, see everything. Make a gross display of all that was conjectured under the dalmaticas of visiting matrons on the feverish evenings of baffled childhood, all that the young lover, in decency and tenderness, forbore to look upon. See it—deal with it in violence. "Get onto the bed."

"When I'm ready."

"You're ready. Get onto the bed."

She yielded, she stepped backward, and it was he who was the high-priest of the world's-end Saturnalia now, tormenting her body, invading and withdrawing where he chose, postponing consummation, always striving after the extreme, the thing of shame. But he did not stay long with the body. For the ultimate degradation, he always came back to the face, the daemoniac face—

And then suddenly, when his urgency was at its highest pitch, the face went blank. Quiet, the eyes alert, it turned slowly to one side. "Just a moment," she said in a self-possessed voice. "I thought I heard—yes, I'm sure of it—somebody's at the door."

But it was pain now, it was such pain that he could not drag himself up to throw the bolt, could only lie clutching at the coverlet while the hinges creaked and the band of faint yellow light widened across the confusion of their clothes and the raw ugliness of their partial nakedness.

"I told you," she said with maddening self-possession. "Somebody's followed us."

Not Charis—it was only the Syrian who was shadowed forth against the dimly lighted hall. A bird with an emerald eye shone on the skirt of her dalmatica, a bracelet shone on her upper arm, her teeth shone between her parted lips, and horrified fascination shone in her eyes.

"Close the door!" He had heard a slave under the lash bellowing like that. "Go away and close the door!"

She did not move.

"Stop it, you fool," said Orbiana in a whisper. "Tell her to come in. With all the old man's been doing to her, there's enough there for us both."

"No!" It was a scream. Even in his extremity, he had to protest. Not that one—that one he could not make a celebrant of the obscene rites, not after she had tenderly brushed the crumbs from the old man's chin, not after she had pitied his own torment and sealed up his eyes.

"Don't be ridiculous." The hard fingers closed on his wrist.

"No!" He had torn himself away, he was out of bed, he was crossing the threshold—gasping, dragged down by a gnawing, unbelievable ache. Then suddenly he could not move—the Syrian had flung herself upon him. Her arms were clinging around his neck. Her cheek, hot and wet with tears, was pressed against his naked chest. And such a torrent of wild and mournful Syriac was pouring from her mouth—such a fierce, incomprehensible plea for deliverance—that only the world's-end daemon within made it possible for him to tear her clasped hands apart and thrust her against the wall and go.

"Let him go, we can do without him," said the loathsome voice behind him. "Just shut the door."

He wandered then, holding his head—split head, split world—he wandered, stepping over bare thighs and listless hands, from one room to another out of areas of light into areas of dark, through spurts of laughter into gasping, panting silences, and how long he wandered, he did not know. Here and there, on a table, in a niche, in the hand of a sleeper, he came upon a goblet with a little wine left in it, and drank where other hateful lips had drunk, and tasted the wormwood, and waited, standing still, to feel whether the lukewarm, lethal stuff had done anything to lessen the fearful knocking of his heart. It will grow quieter, nobody ever died of this sort of thing, he told himself. It will grow quieter, and I will find an empty place and go to sleep. Meanwhile, look for the kitchen, go to the kitchen and purify the defiled mouth with cold, clean water. Then upstairs to the bath, to relieve the intolerable pressure on the bladder. But whoever was lying against the door was immovable. He was forever returning to the dining room, where the monumental sculptress sat on the floor with Memphius lying asleep in her lap, his head hanging backward over her thigh and one hand thrust into her enormous breast. He was forever stumbling back into the sitting room, constantly excusing himself to two equestrian strangers who were speculating in semi-whispers about ways of evading the censorship, always stepping over the befouled and insensate face of the defender of Pythagorean mysteries . . . When he finally made aged to push open the door of the bath, dawn was pale at the windows, light was grey on the floor. And in that light he saw, lying in a heap at his feet, the fine embroidered dalmatica of the Governor of Moesia, and a second dalmatica that would have been rose-colored if the greyness had not bled all color from it, and that other sight—hideous, intolerable, a sword in the heart, a sword in the heart—

Flee—if it is impossible to flee the loathsome body, the putrefying City, the collapsing world—then flee at least this house, this filthy place. Grey garden, cold, moist, with a few carnival lamps reeling still like swollen moons above the top of the wall, dark expanse of lawn, with a shape— Male? Female? Never know, refuse to know—coming slowly, inexorably out of a clump of shadowy trees—Seducer? Deliverer? Do not ask yourself, take and be grateful for any remedy for pain. And the mute shape kneeling down in the grass, and the unasked question, the bowed head and the seeking hands, and the willingness, the burnt-out, weary willingness. . . .

When the thing was finished and he was left alone, he sat on the ground for a long time, bent over, feeling the downward drag of the earth, his forehead on his knees. Another morning broke unbelievably—there should never have been another morning—one bird began to sing and another answered, and the dew came down around him like a light and misty rain. I must go in, he thought, I must go in or I may take a chill and die and be burned in the Forum and reduced to my original elements—earth, air, water, fire . . . But he did not move, he was not disquieted. To die—to accept the perpetual invitation of the earth—today, tomorrow—it made no difference. If only yesterday they had come with coins to seal up his eyelids. But since it had not been yesterday, any time would serve—today, tomorrow, he did not care.

Chapter 13

THROUGH THE dream—he was dead in the dream, in the dream he was lying just as he had seen his father lie on a bier in the Forum, with the powdered incense strewn over him, with the sand-colored incense-powder on his sealed eyelids and in the cracks in his hands—through the dream, he heard distant voices shouting his name.

"Favorinus!"

"Favorinus Herennius, my lord and my master!"

"Where in the name of all the gods have you hidden yourself, my dear boy?"

And that was ridiculous on the part of the Governor of Moesia. If a man was lying in his burial clothes directly beneath the rostrum in the Forum, he could scarcely be called hidden—nor, for all that matter, if he was lying obliquely across the cold marble floor of Charis's vestibule, with the burnt-out carnival lamp hanging black between him and the morning street.

"It's begun to rain," said the voice of Charis.

"Let's thank the gods for that, my lady, that'll lessen the chance of fire."

But why should his mother's steward, in charge of the City property of the Herennii, want to lessen the chance of the fire? Let it burn. Let it rise in one great, golden sheet, let it consume the tainted flesh and the river heart. Let it usher in the Last Great Day foretold by the Stoics, the Day of Fire, when all things shall be devoured by the cleansing flames, when the seas shall be lapped up and the mountains shall fall to ashes, when the whale shall die in the boiling eddies of the ocean, and the deer shall faint in the forest, and the bird also shall be consumed in the upper air, because the air has turned scarlet with heat, and all living things are delivered from the burden of the flesh—

"Don't frighten him, don't even mention the possibility of a fire."

"I'll go and look for him in the garden," Trebonianus Gallus said.

Go and look, he thought, smiling against the damp marble floor. Go and look, you won't find me there, afterward I came round to the front of the house, I remember coming as far as the door. Go and look, you filthy dog, you won't find anybody—

"But there he is, my lady—out there in the vestibule."

His mother's steward, undoubtedly the voice of his mother's steward— and what was *he* doing here, at Charis's house, in the dank after-morning of the world's-end Saturnalia? Sit up, wipe the dew from the face and the salt deposit of sleep and tears from the corners of the eyes. Open the eyes and see.

"My lord and my master Favorinus Herennius," said the steward, standing under the burnt-out lamp and wringing his hands like the messenger in a Greek tragedy, "I'm forced to tell you a dreadful thing, a dreadful thing—"

But what could be more grievous than that which had already come to pass? *She* stood on the left side of the steward, with a man's cloak gathered over her nakedness, and her white face, ugly with sleep and annihilatingly pitiful with remorse, begged for an impossible absolution—

"You must go down to our tenement in the Via Trajana, my lord and my master—"

"Why should he go down? What good can he do there?" she said, weeping. "Let him stay here. If anybody must go, go down yourself—"

"But they know me there, my lady. They know me there—it's I who have to collect the rents—they'd murder me—"

The heaviness of drunken sleep was completely gone from him now. He leaped up and took the steward by the shoulders. "What is it? What happened?" he shouted into the steward's face.

"The front wall gave way—the wall of your tenement in the Via Trajana, my lord and my master. Early this morning, near dawn, before the time of rising, half the building caved in—"

"But where are the tenants? Did they get out?"

"It was before the time of rising, as I told you, my lord and my master. They say that half the tenants are dead."

All the way to the Via Trajana, behind the drawn brown curtains of the hired litter, he kept trying to envision the tenement. It was difficult for him to see it as a whole; from his childhood he remembered it chiefly as a putrid smell, a dark and filthy staircase, a long and lightless hall. It was—or at least he thought it was—a long five-storey structure with an entrance at either end of it. The front—it was the front end that had fallen away in the collapse—faced on a grassless court; the back door opened on a narrow and dirty street. The litter had already moved into the neighborhood of the accident before he realized he would not see it as he imagined it: it would be a heap of wreckage, a ruin enveloped in flames. But, try as he would, he could not conjure up the picture: he found himself contemplating the three wine stains on the skirt of his dalmatica instead.

Tired, burnt-out, utterly incapable of taking the full impact upon the naked spirit—so he was saying to himself when the litter stopped in front of a cookshop opposite the tenement of the Herennii. They could take him no closer, the litter-bearers explained; City Guardsmen were blocking the street. He paid them, stepped out into the drizzle, and stood staring blankly at a sight that was not horrible—merely drab. He was looking at the long side of the building—grey stucco walls, rows of narrow windows, the black tendrils of a sickly vine, all ending in a jagged profile of colorless disaster—the uneven line of violent partition, powdered greyish white with a rain of plaster dust, so that it was hard to see where the structure ended and the glaring sky began. There were no flames. "Wasn't there a fire?" he said in a phlegm-clogged voice, walking over to the beefy, City Guardsman who was standing on the stoop of the cookshop. "Somebody told me there was a fire."

A negligible fire, put out almost at once, the City Guardsman said, astoundingly unaware that the man beside him had anything whatsoever to do with the building, taking him for a Saturnalia reveller who had happened, in the numb aftermath of carnival, to wander onto the site. Those people over there, crawling around on the pile of wreckage—the Guardsman pointed them out with a thick finger, eager to hold forth, taking a kind of official pride in the calamity—those people over there were the tenants. They had carried the last of the wounded out of the building half an hour ago, and now that they were forbidden to go inside they were digging out here for their dead, though that was dangerous, too—there was no telling when the rest of the rotten structure might cave in.

Those people over there . . . Why it was difficult for him to experience their distress with any degree of immediacy, he did not know. It was true that he could make them out only dimly from where he stood: some twenty of them, high up on the pile, so powdered over with the plaster dust that like the torn end of the building, they were almost one with the whitish sky. He told himself that what they were scrabbling for in the wreckage was matter utterly alien to the stone and wood they clutched and pulled at, but even when a shriek, a woman's shriek, tore up from the rubble, he could feel it only as he had felt the falsetto voice of Memphius last night: as a wheel of pain turning at the back of his head—

"Was your Illustriousness looking for somebody in particular in this neighborhood?" the Guardsman said.

"No, nobody in particular." Clasping the nape of his neck with his hand, he asked himself why he *had* come here. To see the property, to go home and give a dependable report on the property—his errand here had nothing to do with the wretches on the pile of rubble, nothing to do with their dead. In the hushed and polished decorum of the little office, his mother would be waiting for him with a series of questions: How much of the structure remained intact? Could the front of it be rebuilt? Or had they better resign themselves to a total loss?

"In that case, your Illustriousness," said the Guardsman, looking at him obliquely, "I wouldn't stay around this neighborhood too long, if I were you. They're likely to get nasty, if you see what I mean. Any little thing can stir them up. I've seen it happen. Why, a couple of years ago, I was on duty in the Suburra when there was an accident like this, and some of the survivors turned on a poor equestrian gentleman who happened to be standing around. It was an awful business, I can tell you. Afterward I heard he lost an eye—they stepped on his face."

He saw a vision of himself in besmirched saffron silk, lying in the street with his head trampled under the plaster-whitened sandals, but that also failed to stir up any sensation in him. When he moved at last, down from the stoop and into the drizzle, it was only because he wished to spare the big, awkward fellow the embarrassment of telling a patrician outright that he'd have to move along.

Once the Guardsman had turned and walked away, he felt deserted, miserably alone. The tenants on the pile of wreckage were unaware that he was in the street, and the guards were conspicuously refusing to turn his way, thinking no doubt that if the drunken patrician were left to himself he would wander off out of sheer boredom. I could go over to the Tribune of the Guard and tell him the building belongs to me, he thought. But such a move might confine him, might interfere with something else he felt impelled to do, something unformulated that was striving to take shape in spite of the exhaustion and the wine. Behave like the drunkard they think you are, he thought: and he walked unsteadily up the Via Trajana toward the rear end of the tenement, glancing back at another pair of guardsmen who were talking with a distracted woman. No, he thought, they're not taking the full impact of it on their naked spirits, not by any means— their masters at the training-school and their exposure to repeated scenes of violence have provided them with appropriate masks: serene attentiveness, detached politeness, remote gravity . . . They did not see him, and he walked without interference across the Via Trajana and down the by-street, as far as the two grimy lions on either side of the open and unguarded rear door.

The lions—he stood with one hand on the greasy mane of the left-hand lion and remembered how he had come here with his father on collection days, how, while Celestus Falconius walked through the stinking corridors with a violet-scented handkerchief at his nose, he sat astride the stone beast, watching, with vague incredulity, the filthy children playing in the filthy street. I never went in, he thought. Those halls and stairways that I thought I remembered—I built them in my mind from what my father said to the steward and what the steward said to my father. No, even when I was too big to sit on the lion, I stayed out here and leaned against it. I never went in at all . . . He mounted the two shallow steps and paused for a moment before the open door. A dank smell came out of it—it was a mouth breathing an unwholesome breath—charred wood and old plaster and ancient filth, poverty and sickness and bottomless discouragement . . . He started because something had moved in the grey hall beyond the doorway. Nothing—a sleek rat scuttling over the cracked green tile on the floor—nothing to keep him from going in. There was rubbish in the hallway, not the momentous rubbish of catastrophe, only the wretched, usual rubbish: greasy papyrus squares on which they had brought their slabs of bacon back from the cookshop, the brown core of an apple, a puddle of urine, a Saturnalia rose . . . But where was the heart, the living heart? Why was it that everything he breathed and saw passed through him as though he were an insubstantial ghost? Where was the naked heart that could experience this, that could grant the accusation and accept the pain?

A long corridor, narrow and crossed by bands of daylight from the apartments, stretched in front of him. A rotten building, the Guardsman had said: it was against reason and the law to wander around in it; at any moment the roof might fall in. He shrugged as if there had been somebody there to see him and stepped into one of the rooms—the lintel was so low that he gave himself a blow on the brow. He blinked and rubbed his forehead and looked about him. Cracked pitcher, basin of lentil soup, smaller basin of bones on the floor, probably for a dog—the dog, had he fled when he heard the thunder of the falling wall? A bed with a tunic for a sheet and a cloak for a coverlet, and the imprint of the body plain where the cloak had been hurled back—shameful revelation of a stranger's vulnerability in sleep. Had Pythagoras wandered into a room once and pondered such a sight? Was that why he forbade his disciples, chaste rejectors of everything but calculation and contemplation—to leave the record of their mortality in their beds?

He left that room and wandered into several of the others, crossing the corridor and crossing back again, seeking something, anything that would cut through the numbness, always forgetting how low the lintels were, repeatedly striking his head. But one place was much like another—to see one was to see them all. Whenever he came upon some object that broke the bleak monotony, he stopped and pondered it: he touched a coil of false hair lying among the paint-pots of a prostitute, he read a letter written home from the Gothic frontier by a legionary, he picked up a little book—some twenty pages stitched together and unbound—from a folded dalmatica that had served as a young woman's pillow, and stood turning over the pages. There were line-drawings here and there in it, and he judged by them that it was the story of the life and death of some plebeian hero or demi-god— Tiberius Gracchus or Hercules. But no, the hero was definitely Eastern. He wore his beard cut long, in the Eastern fashion; and on the last page, where he sat on a throne among winged messengers, his flowing hair was circled with a strange thorny crown.

The silence was suddenly alive with small sounds—creak of wrenched boards, slipping of dislodged stones, intermittent rains of plaster and dust, brief and soft, like sighs. I should go now, he thought, laying the book carefully on the folded dalmatica. Nothing here will make me other than what I am, a wraith that wanders bodiless through their poor rooms; nothing that they suffered can give me back my living heart . . . But when he came out of the hall again, he did not turn back to the entrance by which he had come; he walked slowly up the corridor toward the front of the building instead. Walked into shadow, into deepening gloom, into total dark. Continued to walk, blind, until he stumbled and put his hand straight out before him and felt a rough surface—broken beam, shattered stone. This, then, was as far as he could come. Here it began—the pile of wreckage in which they were digging for their dead. He groped to the right and felt smooth wood—a door, a closed door. Sophocles might have opened it, Sophocles might have performed some humane office over whatever lay within— two handfuls of dust would have been enough, two handfuls of thirsty dust . . . He stood for a long time with his hand on the latch, steeling himself. But he was not Sophocles, he could not bring himself to open the door.

Not Sophocles, and yet not Pythagoras, either. He went back to the entrance, yes, but not into the street. A staircase rose from the entrance, and he stood looking up at it, remembering how he had noticed from the stoop of the cookshop that the pile of wreckage did not reach as high as the third floor: the hall of the third floor would end in a gap. If he went up and looked out from there, he could see the tenants on the pile; he could watch, without being seen, the terrible business going on below.

But he could not make up his mind to ascend. He continued to wander about, impelled to do one meaningless thing after another: he went back and closed the dripping water-cock on the common pipe, he picked up a cloak and hung it on a peg, he picked up a headless wooden doll and laid it on one of the beds. Then, with the slow wheel of pain turning again at the nape of his neck, he went up, wondering at the smoothness of the bannister: it had been worn to a silky texture by generations of hands.

In the third floor hall, the stench of charred wood and ancient filth came pouring at him. Light, white and painful, streamed through the cavernous gap at the far end of the corridor and cast its glare on the confusion there—inner walls between rooms and hall ripped away, white plaster raining down on everything. Stop, wait a moment—yes—this *is* a corpse—corpse of an old woman sitting open-mouthed in a chair, her skull crushed in, her forehead black with clotted blood. This heap of fur and guts is a cat. And this—this white thing between the two charred beams that block the way to the glaring gap—this is a child—dead, naked child—

Why he should want to do it he did not know—the child was dead, nothing could help him now—and yet he was impelled to grasp the end of one of the beams, to heave, as if a spirit were imprisoned and he could set it free. But when he closed his fingers around the end of the shaft, he dropped it and cried out in pain. The underside of the beam was a living coal—red sparks flew from it when he let it fall—he had seared the palms of both his hands.

No, do not deceive yourself—the tears on your cheeks are niggardly tears, squeezed out of inner aridity by the intensity of the pain—not tears for *him*, not the liberal offering of the living heart. Come closer, kneel where the beams cross over the body, kneel so close that the icy feet dangle against your chest . . . Open-eyed, open-mouthed, the child stared up at Chaos breaking over him, and his brown eyes were wonderstruck and terrible in their unbelief, and the sweat of his broken sleep still held his curls to his puckered forehead. Lean closer, see, look as you looked behind the trembling eyelids at the daemoniac fantasies last night—see the world that existed once in this quenched brain. Wondrous flash of yellow on a standing pool of urine, green and azure shapes blooming at the bottom of an old copper basin, dreadful centipede dashing down the wall, white gleam of a rat's teeth in the dark hall by night. In one of these rooms, he had brooded over the gnawing hunger at the pit of his stomach and known the ambrosial taste of a slab of bacon brought back from the cookshop on a greasy papyrus square. From one of these windows he had watched the morning flight of swallows and the evening flight of doves. And now all that he had been and known and dreamed was obliterated like a trampled fire. No striving, no heaving, no burning of the hands would create again the cramped, crazy magic that had glimmered behind his small domed brow.

He did not weep. He reached behind him and gathered, in spite of the burning pain, a handful of plaster-dust, and let it trickle slowly over the hanging head. "Rest in peace everlasting," he said, and knew that it was not enough, that there must be something more than this and other than this which must be said. "Forgive me," he whispered into the stillness. "I was I and mine that took your life. For a few denarii—not enough to feed a hound, not enough to grow ten figs in winter under glass—we bought your death."

"Forgive me. We bought your death." He repeated it over and over, until the shards of stone and plaster had ground into his knees, until the white dust had gathered on his clothes like snow, until the words had lost every vestige of their power, had become as barren of meaning as the archaic formulae that the priestly augurs mouthed before the sacrifice. It was useless to kneel here any longer. It was useless to go to the gap—if this did not serve, then nothing would serve; but he stood up and stepped over the beam and started for the opening nevertheless. To try to walk across this precarious floor would be foolhardy—he lay down on his belly and dragged himself along, holding up his burned hands and testing the loosened boards with his elbows, feeling a vague surprise that the rotten wood did not break through. He did not stop until his head was beyond the edge of the gap and he could see every part of the scene below.

For a while he watched it as he might have watched the cleaning of a colossal statue or the construction of a dome, with nothing more than a dull curiosity. Some seven of them down there were straining to dislodge a big beam from the rubble. Two others were carrying a covered thing on a stretcher—it was a body of course, but he could not conceive of it as a body— toward a line of other covered things at the foot of the pile. Five or six more, two of them women, were on their knees, pushing shards and gravel aside; and the rest were merely standing about, much as he had stood near the wall of the cookshop, with hanging hands and empty eyes. There was nothing there to distract him from the fiery pain that was shooting upward now, higher than his wrists, and he might even have started back down the corridor if he had not been startled by a low, almost musical cry. The ones who were pushing aside the rubble had stopped and sat back on their heels. They had found something there—two of them, a young man and an ageing woman, were facing in his direction, and he could tell that they had found something there by their open, uplifted hands and their upraised faces. He had never seen such faces before—the eyes wide and luminous, the cheeks washed in freely flowing tears, the mouths parted in pity and awe and love. Whatever they had found, their spirits had risen up within them to accept it; the loss and the pain—they had taken the full impact of it upon their living hearts.

"Linus the cobbler, Antonia's son," somebody said.

"Yes," said another voice. "Where is she?"

"In the cookshop. Moyses sent her over to the cookshop."

"Shall I go and bring her?"

"No, not yet, not until we've taken him out, not until we've covered up his head."

The voices—he had never heard such voices, either—there had been no such voices at the funeral of Celestus Falconius. Unashamed, at once decorous and tender, they rose in a grave antiphony, beautiful, almost musical, like the cry. "Shall I go and bring Moyses?" said a girl scarcely out of her childhood, rising and brushing the rubble from her knees. Several of them nodded, and she went toward the group that was struggling with the beam, quickly, but with a dignity that was not lessened by the urgency. The others made a circle again around the horror which they had not found horrible, diligently working to free the body from the stones.

A wail broke the seemly stillness, a helpless, piteous sound from one of those who merely stood by. Now all of them, all the onlookers, had turned hysterical at the sight of the corpse. They were wailing, whimpering, thrusting their fists into their mouths; but the noise went on only for a moment; in a moment they were as they had been before—idle, empty—two of them sat down in the rubble and put their heads down on their knees, just as he had done in the damp garden at dawn. Strange, he thought, that they should be divided into two groups like that—the laborers and the onlookers, the ones with the shining, grieving faces and the ones who were horrified and stunned in the face of death. Strange, stranger still, that the men among the horrified ones should all be shaven clean and that the others should have beards—long beards like the hero in the unbound book, the one with the winged messengers and the thorny crown—

The girl was coming back now, arm in arm with another bearded one, a man in his fifties. Her grandfather, he thought at first, but that was impossible—the girl was the pale daughter of some Briton or Galatian, and the old man was just as plainly a Jew. There was a certain authority about him in spite of his short stature and casual bearing. The mobile face was heavily lined: wrinkles across the forehead, deep furrows in the cheeks, dark concentric circles around the quizzical eyes. But these lines, which recorded some long inner torment, had lost all their bitterness, and suggested only a good-humored ruefulness.

He moved into the circle of the kneeling ones and stood above them, staring down at the corpse, blinking and shaking his head and thrusting out his underlip. "Too bad, too bad," he said, pronouncing his Latin with a soft Semitic accent. "Better see that the blood is washed off before anybody calls Antonia. Turn him on his side, too—you'll do that, won't you, Jovianus?—so that she'll see the good side of his face."

But what was a Jew doing here among these others? They were an aristocratic brotherhood, they always held themselves aloof, the sons of Abraham. The little monkey-faced Secretary of the Privy Purse, even though he had moved in court circles for years, obviously still found it difficult to give the kiss of greeting, always touched the proffered cheek with his lips as though he were coming into contact with unclean meat. And this one made a point of touching the others: he had walked up hand-in-hand with the girl; he patted the head of the kneeling woman; he put his arm around the shoulders of a stocky laborer to steady himself while he bent close to the corpse and made some sign above the bloody head.

Some sign—some sign that he remembered—a sign that he had seen once before in the garden of the Herennii. Prisca had made such a sign, looking up and asking her God to help her find the chip of marble. They were Christians, then—all the ones who had bared their living hearts to the catastrophe and survived the blow of it, all the ones who could look on death and deal with it, all of them were worshippers of Jesus whom they called the Lord. The Jew also, he was a Christian; he had exiled himself from the clean meats and unleavened loaves of his tribesmen's table for—as they said in that strange phrase which they had been casting for generations into the teeth of provincial prefects—"for the Name's sake." The crucified Nazarene who, according to their childish legend, had stepped alive one morning out of his sepulchre—He was just as dead, of course, as the millions who had died before and after him. And yet some vital recollection of Him still walked the earth, moving through the corridors of such tenements as this, stopping at one door and another and summoning the living dead to rise again, turning ghosts into men. . . .

"Rest in peace, Linus, son of Antonia," Moyses said. "Your head is whole this night in Paradise. Lay it in the lap of Jesus Christ, your Saviour and your Lord."

They all said something else then in a chorus, but so softly that he could not hear. He felt deprived and shut out—*they* were together, all of one fellowship, and he was alone—they had not even seen him watching. "Amen," said Moyses, loudly and with conviction, and, though he had never heard the word before, he knew that it signified finality. His vigil also was finished, and he crept backward, blowing on his fiery palms, until his feet touched the beam that lay across the child.

It occurred to him then that he ought to take this body with him. I could find another piece of wood and wedge up the shaft, he thought. I could carry him down and give him to them for washing and burial. They would put him out of reach of the rats, at least . . . But he knew that he would not do it, not because of his burns, but because his flesh crept hideously at the thought of hoisting the naked corpse over his shoulder or holding it against his chest. "Forgive me, I cannot take you," he said aloud, and walked quickly past the old woman, because a rat was sitting in her lap, to the top of the stairs.

There the wheel of pain at the back of his head began to turn again, this time with a frightening speed. He stood swaying at the top of the flight, sick and giddy. Maybe I will make a ridiculous end of myself here, he thought. Maybe, now that I have not been crushed by falling stones or consumed by fire, I will fall down the staircase and break my neck and lie there for rats to gnaw at, with my head in a pool of urine and the grass stains and the wine stains on my clothes for everybody to see . . . But, even though his hands were so sore that he could not cling to the bannister, he kept his footing. So I am still alive, he thought, standing in the stench of the entrance way. What am I to do now? Nothing, nothing, hiss and stamp at a rat, step over two papyrus squares, kick aside the Saturnalia rose. . . .

He walked out of the building into a cool and misty drizzle, and stood for a long time near the grimy lion, waiting for the dizziness to pass and holding up his face to the delicate rain. Go home, then, he thought, find a litter and go back to the palace and tell the old woman that her tenement is utterly done-for . . . But he could not bring himself to leave—he wandered instead through the gentle rain to the corner of the building past the backs of the few Guardsmen left on duty, along the cracked stucco wall at the side . . . Why should I be going to *them*: he asked himself. What can I do? I am sick, I am weary, I could not lift so much as one little stone, not with these hands . . . But he started nevertheless up the long grey slope of rubble, stumbling and flailing with his arms because the shards kept slipping under his feet.

As he came within sight of the top, he saw the corpse of Linus the cobbler, Antonia's son, lying on a stretcher. Somebody was being sent to fetch the mother. Somebody—yes, it was the stocky young workman—was coming straight in his direction, stumbling and sliding down the side of the pile. Am I a ghost, have I been robbed of my substance that he should look straight through me? he asked himself. Then, just as he was passing, the plebe spoke to him softly. "Go away, your Illustriousness," he said, continuing on his way, so as not to attract the attention of those on top of the pile. "Go away," he said again, over his shoulder. "It's been peaceful until now, and we want to keep it that way."

He could not and would not endure it. Nobody could cast him out as if he were some baleful and unwanted spirit wandering about. He turned and pursued the workman until he caught up with him near the bottom of the pile. "Wait," he said.

The plebe turned round and faced him. "Are you drunk or have you lost your mind, your Illustriousness? There are people up there who wouldn't need much urging to tear you to pieces—"

"I mean to go up on the pile nevertheless."

"You mean to go up on—"

Somebody had heard them and was coming down the slope. Bits of dislodged gravel hurtled down and struck against his ankle. He looked up into the rueful, quizzical face of the Jew.

"What's this? What have you got down here now, Jovianus?" It was said in an almost bantering voice, like that of a pedagogue coming upon two lads who have fallen out in their play. The brown eyes, looking sharply, almost merrily, from one of them to the other, were authoritative but kind.

"God only knows," said Jovianus, flinging up his hands. "A senator, either drunk or out of his head. He says he wants to go up on the pile."

"Up on the pile? Now why would you want to go up on the pile, my son?

Look at you, you're sick, you can scarcely stand on your feet." He put out a steadying hand. "Why don't you go home and go to bed?"

"Because their blood is on my head—"

"What blood are you talking about?"

"Their blood—all this blood—"

"How's that? How's that? He's sick, Jovianus, he's not drunk, he's delirious. Get him a litter. We'll get you a litter, my son. Go home and go to bed."

"No!" It was the same loud, wild protest that he had uttered last night against the seduction of the Syrian. It summoned dark shapes—inimical, faceless shapes—to the ridge above him. They stood staring down—the Christians and the others. And the little Jew, casting a furtive glance at them, stiffened and drew a sharp, audible breath.

"Shall I call the Guardsmen?" said Jovianus.

"No, no, there's no need to call the Guardsmen. He'll be going on his way in a moment now, won't you, my son? Why should you want to stay around here, sick as you are? Why—"

"Because I am the owner of the building. The building belongs to me," he said.

If he had imagined that there would be any relief for him in the saying of it, he had been mistaken. Nothing had changed—nothing except the faces of those who were coming down from the ridge—solemn, remonstrating Christian faces and the faces of the rest, vacuous before the enormity of the situation or fiery red with fury—all of them advancing, closing in. . . .

"Get back," said Moyses. "I command you to get back, in Jesus' name."

"Let us obey our elder." It was the voice of the ageing woman whose transported and loving countenance he had seen from the gap in the wall. "Our dead are lying in this pile. It would be a dreadful thing to do any violence here. None of us would want to commit a mortal sin over the very bodies of our dead."

The line of advancing shapes was broken. The Christians paused and fell back a little. Only six continued to advance—clean-shaven ones with menacing eyes and clenched fists.

"And you, too," said Moyses, turning to these, "you who have broken with us at least the bread of this common sorrow, none of you is going to be guilty of any insane or unbecoming thing. He who takes up the sword will die by the sword. Read it—it's written in the Book. Besides, it will be useless. No blood can bring us back our dead."

"Save only the blood of the Lord," said an old man, weeping. "Save only the blood of the Lord."

One of the six, an emaciated government worker whose face had the earth-spotted whiteness of a mushroom, spat on the ground. "There were rotten beams in there," he said. "The beams were rotten, and the wall was nothing but a little chipped stone in plaster stuck onto a lattice of green wood. It was cheap to build, this filthy tenement. The Herennii got their money out of it long ago. They haven't lost anything, you can be sure of that."

"My son," said Moyses, refusing to look at him now, gazing down at the rubble, "did you know there was a lattice of green timber in the walls? Did you know the beams were made of old wood—used wood?"

He also stared down at the rubble and saw such a beam and touched it with the toe of his embroidered sandal. "No," he said, unable to keep himself from sighing. "No, I didn't know, but I should have known."

"He should have known!" It was another raging voice, hurled out of an unseen mouth. "Much good it'll do the dead down there in the wreckage to hear that he should have known!"

There was a murmuring then and a scuffling. Something came hurtling at him—the first stone. But it did not touch him. Moyses had sprung out in front of him, Moyses had taken the blow.

"That was a foolish thing to do," said another one of the six. "What's the good of all this? Now you've hurt the old man."

Moyses spit on his forefinger and wet a small red cut above his eye. "You see how it is, my son," he said. "We're not all Christians here, and I wouldn't take it for granted that even the children of Jesus are all perfect in humility. There's bound to be trouble as long as you stay. And what can you do here? Nothing, nothing at all. Do go and find a litter for him, Jovianus—"

"I can find a litter for myself." Who had said that? Charis had said it, standing like a beaten slave in the dancing-master's doorway on the Via Sacra. Rose-colored dalmatica lying on the floor in the bath, bled of all color by the grey light. World to be returned to, unbearable world . . . "I can go back alone," he said.

"No doubt you can, no doubt you can." The sturdy brown hand was under his elbow, guiding him inexorably down the slope, onto the street. "There are usually plenty of litters three or four streets up from here on the Via Trajana—" The warm voice came to a sudden stop. For an instant the brown eyes, set in their dark, sad, concentric wrinkles, looked at him with understanding and pity and tenderness. "Go now, my son," he said, giving him a little shove. "Go now, and God give you peace."

Chapter 14

MONEY—LARGE sums of money—would have to be distributed immediately among the survivors. He had come to that decision on his way home in the litter; he had clung to it as the one piece of sanity in a welter of waking nightmares; he was not to be diverted from it by any of his mother's arguments—not by the fact that the blameless Glabrii had handed out a very modest sum on a like occasion, not by the accusation that he was setting a standard which could ruin other unfortunate landlords, members of his own class, not by the unanswerable objection that there was really no way at the moment to distinguish false claims from real ones, no way to reach the eighty-some families, doubtless scattered by this time over all the seven hills. It was the lady Sabina Herennia herself—quite unintentionally, of course,— who had given him the idea of taking the money to the house of his cousin Paulina. There was more to this matter than merely wasting one's patrimony, she had said. He might take the money if he liked—after all, she'd scarcely drag him up before the law—but he'd better think twice about the people he was going to hand it over to. There were the Christians, for instance—according to the steward almost a third of the tenants belonged to that crazy sect, and this was not exactly the time to show any tender concern for them. Why not? he had shouted, half in fury at the tight-lipped, knowing mask she had put on, half because he was almost out of his mind with the pain in his hands. Because, she said, the Christians stood in the way of the Emperor's plans for a religious revival; measures would be taken against them one of these days; at a banquet in the house of Caecilia Rubria only a week ago, the Pontifex Maximus had hinted as much . . . Rumor, he had screamed at her, baseless rumor—the yellow-faced old fanatic was deluding himself—if there had been any such intentions, he would have heard of them long ago. And then he had fallen silent, seeing that she had solved his dilemma. The Christians, of course. They were organized, they visited the elect and the uninitiate alike, they went to every tenement in the City, so Paulina had said. And Probus held some official rank in the society, would know exactly what to do . . . "Don't distress yourself, I'll see that anybody I deal with is perfectly trustworthy," he assured her. "Now I've got to go to a physician, I've got to do something about these hands."

But nothing had eased him, nothing had lessened the rapid beating of his heart—not the herb salve nor the cool bandages, not the warm bath nor the slow rubbing down with oil of balsam, not the syrupy drug they had found for him in Drusilla's bedchamber, not the goose-feather pillows put under his neck and arms. Between noon, when he left his mother's office, and a little after the evening meal, when he set out in rain and darkness for the house of his cousin, he had not been able to swallow a bite of food or get so much as a few moments' sleep.

It was only his feverish nervousness, he told himself, that could account for the care he took in transporting the two bags of money from the Palatine to the Aventine. It was fantastic to regret that he was forced to take his body-slave Baubio with him, that his burns would not permit him to carry the bags himself. It was mad to imagine all sorts of impossible eventualities, to wonder whether it wouldn't have been better to take a freedman or a friend, since the law permitted the use of torture in the questioning of slaves. It was preposterous for him not to go in his own litter, as if he were actually engaged in some traitorous enterprise and wanted to involve the least possible number of others. Yet he did hire a litter—the cushions smelled faintly of Saturnalia vomit—and during the entire trip he could not bring himself once to look Baubio straight in the eye.

By the end of the journey his uneasiness had risen to such a pitch that he got out a hundred paces from his cousin's house, at the bottom of the sloping street. Large, spattering drops of rain were falling. He stood staring at the broad black chest of the Aethiopian in the yellow light of the lantern that hung on one of the poles of the litter. "There's money here in my belt, Baubio," he said. "Take some—three or four denarii. Engage the litter for yourself, but don't go all the way back home. Go to some wineshop and have a bowl of wine."

"Go and leave my lord and my master?"

"Put the bags under my arms. I haven't far to walk—I can carry them like that."

"But how can I leave my master alone, with such hands, in a dark street?"

There was more devotion in that than he could use, raw-nerved and ill-at-ease with his conscience as he was. "I know what I'm about. Give me the bags and go back," he said.

But when the litter and the light were gone, he called himself a fool for having given way to ridiculous imaginings. The street was poorly paved and slippery; he kept stepping into puddles, and his arms ached from pressing the heavy bags against his sides. The houses on both sides of the street were either lightless or so thickly curtained that only the faintest gleams seeped through. As his eyes grew more accustomed to the dark, he could see their dull black pediments and balconies dimly outlined against a murky sky. Then there was a sudden break, and he realized that he had reached the sculptor's yard. We sat on a slab of stone there, she and I, he thought, and her hair kept blowing across her cheek, and I saw the mortal, netted veins in her wrists . . . It was as if that hour had been set apart from the rest of his life and remained untouched by yesterday and today, untainted by the filth and the horror and the sickening remorse. Looking up, he saw that every window of her house was lighted: the street before it and the damp and misty air around it were tinged with a yellowish glow. Is she having a reception—do Christians have receptions? he asked himself. Of course she has receptions—she and her husband can entertain if they want to, like anybody else. And I am blundering in on one of her reception nights. . . .

For an instant he thought of turning back, but the prospect of going down the black street and looking for another litter was disheartening: his arms ached so intensely that he would be certain to let one of the bags slip—and how could he pick it up again? She will come to me away from the others, he thought. She came once before when she was otherwise engaged; she came out smiling and picking the lint off her dress and out of her hair . . . He could not use his hands to knock and kicked the door instead, trusting that the sound would be dulled by the chattering within. But when the ancient and decorous steward opened the door, he opened it on utter silence. The grey curtain between the vestibule and the inner chamber was drenched with light; he sensed that there were scores of people in the room beyond, but nobody spoke, nobody moved, and the old man stood on the threshold with a warning finger pressed against his lips.

"I am the cousin of the lady Paulina," he said in a whisper.

"Yes." The word made no more sound than the spatter of the rain. "I remember you, my lord. Will you step in and sit down? She's engaged, I can't call her at the moment, but she'll come out to you in a little while."

He did not dare to drop the money bags on the bench for fear they would jingle. "Take them," he said, still whispering. "Lay them here on the bench. Watch, they'll make a noise."

In the light of the lamp hanging on a black chain, the steward saw the bandaged hands and the inflamed wrists, and drew a hissing breath. "Sit down and rest, my lord," he said, and his concern rang through the whisper. "They're breaking the bread in there. She can't come at once. But I'll tell her, and she'll come as soon as she can."

When the steward was gone, he let himself down onto the bench beside the money bags and rested his head against the wall. The chill of the plaster penetrated to his body at first, so that he shuddered; but almost at once the warmth of the crowded house impinged upon him, a warmth at once soothing and enervating, so gratifying that he thought he would be quite content to sit here gazing at the glowing curtain for hours. The air was fragrant with the smell of the evening meal—fried fish, hot bread, sour wine—a mingling of cooking odors that would have been distasteful to him on any other occasion. But now it was delectable—he remembered that he had taken nothing but a little medicine into his stomach all day long, and he drew his breath in deeply, as if he could be nourished and strengthened by the smells, especially by the smell of the hot bread. Then let them take as much time as they please, he thought, over this business of "breaking the bread". I'm comfortable enough, my heart is quieter now, even the pain is less . . . And he closed his eyes and saw an image of his flaming hands wound in white bandages. Wrapped in peace, he thought, swathed in white peace. . . .

"The Lord be with you."

He started because the unearthly voice—it was the thin, silvery voice of an old man, human only because it spoke in the rough accents of the countryside—seemed to be speaking straight into his ear. He looked up and saw that nobody was there. The voice had spoken on the other side of the curtain, and a multitude of other voices answered it in unison. "And with your spirit," they said.

"Lift up your hearts." It was the silvery, solitary voice again.

Quietly, but with conviction, the chorus responded in a kind of chant: "We lift them up unto the Lord."

The philosopher Cleander had described this ritual once—plump little man, lying on the floor of Charis's living room, with his swollen belly sticking up and his beard foul with vomit—had explained how, when they broke the bread and drank the wine together, they thought they were eating the flesh and drinking the blood of their crucified Jew. There were other tales about it—nobody but the most ignorant among the plebes believed them anymore, but for something more than a century people had been stirred up to violence against them in many of the provinces on the grounds that they came together secretly by night and ate bread made of flour mixed with the blood of a murdered child. . . .

But I am the child-slayer, he thought, seeing it again with a terrible immediacy—the dead white body wedged between the beams. Then the ancient voice drove it away, the ancient voice was calling upon the assembly to give thanks unto the Lord, and they were responding that it was meet and right to do so, they were responding with such loud and joyous assurance that any passer-by in the dark street must surely hear. And that was unwise, unwise—he almost rose to go and tell them so, then stopped himself, knowing that it was a ridiculous notion—unthinkable that spies should be watching, listening in the rainy street . . . Then there was a general rustling, a settling and a congregated sighing, and the silvery voice proceeded to what was evidently the heart of the matter:

"We thank Thee, God, through Thy beloved Servant, Jesus Christ, whom in these last times Thou hast sent us as Saviour and Redeemer and Messenger of Thy council, the Spirit who comes from Thee. . . ."

There was more, but he did not hear it. A single phrase, *in these last times,* hung suspended in his mind and curved his mouth in a secretive smile. "In these last times, in these last times," he whispered. Then they know it also. My cousin Paulina, she knows it also. Looking up from the yards of white linen and seeing the clean, bent, adolescent heads, she dreams what I dreamed in the grey garden, she also sees the ultimate fire lapping round the cracked orb of the world . . . And the thought that this bitter knowledge was not his to bear in secret and alone, the realization that thousands of these Christians in all the provinces of the Empire lifted up their voices and gave public recognition to it as often as they came together for the "breaking of the bread"—this thought was nourishing and sustaining to him. He renewed himself upon it; in his dreaming weariness it was somehow compounded with the glow that came through the curtain, with the warmth that coursed through his body, with the smell of fried fish and sour wine and hot bread. "In these last times," he whispered, and allowed his heavy head to come down so that it rested on his chest. And the silvery old voice was like a dream, was a voice speaking in a dream of peace:

"And when He delivered Himself up to a voluntary passion, to loose death and to break asunder the bonds of the devil, and to trample hell and to enlighten the righteous and to set up the boundary stone and to manifest the resurrection, He took a loaf, gave thanks, and spake: 'Take, eat, this is My body, given for you.' Likewise also this cup, and said, 'This is My blood, poured out for you. So often as you drink this cup, you commemorate Me. . . ."

In the dream he saw this Jesus of Nazareth standing at the head of a long table, his long beard cut in the eastern fashion, his forehead bleeding under a thorny crown . . . Yes, he thought, trying to open his eyes, that must have been one of their books I found in the tenement. . . .

"Remembering therefore His death and His resurrection, we offer to Thee this loaf and this cup. . . ."

It is coming to an end, she will come out to me soon, he thought; and tried to lift his head.

"And we beseech Thee that Thou send down Thy Holy Spirit upon this offering of the Church. Unite it, and grant to all the saints who partake of it their fulfillment with the Holy Spirit, their strengthening of faith in truth, that we may praise Thee and glorify Thee through Thy Servant Jesus Christ, through whom to Thee be glory and honor in Thy Holy Church, now and forever, Amen."

The "Amen" that broke from the assembly was resonant enough to make the wall vibrate behind him, but it did not unseal his eyes. I'll sleep, he thought. What harm could come of it if she should find me here asleep?

No harm, no harm . . . Two young women with new-washed hair appeared in the moist dark behind his eyelids, holding between them a length of linen rolled like a scroll. They began to step away from each other, unrolling the scroll as they went. Backward and backward, with the white web always growing between them, and backward still, and the cloth still rippling and flowing, more and more cloth, more and more white lengths of peace, over green glades, over mountains, over cliffs, over dark waters, out and out to the edges of the world. Then they turned the linen upward, and it became a seemly snow-white table, and there were innumerable plates, and there was a silver plate before him, and on the plate was a fish, laid open so that all the exquisite bones were to be seen, and beside the fish was a rusk of steaming bread. Knowing that all this was his to take, he stretched out his hand to take and eat. But just as his fingers touched the flakes of fish, the dream was broken by a little cry.

He opened his eyes. They were swimming with moisture. He stared for a long time before he knew it was his cousin Paulina standing above him—the whiteness was her intricately tucked dalmatica, the brown shining was her hair. Even when his sight had cleared, he continued to stare, asking himself what transmutations had taken place within him, what dry husk had fallen away from his spirit in sleep that he should look at her as he had never looked at another being before. Then a shadow, as of fright or wonderment, passed across her clear gaze, and she glanced down with dark, compassionate eyes at his bandaged hands. "I'm afraid you have a little fever," she said, laying her fingers across his forehead and then drawing back at once. "It was unwise for you to come, sick as you are, on such a night."

"But I had to come. Our tenement in the Via Trajana—"

"Yes, I know. Probus was there this afternoon. As many of the tenants as this house can hold are here for the night. This evening we're holding an *agapé* for them—" She flushed and looked down at the blue paint that covered the mosaic at her feet. "An *agapé* is a feast of love—a feast and a ritual—it's gone out of fashion now—unfortunately we use it only in times of trouble—I can't quite explain it—the congregation eats together, as one family, and there's a breaking of the bread. But can I bring you anything? Wine? Wine-and-water?—" And suddenly she broke off, she was on her knees before him, laying her cool fingers on his burning wrists. "Oh, my poor cousin," she said, and her mouth trembled, "what have you done with your hands?"

His mother, the steward, the physician—each of them had asked him that question, and all he had told them was that any idiot could see he had burned himself. Now, to his amazement, he found himself giving her a minute and circumstantial account of his doings in the empty building, speaking softly but not in a whisper, since the ritual was plainly over and the feast had begun, with a quiet rise and fall of conversation, a light clinking of pottery and silverware. She listened, nodding now and again and looking up with grave, steady eyes; in her earnest attention, she had so far forgotten herself as to sit back on her heels, and, with her wan, unpainted face tilted upward and her tucked skirt spread wide around her, she looked singularly like a child. He did not mention his encounter with her Christian associates on the rubble heap, but he had an uneasy suspicion that she knew of it nevertheless. When his voice trailed off, she continued to sit before him as if she were waiting to hear more of the story; and when he made it plain that nothing else was forthcoming, he saw a kind of disturbance, as of stirred waters, in her glance.

"You must be very tired," she said at last.

"A little. But I wanted to come and bring this money. I thought that you and Probus might know some way to get it into the hands of the tenants—"

"So much! All this!" She leaned forward, and for the first time he saw her make a gesture of delight. Her thin hands, ringless and veined, passed over the bulges in the leather; her weary face was made tremulous and radiant by a smile; and he could not bring himself to spoil her pleasure by saying that the money should under no circumstances be given in his name.

"I understand that this is nothing," he told her instead, looking at her white forehead, unable now to encounter her eyes. "I know I can never discharge my responsibility in this. Even if I brought you all the holdings of the Herennii, the maimed would still be maimed and the dead would still be dead. To try to pay is useless—"

"Oh, but you tried to pay in the tenement, my cousin. You tried to pay, as if you thought that God was merciful and would accept whatever you had to give. You burned your hands."

He smiled at her quaint reasoning, and shook his head. "No, I never thought of any such thing. I simply couldn't bear to see the beam lying across the child."

She rose and pressed the wrinkles out of her skirt and stood against the glowing curtain. "We'll speak of it another time," she said. "They tell me I'm a tireless preacher—that I use every occasion as an excuse to preach—but I'll not preach to you now, sick and tired as you are. Are you thirsty? They say that burns always make a person thirsty. Let me bring you a little wine."

"I would be drunk in your vestibule if I swallowed a bowlful. My stomach is empty, I haven't eaten since last night."

"But why didn't you say so? There's fresh bread and fish and a sauce of herbs—"

He was ashamed to tell her he doubted he could feed himself. It seemed to him that there had already been far too much talk about the condition of his hands.

She turned and drew the curtain apart a little, so that he caught a glimpse of the inner room: a long table covered with a white cloth, and some forty people sitting in the glow of wax lights—men, women, and children.

"Let me bring you the food while it's still hot," she said, and passed through the opening in the curtain and was gone.

At first he listened to the conversation around the table. They were talking in serene voices about the burial of their dead. Some thirty of those who had departed—may they rest everlastingly in the Lord's peace!—were to be given places in the new corridor of the catacomb. The others were to lie in a field outside the City, given to God by the Anicii—no need to thank them here, the gratefulness of angels was laid up for them in heaven. Had the Bishop Fabian yet visited the new field? Yes, said the old voice, the silvery voice, he had been there this afternoon; everything was in order, the ground had been duly blessed . . . Then he listened no more—it so happened that he rested his head against the wall again, as he had rested it in sleep—and he saw what he had seen at the instant of his waking: his cousin Paulina's dark, compassionate eyes. He continued to brood over them until he heard footsteps approaching the vestibule. Two people were coming out to him. She is bringing Probus, he thought with disgust. But when the curtain was drawn back—it was she who parted it, stepping back in an attitude of respect to let her companion pass—he saw that it was not Probus. It was an old man, a farmer with split nails and earth-stained fingers.

"This is the Shepherd of our flock, our Bishop, our Papa Fabian," she said, pulling the curtain closed with one hand and holding a dish of food in the other.

"Peace to you, my son," said the voice that had spoken alone at the breaking of the bread. "We have lived out a hard day, and you also. We have done what we could, and you also. Now, burdened as we are with the flesh, we must eat and sleep, and you also. He that is risen—sometime I mean to count in the Gospels how many times He told us: Be comforted."

He made as if to stand, but the earth-stained hand signalled him down again. The sunburned face above him, crowned as with a garland by a thick ring of wiry, snow-white curls, was as merry as the face of a grandfather at a wedding feast. And how could that be, since he had visited the earth in which the dead were to be laid, and had doubtless been laboring among the maimed and the mourners since dawn?

He answered the unasked question, fixing his small black eyes on the eyes of the uninitiate. "We don't grieve, we don't permit ourselves to grieve," he said. "So many of the dead who were asking themselves last night how they were to come by today's bread are sitting together this evening at the ample table of the Lord."

He rejected both the assertion and the look. "It must be comforting to believe such things," he said.

"It is, it is. And you are without this comfort—we remember that. My daughter here tells me that you are sick, too, and have eaten nothing since last night, and have blistered your hands. Come, eat while the food is hot. Here, my daughter, come and feed him. He won't object to being fed. Like all of us, he was an infant once, he's been fed before."

Her wan face bent over him, alive with a flush and a smile; and the food that he took at her hand after his long fast did not taste like any other food that had ever passed his lips—the flakes of white fish, the small morsels of hot bread were delectable materializations, light and evanescent, of the odors that had floated through his dreams.

"My cousin has brought money for the tenants, Father," she said.

"Yes, so I see, and a great deal of it." The rough hand with the split nails passed appreciatively over the bulges in the leather. "Have you any wishes about the distribution of the money, my son?"

He swallowed a bite of fish and wet his lips with the tip of his tongue. Here was the occasion for saying it, and yet he could not bring himself to say it, he could not mar the moment with such a harsh and niggardly phrase as *Not in my name*. "Distribute it as you see fit," he said to the Bishop. "You know best." But even while he said it, he thought of the consternation he would stir up in Ummidius Pessinus and the Secretary of the Privy Purse if he told them—he had half a mind to tell them—"I put a small fortune the other night into the hands of the Bishop who presides over the Christians."

"Then we will distribute it according to their needs, my son. You know, of course, that the Lord's charity is dispensed to all, whether or not they are Confessors of the Name." He straightened and stepped back toward the curtain and parted it, but then turned again, smiling a thoughtful smile. "The Lord bless you and keep you and cause His countenance to shine upon you," he said. "The Lord is a tireless seeker, and He will find His own." And, before he left them, he made the sign of the Cross.

"He made the sign of Jesus upon you," she said, and her eyes were vague with wonder, and the hand that was carrying the morsel of bread paused on its way to his lips. "That was the sign of the Cross."

Neither of them said anything more until the plate was empty, and when she spoke to him again there was a certain rigidity about her: it was as if she had been thinking out carefully in the interim everything that was to pass between them before he took his leave. "He's a simple man, he came to us from a little farm in the Campagna, our Papa Fabian," she said. "When the Bishop Anteros left us, there was a convocation to choose a successor. There were a great many candidates, you can imagine—saints and scholars and sons of high patrician houses. It was very difficult to choose. But while the Church was pondering the issue on earth, the matter was settled else-where—our Papa Fabian was chosen for us by the Lord. Just when the names were about to be presented to the convocation, a dove flew into the basilica and passed over the heads of the saints and scholars and patricians, and came down far back, among the lesser tenders of the flock, and perched on our Father Fabian's head. And even though very few of the elders and deacons knew him—he had broken bread only for a few rural families—there was no argument. God sent him to us, and for no small purpose. He's a kindly man, more fitted to comfort the flock than to build the Church, and we say among ourselves that He who sent him saw a time of trouble to come."

He nodded, not knowing what to say. Does she believe it? She's an intel-ligent, well-educated woman—how could she believe it? he asked himself. And yet he was not in the least exasperated with her: as she wiped a fleck of sauce from the corner of his lip and set the dish down on the bench beside him, he thought of the naming of the censor, and smiled. A dove could scarcely have done worse than Decius, he thought. Given a dove flying at random around the Emperor's dining room yesterday morning, there's small likelihood that it wouldn't have lighted on something better than Vale-rian. . . .

"Are you laughing at me?" she asked, standing before him with her thin fingers twined together.

"No, really. I was thinking of something else."

"You must have a great deal to think about. We've kept you here for a long time—"

He rose. "It was I who kept you away from your guests."

For an instant she looked straight at him—the same unveiled, compas-sionate look to which he had opened his eyes in the beginning. Then sud-denly she was close to him—she did what she had never done before—she held up her cheek for the cousinly kiss. Her face was cold and fragrant, like a flower carried in out of rain. "How cool you are!" he said, laughing un-easily. "Is that because I have a fever? Or do you have a cold heart?"

"I think you have a little fever." The faint flush spread over her cheeks again, and as if to hide it she turned her back on him and opened the door on the drenched street. "Look after your hands," she said.

"The last time I came here, you asked me to come again."

"Come again. Our house is yours. Come whenever you can."

Breathing the damp air and seeing the gleam of puddles on the black paving stones in the light from the vestibule, he wondered why she had not offered him a slave to go before him with a lantern, at least until he could find a litter on some more frequently traveled street. Then it occurred to him that she would never have thought of his coming unattended. As, on the day when he had come to her with the business of Drusilla and Herennius, she had believed him capable of running to warn her of a persecution, so tonight she attributed to him more courage than he possessed: she believed he would disregard all eventualities, she took it for granted that a litter, ornamented with silver and attended by the Nubians of the Herennii, would be waiting for him at her very door. And if it had not been for the fever, he thought, I would have come in my own litter. Only a man in a state close to delirium would imagine that imperial spies might follow him and his money-bags from the Palatine to the Aventine, that his body-slave might be taken into the chambers below the office of the Urban Prefect and questioned about his master's whereabouts on such-and-such a night. . . .

And yet, when the soft voice of Baubio addressed him out of the blackness beside the sculptor's wall, he felt an inward sinking. "What are you doing here, you fool? I told you to go back to the palace," he said.

"But I couldn't leave my lord and my master on a dark street like this without protection. I went to the bottom of the hill and drank in a wine-shop, and the more I drank, the more I was sure he'd be set upon by thieves, helpless as he would be with his hands. And I thought: What can he do to me but have me beaten?"

"Did I ever have you beaten?"

"No, my master." He thought he could discern a slight smile on the thick lips. "That was what I told myself."

Chapter 15

THE DEACON Probus went up to his bedchamber early, as soon as the last of the guests had risen from the table, leaving it to his steward to see that those who were to stay the night would be assigned to the proper beds. But the mistress of the house stayed long on the lower floor, directing the slaves as to the whereabouts of pillows and coverlets, wandering around the big room and picking up crusts and bones with her own hand. Always, after the house had been emptied of visitors, a driving restlessness took hold of her, and that restlessness was stronger than ever tonight. She could not bring herself to leave the room, hushed and shadowy now, lighted only by a single wax light in the middle of the table, until everything was in irreproachable order, until she could say to one of the slaves, "Look, it's as if nobody had been here. Who would guess now that we'd broken the bread with forty guests?"

But tonight, even when every crumb had been swept from the floor, even when every stray piece of silverware had been consigned to its proper place in the sideboard, she could not rest. A sense of something forgotten, something left unfinished kept her moving round and round the room, and as she walked she repeated her most frequent prayer, "Lord, give me peace.

Give me peace—did I offer condolences to Sullia on the death of her daughter?—yes, of course I did. Bless me, Father, with the peace that passes all mortal understanding, the abounding peace that stills the hands and quiets the heart. Are there pitchers of water in the upstairs hall? There should be pitchers of water—so many little children—some of them certain to wake up thirsty in the middle of the night. But the steward will look to it—when will I learn to trust the steward? Teach me, out of Thine everlasting patience, teach me. Let me see that it is not all in my hands, but all in Thine. . . .

And yet she lingered, walking around the table, pausing to scratch a little accretion of wax from the cloth—she lingered until she knew what it was she had left undone. One of the plates—the plate from which she had fed her cousin Favorinus—was still on the iron bench in the vestibule. The money-bags had been carried away by the Bishop Fabian, and the light in the hanging lamp had been extinguished, but the plate was still out there in the dark. And an aching fullness rose around her heart when she remembered it—the same ache that she had felt when she had gone into the kitchen to fetch him fish and bread, being unable to take the consecrated food from the table because he was not of the congregation of the Lord.

She stepped through the divide in the shadowy curtain. The cloth, brushing against cheek and shoulder and hip, sent a creeping sensation through her body. In the closed cubicle of the vestibule, her heart began to race—it was as if somebody were waiting there, looking at her with moist and earnest eyes . . . She snatched up the plate and went back with it into the lighted chamber. "One more plate, there's always one more plate. Well, here it is, and now we'll have to wash it," she said, handing it to one of the slaves. But almost immediately she was mournful again, assailed by a poignant regret that she had not taken it out and washed it herself. And when the slave brought it back clean she took it with an eager, nervous gesture. At least, she thought, I can put it into the sideboard with my own hands. . . .

She got down on her knees with it in front of the old cabinet. Apples were stored in one of the compartments, and a fragrance as of summer orchards was in the ancient wood. She could not bring herself to close the door at once, but continued to kneel for some moments, watching the guttering light behind her shimmer on the piled silver, breathing the smell of apples—winy, earthy, sweet.

Give me peace, she thought again, walking up the stairs. But in the upper hall there was no promise of serenity. The floor of the corridor was cluttered with improvised beds; children were whimpering; women whom she scarcely knew were whispering together with more liveliness than was becoming in the victims of a calamity; and those who had fallen asleep were making uneasy sounds—grunts, indistinguishable words, heavy sighs. Those sounds will come in to us all night, she told herself. He will be unable to sleep, and I will be worried for him . . . But when she stepped over the threshold of their common bedchamber and closed the massive door behind her, all noise was shut out, it was as quiet as the grave.

She rested her back against the door and looked at the familiar room—broad bed with two pillows, drawn curtains of deep blue woolen, table strewn with scrawled sheets of papyrus, and he at the table with the new-trimmed lamp beside him, looking up from the page and seeking some answer in her face. He was at work on his *Journey of Barnabas*—he felt that a day was lost unless he had added a few lines to his poem, and this evening, because of the *agapé*, he had not had a moment to call his own. Usually it touched her to find him brooding over the unwieldy thing, but tonight she was somehow nettled by the sight of him sitting there with the quill in his hand. For once, she thought, for once, with so many dead and maimed and with so many taking refuge in the house, he might have let it alone.

The usual joy in their hard-earned solitude refused to rise to her face. "I've never been as tired as this, not in all my days," she said.

He laid the quill among the scattered papyrus sheets and folded his hands on the table. His curly beard and hair shone red in the light of the lamp. Under the folds of his white dalmatica, she saw the outlines of his long, crossed legs, one bony knee thrust out against the cloth. "I wanted to thank you," he said earnestly, "for taking my part in the argument with Moyses."

"You were right, and he was wrong. . . ."

The sentence hung in the stillness, dubious, incomplete: it was as if she had appended a "but" to it. He waited for more, then took up the pen and crossed out the last line that he had written.

She sat down on the edge of the bed with her back turned to him and took off her shoes. You were right and he was wrong, she thought, chafing her feet—they were aching and cold—and if you had upheld your opinions casually, freely, man-to-man, there would have been no argument. What is it in you that makes you always state truth and wisdom in a testy voice? What the elder Cornelius would say with calm assurance and the elder Moyses would say with God-given authority—why must you give it out so coldly, with such uncomfortable officiousness? If you had laid a manly and companionable hand on the shoulder of your opponent, if you had said in an easy voice, "But look, my friend, we have to think of it like this. . . ."

She straightened and crossed herself. Forgive me, Lord Jesus, she said voicelessly, forming the words only with her lips. I was reared in a household of heathens, and the poison that I drank in my childhood is still in my veins. Forgive me that I should reproach my husband, my yoke-fellow in God, my soul's companion, because he is lacking in heathen manners, heathen grace. . . .

The scratch of his pen stopped behind her, but he did not speak. He knew—ten years had taught him to know by the line of her back and the set of her head—that she was praying. He was waiting for a word with her unwilling to break in on her devotions. She let her shoulders drop and began to unfasten the knots in the cord of her girdle.

"But I could have put it more graciously," he said.

And suddenly it was as if her spirit went out to him, like a bird that flies to its nestling, to nourish it, to brood over it, to cover it with warmth from the inimical world. "Ah, love, what difference does that make?" she said, trying to keep the fullness of tears out of her voice, not daring to turn her head. "Tomorrow all of them that heard the argument will waken with clear heads and say among themselves that you were right—wise and just."

He did not answer, but she thought she heard him sigh.

"Once they have time to think it over, they always see that you were right." She was not committing the sin of falsehood, even to comfort him—this much at least could be said of him in white, unblemished truth. How many times had the members of the brotherhood come to tell her, after just such a disturbing difference as this, that he had been right, that the wisdom of God was surely established in his heart?

She began to strive with the second knot—the stubborn one, the one she had tied too tightly in her anxiety to see that the *agapé* table was properly set. Her nails were brittle and her fingers had never been strong: from her childhood she had never trusted herself to carry anything heavy and precious; once—she blushed now to remember it—she had dropped a basket of Eucharist bread. She rose, still striving to open the knot, crossed the cold and gritty floor—they had sold their rugs and all other useless ornaments as offences against Christian simplicity—and came and stood beside him at the corner of the table. "Will you unfasten my girdle for me, Probus?" she said.

But that was tactless, appallingly tactless, far more embarrassing than anything her husband had said to Moyses about the questionable *Gospel According to the Hebrews* that the younger members of the congregation were reading with such regrettable avidity. Unfasten my girdle . . . Unloose my girdle . . . In the Greek and Latin poets, whose works they had both been nourished on in their benighted days, such phrases signified the act of love. She stared down at his red curls and remembered the uneasiness let loose in the classroom whenever such phrases were read aloud—the mocking, knowing faces of the boys, the girls' lowered heads and bright, averted eyes. Children—deceived, dream-dazed children—imagining that love was what the poets said it was, seeing themselves as Mars caught with Venus in a golden net, fancying themselves as Juno preparing herself for her blissful couch of hyacinth . . . His fingers—flat, bony, inelegant—struggled with the knot. Then suddenly, without passion, in grief and tenderness, he put his arms around her and laid his head against her breast. "Are you very unhappy, Paulina?" he said.

"Unhappy?"

"Yes. I thought you were crying."

"Was I?" The tears of her brooding love for him were still on her cheeks—

she had forgotten to wipe her face. "If I was," she said, feeling his arms relax and stepping backward a little to show him that he had in no way wounded her, that she also was ready to conclude the embrace, "if I was, it was only because something strange came over me when I was sitting there on the bed—"

"What, beloved?"

"Nothing—I don't know—only all of a sudden I loved you so much."

"And I love you, Paulina."

Knowing serenely what she had learned with bitterness in the early months of their marriage, knowing that a protest or a disagreement was the only thing he could utter with any fervor, she could not take it ill that the words had come out of him in a flat voice, or that he had turned again to his *Journey of Barnabas* as soon as they had been said. He was no longer looking at her, and she wondered why she should be so painfully aware that she was undressing in his presence. For years now, her body had been to her like some light and extraneous thing, a chrysalis spun of almost weightless filaments—again and again her spirit, her essential being, had slipped out of it in dreams, meditations, ecstasies. But tonight—because I am so weary, she told herself—tonight the flesh was flesh, emerging out of the decent folds of linen alive and warm, so that she could not refrain from glancing down at her breasts, small as a girl's and luminously white. To pull the cold, rough linen shift over her body was somehow to do that body a violence. Decently covered, but shivering now, she sat on the edge of the bed again, turning her back to him and brushing the gritty dust from the soles of her feet.

"Paulina," he said, breaking a stillness that had grown almost sepulchral, "I wanted to ask you something. I was wondering—have you ever regretted our vow?"

Their vow—their vow to live chastely as brother and sister in Jesus Christ, in readiness for the Last Day and the coming of the Kingdom— what had come over him that he should mention it tonight? Nine years and more had gone by—all swift and strangely bodiless—nine years and neither of them had ever said a word concerning that April evening when they had given their marriage to God. Silence had kept it so clear and shining that she could still see the two of them walking home through the April dusk after the Easter Eucharist, walking hand in hand past yards in bloom with crocus and violet, walking in a kind of daze, awed by Christ's open grave and unwound cerements, utterly satisfied on the bread and wine of the Lord. Then, of a sudden, they had fallen to talking—which of them first, she did not know. As birds sing on separate boughs, first out of the abundance of their own spirits and afterward answering and emboldening each other, so, holding hands in the sunset street, they had spoken of their utter completeness in His love. They were fulfilled, they did not even grieve that her womb had not been quickened—the flesh and the joys of the flesh were nothing, nothing—the crocuses were in bloom and the evening stars hung white above the darkening pediments and Christ was risen—risen and beckoning them upward with His pierced and tender hand. They would take the vow of chastity, they would join the saintliest members of the flock, they would live on earth as angels live in Paradise—and then the April street had grown a little less radiant, they had walked a little more slowly, because at the crest of their shared ecstasy it had come again as it always came, the sense of tears. Should they tell the Bishop? he had asked her, stopping and turning to look into her face. No, she had said, seeing the "No" foreshadowed in his eyes. To go to the Bishop, to make a vow of chastity in public, to declare themselves before the congregation would be ostentatious and dishonest, since it was such a sorry love—wounded, awkward, shameful to them both—that they were laying down at the foot of the Cross. . . .

He cleared his throat to let her know that he was still behind her, embarrassed and waiting.

"No, oh, no," she said, looking at him earnestly over her shoulder. "No, I never regretted our vow." She lay down and pulled the coverlet up to her chin. The bed was cold, even colder than the shift—cold linen, damp with a day of rain, hardening her breasts. She shivered and shielded her eyes from the light with the back of her hand.

"I'll blow out the lamp in just a moment," he said. "One line here—I almost have it now, and if I leave it until tomorrow I may forget."

She nodded without uncovering her eyes. I've seen you striving with a line before, she thought. You may very well be striving with it, and the lamp may very well be shining in my eyes, for half the night . . . Then suddenly, like a casing of ice forming around her heart, came the old thought, the old fright: How would it be with me if the lamp were extinguished forever, if they had taken him away to the executioner's block or the beasts or the fire, if I should lift my hand from my eyes and look in vain for the hunched shoulders and the pitiful sheets of papyrus and the dear head? And she almost said his name aloud, so strong was her fear, her longing to have him come and kiss her, her need for the touch of his mouth on her brow.

She lay still until the weariness began to work upon her, relaxing the stiff grasp of her fingers on the coverlet. Gentle Jesus, merciful Jesus, give me peace, she prayed again, forming the words with her lips, as if the act of whispering them could give them more strength, more fervor. Teach me to know in my frozen heart that those whom Thou hast joined together can never be put asunder, but will be united again on the Last Day, by Thee and in Thee. Give me Thy blessed assurance that Thy clear shining will not be dimmed for us by a veil of tears on that Last Day when all who have kept their faith with Thee kneel together at Thy throne. Tell me that howsoever our hearts have been wounded in this world, in this house, in this room, they will be whole and acceptable in the hour when we lift them up to Thee. Deliver me from the devil, and from faint-heartedness, and from loneliness—for who is alone, being with Thee?—and from a nameless sense of sorrow, and from much needless self-torment, and from futile anxiety. Teach me to trust the steward; teach me to leave the slaves' work to the slaves; let me go on no more unnecessary errands into the vestibule in the dark of the night—

And suddenly, before she could ward it off, she was seeing a vision of her cousin Favorinus sleeping under the hanging lamp, with his dark curls fallen over his brow. She saw his ardent, beautiful, and suffering face, with the shadow of the lamp-chain moving across it, shadowy links passing over the hollow temple, the stubbled cheek, the young, parted lips. Lord, Lord, she whispered, driving her hand into the pillow, never let me see him again when he is waking out of his sleep. Give Thine angels charge over me, to bear me up, lest I dash my foot against a stone. Never let me see his naked eyes.

Chapter 16

FOR A long time he was sick, desperately sick, and there were torments and visions—visions glaring and dark, hot and cold—but chiefly there was the dream of the decision between the fish and the tenement. Concerning that matter, the need for a decision was urgent, and because of it he made an affliction of himself: he beat the pillows and strove with the coverlet and made certain harsh pronouncements to those who stood about remonstrating and weeping—Drusilla, his mother, Ummidius Pessinus, the Greek physician. The fish and the tenement—it was elusive, and he tried to explain it to each of them in spite of the terrible weight on his chest, but none of them understood, although each of them pretended to understand.

He was forced to decide immediately, since time was short and the Last Day was quickly drawing on, between taking a piece of white fish to his cousin Paulina's house and laying it down among the brethren at the breaking of the bread—only it was not a piece of fish, it was his own heart, pulled out of his raw chest and wrapped in a piece of oily papyrus, and he could not do it, he could not show his cousin Paulina how small it was, how small and shriveled and dead—he was forced to decide between this unendurable exposure and a task so tremendous that he knew he could never perform it, especially now, with the hot pain always under his ribs: the impossible task of rebuilding the tenement in the Via Trajana with his own hands.

But the whole business was unreal, insane. The real decision was, of course, the one the Greek physician posed to him in a stern voice: Either he would sit up, like the grown man that he was, and try to cough up the strangling accumulation of phlegm in his chest, or he would be pulled up and beaten over the back—all of which was sensible enough. He raised himself with a terrible lurching of the room and a wrenching and a gagging, and the stuff he spit into the napkin that they held to his mouth—they tried to hide it, but he saw it—was a strange, rusty red, and his mother put her exquisite hand over her soft mouth and uttered a hoarse, unmusical, human cry. He listened then, with the pain of the coughing like a bleeding rent in the clogged and mortal stuff under his ribs, to what the physician was whispering to his mother about his case: A fever of the lungs, decidedly—the violent and rapid sort, brought on by exhaustion and dampness and plaster dust. . . .

Feverish sleep, and faceless forms coming and going in evil dreams, and slow waking to an alabaster lamp burning on a table beside his bed. On the other side of the flame, Drusilla sat brooding, her face so fixed and solemn that it might have been carved out of stone.

"You, too—I have betrayed you, too," he said in a hoarse whisper.

"Hush, lie still, sleep if you can."

"No, first I have to tell you how it was that I betrayed you."

"Go to sleep."

"I said to myself, 'Let her go to Epidaurus, give her to the sand, give her to the waters, so long as I have an answer for the Decii—'"

"Forget about that and try to rest."

"But if I live, if I live to go in to him behind the curtain again, you will have to go to Epidaurus."

She rose then and stood over him. There was an insane and terrifying joy in her face—she leaned forward and smiled a madwoman's smile. "Send me to Epidaurus!" she said in a triumphal, hissing whisper. "By all means, send me to Epidaurus—I'll be that much closer to *him* in Epidaurus—"

He propped himself up on his elbows and looked into her eyes. It was like looking into two pieces of polished granite—no depth, no light. "Oh God," he said, "you sit here and think of lying with him while you watch me dying. Go away—stay away from me—send me Baubio—"

They did not send him Baubio. Others—his mother, the steward of the house, and the Greek physician—came running into the room because he was coughing again. The steward held a basin for him, and the Greek physician stood behind him, beating with fists on his back—inexorably, hatefully loosening the strangling stuff within. Phlegm came, and blood came, and his mother stood at the foot of his bed, running her hand through her sparse, disheveled curls and wailing as loudly as a hired mourner, and that was strange, since she had never before shown the slightest concern over Baubio. For it was dark again, with the dank, dripping darkness of the prison chambers under the Urban Prefect's office, and they were doing some horrible thing to Baubio's back. "On the evening of the day following the feast of the Saturnalia, it is true, is it not, that your master Favorinus Herennius carried two bags of money to a certain Christian household on the Aventine?" the voice of the Greek physician said. But Baubio was past all speaking, Baubio was plainly dying, could make no sounds but the tearing, rattling coughs and the short, exhausted cries . . . "God help poor Baubio," he said, raising his face from the basin. And suddenly the black, musky body, living and whole, was lying across the bed, and the warm arms were cradling him, and the shaking fingers were wiping the spittle from his lips, the sweat from his brow. "God help my dear master," said Baubio, weeping. "God help my dear, kind lord."

After that, there were no more horrible dreams. A grave, sad quiet came upon him, and it was always evening—whenever he opened his eyes and saw the ceiling, the red of the setting sun was upon it and he was weary as with a long day's labor, too weary to lift his hand or turn his head. There were times when, because of this stillness and emptiness, he would have thought himself dead if it had not been for the hoarse whisper of his breath coming up through the torn rawness of his chest and for the tears— slow, effortless, blessedly cooling—that kept coursing back over his temples out of the corners of his eyes. If he dreamed then it was because he wished to dream. He returned to the fish because it was his will to return to the fish; the vision of the fish he built piecemeal and always in the evening, so that there was one glow or another upon it, either the glow of the last sunlight or the glow of the newly-replenished lamp beside his bed.

The fish—how far had I gone with the matter of the fish? he would ask himself when the last indignities of the day were over, when Baubio had seen to the shameful necessities of his body, and the Greek physician had fed him the broth of herbs, and his mother, smelling of cassia, dryness, had kissed him on the brow. In yesterday's dream I suddenly realized that I could not take the parcel of fish to my cousin Paulina because it was not here in the palace at all. Yes, I had left it at Charis's house, together with some raisins for Cyrillus and a bunch of myrtle—where did I get the myrtle? —oh, yes, in the market, because the season was late, and I wanted roses, but there was not a single rose. . . .

Opening his eyes, to bring the glow of the lamp back upon the dream, he saw the slave-child Prisca standing at the foot of his bed. She was standing shyly, with her head on one side and her hands behind her. On her milky cheek and along the curve of her breast there was a line of yellowish light. "Ah," he said, "I'm glad you came," and was on the point of drawing her into the dream by adding that she should go at once to the house of his mistress and ask there for a certain package of fish wrapped in oily papyrus, which was not actually fish, but his dead heart.

"I've prayed for my lord and master twice a day, every morning and evening."

"Really, Prisca? Whom do you pray to?" he said. And he was ashamed to have asked her such a question: he knew perfectly well to whom she prayed; it was only that he yearned, as a sailor yearns to hear the name of his own city mentioned in a distant port, to hear one of the phrases that had been uttered when he had sat in the little vestibule and waited through the breaking of the bread.

"Oh, I always pray to our Lord Jesus directly, never through angels. There have been some among us who've taken to praying to angels, but our Bishop Fabian said very emphatically that we—" She shook her head at herself and fell silent, her eyes dark with self-reproach. "But God forbid I should talk at you and make you tired. I only came to see whether you were asleep," she said. "The Lord watch you and keep you and cause His countenance to shine upon you through this night."

As she passed his bed on her way to the door, he saw that her nails were dark with earth: she had been helping her father with the bulbs or some such winter garden task. He pondered remotely the realization that he might not have lived to see the resurrection of whatever it was that Prisca and Sylvanus had laid in the dark earth, and he thought vaguely of flowers and the delicate names of flowers—crocus, narcissus, hyacinth, violet. He could hear her humming somewhere outside. Doubtless she was out there in the corridor where he had seen her that morning in the growing, pulsing brightness of the dawn, and it was good to have her there, to think of her scrubbing the combs or polishing the rings. . . .

The world had begun to impinge upon him. His mother, flushed and a little giddy with an unequivocally favorable report from the physician came in one morning and said there had been three days when nobody had expected him to live, three days—she mentioned it with something of the old, abused self-righteousness in her face—when she had gone so far as to ask him whether he had wanted to see Charis, and he had repeatedly refused. Had she asked him, and had he rejected the offer? He remembered nothing about it, and yet there was that in his heart which kept him from calling her a liar. Now that he searched back over his nightmares, he thought he could recall a recurring image of Charis, with a man's cloak cast over her nakedness, and her face swollen with drunken sleep and pitiful with regret. "What did I say when you asked whether Charis should come?" he asked. And now that she was no longer seeing him on his funeral bier malice triumphed; malice narrowed her eyes and tightened the corners of her soft, pale lips. "Nothing much," she said, carefully tucking the coverlet around his feet. "Only that you wouldn't see her. Only that you hoped you'd never see her as long as you lived."

But that was the violence of some vision, he thought, staring at the noonday ceiling. That was the harshness of pain. If God had eyes and could see my heart, He would know that I do not reject her. It is only that I cannot deal with her now, not in this weariness. . . .

And in the late afternoon they brought him a visitor, Ummidius Pessinus, who began by pretending that the sickness had been very light, of no concern to anybody, really, and ended by shedding tears over the blessed and unbelievable recovery. During the first half hour their talk was lively enough—there were warm good wishes from the "clever ones" and polite good wishes from the others; there was the report that two legions had been ordered into Dacia out of Thrace; there was news of the censorship, if one could call it news: the old lump of fat was doing what everybody had known he would, was procrastinating and equivocating and suggesting that nothing excessive be done at the moment—a few of the most blatant offenders dragged into court and used as examples ought to be enough . . . But then the conversation turned halting and desultory. Possibly because both of them were studiously avoiding any mention of Decius, they found themselves discussing such trivialities as the vast amount of incense the Pontifex Maximus had bought at the State's expense for the festival of the Deified Emperors and the squabble going on between the Empress Etruscilla and the wife of the Secretary of the Imperial Treasury. And when the visitor withdrew—he had stayed too long, shamefacedly, wistfully, plainly hoping that some miracle would release the old vital exchange between them—it was good to go back to silence, to be weak and to know that the day of returning to the little dining room was a long way off, to ask that the curtains be drawn again and to fall into a semi-sleep.

After the evening meal—they allowed him a little shredded lamb and bread for the evening meal—he exasperated the physician and drove Drusilla out of the room in distraction by insisting that he was well enough to read. To strain one's eyes when one was tired, said the physician, was to do permanent damage to one's sight. There were six members of the household who could have read aloud to him in either Latin or Greek, but he rejected them one by one, making petulant complaints to his mother about this one's stance and that one's voice, unable to admit his real reason: that nobody but Charis had read to him in the last three years and that to accept this service from anybody else would be a kind of betrayal. He abandoned the whole idea of reading when his mother suggested another sort of diversion: more than a dozen gifts had been left at the palace for him during his illness, and three slaves were dispatched to bring them up from the atrium and arrange them on one of the carved chests. There was essence of balsam in a vial from Cleander and essence of cinnamon in a box from the Secretary of the Privy Purse. There were fleece-lined boots from Berosus, and there was a leather scroll-cover from Valerian, and he was sick of it as soon as it had begun—the unwrapping and the showing and the forced and excessive praise, every name a new burden to him, another reason to wish himself asleep. And yet, when the exhibition was over and he had driven his mother out with yawns and sighs of boredom, he grew inordinately curious about the packages that stood, still unwrapped, on the chest. "That thing behind the lamp—that little thing—what do you suppose that could be?" he said to Baubio.

"It looks like a jar of some kind, my lord and my master. Shall I bring it? Would you like to see?"

"No, it makes no difference. Do you know who sent it?"

"Yes, your cousin Paulina. She sent it with the lady Drusilla. The lady Drusilla went to visit her yesterday afternoon."

Did they talk of me? he thought, and suddenly his heart began to race, out of an unaccountable mingling of fright and exhilaration.

Once the wrappings were removed—he would not permit Baubio to take them off, he untied the string and laid back the folds of the papyrus himself—once the wrappings were removed, he saw that it *was* a jar, a little unglazed pottery jar, sealed at the top with wax. It was filled with honey, to judge by the faint tang of sweetness that could be sniffed around the lid. It was strangely gratifying to touch; and when Baubio's back was turned, he brushed it slowly across his mouth, and the smoothness of it was like the cool smoothness of a cheek.

"Shall I take away the wrappings, my lord and my master?"

"No," he said irritably. "Why are you always cleaning up everything? Let them alone."

"Would you like me to open the jar for you? If it's honey, maybe you'd like a little of it on some bread."

"Maybe. A little later. I'll hold it. I like the feel of it."

And he turned over on his side and pretended to drowse off, but not before he had put the papyrus under his elbow and the jar between his shoulder and his chin, so that nobody could take them away without rousing him out of his sleep.

He returned then to the dream of the fish. He began close to the end of it, since the time of quiet exile was growing short, and he was justified now in dreaming to the conclusion because the little jar was there under his chin, yielding not only the fragrance of honey but also the delectable fragrance of that remembered hour. He had come on a world's-end evening to the house of his cousin Paulina. He and all the rest of mankind knew that it was evening only because somebody had been appointed to count off the hours; the sun had already been quenched and the moon had gone out and all the hours of the day and the night were the same—a blackness broken only by the light of a few remaining stars, a silence broken only by the distant rumble of falling mountains and the slowly advancing roar of the sea.

Behind the curtain that divided the vestibule from the inner room, there were sounds of preparation. Some were going forth out of the ruin of the earth—how and where, he did not know—and those of the household of

224

Probus and Paulina were among the ones who were to depart. "By and by," said the ancient steward, "she will come out to you, as soon as she has distributed the shrouds to those that are to stay behind." And he sat on the iron bench and listened for her voice among the other voices and stared through the open door at the black sky crossed now and then by the white trail of a falling star.

But he hoped, he earnestly hoped, that she would not be too long about it. In the unstirring air of these Last Times, the piece of wrapped fish that he held on his knees could not long escape decay. Her hands are delicate, like a child's, he thought, and they are scrubbed, too, for the setting forth, and it would be a great pity if any unseemly odor came through the papyrus onto her fingertips . . . But when he bent over and sniffed the package, there was only the scent of wax and honey.

The curtain parted and a procession passed through the vestibule: the Bishop Fabian, the elder Moyses, twelve virgins in white with crowns of myrtle on their new-washed hair, two young men carrying baskets of bleached grain, another young man carrying a trussed sheep. His cousin Probus, bringing up the rear, stopped in the middle of the blue pavement and drew a deep breath. "There is a strange smell here," he said, "a sweetness with an under-odor of decay. Ah, well, it scarcely matters now." And he stepped with the others into the all-obliterating night.

Now she was coming—he knew she was coming because the silence was suddenly alive with innumerable small and silvery sounds—beetle-sounds and cricket-sounds, such as one hears from the window of a villa in Tibur when one listens to the stillness in the night—and that was very strange, for the last of the grass had withered and all the creatures of the grass were long since dead. She was coming—the light from the inner room lay on her veined temple and her wan cheek; and, in mortal shame at that which he had brought into her house, he covered the parcel with both his hands.

"You must excuse me, my cousin," she said, picking the lint out of her hair. "The shrouds are finished, but the snowy vestments are still to be sewn—three hundred thousand snowy vestments for the saints and the winged messengers around the Throne—"

"Is there one for me?" he asked.

"Two," she said, smiling. "I thought of you while I was sewing, and I laid two aside. Take whichever you like, a vestment or a shroud."

"I also brought you something—"

"I can hear it—it sounds like a cricket. Is that what you brought me?" she asked, holding her head on one side and smiling a child's expectant smile. "Is that what you have there under your hands?"

He remembered then that it was only a piece of rotting fish, and he could not answer in his embarrassment, and the silence that was between them was broken by the rolling, muttering sound of another collapsing mountain—the mountains of Africa, he thought, are falling into the sea. . . .

"You must show it to me at once, whatever you have brought me, my cousin," she said. "Let me see it before the hills are made low and the valleys are made high and the last of the stars have fallen onto the earth."

"It's nothing, my cousin. It's only a piece of fish—"

"But I would like to see it nevertheless."

"No, I beg you. I should never have brought it—"

She bent over him then and laid her hands on his shoulders, and begot a stirring in his body, painful and sweet. She smiled without closing her parted lips, and her breath was in his face—wax and honey and rain and flowers. "God knows," she said with childish earnestness, "my own heart is by no means what it was. In these Last Times, we bring what we can—" She started, because there was another rumbling as of faraway thunder, and the tiles of the pavement shuddered under their feet. "Those were the mountains of Africa," she said, sighing.

"Then kiss me, my cousin. Not on the cheek. On the lips."

As her mouth touched his, he felt, under the oily papyrus, certain faint, almost impalpable undulations, and knew that what he had there was a living heart. "Look what I have brought you," he said in wonder, not taking his lips from hers, saying the words into the wax and honey fragrance of her breath. And, as the pressure of her mouth on his grew stronger, the tremulous motions under his palm also strengthened, became a measured beating, so loud that it sounded above the thunder of the falling heights and the murmur of the incoming sea. . . .

All that night he slept profoundly, serenely, as if all doubts, all questions had been cradled to sleep within him. But when he woke in the glare of the cloudy mid-morning, he woke in a state of sensitivity and alertness so acute that it was soon transformed into irritability. That day he was more capricious than he had ever been in his life: he ordered lamb broth and found that he had an appetite for mussels instead; he sent for a novel and promptly sent it back again, feeling that what he had actually wanted was poetry; he got up and put on a new dalmatica of olive-green silk, meaning to leave his room and wander through the house; then, deciding on the threshold that he was too weak to walk, he left the splendid garment in a heap on the floor, and went back to bed. "It's useless trying to do anything for you. You don't know what you want," his mother said. And suddenly he did know: those mysteries which had taken place behind the glowing curtain—he wanted to understand them; he wanted just such a little book as he had seen in the tenement; he wanted it urgently, at once, so that its contents could be fully known, fully comprehended, before he was left alone with dreams again that night . . . "Where's the gardener Sylvanus? Come to think of it, I haven't seen him in weeks," he said.

"Sylvanus? He's out in back of the house, cutting me some myrtle."

"I'd like to have some myrtle for that vase by the window. You're going down to your office, aren't you? Have somebody tell him to bring me a bunch of myrtle," he said.

As soon as she was gone, he got out of bed in his tunic and began to pace the floor. The room was empty at the moment, but somebody was sure to blunder in before the gardener could come—the physician, Drusilla, Baubio. He picked up the olive-green dalmatica and laid it in the chest, he set the jar of honey on a table, he folded the papyrus wrappings and laid them under a jewel-box, he puffed up the pillows and straightened the coverlet. Now, he thought, nobody can use the everlasting business of straightening up as an excuse for coming in . . . And nobody did; there was nobody there when the gardener Sylvanus, his mobile, sun-burned face showing above an armful of myrtle, appeared at the door.

He could hardly restrain himself while the slave was making the usual speech of gratification over the master's recovery. I'm behaving very strangely, he told himself; he'll wonder why I should be walking the floor like this; and he sat down on the side of the bed. "It was a fever of the lungs," he said, and knew by the question in the vague Celtic eyes that he had not answered to the point.

"You'll soon be yourself again, my master and my lord. Where would you like me to put the myrtle?"

"Over there by the window. Now that my eyes aren't sore anymore, I suppose I'll sit there and read."

"It's a good thing that my lord can read again. It helps to pass the time."

"It hasn't helped at all, really." He waited, watching narrowly, until the slave's back was turned, until the myrtle was in the vase and the blond head was bent critically over the dark sprays. "Everything seems unspeakably boring, to tell the truth. No matter what I'm reading, I keep wanting something else."

"Is there something I could get for you in the library?" The tendinous, earth-stained hand moved expertly in the foliage.

"No . . ." His heart was actually pounding at the base of his throat. "In fact, I thought I'd borrow a book from you, if you'd be kind enough. There's a certain little book about Jesus of Nazareth—it's in Greek, it's sewed together with a string—"

But the slave had straightened and wheeled round, his face blank with fright. "A book about Jesus of Nazareth? I don't know what you mean—"

He was mildly exasperated. "Oh, come now, you know it makes no difference to me if you belong to that cult," he said. "I'm only asking for the book because I'm curious and want to read it. It's just the same to me as if I asked for the life of Appolonias of Tyana at the Library of Trajan."

"No, my lord and my master." He raised his hand and picked at his trembling lip. "No, it's not quite the same."

"Why not? Surely you're not expecting a persecution?" He felt the same reasonless anger as he had given way to when his mother had warned him against giving money to the Christians. "Nobody who knows anything about it believes there's going to be a persecution."

"I wish to God," said the gardener fervently, "that all of us were as much at ease on that score as my master and my lord."

"People are always upsetting themselves. It's almost as though they enjoyed being frightened. There hasn't been any trouble of that sort in Rome for sixty years. Besides, I would have thought you could trust me—"

"Oh, I trust my master, it isn't anything like that." It was said in a flat voice, without conviction.

"Then, if you own one of those books, I wish you'd let me have it."

The slave plucked a dead leaf from one of the sprays, wiped his fingers on his tunic, and came and stood near the bed. "I have a Gospel according to Saint Luke," he said in a whisper. "I'll go and get it for my master, since he wants it. But I'll not be at peace until I have it back again."

"I promise you I'll not show it to anybody. If anybody happens to come in, I'll hide it. You can come and take it away before sunset. I'll finish it by sunset, so that you can eat your evening meal in peace."

It was a good half hour before the Gospel was brought in—long enough for his nervous excitement to change to a charged expectancy. The strong and living sorrow of the mourners on the rubble heap, the delectable conviction of utter peace that had come upon him in the vestibule, the glow, the fragrances, the vibrant certainty of their voices lifted up in the breaking of the bread—it was as if the little book could yield them all. If it was a grimy book, egg-stained and wine-stained and marked by many unwashed hands, if the Greek was crude and the penmanship was childish, he touched it nevertheless with reverent fingers, as one touches the rough bark of the cinnamon tree, knowing that an exquisite essence will arise. For a long time he paced the length of his chamber, unwilling to give up this first rich savoring, stopping now and again to spell out a strange eastern name— Zacharias, Elisabeth, Joanna—closing his tired eyes and evoking an image— fisherman's net in the shining waters, madman walking among the whited tombs, thin hand over the eyelids of the blind, a solitary Mourner grieving over the foredoomed destruction of Jerusalem. . . .

It was only after he had settled down and begun to read from the beginning that the radiance fell away. He sat up in bed with his back against heaped pillows and the Gospel on his knees—shaken, embarrassed, knowing that he had been cheated, more than a little ashamed of himself. The opening paragraph—somebody named Luke had written it to somebody named Theophilus—had a certain fervent earnestness. But that was short-lived; with the coming on of Zacharias and Elisabeth it was gone. This was only another account of miraculous doings in a far country: the world was intolerable, and those who claimed to be able to save it were coming on by the dozen; every year or so another winged messenger appeared to another just man in Thrace or Phrygia or Galatia to say that the awaited Healer was about to be born. And Elisabeth and Zacharias had not even begotten this particular Savior: their son John was only a forerunner, dispatched by God to say that His authentic Offspring was about to appear. There was still another angel and still another annunciation—a certain Mary was informed in so many words that she had conceived by Divinity—and it was difficult to read about her protests and her wonderment without impatience. Was Bethlehem so far from the highway that she had never heard of a single one of all those saints and prophets born of the wombs of virgins for the saving of the world?

No, it was nothing—he would have laid the book aside if he had not been drawn on in spite of himself by the Son of Man, by the suffering of the driven dedicated spirit. The white veil of magic that Luke had spun around Him—it could not contain Him, He wrenched it apart. His voice, His look, His exhorting hand tore through the fibrous fabric on almost every page. Tormented with knowledge and desperate with the need to teach, He was a perpetual wanderer: foxes had holes, and the birds of the air had nests, but the Son of Man had nowhere to lay His head. He could not hide Himself—the needy ones were always pressing upon Him; His yearning soul went out of Him to the benighted and the forgotten and left Him depleted; He ate His harried meal among publicans and sinners, and was forever weary, and prayed, and could not sleep. Unlike the other Healers, He was seldom renewed with the bread and converse of angels. If the Spirit of His Father in Heaven sometimes descended upon Him, it was only to give Him strength to go on with the everlasting spending of Himself. From the doorsills of cottages, from hillocks in the wilderness, from the rocking prows of fishermen's boats, He flung out His terrible knowledge as the husbandman flings grain—and His words, spoken in urgency to His little ones, had the ring of absolute authenticity. They had not been muted, they had not been tampered with; they were all of one pitch, one mode; the impact of the world had wrung them all from the same strong, living heart.

Yet when he took these pronouncements out of their alien and strangely moving context, when he tried to see them arranged, like the Stoic rules for the decent life, in a column on a page, they also lost their power. What do they have to do with me? he asked himself. I do not have the sins that Jesus of Nazareth came to pluck out of the hearts of men. I am not a hypocrite—not that it is any credit to me: the son of Celestus Falconius was bound to be pushed by sheer disgust onto the side of simple truth. I am not covetous nor vainglorious, either. The money-bags in my mother's office, her insatiable hunger for prestige and power—these, too, I detested and deserted long ago; my soul found another home for itself in the frugal household of the Decii. I am not to my clients what a certain rich man was to the beggar Lazarus who asked for the crumbs under his table. I am not to the peasants of Egypt what the Levite was to the man who lay dying on the road to Jericho. Nobody ever asked me for bread and was given a stone. Whatever is called for here, I have known and followed beforehand, and still I wander like a bloodless spirit through the mazes of a life that has become a meaningless dream. . . .

He fell to pondering then why it was that thousands had committed themselves to this Gospel, why hundreds had given themselves over for the sake of this Gospel to exile or the rack or the beasts or the fire. Surely, he thought, not all of them were recalled by it from cruel indifference. Surely not all of them were hypocrites, taught for the first time here to look upon their naked hearts with unsparing eyes. Prisca, Paulina, the evasive Sylvanus, the rueful little Jew, the self-distrusting Probus and the serene Fabian—it had taken something more than a set of moral precepts to draw so varied a company to the table of the Lord. And he turned again to the story of the Son of Man Himself: that and that only, so far as he could see, could have moved them all. He began at the triumphal entry into Jerusalem—the palm-strewn streets, the Hosannas, the Passover pilgrims shouting "Blessed is He that cometh in the name of the Lord." And, having begun, he could not turn aside; he must follow Him again to the end of His bitter, foreseen, and accepted destiny, through the final supper eaten with friends in a borrowed room, through the sweating agony on the Mount of Olives, through the senseless travesty in the courts, to the desertion and the loneliness and the thirsty torment of the Cross. He saw now that the story of those final days was told not with disillusionment but with exaltation. Not Luke alone—He also, He Himself—had transmuted that shame into a triumph, had made a mystic consummation of the death-walk to the hill outside the city walls. And here, here—he got out of bed and carried the book to the window, as if the cloudy light at the window could help him see to the core of the mystery—precisely here, in this capacity for turning the wreckage of His life into glory, lay His power with a generation of vipers, with all the blind and leprous children of a perishing earth. To be despised, to go hungry, to go naked, to suffer all that those who inhabit a collapsing world are bound to suffer—these misfortunes are to be received with rejoicing, since he who has nothing on earth lays up treasure for himself where there are neither moths nor rust. Lose your child on earth and find him again clothed in splendor at God's footstool. Be spat upon in the streets of Rome and gain for yourself the greetings of angels in the streets of Paradise. Throw away a clouded, transitory life and receive in return an everlasting morning, when they that have mourned are comforted and they that have been cast down rise up in joy before the crucified Son of Man, crowned now with a starry crown. . . .

But, resting his head against the window frame and gazing at the coppery light of the sunset on the upper branches, he knew with a terrible certainty what he had known first as a child when he had seen a dead horse dragged out of the stable: that death was inescapable and absolute, that all that he was, both his flesh and the bright images begotten in his brain, were destined to be obliterated in the shut darkness of the tomb. The Kingdom of Heaven was for those fortunate ones who were able to deceive themselves. He knew what he was, he bore about with him the knowledge of his own mortality; and nothing—no miracle, no revelation, no host of witnesses, no ecstasy—could give him any portion in the Kingdom of Heaven. The hour of the evening meal was drawing on, and, staring across the garden at the distant hills, he thought how thousands were sitting down to their bacon and lentils in sufficiency and peace, telling themselves that man does not live by bread alone, receiving in their hearts the immaterial food of a promised Paradise. And it is good for them, they are happy, he thought. All that was futile and tawdry in their lives is given purpose and dignity. What insight He must have had to discover so potent a formula for His little ones! How soundly He wrought for these Last Times! The apotheosis of suffering—what an unassailable thing it is and will remain, even when the stars begin to rain out of the sky, even when the mountains of Africa fall into the sea, even unto the end of the world. . . .

A single cricket chirped from the dry, clipped hedges. A rack of clouds showed pink behind the metallic leaves of the sycamores. He saw an image of the two of them—Probus and Paulina—floating hand in hand above the garish branches, and the vision was like the slow coming on of a sickness—a clouding of the sight, a vague nausea, an ominous slowing of the heart. He saw her face, rigid with enforced cheerfulness; he saw her wan cheeks and her heaven-drawn eyes, and he asked himself: What was it that came over me that I should have given her so much grace in a dream? The other faces also—the tear-drenched faces of the mourners on the rubble pile— passed one by one across his consciousness, and all of them were equivocal, disturbing, weakly and softly sweet. . . .

And quickly, fearfully, as he had stepped back from the edge of the Aventine plateau when he sensed that the rank sweetness coming up from the Murcia valley was the sweetness of decay, so he stepped back from the window. The Gospel, the cricket-sound, the jar of honey—he rejected them all, and with them the shimmer of the dying world made bright by tears. He was tired, he was actually trembling, but for the first time since his illness he seated himself upright in a chair. What have I to do with them? he asked himself, closing his fingers hard on the ivory heads of the carved lions. She and Probus and all the rest of them—what do they do but nourish themselves on human wretchedness? How would it be with them if a golden era of peace and plenty were to come? If no tenement ever collapsed, if the vine and the olive flourished, if wars and rumors of wars were utterly silenced, if heralds bearing good reports came upon one another's heels out of the provinces—then what would they do with themselves? If justice and mercy were meted out to all the citizens of a happy world—then what would become of their Kingdom of Heaven?

This life that I labor through with such perplexity and pain—how easy it is for *them,* he thought, still sitting tense and upright in his chair. Always the same answer—for the cities that stand in the shadow of the Gothic forests and the peasants that starve in the province of Egypt, for the sinners who have lost the savor of their sins and the lovers who can no longer love and the poets who have ceased to write poetry—always the same answer, sovereign and simple: Die and inherit the Kingdom of Heaven. A child's answer, a coward's answer, he thought, letting his fist come down on the lion's head. Such an answer as would convince nobody but ineffectual men and unfulfilled women, poverty-stricken artisans and hopeless slaves. And if any rational man accedes to it, he accedes to it only out of utter weariness, only because he has been so confused and tormented by the terrible complexities that he is willing to abandon everything, willing to agree to anything that can give him peace. . . .

And suddenly he could sit still no longer. A growing exasperation made him pace the length of the room and gnaw at the fever-dried skin on his lower lip. Take, for instance, this matter of the tenement, he thought, going over to the clothes chest, pushing up the lid and snatching out the green dalmatica that he had laid away three hours ago. Our tenement collapses in the Via Trajana. I hold myself responsible, I try to make amends, and to some extent I conduct myself like a man in his proper senses: I take a decent sum of money and arrange to have it distributed among the houseless and the maimed and the relatives of the dead. But there, just there, I flounder in weariness or something worse than weariness because I cannot force myself to look steadfastly at the fact of death. I let my reason be lulled into a false and debilitating sense of peace by God knows what—a fragile face, a chanted ritual, the smell of fried fish and baking bread. And while I immerse myself in the glow of the miraculous, the impossible, I am blind—stone blind—to certain obvious possibilities. Why did I never realize until this instant that some general good could be wrested out of that piece of evil, that laws could be passed against the use of green wood lattices and rotten beams, effective laws to forestall another such calamity? How has it been with me? How could I have failed to see what any fool could have seen at once: that I, the Emperor's nephew, a member of the inner circle of the new regime, could go and say to my master and my lord, "Give us such-and-such a building law, and hundreds will be saved"?

He was dressing now, he was hastily, vigorously dressing. He was draping the folds of the olive-green dalmatica, he was girding in the waist with a white leather belt, he was jerking the sleevebands deftly into place as if, by putting on such clothes as a man might wear in the street, he could guarantee his return to the world. Oh, I have been a child and a fool, he thought, looking about him for a certain pair of soft sandals. To turn against

232

him in bitterness, to close him out of my mind because he chose Valerian, to fling down all my hopes with the one hope of the censorship—that was the petulant, self-destructive violence of a sick man or a child . . . The thought of the unsettled affair of Drusilla and Herennius, coming suddenly upon him, clouded his ardor. But she's going to Epidaurus, she said she would be glad to go to Epidaurus, he told himself. One way or another, in mind or in body, the girl is sick, and he can scarcely blame me for that. In fact—he smiled a little at the thought—he may very well regret the way he has behaved to me since the feast of the Saturnalia: silence, utter silence —no gift, not so much as a stick of cinnamon, no kindly letter, no imperial good wishes—nothing at all these last three weeks from the Decii to the Herennii—

Now that he was dressed, he found himself very tired, so tired that he had an almost irrepressible impulse to stretch himself across the bed. But he did not permit himself any such indulgence: he sat in the ivory chair again and called for Baubio and ordered the evening meal—not the minced and watery garbage they had been sending up to him for weeks, he said. He was better, he was completely recovered, he wanted roast pheasant, some beans done in vinegar, three or four hot rolls, and a cup of undiluted Cretan wine.

Night came, and Sylvanus came to take away his Gospel. "It's there under the pillow. Nobody saw it," he told the slave. "You could have had it an hour ago—I was finished. I told you I'd hurry so that you could eat your evening meal in peace."

"But I haven't sat down to table yet, my lord and my master. We eat very late, after everybody else is through."

"I should think you'd be very hungry by this time," he said, and told himself sourly that it scarcely mattered. Why don't you put it off until midnight? he thought. Why don't you work up a really agonizing hunger in your guts? That'd be a way to lay up treasure for yourself in the Kingdom of Heaven.

"May the Lord keep you and cause His countenance—"

"Oh, don't deceive yourself. I'm not a Christian, nor likely to be one, either," he said.

Chapter 17

THE EMPEROR Decius could not imagine himself getting up from the table and ushering the censor Valerian out of the little dining room with the expected cordiality. The private conversation between them had gone on uselessly and far too long—the Dean of the Senate was still insisting, as he had insisted two hours ago, that there was nothing to be gained from entering a suit for violation of the censorship against one of the more truculent members of the influential house of the Glabrii. The air of the closed chamber was stale and heavy with unsettled differences. The red light of the January sunset lay on the legal documents spread out between them, on the plump hands folded with exasperating complacency on the edge of the massive table, on the big body, as impressive and imperturbable as the effigy of a dead Republican carved in stone. And on the opposite side of the closed door, others were waiting—the Pontifex Maximus, somebody else whose name he had not even caught when the sickly steward had looked in to announce it, because he had been telling himself in something close to desperation that he must not shout, that it was utterly useless to shout at Valerian. . . .

And why should I want to shout at him? he thought, filling the baffling silence with a show of business—rolling up scrolls, putting the flat sheets of papyrus into a neat pile, taking the quill out of the ink and laying it

234

on the dented wood. Why should I feel, every time the two of us sit face to face like this, that I was cheated? All those virtues, all those singular qualifications that I found in him when I named him censor, he has them still: the years of accrued experience in the Senate, the Roman blood—pure Roman, not mixed and watered down like mine—the unexceptionable life, the serene outlook, the self-assured and dignified bearing, the ancient, almost sacred name. I wanted the perfect patrician and I got the perfect patrician; and if I was so carried away on a disintegrating tide of emotion that I failed to see that the perfect patrician was bound to have patrician interests at heart, I have nobody to blame but myself.

"My lord and my master knows how deeply I am committed to the censorship."

He nodded—there was no reason to doubt it. Hadn't he stored away the famous silver dishes of the Valerii? Hadn't he sold one third of his slaves? Hadn't he seen to it that his young son Gallienus stopped bathing in oil of cassia? Hadn't he talked his brothers and his sisters, his nephews and his nieces out of Chinese silk dalmaticas and embroidered shoes? If he cringed at the notion of upsetting the Metelli, inconveniencing the Reburri, infuriating the Glabrii, that was to be expected. Anybody would have known—anybody but a turnip-farming Pannonian. . . .

"Only it seems to me that it might be wise to wait a few more days."

"No, I'd rather you'd enter the suit tomorrow." It was unfortunate that he had to force the matter. The patrician prejudices of the Dean of the Senate were, like the rest of his qualities, amiable and mild; and probably he could have been argued out of them without offense, if there had only been time. But there was never any time: everything was urgent, everything was desperate; the Pontifex Maximus and somebody else were pacing the atrium, the government offices were in confusion over two pieces of bad news—the Thracian legions were making appallingly bad time on their march to Dacia because of the deplorable condition of the roads, and the legions of Gaul were on the point of mutiny because somebody was tampering with their supplies. No bacon, they complained, a meatless diet for the past three weeks. . . .

"But it'll be hard to find time to go to court tomorrow."

"Find time somehow. Enter it tomorrow and have it over with," he said.

"And yet I have the impression that, if we gave the poor fellow a little more time to think it over, he might mend his ways without a suit. One member of the family—the old lady, Livia Glabria—told me the other day she thought she could argue him into an official apology."

The Emperor stood up, wiped the dust of the scrolls from his fingers, stepped back a little from the table, and shook his head. These procrastinations, these well-meaning equivocations, these bland implications that things would come right if they were only let alone—they had to be countered constantly, they forced him to change suggestions into requests,

requests into downright commands. "Tell the Glabrii it's too late for that sort of thing," he said, and was painfully conscious of the Pannonian dialect that he had used in giving one patrician to understand what he was to tell another. "Enter the suit. Nobody's exempt. They're not above the welfare of the State—not the Glabrii or anybody else."

"As you say, my lord and my master." He heaved himself out of his chair, resting his weight on the edge of the massive table; and his pink and fleshy face, coming up into a slant of reddish sunset, looked, quite unbelievably, baffled and tired. Slowly—more wearily than ponderously now, weighed down by the ill feelings of the best families—he made his way to the door.

Now that he was alone, the Emperor sat down again, resting his forehead against his closed fist. He could imagine the Pontifex Maximus pacing the colonnade in the atrium, his jaundiced and sanctimonious face more pained than usual because he had had to wait so long. He could have come unannounced this afternoon only because he meant to make a plague of himself about his accursed edict—it hadn't been written, it hadn't even been properly considered. A month ago, so he told himself, he could not have imagined a time when he would wish to avoid a talk with the Pontifex Maximus. His exasperation with the man dated back to the feast of the Saturnalia; one of the events of that too-eventful day had led the jaundiced scholar to say a good many things that should have been left unsaid. He had drawn far-reaching conclusions from the plebes' complaints about the fare on the imperial table; he had implied, with a glint of satisfaction in his unhealthy yellow eyeballs, that something exciting, something drastic ought to be done to capture the imagination of the lowest class. At breakfast he had suggested a religious revival with a public banquet and sacrifices to the genii of Rome and the Emperor. By the hour of the evening meal, hectic and belligerent with the wine that always aggravated his condition, he was hinting at a persecution of the Christians.

And why, why, the Emperor asked himself, had they ever discussed the miserable sect? Unmentioned, they had remained for him only a part of the vast multitude of misguided idiots who wasted their energies on foreign gods. Singled out, they were—as he had been forced to admit—quite different from the worshippers of Mithras and Isis and Cybele. The Pontifex Maximus and his priestly associates had plenty of proof that they held the authority of their Scriptures over and above the authority of the State: very few of them used the courts anymore, and some of them in the legions, confusing war with murder, had been known to throw down their swords on the battlefield in plain sight of their centurions. And, in the confusion of the Saturnalia feast, he had somehow permitted himself to be maneuvered into saying he would issue some sort of edict that would serve to test their loyalty. The worst part of the whole affair was that the Pontifex Maximus, by his irresponsible blabbing and his awkward timing, had made it seem that he, Decius, was willing to persecute the Christians out of political expediency. Such an edict as he had promised would inevitably look like a sop to the plebes—an equivocal promise of games, Nero's kind of games, to pay off for the poor Saturnalia table, the beef and sour wine and home-made bread.

No, he would not see the man this afternoon, not raw and out of temper as he was, not harried as he was by the bacon mutiny and the reports of the bad roads . . . He went to the door and jerked it open with such sudden force that the steward, who had been resting his weary back against it, stumbled and turned and gave him a long look of affronted dignity.

"I'm sorry to inform the Lord of the World that the Pontifex Maximus could not wait," said the steward. "I believe his feelings were a little hurt."

"I'm tired of his and everybody else's feelings." He was suddenly conscious of a trembling at the back of his knees. "I'm going to wash my face. There's half an hour left before the evening meal, and I think I'll sleep."

"But there's another visitor, my lord and master, as I told you—"

"So you did. But so save my life I can't remember his name."

"Your nephew, the illustrious Favorinus Herennius."

He sank down into the chair again and smote himself twice in the middle of the brow. "Not now, not at the end of such a day," he said, less to the steward than to the gods. And yet if the young man, only lately out of his sickbed, had come, uninvited, like a common pleader—"Well, if he's here, he's here," he said, rubbing his flushed and itching face on the sleeve of his toga. "Naturally, I'll see him, only he'll have to wait. Not long, just until I've cleared my mind a bit. Give me about a quarter of an hour."

Left alone now, he gave way completely to his weariness; he folded his arms on the top of the table and rested his head against them, trying to ease his tired eyes in the closed area of dark. But there was no ease, no quiet, no sense of renewal. He could only accuse himself and his raw and touchy pride. To have stayed away from the palace of the Herennii the three long weeks of his nephew's illness, to have inquired about him only in a roundabout fashion—that was unnecessarily harsh, that had indicated downright enmity. And yet, since the young man had seen fit to go down into his sickness without a word about Drusilla, there had been nothing else to do— he could scarcely have presented himself, as if he excused everything, at the foot of Favorinus's bed. What it was that he had to excuse, he could not define with too much clarity. If the Drusilla affair had gone awry, Favorinus could scarcely be blamed for that: if there were objections, they had probably come from the girl herself. So his wife Etruscilla had told him, suggesting in that frightened, tentative, annoying way of hers that it would be only common decency to make a call or send a slave. And now the time for it was past, and the poor young man, sick as he was and probably apprehensive, had been out there in the atrium for the better part of an hour.

He raised his head because a yellowish glow had invaded his area of dark.

The red tinge of sunset had faded from the room, and the steward had been in and out again to set a lamp on the table. It was some moments before he became aware of the figure standing in the doorway, a little beyond the reach of the lamplight—emaciated, strangely stern, and markedly changed.

"Favorinus?"

"Yes, my uncle."

"Come in, come in and sit down. You must be tired."

The young man walked deliberately round to the other side of the table. Perhaps he was afraid of taking liberties because he considered himself in disfavor; perhaps his wounded feelings prompted him to keep his distance—from his stiff and formal bearing it was impossible to tell. His face, with the light of the lamp falling full upon it now, showed almost frightening transformations: the cheeks were as hollow as the cheeks of some self-starved devotee of Isis: the eyes were bloodshot and seemed to have sunken into their sockets; the lips had lost their chaste and precise outline, were indefinite and fever-dried. And the eyes, staring into his across the flame, were eloquent only of things lost. He waited until he had been given the imperial nod before he let himself down onto the edge of one of the dining couches. "How has it been with my uncle these last weeks?" he said.

"Well—well enough, I suppose. I've had my troubles—" He knew of a sudden that he wished desperately to speak of these troubles, that there on the other side of the table was the one man left to whom he could still speak freely, openly, from the heart. "The news from the north is as bad as it was when you left. It seems to us now that Kniva will probably attack early this spring—" He broke off, partly because any mention of the Gothic frontier seemed likely to evoke the painful subject of his son Herennius, partly because he remembered that he had not yet spoken of his nephew's illness or of his own stubborn refusal to show his face at the palace of the Herennii. "But how is it with you? I had a day-to-day report on you from Pessinus. Are you completely recovered now?" he said.

"Oh, yes. They tell me I'm completely better, and I suppose I am. I think I'd have been better long ago if it hadn't been for the shock of that business on the Saturnalia—"

He started. Surely his nephew was not tactless enough to ask him outright why he had chosen Valerian. "The business on the Saturnalia? What business was that?"

"Our tenement in the Via Trajana—it collapsed, you know. The front wall came down in the middle of the night."

He found it hard to keep himself from striking his forehead again. He had known, of course—Etruscilla had drummed his ears with the details of the affair for days—and yet he had completely forgotten, probably because he had chosen to forget. Now he recalled that he had reacted to the news with a surly comment that there was no need to talk about it so much—

knowing, no doubt, that the young man would talk about it endlessly, would weary one with his burden of guilt for the houseless and the maimed and the dead . . . Some other time, not now, he thought, some other time, when I'm not so harassed, not so tired . . . And yet the silence demanded some sort of answer. "Yes, that was very unfortunate," he said. "But you distress yourself too much about these things, Favorinus. It's like those gladiators at your father's memorial games last September—"

"No, really, my uncle. This is something quite different. This time it was clearly my responsibility."

He sighed and looked down at his fingers and saw that they were tapping out a rhythm of hard-maintained patience on the scarred wood.

The young man's glance also settled on the hand, and he also sighed. "My uncle is annoyed with me," he said.

And there it was between them—the three-week-old dilemma. It was impossible to say, "No, not in the least"—that would imply not only that there was abundant leisure in a world like this for grieving over toppled buildings, but also that the Decii were willing to wait endlessly for an answer from the Herennii.

"My uncle is annoyed with me because I never brought him an answer." The eyes forced themselves up to encounter his for an instant, and then withdrew. "For weeks now I've owed you an answer—"

Suddenly he did not want it. He had a ridiculous impulse to request that it be put into writing and brought to him by a slave.

"My uncle will know how bitterly disappointed I am to tell him my sister is in no condition to consider marriage—"

"No? Why not?" It was loud, it was harsh, it was altogether pointless—it only exposed his own agitation and made the young man start.

"Because she's sick—"

"Sick? I hadn't heard anything about it."

"No, I realize that. Nobody could have told you but I myself, and I was ill. Besides—" There was a lifting of the chin, a proud stiffening of the shoulders. "Besides, it's not the sort of sickness we would want to publish from the housetops, my master and my lord."

"Then I'm not to be informed about the nature of the sickness?" He asked it sharply, coldly—and reproached himself at once. If the girl was ailing, which might well be the case—since by his own will he knew nothing of recent goings-on in the palace on the Palatine—then he ought to feel some concern, some regret. But he felt nothing—nothing but rage at the Herennii, who never showed their weaknesses, who always presented themselves as sound and self-sufficient.

"Certainly you're to know, my uncle. I had every intention of telling you, but how to describe it I don't quite know. It's not a sickness of the body, though she's quite thin—emaciated, really, and that's no wonder—she scarcely eats, she almost never sleeps. It's a sickness of the mind, a sickness of the spirit. I wouldn't call her mad or possessed—that would be stating it too strongly, but more and more she seems detached from the world. During the time I was sick, it grew much worse, so bad in fact that there isn't anything left to do but send her to Epidaurus for the change and the cure and the rest. Maybe the priests there can help her—they've been known to help others. We—my mother and I, I mean—feel utterly helpless—"

For an instant he saw an image of the young woman's face as he had seen it on the evening of Celestus Falconius's memorial games—a drained, white, rigid face, less living than the ostentatious display of pearls in the ears and at the brow. Had there been madness in it? Probably, very probably. It was preposterous to think that her brother could have invented so distressing, so terrible a lie. And yet, and yet—he rose and turned his back and walked to the open window—he could not, he did not even wish to rid himself of the notion that he was being affronted, led about, played upon. "When I brought the unfortunate matter up, back there in the beginning," he said without turning to look over his shoulder, looking instead at the empty garden, "how far gone was she then?"

"It's hard to say. It takes a long time before you begin to notice. Now that we know, we look back and remember all sorts of things that didn't seem particularly strange when they happened—"

It was sad, it was raw, somebody was bound to be hurt and humiliated unless he abandoned it at once, unless he turned back from the window and said some kind, conciliatory thing and led the conversation on to something else. And yet he could not help himself. "Was she so far gone that you decided not to consult her about the matter I mentioned?" he said

"No, my uncle. No, she was consulted. That same week, I asked her about it myself."

"Really?" His anger leaped out and fastened on a technicality. "I thought I'd said specifically that some woman friend of hers was to introduce the business. What made you ask her yourself?"

"I don't know. I suppose I thought it would be better—"

"Why?" He was shouting, he was shouting out of the window into the garden. "To save the Decii an additional embarrassment in case she should refuse?"

"I didn't know that she'd refuse—I simply thought—"

He could feel the blood of his anger pulsing in the swollen vein in the middle of his forehead. "Then I'm to take it that she *did* refuse?"

"Yes, she refused, my lord and my master. She refused because nothing's real to her anymore, nothing except the past. She refused, and I couldn't bring myself to come and tell you at once, because I was afraid, and afterwards I was sick—"

"Afraid?" He wheeled around and saw the hunched figure as a blur of whiteness—his fury was actually clouding his sight. "Why? Because you thought I would be hurt? Put yourself at ease—there are plenty of women in the world who would be only too glad to marry the heir to the purple, even if nobody is available from the house of the Herennii—"

"I know that, my uncle."

"I hope you know it." He forced his eyes to focus on the young man's face. There was pity in it—insulting pity, and a false, scared humility. "To tell the truth, the more I see of you the more I'm convinced that you know absolutely nothing. One gives you a simple errand to run, and you blow it up out of all proportions, you blunder, you make a mess of it—"

"Everything you say may be perfectly true." The fine, narrow body drew itself up in all its patrician elegance. "And yet there's no reason for you to shout at me as if I were a galley-slave."

But there was no reason for him to tolerate such insolence, even from the most highborn of the patricians. "I take it you've told me what you came to tell me? I take it you're ready to go now?" he said.

"No, I haven't told you what I came to tell you—"

He could not find the voice to answer; he was stricken speechless by the arrogance. The young man knew perfectly well that the question had been hurled at him in rage and irony. That he should have the effrontery to reply as if it had been asked in good faith, to sit straight-shouldered on the other side of the table, showing no sign—no, it was unbelievable, nobody but the son of Sabina and Celestus Falconius—

"There was another matter, a very urgent matter—"

Urgent indeed, he thought, if the rejection of an imperial marriage is to be relegated to second place for it.

"It grew more or less out of the business of our tenement in the Via Trajana—"

"Your tenement?" He was shouting again. He was standing directly opposite his nephew, with only the carved back of his own chair and the breadth of the table between, but he was shouting as he might have shouted from the rostrum of a camp. "I'm sick of hearing about your tenement. Nobody, not even the Herennii, can raise the dead. So resign yourself to it, accept it like a man—accept it as I had to accept the legionaries left on the battlefield and the Egyptian peasants who starved to death or hanged themselves. And, if you can't accept it, go reason it out with one of your Stoic idiots, go find some priest of Mithras and have it washed away in bull's blood. Only don't bring it to me, I don't want it—I haven't the heart, I haven't the time. Not with six Gothic tribes united under Kniva, not with the Gallic legions in revolt over their stolen bacon, not with the censorship bogging down in a mass of delays and excuses and lies—"

"What you say is perfectly true, my lord and my master." The grave voice, breaking into the first breathless pause in his ranting, reproved him with its control and dignity. "Those who died in our tenement—they're buried and done with. But there are others, thousands of others, all human beings like ourselves—young women who read their foolish little books

241

before they go to sleep, artisans who hurry out of their rooms every morning with no time to erase the hollows of their bodies from their beds. Children, too—thousands of half-starved children, and every one of them with a world of his own locked up in his head—unique, never to be found again anywhere else. And at least a tenth of them, if I know my City, lie down in mortal peril every night because there are rotten beams in their ceilings, because it's cheap and still within the limits of the law to paste a little plaster on a lattice of green wood and call it a wall—"

"What has all that to do with me? Your mother's friends—the Glabrii, the Metelli, the Reburri—*they're* the ones that own the tenements. Go sing it to them, your little song. *I* never had the wherewithal to buy a rotten five-storey building and crush a crowd of plebes to death in it. *My* trade was less elegant. I'm a Pannonian, of the house of the Decii—remember? We made our living in turnips and hay."

"The families you mention would never listen."

"Oh, then I'm mistaken. I thought everybody would listen to the Herennii."

"A person with his fortune at stake listens to nobody. Nothing will serve—as my uncle knows very well—nothing except the law."

"Then forget it, it's hopeless."

"Why is it hopeless? What's to prevent your legislating such buildings as ours out of existence? Why couldn't we have a law that prevented anybody from building or renting a tenement unless it met certain standards, certain requirements?"

"Now? At a time like this?" His laughter was coarse and cruel, but he could not help it. "A building law—so that's what you're here for? I'm to brush aside such minor matters as the Goths and the censorship and settle down to something practical, something pressing, like setting up standards for mortar and wood?"

"I came to ask for a building law, yes, my uncle. A calamity like the one in the Via Trajana has its importance, even in times like these."

"In the name of all the gods, man, I could swear you're not completely recovered. The most charitable conclusion I can come to is that you're still a little out of your head."

For an instant the long, thin face went white with anger. It was with a visibly painful effort, consciously opening his hands and laying them out before him on the table, that the young man controlled himself. "Perhaps it isn't as ridiculous as my lord and my master thinks," he said. "Even from a purely political point of view, it might be a good move to make."

"How? I'm dull, of course, but I fail to see it."

"It would be popular with the plebes. They'd be certain to line up behind the first Emperor who ever concerned himself about the roof over their heads."

He held his peace and pondered, wishing to believe it. Not that he imagined for an instant that such a law would strengthen his regime—even if it gained a few of the plebes, it would alienate forever the most influential among the senators. Still, it was strangely moving to entertain even briefly the notion that the masses could be grateful for a piece of humane legislation; and he permitted himself to remember what he had forced himself to forget: the pile of gifts on the imperial lawn—the bags of herbs, the singing-birds and monkeys, the belts and sandals, the splintered sticks of cinnamon . . . But afterwards, he thought, afterwards it was another matter—they shouted insults into the palace windows on Saturnalia night; they wrote obscenities on the shrines and the arches; they emptied their bladders against the walls. They said I was a miser, they said I fed them horse-meat at the feast. And it wasn't horse-flesh, it was good fresh beef, and they threw it into the streets, they left it for the dogs, while the Egyptians starve and the legionaries in Gaul are on the point of mutiny for want of meat—

"A law like this, my uncle—a law that comes directly into their lives—don't you think it might very well capture their imagination?" the young man said.

"Imagination? Can you conceive of plebes with imagination? What did they imagine they were doing to the Privy Purse when they took good meat and threw it to the dogs? What did they imagine they were doing to me when they pissed on the walls? Don't tell me about their imagination. Their imagination can be captured by dung and carrion, like the imagination of maggots and flies. Give them burnings, crucifixions, chests tramped in by elephants, legs chewed off by lions—that's the way to capture their imagination!"

He stopped short because some daemon was at him again, had made him say what he would never have said in a moment of sanity. Now, if there were to be an edict against the Christians, if the edict should lead to the usual arrests and the plebes should make the usual demand that the prisoners be used in the arena, there would be one man at least who had heard him say in so many words that games—tyrants' games, Nero's kind of games, would serve his cause.

But—the face on the other side of the lamp showed no surprise, no accusation. He had not heard; after the first sentence, he had simply stopped listening; his eyes, staring directly into the flame, looked almost stupid in their expressionlessness. "Well, then," he said after a long, flat silence, "I've done what I could. I know how harried my lord and my master is, and I'll not take any more of his time."

But he could not send him off like that, shouted at and abused. Not now, not when his patrician poise had collapsed and he sat slumped in his chair with one emaciated hand open before him. "Don't go yet, wait a moment," the Emperor said.

"Yes, my lord and my master?"

"Look, Favorinus—" He pulled out his chair and seated himself, wanting to see the face, unwilling any longer to fling his comments down at the bent head. "Let's say I've handled this badly. Let's say that I'm touchy, raw, out of sorts, almost impossible to deal with this afternoon. But you don't know how it is with me these days—nobody asks himself how it is with me— nobody cares. All day and half the night I sit here facing out the things the rest of you can't bear to face—mutiny, the failure of the crops, the breakdown of the supply lines, Kniva and his six united tribes of Goths. And one after another you come in here to me, not wanting to help, not willing even to listen, every one of you meaning to further some little project of his own. *You* want a building law, and the Secretary of the Privy Purse wants an investigation of the tax-collectors, and Valerian wants to keep on visiting terms with the Reburri and the Glabrii, and my wife wants me to come and eat my supper, and there are times when I can't listen to it anymore."

"I know, my uncle."

"No . . ." He propped his elbows on the edge of the table and pushed his chin down on his closed fists. "No, you don't know. Nobody knows. There's nobody I can talk to anymore, there's hardly anybody I can trust—"

The young man drew himself up, suppressing a sigh. It was plain that the sigh rose from exhaustion, not from boredom; there was genuine sympathy in his face.

"The fact is, I've gotten myself into difficulties, with the expert assistance of the Pontifex Maximus—" The jest was feeble, but his nephew gave it a wan smile. And nothing more was necessary, the smile was enough; of a sudden he found himself giving an account of the whole equivocal, embarrassing business, talking without fear of exposing himself, even stopping now and then to point out how thick-headed he had been, how cleverly and with what daring tactics his adversary had driven him against the wall. And for the first time in weeks, he had a listener: the young man on the other side of the table could not have listened more tensely, more avidly if his life had been at stake in the wretched business. In fact, he was so agitated that he did not even hear his uncle out, but broke in at the first mention of the edict. "Did you go that far, really? Did you promise him that?" he said.

"I suppose you could call it a promise."

"But you don't have to keep it. You can tell him you've changed your mind."

"But I'm not at all sure that I ought to. The arguments are all on his side, you know. The only objection I can think of is a purely personal one: I don't want to see myself in the role of a persecuting tyrant, I intended my reign to revive the old Republican principles, I hate to think of some historian making a kind of Nero out of me. But then I ask myself, what do the Christians care about Republican virtues? The Empire may be facing disaster, but they've washed their hands of it—a person might say they'd secede from the State. And the worst of it is that they make a point of their secession. They've deliberately cut themselves off from any connection with the Empire. I have my evidence, I know. When they have to choose between their Gospels and the Roman Law, they choose their Gospels. They go up before their Bishop with their quarrels—none of them take their cases to our prefects anymore. They even refuse to be recruited in the legions. There have been instances—recorded instances—when Christian legionaries simply wouldn't fight. It's a kind of by-word with them that they have no part in the City—they say their only City is the City of God. What we're dealing with here is actually a kind of open defiance—"

"Oh, but you're wrong, my uncle." One thin hand was pulling at the other, wringing the knuckles, making a cracking sound. "Somebody has deliberately misinformed you. They're not like that—they're an inoffensive lot. They believe a good deal of nonsense, of course, but they're not defiant—in fact, they have a kind of tranquility about them."

For an instant he was left wordless by a weird and incongruous image. He saw his nephew Favorinus Herennius standing with a crowd of plebes in a cemetery, watching attentively while some bearded fanatic broke a loaf of bread in two. It was preposterous, as preposterous as his earlier notion that the poor wretch could have invented the story of his sister's insanity, and he dismissed it at once, but it left him a little shaken. "Tranquil or not, they could be dangerous," he said. "They could be dangerous, and they ought to be broken up, as the Pontifex Maximus insists. An edict against them would give the rest of the population to understand that treasonous groups will be dealt with severely. Even a persecution would be to some purpose. It would give the plebes and the government one thing in common —the only sort of thing the plebes can understand—a common enemy."

"But I can't agree with that," said the young man in a consciously modulated voice. "I simply can't believe that the State can profit by the sacrifice of any part of it. Probably it's some flaw in my own thinking, but the fact is, I've never been able to conceive of the State as a whole—now that I think of it, that's probably been the reason for many of the differences that have come up between you and me. When a Christian is burned at the stake, I can't see it as Justice, or the Good of the State, or Political Necessity. All I can see is a mind blotted out, a body going through unimaginable agony. No, no matter how hard I try, it's always been impossible for me—"

It was no subject, certainly, for a sick man to deal with; he was giving the abstract issue the lurid immediacy of a fever-dream. It would have been better to put off the discussion, to offer him a cup of wine-and-water and send him home to rest. And yet one nagging question would not be downed, must have its answer. "Tell me something, will you? Why are you always so tender with the enemy?" the Emperor said.

"With the enemy? I don't think it's that, not really. What you call my

245

'tenderness'—I believe it's more or less general. No, I don't believe it goes out particularly to the enemy—"

"Oh, but it does, I beg your pardon. I've never seen you upset over the legionaries—" He was thinking of his son Herennius, blue in the face with the marsh-fever, waiting in the draughty house at Apulum for the all-healing letter that would never arrive and the Goths who assuredly would. "They're a sacrifice, too, aren't they? It's an agony, too—isn't it?—to have your brains dashed out with a mace? But you don't come in to protest to me about that. Those sixty thousand up there on the river—with my son among them—they don't seem to worry you at all."

The eyes went dull again, and the mouth fell open. It seemed to him that he was about to receive what his nephew had never given him before—a full capitulation. Then the dry lips closed and were curved in the faintest suggestion of a smile. "Oh, but wait, wait—that's altogether different," the young man said. "The legionaries up there on the river—according to my uncle's own beliefs they'd be dying the deaths of ancient Romans. A soldier killed in action on the frontier—that chastens us, that purifies us and ties us all the more securely to the State. But a Christian burned in the arena—that's a different matter—that degrades us, that turns us all into dogs."

The Emperor rose with such violence that the massive table shook and the lamp-flame quivered. "Listen," he said, and he knew his voice was coarse with fury, "see that you don't come here preaching to me anymore. What I said back in the beginning—when I still had hopes, before I knew what lay in store for me—see that you don't come throwing it back in my face. I've made my honorable gestures. I put my son in the path of the Gothic army, I gave them the censorship, I stripped my house and my table, and look what they've done to me! It's useless, I tell you—useless. It's late now, the Goths are at the border, it's a good deal later than you or anybody else can afford to think. There's no time left for worrying about anything but survival—all I can do now is unify this rotten generation to stand against the shock when it comes. To survive, to get through it somehow, at any cost—that's the most we can hope for anymore."

He should have been shattered, he should have bowed his head, but he continued to sit erect with his hands spread out before him; he even lifted his chin and fixed his bloodshot eyes on the Emperor's face. "Then let me ask my uncle one last question? What are we to survive for?" he said. "Three hundred years of tyrants—one Nero after another? The free spirit trampled out of existence? Every generation less alive than the last? The whole world inhabited by the living dead? Fear in the City, fear in the provinces, no place on earth for a man to hide, one half of the population hired to spy upon the other? More and more games to keep the people from seeing what's being done to them—more and more victims to be sacrificed, because there will always be a certain number of fools who would rather die on their feet than crawl around on their bellies in such a world?"

It seemed to him then that never in his life had anything been so hateful to him as that white, unterrified, incorruptible face. He could have hurled the lamp at it—he would have hurled the lamp at it if there had not been another way, a better way. "I'm to take it then that you'd consider an edict against the Christians an act of tyranny on my part?" he said.

"Yes, my lord and my master."

"Have you anything else to suggest that would serve the same purpose? Anything, that is, in addition to your remarkable building law?"

"No." He also had risen. The corner of his mouth was twitching, but there was no wavering in his eyes.

"Well, let's save time, then. If I'm to live out the rest of my reign with nobody by me but soft-livered idiots who consider every forthright action tyranny, I might as well be a tyrant at once. There's an edict to be written— an edict to test the loyalty of the Christians. I'm in a hurry for it, I'll want it day after tomorrow. I'll have a slave bring the notes for it up to your palace. You'd better start work on it tonight."

"My lord and my master must not ask me to do it. Surely he can find somebody else—"

"Not you? Why not? Has their crucified Jew caught your fancy? Have you been creeping about in cemeteries and such, eating their sanctified bread?"

The eyes were level now—level and scornful. "No, my lord and my master. I have not been creeping about in cemeteries. I do not make a habit of eating sanctified bread."

"Then go and write the edict, as I told you."

"But it's impossible for me to put my hand to it."

"You'll put your hand to it, and we'll not discuss it anymore. If I'm to take full responsibility for every stringent piece of legislation, if I'm to carry the whole filthy load with nobody to help me, I can't sit around and talk about it, I haven't got the time."

There was no answer, there was only a profound obeisance, a bow too low to have been made in earnest and yet not quite low enough to be taken for mockery. When the young man straightened, his eyes were fixed and expressionless. Walking backward, after the manner of the eastern courtier, he reached the threshold, put his hand behind him, fumbled for the latch only for an instant, and passed without the flicker of an eyelid through the door.

For a long time the Emperor stood motionless except for the trembling in his knees, staring at the open doorway, thinking how his nephew had probably found his litter by now, was probably being borne into the evening traffic on the main street. Then, like a flash of lightning tearing across the dark, the thought cut through him: He is in league with the Christians, he is going now to warn them, somewhere on the avenue he will get out of his litter and walk to some Christian house and tell some bearded deacon that

247

the sword is about to be loosed against the treasonous dogs . . . It was preposterous, and yet he could not dismiss it. Twice he walked to the door of the little dining room, thinking that he would simply go upstairs now and eat the evening meal; and twice he turned back again, to listen as if the air in that place were pulsing with supernatural warnings, to see again his nephew Favorinus Herennius watching by torchlight the breaking of the bread.

And in the end he called in his steward. "Send to the Urban Prefect," he said, rubbing at a scratch in the wood, unable to look the sickly eunuch in the face. "Send a slave to the Urban Prefect, and tell him I want a spy assigned to follow the one that left here last."

"The Illustrious Favorinus Herennius, my lord and my master?"

"As I said. Tell the Urban Prefect to have the spy report the young man's doings directly to me."

"The doings of your nephew?"

For an instant he saw the comely and incorruptible face as it had been in childhood—earnest, pure, lifted in rapt attention to hear the readings from Livy in the atrium of the house on the Esquiline. A mist rose into his eyes, but his voice did not falter. "Yes, as I told you. The doings of my nephew," he said.

Chapter 18

WHEN HE left the imperial presence that evening, Favorinus Herennius never thought for an instant that a spy would be assigned to follow him. If he did not get out of the litter and go to his cousin's house, if he ordered his Nubians to carry him to his mother's palace by the shortest route, it was only because he was convinced his fever had come back; he would be a corpse by morning, he told himself, unless the frightening symptoms were dealt with at once—the quick transitions from burning heat to clammy cold, the tension closing like an iron circle around his head, the loud, irregular pounding of his heart. In fact, during the whole journey through the almost static traffic—it was a reception evening, and the streets were packed with litters—he was certain that he was already passing into delirium. When he put back the curtain, unable to breathe for the stifling heat, everything was bathed in a somber, yellowish, malevolent glare; faces that he did not recognize made familiar talk at him from the shadows of other litters; and, try as he would, he could not remember with any clarity or continuity what had passed between him and the Emperor Decius. Words, phrases—extreme, unbelievable—clanged like gongs and cymbals above the roaring in his head.

He avoided the small reception that was going on in the atrium of the Herennii by entering at a side door, and got to his chamber without encountering anybody but a couple of slaves. Baubio was waiting for him, and the alarm in the black face confirmed and increased his own. He could not restrain himself, he had to go to the carved chest and pick up the mirror, he had to see for himself the flushed skin, the trembling jaw, the distended pupils, the bloodshot whites of the eyes. "I've taken a chill, I should never have gone out, anoint me with heated oil," he said, and the words came out of him blurred and shaken, in a voice that was not his own. Sitting on the edge of the bed, he watched the preparations and assured himself that here were all the necessary remedies—two braziers brought in glowing and set at the head and the foot of the bed, oil of balsam exuding its healing scent in the heat, a great white woolen cloak which Baubio had the skill to keep at every stage of the anointing between the naked body and the cold. But when he lay on his belly, with all these remedies applied, when the heat of the braziers was flowing in waves over his head and the bare soles of his feet, when the adept fingers were kneading the oil into his back, his flanks, his sides, he was seized by a sudden panic conviction that nothing could help him, nothing at all. I will die, he thought, I will die in this terrible confusion—I will be flung into black Chaos . . . And suddenly they were all intolerable—the pressing hands, the oil, the wool. He had to fling them off, he had to dress again and pace the room. Oh, come, now, he told himself, if I can walk like this, it's plain that I'm not yet ready for my grave.

Somebody came stealthily through the hall and knocked with terrifying precision on the bedroom door. But it was nobody, it was only one of the household slaves with a sheaf of papyrus sheets in his hand. He recognized them at once as the notes for the edict, and dismissed Baubio along with the other slave so that he could examine them without distraction. But when he took the wrinkled, cross-hatched document to the lamp on the chest, he found that he could not read the notes; either they had been written by so furious a hand that nobody could make them out, or his vision was distorted by the fever again. And the sight of the violent pen strokes brought back the violence of the argument. Certain phrases— "Have it washed away in bull's blood" . . . "Something pressing, like setting up standards for mortar and wood . . . Creeping about in cemeteries and such, eating their sanctified bread"—certain phrases recurred to him now with such immediacy that they made him clench his teeth and drive his nails into the palms of his hands. And when the frantic fit had subsided, his exhaustion was such that he stood in the middle of the room, pressing his thumb down on his pulse, scarcely able to find the weak, erratic beat in his wrist. He thought then of calling Baubio, of sending Baubio to the Via Sacra to implore the Greek physician to come at once to the palace of the Herennii; and he would have done so if he had not been stopped by an incomprehensible unwillingness to have the slave wandering about in the streets at this hour of the night and a superstitious conviction that to call the physician was to give the sickness more actuality, more power.

And I'm not sick, I'm merely overwrought, all I need is something calm me down, he told himself, walking back to the chest and picking up, from among the combs and the rings and the bracelets, a little vial of crimson stuff. The physician told me I would feel feverish if I exposed myself to any excitement; he left this here for just such an occasion.

He went to the door and shouted at the top of his voice for Baubio, panic-stricken that the fellow was not sitting in his usual place on a reed mat in the hall, but had gone off to play dice with some other slaves at the top of the stairs. "How is it a person can never find you when you're wanted? I need my sleeping potion. Go get me a cup of wine-and-water," he said. While the slave was gone, he turned down the coverlet and got into bed, partly to indicate that Baubio was remiss, partly to ward off a hideously clear image of his uncle's face—red patches of anger on the cheeks, the pale eyes blazing, a white vein standing out on the florid brow. It was so persistent, so hateful, so shattering an image that he could not believe an ordinary dose of the sleeping potion capable of exorcising it—he ordered his slave to put an extra spoonful of the red stuff in, and when the poor wretch protested, he got out of bed and snatched the vial and the spoon out of the black hands and mixed the dose for himself. Suppose it's really too much, he thought, lying down again and pulling the covers up to his chin. Suppose it's really too much and I die of it . . . But of a sudden the thought of death had lost all terror for him: he lay warm, watching the lamps being quenched, staring with an infantile belief in utter comfort, utter safety, at the soft red glow of the brazier on the wall.

"If my lord and my master wishes it, I will bring in the mat and sleep at the foot of his bed tonight," said the low and sibilant voice, speaking through fibrous darkness.

"Yes, do. Ever since we went up there with the money-bags that night, I've been uneasy about you, I've . . ." But he could not say the rest of it. His jaw was loose and his tongue was tingling. A dreamless sleep, he thought. It was Socrates who said that death was only a dreamless sleep. . . .

He wakened in the bright mid-morning to a still and empty chamber. Small blades of light were cutting in at the bottom of the drawn green curtains; keen edges of silver lay along the mirror, the vial, the spoon with which he had measured out the potion, the bracelet which, in the stifling panic of the preceding evening, he had forgotten to take from his wrist. That morning there was no intermediate stage between his sleeping and his waking. All in an instant he was awake, aware, and he knew with a grave clarity everything that he had hidden from himself in fear and confusion last night. He knew that he and his uncle had said the unsayable and the unforgivable to each other in the little dining room, that never in this world—and he did not believe in the existence of any other—never in this world could they be reconciled. He knew, too, that he would not write a word of the edict; before he left the house this morning, he would dispatch slave with the notes to the office of Pessinus—he would tell the slave to ask the Secretary of Petitions to return the papers just as they were to the Emperor in a day or two. Such a piece of audacity would not, of course, go by without imperial punishment; it would be better to go away, far away, to one of the orchard estates in Africa or to one of the farms in Bithynia—a matter that he could decide upon later—there was no time for pondering it now. He knew also, and with a sudden dilation of his heart, that as soon as he had taken some breakfast he would go in a hired litter to his cousin's house to tell her that an edict against the Christians was about to be published, to warn her that the time of the going-forth had come.

Concerning his reasons for this particular decision, he was too lucid, too solemn to deceive himself. He was going over to the Aventine to tell the innocents that evil was being plotted against them, because the edict *was* evil and they *were* innocent—but that was only a minor part of the truth. He was bound to go to her because, on a certain wan and seasonless afternoon, she had been foolish enough to imagine him capable of such an act. Remembering the look of utter trust she had given him then, he found it impossible to do otherwise.

He dressed alone—according to one of the other slaves, Baubio had been called downstairs by the mistress of the house—he dressed alone, with great care and precision, choosing a slate-grey dalmatica with a dark blue girdle, not because he wished to be inconspicuous in the street, only because the sober colors seemed suited somehow to the occasion. His jaw was still shaking a little, but he was not disturbed by that: he knew now that the fever had not returned and would not return: his spirit, not his flesh, had been in revolt against him last night. Once downstairs, he conducted himself with what he knew to be a slightly self-conscious dignity. He ordered and ate his breakfast with dispatch, but without the slightest suggestion of haste; he asked the steward to deliver an elaborate apology to two of his clients who were expecting to see him in the atrium at noon; he did not permit himself to show any sign of annoyance when he learned that his mother had sent Baubio out of the palace to return a certain silver sauce bowl that she had borrowed from Flavius Labeo.

"When do you expect to come back, my lord and my master?" the steward asked him as he started out of the front door. And the casual, customary question took on a strange, almost philosophical weight, posed against the clear blue shining of the morning. He did not know, he said, and thought on his way down the avenue of sycamores that it was a vain question: the world and mortal life being what they were, how would a person ever know

On the way to the Aventine he kept the curtains of the hired litter drawn—not, he told himself, because of his ridiculous and persistent impression that he was being watched and followed—simply because the brilliance of the winter morning, high and vibrant like the shrill upper tones of the flute, was too intense for his eyes. He had looked over the notes for the edict while he was dressing, and now he rehearsed each provision in

calmly, without any sense of personal involvement, as a schoolboy re-
hearses his lesson on the way to school. It seemed to him that he would be
less embarrassed before his cousin if he could give a detailed and coherent
account of the Emperor's intentions. So far as he had been able to gather
from the disorderly manuscript, no specific mention of the Christians was
to be made at all. There was to be a general religious festival, a universal
attempt to invoke the good will of the gods upon the troubled Empire, a
formal request that every Roman citizen at home and in the provinces
should burn his few grains of incense on the altar of the genii of the City
and the Emperor. Those who had duly fulfilled the requirements would
receive certificates, those found without certificates after a certain unspeci-
fied date would be taken into the court of the Urban Prefect and dealt with
in a matter as yet unclarified, so far as he could see. It could hardly be called
a tyrannical edict: nobody but a fanatic would refuse to burn a little incense for the prosperity of his country and the safety of his Emperor. And
yet, so far as the Christians were concerned, it would bring the same results
as the most outrageous demands. Christians had always preferred exile or
the beasts to the slightest compromise; in Rome, in Africa, in Lyons, in the
Bithynian wilderness Christians had run head-on to their ruin on less prov
ocation before. . . .

He had meant to have the carriers bring him straight to her door, but he
told them to stop a little short of it because he was inexplicably disturbed by
what should have seemed an ordinary sight. Just as the litter came to the
end of the sculptor's stone wall, her door swung open and a kind of procession came out and crossed the street—three young men balancing bundles
wrapped in linen on their heads; and why that sight should have deepened
his gravity, he did not know. How strange, he thought, paying his fare
without glancing at the coins in his hands, looking instead at the high, chill
radiance streaming down on the statues and sarcophagi. How strange that
his, the third time I have come here, should round out a cycle, so that I have
been here once during each of the three divisions of the day—afternoon,
night, and morning. And this obvious observation gave him the same sorrowful sense of fulfillment that comes when one recognizes by the fall of the
notes and the slowing of the rhythm the approaching conclusion of a song.

There was no need to knock—the ancient steward, his face tremulous in
the sunlight, was holding the door wide, perhaps simply to enjoy a breath
of the crystalline air, perhaps to clear the way for other bearers of bales or
grain or white trussed sheep who might come walking through. But that's
strange idea, he thought, nodding and smiling vacantly as he passed the
steward. Bales of linen, yes—bales of linen are always being taken out of
here to the poor in the tenements. But what would an urban household like
this be doing with grain and sheep?
"One moment, your Illustriousness—"
He had omitted the amenities. Wholly taken up with asking himself why

he should have peopled her little vestibule with a rustic procession, he had crossed the blue floor and laid his hand on the curtain without so much as asking whether the lady of the house was in. And the old man was plainly distressed by his forgetfulness; he looked at the visitor with troubled, red-rimmed eyes. "If you'll wait for just a moment—"

"I beg your pardon, I was in a hurry. Is my cousin Paulina in?"

"Yes, your Illustriousness. Only our house is in dreadful confusion just at the moment—"

Dreadful confusion . . . It was only the conscientious steward's routine formula for preparing the unexpected early guest for a table cluttered with this morning's dishes and last night's faded flowers. Then I have come early, earlier than I thought, he told himself—early enough perhaps to see her in her morning guise, some loose and casual robe laid lightly on her body, her hair still hanging down her back, her face still soft and warm with sleep. And he did not think of the heavy import of his news; he could think only, and with a solemn happiness, that he was about to say what she had expected him to say on that wan and seasonless afternoon when she had looked at him in utter terror and utter trust. I will tell her, he thought, what she blushed to have believed I would tell her. I will wipe them both away—my insufficiency and her disgrace. And, since I come with this intent, it is meet that I should be shut out no longer, that I should enter this room where the adolescent girls bent their clean heads over the lengths of linen, and the congregation of the faithful ate in seemly silence of the consecrated bread.

This room? He stopped on the threshold, appalled at the disorder. The benches had been pushed aside, and the table was piled with dishes and pans. Bales, baskets, potted plants were set about in a scatter of packing straw all over the floor. And she was not alone here—why he should have been so sure he would find her here alone, he did not know. On the opposite side of the big, bare chamber, under a blindingly bright and curtainless window, she and her husband were kneeling together on a recalcitrant bundle, their cheeks almost touching as they strove with a knot that was coming undone. At the sight of him she uttered a short cry—not a cry of welcome, a cry of fright. And, seeing her in that pitiless brightness, he found her person as alien, as unbeautiful, as bleak as this disordered chamber: her tucked dalmatica was pulled awry; her eyelids were red either with sleep or with weeping; her face seemed whiter, more childish, more meager than ever because she had completely covered her hair with a strip of white linen, probably to protect it from the clouds of dust visible in the broad shaft of sun.

They loosed their hold on the string and stood up together, and the bundle heaved open and settled against their shins. But he could produce nothing more than a feeble greeting; the words that he had meant to pour out for her were all discredited now; he could not even look at her; he stared instead—stupidly, he knelt at the reddish gleam on her husband's beard and hair. It was Probus who broke the dismal silence. "So you're up and about again, my cousin?" he said. "That's more than we'd expected. The last time Drusilla was here, she said it'd be weeks before you'd be on your feet."

"Oh, yes, I'm up and about." Husband and wife, shoulder to shoulder, arm against arm—his voice was tight with the unexpected, the unprepared-for pain. "I've been up and about since yesterday. I know I shouldn't have come so early in the morning, but yesterday I—"

She did a strange thing then—without a word she stepped around the bundle and crossed the room, never once looking down at the bales and the baskets and the potted flowers that lay in her path. Now that she stood directly in front of him, she gave him a long, unguarded, all-recording look —the look of one who means to have much to remember, much to brood upon in months of absence, months of loneliness. Then, still gazing, and moving with the slow ineptitude of one who moves in sleep, she raised her arm and pushed the band of linen backward with her wrist, so that it fell behind her, loosing her brown and silky hair. How long they might have stood staring at each other if the noise from the street had not broken in upon them, it was impossible to tell. It was a hideous noise—a clanging that hurt his ears and a thud that shook the heart in his chest.

"Oh, they're at those stones with the chisel again, they're working at the aqueduct, they did it all day yesterday," she said, covering her ears with her hands and gazing at him still.

No, my cousin, he thought, it's something else. It's the mountains of Africa cracking apart. Wait a moment, wait, and kiss me on the mouth, and the two of us will hear them crash into the sea . . . And he continued to stare until the last echo of the sound had ceased, until his heart was moored and still again, until the master of the house had come up behind her and covered her shoulders with two bony, proprietary hands.

"I'm sorry you find us in such a state," he said to his visitor over his wife's head. His voice was strident with an attempt at cordiality; the old uneasiness was in his shifting eyes. "You'd like to know how we distributed the money, I suppose, and I'm sorry to say I can't give you that information now—I had a complete list of everything we handed out, of course—but we're going, you see; we're packing up, and all our papers are already gone."

"Oh, the money—" It had taken him some moments to understand what money his host was talking about. He made a jerky, depreciatory gesture with his right hand.

"But there's nothing to worry about—the brotherhood never mislays its records." His raw fingers were trembling on her shoulders now; obviously he was suffering from something more than his usual awkwardness. It was woundingly plain, too, from the way his glance kept flying from one bundle to another, that he wanted his visitor to state his business and depart. "I'll tell you where you can find Moyses, he can account for everything. Meanwhile, if you'll excuse me, I'll get back to these bundles. I can do that while we talk. As I said, we're in a terrible hurry. We're doing everything we can to get out of the house by tonight."

"But why? Where are you going? Nobody said that you were going south—"

"Going south? No, it's not like that—not a vacation. Paulina, here—" He stepped back a little and stood with hanging hands, and his fleeting, unquiet glance came to rest for an instant, rueful and tender, on her silky head. "Paulina's going to a villa in the Campagna—it's not too far from here. Myself, well, I can't quite say—I'll be in the City for a little while at least, at a house I'm not at liberty to name."

"Is something the matter?"

His look shifted again. "Not exactly—that is, there've been rumors—political rumors, I mean. We've gotten reports about certain changes in the Emperor's policy—"

Her voice broke in, breathless and loud, to disclaim the caution, to assert her trust. "There's to be an edict. The Emperor is going to publish an edict—"

"But how did you find out? That was what I came to tell you. He mentioned it to me for the first time yesterday afternoon."

"We were told about it yesterday evening," said Probus, starting back toward the window. "The congregation of the Lord has its servants everywhere in the City, even in the household of the Emperor."

If there was un-Christian pride in that—a deacon's pride in the efficiency of his organization—he must have known as much and duly reproved himself. He looked a little crestfallen, getting awkwardly down on his knees beside the bundle to fasten the knot and cut off the string. And the silence that he had left to them was a strained and disheartening silence. They could only stare at the floor—at the strewn straw and the potted violets. "It was very good of you to come," she said at last.

But I have only made a fool of myself, my cousin. I have only made a fool of myself and given you and your husband more trouble, more pain. Like an over-eager actor rushing in before his time, I have intruded myself upon your last aching hours of privacy, and the line that I deliver is ridiculous—I tell you something which you already know. You have your spies in the Emperor's house, as any fool would realize—Christians have spies like anybody else. And now you will think, with considerable justification, that I see myself as a man of importance, a whisperer of imperial secrets— "No, it was foolish of me. I should never have done it. I should have known you would get the news through channels of your own," he said.

The long bony shape on the other side of the chamber darted at a second bundle. "Don't imagine for a moment that Paulina and I aren't grateful for your kindness—"

"Grateful?" Her voice rang out above the sound of the chisel in the street. "Dear Christ—is that all you have to say to him—grateful? Do you realize what he risked in coming here? God knows who may have followed him! God knows what he may have to suffer before the end of this, for you and for me!"

No, my cousin, he thought, looking at her sandalled feet, pale and narrow on the strewn straw, delicately veined like her hands. No, not for the both of you—tell yourself no such lie. If I am followed, if it so happens that I suffer much, then know at least that it is for you and for nobody else. It is because I felt the shape of your mouth in a dream, knew in a dream the pressure of your kissing mouth and nothing more, not the trailing planets nor the extinguished sun nor the mountains of Africa going down into the sea. . . .

"Pardon me, my mistress." It was the quavering voice of the steward speaking behind him.

He did not turn. He merely raised his eyes to her face. It was very white, such brightness lay upon it now that he thought he could see, behind the thin flesh of the cheeks and brow, the fragile contours of the bones. He shivered and did not understand why he should shiver. If there was suddenly more light in the room, it was only because the curtain between the vestibule and the inner chamber had been drawn aside so that the cool brilliance of the morning could stream in unhindered from the street.

"Those men out there at the aqueduct, my mistress—one of them wants to know if he can step inside. He says there's a leak in the line, he'd like your permission to look at our water pipes—"

"Which one? The old one? The little old Italian?" Her voice had fallen to a whisper.

"No, this is another one, a new one. He started working just a little while ago."

"We can't let him in, he's probably from the Urban Prefect's office. Don't under any circumstances let him in."

"But what am I to tell him, my lady and my mistress?"

"Anything, anything. Tell him there's sickness in the house. Keep him outside."

"No, stay here. Don't do that, my darling, don't send him off like that," said Probus from the other side of the room. The tender and sustaining words were strangely moving—all the more moving because they were uttered in a flat and nasal voice and accompanied by certain graceless, ineffectual movements of the hands. "If you keep him on the doorstep, he'll be all the more suspicious. And what's to be lost by letting him in? People like us—they have their notes on us already. There's nothing he can see here that the Urban Prefect doesn't already know."

She did not see the reassuring eyes and hands. The assertion of their fellowship in danger—she let it pass unrecognized: her look was elsewhere, her look was on her cousin's face. "Yes," she said, "that's true enough, but what about our cousin? What if they sent him to get a report on our cousin?"

His raw and bony hand fell limp, like a bird transfixed by an arrow. "Yes, I suppose you're right about that," he said. "I forgot for the moment what a pass we've come to. I would have thought a person could call on his relatives without being followed by one of the Urban Prefect's spies. But, since the honorable Decius has turned out to be the Anti-Christ after all, we'd better take no chances. Take our cousin upstairs, Paulina."

"But I'd rather not hide. I'd rather get out of here altogether." It was harsh, it was rude, but he could not help it, confused as he was by a sudden assault of embarrassment and pain. That he should have drawn the eye of the Urban Prefect to their front door, that his uncle Decius should have been insulted, misunderstood, transformed into a monster—no, it was intolerable, he could not stay— "Can't you get me out of here by some other door?"

"Oh, no." She caught at his hand with her cold fingers. "There might be others. There are probably others waiting outside."

"But the man's at the door—have the two of you forgotten?" said Probus in a hissing whisper, flinging up both his hands. "Every moment we stand here talking about it, he's growing more suspicious. Go up, go up as fast as you can."

"Of course, you're right, we're going at once." With the quiet, conspiratorial air of a child who leads a companion-in-mischief away from a brewing parental storm, she drew the visitor aside; she led him out of the room and through a little hall and up a narrow staircase, still holding him by the hand. The pressure of her fingers was dry and very light; the spareness of her flesh made her touch all the more intimate and eloquent. They were silent on the stair, and he was grateful for that: no words would have been as unguarded as this mute exchange between their hands. Everything else—even the nasal voice of Probus and the voice of the intruder, unctuously polite—seemed remote and unreal to him now.

"To the left, into the bedchamber," she said in a whisper as soon as they reached the top of the flight; and she turned and gave him a smile as she withdrew her fingers to open the door. It was a strange smile, incongruously blithe, almost light-hearted—it loosed a flock of wild hopes in him like imprisoned birds. She stepped across the threshold, and he walked in behind her, watching her body in motion, tremulously aware of her person shadowed forth now and again through the folds of the white pleated cloth.

"Close the door," she said, still smiling.

He closed it and stood some five paces from her, staring into her face and feeling his whole chest crazily shaken by the knocking of his heart. It seemed to him that in an instant they must clasp each other close, that some inexorable force would have them knee to knee, breast to breast.

But, seeing her there before him, with her hands clasped in front of her

258

and her eyes fixed earnestly on his face, he knew that she was offering him only compassion, only solicitude. "Tell me, my cousin, is it well with you now?" she said, out of breath and speaking very fast. "Are you really recovered? I know how sick you were—Drusilla told me. She said you were dying one day when she came here. You'll never know how terrified I was—she told us you were coughing blood. But it's gone now—you're better? You haven't any fever anymore? You haven't any pain?"

"No pain—no fever—" Something in the gentle inclination of her body let him know that she wished she might unclasp her fingers, might touch him on the forehead, might touch him on the chest.

"And your hands—did they heal? Are they altogether better?"

He had forgotten the burns. That particular misery, like the crumpled rose-colored dalmatica on the floor of the bath, like the seeking hands in the grey garden—that particular misery, like all the others, had been ground away by the nightmares and the pain. He looked at his palms, he opened them into the sunlight and stared down at them, and saw for the first time that there were patches where the skin was pink and unlined like the skin of a newborn child. "Look, like a baby's," he said, taking one step forward and holding out his hands to her. "I forgot all about them. After I burned them there was so much else. Until you mentioned them now, I completely forgot."

And slowly, awkwardly, with the same dazed and dreaming look that she had given him when she had pushed the linen back from her forehead, she traced the scar on his palm with one cold fingertip. Do not withdraw your hand, he thought, and I will dare to tell you what I dreamed: how you came into the vestibule with lint in your hair, how—very strangely, because the grass was long since withered—the music of the creatures of the grass came with you, beetle-sound, cricket-sound, the ringing of minute and innumerable bells. . . .

"It was good of you to come—but I told you that before," she said after an attenuated silence, taking away her hand.

"It was foolish, my cousin. I only brought you more trouble."

"No, no, never think of that. It was good, it was sweet." She smiled at him again, but only for an instant. Before the smile could change the contours of her wan and earnest face, she bit the corner of her lip and sighed; and he wondered whether the room in which they stood had begun to impinge upon her also—table strewn with the sheets of his sterile manuscript, bench where a man's dalmatica and a woman's traveling cloak lay side by side, shared clothes chest, shared bed.

"It never occurred to me that I could bring you so much trouble." Nor myself, he thought, such pain.

"But you're in dreadful trouble yourself, my cousin. I knew it the instant I saw your face."

"Not dreadful trouble, not really. I had a difference—maybe it was a violent difference, I don't know—at any rate, I had a difference with the Emperor. He asked me to write the edict, and I refused to write it. But if it's really a spy from the Urban Prefect's office that your husband has down there, then matters between me and my uncle are a little worse than I've allowed myself to think."

"What will you do? Where will you go now?"

"To Bithynia, to Africa—I haven't made up my mind."

"Don't make up your mind, not until we've talked to Probus," she said, touching his sleeve. "He knows more about such things, and he'll be able to advise you. I'm sure he'll tell you that you shouldn't go to any of your own properties."

"Why not?" His voice was harsh. It was as if, by mentioning her husband, she had actually summoned the bearded, bony presence into the room.

"*He* would be sure to send after you and find you there, my cousin. Go somewhere else."

He—the horned and slavering beast, the devourer of martyrs, the drinker of blood . . . He straightened and drew back from the light, dry pressure of her fingertips. "You learned that from your husband—just like your husband, you see him as a monster," he said. "But let me tell you this—there's not the slightest trace of cruelty or malice in his body. Whatever you think, I doubt very much that he'll be sending into Bithynia or Africa for me."

"I hope not, I pray not." She had put her rejected hand behind her. Her voice was flat now, drained of all warmth and womanliness. "I keep forgetting that it's not the same with you as it is with the rest of us. You're not a Christian—and besides, he's fond of you. All you have to do is get out of his sight for a little while—he'll be glad enough to let you alone. But with us it's another matter. He'll seek us out, he'll hunt us down, he'll send after us to any place we go: there'll never be any peace for us anymore, not until we're in our graves. Every stranger we see from this day forward will look like a spy—" She broke off and stepped backward, her face suddenly wild and distorted with fright. "Dear Christ, what am I doing here? Probus is all alone with him down there," she said. "Are they still talking? Can you hear them?" She ran forward, opened the door, and stood on the threshold, looking into the hall. "Wait—yes—now I can hear them," she said in a whisper, never turning her head. "I'm so confused, I don't know where I am. God forgive me, for all I know they could have taken him away. I must go down now. I would have gone sooner, only I'm so tired I don't know what I'm doing—we didn't sleep, we had to pack, the two of us were up all night."

"You'll do him no good going down like that," he said, and his voice was acid with impotent bitterness. She was no longer thinking of him, and that was only right. "You're white, you look as if you'd been scared half to death. You'd better take hold of yourself."

"I will, I will." She pinched her cheeks between forefinger and thumb until two red patches burned above the thinly-fleshed bones. "There, is that any better?" she said. "My dress, too—my hair—" She straightened her skirt, pushed a loose wisp of hair back from her forehead, and was gone.

And now he could only walk to the bench and sit down beside their traveling clothes laid out together. Since she was gone, there was nothing to shield him from the shattering impact: he was forced to accept the enormity of his situation. That unctuous voice coming in to him through the open door would actually whisper his name in some chamber of the Urban Prefect's office. He would have to go down to the Port and arrange for his passage; he would have to deal with ships and accounts and money-bags, make hurried explanations, hasty and insufficient farewells. Letting his forehead sink down on his clenched hands, he saw a vision of an African orchard, glossy, opulent, sickeningly oppressive, distorted by shimmering waves of heat. He saw himself standing at one end of an avenue of lemon trees, the brazen sun beating on his head and the powdery, brick-red soil crumbling under his shoes. And, terrible through the succulent foliage, there were pairs of peeping eyes—burnt-out eyes of the exile, cruel eyes of the overseer, mute, ox-dumb eyes of the African peasants—hundreds of pairs of alien eyes . . . "I will never bear it," he said in a whisper, as if those who had brought him to it were at hand and could take the sickly-sweet poison of exile from his lips. But nobody was at hand—there was only her traveling cloak, made of some soft grey woolen stuff; and this he snatched away from the dalmatica that lay beside it, this he pressed against his chest, his neck, his face. Such a shuddering seized him then that the bench shook beneath him, and it seemed to him that his heart had gone out of his body to brood upon the light and sorrowful fragrance lingering in the cloth.

But all that he sought for in the folds of her garment was vulnerable, transitory, exposed to mortal danger. He knew of a sudden that in a day or two the statutes of the land would be such that the living essence of her could be shattered or consumed, and this terrible knowledge shamed him into laying her cloak aside. It was out of his hands none too early—there were footfalls on the stairway, the slow, uneven footfalls of the very old. The steward—not she—was coming up to call him back to the lower chamber; and he suppressed the last of the shuddering while he waited, sitting as casually as he could, his head tilted backward and his hands clasped round his knees.

"Will you come down now, your Illustriousness? It's quite safe. My master and my mistress are down there by themselves."

Yes, down there by themselves, he thought, following the bent back and the stiff legs over the threshold and down the stairs. Alone together with their terror and their grief and all the stored, small tendernesses of their mutual years. Alone together as they were before I came, and as they ought to be . . . And yet, through the sober assertion, like an unseasonable flower thrusting up through frosty soil, like the laughter of an infant rippling over the chanted ritual of a solemn sacrifice—broke the recollection of the light, dry pressure of her hand, the incongruous blitheness of her smile.

"Stay out in the hall, cousin." It was the voice of Probus—controlled, almost cheerful—shouting to him from the big, bare room. "You can be seen from the street in here—there aren't any curtains, you know. Paulina wanted them packed, she insisted on taking them with her because they happened to be a present from her novices. So here you are, exposed to danger, and all because of my wife's sentimentality."

The steward had gone back to his post in the vestibule, leaving the visitor to wait for the others in the dark little hallway at the foot of the stairs. Only two patches of light came in from the adjoining chamber—one on the bronze dolphin that adorned the water-cock and the other on the floor near the pipes—white tiles, damp and muddy with the imprint of the intruder's feet.

"He's from the Urban Prefect's office, there's not the slightest doubt about that," said the master of the house, striding into the hall, one hand set almost jauntily on his hip. "He's gone, he isn't even pretending he's working on the aqueduct anymore. But if you'll take my advice, you'll go upstairs for a while, just to make sure he's not outside."

To be irritated at the man was unjust; he was only trying to be helpful. And, considering how ill at ease he was in every ordinary circumstance, it was no great wonder that his self-possession should go to his head, that he should feel an actual exhilaration at finding himself so cool and efficient under stress . . . And yet it was difficult in this raw and shaken state to bring oneself to answer him even with courtesy. "No, I won't wait, I'd better be going," he said, and his voice came out of him remote and cold. "The fact is, I should have gone before. I should never have gone upstairs."

She had come up and was standing a little behind her husband. Her face was in the shadow, but he thought he saw pain in it—the same hurt, childish, wondering look she had given him when he stepped out of reach of her hand. How could I say such a thing? he thought. How could I give her to understand, on the instant of departing, that it was nothing to me that she and I stood face to face, that her finger traced the scar on the palm of my hand?

Still lively, still impervious, her husband went on, his eyes still forcing themselves to focus uneasily on his visitor's face. "If you don't mind my saying so, you're being very foolish about this. To walk out of here while the fellow is still hanging about the neighborhood—"

He hated the voice. It was an offense to his spirit and his ears. "Let him see me if he wants to! I don't care! I'm going into exile—I have nothing to lose."

"So you say, but it's quite possible you're wrong. If he went so far as to set a spy upon you—and that was a spy, cousin, obviously a spy—"

His eyes, in avoiding the insistent stare of his host, had lighted on the muddy footprints on the floor. Something in the streaked brown immediacy of that mud forced him to ask what he regretted before it was out of his mouth: "What sort of fellow was he? The spy, I mean."

It was she who answered, and for the first time he heard loathing in her voice. "He was a Gaul—a fat, red-headed Gaul with white skin and small eyes, like a pig."

"If he's gone so far as to set a spy on you, as I say, I don't know why you should consider yourself more immune than anybody else."

"But I'm not a Christian, I never was a Christian! The law has nothing to do with me."

"But why do you insist on taking chances? Your affairs can't be so urgent that you can't wait around for an hour or so."

To be imprisoned in the tormenting intimacy of that upper chamber—he could not even bear the thought of it now. He looked at her white, shut face beyond her husband's shoulder, and knew that she would not come to him up there again—fear and pity had reasserted themselves, would keep her shackled to her one dear yoke-fellow in sorrow—fear and pity, which had nothing to do with love. "No," he said, "it's ridiculous, I'm going. I'll go into exile, and he'll let me alone. I'll go as soon as I can get passage, I'll stay at our property in Africa—" He announced it loudly, distinctly, despising caution, thinking scornfully of the house in the City that Probus was not at liberty to name. "I'll leave you—it's better—I've caused you too much trouble. A good journey and a safe return to both of you—" He walked past them and into the bright disrupted room, and could not look at her, and could not say "Farewell."

In the blinding brightness of the street he saw two men, two government workers—a little Italian and a young Levantine. They were sitting near a jagged hole in the paving stones, eating their noonday meal of black sausage and cabbage leaves; and their aspect was so ordinary, so innocent that he sighed and straightened and began to walk at a steady but unhurried pace alongside the sculptor's wall.

If he stared curiously at what lay on the other side of the wall, it was not out of any uneasiness, it was only to test the powers of his strained and watering eyes. Busts, statues, sarcophagi, enormous slabs of raw stone—the dazzling lines of light around them were almost blinding at first. And then he stopped and remained standing in the same spot, staring down at an unbelievable thing, a strangely fascinating thing—two white, fat hands, with fingers like enormous maggots, spread against the grey stone on top of the wall.

"A beautiful morning, your Illustriousness," It came up over the wall to tell him so, the bloated and porcine face, topped with its cropped red hair. The foreknown turned incredibly into the actual, and that was frightening enough to set his heart knocking fiercely against the walls of his chest. But more hideous still was the glance that passed between him and the stranger

—knowing, familiar, as if to seal some bond between himself and this loathsome thing with the moist and infantile mouth and the small, glittering hog's eyes.

"Yes, a beautiful morning." It was appalling that the thing could force him to answer, that he should stand here, reduced to immobility, letting the little, bead-bright eyes take him in. They were thorough—they took stock of everything—the convulsive swallowing movement at the base of his throat, the heaving struggle in his chest, the wisp of packing straw caught on the hem of his dalmatica, the clot of mud and straw sticking out from the sole of his shoe.

"Cool and lovely, very cool and lovely." It was the unctuous voice that he had heard downstairs, but now it was almost tender. "Unusually fine for this time of the year."

Break in his mouth for him, he thought. Smash in his filthy mouth with your fist. But the round head went slowly, significantly from side to side, the wet lips gave him a comprehending and indulgent smile. And utterly against his will—it was nothing, he told himself, it was only the result of a nervous spasm in his face—utterly against his will, his own mouth curved upward in what must have seemed an answering smile—shameful and a little obscene.

The beady eyes shifted to the left, informed him confidentially that the wisest thing to do under the circumstances was to proceed without further discussion down the street. It was solely because he knew that he must rouse himself enough to shatter this hideous pattern, must not do what this instrument of annihilation willed and took for granted he would do—it was solely because he must perform some signal act to prove that his spirit was still alive and unfettered within him that he turned on his heel and started wildly for her door. He was up the steps and half way across the vestibule before he saw that she was standing against the heavy curtain, her thin arms extended, pity and mortal terror and unguarded love in her face. "He saw you then? He actually saw you?" she said, and took his shaking hands in hers, and held them against her, in the hollow place between her breasts.

"Yes—he was out there waiting for me. He was hiding, crouching down behind the sculptor's wall."

"The two of you had better get in behind the curtain." It was her husband's voice—judicial, censorious—but it had no power to destroy the solace of her shielding hands and breasts.

"Yes, in a minute. Only wait a minute," she said, and did not loose her hold until the first assault of the shuddering had passed.

"A red-headed Gaul, just as you told me," he said in a whisper. "I can't understand why he should have had such an effect on me. It wasn't that I was afraid to have him see me—it was something about his face."

"Come," she said, turning and taking him by the elbow. "Please sit down, my cousin. You can sit down inside."

A bundle of clothes wrapped in a brown mourning-cloak had been shoved in his absence to a spot just inside the heavy curtain, and he let himself down upon it, unable to suppress a long and audible sigh. There was a crazy and uncontrollable twitching in the muscles just behind his knees. He wanted to speak, but there was no voice left in him; and they also kept their silence, probably to give him time to steady himself. She was somewhere behind him—he could not see her—but her husband stood directly in front of him, near the table, with a basket of straw before him and a wine-cup in his bony hand. Everything that had been offensive in his manner—the exhilaration, the exasperation, the censure—was gone. Christian forbearance only was manifest now in the forced steadiness of the eyes and the stern but quiet line of the bearded lips. "What do you intend to do now, cousin?" he said at last.

"I don't know. I'm not sure anymore."

"Then, in the name of Jesus, let me entreat you not to do anything so rash as starting out for one of your properties. I would take you with me, but that would be foolish—the Bishop and the deacons will be the first to be hunted down, as you can see for yourself." He put a broken wine-cup into the basket and took it out again. He wet his lips with the tip of his tongue and forced himself to look more honestly into his visitor's eyes. "Since you came here to tell us—since you put yourself into this danger by coming here," he said, plainly making an effort to be just, "it's our obligation, of course, to find some safe and decent place where you can hide. That much we can do, and do it better, perhaps, than anybody else—we're used to these exigencies, we're prepared to lose ourselves, the Brotherhood of Jesus has been dealing with this sort of thing for two centuries, and we know our way about. We know, for instance, not to send our wives and children to the provinces at a time like this—Paulina can be safer here in Italy than anywhere else. They'll watch the Port, they'll watch the roads—they haven't started to as yet, but you can expect it in a couple of days."

She came and sat down on the corner of the table and looked earnestly into her husband's face. "Shall I take him to the villa in the Campagna? Shall I take him with me?" she said.

A warm somnolence was settling in after the shuddering. The raw and bony hand, reaching for another wine-cup, moved slowly, like a hand in a dream.

"Yes, that was what I was thinking. He might as well be there. He'll be safer there than anywhere else. Only, it would be better if the two of you went separately. You go tonight, and he can follow tomorrow night."

"How will he find me?"

"Oh, that's easy. We'll send somebody to bring you, cousin—one of the lads, one of the catechumens who knows the way. And while you're about it, you might as well bring some others with you. I think there are two Christians in your household—a gardener and his daughter—their names are on our rolls, and you might take them if you can. It'd be a kindness, a very great kindness, especially to the child."

"Yes, I could take them . . ." But what am I saying, what am I doing? he thought, struggling only faintly against the numb and drowsy passivity.

"Come with me, Favorinus." She did not look at him. She merely stretched out one thin hand in his direction, mortal and beautiful, the blue veins crossing on the wrist.

And all questions, all impossibilities dissolved before the inexorable necessities of his spirit. "Yes, I'll come with you," he said.

Chapter 19

WHEN HE was alone again in the cool brightness of the street, he was borne up on such a surge of exaltation that he did not ask himself once whether the red-headed Gaul could be walking behind him. And this exaltation—so exquisite, so intense that it was not easily distinguishable from pain—did not lessen as he had imagined it would when he left the stoops and doorways of the shabby neighborhood and brought his mind to bear upon all that must be done before he could honorably depart. The necessary interviews with his mistress, his mother, his sister—he was almost ready for them now. He no longer felt that to touch any of their lives again was only to add confusion to confusion. I must carry my living heart to all of them, he told himself. I must give them such tender and honest words that all resentment, all bitterness will fall away, and we can remember the life that is finished now with nothing but respect and gratefulness. . . .

Since it seemed to him that he ought to accomplish the most difficult of these tasks while the tide of his spirit ran highest, he hired another litter and set out for the house of Charis, to make a decent end at last of all that had been between him and his poor love. He accepted—or at least he was willing to accept—the pain that threatened to assail him when he gave the directions to the litter-bearers and realized that he was going to that house for the last time. But he had not reckoned with the possibility that she might not be alone, and he felt baffled and incapable when the Levantine led him into the elegant little room and he saw that Statilius and Memphius were with her. Before he caught sight of her on the couch near the window, erect in folds of sand-colored silk and with her hands crossed in deliberate repose over the flute on her knees, he was aware of the poet lolling in a chair and smiling the knowing smile of one who waits for a choice episode in the human comedy; before he met her glance, he saw that the little dancer, sitting on the floor beside her and playing with the embroidery on the hem of her skirt, was doing his best to suppress his excitement over the scandalous and revealing things that would undoubtedly be said. But she transcended the tingling, tittering atmosphere around her. She gave him a formal greeting without changing in the least her attitude of quiet dignity. And such a light flooded into her pale grey eyes that he told himself: In spite of the other two, this can be honest, this can be kind and deep.

"You look ghastly, if you don't mind my saying so," said Statilius.

"He's been sick, as you know very well. Let him alone."

Bird-voice, flute-voice, he thought, coming as it has always come to my defense, vibrant with a loyalty unmerited now. "Yes, I was very sick. I almost died," he said.

The light that suffused the faded grey pupils of her eyes was intensified; the mouth parted in a tentative smile. Oh, she would believe anything, anything—he had not thought of that! She would believe that nothing but sickness had kept him from her, she would tell herself all the plausible lies about undelivered messages, her starved heart would nourish itself on an imaginary store of love kept back at the palace door by his mother's spite—

"Sit down, my darling, and let me get you a cup of wine."

"No, I'll have to go in a moment." He could not bear to hear her compromise herself by uttering lovers' names before these other two. "Everything is changed with me. I'm in trouble, I'm in very serious trouble. I only came to tell you. I only came to take my leave—"

"To take your leave?"

"Yes, I'm going away, into exile. I'm going tomorrow night."

"Into exile? Let me go—" She fell silent, seeing the consternation and rejection in his look. She rose and let her eyelids down and laid aside the flute. "Let me go with you into some other room," she said. "Our friends here will excuse us—" She straightened her shoulders and smoothed the folds of silk over her bosom; she moved with a jerky travesty of her usual quick grace. "Here," she said, picking up the flute again and laying it in Memphius's lap, "you can amuse yourself with this. As for you"—she crossed the room and laid her hand with studied familiarity along Statilius's sallow cheek, "you can decide for me what I'm to read at Berosus's tonight."

He had thought she would lead him into the dining room. Instead she went before him through the hall and up the narrow outer stairs, taking him to the bedchamber, possibly because she meant to make sure that no word between them would reach the curious and delighted ears of her guests, possibly because she had conjectured what odds had been marshalled up against her and had chosen the ground on which she could summon her only allies, the hosts of wounding memories. For an instant, at the top of the steep flight, he entertained the thought that everything could be postponed: he could allow her to believe a little longer that some arbitrary circumstance had kept him from her, and day after tomorrow he could send a long and well-considered letter from the villa in the Campagna, a merciful and eloquent statement of the truth. But he rejected that; it belied the high and serious heart he had carried to her; it was an affront to her and to himself. She did not come, as he had feared she would, to ask for an embrace; she went instead to the other side of the room, leaving the bed between them—the remembered coverlet marked with the print of Cyrillus's feet. And those marks so unmanned him that he could not find the proper thing to say: he groped for words until she could not bear the sterile stillness anymore. "What is it? Don't stand and stare at me. Tell me what it is," she said.

"I came to tell you what you must already know—"

She would not accept his look but gazed down at the marks on the coverlet. "I don't know anything. All I know is that you were silent, utterly silent —I never had a word from you in all these days. How sick you were—when you almost died—when you began to recover—I got all that from Antisthenes, whose secretary got it from one of Flavius Labeo's slaves. And yesterday, only yesterday, it occurred to me that your mother—"

"No." He took the sword to that doomed and suffering hope; he looked straight into her eyes and shook his head. "No, I didn't write to you, I couldn't bring myself to write to you. What I had to tell you couldn't be written, had to be said—"

"Because you were being spied on?"

Oh, God, he thought, how many lives does this sort of hope possess, how many horrible blows will I be forced to strike before the thing is dead? "No, not that either. There have been changes—a great many changes took place in me while I was sick. Everything is changed now, everything—"

"Everything?" The faded grey eyes were straining out of the rigid, carefully painted face. The hands came together, were clenched together until the knuckles shone.

"Yes, everything." It came out of him in a miserable whisper, without conviction, without dignity.

"Even our love, Favorinus?"

"Yes, even our love."

The sound she uttered then was like the last feeble cry of a dog run over by the wheel of a carriage. "Don't do that, don't make that sound, I can't stand it," he said. "What do you want of me? Do you want me to lie to you?

269

I'm going away, I may never come back again, I have to tell you the truth."

"Yes, of course," she said in a quiet, bitter voice, smiling a sick smile at him. "You're a truthful, honorable man, aren't you? You can't sleep nights unless your accounts are in good order. Keep everything clear and plain, by all means, or the horrible confusion you're so afraid of will come rushing in. Well, tell me the truth, I'm ready—" she stood with her hands behind her, like a slave at the whipping post. "See, I'm ready, tell me the truth."

"Listen, Charis—"

"What's the matter? Haven't you got the courage to say it? Do I have to say it for you because you're afraid? What do you want me to say, my lord and my master? That we're finished, that nothing is left between us now? It's easily said. Only, once you've said it, you can't leave this room at peace with me and yourself and the gods. Maybe you can treat kitchen slaves like that, but I'm different, thanks to you and Marcellinus. Let's say you're finished with me—that's plain enough. But before you walk out of here, you're going to tell me why."

"I can't tell you why. I only know it's happened—"

"Very well, then, let's not inquire into the cause, let's confine ourselves to the occasion," she said, using the terms of philosophic argumentation, implying by her jeering voice that he was the sort to deal with a mangled heart as coldly, as rationally as if it were a geometrical proposition. "Could the occasion by any chance have been what happened here on the evening of the Saturnalia? Might I suggest—only hypothetically, of course—that you found the filthy whore you lay with on that particular evening a little more diverting than my used and stale and somewhat limited self?"

"I didn't lie with her." But he blushed to have said it. He blushed because it was so specious, so sophistical—such a shameful twisting of the truth.

"No? Excuse my innocence. I should have remembered that her inventive powers are extraordinary—better than nature's, certainly better than mine."

"Must we talk about that?"

"Oh, no, certainly not, not if you don't want to. And I can imagine you wouldn't want to. You, of all people, going like a pig in rut after Orbiana Festina—"

"You also—"

"I also?" The laughter that came out of her rigid mouth was as disintegrating as the cry she had uttered a while ago. "What did you want me to do? Watch and applaud? You had an audience. Memphius was entranced. He should have been enough."

"Oh, God," he said, sick with the hopeless conviction that he would never be able to extricate himself from the sordid doings of that night. "Let's get clear of that, let's forgive each other for that. It was something else, it was something entirely different that I wanted to say—"

"It's not a matter of forgiving, don't lie to yourself. Maybe I forgave you, but you didn't forgive me, not in the least—you couldn't look at me that morning when they woke you to tell you about the tenement. If you don't think about that anymore, it's not because you've forgiven me, don't deceive yourself. It's only that sometime between that morning and this afternoon something else happened—something that made you see you didn't care."

He could not look at the pale, glaring eyes. He stared instead at the bolster where their heads had pressed the wadding down through a thousand nights; and this mute record shamed and wounded him more than her accusing eyes. "I cared enough to come. I could have written to you. At least I cared enough that I had to come, I had to see you one more time before I went away," he said.

She had completely forgotten the matter of his going—he knew it by the sharp and sudden intake of her breath. "What's happened? What's the matter?" she asked him, and in so usual a voice that he had to look up, and, looking up, was profoundly disturbed by the sight of her face. All in an instant, it had been transformed, it was innocent now of all fury; only the old concern was there, the loyalty and the tenderness. And he knew with fright that she refused to recognize the breach between them, that she had successfully defended some citadel at the core of her being against every word he had said.

"I told you—I tried to tell you. I quarreled with my uncle. I'm going into exile," he said.

"But surely it's possible to have a difference with him without going into exile. He's not a tyrant—you could explain. You could apologize."

"That would be useless, my darling—" Old habit and her quiet, customary manner had betrayed him into using the term; and, seeing the light brimming into her eyes again, he was appalled. "I've broken with him—he's made up his mind to persecute the Christians. I can't be responsible for that, I won't be part of his following anymore."

"Of course not, I see that. But that doesn't mean you have to go and hide. You could simply withdraw and live quietly here in the City—couldn't you, love? That's a good life, too. You used to like it before he came back from Verona with the purple. That's a good life—we always said so, you and I—"

"No, I couldn't stay. Even if he let me, I wouldn't want to. Everything here is finished for me now."

Her face assumed a false and exasperating puzzlement—the brow furrowed, the lips twisted to one side like the lips of a sulky child. "What are you talking about?" she said.

"Oh, God!" He shouted it, pressing his temples with his clenched fist. What do you want of me, how many times will you force me to say it? Everything is finished between you and me. I don't love you, I can't love you. That's the cruel part, and you keep making me say it over and over until I think I'll go mad. Won't you ever be quiet long enough for me to say the rest? Listen, whether I love you now or not, it's still true that once I loved you, loved you more than I loved anybody else on earth. I'll be grateful to you for every day and every night we ever spent with each other."

"Grateful? Don't bother to be grateful. I never counted the number of times, but I'm sure you paid me well enough. You could scour the city from one end to the other and never find a better-paid whore. In fact—" she flung herself round, she flew from the bed to the chest so suddenly, so wildly that he started back in fright— "in fact, I'm the one that's indebted to you—" With hard hands, with a jangling of bracelets, she grasped the massive jewel box and brought it back with her, the tendons in her neck and arms standing out with the weight of it, the curls nodding crazily on top of her head. "Here, take them, take all of them," she said, gasping and pouring the jewels onto the coverlet. "Nothing I gave you was worth such a price. Whatever I gave you, you could have had at any bawdy house in the Suburra for a couple of denarii."

"Don't do that, my darling, don't do that," he said. "I loved you when I gave you those. Whatever you may think, I have a great affection for you still."

"Affection?" She flung a bracelet at him, and he felt unmanly and ridiculous because he automatically jerked aside. "What do you think I can do with your affection? What good will your affection be to me when I'm here by myself, and my whole body is hungry for your body?"

He could think of no answer, and yet he had to fill up the wretched silence. "Maybe," he said miserably, after a long pause, "maybe there'll be a time when you'll find it possible to forgive me."

"Nobody forgives until he's stopped loving. I'll not stop loving until I'm in my grave. Why don't you take yourself off? What do you want with me? Everything's done, everything's said. Pick up your property, my lord and my master, and get out of this room."

"No, keep them, I don't want them. Sell them, throw them away, do what you like. What would I do with them now?"

"You could always give them to my successor—" She stopped so sharply that he could not refrain from raising his eyes, wet and abashed and shameful as they were, to see what she was about. Her face had undergone another frightening transmutation. It was uglier than he had ever seen it; it was knowing and crafty, with narrowed eyes and compressed lips. "Who is she—who is my successor? Who was it that your mother forced on you when you were too sick and weak to refuse?"

"Nobody. I'm not going to be married. I'll never be married."

"No?" White rage flashed into her faded eyes. "Then it's another mistress? Then it's somebody you chose for yourself?"

"I didn't choose anybody." Again, it was tawdry and sophistical, and he was ashamed to have said it, so ashamed that he was unable to withstand her steady glare.

"Then who was chosen for you?" she asked him, jeering. "How do you find your women? Answer me—answer me one simple question—" she leaned across the bed and shrieked it into his face. "Where have you been since I saw you last?"

No, I'll not lie to her a second time, he thought in his weariness, and wearily mocked at himself, knowing that his willingness to state the facts did not arise out of any moral valor, arose only from his certainty that the truth was so preposterous that she would never see it, even if he laid it before her eyes. "Since I saw you last," he said, "I've scarcely been in situations where I'd be looking for women. Let's see—first of all, I was in a collapsed tenement, and the only women there were dead. After that, I took some money to the Christians—I took it to them because they were the only ones who knew how to reach my tenants. And after that I was at home, sick, as you know—confined to my room, confined to my bed. Nobody came to see me—nobody but the Secretary of Petitions and some old friends of my mother's. When I got up, I went to the Emperor's palace. Matters between me and my uncle were such that I'd hardly have noticed if Venus had been there stark naked. That was yesterday. Today—this morning—I went to my Christian relatives to warn them about the persecution—"

"What relatives? Probus and Paulina?"

"Who else? There are no other Christians among the Herennii—"

"Oh, no!" she said, shaken all over with crazy laughter. "Then that's the reason—for *that* you got yourself into trouble with the Emperor, for *that* you made yourself chief advocate for those idiots and got yourself sent into exile—for that washed-out, sexless thing that nobody else would look at twice. But, of course, you were always dragging her into the conversation, you were always finding reasons to talk about her—but it's too ridiculous, I couldn't believe it, I never guessed. A stick—a dried-up stick in a dress like a vegetable sack—and that look on her face, that never-touch-me look— nobody ever would, she needn't worry—who'd want her, who but that other piece of wood she's married to—him and her crucified Jew? Wait till you get a good look at the dried up thing—you'll see!"

And strangely, out of that coarseness a vision rose and detached itself, a vision so delicate and consoling that he could not suppress a smile. For the first time he pondered her body, all of her body—meager flesh and cloudy hair and netted veins—white and pale brown and bluish violet. "I'll never touch her—it isn't like that," he said, still smiling. "She'll have no part of me. No, I'll never touch her, put it out of your mind. Don't imagine things, don't torment yourself."

"If *that's* where you're going, you'll be coming back."

"No, I don't think so—"

273

"*I* do. You'll be sick of it after a while—taking your dreams out on a wooden idol and taking the rest of it out on whores—"

"Let's stop this. What's the good of it?"

"No good. No good at all. I'm patient—a slave learns patience—I can wait. A couple of months—I'd give you a year at the most—I'm patient, I can bide my time."

"Listen, Charis—"

"I've heard it all, there's nothing more for me to hear. Let's go down to the others."

"I told you to listen!" He grasped her by the shoulders as she started for the door. "It's useless to wait for me, I'll never come back. I can't love you. I'll never be able to love you. Believe that, accept that—you're young, I'll leave you rich, you can make some other life for yourself."

She lunged at him then, she threw her arms around his neck. Her kisses—strong, imperious—assailed his neck, his cheek, his mouth. He stiffened and closed his eyes, holding himself rigid, unseeing, unfeeling, until she drew back and gave him a shattering blow across the face. When he recovered himself he saw that she was over the threshold, out of the room, running down the stairs.

He had meant to follow her, but he stopped at the door, remembering that there were two guests in the room below. He would have to wait for the mark of the blow on his cheek to subside; she would not want them to know that there had been any anger, any violence; mean as it was, he had to admit that the presence of Statilius and Memphius was a fortunate accident, would reduce to a short and decent formula what would otherwise have been a protracted and agonizing farewell. And when he stepped out onto the stair, he was astounded to hear that voice, ranting like the voice of a fishwife, those words, pouring out of the window for all the neighborhood to hear—a voice that was not the voice of Charis, words that were not the words of Charis.

"Tell them at Berosus's place tonight that I'm available again—and cheap, too, used and cheap," she was saying as he entered the room. "He's finished with me—he's found something more to his taste—a Christian matron—not that he means to pick up the skirt of her holy dalmatica—she's above all that sort of vulgarity, they're going to have a lovely, holy time of it, collecting alms and baking sanctified bread. No, don't get any wrong ideas where he's concerned. He's perfectly pure, I can assure you. He draws himself up like a virgin when he's kissed—he's undergone the most amazing change since he tore the clothes off Orbiana Festina on Saturnalia night!"

She was standing in the middle of the room, addressing herself alternately to Statilius and Memphius. The poet had risen hunched and awkward and appalled out of his chair. The little dancer was still sitting cross-legged on the floor, his girlish face twitching and crinkling with fear and delight.

"He's here, he's right behind you," Statilius said.

"What do I care? There's none of it I wouldn't say to his face. He's used me and thrown me away—he knows it himself. How else could it end between a patrician and a slave?"

"Will you be quiet for a moment?" he said.

"To hear more of your rhetoric?"

"No. What I want to say should take no time at all. I forgot to tell you upstairs that the rents will be brought here as usual—my steward will bring them—"

"Oh, no, he won't. If he comes here with your filthy money I'll throw it into the street."

"Oh, now, Charis, that's no way to talk," said the little dancer. For the first time, he was sighting the end of mussels in fish-sauce, and the prospect left him scandalized. "He's doing his best to be nice about it—why don't you let him be nice? Wouldn't it be better for everybody concerned if the two of you parted good friends after all this time."

"Shut your mouth, you little—" She screamed it, and added an epithet that had never before been uttered in this room, a loathsome epithet, begetting a hideous image—an affront to taste and human decency. "Shut your mouth and keep it shut until I come back! I'm going to get his jewels—"

As soon as she was out of the room he started for the door. Stay through another scene he could not—he had borne as much as he could bear. But what a way to leave her, he thought, unable to sustain the stares of Memphius and Statilius, hurrying with bent head toward the doorway. What a way to leave her, after all those mornings, all those nights . . . Nor could he dispel the churning sickness and the shame within him by telling himself in the crowded street that what he had done this afternoon he had been forced to do to fulfill the inexorable necessities of his living heart. Even while he reasoned that to have remained with her, or to have pretended to love her still would have been a kind of corruption, he could not cease condemning himself. The change he had wrought upon her was so heavy on his spirit that he could not keep the stricken aimlessness out of his walk, could not suppress a succession of shaking sighs. When I had a dead heart, he thought, she spoke like a singing bird and moved like a bird in flight, and all the old scholars in the Library of Trajan lifted their rheumy eyes from the scrolls to see her pass. While death was in me, she lived and was as kind and chaste as any faithful wife, and now that I live she is dead and cruel and worse than a whore. . . .

He began to ponder then, to ask himself what sort of harvest this resurrection might yield, seeing that the first fruits of it had been so bitter. Charis was deserted, and the Lord of the World had been deserted in his most pressing hour, and others also—his mother, Drusilla, Baubio—would remain behind to suffer while he looked to the needs of his living heart. It was as if, in rising from the dead, he tore his life out of other men's dying bodies, leaving ruin all around him. And the thought was terrible to him, as terrible as the thought of black Chaos, so that he cursed himself and began to look wildly for a litter, knowing that he must go at once to the palace of the Herennii while there was still some residue of failing valor in him, while he yet had strength enough to do what must be done.

Chapter 20

HALF OF the remaining obligations—the more difficult half, or so at least he told himself, turning his back on the bronze Mercury and the money-bags and the white head bowed on the table—half of the remaining obligations had been discharged. Before he could take anything else upon himself, he would have to eat, he would have to rest. And, in spite of the sobs, in spite of the petty recriminations and the insinuations and the afterthoughts, the encounter had not been entirely fruitless: before the end of it, the real issue had emerged in strength and dignity.

She had asked him all the contemptible questions, yes: Why should he sacrifice himself for a pair of worthless outcasts? How angry *was* the Emperor—angry enough to confiscate the property? What sort of effect did he think a scandal like this would have on the prestige of the Herennii? But in the end she had faced—and mourned—the actual loss. "You're leaving me," he had said, letting her disheveled head come down on her withered arms. Both of you are walking away and leaving me. I'll have nobody now, I have no friends—nobody ever really liked me, you know. The two of you were all I had, not because either of you actually cared for me, only because children are tied to their mothers in spite of themselves. Now that's gone, too, and what do you think I'll do with myself—an old woman, a widow, childless now, not even a grandchild left with me—an old woman wandering around an empty house alone?"

He had honored the question enough to leave it unanswered. Now, turning back for an instant, he saw for the first time in many years the crown of that old head: the silvery veil thrown back, the pink of the scalp showing through the sparse white curls. Somebody else—one of the Nubians —was staring at her also from a shadowy part of the hall, and curiosity and satisfaction shone in the avid, alien eyes. "What are you doing here, you idiot?" he said. "Be about your business, or I'll give you reason to regret it." And he closed the door with a bang and started for the stairs.

Dusk was settling in on the palace. Seen from the staircase in the oblique and fading January light, the atrium had the abandoned look of some forgotten Aegean temple left to the encroachment of the centuries and the sea. A slave on a ladder was taking down the garlands put up for the last reception; detaching them by twos, he dropped them on the floor, where they landed with a dry, rustling sound. A slant of sunlight lighted up the cupboard of the ancestors. There was something awesome, something final about the closed, smoke-blistered doors. "Not even a grandchild left"—so the old voice had said, bewailing the lost seed, the empty womb, the power and the glory heaped up for nothing. And he felt a dynasty come to a dead stop within him.

He fell to wondering whether his sister had ever felt the same annihilating conviction of finality. Her childlessness, like the doings of her husband, had been so minutely discussed, so exhaustively grieved over and brooded upon that every time it was mentioned he thought of something else: none of her afflictions could move him anymore to anything but exasperation. And yet, he told himself, going upstairs, since she is a woman she would feel these things more poignantly than I; once in the course of every moon she must know in her vitals this same reproach, this same futility . . . The wraith that he had made of her almost came to life: she was a woman and deserved at least her share of his general pity for womankind. And if he did not go to talk to her at once, before the customary impatience set in, it was only because he thought it would be better to come to her refreshed and self-possessed, after a little meat and a little wine and the soothing ministrations of his body-slave.

But when he opened the door of his chamber, he was appalled at the sight of the room. Everything was exactly as he had left it in the morning— the unmade bed, the open chest, the clothing strewn on the chairs. "Baubio," he said, and the voice came out of him in a sick whisper. "What's the meaning of this? Where are you? Baubio!"

"Forgive me, my lord and my master," said the steward of the house, looking in at the door. "I should have assigned somebody else to set your room to rights. Your Aethiopian—didn't they tell you?—he went out on a errand for the lady Sabina this morning, and we haven't heard from him since, though we've been looking high and low."

"Gone since morning?" He stepped back and let himself down into a chair. He was seeing the naked black figure being beaten with leather thongs; he was seeing the strong, ministering hands being dragged into the fire. "Gone since morning? Oh, God!"

"We knew you'd be distressed to hear it, my lord and my master. But we're looking, we're still looking, and sooner or later we're bound to hear—"

"Hear? What would you hear?" What news could you hear from the subterranean chambers under the Urban Prefect's office?

"We're doing everything we can, my lord and my master. Meanwhile, allow me to send you another slave."

"Send me nobody," he shouted, pressing his forehead down upon his closed fists. "Get out of here and close the door!"

But as soon as the door was closed he rushed at it and flung it open. It was unthinkable that he should have to endure such a thing at the hands of the Urban Prefect. He would go to him, he would face him out with it at his banquet table before his guests, he would beat his fist on the table and demand the immediate return of his slave. And he had actually crossed the threshold of his chamber before it broke upon him that he was nothing, a man suspected, a man that must go into exile, with no influence at all. He thought of force then. He thought how it would be to take his slaves and his clients and storm the prison doors—but that was childish, and he knew it at once. He was no Caesar, no Marius to beat down the State with the number of his armed retainers. The tribune in charge of the Urban Prefect's prison could summon up at a shout enough City Guardsmen to lay low whatever force any Roman citizen could hurl against the filthy place. And for the first time he felt the meaning of tyranny—felt it in his fiery nerves, felt it in his seething blood.

Then suddenly the fire in him sputtered out, leaving him so weak that he had to sit down on the edge of the bed, so listless that he could not even bestir himself to close the door, though anybody passing in the hall could stare at him in his distress. The slave would die—he knew with bitter certainty that the slave would die without uttering one implicating word, and therein lay the irony: uselessly, to prevent what had already come about, the musk-scented presence that had moved so apt and hushed and gentle in this room would touch and whisper and smile no more. How was it with my slave and me when we were together for the last time? he thought. Was I harsh and hateful with him? Those curses that I shouted at him when he refused to put the double portion of the sleeping potion in my cup—were those the last words that passed and will ever pass between him and me? And when he remembered his own voice saying something else, making some companionable remark to the dusky presence through the fibrous cloud of sleep, it was so blessed an indulgence on the part of destiny that he flung himself down on the pillows and wept.

How long he had been lying there, with his face buried in the pillows, before he became aware that hostile eyes were staring down at him, he did not know. But he knew it was his sister, even before her voice, curt and incisive, came down at him from the foot of the bed. "*You* crying? I never thought I'd live to see the day. What's the matter with you?" she said.

"Baubio's gone." He sat up and groped for a corner of the coverlet and dried his face with it. "He left this morning, and nobody's heard from him since."

"Yes, somebody mentioned he was missing. But aren't you overdoing it a little—your Stoic concern for your slaves?"

He did not look at her. He knew that the grime of the day was streaked across his cheeks, that his eyes were red and swollen. "It's not a matter to make light of," he said in an angry voice. "I'm afraid he's dead."

"Dead? Not very likely. He's probably lying around drunk, in some tavern. He'll probably come reeling in and wake me up just when I've got myself to sleep."

"On the contrary. They have him at the Urban Prefect's office." He looked up for the first time, expecting to see her in consternation. But the implication of his words was apparently lost on her; she continued to stand above him in a rigid and hieratical position, her hands clasped between her breasts, the dimple in her cheek deepened by the old malicious smile.

"Why don't you go and get him then? You're the Emperor's darling. You can get anything from anybody," she said.

He had meant to tell her gently, after a long and reassuring prelude; but her utter unconcern—the smile, the taunting eyes, the unbending body under its veils of sea-green Egyptian linen—goaded him on. "I can't get him. I can't get anything. I'm in trouble, desperate trouble. I've had a quarrel with the Emperor."

A low, incongruous spurt of laughter issued from the curved lips without changing their contours in the least.

"What's there to laugh about?"

"You had a quarrel with the Emperor—that's vastly amusing! Well, considering how much the two of you needed each other, considering that a person couldn't get a word with you for months because you were always running here and there and the other place to be with the Lord of the World, I imagine it's a lover's quarrel, I imagine you'll make it up in a week," she said.

"I tell you, it's a desperate matter," he shouted at the top of his voice. "I'm going into exile. He's finished with me, he hates me, I'll have to get out of his way at once—"

"Why? Why?" She said it in a whisper. "Because I wouldn't climb into bed with that sickly virgin the two of you picked out for me? That's a pity that's a dreadful pity. But he'll forgive you, he'll get over it—wait and see."

"Please try to pay attention to me," he said, and knew with a shock that traveled up and down his spine that he was speaking to her as if she were an irresponsible child. "I had a quarrel with the Emperor. It had nothing whatever to do with you and Herennius. We quarreled about policy, we quarreled about the Christians."

"About the Christians?" A vertical line of concentration—and concentration seemed to be difficult, even painful—stood between her two carefully plucked eyebrows. "What have you got to do with the Christians?"

"Nothing. It was only that I found out there was going to be a persecution." The little, lucid sentences with the long pauses in between—they should have offended her, but she only nodded and sighed. "I found it out from the Emperor himself, and I went to tell them to be prepared. A spy followed me—he saw what I did. That's why I'm leaving—I'll have to leave at once—"

"Why should you do a thing like that?" she said, playing with her fingers, pulling at the tip of one of her fingers until a knuckle made a cracking sound. "That's so kind—so foolish and so kind."

"Do you mean that usually I'm wise and heartless?" he asked, disquieted because her eyes, wide open and luminous now, were staring at him through the growing dark.

"Wise and heartless—yes, that's it. That's the way you are, at least to me. You never went to Eugenius. You never told him he could come back and be forgiven, and any decent brother would have done at least that much. He might have come back if anybody had asked him. How can you know until you've tried? Wise and heartless, and yet you did a kind and foolish thing. Tell me—" she bent forward, she spoke in a whisper, straight into his face— "who were those Christians? Who were the ones you told?"

He drew back from her in spite of himself. His attempt at an offhand gesture was self-conscious, unconvincing. "Probus and Paulina, of course. They're the only Christians I know," he said.

"Probus and Paulina?" She straightened and went back to the business of wrenching and cracking her emaciated fingers. "Yes, of course. They'll be involved in it, they're bound to be involved, because he's a deacon. What'll they do? Where will they go to hide?"

"Probus won't leave—he'll go into hiding somewhere in the City."

"But Paulina—they'll send her away, won't they?"

"Yes, to a villa in the Campagna," he said.

"And you—I suppose you'll go to Africa."

There was an instant when her darting looks and her quick little questions so hemmed him in that he was on the point of telling her a lie. But that was insane: she would be certain to learn the truth from her mother. "No, not to Africa, not anywhere outside of Italy," he said. "Probus advised me not to take ship. He says the ports are being watched, and I suppose he knows

281

what he's talking about. In fact, they made me a very hospitable offer, and I accepted it. I'm going to the Campagna with Paulina."

"With Paulina? You and she—nobody else? You and Paulina, in a villa in the Campagna, all by yourselves?" She laughed again, and the laughter brought on a fit of coughing. She laughed until the tears stood in her eyes.

"Stop that! Stop laughing!" he said, and his voice was loud with the unbearable uncertainty. "What's the matter with you? What is there to laugh about?"

"Nothing, nothing." For a moment it seemed to him that she was about to depart as abruptly as she had come. Stifling her laughter, reassuming the old hieratical rigidity, she walked round the side of the bed and started for the door. But on the threshold she turned and stood in the shadow of the open doorway, invisible except for the moist shining of her eyes. "I was only remembering what you used to think of me—eaten up with love, sick with love, disgustingly in love. What sort of person is it that would throw away everything—self-respect and money and common decency—and all for a morbid infatuation, that's what you used to think about me. I was the one who made a public spectacle of myself. I was the one who disgraced the name of the Herennii. I was the one who turned my back on the purple and insulted the Emperor. And all because I had a disgraceful itch in my blood, as you and Mother kept telling each other behind my back, no doubt. So now you're going to the Campagna—isn't that nice? You and Paulina— well, I like Paulina. I hope you both enjoy yourselves."

"What do you mean?" he said in a whisper.

She did not answer, and in the silence his mind veered between two possibilities: either she had acquired in her total isolation a more-than-human wisdom and knew that he had rendered himself up utterly and therefore laid claim to as much indulgence from him as he demanded for himself, or she was catching scents in the air with animal keenness, with the less-than-human shrewdness of the mad.

Then suddenly the hall behind her was flooded with a yellow radiance. The slaves were bearing the wax lights into the darkened rooms—great candelabra, dripping with wax and tipped with streaming flames. "Kindl my lamps!" he shouted to the Nubian who stood behind her in the corridor and saw in the advancing brightness that she had not stirred, had neither heard his shout nor seen the light. "Forgive me, my lady," said the Nubian behind her, and coughed discreetly because she did not make the slightes move to let him pass. And, with the resigned sigh of one who has learned certain unconventional ways of dealing with such strange behavior, h lowered the candelabrum and waved it near her elbow, so that her pearls the line of her cheek, her brooding eyes, and the dry black braid on top c her head seemed to take fire.

"Oh, yes, you want to come in, you want to light the lamps," she said stepping forward jerkily. "Hurry, will you? I can't bear more than one light at a time anymore. Those candelabra always hurt my eyes."

While the Nubian kindled the lamp on the chest and the lamp on the table, he rose from the side of the bed and stood before her, composing his face into the cool and friendly mask suitable before the mad. And, when the slave was gone, he told her in more of the little, lucid sentences that there were good things to be found in every bad situation, that at least she needn't go to Epidaurus now that he had fallen out with the Emperor, that she could stay at home in comfort—

"Oh, no," she said, breaking in upon him, her brows contracted, her forehead divided again by the vertical line of thought and pain. "Everybody's going away, and so am I. You can't leave me alone here in the house with the old woman. I'll tell you something about her—something you may not know: when she's furious with you and me, she pinches the slaves. At Epidaurus—Flavius Labeo was telling me about it the other day—the windows are always open and the wind comes in from the sea. Nobody's ever alone there, there's always somebody you can talk to, even the beds are set in rows, close together, with nothing but curtains between. All night long the priests come by with lamps to watch over the sleepers. 'Sleep, little one, sleep soundly in the bosom of the god'—that's what the priests come and whisper in your ear in the middle of the night."

The long corridor, peopled with the dreaming multitude of the sick and the lost and the rejected, the moving lamp and the sea-wind billowing the curtains, the whisper and the breath of the whisper stirring subtly over closed eyelids—she was thinking of them, and for an instant the thought of them erased the line between her brows. Then, all at once, the agitation set in again: she bit at her lips, she pulled at her fingers. "But it isn't the peace and quiet I care about, that isn't the reason I'm going," she said.

"Then why are you going?"

"Because it's the only thing I can do to make Eugenius come back to me. You know how it is with him and the old woman. She hates him, and he knows she hates him. While I'm under the same roof with her, he'll never come back. She wishes him evil—he can't live, he can't breathe, with all those evil wishes in the air. And for that I can't blame him—can you? No, I'm going to Epidaurus in any case, there won't be any arguments. And Prisca's going with me—not the old woman—nobody but Prisca—"

She stopped, because he had opened his mouth to speak. "What's the matter? Don't you want me to take her? Do you need her here?" she said. "I have so much trouble with my hair these days—it's too thick, I can't braid it anymore, something's gone wrong with my fingers. She's the only one who can make this braid of mine."

"I have to take her with me because she's a Christian."

The incongruous laughter shook her again, stirring the Egyptian linen draped over her emaciated chest. "Is she a Christian? Is she really a

Christian? That's wonderful, Mother'd be furious if she knew—a Christian living under her roof—"

"Sylvanus, too—I've got to take Sylvanus—"

"Marvelous, marvelous! Mother sets such store by Sylvanus. She says she wouldn't give him up for anything in the world. And now you're taking him away—and Prisca, too—because they're Christians. That's rare, that's marvelous—that they should be Christians and Mother never knew it, I mean. Wait—I'll send you Prisca—I'll tell her where she's going. To the Campagna, isn't it? To a villa in the Campagna. Nobody else, only you and Paulina. Stay where you are and I'll send her to you—" She turned, she darted down the corridor, stumbling over the folds of her dalmatica, steadying herself against the wall. "Stay where you are—she'll come."

And now that he had turned back to the empty room, mercilessly exposed in the light of two lamps, now that he saw again the strewn clothing and the rumpled bed, it sprang at him again like a beast with claws—the thought of Baubio. In utter misery he let himself down on the edge of the bed. His hands lay limp and grimy in his lap; his body smelled of sickly sweat; he shivered with the cold. And such minor comforts as fire and water can bring to the wretched—these, too, he denied himself, inasmuch as he could not bring himself to call another slave to serve him, could only keep thinking over and over: He is dying for my sake, my bringer of water, my kindler of fires. . . .

How long he sat there with his grime and his guilt and his grief upon him, he did not know. It seemed to him that half an hour had passed before the sounds came—the quick, firm step, the little creak of the door.

"Are you sleeping? Have I disturbed you, my master?"

It was the slave-child Prisca. The dim hall was behind her, but his lamp lighted up one side of her—the sturdy bare leg, the white translucent tunic the fresh, freckled cheek and the new-washed hair. "No, no." He sighed and drew his hand across his forehead. "Come in, I'm very glad to see you," he said.

"May I ask you a question, my lord Favorinus?" She stepped into the room, and, automatically, without taking her big and serious eyes from his face for an instant, set herself to reducing the petty confusion—straightened the coverlet, shook the pillow, gathered up a tunic, a belt, a scroll and laid them in a neat heap on top of a chest.

"Yes, certainly," he said after a silence so long that he could not quite remember what it was that he was assenting to.

"My lady Drusilla tells me you told her something. Sometimes—you know how it is with my lady and my mistress—sometimes she imagines people say things that they haven't said at all."

"About going away with me—was that what she told you?"

"Yes, my lord and my master—"

"No, she didn't make that up, it's perfectly true," he said.

She had bent over to pick up a sandal. She came up without it and such delight as he had forgotten could exist in this world broke in her crinkling, freckled face. "Am I really to go on a journey? Am I really to be your slave?" she said.

"Yes, you and your father also."

"My father also?" Her eyes, wide and shadowless, shone at him like water in sun. "Oh, if you knew what you're saving us from, if you knew how blessed—"

She made a wild upward gesture of rejoicing, striking her hands together above her head, and even his stiff and weary mouth was able to smile. "I do know. We'll hide—we're going into the Campagna. It'll be safer for you there," he said.

"Dear master, deliverer!" The words leaped out of her strong and unconstrained, ringing with exultation. She knelt on the carpet at his feet, she clasped his legs, she pressed her face against his knees. "The angels will hear of it, God will reward you. I love you, I'll pray for you, I'll serve you with all my heart as long as I live!"

"Get up, get up, it's nothing—"

"God knows what it is." She raised her head and offered him, like a draught of crystalline water, all the radiant, innocent happiness in her face. And his living heart rose up to take it. This good at least had come out of all the evil, this flower at least flourished among the ruins, she at least had been salvaged from the sick and the deserted and the dead—so he told his living heart.

Chapter 21

"Dear wife, dear sharer in the hope of the Kingdom that is to come," wrote the deacon Probus on the third sheet of papyrus, and then looked up at the other two sheets, crushed into balls and still crackling open in the light of the lamp. It was a waste of time, it was a waste of papyrus—the words in all three of the salutations were more or less the same. Nor was it necessary, he told himself, to turn out an eloquent and unassailable document. He was not writing his epic on the wanderings of Barnabas; he was writing a letter, a simple letter, to tell his wife that he loved her and that the old man, the shepherd of the flock, whom the two of them had loved together, was dead, had gone before them to sit at the throne of God. "Dear sharer in the hope of the Kingdom that is to come" was perfectly suitable for the occasion. Only, he wished now that he had inserted another phrase before it, something like "Dear sharer in my cup of the tears of this world."

"I write this at midnight, in the cellar room of one of the smaller tenements in the Suburra. It is damp and bare, but it serves well enough as a dwelling place for the elders and the deacons and as an office for the business of the Lord. We have food, we have oil for the lamps, we have tables and drawers, and our beds are made up of old tunics and cloaks spread out on the earthen floor. The owner of the tenement, a Christian of the house of the Aemilii, sees to our wants with understanding and diligence. We suffer not

286

ing but minor inconveniences, and, since we have been coming and going circumspectly, dressed like artisans and entering and leaving at the usual workman's hours, nobody in the neighborhood has shown the slightest curiosity."

He re-read the whole first paragraph and shook his head. I should have begun with something else, he thought. I should have told her: I miss our house, I miss our room, I miss our bed; it seems intolerable to lie down without your hand reaching for mine in the dark . . . He dipped the pen again. "Believe me," he wrote, "I feel the lack of you. The greatest burden our Lord has put upon me yet is this burden of loneliness.

"As I write this all the brethren are asleep, save only the respected elder Novatian and myself. The rest retired early, worn out with the rich fulfillment of God's purpose to which we bore witness this day, when the most worthy of us all was taken up to the arms of his Saviour . . ." It was easier now, it was always so when he gave up the stubborn striving to write what he actually felt, and immersed himself instead in that river of prose, warm and ambient and faintly clouded, which had been pouring now for two centuries from the pens of the scribes of God. He did not look up: it would be better not to intrude himself, even by a glance, upon the vigil of Nova tian. "For this is the day of the martyrdom of the blessed Fabian, our shepherd, chosen for us to such high purpose by God and His dove. We were with our blessed one, we beheld it all from the beginning, but there was not one among us who marred the glorious moment with our tears. And, remembering how many times in the course of his life with us he bade us not to weep, we will sleep soundly through this night in the sure knowledge that he is with the Lord.

"Our Papa Fabian was the first to be taken. With him there was no tarrying. Day before yesterday he was led from his house by a tribune of the City Guard; yesterday he confessed the Name, joyously and with a sweet simplicity, in the court of the Urban Prefect; and before the sun was fully up this day he was in Paradise. God's just wrath will descend in fire on the Last Great Day upon the heads of those who took our father unoffending from his sheep and shed his guileless blood. . . ."

And yet to write half a dozen vituperative, apocalyptic phrases concerning the atrocities committed by the Beast would not be to tell her the things she would want to know. Laying the pen aside and running his fingers through his beard, he knew that there was no specific complaint to be made against the servants of the Anti-Christ—they had dealt decently, even courteously with the old man; they had in no wise outraged his person or detracted from his dignity; and to those of the congregation who had come to see him beheaded on the hill beyond the limits of the City they had extended something more than indulgence, something that might even have been called charity. They had accosted nobody, arrested nobody, asked nobody to show the certificate of proof that he had rendered the required sacrifice to the genii of Rome and the Emperor. They had left the body and the head lying on the grass near the block, to be taken away by anybody who chose to claim it; and they had not even turned to stare when the elder Cornelius had said in his resonant tone that he meant to take the corpse to his home and prepare it for the grave with balsam and cinnamon. No, it would be difficult to find particular charges against the bondsmen of the Beast, and the official formulae were scarcely what she would be expecting to hear.

"Knowing, then, that you would have desired above all things to be at hand when he whom we loved together came to the block for Jesus' sake, and wishing furthermore to give you your just portion in this, I set down in all truth and simplicity what we beheld. Would that an angel might guide my hand! For I am, in honesty, as I have said to you many times, lacking in grace. Whatsoever I set down, as you know, comes crabbedly, by much desperate striving. And that which we witnessed on the hill this morning should come to you like the flow of living water from the rock at the stroke of the miraculous rod."

He laid his pen aside again and rested his face on his hands, partly because his eyes were weary with the light, and partly because he kept feeling himself impelled to stare across the long, low cellar into the ecstatic face of his superior, the elder Novatian. *He* is the one who ought to be writing this letter, he thought. *He* is the one whose pen the angels move. *He* opens his mouth to tell a teamster that no decent Christian would ever beat a horse, and the congregation is stricken with wonder, it is pure poetry . . . In spite of himself, he looked through the crack between two of his fingers. The elder Novatian was still sitting, as he had been sitting for the last three hours, on a three-legged stool against the opposite wall, his head tilted backward, his thin and passionate lips softened by a melting smile, his arms extended on either side of him to imitate and symbolize the Lord's suffering on the Cross. An austere man who had lived close to half a century without making a single compromise. A self-denying, self-consuming man, without one ounce of unnecessary flesh to mar the awesome beauty of his frame. Everything about him was exquisite—the soft hair streaming back from the white forehead, the deep-set eyes in their shadowy hollows, the fine teeth gleaming between the parted lips. Even the nose, sharp and spare, with narrow nostrils that were always a little distended, was less a thing of the flesh than the noses of other men.

Tomorrow he will be sick again, thought the deacon Probus. Tomorrow worn out with this ecstasy, he will fall on the floor in a fit, and all his labors will be left to me, and nobody will think to reproach him, because God's grace is in him—even his sickness is made beautiful by grace. When I am sick, it is always with a disgusting sickness, but his afflictions are holy afflictions: the elder Novatian tosses like a dying hero in his fit; the foam

288

of prophecy is churned up on his lips, and he speaks wonders while the deacons stand around him in a ring and the virgins of the congregation contend for permission to support his head. While the seizure is on him, they will bring their troubles and their questions to me, and I will answer them as well as I can, with hard reason and hard justice—all that I have to offer to my Lord and to the frightened church of God. I will tell them the truth, which no man likes to hear; and the fruit of my labors will be dissensions between them and me—bad blood, I always make bad blood. And then he will return again, in a fresh white tunic, clean and beautiful and purified. He will come back and set us all to rights with a gesture, a sigh, a smile. . . .

He straightened and crossed himself against all evil thoughts, and reached for the small indulgence that he had set out for himself an hour ago: a cluster of yellow raisins and a cup of water mixed with wine. Now that he had come to the very core of the letter, he had no will to write: he was dragged down by the old conviction of insufficiency. The high event, the charged moment, the significance and the intensity—he always collapsed before them, he had no heart for this, no heart . . . And, having no heart for it, he drank a little of the wine and ate a few raisins. He set the seeds in a row and licked the stickiness from his fingers and noticed that one of his fingernails was split. A phrase, find a good phrase, he told himself, and that will beget another and another. But, much as he set his teeth and clenched the pen, no phrase would come.

And yet all afternoon the dank air of this cellar chamber had blossomed with phrases. For more than an hour, before he had fallen into the ecstasy, the elder Novatian had described the martyrdom of the blessed Fabian to the assembled deacons in ornate, rhapsodic phrases—the fact that all of them had seen it themselves had not deterred him in the least. The holy gift of innocence—that had been his theme. The Bishop's simple-mindedness, his unlettered speech, his rustic manners—characteristics which the elder Novatian had borne with a somewhat conspicuous Christian patience during the Bishop Fabian's stewardship over the flock—had become material for an exquisite pastoral, now that the old man was dead. Our Papa Fabian, so Novatian said, had come to the block joyously, as a shepherd hastens at the hour of midday to cool well. He had bent his head swiftly to the ax, eager to drink the draught of pain, since pain itself had been sweetened by the suffering of the Lord. Doves had gone up—*some* birds *had* gone up, the deacon Probus was forced to admit—doves had gone up at the ring of the ax; just as it was a dove that had called him first to the service of the congregation, so now doves innumerable had sprung up to lead his soul to Paradise.

If he had been writing an account of the event to the congregation at Corinth or Palmyra, he would have used some of those phrases, giving due credit of course to the elder Novatian, whose tongue, inspired by angels, had uttered them for the edification of the deacons and the greater glory of God. But there was nothing in them that would compensate his wife for the fact that she had been denied her just portion in this high and holy hour. For the elder Novatian had not really borne witness to the sufferings of the Bishop Fabian. The stark horror of the moment when the old, shaking head had brought itself down upon the block—he had escaped that by transforming the block into a well. The head—hideously, unbelievably separated from the body—he had been borne up and away from it by the ascent of doves.

And she—what would she want to know if she were here with me now? he asked himself. Of one thing he was certain: she would be eager to hear exactly what the Bishop Fabian had said. His words had been few and simple—too simple for the elder Novatian to elaborate upon, no source of doctrine, no well-spring of poetry. Stopping and turning a little just in front of the block, the old man had said softly, with a nervous catch in his voice and with a jerky smile, "Well, I am departing from you now, as you see. Love one another, and try if you can to remember me with love." Halting words, commonplace words, said in the earthy tone and the accents of the countryside . . . The deacon Probus said them over to himself voicelessly, forming them slowly with his lips, and knew that, for her, there would have been no need for him to say anything else.

"They brought him to the place of execution without any chains upon him," he wrote. "There were some fifty of us, all sons and daughters of the Crucified, at the crest of the hill when he and the City Guardsmen appeared at the foot of it, and we parted into two groups to make way for him and the others to pass, like the waters of the Red Sea dividing before the children of Israel. So far as I can remember, he did not look at any of us, although he did lay his right hand—absent-mindedly, I think—on the head of a very young child. When he came to the block—it was low and covered with a length of linen woven by the wife of the deacon Solonius—he made a kind of half-turn and spoke to us in an uncertain voice, low, with his head bent down so that we were unable to see his face. 'Well, I am departing from you now, as you see. Love each other and try if you can to remember me with love'—that was all he said. But, if I remember rightly, he smiled.'

What else? he asked himself, stripping the last, most shriveled raisins from their stems and drinking the lukewarm dregs of the water-and-wine. Actually, one could bring it to an end with a single sentence: "Having so said, he bowed his head on the block and was mercifully dispatched at one stroke to his everlasting blessedness." And yet he could not do it, even empty-hearted and tired as he was. She would want something more; she was always wanting; her seeking face—in spite of the ache of their separation, he had to admit it to himself—was a reason for exasperation, a nagging reproach, asking as it always did for something more, something else . . . What else would she ask? What would she want to know?

Whether the old hand had trembled as it came down on the little one's head—whether the moist eyes, gazing over the assembled flock at the doomed City, had been dry or moist with tears—whether it had been love or terror that had cracked, for this one and only time, the ring of his voice—these were the things that she would want to know. But I cannot tell you, he thought, I did not see. You would have seen, you would have told me later, when we lay hand in hand in the dark, whether or not, after the head was severed from the body, the face still wore the old half-merry look. You would have kissed the hands and let your head come down upon the bloody breast. But I am not such a one as can bear witness to these things. If the elder Novatian escaped out of them into ecstasy and poetry, I also am found wanting, I never even entered in. My flesh was present, but my soul was elsewhere. My soul had no dealings whatsoever with the sufferings of the Bishop Fabian.

"I was standing nearby, I was not more than seven paces from the block," he wrote, "but if I am to speak the truth, I must set down that I saw little enough. At such moments—I admit it to my own shame—it is as if a casing of crystal surrounds my spirit, sealing me off, coming, as it were, between my spirit and the event. I saw him bow his head, but the rest I did not see I looked up after I heard the ring of the ax and watched the ascent of a flock of birds that went up because they were startled by the sound—our elder Novatian saw them also and says that they were doves. And when I looked down again, I saw that there was blood on my tunic, near my knees. I had been spattered with some of the blood of the blessed Fabian. This tunic I will lay by for you, knowing that it will be dear to you, both as an earnest of salvation and as a keepsake whereby to remember one whom you loved."

That spattered tunic—he looked covertly over his shoulder and saw it lying on a bench behind him, neatly folded, with the dark, stiff spots turned outward, so that the deacons might see and be edified. Edified he was not, nor, if he remained in his present state, would ever be. He had been horrified by the blood; he had felt a crawling sensation in his stomach when the wet and sticky cloth had clung to his knees. And a kind of baffled anger rose in him when he thought how, with her, there would have been neither horror nor disgust. If she had been with him now, she would have held the tunic in her lap; her hand would have passed tenderly, without revulsion, over the brownish stains. And this is not right, either, he thought. She wants too much, she loves too much. She is bound forever to gardens and streets and houses and men. She is so inextricably caught and held to earth by the clinging hands of the children of God that she will never tear herself away and go to God himself.

And suddenly, for no reason that he could fathom, he was overcome by yearning for her: he had to make a futile, reaching movement with the fingers of his left hand. "Would that you were here with me!" he wrote at the bottom of the page. "Would that the courier who carries this letter to you could tarry until you had written me an account of yourself! My Redeemer must find me a slow and erring pupil indeed if He is striving to teach me to live without you. I have not yet been able even to pray that you are more at peace than I, that you do not suffer this same loneliness."

In fact, now that he came to consider the matter, he knew that, whenever he had imagined her at that ramshackle villa of the Cornelii, he had seen her walking alone. It never occurred to him that a patrician cousin of hers—comely and tormented and tender—was there with her at all hours of the day. At this very moment, he thought, she may be striving after the salvation of his soul; the two of them may be conversing earnestly in the light of a single lamp, with the living, rural darkness pressing all about them . . . And suddenly the reddish hair rose on his forearms: it was as if some many-legged creature of the earth had scuttled over his flesh. He is a fool, *her* kind of fool, he thought, the sort of fool who carries his heart in his hands and rushes with it over the precipice. He came to us on a fool's errand, and now he must be hidden and watched and tended like the fool that he is. *I* sit solitary in a damp cellar, and *he* is with her. How is it, my Lord and my Saviour, that there is never any indulgence for the circumspect, only for the rash ones, only for the fools?

"Ah, well," said the elder Novatian, coming out of his ecstasy. The words were uttered on a long suspiration, shaken and musical, like the deepest sounds of the flute.

He glanced at the saintly figure in the dark corner. He would have a few moments for finishing his letter—the elder Novatian had only begun to stir. The fine head with its plume of silky pale-brown hair—not a streak of grey in it, in spite of his forty-eight years—moved from side to side. The long white legs came slowly forward, and the arms descended gradually, gracefully, like the folding wings of a butterfly. "Yet if I am absent from you in the flesh," he wrote in haste, "what is the flesh to us? Are we not everlastingly united in God? I lay the holy kiss of greeting on your forehead. Pray for me unceasingly, my beloved in Christ. Probus, a deacon, an under-shepherd, the least among the children of the Lord."

"Still watching, Probus?" The voice was self-possessed, quiet. Always, between the ecstasy and the foaming fit, there was a period of precision and clear-headedness. Tonight the elder Novatian would not sleep. He would labor diligently in the Lord's service, making notes, writing letters, taking care of neglected business.

"No, my father, I have not been watching. Since you said this morning that I might send a letter to my wife by the courier visiting the rural congregations, I have been setting down for her an account of the martyrdom of the blessed Fabian."

He did not ask to see it. He rose—holy and beautiful and tall, so tall that his cloudy hair almost touched the cobwebbed rafters—and smiled pondering, no doubt, the account that he himself had already begun, an epistle to Cyprian, bishop of the Church of God in Carthage, his only living rival in subtle reasoning and rhapsodic poetry. His eyes were usually vague with meditation. When he forced them to focus on another man's face, it was a conscious effort, and the striving was evident in the contraction of his brows. "Well," he said, bringing his look to bear sharply on the face of his deacon, "finish it and sleep."

"It is already finished, my father."

"Sleep then. Today we were fed the bread of angels. Tomorrow, out of gratefulness, we must labor with a double diligence."

"Yes, I know." But, thinking how Novatian would lie in the grasp of visions all through the coming day, he found it difficult to suppress a smile. "Send the peace of the Lord to our cousin Paulina."

He nodded and took up the pen. "I have been wondering," he said while he added the message in a jerky scrawl, "whether the courier might pause at the villa of the Cornelii long enough for my wife to write me a reply—"

There was no need for any answer. The return of the vagueness in the eyes, the slow elevation of the pale eyebrows were enough. "When the blight is on the vineyard, when the locusts are in the wheat, is it well that any of the laborers should tarry on any errand?" he said.

"No, my father." Every time he was forced to confess himself in error in so many words, his gall spilled over. The tacit admission, the hot retort strangled—these were difficult and degrading enough.

"Well, go to sleep. May the Lord watch you and keep you and cause His countenance to shine upon you."

"And upon you also," he said, in no gracious voice, and walked gladly out of the circle of lamplight into the long, protecting strip of darkness against the wall.

The locusts in the wheat, the blight on the vineyard . . . He pondered the phrases as he kicked off his sandals, unfastened his belt, and laid himself down on the pile of tattered cloaks and tunics that served as his bed. He wished to God that he could see the dilemma of the Church of Christ with the eyes of Novatian, that it could appear to him also as some great consummation, worthy to be described in terms drawn from the books of the Law and the Prophets, like the slavery in Egypt or the exile by the waters of Babylon. But to him it was nothing of the sort; the snarling dogs— so *he* would have described it if anybody had asked him—are hot on the trail of the fleeing hares.

For, if the Bishop Fabian had refused to sacrifice to the images of pagan daemons, the same could not be said for many of the rest. Hundreds of others had already gone boldfaced to the Forum to burn their grains of incense for the Genices of Rome and the happiness and safety of the Emperor. He and his fellow-undershepherds had made themselves hoarse with reprimands and exhortations—and for the most part their strivings had been in vain. Some twenty of the most excitable of the congregation—part of them driven by the extremity of their terror and part by a reckless yearning for a martyr's crown—had seen fit to give themselves up to the City Guard and were waiting judgment in prison; but their precipitous sacrifice had not stirred any of the others to emulation. The state of a good half of the Church was appalling, unbelievable. Members of the congregation had been buying certificates of sacrifice from corruptible City Guardsmen. Women whom he had seen at the altar in the Forum were swearing in the presence of the sanctified bread that they had never set foot in the place.

The blight is on the vineyard, the locusts are in the wheat . . . The rats are running out of the burning building, he told himself, sneering into the dark. And it did no good to brood upon it; better to use the interim between labor and sleep as he had been using it night after night, to add a line or two to the *Journey of Barnabas*. Since the beginning of his sojourn in this cellar, he had not been able to reread any of his work—the pages lay damp and creased in the wool under his body—no Christian deacon would be seen working on a poem at such a time as this. And the inability to reread what he could not completely remember was a loss and a sorrow to him; the lines that he produced at the end of the day hung isolated in his mind, not borne up by the sweep of that which came before them, and, hanging so, seemed thin and paltry, devoid of life. There were times—times when his blood ran even and warm and none of his minor illnesses or worries affected him—there were times when the epic of *Barnabas* seemed to him to accomplish a magnificent feat—to combine pure Christian themes with the noble forms and exquisite diction of ancient poetry. And yet there were other occasions, like last night and the night before that and tonight, when even the best of his lines failed to move him in the slightest and he could not tell whether the poem itself was drab and un-convinced or whether the taint upon it was due to his own dulled mind, his own unresponsive heart. It is true, he told himself, that at such moments as these neither Virgil nor Homer can move me. When I rise tomorrow, the same lines that seem mawkish to me now may soar and sing . . . And, com-forting himself with that thought, he turned on his pile of rags and slept.

Chapter 22

HE HAD come in good faith to be with her at the villa of the Cornelii—so he told himself in the first sterile and tormenting weeks of his exile there, and so he continued to tell himself for the rest of his days. Perhaps if he had come without the unhappy aftertaste of accomplished love in his mouth, it would have been otherwise; perhaps the dry perfume of the burnt stubble and the generative warmth of the new-turned furrows and the neighing of the stallions and the mares would have transformed the vague images of his sleep into waking visions definite enough to demand fulfillment. But he had come in good faith, still sick to the heart with the ruin he had wrought; he wanted no more of his cousin in these deserted porticoes, these empty chambers dappled with the thin light of a February moon than she had given him freely in her own house under her husband's eyes—the touch, the look, the smile. And if any of these had been forthcoming—so he told himself a dozen times a day—he would never have been driven to spoil the sober peace of their meals together with equivocal arguments or to break into the meditative quiet of their evening walks with questionable lines of pagan poetry.

In his bafflement and his bitterness he told himself that he would never be able to understand how so complete and disconcerting a change could have come about in a matter of some thirty hours. He could establish no connection in his mind between the woman who had stood in the doorway of the house on the Aventine, holding his shaking hands in the hollow between her breasts, and the one who had come to greet him in the atrium of this country house—consciously pleasant, filling up every silence that threatened to be significant with forced sallies of amiability, holding the lamp always between herself and him, granting him nothing more than a brisk and friendly pressure of the hand. That strange mutation in her spirit left him with the same impression of meagerness and unloveliness that he had felt on the day of her departure, when he had seen her with her hair bound up in a linen band. And when he thought how she had gazed at him then, pushing the band back from her forehead, when he remembered the raised arm and the silky hair and compared all this with her present bearing, he abandoned the hope that she would ever lay a hand on his person again, ever look at him as she had looked at him when the chisel had clanged against the paving stones and the mountains of Africa had fallen into the sea.

He no longer could hear the thunder of that collapsing world reverberating around them. The conviction that they ought at least to hold to each other and cherish each other in these Last Times—that, too, was gone. Only in his rational mind could he believe that they were moored here in this rambling villa—he and she and her ancient steward and the slave-child Prisca and the gardener Sylvanus—for any sensible reason. He had to remind himself regularly that necessity—a persecution, an edict copied out by government slaves and posted on pedestals and walls, a written threat to her life and to his liberty—detained them in these sad, low rooms that smelled of dust and last year's apples and disuse. If heads had fallen on the block, if bodies had been mauled by beasts or torn on the rack or consumed in the fire, he had no word of it; nobody crossed the blue rim of the Campanian hills, nobody broke through the screen of hedge and thicket to bring news; weeks had gone by and not so much as a rumor had been borne up from the adjacent villages along with the pickled meat and cheese. Once and once only, seeing her by moonlight from a high window opening upon an untended garden, seeing her standing in prayer or meditation among the dried and fibrous blossoms of last autumn's weeds, he had felt for an instant the aching conviction of her mortality. But it had been only for an instant: she had seen him, she had waved to him casually and had gainsaid her earnestness with a consciously amiable smile.

She could be grave enough, she would be solemn and ardent for hours on end during those portions of the day she allotted to the saving of his soul. She had told him once that she was a tireless preacher; she had spared him a sermon one unforgettable afternoon only because the late sun had lain red across the statues and sarcophagi, and had held her tongue on an even more memorable occasion only out of consideration for his burned hands. Now she came to him always with a scroll or a little book. Over the rumble of the two-wheeled ox-carts furrowing the fields, over the snap and crackle of the burning brush, over the songs of the tenant farmers digging up the earth around the vines, she read him the letters of Cyprian and the orations of Tertullian. At the spread table between the courses, and at the empty board when the last edible diversion had been borne away and he had nothing to toy with, nothing to give him the right to a show of distraction, she took some passage from one of the Gospels and gave him quoted comment by the elder Cornelius, the elder Novatian or, most infuriating of all, by her yoke-fellow in the Lord. Sometimes he listened with a display of attention and felt like a fool. Sometimes he took exception to a point in her discourse and was frightened by the excessive protest in her voice and face. Sometimes he fabricated a pretense of agreement, and saw her disproportionate delight, and called himself a hypocrite, and was duly ashamed of himself. And, if the lecture went on for longer than an hour, he found himself profoundly tired, yearning to be rid of her and her apostles and her angels and her saints, thinking with longing of the closed room and silence and his bed.

Lying on that unfamiliar bed, with the alien room and the impenetrable night pressing around him, he would try to obliterate the recollection of those interminable harangues. He was only partially successful: he could forget the words—he had never really listened to the words—but not the hounded presence on the other side of the table, the eyes straining to maintain a steady gaze, the thin hand fluttering through the pages of the book, the teeth set into the trembling lower lip. And, one unquiet, wind-ridden night, when he was suddenly pulled out of that vague and perilous province of causeless starts and sane incongruities that lies between waking and sleeping, it suddenly came to him like a momentous revelation: Not because of her zeal to preach was she driven to exhort and quote and elucidate, but only because her preaching kept her from coming face to face with some nameless, unthinkable thing. Sitting in the windy darkness, with his feet on the dusty floor, he tried to see what that unthinkable thing might be, what interdicted activity of the mind or the heart had driven her to argue peremptorily with him long after sunset that it was only Stoic stubbornness and Stoic pride that made him close his ears to the voice of her God. What drove her on tonight and all those other nights? he asked himself. A need to strangle some persistent doubt of her own? He did not know, he could not tell. Much later, after he had lain down again, he told himself that her motive was probably an obvious one, that she was undoubtedly using her contest with him as a means of diverting her attention from whatever unbearable things were going on in Rome; and this solution—not entirely satisfactory to him in the whispering blackness of that night—seemed very plausible when he encountered her again in daylight, over the morning fruit and bread.

That whole day was awkward, painful, filled with embarrassing mischances. Perhaps because he was raw-nerved and vulnerable with lack of sleep, he found himself unable to respond to her attempts to be pleasant. When she remarked on the fine texture of the new bread and the sweet smell of burning brush, he could not summon up the usual empty and enthusiastic reply. Seeing him lying on his face on a bench near the dairy—the sun was warm for the first time, and he had always had an almost mystic belief in the power of the sun to heal all sicknesses of the flesh and of the spirit—she came out to inquire whether he was ill by any chance; and her solicitude was so detached that he could not help comparing it with the compassion she had shown for his burned hands, could not keep himself from saying in a testy voice that there was nothing the matter with him, that all he needed was to be let alone. For four hours thereafter she let him alone in so marked a manner that it was obvious to everybody in the household; and, since the household was so newly formed, so haphazardly and tentatively held together, it almost cracked under the strain. The ancient steward walked about like a physician in a dying man's chamber, the gardener Sylvanus seemed to feel that he could be loyal to his master only by showing his temporary mistress certain subtle incivilities, and the little Prisca fled the tense atmosphere of the villa to walk by herself in the hills, and came back tired and dirty in the waning afternoon, with a sun-flushed face and bramble-scratched knees.

The sunburn, the scratches, the taint of unhappiness spoiling a child's first afternoon of spring—he charged himself with them all, and so did his cousin Paulina: she could not keep her eyes from the child, she bent down half a dozen times to test the warmth of the flushed forehead with her lips. Once, in a crossing of glances, the two of them acknowledged their common guilt. It was only for an instant that their eyes met across the sunny dining room, but even so slight an exchange made it again possible for them to sit opposite each other at the evening meal, weary and chastened and eager for peace. "The hare is nicely spiced, isn't it?" she said in a weak and tentative voice, staring at her plate and trying to smile. "Excellently spiced," he said, holding forth at some length on the merits of the various spices, and adding that the bread on the table tonight—and this morning, too, for all that matter—was very fine in texture, as fine a loaf of bread as he had ever eaten.

The meal would probably have passed as uneventfully as any of the others if one of the tenant farmers had not chosen this particular hour for airing one of his grievances in the atrium. All at once his voice, rough and resentful, was lecturing the old steward of the house on the subject of lamb: lamb was scarce, lamb was expensive, lamb was not to be produced at a whistle, he said; and his aggrieved pronouncements reduced their carefully constructed conversation to a pitiful heap of inanities. Nevertheless, she made a valiant effort to drown out the dissension in the atrium: the almond cake, she was afraid, had been overdone—her steward was too old to make out what color a cake was in the red light of an oven—last week he had burned a partridge to a crisp . . . "And if you think," said the surly voice of the tenant farmer, "that this villa is prepared to serve you like a resort hotel in Baiae, you'll be disappointed in more ways than this . . ." Her thin hand reached across the table to refill his cup. White, veined, pitifully insufficient, it was dragged down by the weight of the cruet, and the wine splashed over the cloth. "What's going on between your steward and that insolent farmer out there? Shall I go out and put him in his place?" he said.

"Oh, no, please don't—" For the first time—doubtless it was only because she was timorous by nature and miserably afraid that he would multiply the anger and the noise—for the first time and very briefly she let her hand come down upon his hand. "It's my fault—it was I who asked him to bring us the lamb. But when the elder Cornelius told us we could have this villa, he said we could ask the tenant farmers for anything we wanted—he hadn't collected his tithes from them in the last three years—that's what he said. Still, they're poor, and they're annoyed to have so many of us here—not that I wish we were fewer—I'm glad you're here, I think I'd go mad if I had to stay here by myself. And now that I know he's so sensitive about lamb, I'll just never ask him for any more lamb—" And, in the midst of a wan attempt to smile, she lost control of herself; her face became the wrinkled face of a prematurely aging child, and she cast him one shamed, tender look and covered her eyes with her hands and wept.

"Don't cry, don't cry, my darling—"

The epithet was lost in the tenant farmer's loud assertion that yesterday it had been chicken and today it was lamb and no doubt tomorrow it would be cranes' tongues. And the sarcasm was unbearable to him; he could not permit the rude voice to continue its assault upon the fragile dignity of her spirit. He went to the door and shouted into the atrium that the argument should be carried out into the pigsty where it belonged, that never in his life had he heard such talk out of a serving man, that henceforth the fellow would never set foot in the house if he knew what was good for him. . . .

After the shouting, quiet—spent and gentle quiet—settled upon the room. By the time he returned to the table, the dissension had been borne away into the dusky yard and her sobbing had ceased. Not that she had taken hold of herself—her shape, grey and shadowy against the evening glow beyond the window, was bowed over the table; her face was hidden in her arms, and her hair was spread against the whiteness of the cloth. But it was a blessed thing that she should weep before him. Tears from her—so he told himself, hard put to it to refrain from going around the table and kissing the top of her bowed head—tears from her were an earnest of intimacy more telling than another woman's lifted mouth or bared breast.

It was as if she had sensed the sweetness of the moment and wished to prolong it. She did not move even when Sylvanus entered the dining room with the five-branched candelabrum and set it in the middle of the board, whispering the formula that every slave uttered as he bore in the evening light: "I come to conquer the dark." For no reason that he could fathom, he thought of other lights being brought into other rooms: the pottery lamp placed on the cluttered desk in the library of the imperial palace, the wax lights carried by Nubians into the vast, deserted atrium of the Herennii, the priest-borne lamps passing slowly down the corridors of the Temple at Epidaurus, the alabaster saucers set in niche and corner in the known chambers in the house of Charis; and, thinking of these rooms, he felt his heart dilate within his chest. I have left much, lost much, he thought, and reached across the table, and touched a strand of her hair. She did not stir, she did not draw away; and the living silkiness under his fingertips was precious and he knew in his heart that every lost hope and room, every lost touch and face and voice was well lost. . . .

Yet, when she raised her head and brought her wet and vulnerable face into the light, he felt disintegrating pity for her. It would be doing violence to force this intimacy upon her, frail and assailed by nameless troubles as she was. He could not let her see that he had been touching her hair; he pretended instead to be rubbing at a wine-spot on the cloth. And when the silence between them became unbearable with the threat of revelation, he cleared his throat and took the customary pupil's attitude, his elbows on the edge of the board, his fists supporting his chin. "Well, where is your book?" he said. "Didn't you bring your book tonight?"

"No," she said on a sigh, implying futility, admitting to what he saw now had been a long and disheartening series of failures for her. "What's the use?"

"You do very well without one, that much is certain. I like it best when it comes directly from you."

She smiled feebly and shrugged her shoulders. "So far as I can see, you haven't liked any of it. And if I failed to interest you in the past, I haven't the slightest hope of interesting you now. Tonight I'm utterly tired."

"Then tell me something simple, something you can tell me easily, without any strain." Much as he pitied her, he could not relinquish her presence, must hold her longer there on the other side of the table, where, in the light of the five wax lights, he could look at the tear-streaked face, the veined and mortal hands.

"Nothing is easy. Nothing is ever simple any more." Her voice carried with it a vast, melancholy bafflement over the complexity and multiplicity of things. "I wish I were a child again," she said.

He thought how, as a child, he must have seen her standing on feast-days with the other undistinguished members of the family at the outer edge of the atrium of the Herennii. But, so far as he could remember, he had never singled her out. There had always been so many children; if he had seen her standing, silky-haired and timid and slight, with a Saturnalia doll clasped to her scarcely-budded breast, he had lost the image; and this seemed to him an aching and irreparable loss.

"But that was an impious wish," she said, crossing herself against it.

"Why, Paulina?"

"Because, when I was a child, I was a pagan. I might even say I was an ardent pagan, in a ridiculous way. I had a kind of obsession with the she-daemon Proserpine. I was lonely, and I suppose I'd heard that she was lonely too, in the kingdom of Hades, and I used to go to her altar every week to leave her a present—fruit or wine or flowers. I was a pagan much longer than Probus was." She had hesitated almost imperceptibly before saying her husband's name, and the pause had given the name a certain disquieting stress. She withdrew her glance and stared at the old-fashioned, ornate silver candelabrum, and took a deep breath, and hurried on. "I was all of eighteen," she said, "before I came to know my Saviour and my Lord."

"Who was your teacher?"

"Probus. Everything I learned in the first two years I learned from Probus." There was an assertion of loyalty, at once touching and disturbing, in the emphatic repetition of the name. "The Lord brought us to each other," she said, forcing herself to lift her chin and fix a strained look upon him. "He met me in the house of a friend and came to love me. At first he didn't know that we could marry if we liked—he thought my family was utterly out of his reach because we belonged to the Herennii. He taught me better than anybody else could have taught me. He taught me tirelessly, learnedly, with great devotion, because it seemed to him we could never be united in this world, and it consoled him in those days to think I might at least become his sister in the Lord."

"That's a strange story," he said at last, not knowing what else to say in his embarrassment and pain.

"No, no, it's not." She spoke with an agitated earnestness now, her eyes seeking his across the flames, her thin hands clasped so tight that the knuckles shone. "Many of our novices have come to us like that. Thousands of women, renouncing things they find it impossible to possess in the flesh—don't laugh at us, don't say it's self-deception—console themselves by bringing what they love to God."

"But what satisfaction can they find in that?"

"Profound satisfaction—the only lasting satisfaction," she said. "You see"—she was choosing her words carefully, she was seeking them in the secret chambers of her heart—"what God possesses, we all possess—in some way, in some measure, it's hard to tell you how—but each of us has his portion of it in God."

It seemed to him that if she had dared to speak she would have said: "I loved you, my cousin, when we sat together on the unhewn stone in the sculptor's yard, when you opened your eyes out of sleep to me in the vestibule, when, in the presence of my marriage bed, I touched the scar on your hand. I loved you, my cousin, and I love you still. One change and only one has taken place in me. I renounce you in the world and strive with you day and night because there is only one possibility left to me: that I embrace you in the Lord."

If what he imagined in that charged moment of silence was so, she must think hard of him that he should sit and stare at her and hold his peace. And yet he could not hazard a gesture or a word: he had a vision of her walking out of the room, not in an impenetrable aura of Christian dignity—he could have sustained that—but confused, wounded, reduced to tears. Other sounds, the usual sounds of an ordinary rural evening, came in to fill the hush and ease the tension: splash of water and clink of pottery in the adjoining room, the lowing of oxen being driven back to their stalls, the wild, high whinnying of the mares. Say something, he thought, say anything to her now. Since you cannot say, "Do you know, beloved, that in a dream you gave me back my living heart?" nothing is right and anything will do. . . .

"Did I ever tell you—the time when I was sick I read one of the Gospels. It was because of you that I read it," he said.

She plucked off a long, warm string of wax from the silver side of the candelabrum and kneaded it slowly into a pellet between her two thin hands. "No, you never told me. Which Gospel was it?" A faint, brooding ghost of the remembered smile deepened the corners of her lips.

"I believe it was Luke."

"Saint Luke? You read it? And because of me?" Slowly, tenderly, she was shaping the wax with her nails and the tips of her fingers, turning it into something that resembled a blown white rose. "I must read it again tonight so that I can imagine how it must have sounded to you."

No, he thought, no, I'll never be content with that. I am no Probus, looking for a sister in the Lord, nourished on the bloodless ecstasies of renunciation. My living heart demands at least the gaze, the smile, the touch . . . He looked at her half sternly, half mockingly across the wavering flames. "Do you think *that* will bring you peace, my cousin?" he said.

She sighed and laid the waxen rose on the board and looked at it long and ruefully before she pressed it into a flat white disc on the cloth. "My Lord and my Redeemer—He is the only one who can give us peace. I know that now. Maybe that's the only thing I know," she said.

"Then I'm to take it that He *has* given you peace, Paulina?"

She flushed and straightened. "Assuredly, He has given me peace." She threw him one quick, wild glance, and he was ashamed of himself that he should have driven her to so unqualified an avowal. She flicked the flattened bit of wax away, and it seemed to him that she was dismissing all threatening intimacies, all equivocal sentences exchanged between man and woman at dusk on an early day of spring. "And you—what did you think of the Gospel?" she asked, settling herself with conscious dignity on the edge of her dining couch, looking at him with empty, attentive eyes and folding her unquiet hands.

"I was disappointed." The sentence hung between them, harsh and in-complete, since he could not tell her what it was that he had sought in the soiled pages, could not say to her: "But I was bound to be disappointed, since I wanted nothing of it but whatever was between you and me in the vestibule that rainy night, and in my dreams."

"Disappointed?" She was the pedagogue again, the patient teacher, keep-ing her hands reposeful, striving to erase the querulous line between her brows. "But perhaps you read it too superficially, too quickly. Perhaps if we read it slowly, together—I have a copy—I could go and get it—"

"No!" It was loud and unseemly in the decent room and the rural hush; and yet he must disabuse her forever of the notion that his living flesh and his uncompanioned heart could be satisfied with such bodiless, savorless wafers as she was holding out to him tonight.

"Why not, my cousin?"

"Because I am not a child, because I cannot be put to sleep with a legend or a magical tale." He was appalled at himself that he should say such an annihilating thing, and yet he could not stop, he could not even lower his angry voice. "I know that I was nothing once, and am something now for a little while, and will be nothing again in my grave. What I love in this world, I must possess in this world. There may be those who can deceive themselves. There may be those—" he thought of Probus and felt the blood rush into his face—"there may be those who can find a counter-feit peace by saying to themselves: I will eat this bread or love this woman or write this poem in the Kingdom of Heaven. But I am not such a one as that. I would rather accept the fact that I will go unfulfilled and starving into my tomb than feed myself on a non-existent Kingdom of Heaven."

She did not answer at once, and he did not dare to look at her. In the disquieting interim he asked himself who else had heard, what other heart he could have bruised with his violence. Prisca was in the adjoining room, Prisca might have heard him; and it was cruel to besmirch a child's bright faith, cruel to force the black finality of death upon the tender reason of a child. . . .

"The Kingdom of Heaven?" she said at last in a quiet, puzzled voice. "You mean Paradise? Do you know—" she inclined her body toward him, so that her wide-set eyes shone clear and childish in the light of the five flames, "I almost never think of Paradise. The Kingdom of Heaven is strange and new to those of us who were brought up in the old philosophies. To tell the truth, I have to keep reminding myself that it exists—I always forget. Our children—those who were born to it, those who drew it in with their mother's milk—they'll be the native citizens of the City of God. Little ones like Prisca—" her voice dealt with the name tenderly, as a hand might deal with the first apple blossom of a wintry spring— "little ones like Prisca will possess it, will take it all for granted. But we—it's otherwise with us—there's not one among us who won't be wonderstruck to find himself in the King-dom of Heaven."

"Take that away, and what's left, Paulina?"

The remembered smile, at once innocent and infinitely wise, indented the corners of her lips. "Why, love," she said, almost in a whisper. "Many things, of course, for many people. But for me, love above everything else—the right to love, the dignity of love. There are those who are born with extraordinary wit or beauty, with wealth or high names or a kind of glowing, inexhaustible vitality. But I—God help me—I was born with none of these. I was plain, I was poor, I was always sickly, always tired. Now that I look back on it I can see that the only talent I had was a great capacity for love. If anybody so much as held out a little finger to me in kindness—a tutor, a visitor in the house, a friend—I loved him, I consumed myself with gratefulness and yearning, I wanted to be the slave that made his fire or the dog that slept across his feet. And anyone who obliterates himself with such love in a world like this is bound to be humiliated, rejected. So it was, and over and over again, with me. They told me I was a fool, and I came to believe them. My only gift, my only talent—after a while I learned to despise it, I locked it up, I laid it by to rot in my heart. Love unspent is poison, a very strong poison, my cousin. I was sick with it, I was feverish and restless, I never had a moment's peace. Never a moment's peace until I heard, almost by chance, how God so loved the world that He gave His only-begotten Son to die so that those who wanted no salvation might be saved. And if my Lord could scatter such love as His to a world that neither wanted Him nor listened to Him, if my Redeemer could knock always at the closed doors, if He could take in return for His boundless giving a crown of thorns and loneliness and death in agony on a Cross, then who was I—who was I—? You see then how it has been with me, my cousin. I needed only to open my heart and love, and I was at peace."

But the look, the touch, the smile—he would not believe that they had flowed over him merely by chance, out of a general bounty. "I'm confused now, I'm afraid I don't follow you, Paulina," he said, regretting the annoy-ance in his voice but unable to stifle it. "I don't know what you mean when you speak of 'love'. Love—at least in my language—means an involvement with a single person—an obsession, a need so desperate that life would be meaningless, even impossible, if that person were gone. Love—in that sense of the word has no place in your doctrine, no place whatsoever so far as I can see."

She continued to bend forward, untroubled by his querulousness, her eyes still shining. "I see what you mean, there *is* a difference, the sort of love I mean mustn't ask for anything in return," she said. "If I should ever become so perfect in Christ as to love according to His commandments, would love with all my strength and never think of asking for so much as the shadow of an answering smile. Love itself—the very process of loving—

love unanswered, even unguessed, would be enough and more than enough."

You do not believe it, he thought, not in the secret places of your heart. You talk of abnegation in too warm and womanly a voice. The living flush suffusing your cheeks and your temples under your loosened hair, your gesturing hands with their instinctive eloquence, the soft and telling indentations at the corners of your mouth—these are the actualities, and they belie the rest. . . .

"Of course," she was saying, "not all of us are capable of that sort of love. . . ."

"Oh, no, of course not, that's one thing I'll agree with completely!" There was a crazy ripple of laughter under his voice, and he was speaking far too loudly; but he had ceased to concern himself about the child out there in the other room: if this was the sort of thing she had been hearing since her infancy, it was high time to acquaint her with something else. "As you say, not all of us, my cousin. Only the elect among us. Only the outworn, the savorless, the sickly, the hopeless, the tired—only the ones of us who have the honor to belong to the growing society of the living dead. If we are alive, if the blood persists in running through our veins, we'll ask for other things, crasser things. We'll want the long look and the touching hand to waken all the slow music of desire in us. We'll want the one voice, the only acceptable voice saying the unsayable, promising everything. We'll want—to our everlasting weakness and our everlasting glory—the flesh, the sweet flesh itself, all the dearer to us because it is with us only for an instant in eternity—"

"Yes, my cousin, I know," she said, and her eyes were moist. "I know such love exists, and has existed, and will exist again. Only, in such a world as ours, we make too much of it. It's doomed to be overblown, since it's the single blossom on the stem, with all the rest gone. Pampered and over-rich as it is, it's sure to sicken in the end—believe me, my cousin, I've seen, I know. No, as I said, we make too much of love. It sickens—it's sure to sicken in this world."

"Then what shall we do with it? Throw it away? Tear it to bits because it's more beautiful than it ought to be? Trample it in the mud because it's the last thing left?"

She did not give him an immediate reply. She was making ready—but without the haste of flight—for her departure. She was gathering up from the dining couch such things as she always brought to table with her: a linen stole, a crumpled handkerchief, a ribbon strung with keys. "Let it alone," she said, smiling, using the tone in which a mother cautions a child whose curiosity is leading him into some negligible danger. "It'll die of itself, if only we let it alone. If it is as the Fathers say it is, if the sea is less purple and the tide less strong than when Aeneas sailed, if the fields are failing, if the birds are fewer in the air and the light is failing in the moon and the heat is lessening in the sun—if everything faints and passes—

this, too, will faint and pass, if only we let it alone." She rose and bent over the wax lights and blew at them. Her breath was light and strengthless—it scarcely stirred the flames—but it seemed to him that he could feel it pass across his face.

"There are some things," he said, looking straight at her, "that I would want to possess even if the earth were cracking under my feet."

"Yes, I know, my cousin." She looked away from him, she looked at the rusty keys in the white hollow of her hand and managed to smile a rueful smile. "Only, I tell myself what the Fathers tell me: that these desires will dwindle as the Last Great Day draws on. When the heavens open and the Son of Man descends to us, no bird or beast or creature made in the likeness of God will be afflicted with such longings anymore—so my Lord and my Redeemer Himself has said."

"Has He indeed, Paulina?" He strove for her eyes, but they would not look at him. They fixed themselves gravely, sorrowfully upon the harsh iron and the rust.

"Yes, my cousin. When it was asked of Him when His Kingdom would come, this is what He said: 'When the two shall be one and the outside as the inside, and the male with the female neither male nor female.' "

He rose—he startled her by rising. "What does that mean?" he asked, coming close to her now. Only the five flames were between.

"That the Day of Doom will not come until all yearning between men and women has faltered—as I said."

"For me that time has not yet come, Paulina."

"No . . ." She settled the stole around her shoulders and started for the door, closing her parted lips on a long and shaking sigh. But on the threshold she turned and gave him such a look as he had never had from the eyes of a woman—utterly honest, and without the slightest taint of shame. "No, for me also, my cousin, that time is not yet come," she said.

Chapter 23

Fon THREE days it rained the first warm rain splashing on the winter-dulled foliage of the Campagna, washing the leathery leaves of the laurel, streaming down the trunks of the sycamores and beeches and wild olives until the bark took on the sheen of silk. Sometimes the clouds would be drawn apart—never for long, only for a short space; but what came to pass in these short spans of time—the multiplying chorus of birds, the leafing above and the sprouting below, the scent of green shoot and sticky bud suddenly disseminated on the drenched air—made it seem as if a month's growth and change had come about, as if the next rent in the brooding greyness would let summer itself descend upon the world. So she thought, busying herself always with something that wanted tending in the neglected villa: bronze pot stained with a green patina, oleander plant in need of digging and pruning, crystal cruet filthy at the bottom with dust and the dried lees of long-standing wine. Rainy days—she had loved them in the City, they had prevented the usual round of visits to the poor and the sick and the imprisoned, they had given her time for stitching and scouring and making corners clean; and it eased her mind a little to employ them in the same fashion in this alien place. There were moments when, absorbed in the task at hand, she forgot where she was and what gnawed at her heart. There were moments when she believed herself in her own house, expect-

307

ing a known door to be opened by a known hand, waiting for the air to be filled with the blamelessly gratifying smell of her husband's wool cloak drenched by the rain.

But it was different now, everything was altogether different. To yearn for those innocent times was as futile as to yearn, like the pagan poets, for the lost and guileless Age of Gold. She had thought certain thoughts, no matter how unwillingly; she had seen certain images, no matter how fleeting; she had come to the table without her book and had known herself and committed herself—and henceforth nothing could ever be the same. And if she had wept unremittingly, bringing her mind constantly to bear on whatever might have offered her salvation—her crucified Lord, her dear yokefellow in Christ, the blue woolen curtains in their bedroom at home, the pitifully few pages of the manuscript on Barnabas—if she had wept unremittingly, she might have hoped for a return to peace and grace. But there was the sun again, there was the shining world again, netted in crystal drops and flashing with rainbows; there was his voice, his face, his seeking look. And, against them, nothing was strong enough but the thought of the beasts and the rack and the fire, and she would go mad, she would go screaming mad if she lay awake another night thinking of the beasts and the rack and the fire. Take the brush to the cluttered corner, take the shears to the disorderly vine, take the needle to the raveled tablecloth. This also is virtue of a kind . . . But always, while her cheeks were still stiff with her penitential tears, her lips would do exactly as they pleased: her lips would shape themselves into the slow, still smile.

She could not hide from herself, either, the appalling realization that in these last three days her spirit had been tainted with something uglier and meaner than her involuntary happiness. All at once she would find herself in a dire and destructive humor, so alien to her nature that she could not even find a means of dealing with it. She would fly about with her cloth raising an unnecessary cloud of dust, she would bang the crystal cups and clatter the silver dishes; and all because the child was coming in again—the blithe, warm-hearted little slave whom all her Christian charity and all her natural inclinations should have prompted her to love. But it was useless now to wait for *him* to come down from the library or in from the kitchen garden. If the child was there—and the child was always there, following him, watching him, claiming his look with her clear and beseeching eyes—whatever he wished to say, whatever he wished to add to the halting conversation that they had made that night over the evening meal must remain unsaid. There was no escape from her now, no casual wandering out together, not with the rain descending past the windows in silvery sheets, not with the earth so sodden that the slaves came barefoot into the house leaving their clotted sandals on the mat at the door. She could not make an occasion, could not be so crass or so devious as to contrive an encounter with him in an upper corridor after the others were asleep, could not be so cruel as to send the little slave to wipe the cobwebs from the wine jars in the cellar or sweep the dust and old accumulated leaves from the balcony. For the child was to be pitied—in Christian charity or in mere human decency the child was to be pitied. It was tormentingly obvious that the child had no power over herself, was drawn to him as inexorably as the young shoot is drawn toward the sun, was humbly and hopelessly and wretchedly in love. . . .

But there was not a trace of pity in her. There was nothing in her now but hate and fury. She who had always loved the youth of her novices, she who had yearned over their silky heads and blunt, childish fingers, she who had listened with earnest attention to their confidences and wept alone over the doomed dreams they allowed her to see in the secret places of their hearts, she, even she—oh, it was unbelievable and shameful!—she hated the little thing, was in an uncontrollable fit of anger with the little thing because she was so young. She did not want the child beside her in his sight; she could not bear to think how those two faces, Prisca's and her own, must look to him in the brightness of a lamp or the sun. Round cheek and sunken cheek, clear eyes and tired eyes, sweet mouth parted in eagerness, wan mouth closed upon too much unsatisfied longing—how could he want her leanness and her weariness? And if she had stopped at envying the tender freshness of the girl she would have waded into evil far enough, but she went further still. Let him tease the child or touch the child or give the child a flower, and she slandered and soiled the loveliness, she turned it into a cheap and meretricious thing. A dozen times a day she found herself thinking how the mouth was stupid, always hanging open like that, how the smooth whiteness of the face was sheer vapidity, no more expressive than a puddle of spilled milk. What ugly hands she has, she told herself. Those stubby fingers, those grimy dimples in the fat, those rings around the wrists. . . .

Then of a sudden the child would fall into deep thought, letting her eyelids down and resting her round elbows on the edge of the table. With the brief and watery sunlight drawing a line around her silky hair, the child would assume an attitude and an expression so earnest, so guileless, so pathetically beautiful that hate would falter and fury would melt away and nothing would be possible except self-condemnation and love. Seeing the child from the other side of the table, she would feel a heart-dissolving yearning to take her in her arms, to beg forgiveness, to kiss the lineless eyelids, the unblemished cheeks, the parted lips. Like an angel, like an angel of God, she would say to herself, rubbing the tears out of her eyes with the back of her dusty hand. And He has sent her, He has given this one of His angels charge over me, to trail after me from room to room, to gaze at my shameful wishes and thoughts with innocent eyes, to bear me up lest I dash my foot against a stone. If it were not for the rain and her, who knows

309

what I might have said or done this day, what new causes I might have for reproaching myself, what new terrors might be visited upon me, and justly, when I lie down tonight to think of the beasts and the rack and the fire? And, moved beyond the practise of the virtue of industriousness, she would push aside the silver or drop the brush or the cloth. She, also, would sit at the table and rest her head upon her arms and conjure up a vision of her husband's face. There in the darkness, with the sound of rushing runnels and splashing drops in her ears, she would thank her Lord and her Saviour from the depths of her heart for the constantly-present little one and the confining rain. . . .

But on the fourth day the rain was over. It had stopped in the night; and by mid-morning there was no excuse for remaining indoors; even the moisture underfoot had been drawn up for the most part in a light and wholesome mist. He was eager to be out of doors again, that much was plain: he left immediately after the noonday eggs and cheese and came back in half an hour, the whiteness of his forehead and the sharp ridge of his nose made ruddy by the sun. Oh, it was unbelievably fine out there, he said, following her around the atrium, where she was dusting the grimy faces of the statues. The almond trees were out, the wild plums were out, it was impossible to imagine the smell in the air—buds and blossoms and wet pine. But she went somberly on with her dusting. There was work to be done, she told him in so many words. After all, *somebody* had to make some return for the hospitality; it behooved all of them to remember that they were indebted for the food on their table and the roof over their heads. He found a dust-cloth and followed her for a little; but she was silent and he grew sulky, and before she could think of anything to say that might entertain him he was off again, taking Prisca with him, into the shining, dripping woods. And it was dreary, dreary and wounding, to think of the two of them out there, chattering and laughing while she labored alone in the alien house—uneasy and jealous, sour with unwilling work, sweaty and covered with dust. So, after supper, when he said that he meant to go back to the grove again, when he stood up on the other side of the wax light and gave her that long, pained, beseeching look, she could not help herself, she could only say, "Wait a moment, I'll go with you, wait till I get my cloak." But there was bitterness in it, like the faint, bitter tang under the fragrance of the green almond blossoms. Her husband had given her the cloak that *he* was laying over her shoulders; her husband had bought it at a bargain and had been memorably pleased both because he had been clever enough to make such a find and because she had shown so much delight. And the child had to be told outright that she was to stay behind. She trailed along with them as far as the dairy-house before they could bring themselves to make their meaning plain. "You've been running around all day, you really ought to get some rest," he said. And the little slave turned around and went without a word, smiling against wounded dignity, blinking against tears.

And the woods—she was as silent with him in the woods as she had been in the neglected atrium. No Christian graveyard, no shadowy labyrinth in any of the catacombs could have been a less felicitous place for him to choose if he meant to brush lightly against her as they walked, if he meant to allow his hand to graze her hand. For her, a woods in spring would always be an Easter woods: the birds sang "Benedictus" and "Hosanna" in the glowing dusk; that crocus breaking out of the cleft clods was Christ Himself arising from the tomb; among the other winter-darkened boughs the flowering plums and the almonds hung, pale Pentecostal clouds of light.

Yet there was the stump again, changed in these last four days. There were frail red tendrils of new ivy on it now, and the moss on top of it had been washed bright green by the rain. "Watch, don't run into it," she said, remembering how his wide and nervous gestures had carried him straight into it not many days ago when he had been protesting with his voice and his body against the charged stillness that had brooded over them so long.

"I see it, I'll be careful. I assure you I have cause to remember it," he said, making a face and touching his hip bone.

And she remembered how she had thought that other time: Ah, God, he has a bone there, like any other man, and he is made in such-and-such a way, and the skin under his tunic would be paler than the skin on his neck and face, since he is a scholar and never goes to the gymnasium, never lies naked on the sand in the sun . . . The image that she had seen that afternoon—she covertly crossed herself against it now, and yet it came again, in spite of the prayer, in spite of the holy sign. She raised her face to heaven to be delivered from it, and still it hung before her, evanescent as the clouds of blossoms on the trees, and when the tears stood in her eyes she did not know whether it was for her sinfulness or for his mortality that she wept. Behold, all flesh is as the grass, she told herself—yours also, your sweet flesh also is only as the grass, my cousin and my beloved. . . .

"The Cornelii don't seem to take very much trouble with this place," he said, flinging his hand in the direction of a wild olive tree whose silvery leaves and fantastic trunk were scarcely visible anymore under the coils of a strangling vine. It was trivial and incongruous, that remark, coming as it did into the fervor of her meditation. These walks were useless, nothing came of them—nothing but a sore conscience and a bruised heart. Always, unless she preached to him, he talked about inconsequential things; and yet, poor wretch, what else was there for him to talk about? He could scarcely stop of a sudden and take her by the wrists and say to her: "Listen, this silence is unbearable, I will not have it anymore. You know and I know how it is with you and me, what must be said, what must be done before we can possess our souls in peace" . . .

"Look at it—weeds all over the lawns, vines all over the trees." His hand described another wide arc across the dripping green.

"Yes, it *is* a pity. It's terribly neglected, and it could be so beautiful," she said.

"The laurels need pruning."

She did not answer him at once. At the end of the grove, a plum tree stood, pale and separate among the glossy mulberries and peeled sycamores, its upper branches still effulgent in the last of the sun. They had never walked beyond that tree; they had always turned back there and started toward the pale cloud of smoke that hung above the roof, sent upward from the kitchen by the dying supper fires. If we turn backward from that flowering plum tonight, she thought, if there has been nothing between the two of us when we turn home again—nothing more than this grazing of bodies, this touching of hands—then I will say to myself: It was a dream and I have awakened. Then I will kneel in penance for three hours on the floor beside my bed, and pray for Probus with all that is left of my dead heart, and bury my dead heart and sleep. . . .

"Do they stay in this villa very often, Paulina?"

"Somebody comes here almost every year. The elder Cornelius usually comes in April—"

She stopped, on the point of adding that he would scarcely come this year, seeing how it stood in the City with the children of the Lord. That, too, was impossible; that, too, was a matter for silence, a matter to be covered up with trivialities and incongruities. For you know and I know, she thought, glancing sidewise at him, how it would be with whatever transitory, nameless thing exists between us if we admitted the stark, inadmissible actuality, if, brushing hands, brushing hips, breathing this vernal incense, I were to say to you or you were to say to me: "What goes on in Rome tonight? How is it there tonight with the Confessors of the Name?"

"That plum tree there, at the end of the grove—if the place were mine, I would put a half-circle of benches around it. I was saying so to Prisca this afternoon."

She turned her face away from him and blinked against the stinging tears. Bitter, bitter—to be an ageing woman walking with a young man through a springtime woods, to know nothing, to be certain of nothing, to say to oneself: But none of it was so, I invented it all, I told myself a foolish tale in my loneliness and my emptiness. He loves his mistress, he will marry some exquisite young patrician, he loves that child, that little slave. . . .

"You're very silent, my cousin."

"Am I? Am I really?" Her voice was hard with an attempt to hide the quavering and the tears. "I'm silent by nature, I suppose. I've lived for close to thirty years, I've worked like a slave and worn myself out and beaten myself. I don't see much to chatter about. I can't keep talking nonsense. I'm not lighthearted, I'm not a child."

He had taken it that *he* was the childish, inanely lighthearted one, intruding upon her Christian solemnity and her wifely sorrows with his insignificant talk of benches and weeds and vines. His face took on a look that she remembered: so it had been—bewildered, vulnerable, dreaming—that night in the little vestibule when the shadow of the chain had swung across the parted mouth, the wide and wondering eyes, the white brow. If I had been a divine being, she thought, aware all the while of the sinfulness, the unforgivable arrogance, those are the lips between which I would have breathed the breath of life with my mouth, those are the cheeks in which I would have kindled the blood with the fire in the palms of my hands. . . .

They had come thus far without a sign or a meaningful word, and there, hanging directly above them now, were the drenched and rosy masses on the outer branches of the plum tree, and the time for turning back was upon them, and yet she could not turn, not at once, not without reaching up to feel the moist coolness of one dripping cluster with her fingertips. But they were too high to touch—this gesture too was futile; and she stood staring down at her own feet, thin and veined in the wet grass, knowing that one ungentle word from him would be enough to make her weep.

"Did you want a sprig of them to wear, Paulina?"

"Not to wear. To hold. They look so fresh, so wet, so—"

"Wait a moment, I can reach them for you—"

He leaped and caught hold of a flowering twig, but it was moist and slipped out of his fingers. The branch snapped back, and the shaken pink clusters shed a shower of petals—her hair, her cheek, her dalmatica, her forehead were spattered with petals and rain.

"Ah, now, see what I've done. You are covered with flowers," he said.

Slowly, mechanically, she raised her hand and began to pick off the petals, scarcely knowing what she did, gazing at him because some strange transformation was coming to pass in his eyes.

"But wait, wait, let me help you," he said, bending over her and beginning to breathe very fast, like a man in a fever. "It's strange, it reminds me of something, your doing that—don't move, let me think, please stand still. Yes, I know now, you were doing something of the sort that afternoon when I came to ask you about Drusilla. You were picking lint off your clothes—you'd been making shifts or shrouds or something. And afterwards, when my sickness was beginning to go away, I dreamed that you came out to me again—I dreamed that you came out to me, and you were picking the lint off your dalmatica, and you were in a hurry, a dreadful hurry, and no great wonder, either, because everything outside was changed, the stars were falling down, the time had almost come for the end of the world. There were sounds that came with you—sounds of insects making music, which was strange, too, since the grass and all the creatures of the grass were dead. Here, let me wipe this drop of water off your cheek. And here's a petal in your hair, and here's another, here—no, here in the corner of your lips—"

And suddenly they were standing against each other, with the water of the shaken branch still dripping down upon them. His arms were around her waist, and hers were about his neck, and he bowed his head and pressed his cheek against her face. They stood so, unmoving, for what seemed a very long time, until he drew a little apart and opened his eyes and looked steadily into her eyes. So profound a stillness came upon him then that she could not exorcise the thought of death. And, thinking of the world's end and mortality and loneliness and empty nights, thinking of these things and knowing well what she did and at what cost, she held him to her with all the strength in her body and raised her mouth and knew the pressure of his lips.

There was no reason for them to start—they had stepped away from each other, they were gazing at each other and trying to know what it was they had done—there was no reason for them to start when the white figure appeared at the end of the clearing, emerging swiftly out of the shadow of the trees. Prisca—and it was plain she had been running all the way: she was panting, and her hair was sticking to her cheeks and brow. But the instant she sighted them she stopped short, and then came on at an uneven, halting pace, her eyes fixed on the grass, her head down, her arms pressed close to her sides.

"What do you want?" he called to her while she was still some twenty paces off. There was no trace of irritation in his voice, and yet she stopped again, big-eyed and rigid, as if she sensed that he wished to keep her away.

"My lady—I had to come to tell my lady," she said.

"What did you want to tell me?" Something portentous, something terrible—the villa was afire, the first star had fallen, the sky had been riven by the trumpets of the angels of God.

"About the messenger." She folded her arms behind her and advanced There was something stubborn, something almost truculent about her bearing and the look on her face—the marching walk, the clasped arms, the lower lip thrust out, pink and petulant.

"What messenger?" She glanced again, with witless apprehension, at the pale cloud of smoke above the distant roof of the villa. It was nothing, nothing—it was only the last of the supper fires. "Who sent a messenger?"

"He came from the City, my lady." The child had stopped and was staring straight into her face. The eyes, wide and luminous, grew unsteady of a sudden, were tender with pity for what they saw—the terror, the guilt, the shame. "He came from the City, with a letter for my lady from the deacon Probus—"

The name hung suspended in the stillness, and before she could summon up her voice, before she could break the intolerable quiet a thrush began to sing, sang far away, out of sight, on some flowery bough gilded with th last of the sunlight—sang as if his heart were too charged, too swollen to be contained in his speckled bosom, sang as if his heart must break.

"Where is the letter? Did you bring it?" Listening all the while to the bitter music of the thrush, she slowly put out her hand.

"No, my lady, I didn't bring it. I thought it might be torn, I thought it might be lost."

"You were perfectly right," she said, meting out cold justice, rejecting the eyes now, staring instead at the round, clear brow. "You could have torn it. It might have been lost."

And suddenly, partly because of the song of the bird and partly because of the thought of the letter wrinkled and trampled—it did no good for her to tell herself that it was safe—suddenly she began to weep, not loudly, not with her body, not with the rest of her face, only with her eyes. Tears, copious, uncontrollable, fell in quick succession on her sleeve, her arm, her breast.

"Paulina," he said.

She looked at him through the blur of tears. He had raised his hand in a tentative gesture toward her, and his face seemed to her immeasurably beautiful and desirable, and yet at the same time so alien that she thought she would shriek if he touched her.

"I'm perfectly calm now, my cousin," she said, stepping further away from him. "I'm completely in possession of myself. And now"—she looked at the child's blank brow again—"now I had better go back and have a word with the messenger. He'll have news, he'll wait while I write an answer to Probus—"

"But, my lady," said Prisca, "he's gone, the messenger is gone."

"Gone?" It was so loud a cry that it rang through the forest. "Gone?" It was not she who had said it, no, nor he, either. It was only an echo—some hollow hillside had flung it back into her face.

"Yes. The elder Novatian charged him expressly not to tarry. Even if my lady had been there, he would have gone at once."

She laughed. Have I lost my senses, she asked herself, that at such a moment "charged expressly" and "tarry" should sound quaint and laughable to me in the mouth of a little slave?

"Paulina," he said again, putting his arm around her.

"But the letter—I must get back to the villa and see the letter—" And she wrenched away from him, ran on ahead of him, as in the dreams of her childhood she had run from the terrible beast or the great white cruel bird or the faceless pursuer whose name is Death. She ran over knoll and through thicket, turning her ankle, scratching her shins, her hair snagged on blossoming twigs, her cheeks stung by sharp whips of pine. For a while he followed—she could hear the crackle of the brush behind her, and the thud of his feet. Then he fell back, and it seemed to her that the whole grove was shaken by a long sigh. Once and once only, like Lot's accursed wife, she turned back to see him. Under the dusky pine boughs he was walking slowly—disconsolate, but not alone. And the taste in her mouth then was salt, the salty taste of her tears, when she saw that the child was with him, that his arm was laid across the shoulders of the child.

Chapter 24

WHILE THE light had lasted, she had read the letter a dozen times. If Prisca had actually dropped and trampled it in the woods, it could not have been in a more deplorable state. It was wrinkled, creased, limp at the edges with her tears—she stroked it, she straightened it, she pitied it as she sat there on the edge of the bed in the humid dark. But, wring it as she would between her hands, press it as she did against her mouth, the essence that emanated from the words was no more than the dry scent of some desiccated flower.

But he is dead—the old, dear Shepherd of the Flock is dead, she told herself, pressing the swollen fullness out of her heart with that thought, using that thought to bring on more weeping, more release. He is dead, and we loved him together—this at least you have brought yourself to write in so many words on a sheet of papyrus; and if it would be little enough from an ardent man, a giving man, still, coming from you, it is much. Look, I remember how we loved him together, how, when the others grew impatient with his slowness or raised their eyebrows over his simplicity, we smiled and nodded at each other, sharing the knowledge of his indisputable worth. He is dead now, washed and clothed in linen and sprinkled with spices, and I weep for him here in the dark Campagna, and you weep for him in a cellar in Rome, and we are one where we have always been one—in the sharing of a common cup of tears.

Voices came from the garden beneath her window. Prisca's voice and

317

Prisca's father's voice and *his* voice broke in upon her thoughts. But they were not thoughts, really; they were only images—she kept seeing the old body laid in the grave, the arms crossed over the chest, the silver hair decently combed, the severed head placed on the neck again, bound to the neck with a linen band . . . "No stars," said the voice of the gardener Sylvanus. "Very likely it'll rain again tonight." Oh, God, God, God, she thought, cradling the letter, rocking from side to side on the edge of the bed, if only it had rained this morning! If the rain had only come down on the earth, on the woods, on the thrush, on the blossoming plum in drowning, obliterating torrents! Then I could have wept with an untainted heart for the still hands and the silenced voice and the unseeing eyes of him whom the two of us loved together. Then I could have lain down with your letter under my cheek, possessing in full measure that wine which my Lord poured out for me to drink on earth, knowing no stronger wine, wanting no other wine, calling myself blessed, knowing myself at peace. . . .

"Oh, but I'm sleepy," said the little slave, blurring the words in a yawn. Shameful and bitter that even at such a time she should think of the lifted arms and wonder whether the dusky armpits were revealed to him in the damp and generative dark.

"What are you waiting for?" It was the gardener's voice again. "Why don't you take yourself upstairs to bed?"

Yes, what are you waiting for? she thought. To see how it will be with me when I come down again, with all the color drained out of my face and my mouth trembling like an idiot's mouth and the skin on my cheeks worn raw with tears?

"But I wanted to hear the news from the City—"

Ah, yes, you did, of course you did, she thought, rocking back and forth again. And who has a better right than the blameless lamb to hear the news of the mild old Shepherd's death? Those earth-stained fingers, crossed in the final, ritual gesture of renunciation now—how many times did they stroke your silky head, how many times did they bring the blood and the body of our sweet mutual Saviour to your parted lips? And whatever prayer you fashion for the peace of his soul tonight—even if it includes such quaint words as "expressly charged" and "tarry"—will be far more acceptable than anything I can send up out of my labored grief to the place where he sits before the throne of God. . . .

"You'll hear the news tomorrow. Tomorrow will be soon enough." The voice was weak and melancholy and evoked an image of the gardener's face —soft, sad face, with bluish, shifting eyes.

"But it might be good news, Father."

"Not very likely, Prisca." *He* had spoken. How was it possible—in spite of the terror and the shame—that his voice should still compel her heart? "Your father's right, you're tired, you've been running about since morning. You'd better go upstairs and sleep."

And I—what do you think I had better do? she thought, getting up and going to the window, as if she expected him or the vast darkness to yield up some answer to her question, some balm for her pain. The mist was cool on her arms and face; the smell of the blossoms was overpowered now by the stronger, more soporific fragrance of the pines and the dark breath of the drenched earth. To lie insensate, undreaming under the fresh, moist clods is not so terrible a thing, she told herself. And suddenly, without thinking, she crossed her hands on her breast over the letter, and stood for an instant unbreathing, knowing how well it was with her Shepherd and with all the dead. . . .

"Good-night, then," said Prisca. "May the Lord watch you and keep you and cause His countenance to shine upon you. If anybody wants cold lamb before he goes to bed, there's a piece of it laid by from yesterday. Goodnight."

Often, she thought, rousing herself with a shiver, often we used to eat together, Probus and I—a little cold meat, a little cheese, an egg or two—late at night, when things had gone ill with *Barnabas* and he needed some compensation for the lost day, some solace for restlessness . . . And of a sudden she found herself wondering feverishly what had become of the pile of scrawled papyrus sheets, whether the ink would fade in the dampness of a cellar, whether rats would nibble lines away, whether, in the midst of some terror-stricken exodus, the whole manuscript might be left behind and irretrievably lost. I must warn him about forgetting it, she thought, turning from the window. I must tell him to keep it all in one place, close at hand, beside his bed . . . A dozen things that she had meant to tell him came rushing into her consciousness then: she no longer had the appalling sensation that there was nothing to say to him save only "God bear witness to my grief for our Shepherd and to the bitterness of my exile in this alien place." She would write—of *Barnabas*, of the novices, of the eggs and cheese they had eaten together, of the bloody tunic he had saved for her, of everything. The pen was here, the ink was here, she needed nothing but a light—

"With your permission, my lord and my master," said the gardener Sylvanus, "I think I also will go to bed."

"Certainly, certainly." The voice was irritable and weary. "A good night's rest to you. I intend to go in very soon myself."

"No, oh, no!" she said in a whisper, feeling her way across the unfamiliar room. She had never imagined that he might put a violent end to the day without another word, another look, that he might shut himself away behind his door—and she alone outside, assailed all night by sin and death and fright and the smothering dark— "Wait, wait, my cousin," she said aloud, knowing well that nobody could hear her. "Wait and tell me something, anything that will quiet my heart." She hurt her fingers against the corner of a chest, and, reaching over to chafe them, found that she still held the letter in the other hand. And what have I come to, she asked herself, that I should be running to my lover with my husband's letter? How is it with me, in the name of God?

But, just as she was about to step into the corridor, a cool, grave lucidity came upon her—from what source she did not know, perhaps from the Lord. She was not *compelled*, she knew of a sudden, to run down the stairs and seek him in the garden and stand again as they had stood under the dripping tree. She could take up the lamp instead—there *was* a lamp, here, directly under her hand; she could kindle it in the hall—there was a light out there, burning under a wall-painting of the young Shepherd with the strayed sheep over his shoulders; she could sit still—anybody could sit still, even a chidden child—she could sit still here at this table and wear away the night with writing to her dear yoke-fellow in Jesus Christ; and He who had been gracious to her thus far would surely vouchsafe her more grace tomorrow morning, and would make her strong against *his* eyes, *his* words, *his* lips. Phrases which could carry her yearning for reunion and peace into the dank cellar in the City had already begun to take shape in her mind. If they were excessive, if they were too ardent for Probus, that was no great matter: she had hours in which to reconsider them and make them acceptable. She bore the lamp then as far as the Good Shepherd, and thanked the Lord that there were no footfalls, no voices, no tempting sounds to draw her down the stairs. The face in the painting seemed strangely flat and ordinary tonight, perhaps because all subtlety had been bled out of it by the white flame that burned below. Tomorrow it will be different in the sunlight, she thought, and trimmed and kindled her wick, and stared for a long time at the lengthening flame, and sighed.

It broke upon her with consternation that she no longer had the letter with her. Had she dropped it? Had she lost it? No, that was impossible, that was needless self-torment; she had laid it down—she remembered the moment and the movement clearly now—she had laid it carefully down on the bed before taking the little saucer of oil in her hand. I am not worthy to sleep with my face against his writing, not as yet, she thought. Tonight I will put his letter under the pillow, and perhaps tomorrow, when I have made myself closer to him by the very act of writing to him, perhaps tomorrow when my words are on their way to him—

She realized then that she had no slave who could bear her letter to the City; the old steward, the only servant she had brought with her, could never find the way. Then whom shall I send? she thought, walking aimlessly in the wrong direction, going not toward her bedroom but straight to the shadowy stairway. None of the tenant farmers will go, that much is certain. I have no money to bribe them with; and, since we ate their food and increased their labor and brought them no presents, I would not have the face to ask even the most amiable of them to risk his neck for love . . . She caught a glimpse of herself in a plaque of polished yellow marble. Her face was strange in the flickering brightness; why she should suddenly be smiling, she could not tell. And why have I come to the head of the stairs? she asked herself, still smiling. To seek him in the humid, whispering garden? Certainly not. To call him into the lighted atrium, to say to him in the voice of one who remembers nothing: "I have a letter to be taken to my husband tomorrow, and there is nobody to take it but one of your slaves. Much as I dislike making such a request, I must ask you to lend me the gardener Sylvanus. Tell him to be ready to set out at dawn."

Before she had finished constructing the speech, she found that she had come all the way downstairs and was standing on the threshold of the chamber to which she intended to summon him. It was darker here than she had expected; all but one wax light, burning high up and at the end of the atrium to her left as she entered, had been quenched for the night. The yellowish glow, falling from behind her—she had turned to the right now and was walking slowly up the middle of the room—the yellowish glow lighted only the upper rounds of a few of the columns and shone faintly on the foreheads and noses and cheekbones of the stony forebears of the Cornelii. Christians, good Christians, all of them—for almost two hundred years a family of strong, uncompromising Confessors of the Name—and their eyes accusing her now in the shadow, and their harsh judgments written in the creases in their brows . . . I could go back, she told herself. Tomorrow would be time enough to ask him for his slave. But of a sudden, without a word or any other sound to tell her so, she knew that he was in the room. She sensed that he was standing against a pedestal not ten paces ahead of her, alone and watching her, invisible in a patch of dark. Stepping forward a little and raising her lamp, she saw only what she had expected to see: his black curls against the hem of a white marble skirt, the whites of his eyes shining in the trembling light.

"I came because I wanted to ask you—" she said, and fell silent. His face, clear in the quaking brightness now, left her without words or breath. She had never once asked herself what wounds he had received at her hands; and the beautiful eyes were red-rimmed as with weeping, dark as with immeasurable pain.

"What did you want to ask me?" The voice strove to be casual, but the last two words came out quavering and high, and it was as if some vital thing within her cringed to know how ridiculous he must think himself.

"To lend me your slave. I have to send a letter to my husband—" It was cruel, like a slap in the face. But, once she had begun, what else was to be said?

"Prisca?" he asked. "I'll never let Prisca go to the City alone, not in a time of persecution. She couldn't take care of herself, she's a defenseless child—"

"If you'll try to control yourself," she said with cold hate in her voice, "I'll do what I can to make myself plain. I never thought of sending Prisca. We'll keep her here, we'll look after her, we'll see that no harm comes to her—no more harm than might happen to any well-developed girl who lolls about in the woods with a man from morning to night—"

He swallowed and set his teeth into his lower lip. It was impossible to know what thoughts were passing through his mind. His look was blank, almost stupid—she looked at the folds of marble drapery above his head, unable to endure the sight of the drained and helpless eyes.

"It was Sylvanus the gardener that I wanted to borrow," she said miserably. "I would never have thought of sending Prisca. I'd send my steward if I could—he's the one that ought to go, of course. But he'd never get there—he's too old."

"Is it urgent?" he asked, and the dark pain welled into his look, and his hand dragged at his girdle as if the tightness of the leather were the source of his suffering.

"Urgent?" she said, knowing there could be no answer without further pain. "Urgent? My husband and I have been separated for weeks. At a time like this"—she heard and regretted the deviousness of her own voice—"it's very hard to know whether a thing is urgent or not—"

The thin hand kept working at the girdle. The eyes looked down at the leather thong and then flashed up again, startling, peremptory. "Do you love him so much? If you love him so much, then tell me so. I can accept it," he said.

"Yes, I love him." The tears were streaming over her cheeks again, stinging the raw skin. "Of course I love him—how could it be otherwise? How could it be otherwise unless I were less than a beast? Ten years together—ten years—"

"Then give *me* your letter, let *me* take it," he said, abandoning the girdle now, turning his head slowly from side to side against the skirt of the statue, like a man in mortal anguish. "I see now I was deceived about the way things were between the two of you. I never dreamed—not until you broke away from me in the woods like that—I never dreamed you belonged to him so completely that my touching you would be a kind of defilement to you. If you love him so much, then I'll take the letter."

She knew that her own eyes had gone blank now. The angry fire that burned in her vitals every time he laid his hand on the child's silky head—*he* was devoured by it now at the thought of her and Probus; and that was useless, since there was no cause. With so much unavoidable suffering in this sick and insupportable world, it was unbearable to her that he should endure this needless torment. She turned and set the lamp on a pedestal behind her. She walked the ten paces that lay between them, and put her arms around his neck again, and laid her cheek against his chest. "But it isn't like that with us, my cousin," she said, forgetting everything, forgetting her Saviour and the shining Easter evening, and the sacred promise of silence that had been unbroken these ten years. "Don't torment yourself, there's no reason for you to torment yourself. He and I—after the first few

322

months, we never were together in the flesh, only in the spirit. We took a vow, we took a vow of chastity. Nobody touches me, nobody comes near me, never think of that. We live as brother and sister in the Lord—"

He uttered a cry then, low and triumphal. He took her face between his hands and strained her head backward and looked long into her eyes and kissed her on the mouth and laughed and wept. "No, truly, truly?" he asked, kissing her cheeks, kissing her eyelids. "But of course it's the truth—who would think of lying about such a thing? I know, I know." But then the laughter died out of him. He stepped back from her and stroked her cheek with an infinitely tender hand. "Poor Paulina," he said, "poor girl, poor child," and took her hand and raised it to his lips and kissed first the fingers and then the spot where the veins crossed on the inner part of the wrist.

"I must go, I must go now, you must let me go, my cousin," she said.

"Yes, certainly, go and get some sleep. Poor Paulina, I can see you're very tired."

"I must write the letter—"

"Yes, of course." He went and brought her lamp and set it in her hand. "Write the letter and go to sleep."

He stepped back and stood against the pedestal again, nor did he follow her to the foot of the stairs. He also will go to bed and sleep, she told herself, bearing the light before her slowly up the staircase. He is at peace, he is satisfied with as much as he has received from me tonight, it would be crass of me to think of bolting my door . . . But when she stood alone again in the alien room, when she saw the wrinkled letter lying on the bed, such terror came upon her that she did not know what she did: she would have done anything to take back every word she had uttered and hold the dear mutual secret again untold. And there was nothing to do but to wait for the sound of his feet on the stairway—slow footfalls of a man who walks in profound thought, striving to know himself within. And, waiting in unbelievable cruelty until his footfalls were passing her threshold, she sprang from the bed and threw the bolt so that the softness of the night was torn with the clanging iron sound. Jesus, Jesus, ring me round with the swords of angels! she thought. Will I never sleep again? Jesus, will I never sleep?

Chapter 25

CONSIDERING THE fact that he was the only one of the undershepherds honored with an outright invitation to remain in the cellar and hear the discussion between the elder Cornelius and the elder Novatian, the deacon Probus had been holding his peace with too marked a stubbornness. But if they expected him to introduce the charged and perilous subject of their difference—the more serious since the imprisonment of the elder Moyses had left the two of them at the head of the congregation—they were mistaken. So far as he was concerned they could sit on their stools and offer each other excessive courtesies for the rest of the night.

It was the first time the elder Cornelius had visited them in the cellar. Since he was of a wealthy and ancient consular family—from the beginning, the persecution, like the censorship, had been confined to inconsequential victims—there was no need for him to hide. He had offered some weeks ago to share the miserable quarters of the other undershepherds; but the Blessed Fabian had specified in his last days that he stay in his own house, partly because he had weak lungs and partly because it was necessary for him to be close to the Urban Prefect's prison, since his business was chiefly with those who suffered there for the Name. Like all the other patricians of the congregation, he wore a disguise, but the mild and decadent elegance of an aristocratic house belied his rags. The head that emerged from the collar of the dark-brown shoemaker's cloak was the head of a well-fed Jupiter: the lips serene above the luxuriant beard, the brow covered with brown, Olympian curls. Only the eyes—short-sighted, pensive, and tender—seemed out of harmony with the pagan past. The elder Cornelius had almost ruined his sight with copying manuscripts and keeping accounts for the Church of Christ; and now, no matter what he peered at, his eyes had a beseeching, helpless look which spoiled his ambrosial composure and made him seem always a little puzzled, always somehow at a loss.

Now, in the midst of an embarrassing silence, those gentle, ineffectual eyes rested for the first time on Probus's face. "I hope your wife and cousin aren't too uncomfortable in that dilapidated villa of mine," he said—incongruously, since the talk with Novatian that had preceded the silence had dealt with quite another matter. But if the remark had piqued the poet-saint, he did not show it. He clasped his beautiful hands around his knees and smiled the most enigmatic of his smiles while the deacon Probus groped for the gracious phrases that he was never able to find. It was only after he had trailed off into a baffled wordlessness that the elder Novatian broke in.

"Did you bring the letter of the Blessed Fabian?" he asked the elder Cornelius; and the tone of the question was so hushed, so reverent that it implied reproof. It was as if he had said: "Now that we have finished with wives and villas and such, may we take a moment to consider such matters as the last testament of our Shepherd who is asleep in the Lord?"

"Yes, I brought the letter." Unruffled, almost indolent in his motions, he drew it from his leather pouch and unfolded it and held it under the uncertain light of the lamp for the other two to see.

"We must find a safe place to keep it in. It's a very precious document," said the elder Novatian.

You ought to think so, the deacon Probus thought. It relieves *you* of the necessity of laying your head on the executioner's block, though that, too, you could do beautifully, no doubt. The letter contained an express command from the Blessed Fabian that none of the elders should assume the title of Bishop, inasmuch as nothing would be accomplished by such a move at present except to place the new Shepherd under sentence of death. Why he had done it, whether heavenly wisdom or earthly pity had led him to write that sentence in the last thin hours before his execution, none of the Flock would ever know. . . .

"Yes, very precious," said the elder Cornelius in a quiet voice; and it was impossible to tell whether he had been moved to tears at the sight of the familiar handwriting or whether staring into the light had brought water to his eyes.

"It occurred to me—not that I mean to make a point of it, it's merely a suggestion—it occurred to me that somebody less exposed ought to keep it in his possession."

"Yes, we could give it to one of the women," said the elder Cornelius, folding the papyrus carefully again. "We could give it to Priscilla or Aurelia or Livia—" He stopped short. Quite by accident, he had blundered into the subject of the difference that lay between him and the elder Novatian, the whole bitter question as to what the congregation was to do with those who had bowed to the persecution and denied the Name. This same Livia, whom he had been careless enough to mention, was one of several hundred Roman Christians who had given themselves over to the daemon by burning incense to the genii of the City and the Emperor. Her case was well-known. She had discussed it with everybody who would listen. It was sickening to see her—her and hundreds like her—beating on the doors of the deacons' houses, kissing the feet of the martyrs and imploring their intercession at the prison, walking the streets of the City with blackened cheeks and shorn heads. She could not help it, she said, if her fear had forced her to the altar. Whenever she heard a knock at the door, whenever she saw a Guardsman stop a passerby, the milk went to a lump in her breast. At last somebody had suggested that she bring the dilemma before the two elders whom the Blessed Fabian had left at the head of the Flock. From them she had received divided counsel: the elder Cornelius had told her to go and sin no more, but the elder Novatian had insisted that her errors could be wiped out only if she went to the Urban Prefect and confessed the Name. "And if I cannot?" she had asked him, shaking and weeping. His answer had been swift and unmistakable: Those who forsook the Lord must expect also to be forsaken, to have no part in prayers or alms or the breaking of the bread.

Yet now he looked mild enough, hanging his impressive head a little to one side, staring slantwise at the floor and clasping his knees in his emaciated hands. If he did not show the least inclination to initiate the argument, if all he said was "Not Livia—Aurelia," if his voice was meditative and solemn and sweet, it was doubtless because he was motivated by a genuine desire for unity and peace.

But the elder Cornelius would not be put off. "Aurelia, if you like, but what about Livia? What do you propose to do about her and all the rest of those poor wretches?" he said.

"I propose to do nothing." The long foot, white and veined, swung slowly back and forth, and the half-veiled eyes moved with it. "The question is, what do *they* propose to do. The lapsed—those among us who have so far forgotten themselves as to forget their Saviour also—really, dear brother, isn't their fate in their own hands? When they went to the altar to humor the Beast, didn't they render up, quite automatically, their credit with God? And if they repent now, can't they buy their salvation and more than their salvation in the twinkling of an eye? They have only to walk into the Urban Prefect's office and give themselves up. Nobody, not the most austere among us, would deny them the complete forgiveness that falls to him who takes unto himself a martyr's crown."

"And yet," said the elder Cornelius, putting the letter back into his money-pouch, "I wonder what the Blessed Fabian would have wanted us to do in a case like this."

"We have his example, brother. *He* never weighed the matter for a moment. Swiftly, as if the wings of angels had been fastened to his feet, he hastened to the block."

"And never turned back in his going to tell others to come after." The voice was thoughtful; the white patrician hand fingered the pouch. "It's strange how those who confess the Name and die the death are always slower to judgment than those of us who have nothing to complain of but bad food and damp cellars and lost sleep."

"Have I complained? Is there anybody who has ever heard a word of complaint pass the threshold of my lips?" The hands had tightened around the knee until the knuckles shone. The eyes flashed up, and there was a glittering at the bottom of the deep and webby sockets. "God bear witness that I have never complained."

"No, of course not. It is common knowledge with the entire congregation that the elder Novatian never complains. He labors in fortitude until such time as the strength departs out of his body, and then, without complaint, he lies down wherever he happens to be, utterly undone by his supernatural efforts and possessed by the Holy Ghost." The voice was grave, but even in the dark room it was possible to see, above the curling beard, a faint smile.

"Are you mocking my affliction?"

"God forbid that I should mock anybody's afflictions! I have afflictions enough of my own. It's because of my weak lungs that I'm not with the rest of you here in this cellar. But then, too, I think of Livia's weaknesses— a young nursing mother, still shaken after childbirth, coming up as it were out of one death to face another—"

"Are they all of them young nursing mothers?"

"I will not answer that. It seems to me that my brother asks me that in something less than Christian fellowship and charity. I only said that each of us has his affliction. Who knows what dark places, what soft places, what terrible scars there are on another man's heart? I think of that, and it makes me slow to judgment. I think too how Saint John the Divine used to rise at every meeting of the sons and daughters of God in Ephesus and tell them to love each other and be as little children, since that was all the Lord Himself taught while he walked on this earth. And, thinking of these things, I think of Livia—I ask myself: When we turn her away from the Lord's table, are we loving her, is it between her and us as it is between little children? Have you an answer for that, my brother Novatian? I have none, but perhaps my confusion is only the result of some dark and questionable spot on my own heart."

"You think of Livia—" He had risen, the necessity to look up at the Olympian figure had become intolerable to him. Their eyes met now, level with each other—the flashing, passionate eyes and the mournful short-sighted ones. "You think of Livia and I think of Jesus—my Saviour, my crucified Saviour, my sweet, afflicted Lord—He who clothed Himself in our shameful flesh and died the death for Livia and such. And in return for this they betray Him. Like Judas they betray Him—for a scrap of yellow papyrus they sell Him in the marketplace. A Judas, I say, every one of them a Judas— but there are still some among us who love their Lord too much to sit down at a Eucharist table with Judas multiplied a hundredfold—"

He stopped. The creaking of the cellar door had broken in upon his thundering eloquence. A figure stood in the doorway, an unexpected figure; but the young man who stopped on the threshold was familiar, nevertheless: the deacon Probus had seen the slender figure, the blond head, and the pale Celtic eyes of the gardener Sylvanus both in the basilica and in the splendid gardens of the Herennii. But he went with them to the Campagna, he thought, trying to control the racing of his heart. He and his little daughter went with the two of them to the villa of the Cornelii. . . .

"May the face of the Lord shine upon the deacon Probus," the newcomer said, panting. He put up his hand—he seemed to be putting up his hand to brush a lock of hair away from his sweaty brow, but suddenly he covered his face with it instead—covered his face and broke the appalled silence with loud, unmanly weeping. Tears trickled through his fingers; they were bitten to the quick; the flesh around the thumbnails was ringed with blood.

"How is it with my wife?"

Both of the elders started at his voice—he had envisioned her dead, he had known how it would be to look into her blank, unanswering eyes.

"She's well enough—" The words were shattered by the terrible sobbing. "She sent you a letter—" Without uncovering his face, he nodded his head toward a roll of papyrus that showed above the leather at his waist.

"A letter? What about?"

"How should I know? I don't read other people's letters—" He was striving to master his terror by transforming it into fury. "It ought to be important—" He removed his hand at last and took the three of them in, one after the other, with a pale, disordered glare. "God knows it ought to be—considering what I've been through in the last two hours—"

"Why? Were you accosted?" the elder Cornelius said, advancing a little and stopping, held at a distance by the furious eyes.

"No, I was not accosted. But what do you think it was like to come up against them twenty times, to keep thinking: It'll happen now—that one, there, he'll never let me pass? They must have stopped a dozen others before me and behind me. I'm here, yes—but that's only by chance—or, if you like it better, by the grace of God."

"Where is my letter?" It seemed to him that it was not he who spoke, who utterly disregarded this pitiful brother in the Lord, who stood in the presence of his elders demanding his letter, like a child.

"Here, take your letter." He tore the crushed roll of papyrus out of his belt and thrust it into the extended hand. "There it is, and I wish you joy of it. It was for this that I risked my life at every corner in the City from here to the Old Wall and left a motherless child up there in the Campagna. What's to become of her if they take me to the Urban Prefect's office, nobody knows and nobody cares. Jesus Christ died on the Cross to save all sinners, even the lowest—so they say in the basilicas. But slaves are still slaves, Jesus notwithstanding. If you have a piece of dirty work to do, you give it to a slave."

All this was so, and a matter for shame; but he could not think of that now; he could think only that the bond which had been broken between them for weeks was about to be re-established.

"What's in the letter? Why don't you see what's in it?" said the elder Cornelius, laying a kindly hand on his shoulder.

"Perhaps it's urgent," said the elder Novatian. "Perhaps it's well worth the trouble he took to bring it."

But it was nothing of the kind. It was only a letter from a wife to her husband. Holding it under the flame of the lamp, forcing his eyes to race from line to line, he saw that it was of no general import, no public value at all. He saw also certain excessive words, phrases mysteriously intense, one whole sentence that came at him sharp and wild, like a cry. And, terrified lest they should ask to read it, he folded it in two and thrust it into his breast.

"What did she write you, my brother Probus?" The elder Cornelius asked the question in all good faith. Nobody, not even this mildest of the undershepherds of the Flock, could believe that a woman would so forget herself as to send a slave to the City with nothing but a love-letter—if those desperate sentences could be considered the utterances of love. . . .

"Nothing, nothing," he said, knowing that his air was truculent, yet unable to lower his chin or to lessen the insolence in his eyes. "She simply wrote to me—we've never been separated for more than a day in the past ten years, and she saw fit to write to me. It was foolish, it was childish, I know—"

"It was certainly childish," said the elder Novatian, biting his lip and turning his head from side to side. "Whatever could have come over her? She was always trustworthy, always circumspect—"

White fury blazed up in him—all the hate that he had tried to stifle in these tormenting weeks. "It's your doing—not hers nor mine!" he shouted into the face of the elder Novatian. "If you had allowed your messenger to wait for an answer—how long could it have taken, anyway?—if you had kept yourself once from using the occasion to prove that you were an angel on earth, there wouldn't have been any reason for her to send a slave!"

"Children, dear sons of Jesus, undershepherds of the Flock, how can you shout at each other at such a time?" said the elder Cornelius, laying his hands on the shoulders of them both—though it had been only the deacon who had raised his voice. "What can we gain with this sort of thing? What's done is done—we can't undo it now. And while we stand here abusing each other, here's this poor brother of ours, half-fainting on his feet—he ought to have a cup of wine, he ought to have a bed. Come, my son, here's a chair, rest yourself a little. You'll be better in the morning after a good night's sleep."

"Oh, no, that's one thing I don't have to do," he said, pushing the offered chair aside. "My master made me bring the letter, yes—but he didn't order me to stay in the cellar with the leaders. I'll not be here when the Urban Prefect's men break in—who's to say they'll even give a man a chance to sacrifice once they've found him in a hideout like this?"

It seemed to the deacon Probus that he, too, was trapped within these walls, that he also might give way to the senseless and unmanly drive to break away, to rush into the street. "Jesus!" he said under his breath, raising his hand and crushing the crackling letter against his chest.

"Jesus—yes, Jesus . . ." said the elder Novatian, closing his eyes and smiling a sweet, exalted smile. "It is nowhere recorded that He said:'I must flee, since tomorrow they will scourge Me with thongs and press a crown of thorns upon My forehead and hammer nails into My hands and feet.'"

"But there was the agony on the Mount of Olives," said the elder Cornelius, staring stubbornly into the rhapsodic face. "There was the night when He prayed to His Father in Heaven that the cup be taken from Him—"

"And added immediately that He would drink, if His Father so willed—"

"I will not stay in this cellar, I tell you! Let me get out of here—I'll hide under one of the bridges, I'll sleep in a garden, I'll find a place—"

And suddenly, knowing himself to be stronger than this hysterical slave, the deacon Probus assumed that air of complete self-possession which he always managed to acquire in times of stress. "Why should he stay if he doesn't want to?" he said quietly. "Our brother Cornelius could give him a bed for the night. It's late, it's fairly safe now, I should think—the City Guardsmen get tired of the whole business by this time of night. I'll come with you, too, if you like. I need a breath of air myself."

The street to which the three of them ascended, walking up four stone steps from the level of the cellar, was considerably less cool and just as dank as the chamber they had issued from, and the deacon Probus was disheartened to find it so. The heat of the day seemed to cling to the walls of the tenements—palpable, almost visible, though one knew that the reddish glow swathing gate and wall and archway was not actually heat, was only the diffuse light of the unusual number of altar fires coloring smoke and mist. Although nobody of any account was to be seen—all the way down the long, narrow street there was only a drunken woman and a disconsolate old derelict sitting on a stoop with his head in his hands—the gardener Sylvanus, obsessed with the notion that he was walking with marked men, broke away from the other two and lagged some ten paces behind them, keeping close to the walls. At the end of the street, a good sixty paces away, one of the temporary altars stood, with a black archway opening behind it. There were hundreds of such altars scattered through every part of the City, and all of them the same—a rough slab of stone with a plaster head of Decius and a plaster likeness of the goddess Roma coming up white out of a nest of myrtle. The sculptors' association that manufactured the ugly figurines had probably made a fortune—somebody was always bound to profit, the deacon Probus told himself.

"You haven't had an opportunity to read your letter, have you?" said the elder Cornelius.

"I looked over it. There's nothing in it—nothing of any consequence."

"It's of consequence to you, of that I'm certain. Suppose you stop for a little at my house. You could go up to the library there and read it in peace." And suddenly the casual voice grew halting and husky. "You miss her very much, don't you, my brother Probus? Your wife, I mean. I was thinking—you ought to go up there yourself for a couple of days. You've been working like a dray-horse for weeks on end. You and Novatian—if we ever settle this business of the lapsed, or, for all that matter, even if we never settle it—the two of you ought to go up there for a while and rest."

They had passed the altar and were walking under the arch. Surely it was because the prospect of such a rest and such a reunion was too blessed to be believable that he fancied he saw a dark shape lurking there—plumed, with a shining breastplate—such a shape as could take this hope and smash it with a word. But they passed to the other side of the archway un-molested; the glimmer that he had sighted must have been water dripping down over the stones.

"She's not sick, is she?" said the elder Cornelius.

"No, not so far as I can gather. I think she—"

What he thought was never uttered. There was a short, sharp cry on the other side of the arch behind them, and both of them looked wildly into each other's eyes, knowing it was the gardener Sylvanus who had let out that cry.

"Walk on, walk on," said the elder, drawing him along by the elbow.

"One moment, slave." The weary voice made echoes in the archway. "I must see your certificate of sacrifice."

"I haven't got one, I only came into the City tonight, I—"

"No certificate of sacrifice?"

The deacon and the elder stopped short in their tracks. They had walked straight into a wall.

"No, as I said, I came only this evening from the Campagna on an errand for my master. I've been out of the City for weeks—I went before there were any certificates of sacrifice."

"Well, it's easy enough to get one. Throw a pinch of incense onto the pan here on the altar, and I'll give you your certificate."

"Where?"

"Why, there, fool, right behind you. What's the matter? Are you blind?"

331

"Oh, God," said the deacon Probus in a whisper, "he'll do it, he's frightened enough to do it—"

"Hush, of course he will," the elder Cornelius said.

They waited, not daring to turn, their faces to the wall, until such time as they knew the thing had been accomplished. There was no visible sign to mark the awesome instant when the gardener Sylvanus turned into Judas and sold his Saviour in the marketplace; the brightness of the fed flame was not detectable in the general glare, and the scent of incense was lost in the stench of the street. But such a conviction of futility came upon the deacon Probus then that he could not move, might have stayed there for an hour with his forehead resting against the crackling vine on the wall if his elder had not reached down and touched his hand.

"Should we wait for him, my brother Cornelius?" he asked in a whisper.

"No, no, what's the good in waiting? Come along, we'll go home." The words came out slowly, on a heavy sigh. "We're the last people in the world he'd want to see. If our brother Novatian has his way, the poor wretch will never look a Christian in the eye again as long as he lives."

Chapter 26

THE EMPEROR Decius was not in the habit of visiting the prisons. Other Emperors before him—Tiberius, Caligula, Nero, Domitian—had gone with some regularity to those subterranean chambers where necessary information was wrested out of failing flesh; but he had always suspected that the failing flesh had been of more interest to them than the information—the impersonal records on the papyrus sheets had seemed sufficient to him, at any rate. It was enough to read in the morning how the slave Andros had told, after a hundred and twenty stripes, that his master had made a fortune by adulterating the grain shipped to the legions on the Persian front, how the centurion Timotheus had confessed on the rack that his uncle Maximianus was plotting mutiny in Gaul, how the equestrian lady Sybilla Semphronia had accused her brother of violating the censorship at the very sight of a pan of hot coals, how nothing further had been discovered in the matter of the murder of the tribune Arcadius, since the legionary brought in for questioning had died under torture without a word.

Once, and once only in the months of his reign, the Emperor Decius had presented himself at the door of the Urban Prefect's prison during those hours between dusk and dawn when the questioning usually took place, and then it was a family matter, a matter of personal involvement that brought him there: he had been driven by an imperious necessity to come and hear with his own ears whatever was to be beaten and racked and burned out of a certain Aethiopian slave named Baubio. But when the heavy door had been pulled open to him, he had seen that he had come too late; the fires were out, the lingering smell of burnt flesh was all that remained in the oppressively silent room; the mangled body had been put, like the stripped carcass of a steer, near the entrance, to be carted away at dawn. The slave Baubio, the Urban Prefect himself had regretted to inform his lord and his master, had died without uttering one incriminating thing; in fact, whenever they had left off for an instant to catch their breaths or to change their instruments, the big black wretch had smiled at them—a maddening Aethiopian grin. They had been so obsessed with that smile that the Emperor had taken a torch and carried it to the body in order to see it for himself. But it was not there; the eyes had been wide and the thick mouth had been open, round as an *O*; the flesh of the cheeks had been stretched almost to breaking in that final cry.

"Will you bury him?" he had asked, laying his hand on his own stomach because there was suddenly a great emptiness there. "Oh, yes, we'll bury him, we bury all of them, my lord and my master," one of the experts had assured him in a nervous voice, since there was a rumor that the prison attendants frequently sold the corpses to physicians at an exorbitant price. He had stood for a long time then, looking away from the face now, looking at the hands instead—unmutilated, beautiful, serviceable—the skin and the nails pliant and soft with the oil they had trafficked in. "Clean him up," he said in a low voice. "Clean him up and wrap him in linen—I don't want the old woman and the girl upset. Take him to the palace, and tell them he was a faithful slave. Tell them I want him buried, with a memorial stone, in the garden of the Herennii."

And that visit to the prison had been enough for him. He said to Etruscilla that he would never go again, unless, of course, he was forced to by some necessity of the State. Even in the business of the Christians, he knew all he wanted to know from the records—or thought he did until that morning when he overheard Ummidius Pessinus say to the Secretary of the Privy Purse in the little dining room that the much-lauded persecution was proceeding along the same lines as the much-lauded censorship.

Precisely what had the Secretary of Petitions meant by that remark? he had asked, finding it rather strange that he should be talking with the man at all, since for months now—ever since the censorship had fallen to Valeria —Pessinus had been keeping his distance, not in haughtiness, not with the studied coolness of a man who nurses wounded sensibilities, but in his concern, in dreamy remoteness, in lassitude.

For an instant, confronted with the knowledge that his Emperor had overheard, he flushed and squeezed his handkerchief. But the confusion had soon passed; the lassitude, the evasiveness, had come back almost at once into the gentle eyes. He had asked to hear the exact words repeated

334

had pondered them, and had said at last, staring at some distant point beyond the imperial shoulder, that he couldn't imagine what he had meant —possibly that neither the persecution nor the censorship had stirred up much interest on the part of the populace. . . .

Not that they were both impractical, idealistic?

Oh, no, it was too early to make a judgment about that—at least so far as the persecution was concerned, it was much too early to tell. . . .

Had he meant, by any chance, that they were not being conducted with the proper speed and efficiency?

Speed? Efficiency? He couldn't say, he hadn't been following the day-to-day developments—his energies were completely taken up with affairs in his own department—he seldom concerned himself with what went on outside it anymore.

Surely he couldn't mean that the government had failed to arrest the outstanding offenders. He'd heard—hadn't he?—that their Bishop had been taken and sent to the block not more than a week after the edict had been posted on the walls.

Yes, he'd heard that—in fact, he'd been in court when they tried the Bishop. An unlettered, undistinguished man—a petty farmer from the countryside. That's what you'd imagine most of them were—unlettered, undistinguished—judging by those he'd seen when he'd gone on official business to the Urban Prefect's prison. And it seemed a little peculiar, when any man in the street could name you without hesitation half a dozen patrician families who were Christians, that the Urban Prefect and his lieutenants, men who were supposed to be well-informed about such matters, seemed to imagine that nobody but slaves and freedmen ate fish on Friday or carried spices to the catacombs or kept their doors closed to casual visitors on certain nights.

Nobody but slaves and freedmen in the Urban Prefect's prison? Oh, come, now, the Secretary of Petitions must know better than that.

Yes, he had to admit his statement wasn't quite accurate. He'd counted six or seven plebes and a few additional demented wretches who were too far gone in their wits to know *what* class they were in.

Nobody else?

Oh, yes, he had forgotten the most important of them all. From the way the lads were working on him down there it would seem that the most forceful and pernicious character to be ferreted out of the ranks of the Christians was a weaver named Moyses, an old plebeian Jew. This was the one that was being beaten and stretched on the rack day after day.

Late at night and alone, weary with the discharge of other more urgent duties, he had sat at the table in the imperial library, going laboriously through the files of the Urban Prefect's office, looking with mounting aggravation for a Cornelius, an Aurelius, an eminent equestrian, looking in vain for anybody but a plebe or a freedman or a slave. And strangely, in those hours of isolation and bafflement, his rage had not gone out against the Urban Prefect or any of his underlings. The face that kept recurring to him, that made his heart knock in his chest and his veins stand out on his forehead was the mild and benevolent face of Valerian. It was unjust— he knew it was unjust: he had not even given the Dean of the Senate an official position in connection with the arraignment of the Christians, he had merely told him to keep an eye on the Urban Prefect's office and to report any inefficiencies. And yet, when the matter had grown intolerable, when too many papyrus sheets had yielded the same maddening results, when he knew that he must go again to the dark chambers, it was Valerian whom he ordered to accompany him. Whatever appalling favoritism, whatever rank injustice was to be found there, he meant to show to the Dean of the Senate. Whatever curses were to be released, he meant to release upon that great pink mass of noble immobility.

They were conducted to the place in the morning, the bright mid morning, but only a very faint light managed to seep into the great common chamber where the prisoners spent their days. The room, very high and too vast to be crowded, was marked off by beehive arches; its stern emptiness was broken here and there by tables and benches made of raw timber; the rough stone of the walls shone with subterranean moisture, and the floor was earthen and strewn with refuse.

The thought that these prisoners should actually be immured here—one hundred, two hundred, it was too dark for a close estimate—the thought that these walls, this floor, this ceiling should make up as it were a box in which they were inexorably shut away from the streets and the sky and other men—this realization gave him the same sensation of emptiness in his stomach that he had felt on looking at the distorted face of the Aethiopian slave.

"Don't you have Guardsmen stationed here?" he asked the lieutenant who was serving as his guide.

"No, my lord and my master. Their feet are chained, as you can see."

"Which are the Christians?" he asked, keeping his glance moving from one group to another, reluctant to have it settle on any single face.

"Oh, they're all Christians. The others are moved at once to one of the larger prisons. There are more here than you would think at first glance. Only the other night, we arrested forty-three of them."

"Any patricians?" he asked, forcing himself to look into Valerian's impassive face. "Any equestrians? Anybody but freedmen and slaves?"

"We have three equestrians, my lord and my master." He said it with pride, like a boy who boasts that he has three unusual pebbles or three rare butterflies. "We have a schoolmaster who tried to take refuge in the City from the persecution at Carthage, and the wife of a dealer in perfumes, and a maker of flutes."

"No Cornelii? No Aurelii?" He saw a kind of clouding in Valerian's serene and unfocused eyes.

"Nobody like that, my lord and my master. But it's hard to tell who'll be picked up next by the City Guardsmen—"

"Is it?" he said, addressing Valerian. "Is it hard to tell?"

"If my lord and my master means to imply that the Guardsmen have received certain directives from the Urban Prefect," said the Dean of the Senate sententiously, "then it would be only just for him to direct such a question at the Urban Prefect—not at me."

That was true enough, and he turned back to the vast room and the scattered prisoners. They were conscious now of the presence and the rank of their visitor. They were rising from the floor and the benches, they were emerging from the shadows of the corners and the arches, they were coming forward to look at him, slowly, laboriously, because of their chains. "Tell them they needn't rise. Tell them to go back to their places. Tell them to be about their business," he said—and knew sickeningly that they had no business, no concern, no occupation except to wait for death.

With the Urban Prefect's man before him and the Dean of the Senate a little way behind him, he walked among the prisoners, inhaling the odors of sick breath and rancid sweat and earth soaked with urine. Here and there the floor was spotted with spittle. "This floor is filthy. How often do you sweep it?" he said.

"Twice a week, twice a week, may I be stricken by a bolt of thunder otherwise. They're dirty creatures, they can make it foul again in half an hour."

"I came here to see Christians—important Christians. Find me your most notable Christian—he's the one I want to talk to—"

"We do have one very notable Christian," said the lieutenant. "An elder—a fellow named Moyses. An elder's very high, you know, next to the Bishop in the brotherhood."

"He's a Jew, this Moyses, isn't he?"

"Why, yes, he is. You're certainly very well informed, my lord and my master. He's a converted Jew."

He sat, this old son of Abraham, this most eminent among the Confessors, on a low stool, under an arch and against the base of it, his muddy skin the same color as the stones, only much paler than the stones. A woman—an ugly, ageing, and enormously fat woman—was sitting on the floor beside him, resting her head on his knee. Her face, darkened above the thick lip and along the outer margins of the cheeks with a black furze of hair, was empty of all human expressiveness, so vacant that if her eyes had not been open she would have seemed profoundly asleep.

"Believe me," said the Jew, raising his bright and beady eyes as the Emperor approached him, "I would stand if I could. 'Render unto Caesar the things that are Caesar's'—so it is written, so says our gentle Jesus, and

337

I would freely do His bidding and render you your due honor, except that last night they broke my left ankle, and the other knee is bent, too, so that it's quite impossible for me to get up on my feet. As for my little sister here"—he laid his hand with infinite gentleness on her head—"I would tell her that she ought to rise, but she is very halting in her wits."

"Sit," said the Emperor, glancing down in spite of himself at the mutilated foot. It was furiously red and so swollen that it looked like a wineskin, bulging out below the fetter. "Is she your sister?"

"This child of God? My sister in the flesh? No, no, she's a Greek, and I came to Christ out of the house of Abraham. I only meant that she's my sister in the Lord. She came here strangely, almost by accident. She was a charwoman in the Temple of Isis, poor thing, and one hot afternoon she was seized with a terrible gloom and ran into the streets and told one of the Guardsmen there that Christ was her Saviour. Why on earth she did it, I don't know—nobody here knows her, nobody ever saw her in the basilica or in the cemetery or at any of the tables where we break the bread. But if she claims Christ for her Saviour, then surely He is her Saviour. Whosoever knocks, the door will be opened to him, and this head also will have its undying crown. All souls, stripped clean of the flesh, will be beautiful on the Last Great Day. Upright and thin and flawless as a lily she will come before her Bridegroom—eh, Chloe, my sister?" He stroked the cheek, drawing his blunt, mud-colored fingers over the black furze. "God will give you a fresh honeycomb to delight your tongue and golden sandals to bind on your feet."

"And you—how did you come here?"

"I?" The face, netted all over with marvelously intricate crevices, was lifted toward him. "Easily, very easily, like all the rest. I walked past an altar on which there was a likeness of the female daemon Roma and the likeness also of my lord and my master—though it was not a very good likeness, and now that I have set eyes upon you I may state that it does you a great injustice," he said, and smiled.

"You would rather sit in this stinking hole than burn a little incense so that your City and your Emperor may prosper?"

"You must pardon me for plain speaking, but it seems to me that to ask that my City and my Emperor should prosper—things being as they are—to ask the impossible. Besides, I do not always sit in this stinking hole. The Blessed Peter—who holds the keys to everything—he comes and unlocks the door, and I fly forth by night. When they have torn my flesh and broken my bones, when they have done all manner of violence to my senses, then that part of me which is neither flesh nor sense is delivered out of my body and goes to such a delectable land as my master the Emperor would find it hard to imagine. I sit down then at the edge of celestial waters, I listen to the voiceless singing of bodiless angels, I melt, I dissolve in perfect peace. And when I return from that place again, I do not return a stinking hole, I come back to my fellowship with all of these—" His small and shining eyes swept the length and breadth of the chamber with ardor, with tenderness. "While I wait for the cool peace of heaven to envelop my soul, my aching bones are wrapped by these in the warmth of earthly love. Yes, it would be hard for my master the Emperor to understand how we love each other here, how we console and sustain each other, how kind we are to each other, how close, like little children huddled together and watching out the terrible night in one hard bed."

"I understand that you will die," he said, strangely moved, not by the discourse on the delights of paradise, but by the thought of the little children huddled together. "I understand that they will make an end of you if you persist in this foolishness, this insubordination"—he tried, and vainly, because of the emptiness that was in him, to work himself into some semblance of fury—"this treason—"

"My master the Emperor cannot justly accuse me of treason. I cannot commit treason to the City since I am not of the City. I have no citizenship now, save only in the Kingdom of God."

"Yet if you went this moment to the Urban Prefect and said, 'Take me to an altar and let me sacrifice,' you would be restored, you would have full citizenship again."

"So I would, so I would, but I cannot do it. Things better to me than Roman citizenship, things dearer to me than my portion in this toppling City—for it will fall, the day of its ruin is almost at hand—things far dearer, I assure you, I threw away in my youth in exchange for my sweet Lord."

"What things were those?"

"My mother, my father, my brothers and sisters. Mariamne, my betrothed. The Sabbath lights and the unbroken meats and the unleavened bread. My mother—a little old woman—I can see her now, though it is forty years since I laid eyes on her and she died without forgiving me. She cast me forth, all of them cast me forth, and rent their clothes as though they had laid me under the earth, and said the prayers for the dead for me—all because I had been baptized into the congregation of the Lord. And this was bitter to me, this was very bitter, you may believe me. Only, it was lost in the sweetness that was poured out upon me from the pierced hands and feet of my pitying God. And surely you see, if I could not trade Him in my youth for the life which I tenderly loved with all my affections and all my senses—surely you will see that I would not trade Him now, not for a few lonely years, and Roman citizenship, and a portion in a City which is already crumbling and which the Lord our God has doomed to fall."

He could not understand why the repeated announcement of the impending destruction of the City did not rouse anger in him, roused nothing in him but an almost irrepressible desire to sigh.

"What life would I have," asked the old Jew softly, "if these also should

339

cast me out? I would be better dead than without a portion in the congregation—"

"What is your rank?"

"Plebeian. And yet not plebeian, either. I have forfeited my rank in the world, and I do not know as yet what rank I may deserve when I come into my Father's Kingdom. It may be—I have sometimes thought so—that there are no classes there, no ranks at all. . . ."

"And yet I have scoured the records, I have asked the Urban Prefect's men, I have looked about with my own eyes, and I have found nobody here but plebes and freedmen and slaves. When you comfort each other, when you wait out the time like little children in the same hard bed, do you never ask among yourselves how it is that there are no patrician ladies, no illustrious senators, no eminent equestrians in this same bed?"

"No, we never ask it."

"Never wish that the mighty ones, the untouchable ones, the great ones of the earth would also suffer?"

"No, my master the Emperor," he said. "I never wish it, though I remember that I wished it often enough in my youth. It's plain to me now that the great ones of the earth will also suffer. In the besieged cities where dogs and rats and human corpses will be eaten, they will suffer; in their rotting bones and their sick minds and their hollow hearts they will bitterly suffer—they will suffer enough and more than enough. And if my master the Emperor means to ask me whether I wish that certain of my brothers in Christ, those who have denied their power and their glory to kneel humbly with me and the likes of me at the foot of the Cross—if he means to ask me if I wish that they also were here in this prison, then I will tell him no, never, not for an instant. They have already suffered greatly, or they would not have left the world and brought their sufferings to Jesus—surely my master the Emperor sees that for himself. Furthermore, it is sometimes possible for them to serve God and the poor frightened sheep of God better than we lesser ones can serve. Therefore, we rejoice and give thanks when those whom the Guardsmen bring to us are of little consequence in the City. Grant, sweet Jesus, that slaves and freedmen and plebes be the first to enter into Thy Kingdom. Save, if it be Thy will, the others—the senators, the patricians, the equestrians—to be among the very last."

He was lost, he had entered into discourse with that other Jew whom they had crucified on a hill called Golgotha. And somehow he had communicated his ecstasy to the heavy body that leaned against him—she had folded her hands, she had closed her vacant eyes. The Emperor turned away, turned in haste, thinking to see the Dean of the Senate and the Urban Prefect's lieutenant behind him. The guide was still there, but Valerian was standing some thirty paces away. How long ago he had wandered off, it was impossible to tell.

That all the long exchange with this Moyses, so strangely moving and s incommunicable, should not even have sounded on his ears—it was in-furiating, it was insupportable, it was enough to make the blood pound in his head. The Emperor strode across the intervening space, pushing aside an old woman, breaking up a little circle of onlookers. "What in the name of all the gods are you doing? Since when do you walk away without my leave?" he said.

"My lord and my master—"

"It was important! I wanted you to hear it! It was of the utmost im-portance for us to hear what he said!"

"What did he say, my lord and my master? I must have missed the meat of it. What I heard sounded like one of their usual ecstasies."

Something—perhaps the terrible impossibility of ever communicating what had passed between him and the valiant old son of Abraham, perhaps the very sight of this scrubbed and imperturbable presence, clean in the midst of the filth, composed in the midst of the sordid wretchedness—some-thing made his rage burst like a red, exploding sun in front of his eyes. Fools!" he screamed at the top of his voice. "Who is with me—what have I got? Fools, nothing but fools!"

"If my lord and my master has any complaints to make where I am concerned"—the massive body straightened; the monumental head turned proudly on the thick neck, and five centuries of ancient dignity shone out of the glassy eyes—"if he has found my behavior exceptionable, then he might do me the courtesy to tell me so in private. He need not shout it here at the top of his voice for the amusement of plebes and freedmen and slaves."

"Plebes and freedmen and slaves!" His voice was even louder than before. Why is it that we have nothing here but plebes and freedmen and slaves? Where are the rest?"

"My lord and my master might ask that question of the Urban Prefect."

"I told you, you remember perfectly well that I told you to keep an eye on this business—"

"So you did, so I remember. But the gods bear witness that I thought it was proceeding very well. I saw no dereliction, I saw no inefficiency."

"No dereliction? No inefficiency? Where are the Christians that any man the street could name? Where are the Aurelii? Where are the Cornelii?"

"I repeat that this is a question which my lord and my master should address to the Urban Prefect. It's his responsibility—not mine."

"It's yours, beginning at this instant."

"Oh, if my lord and my master wants to make it clear to the Urban Prefect that I'm to serve in a supervisory capacity . . ." The glassy eyes had begun to melt a little. The plump hand unclenched, and the enormous weight was shifted from one pink foot to the other. "I imagine I'll be able to find an hour or two a day. . . ."

"An hour or two a day? To read reports, to interview prisoners, to talk to spies, to keep the Guardsmen in line? Don't be an idiot! Five hours a day would hardly be enough!"

"But my lord and my master knows perfectly well that I'm in no position to give this business my exclusive attention. I'm already overburdened with the duties of the censorship."

"The censorship!" he said in scorn and bitterness. "There is no censorship, there never was a censorship. Everybody laughs at the censorship—in the palace, in the bureaus, in the streets—" It was as if he had thrown down his own vitals and were trampling them into the filthy earth. He stared at that earth, unwilling to permit this son of an ancient house to see the pain behind the fury in his eyes. "Forget the censorship, cease to waste your valuable time on the censorship. Nobody ever believed in the censorship—nobody but I. And the time has come when even I, Pannonian farmer that I am, can't be deceived about it anymore."

"My lord and my master—"

"Hold your tongue. I'm speaking, I wasn't finished. I have orders to give and I mean to give them now. Beginning tonight, your underlings can attend to the trivial details of the censorship. You will be responsible for this matter of the Christians."

"But surely there are others—"

"No others. You and you only. You will do it, and I swear in the name of all the gods that you will do it well. Within ten days, within a week, you'll see that we have another kind of prisoner in this abominable hole—you'll see to it or you'll have more to regret than you think. I want equestrians—rich equestrians, powerful equestrians. I want patricians—senators, consulars. I want Aurelii and Cornelii."

A disturbing change came upon the placid face. It should have looked shocked and blank, but a kind of sprightly slyness crept into it instead. "I wonder," said the Dean of the Senate, "whether it has occurred to my lord and my master that many patrician families—families closer to him and more influential than those two he keeps mentioning—may suffer if we pursue this business as stringently as he would like to see it pursued."

"Let them suffer."

"My lord and my master might regret it. It's quite possible that an exhaustive search might turn up certain of his own connections—"

"What connections? I have no connections! Your Roman aristocrats that tolerated me for the sake of peace and a chance to make money after the battle of Verona, your ancient families who call me the turnip farmer, your consulars who scrape and bow to my face and twist and violate my orders as soon as I turn my back—what are the pack of them to me?"

And still the slyness remained, twinkling in the big pink folds of fat, glinting in the eyes. "But my lord and my master is related to one such family. My lord and my master would certainly not want an inquiry made into the religious predilections of the Herennii," he said.

"Why not?"

"Because your nephew, Favorinus Herennius—"

"My nephew Favorinus Herennius," he shouted, "is under suspicion for insubordination—insubordination and nothing else. He disobeyed my orders —disobeyed them outright, instead of behind my back—which is why he is in exile and you are still in the City, for the time being, at any rate. My nephew Favorinus Herennius was never accused by anybody of being a Christian."

"No?" The face subsided into its customary placidity. "But I was told by the Urban Prefect that Favorinus Herennius was suspected of a close connection with some elder, some deacon, one of the more distinguished Confessors of the Name—"

"Whoever told you that was a liar."

"As you say, my lord and my master. And yet it would be better to consider, before undertaking such a search as you suggest, whether it is your intention that everybody—anybody—even a member of the imperial family—"

He straightened, he drew himself up to all his soldierly height, he looked directly and scornfully into the eyes of this miserable remnant of Roman greatness—and never in all his life had he felt such respect for himself. "I shield nobody, I never shielded anybody," he said, slowly, quietly, giving each word its proper weight. "I never did and I never shall. My property I sold in the Forum. My son—my only son—is not sitting like yours in a kitchen, experimenting with salads and sauces. My son is in Dacia, on the river, waiting for the Goths. When the Empire cracks, it cracks under my feet and swallows my wife, my son, myself. No, I shield nobody, nobody at all. If it so happens that they take my nephew in some Christian holy place, that they show me a letter of his with the name of Christ in it, that they bring me a witness who has seen him eat the consecrated bread, then he will sacrifice or die—like anybody else."

Chapter 27

How FAR he had come, in the dark, in the pouring rain, through the woods
behind the villa of the Cornelii—venting his anguish on his drenched garments and the brush around his legs and the masses of leaves and twig
before his face—how far he had come, and whether the next flash of lightning would reveal the ivy-covered stump or the violet patch or the wild
plum against the purpling sky, he could not tell. But he had come far, he
had been thrashing about for an hour and more, hardly able to keep his
footing for the slippery leaves, before he asked himself what he was doing
in a woods in a thunderstorm—he that had never walked by night in anything less cultivated than a suburban garden before.

Garden—garden at home in the City, he thought, and then there wer
memories also to be wrestled with: the semi-circle of marble seats on the
lightning-whitened lawn and the melancholy insistence of crickets in the
rain. He saw the atrium of the Herennii—unlighted, desolate—and his
mother standing by the pedestal of Hercules, her eyes wild because the
windows had turned suddenly into luminous blue oblongs, the wind snatching the silvery veils away from her withered body and her sparse curl
Another jagged spar tore through the upper branches and brought the
clustered leaves above him into brief being against the bluish light. And
it was as if the lightning were traveling across other forgotten places: the

empty corridors of the Library of Trajan, the little bedroom where Cyrillus crouched and chattered against the pillow, a seaward window in the Temple at Epidaurus, Baubio's grave. "No!" he said aloud, half to these unendurable remembrances and half to the low-hanging boughs that he must thrust aside with both his hands. Not now—he must not think of any of them now—it was enough to have to keep moving through the blackness and the tangle and the drenched unknown, it was enough to have to think of her and of the terrible quarrel between the two of them that had driven him out of the villa into this. And suddenly he let himself sink back against the soaked trunk of a tree; he had been running, trying to exhaust himself beyond all thought; his breath was coming in tearing gasps through his chest, he could not go on anymore.

The flashes of lightning were nearer now, seemed to be crackling in the upper branches of the trees. For an instant he imagined her pacing the lightless atrium of the Cornelii, wringing her hands and thinking that one of these forked purple prongs might dart down at him. But no, that was impossible, she would be sleeping behind the barred doors of her chamber; he saw her face, bled of all life, cold and insensate, locked up in sleep. She has rejected me forever, he told himself. If I were to die here, if they were to find me tomorrow, struck by lightning, her life would be the more bearable for that. She was at peace before I came, I spoiled her peace, it would have been better for her if she had never seen my face—she told me so, he told me so!

A terrible argument—a brutal and annihilating argument. Fragments of it still sounded in his mind, more immediate to him than the reverberations of the thunder and the rushing of the wind in the tops of the trees. Coarse, cruel, and unforgivable—the crassest Epicurean could not have said worse things than he—mocking at her miracles, reducing the quoted statements of her saints and seers to absurdities, shouting into her face that her Jesus was the refuge of cowards that could not bear the thought of death. And she—in the fury of the quarrel she had taken leave of all her reason, all her humanity, had told him in a cold and shaking voice that the life he asked her to live was nothing but an evil dream, that the only good, the only reality lay on the other side of the tomb. She believed—she had quoted the same maddening formula over and over—in the resurrection of the flesh and the spirit, in the risen Christ walking on earth among His children, in the unassailable dictates of the Church of God. Did he find these things incredible? That was all the better—once her petty mind, moving without faith in darkness, had also found them so. But now, like a certain Tertullian whose name she had taught him to hate, she exulted in their very incredibility. Precisely because they were impossible, she knew them to be true.

Nor could he wish, even now—self-exiled from the house and sick with the remembrance of that violence—to turn time backward to the days before the quarrel, to have the quarrel wiped out, undone. Even the coarseness,

even the cruelty was better than the nightmare remoteness that had come
before it. It was seven days since she had confessed her secret to him in
the dark atrium of the Cornelii, and seven days was too long for him to
rejoice in loneliness over jealousy assuaged—after seven days it was no great
wonder that he should begin to ask for more. Better to be one with her
even in contention than to live out another week, in silence, with a ghost.
Seven days, and she had scarcely spoken to him, had kept to her room for
hours on end, had come to the table unlovely and withdrawn, unwilling
to give him so much as a smile or the touch of her fingertips, her eyes
forever anxious, her hand forever wandering to the wrinkled square of
papyrus—that accursed, ill-timed letter from *him*—which she wore now like
an amulet between the folds of her dalmatica and her breast.

The next streak of lightning licked downward with a quivering tongue
like the tongue of a serpent. Something shone pale in the flickering light—
the wet wild plum with its overblown blossoms? Which way was he facing?
He could not see, he could not tell. The thrush that had sung that evening
among the moist and rosy clusters, bursting his throat with exultation and
lament—where had he hidden himself under this riven sky? Remember—for
the hundredth time in these seven lean days, permit yourself to remember
oh, wet pale petals on her wet pale cheeks, oh, warm and giving mouth,
oh, kiss, oh thrush . . . And now it was with him as it always was when
he was in her presence or conjured up in recollection her voice, her hands,
her face. Her person and his overmastering yearning to clasp it to him were
the only realities. All the rest—storms and contentions, exiles and marriages,
lost loyalties and persecutions—all the rest receded and were gone. "Paulina,"
he said softly, as if she were beside him, as if he need only lean forward
a little to touch her. "Paulina, where are you?" he said in a whisper, and
pressed his mouth against his own raised hands, as if his flesh were her
flesh, as if he were kissing the hollow place in her temple, her eyelids, her
parted lips.

But no, he thought, tearing his hands from his face in shame and in
bitterness. She will not have me, she does not want me, I may as well accept
it now. And I cannot tell myself any longer that she turns me away unwillingly, in the name of Christian virtue. Her soul is elsewhere—with *him*
or with her ghostly Jesus. Her soul, devoured by pity, is weeping and will
weep forever over a worthless manuscript or sufferings that were finished
in Judea two hundred years ago. And pity for them makes her pitiless with
me, so cruel that she can say: "I loved my peace and you have spoiled my
peace. I wish you had never come to my house. I wish we had never walked
together in the sculptor's yard. I could have lived my life, I could have
loved my life if only I had never seen your face." It was then that he had
said it: at the door of the villa, on an angry sob, he had told her to go and
live it. And hate, hate and fury, as unpredictable as the lightning, tore up in
him again. Hate for the bed with the familiar hollows in the pillows. Ha

346

for the holy books they read with each other. Hate for the dead old man whom they had loved together. Hate for the very smell of their house—their fish and their wine and their sanctified bread.

There was a blinding flash and a thunderbolt, and the whole sky was lighted up by a dull red glare. Every leaf above him stood out before it faded; he saw enough to know where he stood—not far from the house, close to the ivy-covered stump; it was not the plum tree that he had seen, the plum tree was behind him; the whiteness was the whiteness of a wild olive, its turned leaves silvered by the rain. And then, as the light died out, he heard a wrenching and a creaking—it was a huge limb swishing down through the branches—near him, so near him that the wind of the fall flew past his face and the thud jarred the ground under his feet. I might have died, he thought, I might have died without her, at war with her, unreconciled . . . And now the torrents that poured upon him from the rent clouds seemed healing, blessed. He lifted his face, he let the rain and the tears stream freely over his cheeks. To make peace with her on any terms, to claim nothing of her but his rightful portion of her pity. To kneel by the side of her bed, to kiss her hands, to rest his head against her thin, veined feet.

There were more flashes, more rumblings, diminishing, receding, but he was scarcely aware of them; for a long time he gave himself over to the absolution of the rain. Then that also lessened, until the sound of it was only a splatter and a whisper, until he could not tell whether the desultory drops that fell upon him were coming from the sky or from the leaves; and when he stepped out of the shelter of the boughs he thought he saw the wet, white glimmer of a star. If I could go to her, he thought, if I could lay my hand upon her cheek and draw her spirit back from frozen sleep, if I could say to her: "However fortunate you think I am, I am as much in need of your tenderness as he. He will depart with you in the hour of the great going forth. And look how it is with me—my sun and moon and stars have trailed long since like comets into the dark, and my days are purposeless, and I sit in your vestibule, with my living heart in my hands, listening to the mountains of Africa falling into the sea . . ." But it was useless, useless to imagine it. Coming out from under the dripping blackness of the rest of the trees, coming into the kitchen garden and past the dairy-house and the well, he laughed—whatever vitality remained in his drenched and shaken body rose up to deride such childishness. See her? Weep with her? Whisper out the rest of the night, kneeling beside her bed? That was impossible, she would not have it, she did not want it—she barred the door, she always barred her door.

The entrance at the back of the villa was closed against him—he should have known as much: the steward always locked the door at night. Keeping close to the wet, shining, ivy-covered wall of the house, he walked along the long wing of it. He could make out the balcony—columns and an awning flapping in the fresh, light wind. The wind had torn the clouds apart, the clouds were only pale and tattered streamers now, floating against constellations that shone as if their light had been dissolved and diffused, as if they also had been cleansed and given absolution by the rain. Walking quickly, walking without peril over the smooth starlit lawn, he came round to the front of the house, to the door that led between two tall columns into the atrium. This door was open, but he stopped on the threshold, reluctant to enter the murky darkness, to feel his way through the lightless corridors and the desolate rooms.

And then of a sudden, staring into impenetrable dark, he saw a moving light. Somebody—the ancient steward or the little Prisca, taking the duties of a slave too much to heart—was waiting for him in the atrium, had heard him depart in fury, had sat out the storm, listening for his return. The flame advanced and the form that bore it also came on: vague, unrecognizable, moving like a ghost in a sheath of yellowish radiance, the trailing garment plain, but the features still lost. He crossed the threshold, he moved to meet that hastening figure, and saw *her* tormented eyes, her suffering and rejoicing face.

"Paulina!"

"My cousin—oh, my poor cousin—"

"You waited for me—"

"I thought you were dead. I thought you were dead!"

He took the lamp from her shaking hand and set it on the seat of an ebony chair, scarcely aware of what he was doing, unable to take his eyes from her eyes. He also was seized with an uncontrollable shivering, partly because of the coldness of his drenched clothes, partly because his spirit shuddered within him, in awe and in delight, at all that he saw in her face.

"I thought you were dead," she said again, as if in this and in this only was she explained and justified. And, even as she said it, she came to him, she clasped her arms about his neck, she pressed her face so close to his cheek that he could feel the wild opening and closing of her eyelids, the quick coming and going of her breath. "I thought I would never see you again," she said, and then said nothing more, only gave herself up to the wordless clinging. Standing so in the dark, beyond the circle of light cast by the lamp, they held to each other, brow and mouth and breast and thigh and knee; and he could not tell how long they stood, since time was hourless, measured only by the loud beating of his heart.

It was she who broke the embrace, but slowly, gently, finding his finger, taking hold of his fingers before she drew apart. That seeking hand gave him courage—courage to clasp her round the waist, to lead her on through darkness toward a couch. Groping about in the shadow, he found it and drew her down beside him on cushions that gave off the dry, sad smell of dust. "Kiss me, Paulina," he said in a whisper. "Give me the rest of the kiss we never finished—"

348

"Yes, my cousin. Here, my beloved." She lay beside him, she rested her slight weight against him, sending her warmth through the drenched dalmatica, impatient with the pleated linen that confined her, impatient with the curve of the cushion that rose between their lips. And her slow kisses and the touches of her light and wandering hand were such as he had never known before, issuing out of abundance long stored and shut away, coming sorrowful and exultant out of her vast, unused capacity for love. It was this knowledge that taught him to move slowly, circumspectly, toward the culmination of their oneness, to brood, aching and close to weeping, over her thin feet and her narrow back and her cold and childish shoulders, to value the tears on her cheeks as much as he valued her breasts, to withhold himself long from the ultimate revelation, and to know even this in awe and tenderness. The salt taste of tears was in all of it, even at the instant when the sky spun and the earth divided. Even in their fulfillment they clung together like children in a darkling woods, so that pity was inextricably bound up with love.

Taste of sorrow in the kisses with which they kissed each other into sleep . . . Tears also in his dreams—drops falling slowly, one by one, on the strewn pages of an unfinished manuscript . . . Another basin—no, a chalice -tipped between the earth-stained fingers of the old farmer from the Campagna—red drops—he started in his sleep because he could not tell whether these drops were drops of consecrated wine or drops of blood . . . He walked in the wind and the heavy sigh of the sea along one wing of the Temple at Epidaurus. He looked in, fearfully, at a window with a blowing curtain, and saw his sister Drusilla, naked and emaciated, start out of bed with a lamp in her hand. "Where are you going in the middle of the night?" he said above the desperate sighing of the waters. "To a strange land," she told him, stepping into a pair of golden shoes that were clotted with mud. "To an unknown land." It was night on the bleached rocks by the Temple of Epidaurus, but then of a sudden it was dawn—he saw through the slits of his eyes a solemn shining on the faces and togas and marble feet of the dead Cornelii. And did not open his eyes, knowing that *she* was kneeling on the floor beside the couch where he lay, with her cool hand trailing over his nakedness, with her head heavy on his chest. And in her slow and tentative touch, in the long kiss she pressed upon the spot where his living heart beat out the only measure left for time, there was the same unfathomable grieving that he had known in his dreams. It seemed to him—he started up, supporting himself on his elbows—it seemed to him that she was bidding his body an eternal farewell.

"Paulina," he said, and she rose and stood above him, her face wet with weeping, and such a look of desolation in her eyes that he must negate it at once, must say to her in a whisper, "It's still very early, nobody's awake, come down and kiss me."

"No, no." She took his hand and drew it up and pressed it between her

349

breasts, and he knew, with utter sickness of heart, that she had already prepared herself for whatever lay before her. Her body was shut up from him in the intricately pleated linen sheath; and, even as he stared at her, the old solemnity, the old remoteness settled upon her mouth, her eyes, her brow.

"One kiss—it's still very early—"

"No, my cousin."

"Tonight, then? Let me come to you tonight."

For a long time she stood above him, lost in thought. But he could take no hope from that, he knew with a terrible certainty that she was not weighing the possibility, was only striving to find such words as would fall most kindly upon his heart. "No," she said at last, playing with the tips of his fingers. "You know and I know that between the two of us there can never be one kiss. With us, it's nothing or it's everything—I knew that always, from the start—"

"Then everything, everything—"

"But I have given you everything." She straightened her shoulders to say it—she said it with a sorrowful and childish pride. "God bear me witness here and hereafter also if I am shut out in darkness and fire for it forever—God bear me witness that I was yours, utterly yours in the flesh and in the spirit, and that no love I ever imagined was as much as this, as good as this—"

"For me also—"

"Truly? Truly, my cousin?" A faint spasm of receding happiness passed over her face, and tears stood bright in her eyes.

"Truly. Never—with anybody—never—"

"I'm glad of that. I'm very glad of that."

"Then let me come to you tonight."

"No, Favorinus. No, beloved." She bent her head and brushed his finger tips with her cold lips. She laid his hand among the flattened cushions at his side, and turned from him, and started for the stair.

"When?" he said in a whisper, uselessly, knowing the futility.

"No more, Favorinus. No more, my beloved. Never again in this world.

Chapter 28

IT SEEMED to him that the newcomers had been living in the villa of the
Cornelii for an interminable stretch of time—so long that no echoes of
remembered conversations had survived their theological arguments, so long
that the atrium and the garden and the path to the grove were no longer
suitable habitations for his memories. Yet it was only three days since they
had appeared at the back entrance that evening after the storm—the two
of them standing on the threshold with their lanterns in their hands—as
unexpected and inevitable as the fatal error in the third act of a Senecan
tragedy. Since that night they had shed their terror for him; they had resumed their daily guises; they had again become her husband the deacon
Probus, and his companion the elder Novatian. But when the door had
swung open to reveal them standing with their lanterns against the rural
night, a fist of fear had been driven against his heart. He had seen a man
monstrously sinned against, irreparably wronged, and—standing erect and
staring with burning eyes through a cloud of blowing hair—an avenging
minister of God.

But they knew nothing about it, she had told them nothing. Even in her
consternation at the sight of them, she had given him to understand that
they would never know anything about it, by a slight turning of her head
and distracted signals flashing at him out of her eyes. Nor had there been

any reason yesterday to think that she had changed her mind. Yesterday and the evening before that—he pondered it in amazement: so short a time, so short a time . . . And she passing before his eyes through the stages of the strangest metamorphosis that he had ever seen—less like herself from day to day than the bee is like the larva. He watched her at the table, he met her in the garden, he heard her speak and could not grasp her meanings —he simply did not know her anymore.

On that first evening he had left them early, unable to endure the sight of *him* and *her* together. Not that he was jealous of them—how could he be jealous? Witnessing their rawness, their tenderness, their aching solicitude for each other, he had experienced so overwhelming a pity for them that there was no longer any place in him for jealousy. No, nor hate, either. He had tried to prod himself into hate; he had watched the loose-jointed, uncomfortable presence striding up and down the room and eating blatantly, hungrily, without any manners; but that was useless—the hate was gone, the hate was dead. In fact—it was so disintegrating a thought that he had to walk out into the garden where he could cope with it in solitude—in fact, he knew now that it was impossible to hate what we have abused, that between us and whatever we have mortally wronged there is a morbid fascination not altogether divorced from love. And, back in their company again, listening silent and shut out to their three-way conversation about martyrs and deserters and penances and catacombs, watching her rest her head tentatively, like a fearful child, against her husband's shoulder, he had felt his own yearning for her rise to an intolerable pitch. Her eyes, never fixed on him, fixed always on that bony and unprepossessing countenance in remorse, as if paradise itself were there and she forever exiled from it— her mouth, tremulous, uttering halting banalities, her fingers covertly playing with the hairy red hand—he loved them in their pain, he loved them in their weakness, he loved her as he had never loved in all his days. But it was too much; the heart could be pierced and tormented with it, as the ear is pierced and tormented with the most poignant notes on the flute. And that other one, the ecstatic and sanctified one, was always breaking in, was forever taking advantage of her clinging numbness and her husband's weariness in order to deliver a discourse on the nature of angels, the duties of deacons, and the healing properties of water shipped from Jerusalem. And all the while she had held to a fold of the sleeve of *his* dalmatica, feeling it between her thumb and forefinger, bending toward it, plainly wanting to press it to her lips . . . Too much, too much—and he had deserted. In the first brief pause, he had risen and cast her one wild and pitying look and said goodnight and gone upstairs to lie sleepless in the dark.

All that night, between one disquieting dream and another, he had pondered how he should conduct himself. He decided that it would be better for him to keep out of their way, better to go to the woods or the town and leave them alone in their suffering. He was as useless, even as distressing here as a visitor who bounces about on a sick man's couch, begetting with every movement new apprehension, new pain. He would eat the morning bread with them, yes; he would try to give her some sign of his pity and his self-abnegation in a look or a covert touch; but further than that he would not intrude upon her numbness and her confusion.

But, finding the three of them finished with the meal and ready to rise from the table when he entered the dining room, he had seen the futility of his planning. Some incomprehensible change had come upon her while she had lain beside her husband through the hours of the night, and there was something so alarming in the very completeness of the metamorphosis that he could not bring himself to leave her, but wandered about with them, unwelcome and incapable of taking part in their talk, watching her always with growing uneasiness. She bore herself quietly, graciously, even with poise. She had plainly taken considerable trouble with her appearance: every hair on her head and every pleat in her long white dalmatica was severely in place. Her talk was easy and to the point, but utterly bodiless. One could tell by her eyes, which looked attentive and strained, that she was concerned not with what she or any of her companions said, but with some vast and obscure argument that was going on within. This strangeness, this remoteness had hounded him into questionable behavior: twice he had started for the grove and twice come back, as if in her presence he would be more likely to hear those inaudible voices that were sounding in her thoughts, to catch some glimpse of the unfathomable thing that was lying behind her expressionless eyes. And once, at the evening meal, he had totally lost hold on himself: Seeing her sitting like a statue, with a spoonful of stewed apple halfway between her plate and her mouth, he had asked in a desperate voice, "What are you thinking about?" Her hand had jerked, and her face had gone very white. "I? What am I thinking about? I don't know, maybe about my novices back home. Yes, it was about my novices. I was wondering what they're doing now," she said.

The greater part of that evening he spent in the town, drinking bad wine in the only tavern, trying to follow his elusive and fruitless conjectures above the noises of ribaldry and bickering between tenant farmers and their wives and legionaries and their whores. When he first stepped into the acrid air of that crowded room, he was struck by the thought that he was exposing himself to the danger of arrest; but his apprehension was clouded and be-numbed by the time he had taken three or four bowls of the raw and power-ful wine. It had been late, very late, when the next fit of anxiety had seized him. A hissing voice seemed to be uttering indistinguishable words in his head; her face, intent and strained, came sharp through the fumes of the wine. But a hasty return had been impossible—the mule on which he had ridden was sullen and hostile and stopped at every pool, every tree-shadow, every moon-blanched pebble; and, by the time he reached the villa, all of

them—fortunately, since his eyes were bloodshot and his tongue had thickened—all of them except the ancient steward had gone to their beds.

On the third day he rose early out of a deep and winy sleep. He saw
from the window of his bedchamber that the day would be brooding and
heavy; huge grey clouds were moving across the whole sweep of the firma-
ment, and the air was rich almost to the point of rankness with the smell of
moist foliage and blossoms and earth. Perhaps because the murkiness of the
wine was still upon him, it took him a long time to dress: before he had his
sandals tied, he could hear some of the others walking down the corridor.
He went to the door, a little dizzy with bending over, and opened it and
saw Paulina and Probus moving down the hall. For an instant it seemed to
him that she had slipped back into the childish dependency of the first
evening: her head was resting on her husband's shoulder, and her hand was
in his hand. But there was something formal, almost ritualistic in their
attitudes, and it occurred to him with a small ache that they probably always
walked down to the morning meal in that fashion, that she had been taking
his hand and resting her head on his shoulder, just so, for ten years . .
He waited in the dark hall until he was sure that they were seated, and by
the time he entered the little dining room, all the shapes and colors—the
yellow of the preserved figs, the white of the broken loaf, the purple of the
bowl of violets—seemed to have been intensified in the grey glare of the
morning. *She* sat opposite him, in the full light of a window—erect, alert, no
longer dreaming; and when she turned to ask the elder Novatian how he had
slept, her lover saw in her spare profile such keenness, such self-possession
as he had never seen in it before.

Later, when he looked back on that day with afterknowledge of its bitter
fruits, he saw it all as infinitely pathetic: the sallies of her wit, the sharpness
of her arguments, her willingness to do what he had never seen her do before: to assert herself, to break in upon others, to take the talk by the bridle
and lead it wherever she would. These unexpected skills—remembering
them afterward, he knew them for the ultimate capacities of her spirit, conjured up for a final struggle; and he could recall the driven urgency in her
voice, the desperation in the raised hand and the reared head. But at the
time he only wondered how he could have taken as simple truth her self-
disparaging and Christian assertion that her only capacity was the capacity
for love, could have failed to see how adroit she was—her darting mind always ahead of her husband's careful reasoning, her wit capable of stripping
the elder's rigid dogma of all its colorful veils of poetry.

She showed her mettle before they had been at the morning meal for
half an hour. There was an argument—and *she* had started it—there was
bitter if courteous argument about a certain Phoebe, an ageing Christian
virgin, who was, according to the deacon Probus and the elder Novatian
carrying on the program of educating the novices in Paulina's absence with
commendable success. Commendable success? She begged to differ. H

chin went up, her shoulders went forward, she brought her fingers down on the edge of the table sharply, like a master calling the class to attention. This Phoebe—in her poor opinion at any rate—was unsuited by her very nature to teach anybody, least of all novices. What harm she might be doing now, she shuddered to think. And why? asked the deacon Probus, laying a hairy and restraining hand on her fidgeting fingers. Why indeed? asked the elder Novatian, shaking his head at the proffered dish of preserved figs—to rest here in the country was self-indulgence enough, he need not coddle his gross belly into the bargain—what under the sun was the matter with poor Phoebe, who seemed to him chaste, circumspect, hard-working, and very zealous for the Lord? She paused to take a fig before offering him her answer. She made a point of taking the fig, saying that God had made it and that it was delicious. But now, to go back to this Phoebe, she was chaste, yes; but wouldn't the reverend elder admit that there were two kinds of chastity? Two kinds of chastity? Would the sister in the Lord be good enough to elucidate? Gladly, gladly, if she could have a moment without interruption. Some were chaste because they preferred the love of Jesus above the love of men, and others were chaste because they were so loveless in their dealings with men that nobody could love them excepting God. Her husband chided her mildly: that was an uncharitable thing to say about poor Phoebe, who was scarcely responsible for her figure or her face . . . Oh, but it wasn't her figure or her face—people would overlook such plainness if the heart was loving. And if it was uncharitable to say that Phoebe had a loveless heart, then it was far better to say an uncharitable word about one member of the congregation than to permit all the helpless lambs of the Saviour to be misled. Misled? asked the elder Novatian. How, precisely, could Phoebe mislead them? Why, by her very manner, she told him loudly across the table, assuming a caricature of that manner, stiffening her back and pursing her lips. Nagging and fussing and plaguing and finger-tapping—was that the way to instruct in the name of Him who had said, "Suffer little children to come unto me"? No, she was sure that the elder Novatian himself deplored such teaching—we cannot instruct in Divine Love unless we carry in our spirits at least some faint reflection of that Love. And Phoebe, heaven help her, was singularly lacking in Christian grace. The Blessed Fabian himself had assigned her to the task of sorting linen. Goods and property she could be trusted with—she was conscientious, she was scrupulously honest—but not human hearts, not vulnerable, adolescent human hearts.

And then, of a sudden, with such perfect timing that Favorinus knew the whole scene to be contrived and controlled, she arrived at what was plainly, for her, the goal of the argument: It was she herself whom the Blessed Fabian had assigned to the task of teaching the female novices; her talent lay unused and rotting within her here in the Campagna; she was sick with loneliness and sleepless with worrying about them; three times now she had seen them in her dreams, weeping in the house on the Aventine where they and she—she was certain that she did not flatter herself, this was her one gift, her only usefulness—had spent so many happy and profitable days. "Let me go home," she said, extending her thin, veined hand toward the elder. "My dead Shepherd wants me there—every time I think of his face, I see such a look of reproach on it as I never saw while he lived. My body would be in danger in Rome, to be sure. But here it is my soul itself that sickens from one day to the next in idleness, in fruitlessness."

There had been so much of the conscious and the contrived in her maneuvering that, even when her voice was vibrant with earnestness, Favorinus could not believe in her sincerity. A dozen times in his life he had heard patrician matrons ask, with complete confidence in the forthcoming refusal, to be allowed to follow their husbands to the Persian or Gothic frontier; and he was amazed that the deacon Probus should only sigh. "Our sister Paulina knows," said the elder Novatian after long silence, "that I believe what the Blessed Fabian believed: No other sister in all the Flock at Rome is so apt in caring for the tender ewes, so amply provided with Christian patience and Christian grace. If the Lord and our dead Shepherd have told her in dreams to return, then let her wait only until such time as we can provide a suitable place for her in the City. For who am I to question the Blessed Fabian or the Lord?"

The incredible knowledge that it was actually her intention to return, to walk on a certain day out of comparative safety into mortal danger, left him so stunned that he could not open his mouth, could only stare at her changing face. And that, too, was incomprehensible: even while he looked, it relaxed and softened; a rueful smile deepened the corners of her lips, and a kind of cloudy light shone, not upon him but over him and beyond him from the wide-set eyes.

Through the remainder of the morning, through the midday meal and into the waning afternoon, other arguments moved around him and above him—in the atrium, in the kitchen garden, on that smooth lawn across which he had come to her, on a night that seemed a hundred years departed, in the moist, diffused light of the stars. But for him they were distant contentions; it was as if supernatural legions, invisible, met in the leaden air above him with muffled clangings and the whirrings of unseen wings. Fragments reached him, phrases about a thousand Judases, phrases about penance, phrases about martyrs' crowns; but he could not follow, he could think only: If she is to go, am I to go with her? Where am I to be taken? In what cramped room scores of streets away from her will they hide me? How will it be with me when I do not know from one hour to the next whether they have taken her away to the beasts and the rack and the fire?

Once or twice, following them from room to room—forgotten, not wanted in their company, too stunned to make a single intelligent statement—once or twice he heard them mention the name of his slave Sylvanus: it seemed that the hottest of the arguments was being waged around that unfortunate deserter's head. His master and his grieving daughter had known for three days now that he had sacrificed to the goddess Roma and the genius of the Emperor to save his skin; and the fact that he was in Rome now, probably back at the Palatine where he could be found for questioning—and he no Baubio, he a proved coward—was another reason for multiplying uneasiness. Nor would *she* look at him—not, at any rate, while he was looking in her direction. He might have been a hound following her from place to place, for all the attention she gave him; though once, turning suddenly, he caught her look directed upon him—sad, immeasurably sad, as steady and as desolate as though she were staring into an open grave.

Then all at once, in that enervating hour of the afternoon which comes before the evening meal, the contention ceased. It was as if the invisible legions had put up their swords and retreated—and it was she again who had sounded the retreat; in her drained face and her folded hands, there was an exhausted and hard-won peace. There were only three of them now in the little arbor at the end of the kitchen garden—she and he and the elder Novatian. Several new lines for *The Journey of Barnabus* had suddenly occurred to the deacon Probus; he had gone upstairs to write them down; and silence had settled in at his departure—a somber silence, heavy with heat and broken by desultory remarks and sighs. On the stone bench under the arbor there was room only for two. She and Novatian sat side by side, and the stranger, the uninitiate, sat in the moist grass at her feet. A strange light, at once pale and powerful, was shed evenly upon the garden from the leaden sky. The grass seemed violently green; the tendrils of the vine behind her head were red as fire; and the distant patches of violets, intensely purple, seemed to flicker before his eyes.

He knew that she did not want him there. Her husband had been gone only for a little while when she turned a falsely solicitous look upon her lover. "You seem tired," she said, smiling wanly down at him. "Why don't you go inside and rest? Besides, there's another point of doctrine I want to take up with the elder Novatian, and I'm afraid you'll find us tedious."

"I don't mind in the least," he said, looking up at her quite shamelessly. "If I find you tedious, I can always lie down and sleep here on the grass."

She did not answer. She merely turned away from him and fixed her attention on the solemn and emaciated presence beside her. "You mentioned the crimson Confessors when we were arguing about the lapsed this morning," she said in a low voice. "There was something you said—about the crimson Confessors, I mean—and I want to be quite sure I understand. Did you imply—or did I only imagine it—that a crimson Confessor, no matter what he carries on his conscience, can dispense with both the usual forms of contrition—the private confession and the public penitence? Am I quite clear as to that—did you say that you and the Blessed Fabian were both of the opinion that the crimson confession by itself is enough to give the Confessor complete and unquestionable absolution?"

To the uninitiate, it was incomprehensible. In fact, he suspected her of using the most abstruse language she could summon up simply to keep him in the dark; and he withdrew himself—stretched himself out on his back on the grass and laid his arm across his eyes.

"Oh, yes, the Blessed Fabian and I were in complete agreement as to that," said the voice of the elder, measured and musical. "Whosoever comes to the throne of the Almighty as a crimson Confessor comes without spot and is received without question. His blood is his absolution."

"Suppose he had committed a murder, my father?"

"He is redeemed nevertheless."

"Even if he has never confessed the murder?"

"Even if he has never confessed."

"But suppose he is more afraid of the usual forms of penitence than of the crimson confession. Wouldn't it, then, be a piece of self-indulgence on his part?"

"Self-indulgence? How could it be self-indulgence to forfeit—"

"But wait, my father," she said, breaking in upon him. "Wouldn't it be possible—can't you imagine a situation in which a sinner might feel that the crimson confession was the easier course?"

There was a moment of silence, and, even without looking, the intruder on the grass knew that the elder's fanatical and burning eyes were misted over with meditation. "How is it that you've grown so hard, my daughter?" he said at last. "What better choice is possible than to do as He did? No, believe me, I can tell you with complete confidence that whosoever elects *that* course, for whatsoever reason, will certainly drink of the waters of Paradise."

"Am I plaguing you too much with this, my father? I've been trying to reason it out without assistance, but certain problems keep presenting themselves. Suppose, for instance, a member of our congregation here at Rome committed a sin—"

"A mortal sin, my daughter?"

"Let's say it was a mortal sin. Let's say it was adultery." And, even while she was uttering the word, she moved her foot toward her lover, she pressed the command for silence down upon his knee, so that he did not dare to stir or uncover his face.

"What cleanses the murderer will also cleanse the adulterer."

"But think what the adulterer has to gain by making a crimson confession. All the time we were arguing this morning, I kept thinking of a certain adulteress—not of our congregation—she's been dead for more than a hundred years—she lived in the reign of Titus, a long time ago. But the virgins of the congregation still talk about her—she was the daughter of an illustrious Christian house, and I suppose such stories are hard for women to forget

358

She married early and was chaste and loving and quiet—a decent Christian matron, bred from her childhood in the faith and bound to her yoke-fellow in the Lord with all her mind and all her heart. But then one night she was left alone in the house with a guest of her husband's, and something came over her—lust, the virgins of the congregation say; but to me it has always seemed a very hard judgment upon her to say that she offended through lust. It's possible—is it not?—that she could have offended through something else—through tenderness or pity or wonderment over the very existence of so much fervor. At any rate, my father, whenever they speak of her, I pray for her immortal soul, and I never think 'lust', I always think 'love'. Well, however it was that she offended, she performed the required penances, she confessed her sin to the congregation: and knelt on the deacons' doorsteps and lay across the threshold of the Bishop's house; and after due contrition she was forgiven and restored to her former place at the table of the Lord. But I was thinking of her again as we talked this morning. I was thinking how hard it went with her, and what ruinous things she was forced to do to save herself. She was required to give the name of her lover, and from that day forth he was never seen again at the Eucharist—he was weak in his faith, and would not do his penance, and was cast out of the flock, consigned by the Bishop to the everlasting fire and the dark. As for her husband—he loved her, and his manhood was shamed through her and his heart was broken. And I have been thinking, my father, how unfortunate it was for her that she lived in the reign of Titus, when the flock was left in peace and no daughter of Jesus could cleanse herself with a crimson confession. Surely if she had lived among us now she would gladly have given herself up, so that her husband might be shielded and her lover saved from hell—yes, and she also absolved and justified—"

He lifted himself up from the grass on his elbows, with the whole landscape careening around him. He tried to speak, but could not for the terrible knocking of his heart.

"Are you ill again, my cousin?" she said, bending down and reaching her hand to him and looking at him with loving, admonishing eyes.

"No, no. What are you talking about? What is a crimson confession?"

"But I can explain that to you another time, my cousin."

"No, not later. I want to know—"

"A crimson confession is the ultimate act of faith," said the elder Novatian; and the musical and measured voice seemed far away, because of the roaring and rushing in his ears. "The crimson Confessors are the martyrs—those who have shed their blood at the block or in the prison or in the arena—bearing public witness to their faith in the Name."

It could not happen. Before he had stumbled up from the grass with the help of her two thin hands, he knew that it could not happen. He could more easily believe that time would be turned backward and the deed undone than that she could consider any such preposterous thing. Tonight or tomorrow morning—so he told himself, trying to shake off the dizziness—tonight or tomorrow morning he would draw her apart and show her how utterly mad it was. And if she would not listen, then there were other measures: he could carry her off, he could even go to the deacon Probus and lay the whole matter before him—he had a wild and laughable vision of himself standing in the kitchen garden among the rows of violently green cabbages with the deacon Probus, plucking the sleeve of his dalmatica and saying, "Circumstances have so shaped themselves that I find myself forced to tell you that your wife and I. . . ."

"Sit down, Favorinus Herennius," said the elder.

He forced his veering vision to focus on the long white face with its thatch of cloudy hair; he looked with apprehension into the deep-set eyes. But there was no suspicion—nothing but intolerable Christian concern for the frailties of his flesh; and he shook his head and forced his inept tongue to say, that such fits always came upon him in oppressive weather, that he was perfectly capable of walking back to the villa—now, at once, alone.

But they would not think of it: heaven forbid that he should try to walk by himself, unsteady as he was. Besides, it was time for the evening meal, and there was the deacon Probus, come to summon them in, walking carefully toward them between the rows of cabbages, smiling over the several lines that he had added to *The Journey of Barnabas*. There was an instant, the cruellest in his life, when he cancelled out that gangling figure, when he thought with unholy joy, "If you were dead, if you were only dead!" Then everything subsided, and they were strolling like any four sane human beings over the lawn and around the side of the house—two and two in the narrow places, the deacon beside the elder, and she with him, offering her arm to him in cousinly courtesy and in consideration for his recent weakness, closing her cool and living fingers around his hand. No, he would never believe it; she had only been carried away by some momentary Christian ecstasy; now that she was herself again she would see that it was a wild dream. And so it seemed to him—a wild dream and nothing more—all through the first four courses. He even forced himself to eat a little of the roast duck and a sprig or two of the new watercress, for the conversation was blither than it had been on any evening since their coming, and she more cheerful than he had seen her in weeks—frank and guileless and witty and kind.

And yet, when they had been sitting for a long time over the raisins and the honey-cake, with the grey light fading on the table, there was a moment when he was forced to believe it, when everything else was false and insubstantial and *it* was the only actuality. The little Prisca came into the room with an amphora to refill the wine cruet, and it was as if the awful and unthinkable thing had crept through the doorway behind her—so strange a transmutation took place in Paulina's face. First there was distress, such distress that she sat upright on her couch and stared at the newcomer with haggard eyes. There was a charged and heavy silence while the wine gurgled out of the amphora into the cruet; and during that silence the face of his beloved changed again: the look of trouble gave way to one of brooding tenderness, a look that came to rest on Prisca's bent and silky head and followed her while she made her sturdy, self-conscious march back to the kitchen. Then the pale lips trembled and tried to form a word—perhaps, thought Favorinus, "forgive".

"Has something distressed you, my daughter in Jesus?" said the elder.

"No, no, not in the least." She tipped the cruet over her husband's cup and smiled. "Only it has just occurred to me—no provision whatsoever has been made for the child."

"What child, my daughter?"

"Prisca—my cousin's slave—the girl who just brought the amphora in. I was wondering what would become of her, motherless as she is, with her father cut off now from the Lord's flock and the Lord's table. I was wondering what would become of her if I—if my husband—if my cousin—if all of us three—"

"Oh, but that's a very long way to think, isn't it, my child? Sufficient unto the day is the evil thereof—and none of us has any reason to think that we will not all be here tomorrow to break the morning bread."

"Nevertheless, my father—"

"Your husband will agree with me that you distress yourself too much. You have worn yourself away these last few months taking everything upon your own shoulders. You will grow old before your time with this unwarranted solicitude. When will you establish peace within your spirit? When will you learn to fold your hands and leave these matters in the lap of God?"

"Soon, very soon, believe me, my father. Only let me say that the child would be very desolate, very vulnerable, in the eventuality that I mentioned before. What would she do? Where could she go? Not to her father, certainly—he is exiled from the flock, he has burned his incense. Nor can she take refuge at my cousin's palace where she used to serve. They would find her there, and she is too young to be taken to prison, too young to suffer the questioning."

"But you excite yourself unnecessarily, Paulina," said the deacon Probus. "There are charities to see to such things. The virgins of the congregation would give her shelter, since she is actually an orphan now in the sight of God."

She turned from them both, the elder and the deacon, and looked earnestly across the table at the uninitiate. "Promise me, my cousin," she said in desperate sincerity, "swear to me that if it should so happen that you remain longer than I in this world, you will do whatever you can to help the child."

"There is no reason to think I will remain longer in this world than my cousin," he said, thrusting his shaking hands under the table. "I am in far worse case than my cousin, marked out as I am by the Emperor."

"Yes, yes, that's undoubtedly so. And yet indulge me a little, since I am worn away with worry and well-doing, as they say. Promise, for my sake, to look to the child."

"Of course. I give you my promise."

"Thank you, thank you. I plague you too much, I know. And yet—strange as it may seem to you, considering that I found fault with her in the beginning—I have come to love her. The love that I have come to feel for her is a very strong, a very holy love—" She flushed, she felt herself ridiculous, she made a quick, self-disparaging movement with her hand and toppled her wine cup, and frowned in mock severity at the red stain spreading on the cloth. "You see how it is with me," she said of a sudden, rising and giving each of them, one after the other, a rueful smile. "I have worn myself away with needless worries until I am not fit to sit with decent people at the table anymore. I have grown old, too, very old in these last weeks—would I were a grandmother, with a veil on my head—would I were a reverend old matriarch, sitting by a hearth and staring at a fire—"

"Where are you going?" said the deacon Probus.

She stood behind him and drew his head against her side. She stroked the side of his face—his temple, his cheek, his rough red beard—with the back of her hand. "To bed, only to bed," she said, "because I am old and weary. My father in Christ—" she bowed to the elder—"my husband, my dear yoke-fellow in the Lord—" she bent and kissed him lightly on the forehead—"my beloved cousin—" she put her fingertips to her mouth and sent him a cousinly kiss—"may all of you sleep as soundly as I intend to sleep tonight. Also may the Lord Jesus watch you and keep you and cause His countenance to shine upon you and go with you in all your ways." Then she gathered up the little litter that always lay beside her on the table—the stole, the book, the keys, the crumpled handkerchief—still smiling, she gathered up the little litter and was gone.

For more than an hour after her going he swallowed the black fear that kept heaving up within him. But then he could bear it no longer; he said the sickness was returning; he went, in shameless haste, two steps at a time up the stairs. The upper hall was empty. The lamp flame burned, small and strangely peaceful, under the picture of the Good Shepherd carrying the strayed lamb on His shoulders, and he stood for a long time wondering what it was that he had meant to do and staring into the Good Shepherd's large, black, empty eyes. Looking carefully up and down the hall to make certain that nobody was about, he went to the door of her chamber and knocked lightly upon it, twice, three times, before he heard the stirring within.

"Who is it?" she said on the other side of the portal.

"Let me talk to you, my cousin. Let me talk to you at least—"

"You must go. They will hear you," she said.

"But surely I have the right to tell you what I think about this matter

Surely we can sit down and talk of this together—" In his exigency, he laid his hand on the door, but some reticence kept him from pushing it inward.

"Not now, not tonight. Surely you see that it's impossible, beloved. To-morrow—I could come to you tomorrow in the kitchen garden—"

"But tell me you didn't mean it—tell me tonight that you couldn't have meant it—"

"Tomorrow, tomorrow. We'll talk of it tomorrow. Go now, before they hear you. Go to bed, my darling, and try to sleep."

"How could I possibly go to bed, Paulina?"

But the iron sound rang loud in the quiet corridor, and there was no choice left to him. She had barred the door.

Chapter 29

ALL MORNING the heart of the slave-child Prisca had been borne up on a cool, high tide of happiness. Not that there was any discernible reason for her to rejoice, things being with her father as they were and life at the villa being in such confusion. Nobody knew how much she had on her hands, with the lady Paulina so suddenly gone to Rome to her novices, and the others meaning to follow her as soon as the sun went down, and she the only woman left to do the women's work: to fold the garments decently and pack the pottery in straw and empty the stagnant water from the vases and throw away the wilted flowers. Yet she was happy, so happy that, out of consideration for the grave faces of the others, she had to suppress a persistent desire to sing at the top of her voice, she had to school her crinkling face and chide her skipping feet.

Nor was it because of the fine weather, as the deacon Probus had said, smiling a distracted smile at her a moment ago. It was true that the day was unusually fine—the far hills green and sharp in the crystal air, and every asparagus-frond, every cabbage-leaf clean and precise in the rain-washed kitchen garden, and such a choiring of birds, such a humming of bees, such a buzzing and darting of insects everywhere that the air itself seemed to be peopled with a host of aerial creatures—whole empires of little living beings going about their business between the blue arc of heaven and the green curve of the world. No, though the weather was splendid, it was not the weather that had lifted up her heart; and, if she had not still been somewhat afraid of the rough red beard, she would have told the deacon Probus so. It was actually that the eye of God, long turned away from this melancholy villa, had turned back to it again. Those unwholesome mists, those whispering daemon-voices, those nameless agents of evil that had been creeping round the vine-covered walls and through the groves had been dispersed by night. The place had been cleansed, the place had been made fit to receive the bright influence of heaven; and, waking from a dream of milk-white horses grazing on a daisy-strewn plain, she had felt the face of God bending above the house; His voice had addressed her in the carolings and the murmurings, and the sun on her cheeks was His glance.

And when God's eye was upon her, she could not believe in any of those things that had obsessed her during the days without the sureness and the light. She could not believe that her father would be driven forth from the Lord's table into everlasting fire because in his fright he had burned incense to the daemons. She could not believe that any harm would come to the lady Paulina, even though she had set out for Rome without saying where she meant to stay, had disappeared in the middle of the night, with Novatian's mule, and all by herself. Nor could she see that City to which all of them were going this same evening as the hateful Babylon of which Saint John the Divine had written in Apocalypse, slimy with sin and red with the fires in which the Faithful were to be consumed for the sake of the Name. She yearned to return to it; she thought of its marble balconies and colonnades, rosy like plum blossoms in the morning light, amber like honey in the setting sun; she thought of the streets surging with life and of the known faces, long unseen, that would salute her joyously again in those streets; and, thinking of these things, she could not be afraid.

If there was anything that troubled her that day, it was her concern for her master. He was not, she had to admit, making a proper showing in the matter of bundles and ropes and dishes. His offers to be of assistance were purely perfunctory, so far as she could see. If he was asked to make up a bundle, he sat on the floor and fell into a dream over the scattered articles, until she—to protect him from disapproving looks and to salvage the honor of the house of the Herennii—had to tear herself away from something more important and make up the bundle herself. He was not sick, though the others, in their Christian charity, preferred to think so. He was brooding over some grief of his own—doubtless a dark and noble grief; and yet for the first time in her life she was a little ashamed for him, ashamed that he did not take hold of himself and set to work when the elder Novatian and the deacon Probus were short of breath with running the stairs. Still, in the radiance of the crystalline day, her embarrassment for his idleness was only a minor shadow; she could not even say in simple truth that she would have been happier if he had been more diligent. His uselessness provided her with a dozen excuses to look at him, to be close to him. If he had heaped his own linens and tied his own knots, she could not have crouched close to him, pressing her shoulder lightly against his and letting his beautiful black hair brush against her lips.

O God, Creator of the World, she thought, Creator of the daisies and the violets and the flowering grass, and the dragonflies that shimmer by day and the fireflies that twinkle by night, Maker of clouds and sunlight, Fashioner of glades and hills, what have You made that is as marvelous as my master and my love? Nothing that grows on the earth is as beautiful as his swift feet that walk upon it. His motion is more to be wondered at than the flying of swallows, and his stillness is like the stillness of evening water at the bottom of a well. His body is like marble, but You have breathed the breath of life into every part of it—it is filled with life as the sack of the bee is filled with honey and the globe of the grape is filled with wine. His face is more splendid to look upon than a high meadow open to the sun. Like the shadows of clouds, majestic and constantly changing, his thoughts pass across his face. And his forehead is a Temple, a Holy of Holies, since the mysteries that come to pass behind his forehead are the glory of Creation, intricate and unfathomable beyond anything else that You have fashioned in the world.

And it was something of a pity that there were so many dishes to be packed in the straw, for she also was filled with the breath of life and would have liked to take him by the hand and lead him into the woods, where she could show him what miracles she was capable of—she felt so blessed this morning that she was certain she could produce a whole train of minor miracles, could conjure the sap back into a dying tree, could converse with a squirrel, could tame a butterfly. Once before, when she had felt just such exaltation stirring in her blood, she *had* tamed a butterfly, had found it resting, still wet and sleepy with the juices of the cocoon, on a flowering yellow weed, had held out her arm to it, had induced it by magic and patience to walk from her wrist to her shoulder—oh, the soft trailing of the nether-wings and the light creeping of the minute and exquisite feet . . . Yes, it was a pity that there was so much to do and he so useless. If he had helped, by this time they might have been finished, and he and she might have gone together into the woods to make their farewells to the grove and the wild olives and the bees . . . But she would see him in Rome, she would see him often in Rome; on a day like today, when the eye of God was upon her, she could not believe in everlasting separations. Perhaps they would be given refuge under one roof; she might see him every day and hear his breathing through a thin wall at night and wash the linens for his body and fasten his sandals to his feet. Everything was possible in the eye of God, even that an angel should come to him in his sleep and lead him up out of his pagan error, even that a day should come when he would drink of the cup and eat of the loaf with her at the table of her sweet Lord . . . And quick and joyous with these hopes, she went to the cupboard to bring out the last of the dishes, and, returning, found the corner where he had been kneeling blankly empty—where could he have gone?

So the deacon Probus asked the elder Novatian, plainly regretting at once the exasperation that had come into his voice, adding at once that the young man was not himself this morning, was either ill or preoccupied with some inner striving—one never knew, his wife had been very zealous for her cousin's salvation, perhaps these were the first painful movements of a spirit drawn upward toward the Cross. . . .

"Perhaps so," said the elder Novatian, a little shortly. "But where could he have taken himself off to? I didn't see him go upstairs."

For the first time that day a taint of fear spread across the universal brightness. "Yes, where did he go?" she said, thinking how the lady Paulina had disappeared with neither warning nor farewell. "Maybe he's gone out to get some air. Shall I go and see?"

Not in the dining room, not in the kitchen, either. Not anywhere in the kitchen-garden—though he might have retreated to the other side of the dairy house. She walked quickly between the rows of cabbages and past the entrance of the dairy-shed, whose darkness exhaled moist coolness and the sour-sweet smell of the churn. And there on a wooden bench spotted with curds and milk, behind flowering weeds that grew almost as high as her waist, he lay on his back, still and unseeing. There was something awesome in his fixed stare and his parted lips. She drew a little closer and stopped in terror: he had uttered a moan, he was grinding his fist into the folds of linen over his heart. And suddenly, sensing her presence, he started up, and the look of suffering on his face was such as she had seen only once before in all her days. He looked as he had looked that afternoon when he had come home with scared hands from the ruins of his tenement in the Via Trajana—his mouth hanging open, the flesh of his cheeks fallen in, his beautiful eyes stupid with amazement before the vastness of his pain.

"Are you sick again, my master?"

"No, no—what are you doing here? Go away and let me alone."

Radiant day, flawless and radiant, like a crystal chalice, slipping out of her hands. But before it was shattered, he caught it—he held out his arms to her, he drew her to him, he sobbed against her chest. "God forgive me," he said, miserably weeping. "Oh, Prisca, Prisca, it would be better if I were dead."

She clasped her arms around him, she pressed her lips to his hair—and in spite of the terrible and incomprehensible grief that he wept out against her, the eye of God continued to shine and she could not doubt that its all-healing, all-absolving influence shone also upon this head that lay against her breast. He would be comforted, he would be cleansed and saved, she would meet him on some shadowless morning, crowned and walking in a company of saints and angels, on one of the golden avenues of the City of God.

"Whatever it is that devours my master's heart, the Lord will take it away," she told him, kissing his forehead. "The Lord will give you peace."

"In my grave," he said, bitterly weeping. "In my grave He will give me peace."

She did not gainsay him. Graves were to her neither terrible nor imponderable. It was written, and she had heard it read, that on the Last Great Day all graves would yield up their mysteries, that sight would be restored to the dull eyes, and hearing to the sealed ears, and flesh to the stripped bones. She saw him rising so, in all his beauty, among the ruins of a shattered world, with the slanting rays of heaven upon his wondering face. "That, too, is possible," she said. "Everything is possible with God."

Chapter 30

It was a good camp, said Trebonianus Gallus, standing on the rampart with his arms akimbo, and looking down at the grimy roofs of Apulum, unbeautiful in the wan April sun. It was a very good camp, well situated and constructed strictly according to regulations—the longest side of the quadrangle seven hundred feet, the rampart twelve feet high, the ditch outside the rampart twelve feet deep. He could think of only one drawback: the tents, the headquarters in their midst, the broad streets running from side to side and from end to end—all of them would strike Kniva as lacking the seasoned look of age and use when he came up here for the parley. He would say to himself: The Romans are newcomers to these heights; there was never a camp up here before.

Possibly, thought Herennius Decius, but the rawness and the newness were no fault of his. Spring had come very late to the province of Dacia this year, and he had begun the work at the faintest promise of a thaw and pursued it day and night through a season of bitter frost. Before the snow had even begun to soften on the heights, he had marked out the quadrangle in the most auspicious place. And those comrades-in-arms of his to whom he had assigned the digging were still unable to take part in exercise, incapacitated as they were by frozen hands and feet.

"Unfortunate—isn't it?—" said the Governor of Moesia, "that you didn't build it in the autumn of last year."

But in the autumn of last year the Goths in this region had been six scattered tribes, and the walls of Apulum had seemed strong enough to withstand their desultory sallies. "Better late then never," he said, turning around to take the orderly prospect in; and, at the sight of it, he felt the old irrepressible surge of high heartedness. He never saw a Roman camp above a river crossing or a city without thinking of the hundreds of others like it, strewn these last centuries from one end of the known world to the other—Caesar's camps on the rolling hills of Gaul, Pompey's camps on the Phrygian plains, the camps of Claudius in the bluish mists of Ultima Thule, the camps of Trajan and Hadrian commanding the wildernesses of Raetia and Moesia and Pannonia and Noricum. The very configuration of the camp was for him the visible symbol of Roman power. It was as if the Empire had set its signet here, and here, and here, pressing its ineradicable mark upon the varying line of plateau and hill. And here, set above Apulum, was the camp that *he* had built—his mark, like the marks of Caesar and Trajan and the rest.

And, having harbored one propitious thought in the hour of his exigency —for it *was* a time of stress, this first occasion when he and the redoubtable Kniva would meet face to face—he fingered the folds of the letter through the supple links of his tunic of mail, and permitted himself further high heartedness over one thing his father had written. Along with ill news of the censorship and anxious and insistent directives as to what was to be said or left unsaid in the parley with Kniva, there was something else: Drusilla Herennia was no longer in the vast and inimical palace on the Palatine; she was sick, poor beloved—so sick that the life which had shut him out could not be *her* life anymore. Her life was confined now within the grave and seemly province of the Temple at Epidaurus; chaste priests were her advisors, and other invalids—as sick as she was, as sick as he himself had been and yet might be—were her only companions. And the gain in sheer miles was in itself a thing for rejoicing. In comparison with Rome, Epidaurus seemed almost a neighboring town. Perhaps a week to cut across Dacia and a little strip of Moesia in a season of safety—say, after a truce— two or three days to journey down through the mountains of Thrace and take ship at Eritrea, and less than three days later one could disembark within sight of the Temple. . . .

There was a sound of hammering in the quadrangle below them. The legionaries were setting up the dais on which he would sit during the parley, with the newly-gilded Roman eagle at his right hand and the Governor of Moesia at his left.

"How high are you making that dais?" Trebonianus Gallus said.

"Four feet, with six steps up the middle of it. The drapers of Apulum have sent a crimson cloth to cover it with."

"That's a pity—that it's only going to be four feet high, I mean. You should have made it five feet. You're not that tall, you know."

"You're scarcely the person to talk about height." It was the first retort he had permitted himself since breakfast.

"Oh, but I'm the civil arm, there's no need for me to tower," said the Governor, grinning. "You're a commander—it's different with you. You'd better get yourself a helmet with a prodigious crest."

He had gotten himself just such a helmet, but he did not say so. He started down the sloping inner side of the rampart, hunching a little to counteract an involuntary straightening of his shoulders, and thinking that it was useless to trouble himself further: he had done what he could to make himself a worthy incarnation of the power and majesty of Rome. In the little time left to him before the parley, he would put on his greaves and his helmet; he would fasten the scarlet cloak with a pair of curiously-wrought brooches; he would take his place on the dais in the curved curile chair, whose shape, like the shape of the camp, had sunken deep into the consciousness of innumerable subject peoples from the inland waters of the Caspian Sea to the uncharted waters of the great western ocean. His sword would lie across his knees, and his buckler, covered with hide and studded with brass, would shine in the sun at his feet. And if, through all those century-hallowed trappings, the chieftain-king of six tribes of Goths should see the unwanted suitor, the man too squeamish to go to a brothel, the soldier whose keenest pleasure was the lamplit quiet of his tent at night, then there was no help—it was all in the lap of the gods.

"You're not lining them up, are you?" said the Governor of Moesia, stopping at the bottom of the rampart and waving his hand in the direction of the serried rows of tents where the majority of the ranks had taken shelter from the early April cold.

"The legionaries?"

"Yes—who else? It would be better if you let them loll about, as if the whole parley were one little incident in a busy day, no more."

He flushed because such an idea had never entered his head. He had wanted the evil blue eye of Kniva to be dazzled with helmets and bucklers and swords from the instant of the opening of the gate.

"What's wrong with lining them up?" he said.

"Have you had a look at them lined up?"

"Of course I have. I had them take their positions yesterday afternoon."

"Well, that's good. Then you know what kind of impression they're likely to make. I always avoid lining up my own City Guard if I can. I did it once to my grief, when the Governor of Dalmatia came up to visit me. Such a sorry crowd of beaten-down wretches you never saw in your life."

Beaten-down wretches? But yesterday, seeing them in the declining light of the meager northern sun, he had found them so splendid in their dogged valor that his eyes had smarted with tears. The winter and the fear and the hunger had told upon them, yes; they were some of them as scrawny as eagles; in fact, he had thought then that there was much of the eagle about them—the stern power under the rumpled and irascible look, the cold flash in the red-rimmed eye.

"Did your father have any suggestions about what you should do with the legionaries?"

His hand went instinctively to the spot where the letter crackled under his tunic of mail, and he regretted the move at once. Ever since his arrival this morning, Gallus had been itching to see it, had thrown out a dozen hints to force it out of its hiding place. "No, he had nothing whatever to say about that," he said.

"Well, what *did* he have to say? You never told me."

"About the parley?" He was maneuvering for time.

"Oh, it's easy enough to guess what he said about the parley." They had crossed the broad avenue between the rampart and the tents, and the Governor, stopping at a pile of bucklers, rubbed at a spot of rust on one of them, and pursed his lips. "No tribute. Isn't that it? Gifts, but no tribute."

It was slipping from him now—the confidential information that might have kept the Roman side of the parleying under his own control. "Yes, that's what he said."

"And he specified, of course, that we should under no circumstances give them any hostages, or grant them the freedom of any border city, or allow them to get the idea that they can buy and sell in any of the market towns."

It was so to the last detail, and the young man could take comfort only in the fact that the Governor had named the items backward. "That's about the gist of it. There's nothing else of importance," he said.

"You wrote him—didn't you?—that I was coming over here to the parley."

"Yes, I mentioned that."

"And you mean to tell me—" the knobby finger thrust itself with distressing intimacy into the spot where the folds of papyrus crackled under the mail—"you mean to tell me in the whole of that letter there's not one word about me?"

"No." He could not, for the life of him, suppress the gratified smile. "Now that I think of it, he didn't mention you at all."

"There's a fine example of imperial gratitude! A man spends ten years of his life in a rubbish-dump like Moesia, and what's his reward? Evasions, half-promises—"

He broke off because the air had been ripped by a raucous sound—angry bawl of the ram's horn to herald a barbarian chieftain, less resonant but more startling than the brazen blasts which marked the coming of the mighty ones of Rome. Kniva was early—there were trappings to be put on, there were orders to be given. But his legionaries needed no word from him; they were already streaming out of their tents and taking their positions

Two orderlies were spreading the crimson gift of the weavers of Apulum over the wooden dais. A tribune had issued from the highest of the tents, bearing his commander's greaves, cloak, buckler, and sword; and another was coming out behind him, carrying the curule chair. To an unpractised eye, the shouting and the milling about might have seemed like sheer confusion; but he knew it for what it was: a martial orderliness, a splendid exhibition of Roman discipline. In less time than it takes to count fifty, every man was in his place—yes, and he also, ascending the steps of the dais, waiting for an orderly to fasten the buckles of his greaves, presenting his shoulders for the scarlet cloak. He seated himself in the curule chair, and, while they set the crested helmet on his head and laid his sword across his knees, he permitted himself to look at the legions behind him. Descendants of the legions of Pompey and Caesar, he told himself—and knew of a sudden with a sinking heart that it was not so. Pale Pannonians, pale Illyrians, swart little Asians from whose flat faces even these bitter months had not been able to drive the sly servility of the Levant . . . Mithras, he thought, stuffing a lock of his own yellow, northern hair under his helmet, and staring toward the altar he had built for the god of warriors—Mithras, let him not look at our hybrid faces, let him see the crests, let him see the swords.

They were coming now, some seventy of them, up the broad new avenue that led through the center of the camp to the dais. The old wonder at their height and their comeliness stirred within him as he watched them coming on, their long limbs shadowed forth under their tunics of rough cloth, their fur cloaks swinging out behind them, and the April wind lifting their flowing blond hair. At first he could not single out their captain—they walked in close ranks of ten or twelve, and all of them were armed alike, carrying close to their bodies the notable spear and the still more notable battle mace, black and knobby at the top, hardened in fire. But when they were some twenty paces off, he saw the face and knew that he had envisioned it with close accuracy in his fever dreams. It was the eye that caught him first—hard blue, like a flawless sapphire—filled with loathing, as if it had seen and come to despise the rotting core at the center of the world. Under the eyes there were bluish shadows, unhealthy, like bruises—it was said of him that he had developed an uncontrollable passion for Roman wines. His cheeks were long and spare and without the faintest trace of color. The thin mouth, pale and incapable of the childish Gothic smile, was tightened at the corners in a sneer that gave the whole lean face a look of unbelievable arrogance.

There had been one breath-taking instant when it had seemed to Herennius that they would come straight up the steps and trample him down; but they stopped some ten paces away without deigning to raise their eyes. The blond head of Kniva—he looked down upon it from the curule chair—was encircled by an iron crown, which should have been ridiculous since it looked more like the rim of a Roman cooking pot than anything else. But he could not smile at it: it took an inexplicable majesty from the tilt of the haughty head. Somebody, probably the chieftain himself, had muttered something, not in the pure Gothic tongue, which, after long labors, he was able to make out, but in the obscure dialect of one of the neighboring tribes.

"Did you understand him?" said Gallus in a loud voice.

"No. Did you?" He said it softly, in spite of himself.

"Yes, I think so. He's talking Carpi."

"What did he say?"

"That you are not your father. He's an insolent dog."

No, I am not my father, and my father is not Caesar, and these behind me are not the legions that carried the eagle from Britain to Parthia; but even the shadows of Romans will not tolerate such insolence. "Speak Latin! Whatever you say here, say it in Latin," he shouted, using the Gothic tongue, so that all the chieftain's companions-in-arms might understand. "I know you speak Latin—my father parleyed with you on the river less than two years ago."

He was answered by another volley of Carpi. The hard eyes, unblinking, stared at his feet.

"He says that fashions change. He says the Goths speak Gothic now."

"Then let him speak in Gothic!" All the time-honored, martial rigidity had gone from him in his fury. Like one who haggles over vegetables, he was leaning far forward in the curile chair.

The blue eyes encountered his in a keen and level glance. Carpi—swift, guttural Carpi—continued to issue from the tight and scornful lips.

"He says he'll speak in any dialect he chooses. He says that Goths and Carpi are one people now—blood brothers—at the mead-table and on the field of battle—as we will have cause to know if we are foolish enough to throw our armies—I think he called them our flea-bitten armies—at the invincible Goths."

"Tell him—"

"Wait now, control yourself, he'll pull in his horns in a moment. He's trying to make an impression on his companions. Suppose I ask him if he'd like me to serve as interpreter." But after a swift exchange with the chieftain, the Governor turned back to the commander-in-chief and shrugged. "He wants his own interpreter, one that he brought with him. Let him have his way—it's a small matter. There'll be plenty of time later for you to rattle the sword."

There was more gibberish, and a stirring at the rear of the Gothic ranks, and a ripple of laughter. They were watching his face—their fair cheeks crinkled and their blue eyes narrowed—they were watching his face, as pleased as children at a pantomime. For here, moving strangely, dragging one foot like a crippled bird, was none other than Horatius Tatianus, a tribune of his, lost these five months, sent on an errand to Sarmizegetusa and never heard from since. The Gothic chieftain turned upon him as he came and loosed another burst of Carpi upon his bowed head.

"It seems," said Trebonianus Gallus, "that he doesn't move fast enough to suit his new master."

A long, low groan came up out of the throats of the legionaries. Kniva had thrust the tribune forward so fiercely that he stumbled and had to steady himself, leaning with one hand upon the dais, pulling long wrinkles in the crimson cloth.

"My master Kniva says that you are not to judge me too harshly," he said, stopping to wait for the speech that issued piecemeal in Carpi from his new lord. "He says to tell you that they beat me in the face with willow wands for three days—and still I told them nothing. He says to tell you it was only when they hung me up by the armpits on a sacred tree—and lit a slow fire under my feet—that I gave them any information at all. He says I am no longer of any great value to him—you and he may be able to agree on a ransom—"

Sick pity surged up in him. His hands made weak and unmanly movements, opening and closing on the arms of the curile chair. "Ask him his price. Say I will ransom you at any cost."

"Don't be a fool," said Trebonianus Gallus in a low voice, while a new exchange was taking place between the chieftain and his captive. "What sort of ransom do you think he'll ask for? He wants javelins—Roman javelins to hurl back in your face on the day of reckoning."

The tribune turned round. "No ransom," he said voicelessly, forming the words only with his lips and striving with a shaking and grimy hand to smooth the wrinkles from the crimson drapery. But Kniva had sauntered up behind him, was striking him again across the shoulders. "One hundred Roman javelins—that's what my master, the valorous Kniva, asks for my ransom," he said in a loud voice. "Unless it is more convenient for you to give him instead fifty Arabian bows and twenty unused Gallic swords."

"Remember, no weapons, my dear fellow—"

"Tell him no weapons—"

"Hostages?" said Kniva in Latin, striding to the edge of the dais in his eagerness. "Three hostages? Including a Governor's son? We would use them well."

"Neither weapons nor hostages. Caius Messius Quintus Trajanus Decius, Emperor of All the Romans and Lord of the World, has absolutely forbidden it."

He shrugged, stepped back a few paces, flung up his long white hands and lapsed again into Carpi, smiling an evil smile.

"He says that's a pity," said the tribune Horatius Tatianus. "He says in that case he can always take me back to the sacred tree and light another fire—unless you have something of equal worth to offer in the course of the

375

parley. He says he will take me and—oh, my commander, my dear lord—"

But it was not he, it was the Governor of Moesia who provided what was required. He stepped to the edge of the dais and pointed out in easy Gothic to the chieftain Kniva that neither he himself nor this heir to Roman splendor here had come to discuss ransoms; their time was valuable, they did not trouble themselves with such trivial matters; this meeting, or so he had been led to believe, had been arranged solely to settle on a summer's truce and to regularize relationships between Romans and Goths. If the valorous Kniva wished to discuss the main issues—and in Gothic, since the son of the Emperor in his boundless patience had abandoned the customary requirement that all parleys be held in Latin—then there was some purpose to the meeting, then the affair might end amicably and the sons of the forest might return to their homes with a favorable report to their people and a liberal gift of Roman spices, Roman linen, and Roman wine. If he did not wish to discuss the main issues—he flung up his pudgy little hands and smirked—the Goths might take themselves off empty-handed. The Romans were comfortable enough in their present situation. Their ranks had been swollen during the winter by thousands of fresh legionaries out of Thrace. It was nothing to him—nor to this heir to the purple—if the Goths went home without discussing anything at all.

If the chieftain Kniva kept silent during this long harangue, it could not precisely have been said of him that he listened. While it was in progress, he took hold of the tribune Horatius Tatianus and flung him full force at the ranks of the Gothic companions-in-arms, who parted, laughing, to receive him; he strolled the length of the dais and felt the crimson drapery; he spit on the fingers of his right hand and smoothed the hair that flowed down below the iron crown. And, before he addressed himself to the dignity of Rome enthroned on the dais, he turned his head and made a few more laughter-provoking comments in Carpi to his fellow-Goths. "If the Roman ranks have been swollen by Thracians," he said, turning back to the heir to the purple, "we also have somewhat increased our numbers. Scores come to us daily out of the reaches of the northward forests. *Our* women are fruitful."

"In that case," said the Governor of Moesia, "there's nothing for us to discuss. You may as well go back to your encampment on the river without a truce."

For an instant it seemed to the commander-in-chief that they would do exactly that. They grasped their spears more firmly; they leaned forward a little, peering, trying to read the cold blue eye of the captain of their host. A nightmare sense of unreality settled upon Herennius Decius then. He could not believe that a word or a movement now would decide whether the walls of Apulum would be surrounded by screaming barbarians, whether the inhabitants of such northern cities as Marcianopolis and Philippopolis had only so many months to live before their heads were beaten in by the

Gothic battle-mace. And, before he could steady himself enough to look at the chieftain, they found their answer—some seventy fair, childish faces changing slowly, with childish laughter crinkling at the corners of their bright blue eyes; and it took all the military virtue in him to suppress the unmanly smile of relief, the tremulous sigh.

"Shall we continue the discussion?" said the Governor of Moesia.

"But what is there to discuss?" asked the chieftain, his white and degenerate face suddenly assuming a look of false sweetness and candor. "This princeling here—" the term was less derogatory in Gothic than it would have been in Latin—"this princeling here is plainly under the thumb of his father, and his father has convinced him that we are not to be trusted, has told him that we are to have no hostages, no, nor weapons either, even to ransom a captive—and this is hard bargaining indeed. What *does* he mean to give us at the behest of his father? Something valuable? A promise, for instance, that those eastern cheats and robbers who sit in the bazaars will do us also the honor of selling us a little worthless goods at an exorbitant price? An assurance that we will not be murdered in the streets if we walk into any of your towns?"

"Neither the freedom of the towns nor the right to trade in the markets," said Trebonianus Gallus. "The Lord of the World, who holds the vast armies of Parthia trembling on his eastern border, has absolutely forbidden any such thing."

"Do they tremble?" He turned his face to Herennius Decius—still candid, still falsely sweet. "Tell me, son of the successor to Philip the Arabian—do the Parthians really tremble?"

"They have no need to tremble," he said in a voice more authoritative than he had dared to hope it would be. "Peace, honorable peace, is between the Empire and Parthia. The ambassadors of Parthia drink the wines of Crete and Syria at the table of Caius Messius Quintus Trajanus Decius. His caravans bear gifts in spring and autumn to the lord of the Parthians. Kniva and the sons of the forest who follow him might also enjoy the advantages of such a peace—"

The chieftain wheeled round and made a brief statement in Carpi to his companions.

"He is telling them that the Empire pays tribute to the Parthians now," the Governor of Moesia said.

It was too much—clutching his sword, he started from the curile chair and shouted at the pale impassive face that it was a lie, he had said no such thing, never in the history of the Empire had any Roman paid tribute to any barbarian king. Tribute, like hostages and weapons and access to Roman towns and markets, was out of the question. Caius Messius Quintus Trajanus Decius, Emperor of All the Romans and invincible Lord of the World had absolutely forbidden it.

The chieftain walked indolently up to the very edge of the dais and set one foot on the second step. His thin lips scarcely moved as they pronounced the perfect Latin—distinctly so that even the legionaries might hear. It was not necessary, he said, for the commander-in-chief to keep repeating all the names and titles of his illustrious father, especially since time was so valuable, as the Governor of Moesia had pointed out. His own name was merely Kniva, and yet when it was spoken three million who dwelt in the lands between the desert and the frozen ocean trembled to hear. Even the benighted sons of the forest knew who Decius was without a string of titles. There were captives in the remotest of the Gothic encampments who had told the glorious tale—how Decius, formerly brother-in-arms to one Philip the Arabian, had defeated his Emperor in battle, how thousands of Roman legionaries had perished on the plain near Verona for the security of his house, how Philip's line had been wiped out, even to the last innocent child, how this same Decius, newly arrayed in the purple, had received the cleft head of this same Philip, formerly his master and his lord—

The commander was standing at the edge of the dais now. Somehow he had gotten to the edge of the dais and was shouting down from it, with his sword in his hand. All the words that he had sworn to keep locked up within him were flying out: dog, ignorant barbarian, beast of the forest, insolent dog.

But the Governor of Moesia had come up beside him, was drawing him back, was forcing him down into the curile chair, was saying that this was a parley, not a skirmish, was taking his sword out of his hand and laying it across his knees. And, when the red mist of fury had cleared from before his eyes, he saw the tall and slender body still standing with one foot on the second step of the dais, the face still wearing the cold and jeering smile.

"If you utter one more word concerning the inimitable majesty of Rome in the course of this parley," said Trebonianus Gallus, "this fiery son of a fiery father will send the lot of you back home, without spices or linen or wine. The gifts which he offers you, like the gifts which his father sends in cousinly affection and kingly courtesy to the lord of Parthia, are better than anything you will find in the markets of Dacia. The spices are fresh from Arabia and so aromatic that to open the bundle is to ascend into heaven. The linen is whiter than the untrodden snow on the tops of your impenetrable mountain ranges. As for the wine—the grapes were matured in the amorous sun of Syria, and the amphorae were lodged in the cellars of the imperial palace through the reigns of ten emperors. The valorous Kniva has never tasted such wine."

The valorous Kniva said in Latin, without stirring, that the reigns of ten Emperors made up a short time at best, but added that the wine was worth his consideration nevertheless.

"Come on, my dear fellow," said Gallus in a whisper. "Now's the time for it, make the offer. Six months of peace in return for that load of stuff you have at Apulum."

But nobody needed to prompt him as if he were a child. "For the peerless Arabian spices, for the linens as delicate as silks out of China, for the time-sweetened wines in the ancient amphorae," he said, knowing that his studied Gothic efflorescence was a poor imitation of the Governor's casual poetry, "Caius Messius Quintus Trajanus Decius—" he gave full weight to every one of the names—"and I also, Herennius Decius, his son, heir to the purple and commander of the invincible legions that stand guard at the northern frontier, ask of the valorous Kniva—" he paused, because the conclusion seemed anti-climactic—"six months of peace."

"And these wines, these spices, these linens—in what quantity do they come?" said Kniva.

"Ten bundles of spices, three hundred bales of linen, five hundred amphorae of Syrian and Cretan wines."

"That will be sufficient."

But he had said it so inconclusively that Trebonianus Gallus was impelled to break in. "Sufficient for what?" he said. "State it. Say in the presence of your brothers-in-arms that the gift insures six months of peace."

"Are you uneasy?" The pale mouth smiled. "Any pact will be more secure, of course, if it is insured by the exchange of hostages—but that has been absolutely forbidden by Caius Messius Quintus and whatever the rest of it is. As it stands—" he sighed and took his foot from the dais—"we will have to depend upon each other's honor—I on the honor of the son of the successor to Philip the Arabian, and you, Herennius Decius, on the honor of a barbarian."

Either in wisdom or in impotence—he was far too shaken now to be certain which—he let the insult pass. "Six months of peace, at the end of which we will give you the same gift again, adding a quantity of fresh fruits from the southern orchards—figs, dates, and apricots. Such is the generosity of our master and our lord."

"Sufficient. Quite sufficient." He said it in Latin, smiling and rubbing his neck and his shoulder. Then he turned and addressed himself again in Gothic to the Goths. "A decent settlement—don't you think? A much more generous tribute than his father offered on the river two years ago."

"The gods of my fathers and the gods of the forest bear witness that I never spoke of tribute." His voice was controlled—the anger that had risen in him now was sick with hopelessness. "A free gift, unsolicited, is all that I indicated. There is not one legionary here behind me who would not gladly give his life to prevent one bead from going in tribute to a pack of barbarian dogs."

"Gift then, call it a gift then," said Kniva in Latin.

"Tell them it is a gift, and tell them so in Gothic."

"He is a splitter of hairs," said the chieftain over his shoulder to the snickering crowd behind him. "He keeps insisting that I call his tribute a gift, and I am so weary of all this talk that I am willing to call it almost anything. Let us accept his gift, or whatever he chooses to call it. We can use the summer to drink up the wine and beat out more swords."

"The gift will be ready for you at the gates of Apulum tomorrow," said the Governor of Moesia.

"Let it be as he says—the lord of those miserable cities that lie exposed in the wilderness of the defenseless province of Moesia." He wheeled round again with consummate grace and made a gesture for the benefit of his companions-in-arms. What he did could not be ascertained from the dais, but the Goths rocked with laughter, laughed until their weapons shook and the tears stood in their bright blue eyes. And, when the laughter had died down a little, he spoke to them again in Carpi, his own voice shaken by a wild hilarity. Three times he repeated the same piece of gibberish, and they nodded and struck their shields with their spears.

"What is he telling them?"

"He says it's tribute, whatever you choose to call it. Let it pass, my dear fellow, let it pass—"

"Not while there is a drop of blood left in a Roman body! Let him depart and never show his face to me again, except on the battlefield, where it will be his blood or mine."

He rose, tall in his crested helmet, splendid in his scarlet cloak. He lifted his sword and plunged it through the crimson cloth, deep into the wood, to manifest to Kniva and to all the world that henceforth it was a matter of blood between Rome and the Goths. A thunderous burst of acclaim broke from the legionaries and shook the dais beneath him. Three times, according to the established military ritual—as though he had been Augustus's son or the darling of Trajan—they struck their swords against their shields and saluted him by name. I am theirs and they are mine, he thought. In the knowledge of shared hunger and fear and cold, we are bound everlastingly to each other. . . .

Nothing could lessen the surge of exhilaration that bore him up—not the sneer on the face of the chieftain as he walked through the fur-clad ranks that parted to receive him, not the nudging and the laughter, not their insolently unhurried departure down the broad new avenue by which they had come. Until the gate clanged shut behind them, the heart in his body continued to swell, bringing tears to his eyes, conjuring up in him for the first time in his life an unshakable conviction of valor and magnificence. But, with the closing of the gate, the ranks behind him broke and came forward, and the ritual shouting ceased; and, in spite of all the known weathered faces that surged around him, he felt himself isolated, exposed, cut off from the rest.

All through the remainder of that empty day, he was hounded by this sense of isolation. Whenever the noises of the camp died away into one of those inexplicable stillnesses which settle over multitudes, he found himself talking swiftly, talking a little incoherently, talking about anything in order to dispel the sense of loneliness, the need to think. He slipped his arm through the arm of every tribune and centurion who came to consult him; he tried to break down the new and alarming taciturnity of the Governor of Moesia, who had uttered scarcely anything but monosyllables since the parley, who sat silent at the evening meal, staring with fixed eyes at the gathering clouds and offering no comment on the tough meat or the raw wine.

And at nightfall, when Gallus had departed and the bivouac fires had gone out, he was still so restless that he could not begin the letter to his father, but must stroll out of his tent and as far as the rampart. The lights of Apulum—there were a few lights burning still in houses where the nameless and inglorious waited with lamps for birth or death—the lights of Apulum set him to wondering how it would have been with him if he had been born the son of a weaver or a schoolmaster in a century of peace. To sit by a homely hearth, to see *her* face serene and loving in the changing light of the flames . . . To rise of a morning and kiss one's wife and children and set out for the classroom or the loom with the knowledge that one's labors could last only a given number of hours . . . To know the quiet pleasures of the return—the bath and the soft sandals and the scroll laid open on the table, the gentle, aimless talk and the shared bed and the sleep unhaunted by dreams of a task too heavy to be done . . . I want my life, he thought, breathing the scents of pitch and hide borne in from Apulum. Surely to want my life is not such a shameful and unmanly thing in me. . . .

The guard who was patrolling the top of the rampart started at the sight of him. "Who's there?" he shouted into the dark.

"Nobody to be alarmed about. Herennius Decius."

"My general? Oh, but you told them off magnificently this morning—"

"Did I?" he asked, still thinking how he wanted his life. And he looked back upon the moment when he had plunged his sword through the crimson cloth as one might look on a piece of history that had come to pass three hundred years ago.

Chapter 31

THOUGH THE journey had been a strange and lonely one—she and the elder Novatian's mule and the single lantern, precariously flickering, moving in a confined area of light through utter dark—though there had been only sorrowful sounds to attend upon her sorrowful thoughts—rush of distant and unseen waters, bursting croak of the bull-frog, rattle of a carriage coming up behind her and passing and dying away on its road from the Campagna to the dark environs of Rome—she had not been uncertain or confused, she had never once found herself afraid. It was not that the Lord had walked with her, leading the elder Novatian's mule by the bridle toward the City and her destiny: she had felt no sense of His presence she had been singularly divided from Him though she had thought of Him much, wondering again and again how it had been with Him when He made His last visit on a borrowed beast to the palm-strewn streets of Jerusalem. Looking back on that journey of hers, she could not say that she had made it in a state of grace—her mind had been on earthly matters turning often to her husband, often to her beloved, wondering in the black of the night how each of them looked in his sleep, thinking in the first bleak beginnings of the light that now one or the other of them must have wakened and found her gone. The sense of her own mortality also had been very heavy upon her. Sepulchres, scores of sepulchres, stood white along the road in clumps of cypresses; and, once the rosy streaks of dawn had issued from the edges of the east, she could not ride half a mile without encountering another reminder of death. But a solemn, high determination had borne her steadily on; the tears on her cheeks had been cool and effortless tears; her way had lain before her, simple and plain; and she had thought how the dead, rising out of their sepulchres on the Last Great Day, would tell each other in wonderment how profound, how refreshing had been their rest.

But in the City it was altogether different. She had no sooner entered the City than what had seemed to her foreordained and easy became almost inconceivable. Her sense of stern and significant purpose was dissipated in dealing with a welter of meaningless details; and all her serenity, all her self-possession was gone. Wandering about at mid-morning in an unfamiliar neighborhood near the Flavian Amphitheater, among the booths of fortune-tellers and doll-makers and vendors of clams and oysters and wine, she found that she could neither think consistently about how and where she meant to give herself up nor pray with any steadfastness for strength from the Lord. In fact, when she stepped into the shadow of a doll-maker's stoop to collect herself, she knew with amazement that for the last two hours—during which she had walked aimlessly past a dozen altars, in front of a score of City Guardsmen—she had given no real thought to what she meant to accomplish in the City: her mind had been taken up for the most part with the elder Novatian's mule, which she had been forced to abandon in a filthy carriage-station outside the limits of the City. Beasts of burden —how she could have forgotten it she did not know—were prohibited from entering the City between dawn and dark, and the animal would become City property unless he was redeemed by twilight. She did not dare to show herself at any Christian house in order to arrange for his redemption, and the plight of the deserted little beast who had been her only companion through the long journey brought her almost to the point of tears.

But how is it, she asked herself—looking attentively at the painted faces of the dolls that hung on strings in front of the shop, their hard cheeks shining in the bright spring sunlight—how is it that nobody has asked me for my certificate of sacrifice? Of the twenty-odd Guardsmen that she had passed this morning, not one had made the slightest move to detain her, and two or three had actually looked straight into her face and smiled. There were rumors—Probus and the elder Novatian had told her so—that the Guards had been directed to make no arrests among patricians; and certain parts of her clothing—the brooch on her shoulder, the cloak that hung over her arm, the comb that held back her hair—might very well be indications of her class. Still staring at the dangling dolls, she waited until the crowded street had cleared a little, and covertly removed the comb and undid the brooch, knotting the linen at her shoulder with awkward hands. The bits of jewelry she dropped onto the step and slid with the toe of her shoe until they fell over the side onto a heap of papyrus and sand. But the cloak she could never bring herself to dispose of—she bent her face to it, she brushed her lips against it, she pressed it between her breasts. For the cloak had been a gift of Probus; she had worn it on many quiet walks with him; and one night, a year or more ago, she had wakened to find the weather turned colder and he standing above her, spreading the cloak over her shoulders, tucking the bottom of it around her feet.

She started and walked away because a little girl and her mother, who had stopped to see the dolls, were looking at her with curious and pitying eyes. But I must not let the cloak undo me, she said to herself. The cloak must be a source of sustenance and strength. If I put it around me—she flung it over her shoulders in spite of the April heat—I do what is foreordained for me with his presence about me, I go to the next altar wrapped in his love . . . But the next altar, set at the end of a tawdry street smelling of cheap sweets and frying grease, was almost invisible because of the crowd that had gathered around it. Two artisans were burning incense, and some ten other plebes were standing about, waving their yellow certificates of sacrifice into the face of a flustered Guardsman. Besides, the vast, gloomy curve of the Amphitheater dominated the whole miserable neighborhood, and she knew of a sudden that she could never do it here, must do it in some cleaner, quieter neighborhood where she would not have to think what things went on within the confines of that wall, where she would not have to be afraid that at any moment the air would be torn apart by the roar of a caged lion or the trumpeting of an elephant in some subterranean corridor.

She turned and tried to find her way out of the environs of the Flavian Amphitheater. But it was difficult, she kept losing herself; being a Christian, she had never walked through these garish streets before. And now again she found herself preoccupied with incongruous and utterly insignificant things, wondering how the cheap sugar-cakes tasted to the two lovers who were munching them, marvelling at the glib inventiveness of the fortune-teller, asking herself whether the painted woman who lolled against the barrel of clams was a whore or a public slave—one of the acrobats who walked on a rope or tumbled to fill up the dull interim between the gladiators and the beasts. She felt warm and oppressed because of the weight of the cloak, and her face was covered with sweat, but she did not dare raise her arm to wipe it away, since the knot at her shoulder might come undone and leave her standing in her shift in the street. But slowly the booths became sparser and the noises began to be less. She slipped past another altar and through a huge dark arch—the Guardsman did not see her, he was leaning against the archway, half-asleep—and found herself on an ancient avenue lined with mulberry trees and peopled with half a dozen marble emperors and gods. The tenements here were old and ill-kept; tattered cloaks and wet dalmaticas hung from the windows and the balconies; but here, at any rate, between the heads of the divinities and the leaves of the mulberries, it was possible to see the sky, and the sight of the sky relieved the strange and stifling pressure around her heart.

Some fifty paces beyond the doorway where she stopped to get her breath there was another altar, set between a marble Orpheus and a silver Marcus Aurelius. But there was nobody standing behind it. Plainly the Guardsman had wandered away, and she found herself gravely pondering why he had left his station. To meet his wife in a cookshop? To take some Christian off to the authorities? To go to a urinal and relieve himself? Her own body had been singularly unassertive all morning, but she began to wonder what she would do if she had need of privacy. Walk until she came to a public bath? But that was unnecessary; there were accommodations in the main halls of the tenements. Now that she had become conscious of her person, she found that she was fearfully thirsty—her tongue was too dry to wet her lips. How can I declare myself, she thought, before I have had a drink of water? And with that thought a wave of weakness broke upon her and her knees began to shake. For if I cannot do this simple thing, she thought, if I cannot go to an altar without a drink of water, then how will I ever have strength for all the rest?

He was coming back to his station—a thin and ageing man, unsoldierly in spite of his coat of mail and his scarlet crest. Now, I must do it now or I will never do it, she told herself; and with the thought a sickly cast of unreality settled over the place: the light came wan through the dark mulberry leaves, and the shadows of the gods and emperors lay faint across the grey stones. She watched him from the doorway while he took his post, trimmed the flame on the altar, and broke a seared leaf from the laurel. I will never find a better place, she thought, than this decaying avenue—empty, no crowd to jeer at me, nobody at any balcony or window to see . . . Stepping backward a little, she tightened the knot at her shoulder and smoothed her hair and brought her glance slowly to focus on his face.

But he was an unlikely one to be the dispenser of her destiny. He had walked round to the side of the altar now and was leaning back, lost in some private dream, against the granite pedestal of the silver Marcus Aurelius, his head bent down, his arms folded across his chest. He was not a Roman; he was a bearded, grey-eyed barbarian, probably Germanic; there was a northern paleness and indefiniteness in his thin cheeks and bloodless lips. Go up to him, she told herself, coming to the very edge of the doorway. Go up to him at once, before your voice is gone and your knees are unstrung. Go up and say—but she faltered, knowing she had given no thought whatever to what she would say, and finding it preposterous, unimaginable that she should walk up to the altar and say anything at all.

How was it done? What had she heard about other martyrs? Some of them—so Novatian had told her—had scorned to make speeches, had walked up to the altar and swept the plaster daemons to the ground. But I could never do such a thing, she told herself. I need only declare myself briefly and with dignity . . . Half a dozen possible introductions came into her head: "I am a member of the fellowship of Jesus," "Arrest me and take me to the authorities," "I am here not to burn incense but to confess the Name . . ." She tried each of them, saying them soundlessly, forming the words with her lips—but every one of them she rejected, she simply could not conceive of uttering such excessive things aloud in this quiet street . . . She started, knowing that the Guardsman had moved away from the pedestal and had fixed a curious look upon her. And no wonder, she thought, coming out of the doorway. He has seen me talking to myself, he probably thinks I am mad.

She walked automatically towards him, through the strange dim spots of light, past a Hermes, past a Hercules, past an Alexander Severus. It seemed to her that he did not see her—he busied himself with some dust on the ugly head of his plaster Decius, blew at it, rubbed the bald crown with his fingertip. She stepped directly in front of the altar and turned and laid her hand on the corner of it to steady herself. Whatever beginnings she had rehearsed back there in the doorway had disappeared from her consciousness. "Are you in charge of the sacrifices here?" she said.

"Yes, I'm happy to say." He did not look at her. "We don't have any trouble around here. There are no Christians in this neighborhood."

"But I don't live in this neighborhood."

"No?" He bent over the altar and fingered the dried laurel. "I don't, either. I live in the Suburra—I've lived there for the last three years."

Say it, say it now, say anything, she thought, but his casual melancholy made her incapable of anything but a long and shaking sigh.

"So the lady's not from this section of the City?"

"No. I'm from Istrus—Istrus on the Euxine Sea." She had never been there and could not imagine why it should have come into her head. Yet it was possible that the Lord, more mindful of her than she could be of Him in this hour of her exigency, had put the name into her mouth. If she was to be taken, if she was to be questioned—oh, but she must not think of that, not now, not here—then it would be better that she should hide her identity. Those who came from the far cities—with them it went better in the prison, so Probus had told her. Romans were tortured for the names of other Romans, but nobody would trouble to send a messenger to seek out such-and-such a one in Istrus by the Euxine. . . .

"That's a long journey, from Istrus to the City."

It was coming to nothing—they might stand here for an hour in such talk, and still it would come to nothing. She stepped forward and grasped both corners of the altar and looked into his pale, evasive eyes. "My husband was a cobbler there," she said. "Paulina Thomasa—" she deliberately chose a Christian patronymic—"my name is Paulina Thomasa—"

A flush fired up the pale skin of his cheeks. "My mother was the daughter of a cobbler back in Vindonissa."

"Many confess the Name in Istrus—"

"Do they? I don't doubt it. Well, let them stay in Istrus, it's better for them there."

Do it, do it—help me now, merciful Jesus, to do it . . . Her voice came out of her so small that it was scarcely louder than the crackling of the laurel in the altar fire. "I have no certificate of sacrifice," she said, and felt a blessed relief, and told herself that it was accomplished, that now she might set her soul at peace.

But he only bent forward, baffled and exasperated, and told her that she should go to some other altar, that he had used up all his certificates of sacrifice; and while she listened her heart began to beat with such violence that she had to cling to the altar to keep herself on her feet. I thought it was accomplished, she told herself, and see, it has only begun. I have only committed myself to all the rest of it—the office of the Urban Prefect and the prison and all those other things which I must not think of here or I will go raving mad and shriek in the street—

"Go do it at some other altar," he said. "Go at once, before somebody comes and sees."

She straightened her shoulders and made the sign of the Cross. "No, not at any altar, I will not burn incense at any altar," she said in a high and piercing voice, knowing that he would never take her unless witnesses were summoned out of the houses. "These plaster daemons—I reject them, I spit on them, I utterly deny them. I believe in one God only—the Father Almighty, and Jesus Christ, His only Son, our Lord."

Somebody had come out onto one of the balconies. Two or three faces had appeared at the windows. Just beyond the altar, at a basement window, an old woman had thrust out her head. Above her face, patchy and fiery, stood her white and unkempt hair.

"Have it as you like," he said in his barbaric Latin. "But why do you do it? If you're sick of the world, are there no rivers where you can drown yourselves?"

Oh, God, God, God, she thought in her terror, how sweet it would be to go down into the darkness of a river, how much better than to be dragged into an arena, with fifty thousand looking on!

The woman with the red face beat on the sill with her fist and shouted that he should take the Christian witch, the eater of bread leavened with the blood of little children, and see that she was burned to a cinder. Other faces, looking down at her from the upper windows and the balconies, took up the same cry. Violence, coarse and sickening violence—and she completely unprepared to sustain it, she nurtured so delicately that a heated argument among the deacons had always been enough to unnerve her. "Arrest me, take me away from here," she said, coming around to the back of the altar and slipping her arm through the hairy arm of the Guardsman, looking up at him beseechingly, as if he had been her friend. "Take me away, take me to prison—"

He offered her no pitying look, no encouraging handclasp—his arm remained motionless under her touch. "Get in with you, grandmother," he said over his shoulder to the woman with the unkempt hair. "These matters are in the hands of the Prefect. Get in with you and see that you keep the peace."

A little shower of earth, probably gathered from a flower pot on one of the balconies, came at her, struck her in the face.

"Come," he said, pulling his arm away and taking hold of her by the wrist. "You'll have to go in a chariot. It's a good way from here."

In a chariot? In an open chariot? A prisoner standing beside a Guardsman in an open chariot—shamed, exposed, a target for shouts and missiles, a spectacle for curious eyes . . . "With you?" she said.

"Yes, with me." He still refused to look at her. Once they had come round to the front of the altar, he walked ahead of her, drawing her along, toward the end of the street, where the metallic curve of his chariot shone in the sun and his white horse cropped the grass that grew between the broken paving stones. The shouting behind them had died away, and nobody in the neighboring tenements came out to take it up; the windows and balconies remained blessedly still. I can walk, she thought, at least I can walk, my knees are steady and now I am scarcely thirsty anymore . . . But she was stupid about the chariot, she had never ridden in a chariot. With a sigh of exasperation, he pushed her up into place. "Hold on," he said, "can't you see that you'll have to hold on? Otherwise, one jerk and you'll fall right out."

She had heard tales of other martyrs who had used this shameful journey through the streets of the City for the greater glory of God. In Lyons, in Carthage, in Rome itself some of the sons and daughters of Jesus had borne themselves with so much joyous confidence that those who took them prisoner had come with them to the Urban Prefect and confessed the Name. But the strength of the Lord was within them, she thought, and the glory of the Lord shone around them. And I—it is all I can do to keep myself upright, to keep my cloak on my shoulders, to keep my dalmatica tied. I would not dare to assail him with texts—my tireless preaching has faltered at last. I cannot offend him, I am too bitterly in need of his begrudged kindness. . . .

Spring sun on a garlanded lintel—somebody in that house today was born or betrothed or married. Married, married—oh, first sorrowful, pine scented night on the wedding journey in the villa at Tibur—oh, sandals set side by side on the bare Christian floor—wet cloak, strewn manuscript . . . Red roses, first spring roses out of Africa offered for sale in a wicker basket. Nobody ever gave me a flower. You came to me in an unseasonable hour, my cousin, either too late or too early for roses. Nobody ever gave me a

388

rose . . . Forsaken child crying on a crowded corner. We are all of us children, lost and alone and crying. Where are You? How is it that my spirit cannot find You, cannot be comforted in Your bosom, O my God? Lift me up, cover my eyes, hide my eyes from this cursing priest of Isis, hide my eyes with the feathers of Your wings . . . No, no, for such a one as I am there is no ecstasy, there is nothing but terror—black, disintegrating terror now that we are almost there, now that we are passing the somber colonnades and gardens of the Palatine. For if they use me roughly in the Urban Prefect's office, if they call me foul names and lay hard hands upon me, I will shame my sweet Lord in the Citadel of the Beast. I will weep like an infant, I will surely weep. . . .

Now that they had come to the place, there was an instant when her fear was so overwhelming that she thought she might cling fast to the rail in the chariot, might shriek and fight him off, might force him to wrench her hands free and drag her up the stairs and through the great, forbidding archway of the door. "Will they lay hands on me there?" she asked him, still standing in the chariot, looking fearfully down into his face.

"Come," he said, and lifted her down. "Probably not. It depends on what sort of humor they're in. Usually they're decent enough—but conduct yourself quietly—none of your talk about spitting on the gods."

Idlers lined the stairs—idlers in bright dalmaticas and the striped togas of patricians. She drooped her head awkwardly to one side, trying to hide her face in the collar of her cloak, afraid that somebody who knew her might be there to see. But none of the faces were familiar, and only a few of them were cruel. Now that she was no longer riding, the heat broke upon her again reflecting upward from the stones as she climbed the long stairs. But it was cool inside the building, cool and dark. The stillness of the empty corridor was broken by the purling of water, and in his rough mercy he stepped aside and waited for her to drink. She drank long and dabbled her fingers in the spray; she wet her cheeks and temples and was ready. He took hold of her wrist again, but his fingers were loose and gentle. "Jesus reward you," she said; and as she said it the weak tears, the childish tears, started out of her eyes.

She had expected rows of them, arranged in the stern pattern of justice in a solemn chamber. That there were only two of them, that the room should be so unimpressive, so bright, that there were no other prisoners waiting—all these things brought into her mind a wild and unwarranted hope that the persecution was a false and fabricated thing and could not last. Perhaps, she thought, turning her glance from the centurion who stood looking out of the window to the tribune who sat at a table carelessly strewn with documents, perhaps next week or the week after that the whole flimsy structure will collapse, and the doors of the Urban Prefect's prison will be opened, and the children of the congregation, absolved of their sins for their mere willingness to die, will stream, liberated and rejoicing, into the street. . . .

"What have you brought us?" said the tribune without taking his cheek from his hand or his elbow from the table. He was a sallow young man, and the noonday warmth of the place had plainly drugged him into an unwholesome sleepiness.

"A woman of Istrus, one Paulina Thomasa, the wife of a cobbler."

"The wife of a cobbler?" said the centurion, turning away from the window and clucking his tongue. "We told you—didn't we?—they want patricians."

"Tell me, Paulina Thomasa, when did you arrive from Istrus?" said the tribune, getting up and yawning.

"This morning—I arrived in the City only this morning."

"It didn't take you long to get yourself into trouble—did it? We can get you a certificate of sacrifice, though, if you want it. All that's necessary is to burn a little incense."

"I do not burn incense before plaster—"

"No use, no use," said her Guardsman, clamping his fingers hard upon her wrist. "We've been through all that already, she and I. She's an ingrained Confessor of the Name. She refuses to sacrifice—she did so publicly before witnesses."

"She refuses, does she?" It was the centurion who spoke, strolling away from the window. He was large and soft and smooth of face; there was something of the feline in his walk; and as he drew closer her heart stood still, since violence flickered in his yellow eyes. God help me, she thought, he is going to give me a blow in the face. But he stopped some ten paces away from her and made a sound of disgust. "Look, she's crying like a baby. Get her out of here," he said.

"Come," said the Guardsman, taking her by the wrist again, and she followed him along the interminable and shadowy corridors, down the always darkening stairs. She had begun to retch, perhaps because of the cold water that she had put into her empty stomach, perhaps because of the smell of stale excrement and sweat, always thickening, always growing stronger. She held the sleeve of her dalmatica to her nostrils, thinking it might still be sweet with the scent of thyme and marjoram; but the cloth and her flesh itself seemed already to have taken on the nauseating stench of the place. "Come along," he said, jerking at her wrist a little. "You won't notice it after a while. I was stationed down here once, and you get used to it."

At the end of the corridor was the door to the prison—a great oak portal, heavily bolted and crossed by bands of iron. Only a single Guardsman stood there, his fat body slumped against the frame. In there—I am to be locked up in there, she told herself, stupefied, knowing that for this also she was utterly unprepared: not once had she admitted into her mind how it would feel to be confined, closed in, held until the last day of her life in a vault beneath the earth, away from the air, away from the sun.

"Your name?" said the fat one in a weary voice.

But she could not remember the name she had invented at the altar. She stammered, and he reached out and took her by the shoulder and shook her.

"Your name—tell me your name," he said again. "What ails you? Are you deaf and dumb?"

"Paulina—" And now she remembered. "Paulina Thomasa of Istrus on the Euxine—"

"And your offense?"

"My offense?"

"Why are you here?"

"I am a Confessor."

"Well, in with you then. Tomorrow we will see about your fetters. The smith is sick today. See to it that you behave yourself."

I am not shrieking, she told herself. That is the door, grating on its hinges. I should go in—what is to be gained by standing here and waiting for them to thrust me in? But she simply could not commit herself to that shut darkness, greenish and dank, with an evil glister along the walls, and she lifted one last beseeching look to her Guardsman's pale, evasive eyes.

"Why don't you come to your senses?" he said in his barbaric Latin. "You could still go upstairs and burn a little incense."

"No," she said faintly, and found the strength to turn from them and give herself up to the greenish shadow, staring straight ahead and holding her breath. The door clanged shut behind her, and she moved forward slowly, tentatively, like the blind. One extended sandal came down over nothingness—she stepped back—she was standing at the head of a steep flight of stairs. The glistening lines of the steps, visible near the top, gradually disappeared in the shadow, and the darkness at the bottom was impenetrable, unrelieved by the faint streamers of brightness coming through the barred windows set in the upper walls. She could not take another step; it was as if she were stepping down into her grave; she could only say the name of Jesus and make the sign of the Cross.

He did not come—the Bridegroom clad in shining raiment, descending in a cloud of glory to light the noisome bridal chamber with the brightness of His face. He did not come, but the naming of His Name was enough to dispel the powers of darkness. At His Name and His sign the darkness below her murmured and took shape and moved. People, living beings, poor prisoners fettered and making a clanking with their chains—she knew with wonderment that only these and their sufferings were there at the core of the blackness; and this knowledge was unutterably consoling and sweet. "A sister—it's another sister," said a manly voice, eager and resonant above the general murmuring. And slowly, very slowly, as if they were afraid they might frighten her by any sudden movement, they came in twos and threes—she could make them out, she could see them now in the lessening dark—and stood looking up at her from the foot of the stairs.

A hundred, perhaps two hundred of them, drawn by the news of her arrival from the farthest reaches of the darkness, were coming in the absence of the Bridegroom to welcome her to this last earthly fellowship, to say to her in the Bridegroom's Name: "Lo, I am with you even unto the end of the world." Old women who had risen up from the dreaming quiet of their hearths to confess the Name in the streets, old men who had set down their children's children to give up their lives for the Lord, young wives and husbands who had said an everlasting farewell to the known table and the known bed, gentle girls, bred in cleanliness and used to tender talk and only the mildest of reproofs, young men, bereaved of the manly labor of the smithy and the carpenter's shop and the fields—it was lighter now, she could see their faces. And all of them were inseparably bound to her and to each other even unto the last hour, by the common terror and the common triumph. For all of us have walked up to the altar and declared ourselves, she thought. All of us have ridden through the streets in the open chariot, and confessed the Name to the indifferent officers, and hoped and relinquished hope and committed ourselves to the dark . . . And now, among those who stood below her, she could distinguish in the lessening dark certain familiar faces—this one had slept in her house on the night the tenement had collapsed, that one had helped her distribute money to the poor, and this other one had stood beside her in the basilica one faraway Sabbath morning at the breaking of the bread.

"But look, it's our sister Paulina," said the known voice of the elder Moyses. The crowd before her parted, and he dragged himself, leaning on the shoulders of two young men, to the foot of the stairway. He was so changed that she knew him only by the voice; but love—indestructible love that suffers all things and is kind—went out to her from his ravaged eyes. "Bless me, my father," she said, weeping. And he, and the others with him, said, "May the Lord Jesus walk with you and cause His countenance to shine upon you and give you peace."

And then a young girl—bony, disheveled, half-naked—was flying up the stairs to her, was taking her hands and covering them with kisses, was saying, "My teacher, my teacher—oh, my dear teacher," was holding her in a strong and shaking embrace. But this is one of my novices, this is Constanta; changed and filthy and broken as she is, this is my little one, she told herself, pressing the emaciated body to her, brushing her lips across the oily, stringy hair. And remembering this same child at her stitching in the house on the Aventine, remembering how this same head had bent clean and silky over the white linen in chaste happiness, she felt as if a stone had been rolled away, as if something that had lain dead had risen again within her—

strong to carry her through whatever was to come, bright to dispel all darkness, even the shut darkness of the grave.

"Bring her down, Constanta. If she's thirsty, I have fresh water," said the feeble voice of an old man.

"If she's hungry," said a child-voice, lifted up in the midst of the multitude, "you can bring her here to my mother. We have bread."

And, walking with her little one, embracing and comforting her, she came down among them, knowing that she also could suffer long and be kind.

Chapter 32

LETTERS CAME to her there—two of them, brought in by different bearers though they had been written on the same day in the same dark cellar under the tenement in the Suburra—one from *him*, shattered and passionate and despairing, and one from Probus, which was plainly, by its carefully chosen words and its elaborately constructed sentences, the product of a hard-won serenity. *His* she took from the pudgy hand of Prisca—the Guardsmen never troubled the children, who came and went as they pleased even when there were no visiting hours. And, strangely, there had been no trace of the old jealousy, the old bitterness; in fact, her heart had been less lifted up at the sight of the letter than by the pleasure of hearing the news and seeing the clean, milky, freckled face. Oh, they were safe enough, said the slave-child. The deacon and her master were living in the cellar with the other undershepherds, and the elder Cornelius had found her a place to stay with one of the virgins of the congregation. Her master was sick or strange or something—she couldn't quite say which—and the deacon Probus was being very good to him, was keeping him in the driest corner on the best rags and giving him syrup to make him sleep. At first he had caused a good deal of disturbance by insisting on going to the prison—once he had even stolen out in the middle of the night, and the deacon Alypius had had to go to find him, and had brought him back crying like a child. But now he was calmer and understood that he must not come to the lady Paulina, that any contact with him—marked out as he was—would only subject her to the danger of questioning under torture. He slept much of the day now, probably because of the syrup. She herself was allowed to visit him three times a day, and she always took him a bowl of broth. But today he had asked her to bring the letter, and he had made a great secret of it, had forced her to swear on a Cross made of sticks that nobody, not even the deacon Probus, would ever know.

What a thing to do to a child! she thought, smiling and shaking her head. But afterwards, when the little slave had gone and she had opened the letter, she forgave him everything, even the Cross of sticks, seeing his exigency. Wild words . . . She read them, standing in one of the streamers of light that entered through the upper windows. Black, tormented, filled with self-loathing . . . She had to stop and put the letter into her girdle: a red-haired Germanic slave-woman had begun to have her labor pains; and after she had seen to that there were other things to attend to—an asthmatic old man was choking on a fish bone, one of the catechumens was seized with a fit of hysteria, an old woman wanted a letter spelled out to her son—and she was slow getting about to one and another of them, with the weight of her fetters dragging at her feet. Wild words . . . She pondered them for the second time in the dimmer light of the afternoon, and for an instant her vitals yearned in her at the thought of his suffering—and he without comfort, he without knowledge of what change had come upon her since she had walked down the steps into the welcoming arms of the Lord's children, he thinking that it had been with her all these nine days as it had been when the door clanged shut and she looked out across the dark . . . I should write to him or send somebody to him, she thought, shredding the papyrus and letting it fall from her open, tired hands. I should find some means of making him understand that I do not suffer what he thinks I suffer, that I am at peace.

Such were the thoughts that occupied her until the hour for the arrival of the visitors. They did not enter through the long corridor by which she had come, but were admitted by another entrance, a big portal that opened on a stairwell and a flight of stone steps leading up into the street. They came—some threescore of them with bread and wine and bacon wrapped in papyrus—about half an hour before the time for the evening bread. Inasmuch as all the prisoners had their feet fettered, there were only two Guardsmen stationed at this door, but the visitors were uneasy nevertheless, and there was good cause: during the nine days of her stay with the children of Jesus, seven visitors had been detained, and three of those seven were in the prison now, in chains. She stood a little way back from the entrance, watching them coming down the littered stairs, holding her breath lest she should see her husband. But he was not among them, and she was given no time either to rejoice in his safety or to grieve over his absence.

Along with their gifts, they were bringing news, hard news. There were to be games in the arena: the consuls of the year were giving lions and elephants, and it was rumored also that there were to be fiery Crosses, though nobody, said a level-headed shopkeeper from the Suburra, had heard a single dependable word about a fiery Cross . . . She turned away, recognizing the wormy creepings of terror in her stomach and knowing that she could put them down only by assiduous labors in the vineyard of the Lord.

The Lord, though His face was still hidden from her, had not removed those few poor gifts of grace for which she had been praised before the congregation in other days. She still knew precisely what should be said to the schoolboy who was smitten with panic at the very mention of elephants. Her hand, drawn down the grimy cheek of one of her novices, could still quiet the trembling and bring forth the relieving tears. They clustered about her now—all the young ones and the weak ones clustered about her and kept her from the table. Her words were more nourishing to them than the food taken out of the papyrus wrappings and laid out in the weak light of the single lamp in the middle of the board. And it was in the midst of the little crowd of them—young ones and sick ones and one who was blind—that the elder Cornelius came upon her. She did not recognize him in his plebeian disguise. She knew him first by his voice when he greeted her by name and drew her apart. Near a bench under one of the beehive arches he said that he had come to her from Probus and pressed a square of papyrus and a linen tunic into her hands.

She had never been on really intimate terms with the elder Cornelius; and now, looking at his grave countenance in the dim light, she recalled that none of the members of the congregation had ever claimed to know him intimately. His mild Olympian dignity and his impartial beneficence had transformed him into a kind of figurehead, robbing him of his individual humanity and consigning him to a cheerful loneliness. She took the proffered objects from him a little shyly, afraid to touch his clean white fingers with her grimy hand. He could not quite conceal the shock that he felt; nine days in the darkness was enough to make vast changes; and for the first time, through his eyes, she saw herself as she was—dirty and haggard and in chains. She was confused, too, by the tunic. Of one thing she was certain: her husband had not sent her his tunic simply because it *was* his tunic. And, in her embarrassment, she smiled and asked the elder after the health of an ailing sister of his, precisely as if she had met him by chance on some sunny street.

He did not answer. Above his ample, curling beard, the lines of his beautiful mouth were molded and softened by tenderness. "I saw your husband. Let me tell you about your husband," he said. "He's safe, quite safe, down there in the cellar with the rest of the elders and deacons. You know he grieves for you, I needn't tell you that. But I thought you might be easier if you knew that he is strong in his grief, sustained by an unfailing faith in the Lord."

"Tell him he mustn't come here, my father. Tell him it isn't safe—they're watching for the deacons, everybody says. Tell him he mustn't ever allow himself to come here. You, too—you shouldn't come here yourself—"

"Oh, I . . ." He shrugged and smiled and looked down at his sandals. "The labor in the prisons—that's all I do, you know. Nothing else I do is of the slightest worth. Besides, the blessed Fabian—" he cast a curiously significant glance at the tunic which she had taken from him—"he charged me explicitly to visit the prisons. He spoke of it on his way to the block, in the very hour of his death. . . ."

His casual, musical voice trailed on above the murmuring and the weeping and the chatter, but she did not listen. Suddenly she had realized that this tunic was the one her husband had worn to the martyrdom of the blessed Fabian; even in the dying light she could make out the blackish spots of blood. He had not brought it with him to the villa in the Campagna because the elder Novatian had ruled that it was too precious an object to be taken on so perilous a journey; and she remembered how at the time she had been glad to be delivered from the sight of it, had felt infinitely grateful that she need not take it into her hands. But now it was otherwise, now she would not be smitten with sick-heartedness if she clasped it and kissed it. And, flushing because the brown, short-sighted eyes of the elder Cornelius would not leave her face, she raised the tunic to her lips.

"It's yours to keep so long as you're here in the prison, my daughter."

"Oh, no, I couldn't consider it," she said, shaking her head. "There are a dozen others here who stand more in need of this sacred relic than I do." But it was not entirely an impulse of Christian generosity that had made her renounce the spotted linen, and she could not look into his face. "Besides," she said, "there are some things that we can't permit ourselves down here in the darkness. There are some things—it will be hard for me to make my father understand—that by their very sweetness can be like bruises on our hearts. I loved him—I loved them both—Probus and our dead Shepherd whom we loved together. And if the tunic were beside me in the night I couldn't sleep, and if I don't sleep I'm useless, incapable of any labors for the Lord—"

And now, she thought, in my weakness and my foolishness I have made him weep. A single tear, large and effortless, rolled out of the corner of his eye, trickled over his cheek, and was lost in the ambrosial curls of his beard.

"Come, take it," she said lightly, almost gayly, pressing the tunic into his hands as if she were forcing him to accept another piece of fruit or another cup of wine. "Take it, and let us go to the table where we can be with the others—they'll all be wanting to see you, too. Say a kind word to my novice

397

Constanta if you can—she's very young, and all this is very difficult for her to bear."

"But give me a message first. Tell me what you want me to say to Probus."

"To Probus?" It was strange that there should be so little left to say to Probus, so little left to say, in fact, to anyone who still walked about unfettered in the light of the sun. "Only that the Lord has sent His peace to me, even though He Himself has not yet come. Only that I am greatly comforted and sustained by those that are with me here. Only that he should address himself to God for me, asking that in the last hour I be given strength to make a good crimson confession, with a steadfast heart. Oh, yes, and tell him also that I kiss him on the forehead—" it was the easier to say it because the cheek was dry now, the beautiful face had become again the face of a noble statue. "Say that I kiss him on the forehead and wish him well with *The Journey of Barnabas* and pray every hour of the day that he is being sustained in this by grace out of heaven." He had turned, patrician gentleman that he was, and was leading her toward the others. And his gracious, easy manner made it possible for her to add that he should tell her husband also that she often thought how blessed she had been in him these last ten years, how no woman could have had a better helpmeet, a dearer yoke-fellow in the Lord.

The letter—she could read it only in the most desultory fashion, since there was so much talk while the meal was in progress, and, as soon as the meal was over, the tribune in charge for the evening insisted on the quenching of the lamp. Once the visitors had departed, the place seemed quiet, almost empty. Everything was relative—so she had been telling herself since the day of her coming: the departure of the visitors was enough to give an air of openness to what had seemed stiflingly crowded; a little water to wash one's mouth and fingertips could give an illusion of cleanliness; a morsel of fish and a crust of bread could fill the shrunken stomach and quicken the sluggish blood. Usually she was so exhausted with the labors of the day and the weight of her chains that merely to lie down was to subside into a blessed conviction of rest. But tonight she could not sleep—partly because of the ache in her fettered ankles and the hateful, secretive biting of the lice, but also because of the letter that crackled against her chest.

Not that it was in any way disturbing or surprising. If she had known that she was to receive a letter from Probus, she would have been able to guess in advance most of the phrases which she had read in the weak light of the single flame. But this very rigidity, this very inability to say one passionate, unpremeditated thing—this, together with the stiff, familiar handwriting—begot a vague ache in her, not sharp, not bitter, but quiet and brooding, such an ache as she had felt in her childhood when somebody had read her the tale of Orpheus or Lucretia or Cassandra—all that sorrow over now, all of them dead a long time ago . . . It was not that she accused herself because she had committed adultery: that sin had been atoned for in the sickening moment when she had stood at the altar and declared herself, and whatever taint of guilt remained upon her spirit would be utterly washed away in her crimson confession. But there were other matters— there was the fact that she had found her husband insufficient, that she had needed more than the poor all he had to offer, that she, his only close companion, had for one night at least turned her back upon him and left him to his total isolation from other men. This thought filled her with a mournfulness that was with her still when the bars of the upper windows began to show forth against the faint and glimmering greyness, that lessened only a little when the exhausted and unbeautiful faces of her fellow-confessors were revealed to her again in the uncharitable whiteness of the dawn.

Sitting up, with her aching back supported against one of the beehive arches, she looked, as she always looked now in times of stress, for the elder Moyses. He was lying on a heap of rags directly under a window, and it was difficult to see him because between her and his huddled body there was a moted slant of light. But after a while she could make out his face and could tell that he was sleeping soundly—which was a blessed thing, since he was very weary: he had spoken long and zealously at the table with the elder Cornelius, commending the lapsed to the mercy of the other undershepherds, growing angry enough to say at last that the elder Novatian was at cross-purposes with his Redeemer, was closing the door against the weak and benighted ones, the very ones whom Christ had died to save . . . He had slept all night—no Guardsman had come to take him out for the questioning. They had tortured him so long and so fruitlessly that they had grown weary of it; the last few nights they had come for a younger man, a quarry-slave, instead. And every morning, at about this hour, the quarry-slave would be brought back with broken bones or seared feet or bleeding fingers, and the elder Moyses would drag himself over to him and tend him and thank him, saying, "You went in my place, dear brother in Jesus. It was because of you that I had a whole night's blessed sleep."

Perhaps because he knew in his dreams that it was close to the time for the slave to be brought in that he wakened, moaning when he moved and stifling the moan lest he should disturb the others about him, pulling his wretched rags around his cold and broken old body and rubbing his eyes. He saw her at once—all that were between them lay prone and still sleeping. The innumerable wrinkles in his face crinkled and changed, and, with all the easy warmth of the sons of Abraham, brought up in houses where love and the manifestations of love are taken for granted, he leaned toward her and blew her a paternal kiss.

And suddenly she felt an overwhelming need to be near him, to sit with him between the damp wall and the streamer of light, to engage for one last time in private converse—though what she wished to say to him she did not know. Slowly, tentatively, on her knees and reaching behind her to hold her fetters in her hand lest the clanking should waken the sleepers, she came to him over the filthy earthen floor, past the three novices who always slept beside her, past an old woman wheezing with asthma, past a young mother whose infant whimpered and groped in her tattered tunic for her breast. The way to him was devious, and they laughed together at her maneuvers when she reached him. Making a place for her on the heap of rags, so that she could sit beside him with her back against the wall, he took her hand in his wrinkled, mud-colored hand and played with her fingers. "You had a letter from your husband last night—Constanta told me," he said in a whisper. "He writes a fine letter, your Probus—he's written me two since I've been in prison. I hope it lifted up your heart."

But, scarcely knowing what she did, she fetched up a sigh and shook her head. "No, it made me mournful. It made me so mournful that I found it necessary to come over here to you like a child, to sit with you, to try to find it again—my steadfastness, my peace."

"Truly?" he said, still playing with her fingers, testing their limberness, bending them back against his infinitely wrinkled palm. "But how is that? Probus is scarcely the man to say anything disturbing—"

Her hand stiffened a little. It wounded her for her husband's sake that this elder should know him so well, should see that, even in an hour of extremity, the deacon Probus would never give way to human desperation, would write no wild words, would maintain his stern control upon himself. "No, nothing disturbing," she said.

"And nothing consoling—is that it?"

She had no right to be angry that he should ask her such a question. She looked through the moted slant of brightness at the awkwardly disposed bodies and the ravaged faces; she breathed the smell of their sweat and their excrement in the stale air; she saw the bites of the lice along his old veined arm, and thought how foolish and futile it was to be proud and withdrawn in such a place as this. For all of us, she told herself, walk naked in our spirits now, naked and unashamed before each other and the Lord. "If I was not consoled, it was no fault of his," she said in a whisper. "It was because I was a poor wife to him, not worthy—even now not worthy of the consolation that he sends me."

He shrugged and pursed his lips and went on bending her fingers. Doubtless a dozen innocent wives had come to him with just such talk, troubled in their last days over minor matters—the purchase of a necklace when the family means were small, a harsh word left unforgiven, skittishness, captiousness . . . "You torment yourself needlessly. All that he asked for, you gave him freely," he said.

There was bitter, barren truth in that, and she nodded, looking at him gravely. Yet all the while she was thinking that love should not be measured according to the needs of the beloved, that the only love deserving of the name was boundless love, unasking love, such love as had streamed down upon an indifferent multitude from the face of her crucified God . . . "I should have loved him more than he required. I should have loved him limitlessly, wholly," she said at last. "As the Lord loved us, so I should have loved him, and I could not. I was always restless, always wanting, always seeking—"

"But you were human," he said, as if she were already dead, as if he were saying a kind word for her over her grave.

And suddenly, staring into the moted brightness and seeing the sleepers beyond it distant and unreal, as if they, too, had been gathered to their fathers and had lain waiting through a thousand years for the millennium— seeing all things as far away and long ago, she knew that she might make a confession to him if she chose, since what she wished to tell him had come to pass in the world, and she and he and all these sleepers had already taken their everlasting leave of the world. "Let me confess to you, my father, since I have not made a confession—"

"But that's quite needless for all of us here, my daughter. Besides, I know in my heart that you have nothing to confess."

"Oh, but I have, I have indeed, my father. I betrayed my husband."

"To the authorities? When you came from the altar into the prison?" His hand closed down upon her fingers. She glanced sidewise and saw the flash of reproof stifled in his little beady eyes, and for the life of her she could not suppress a smile.

"Oh, no, nothing like that. They asked me nothing. I lied, I said I was a woman of Istrus—the wife of a cobbler. I mean, I betrayed my husband in the matter of the flesh," she said.

Whatever it was that she wanted of him, she was not disappointed. If he had received her confession in the free, bright world, he would have been forced to ask her with whom. But here it was otherwise, here he only sighed and nodded, both at once, after the manner of the sons of Abraham, and it was as if he had said: "But all that was long ago."

"I loved him, my father."

"Probus? Assuredly. I know you loved him."

"No, the other one, the one that was my lover. I loved him entirely, with my flesh and my spirit." It seemed to her then that in the midst of the dusty slant of light he stood before her. The known and renounced sweetness, the forgone delight plucked at her as if she had been a string on a cythera, plucked and begot high music. Then the tremor died away, and the beautiful flesh grew ghostly and dissolved into the light. "God knows I loved him," she said.

"Certainly you loved him. That also—that together with the crimson confession—will plead for you before the throne. Anybody would know you could never do it lightly, you could do it only out of love."

"That is the worst of it, my father."

"What is the worst of it?" Slowly, with grave concentration, as if he were doing an exercise in anatomy, he traced the bluish vein on her grimy wrist.

"That I should have loved him so much. I took from him what I never had in Probus, and by holding out my hands to take it I made plain that Probus was insufficient, and I—I above all others—" she wept now, resting her head on his knees—"I who leaned on his steadfastness and knew him and the worth of him better than any of the others—I who was his only companion—I should never have let my restless, seeking heart betray me into showing, even to myself, even before one other man, that my dear yoke-fellow in Jesus was not enough—"

"The flesh is weak—the flesh is very weak, my daughter, and all the weaker when we torment it with interdictions—"

He was inviting her to offer her only excuse: that she and her husband had lived most of their ten years together in chastity. She had never spoken of it, and neither had Probus, yet somehow some hint of it must have been communicated to the congregation. Doubtless some of the novices, loving their teacher and zealous to crown her with all the ornaments of Christian grace, had made the conjecture and started the tale . . . And, strangely, the thought that they had chattered of her purity over their lessons and their stitching had about it a kind of unearthly irony. She smiled, she felt a quiver of laughter struggling in her chest, even while her face was wet with tears.

"To live chastely in marriage is very hard, Paulina."

But she could not accept the proffered mercy. The vow was their secret, their dear and intimate secret, and she would not share it again. She lifted her face from his knee and wiped the tears away and shook her head. "My father must not let himself be misled by the rumors of foolish children. I had my husband. We had each other," she said. And so we did, she thought, remembering the wedding journey to Tibur, and the long, troubled nights, and the smell of the pines coming up to the windows through the dark. In the shaft of light where her lover had stood a moment since she saw two pairs of sandals set side by side on the bare Christian floor. "I had him and I loved him. If he was insufficient, it was because my own heart was forever restless and wanting. If you stay behind me after I have made my crimson confession, pray that I may be delivered at last from my restless heart."

"And yet," he said thoughtfully, taking her hand again, "much good much blessedness for the rest of us came in the course of your life out of this same restless heart. The love that drove you to your lover served also for other things. It made your house a home to all the children of Jesus. I drew the weak ones and the young ones to your knees for counsel—and your counsel was always reasonably wise. It manifested itself in tenderness when you labored with the novices—not one, not the tenderest of the shoots in the Lord's vineyard was ever crushed or broken by your hands. And here, too, is with you—it shines in your face, so that we come by the dozens to the light and the warmth of it, to cheer ourselves, to warm ourselves. No, would never have had you loveless, my daughter. That was the best of it—your love."

Far off, in one of the other subterranean chambers, a door clanged shut with a reverberating echo, and the stillness was filled with the resounding beat of approaching feet.

"They're bringing him back, they're coming back with the quarry-slave," he said. "But wait, wait a moment, there's something I wanted to tell you. In the Gospel of Saint Luke there's that story of the woman of the city, the one who poured the precious ointment on the feet of Jesus. A sinner—you know what sort of sinner she was, my daughter. 'A woman of the city' means a prostitute. And even of such a one as she was, He said at His supper, before the disciples and the Pharisees: 'Her sins, which are many, are forgiven: for she loved much.' You also, my daughter—it will be said of you when you have inherited your peace that you loved much. . . ."

The great door at the other end of the prison, the door through which she had come to render herself up to the darkness, opened with a rasping sound. Two Guardsmen dragged the quarry-slave in between them and pushed him methodically, without anger or malice, down the flight of stairs.

"We'd better go to him," said the elder Moyses, putting his hand on her shoulder and heaving himself up. "They've had him on the rack again, he can't stand on his feet. Let's look to him, but remember what I told you. They're the Lord's own words, you can read them in the Gospel according to Saint Luke, about a third of the way through: 'Her sins, which are many, are forgiven, for she loved much.' Oh, these legs of mine—these wretched legs—no, we'll have to call the others. We'll have to waken Theodorus and Apollonius. You're slight, my daughter, and I'm heavier than you'd think. You'll never be able to drag me all that way alone."

It had gone very ill with the quarry-slave out there in the other chamber. The bones of his wrists and ankles had been broken; and these the elder Moyses and a certain Alexandrine who had once assisted a Greek physician were able to see to with splints and bandages. But something else had happened inside him while he was on the rack—a terrible tearing and a kind of bursting, as he explained to them in a whisper; and now he was sick, deathly sick, so sick that his vitals seemed to heave every time he so much as lifted his hand. They were afraid to move him from the bare floor where he had fallen, and, while the two men looked to him, she crept close and raised his head a little and made a pillow for him of her knee. The floor was cold, and the position which she had taken became very hard to maintain because of the cramp that shot along her thigh; but after a while she scarcely noticed the pain, she was so absorbed in staring at his face.

That face—she could have sworn that she had seen it, not once but a hundred times before. It was eastern and delicate, the chin bearded, the nose aquiline, the eyelids heavy over the large brown eyes. It was a mature man's face—the quarry-slave had undoubtedly passed his thirtieth year—yet

403

it was touchingly pure, childishly innocent. And every expression that passed across it while they tended him—agony and relief, terror and gratefulness—merged in her consciousness with some nameless recollection, so that finally she could no longer control her curiosity.

No, he told her, in the intervals between pain and pain, no, she could not have known him in the past. He had been born in Syria, sold into slavery there, assigned to the quarries near Megara in Greece, and sent from that city to Rome for examination, because he had refused to quarry any more marble—it had come upon him one morning in the pit that he was an agent of evil, supplying the sculptors with marble to be made into false gods. But the Guardsmen here in the prison, seeing him always in the company of the elder Moyses, who had greatly sustained him, took him to be some notable member of the Roman congregation and kept torturing him for information which he did not even have. "And that," he said, smiling up at her, "is as it should be. What I don't know can't be forced from me. God forbid that I should disabuse them of their mistake, since every time they take me out they give the elder Moyses a night's rest."

And yet she was convinced that she had known him—if not in life, then perhaps in a picture, perhaps in one of the golden visions which had flamed across her lost hours of ecstasy, perhaps in a recurring dream. And this strange foreknowledge of him made him dearer to her than any she had labored with here in the prison, dearer even than the novice Constanta, dearer even than the elder Moyses to whom she had shown the secret places of her heart. For hours she sat with her knee under his head, taking no food, barely wetting her lips with water lest some need of her body should call her from her place. And in the afternoon, when the fever that had been upon him gave way to a clammy coldness, she called Constanta and told her to bring the cloak, the gift of Probus which she had worn at the altar and brought with her into the prison. "Bring it to cover our brother in Jesus here. It has a lining of sheepskin," she said.

But the novice was jealous and unwilling. She pointed out that once the cloak was relinquished her teacher would never set eyes on it again; and if she had not been in such a pitiful state—the affliction of women had come upon her for the first time two days ago—Paulina would have felt called upon to administer a reproof. As it was, when the grimy and disconsolate little thing returned with the cloak, she could not send her off again. Since Constanta would plainly be discontented until she also lay with her head in her teacher's lap, Paulina invited her to rest against the other knee. So, into the late hours of the afternoon, she sat supporting the heads of the two of them; and if her legs ceased to ache it was only because she was utterly numb. A profound quiet had settled upon her, body and spirit. The girl fell into a drowse, and it was no longer needful for her to divide her attention: she could look as earnestly, as steadfastly as she wished into the sleeping face of the quarry-slave. But her eyelids were heavy, and her head kept drooping toward her chest, and she was able to wrest herself out of sleep only by remembering how the Lord had said: "Could ye not watch with Me one hour?"

Yet she was sleeping—it seemed that she had been striving for hours with uneasy dreams—when the voice of the elder Moyses roused her. The waning sun of the late afternoon shone at the barred windows: Another of my few poor days on earth drawing to a close, she thought. The chamber seemed almost crowded, the visitors had come again—to tell us more about the games, she told herself, to give us the hour and the manner of our death . . . Then she remembered the quarry-slave and was filled with consternation because his head was no longer on her knee. "We lifted him up," said the elder Moyses, his furrowed face coming close to hers, advancing out of the mists of sleep. "Don't worry, your novices are with him. And now you must get up. Your husband has come."

"Probus?" But she had told him not to come, she had never thought how it would be to see him. The old pain, the old poignance carried down here into the darkness—she was not sure that she could bear it. She pressed her fist over her halting heart.

"Here's Constanta, she can take you to him. But wait a moment, my daughter, he never saw you as you are. Smooth your hair a little, wipe your face."

She could not move. It seemed to her that her spirit hung fearful and suspended within her, and the tingling numbness of her body was such that she had to let them drag her to her feet. She stood like a child while Constanta wiped her face with a dirty piece of linen that had once been a napkin. Somebody else, somebody behind her, ran a jagged fragment of comb through her hair. "You needn't adorn me as if I were going to my wedding," she said, laughing to smother the terror. "He and I have been married for ten years."

"There he is, my daughter, over there by the bench under the window."

She saw him then, disguised as a cobbler, in a tunic far too short for his bony body, with a bag of cobbler's tools ineptly held in his hand. And, instead of the disintegrating poignance, something else stirred within her at the sight of him—a tender merriment. "Surely they could have found him a longer tunic. He looks like a boy who has outgrown his clothes," she said.

She was glad he was looking for her elsewhere and did not see her stumbling toward him on her benumbed and fettered feet, supporting herself on the arm of the little Constanta with one hand and using the other to push a disorderly lock of hair out of her eyes. He did not turn in her direction until she was almost upon him, and when he looked so little change took place in her that it was possible for her to give him a ghostly smile. His arms around her, his chest under her cheek, the roughness of his beard—she had no reason to be afraid that they would shatter her serenity. Her stay here in the darkness with the children of the Lord was as a hundred years; and he also, even he, lay on the other side of it, relinquished, forgone, a quieted remembrance out of the past.

In the red light of the approaching evening she sat beside him on the bench—not close, since they had never sat close and it seemed unnatural to do so now. He asked her how it was with her, and she found it difficult to give him any real account: the filth, the lice, the ache of the fetters, the endless labor in the Lord's vineyard, Constanta's ailment, the rip in the vitals of the quarry-slave—she could not speak of such things to him, it was better to spare him, poor broken child of God that he seemed in his cobbler's clothes. So many matters—yes, all the matters that she ever thought about now—ought not to be mentioned to those who still walked in the light of the sun . . . And these interdictions made their converse uneasy and unfruitful. He looked often at the reddish light, and she knew with infinite pity that he was thinking in his heart: "In this also I am insufficient—the moments of our last meeting are running through my fingers—I cannot even say a creditable farewell. . . ."

Yet after a little he gained hold of himself. He took her hand—and that was good, it was blessed in this dank tomb to feel the pressure of warm earthly fingers—he took her hand and addressed her as he had often addressed her at their hearth in the evenings of rest, without looking into her face. He spoke—she knew with gentle irony that he had planned the words, had chosen the words as carefully and uneasily as he had always chosen the words for *The Journey of Barnabas*—he spoke as any good Christian husband, learned and not devoid of eloquence, should speak in such an hour: of the splendor of her courage and the richness of her reward, of the brevity of the earthly suffering that awaited her and the endlessness of her heavenly peace, of the prayers that he would send up for her so long as he lived and the joy that would come to them both when they beheld each other among the hosts in Paradise. She listened less to the words than to the sound of his voice. I have it now, I will never forget it, she thought; for sometimes, waking in the middle of the night, she had striven in vain to remember his voice. And, when he finished his speech, she knew with remorse that she had not heard the end of it and could not make an answer, could only ask him, quite ineptly, whether in all this sorrow and confusion he had been able to add any lines to *The Journey of Barnabas*.

"No," he said gravely, looking for the first time straight into her eyes. "I didn't know whether I ought to tell you, but somehow now it seems I should. It's without any conviction—it's lifeless—I'm giving it up. And now that I'm finished with it, the Lord has granted me a certain measure of peace."

To go to the arena with a heart delivered of at least that burden, to cancel from her thoughts the image of him sitting alone in the bedroom over the pitiful manuscript, to think of him as liberated at last from his impossible task—it would be blessed, and yet she did not dare to smile. "But you'll go back to it. You'll want to work on it again—afterward, when all this is over with," she said.

"No, Paulina. Never. I thought I would work at it, I thought it might be a consolation. I tried to add a line or so that evening when they came and said you had confessed the Name. But I was changed—" he took her hand and raised it to his lips—"I was so changed by that sorrow that I saw everything with new eyes. I knew then that the thing was dead, and I was glad to be delivered from it. I have no consolation now but the consolation of labor, and it's a good season for labor—I labor day and night now for the Lord—"

And then suddenly his voice broke. She had shifted on the bench to move a little closer to him, and her chains had made a clanking sound. He was looking at her feet—his eyes, amazed and suffering, were fixed upon the bruises from the fetters. Oh, no, she thought, pulling her feet back under the bench out of his sight. Oh, no, dear, pitiful Jesus, spare me, spare the both of us, let him go from me quietly, don't let him weep . . . But his bony hands went up and covered his face, his shoulders heaved, and such sounds as she had never heard him make issued out of him—the wild, wet sobs of a heartbroken child. "Oh, your poor ankles," he said over and over. "Oh, God, how is it possible? Oh, poor Paulina—your feet, look at your feet."

"But they don't hurt, you mustn't think they hurt, you get used to it in no time at all." As remote as if she were a spirit risen from its grave to come back and comfort him, without reserve and without pleasure, she permitted herself such liberties with his person as she had never dared to take: she drew his head against her breast and kissed the nape of his neck through his hair. "These are small things—little pains and indignities given only to the body—"

"But it is what happens to your body that I cannot bear! That they should do violence to your body, that your body should in any way be hurt or shamed or touched—believe me, though there was a vow between us, I loved your body, I was tender of your body. No, no, Jesus sustain me—these are the things I cannot bear!"

These others also suffer, she thought, touching him gently, stroking his shaking shoulders. Through us they suffer—the ones who remain behind us in the world. And the future also, like the present, took on the remoteness and the quietness of the past; she saw him far away and long ago lying in his bereaved and lonely bed, she saw him seeking her lost person in a cloak or a comb, she saw him at her grave. Weary as I am, my Lord and my Redeemer, she prayed, You must give me words with which to comfort him—and the words were given. She told him how she was scarcely aware of her body anymore; she told him, stretching truth a little in the name of charity, that she supposed her spirit had already taken leave of her body, borne thence on the pinions of the final ecstasy; she told him that the love which had been between them had had little to do with the flesh and much to do with the spirit—and when that only brought the weeping on afresh, she said he would see her again, unmarred, unchanged, when the sepulchres were opened on the Last Great Day . . . He listened, looking up at her with reddened eyes, seizing her hands now and again, opening her hands and pressing kisses on her fingers, her palms, her wrists. Whether it was these kisses or her slow and quiet talk that eased him, she did not know; but after a while he ceased to weep and sat up and sighed.

She straightened then and saw that most of the visitors were gone. Large patches of the filthy floor lay open, and the reddish light of sunset fell upon them in blurred squares; the little lamp was kindled again in the middle of the table, and the food had been taken out of its packages. But this is the sixth day of the week, she told herself. This is a holy day, and when the others have all departed, we of the fellowship of the dark will sit down together, and the elder Moyses will break the bread, and we will have our Eucharist. She thought also of the quarry-slave, and wondered whether he would live through the sunset and knew that if he survived as long as that he would certainly be with them still at dawn. I will take the Body and the Blood of our Lord to him, she thought. I will crumble the bread into bits, as if I were about to feed a bird, and I will pour the wine drop by drop between his lips . . . And it was only after she had thought all these things that she thought also how perilous it was for Probus that he should be here so late, that he should pass in so small a company between the guards that stood at the door. "Oh, but you must go now, they will look at you closely if you stay any longer," she said, rising and drawing him toward the door.

It was easy, it was mercifully easy. A Guard was standing at the entrance, and to embrace under his alien look was unthinkable. She could only make the sign of the Cross upon him and say that blessed formula which negated all need for invention: "May the Lord Jesus walk with you and cause His countenance to shine upon you and give you peace." Nor was she forced to know and suffer a moment when her eyes beheld him for the last time; others moved in between her and him before he had passed through the entrance—a woman with a basket, a stooped old man carrying a child. As she went back toward the table, she heard little knots of them saying here and there that the games were to be held the week after next, with lions and elephants. A week, two weeks, then, she thought, but numbly, being far too weary to care.

And before she had come to her place at the table, the voice of the elder Moyses was lifted up in prayer: "We thank Thee, God, through Thy beloved Servant, Jesus Christ, whom in these last times Thou hast sent us as Saviour and Redeemer and Messenger of Thy Council, the Spirit who comes from Thee . . ." She tried to see the countenance of the Lord in the light of the weak flame that burned in the middle of the table, but, try as she would, she could see only the face of the tortured quarry-slave. She found the place reserved for her at the board, she sat down and tried to listen, but her glance kept flying to the shadowy corner where he lay, and that, too, was useless, since she could see only the outlines of the cloak she had given him. "He's alive, he seems a little better," said Constanta in a whisper. And it hardly mattered that he, like any of them, might be given to the beasts in a week or two: it was as if he had been delivered completely out of the grasp of death. Peace had descended upon her, the peace of the fellowship of the dark; and she smiled at the elder Moyses as she reached for the bread and the wine, the Body and the Blood of the Lord.

Chapter 33

EVERY NOW and again the Confessors confined in the Urban Prefect's prison had given signs that fear was among them still. None of them, saving only the elder Moyses and the quarry-slave, had ever felt complete confidence in the steadfastness of his own heart. In the middle of the night somebody would utter a shriek because he had dreamed he was being trampled under the feet of elephants. Somebody else would spring up in the middle of a quiet conversation and beg to be assured that he would smother from the smoke before he felt the fire. Novices and catechumens had given vent to their fright in fits of screaming and hysterical weeping; women had driven their nails into their palms and pulled the hair from their heads in their struggles to master the daemon fright; and three or four of the men had gone apart and bruised their fists and foreheads by grinding them against the rough stone of the wall. Nor were there very many in the dark common chamber who had not thought at least once, how, when the final hour came all these half-mastered terrors would leap up again, strong enough to make some of the weaker children of Jesus recant and thereby taint and mar the sacrifice which all of them were bringing to the Lord.

And yet that night when the summons came—when the tribune appeared with the expected and yet unbelievable scroll of names in his hand—there was not one shriek, there was not so much as a whimper among those who stood below. The only sound in the prison was the clink of their chains as they turned to look at him—that and a profound sigh. He paused after each of the sixty names for a protest or a recantation; but he was given no answer save the one that came at the end of the list, when all of them said in unison, as if by prearrangement: "We are here and ready to confess the Name." And the weeping that broke the long stillness which followed his departure—he had made it plain to them before reading the list that they would have an hour or so to make their farewells—was not the wild weeping of the terrified, but the gentler weeping of those who knew that they must now leave this chamber, their last and dearest home on earth, must depart from the companions who had seen their spirits in utter nakedness and loved them nevertheless.

The elder Moyses said almost at once that he thought it would be seemly to have a Eucharist. There was only a little bread left from the gifts of the evening and only a little wine to mingle with the water—enough, perhaps, for each of the sixty who had been called to have a drop and a crumb, but not enough for the rest. So the sixty came to the long table in the middle of the room they were, according to the reckoning of the world, the least of the fold, weavers, tanners, cobblers' wives and such—and the others sat on the floor in a vast, uneven circle around them, sustaining them as best they could, looking steadily into their faces with earnest, streaming eyes. The known words of the service, uttered into breathing stillness by the warm Semitic voice, flowered with a new significance. Many of them wept afresh when Moyses said "In these last times"; and some of them could not refrain from whispering along with him: "Take, eat, this is My Body, given for you . . . This is My blood, poured out for you. So often as you drink this cup, you commemorate Me. . . ."

But the white wing of tenderness and exaltation that had borne them up drooped a little in the interim that was left to them between the service and the setting forth. The time was at once too short and too long—too short for real communication, too long for the sustaining of ecstasy. There was something harried about the last handclasps, the last kisses; they could not find the one revealing sentence to write to husband or child or mother on the little scraps of papyrus held out to them. And when the tribune returned and called their names again, when the flock was actually divided and those who were to see these walls no more were herded near the great door that opened onto the street, they felt forlorn and alone. The torches—some twenty torches streaming in the wind—were painful to their tender eyes, and some of them stumbled over their fetters and fell up the stairs.

But it was better, it was much better when they had been loaded shoulder to shoulder into the carts. The sundered fellowship was mended again; they smiled nervously at each other; they reached for each other's hands. If they were forced to face the inexorable knowledge that the dreaded thing had actually come to pass, they were also relieved of all responsibility.

Henceforth they were, as the blessed Ignatius had said long before, mere "wheat to be ground in the mill of the Lord"—passive, committed, rendered up. And their exhaustion—for each of them had labored according to his talents in the vineyard of God—their exhaustion transformed this passivity into a kind of blessedness.

Not that they were unaware of what went on around them. All the way to their destination—the subterranean chambers under the Flavian Amphitheater where they were to spend their last hours on the earth—they kept asking themselves and each other why it was that they had been given such a heavy guard and taken off so late at night. The riddle was solved when one of them happened to see the mounted tribune pull his horse to a sudden stop and peer apprehensively down a black street. They were afraid—the servants of the Beast were foolishly afraid that others of the congregation would rush out of some dark alley to rescue the captive children of the Lord. They had never heard of the reproof laid upon Peter in the grove above Jerusalem; nobody had ever told them that those who take up the sword will perish by the sword. And this misunderstanding on their part bore good and gentle fruit: since the Guards feared violence and met no violence, since all of them would be able to return to their homes or their barracks without so much as a bruise, they were considerate, they were even kind.

The tribune and the young centurion who were left behind with them once they were herded into the chambers below the arena showed a consideration that bordered on delicacy. It was these two who were charged with the unpleasant duty of making the prisoners presentable for the games, and they explained that it was necessary for the Confessors to bathe and anoint themselves, that a bath had been prepared for this purpose in the adjoining chamber, that they might rest confident that nobody would peer at them while they were about their ablutions, that the women and the men might bathe separately if they wished, the women first and the men after, since the consuls who were giving the spectacle had asked that some consideration be shown for Christian modesty. The Guardsmen went so far as to assure them that nobody would be expected to appear in the arena tomorrow in any outlandish or pagan garment: there would be no impersonation of Hercules or Apollo or Diana or the dryads or the nymphs of the sea. It was the will of the consuls that each of those who were to go to their deaths tomorrow should go decently clad: clean white tunics of heavy linen were to be found on such-and-such a bench in such-and-such a corridor, and, since they had been provided for the occasion by the eldest of the Vestal Virgins, even the shortest of them would fall well below the knee. And finally, seeing that the men and the women showed some signs of distress at being parted from each other, they added that all of them would be reunited in a larger chamber, where they would be left in peace for the remainder of the night.

Among the last of the women to step down into the lukewarm pool made ready for the condemned was the lady Paulina, the wife of a cobbler of Istrus, according to the Urban Prefect's list. Terror—a private and stifled terror—had kept her standing long in her nakedness against the damp stone wall. Since the time they had been ordered out of the carts, each of the Confessors had felt the coming back of fright, some when the curve of the Flavian Amphitheater showed dark against the red and smoky sky, some when they started down the final stairway, some when they passed under the lintel of the last entrance, narrow, like the door of a tomb. If she had been spared until this moment, it was not because she was more steadfast than the rest; it was only because all other thoughts gave way to a vast and mournful wondering as to what had become of the quarry-slave. They had dragged him out, suffering as he was, to the questioning last night; they had taken him away, and where they had laid him she would never know. When the fresh night air had streamed across her cheeks during the ride in the cart, she had thought of his feverish cheeks; when the Guard had struck the fetters from her ankles, she had thought of the load of iron still dragging at his bruised and broken feet. And now, standing on the brink of the pool, with the reflection of torch flames on the water before her, with the novice Constanta sitting on the edge and gazing anxiously up into her face, she thought for the first time of herself. My body, my naked body, she thought—this is my flesh, and I am to wash it, I am to make it as clean and fair as I can for tomorrow, for my death. And the realization that this same flesh, which she was about to lave and anoint, would be rendered up to the teeth of the lions or the feet of the elephants could not be suppressed, was so terrible to her that she could not step down into the pool, and could keep herself from shaking only by bruising her back against the rough stones of the wall.

"Are you sick, my teacher?" said the bony little novice, lifting her peaked and pitiful face. The face itself seemed to have fallen away in the last week. The eyes were enormous, and so childish and unguarded that it was possible for Paulina to read them completely, to see at a glance that the child really thought she suffered from some physical affliction, could not have entertained for a moment the belief that an instructor of novices, the wife of a deacon, could be afraid.

"A little—in the pit of my stomach. I wonder—" she had said it unanswered to the distracted girl at least a dozen times in the course of the last miserable hour—"I wonder where they took the quarry-slave."

"Maybe he's dead, my teacher. Maybe our Lord Jesus, seeing how much he has suffered, took him to his everlasting peace."

"I wish he could have had a decent burial."

"Maybe he will. Maybe somebody will claim him. Maybe he's not even dead."

How much of me will be left for Probus to claim tomorrow? she asked herself. And though she had lingered at the side of the pool far too long, though the shadow of anxiety was growing stronger now in the big, starved eyes, she simply could not bring herself to step down and in. Redeemer, Saviour of the poor in spirit, she prayed, this is the hour of my greatest need—reveal Yourself to me. Walk over these waters, in and out between the heads of Your condemned daughters, as you walked toward the fearful fishers on the Sea of Galilee . . . But there was no vision, there was only a commotion somewhere near the middle of the pool, there was only a general cry that Flavia Corbia, one of the oldest of the women, had been seized with a cramp in the water. It was that and only that which made her leap in.

Yet once she had immersed herself in the pool, she could think only of how good the lukewarm water felt to her grimy body, how gently the soothing warmth of it was untying her knotted muscles and penetrating to her aching bones. By the time Flavia Corbia was taken care of and the greasy locks of the novice Constanta had been rubbed back to their old smooth brightness and the lice had been picked out of the hair of several of the others, she herself was clean—clean and deliciously moist and heavy with an irresistible yearning for sleep. Her drowsiness was such that she forgot where she was. When she stood in the dank corridor, slipping the fresh tunic over her head, it seemed to her that she was in her own upper chamber in the house on the Aventine—she had to remind herself not to step backward and let herself down on the side of the bed. And when all of them, the men and the women, were gathered together in the appointed place, when she had settled herself on a heap of sacks, with the novice Constanta to her left and the wall to her right and the boy who was afraid of elephants at her feet, a grey mist spread before her, and she did not know where she lay. As in a dream she reached out and found a hand in the darkness, but did not know whose hand it was—Probus's or her lover's or the fever-dried hand of the quarry-slave.

How long she lay there, trying in spite of the overpowering numbness to pray or meditate, she could not tell, though there was a way to measure the time: it could be measured by songs. In one of the other chambers under the arena the gladiators who would open tomorrow's spectacle were feasting and singing the songs of their homelands—wild songs out of Thrace, melting and indolent songs out of Africa, earthy and tender songs out of Hispania and Sicily. One of the Confessors—she grieved a little that she could not recognize him by his voice—chanted against that music, countered that music with words from the Gospels, bits of the service, prayers to the Lamb of God that takes away the sins of the world. She knew he intended his music to drown the other singing out, and she tried to isolate it in her own consciousness—into her drowsiness she saw his performance as a kind of wavering white line drawn above the scarlet and purple of the music that came in bursts and surges through the wall. But, sinful as it was, she could not maintain the pattern: before her eyelids came down, the sounds had merged—the shining white thread was woven in and out among the other

414

varicolored filaments. And when the effortless tears ran back over her temples and her hair and wet the empty sacks, she wept for all—the gladiators as well as the Confessors—those who had long since perished and those who were yet unborn—for all transitory flesh, all spirits kindled and put out from the beginnings of time even unto the end of the world. . . .

During the night she wakened only once—but wildly and with a start—because the novice and the boy who lay across her feet were both miserably weeping. One terrible actuality after another closed around her heart: tomorrow was the appointed time and tomorrow was almost here; she would never know what had become of the quarry-slave; she would have to live out the rest of this as best she could alone, since it was plain now that her Lord and Redeemer would not manifest Himself. It seemed to her then that her spirit had been shrunken and drawn back into the narrow confines of herself, where it hunched, sick and rigid, over her fright. It seemed to her that the novice and the boy would have to weep the night away uncomforted—she could not force a word from her tightened throat, she could not bring herself to put out her frozen hand. But then, from the other chamber where the gladiators made their feast, a single voice sang drunkenly in a Thessalian dialect of a father's pride when he beholds his first-born son, and the old brooding sorrow over her own childlessness dissolved the icy terror and set her free.

"What's the matter?" she said in a whisper, still listening to the distant song. And, since she loved Constanta the more tenderly of the two, it was to the boy that she addressed herself, it was toward his wet, thin, beardless face that she directed her groping hand.

He grasped that hand and covered it with kisses, and she knew that the kisses were audible in the sighing, uneasy quiet: the novice stiffened against her side.

"Nothing, really, nothing, my teacher," he said.

"Then go to sleep, my son in Jesus."

The bony little body of the girl actually drew apart from her. "And you, my daughter, can't you sleep, either?" she said, brushing her lips across the new-washed hair.

"Not while he keeps crying about the elephants. And it's foolish—he doesn't even know it's going to be elephants."

He dropped her hand and sat up. "I'll see that I don't disturb your sleep with any more of my foolishness, Constanta," he said in bitterness. "It's well enough for you, you're sleeping on our teacher's shoulder. But I'm down here by myself."

And if I tell him to come up here to me, she thought, then I am hemmed in on either side, and my rest is gone, and there will not be one more night on earth for me to enjoy the blessedness of sleep . . . Yet, remembering again the agony in the garden, and how the Saviour had asked whether those that were with Him could not watch with Him one hour, she took his hand again and drew him up and spoke to them both in whispers, turning her face first toward one and then toward the other, nourishing them equally with the abundance of her tenderness. She told them how easily the blessed Blandina had died at Lyons, how nobody felt anything after the first moment, how surely He who had given Himself up for them to be crucified would come to sustain them in the final hour, how she would keep close to them as long as she could . . . After a little, both of them lay quietly against her, the boy's head on her shoulder and the girl's head on her breast. And, heavy as they were and fearful as she was to sleep lest in her sleep she move and waken them again, she did not see the first greyness of the morning. I have had a husband, she thought, and a beloved, and two children in Jesus, a son and a daughter; and, thinking this, she slept.

There was the morning to be lived through, and they dealt as best they could with the heavy hours. On waking, they had found themselves too wan, too drained to immerse themselves in meditation. It was better to sit in a circle, shoulder to shoulder, and repeat the same prayers over and over in a muted chorus, clinging to the words when it was impossible to lift the weary spirit to the level of the meaning. It was better not to gaze at a single face, to raise one's eyes instead to the one shaft of light that poured into the middle of the chamber through an iron grating that opened on the street. There were four of five among them who had fallen into the ecstasy during the night. Their voices, shrill with conviction, rang above the monotonous murmurings of the others; and one of them, a pale and consumptive scribe from the office of the Privy Purse, who had said scarcely a word during the whole of his imprisonment, broke the ritual every now and again to hold intimate and plaintive converse with the Lord.

There were other interruptions also. One of the gladiators, a thickset, self-conscious Sicilian, came in bearing a basket, with a Guardsman behind him, and said in the stiff manner of one who has memorized his lines that his fellows over there in the other chamber, having been given more food than they could possibly eat, were sending these loaves and these figs to the Christians and joined him in wishing them all good courage and an easy death. He could not sustain their thanks; his heavy, sullen face broke into scarlet patches and he departed in haste, colliding with the Guardsman and slamming the door.

About an hour after he had gone there was another diversion: something fluttered like a bird through the sunny grating—a long, folded strip of papyrus addressed "To those who this day will most gloriously confess the Name." It was signed by the elder Cornelius, and it had probably been his hand that had forced it through the grating, since he had never been one to send other men on dangerous errands. It told them all, very simply, that, if they looked to the middle rows of the last tier directly to the right of the imperial box, they would see the children of Jesus who had come to be with them and to bear witness to their crimson confession, and that some seven of these would be wearing yellow cloaks and would so seat themselves that the yellow cloaks would form the pattern of the Cross. Before the coming of the letter, many of the figs and several of the loaves had remained uneaten, since there were those among the Confessors who could not bear the thought of coming into the arena with food in their bodies—it made a gross and hideous thing of death. But now even these were cheered a little and took their share out of the gladiators' basket, and asked each other how high the middle rows in the last tier would be, and whether it would be possible to see a signal or the expression on a face.

After that, they did not return to the murmurous, convictionless praying. An old man told how in his youth he had walked in a pine forest in Dalmatia, seeking converse with his Saviour, and, receiving no word or sign, had turned back heavy-hearted because of the coming on of night. "And do you know," he said in a querulous old voice, "when I turned again, I saw footprints—not mine, but Another's—very narrow, very delicate, in the needles fallen from the pine trees. And here and there—I have never spoken of it before, but I beg you to believe me—here and there, toward the front of the sole, there were traces of blood." Others among them were also approaching the awaited ecstasy. An old Armenian slave-woman said she could see her five dead grandchildren standing in the beam of light that fell through the grating. A brawny cobbler could make out in the shadows the cloudy shape of a ministering angel. And a faded seamstress, one of the virgins of the congregation, could no longer hear the tender and solicitous questions of those around her—every earthly sound, she said, was drowned out by the whirring of onrushing wings.

It was in the midst of her dazed and quiet discourse that the door swung open. The tribune had come again, brisker and more authoritarian after his night's sleep. He held two lists of names and only two, they told each other, smiling: one for the lions and one for the elephants, and therefore it was certain that none of them would be consumed on a fiery cross. Standing outside of the uneven circle in which they had sat to pray together, he read the names of those who were to go to the lions; and after each name he paused long, waiting as he had been directed to wait for a protest or a recantation, and this pause after each of the names was burdensome and dragging to the spirit. There was one hysterical moment when the beardless boy who stood beside the lady Paulina was called to the lions; but it was later explained that the series of gasping sounds he made were only out of relief that it was to be the lions instead of the elephants; and the irony of that drew from all of them, even from the tribune, a burst of laughter that must have bewildered the gladiators on the other side of the wall. There was no need to read the rest of the names—the remainder were for the elephants, the young officer said. As they could hear, the gladiators were going now, and the ones for the lions would be next, and the ones for the elephants would come after that. The whole spectacle, he conjectured, would take something more than four hours. If there was anybody in the assembly who wished to recant . . . All of them, sitting on the floor and staring at the floor, slowly shook their heads. Well, then, he said, somebody else, the Master of the Games, would come for the first thirty when the hour was up. Stern and white in the face, he strode away, but turned at the door and, like the embarrassed gladiator who had brought the figs and loaves, wished them good courage and an easy death.

It was in that last hour of waiting—a harried hour, broken into meaningless segments, since the Master of the Games came almost at once and divided the flock for the second time and led the first thirty through a dozen empty, lightless rooms and down innumerable narrow halls—it was in that last hour of waiting that Paulina began to ask herself whether she would live to make her crimson confession: something was amiss inside her, something was wrong with her heart. The pauses, the fluttering irregularities, the long and astounding stillnesses between beat and beat made her so short of breath that her talk with her son and daughter in Jesus was constantly being broken by gasps and sighs. Nothing that she said had any continuity or high significance. She talked for a purpose—at first to make them forget that with every step they were drawing closer to the moment and the place, and afterward to drown out the noises: the clank of the chains that were pulling the platform up into the arena, the blast of the trumpets, the muffled brazen clanging of shields and swords. She said whatever came into her mind: how Saint John the Divine used to confer with the deacons with a pet pigeon on his shoulder, how the Lord had risen hungry out of His sepulchre and asked on the morning of His resurrection for a bit of fish and a piece of honeycomb; how Mary of Magdala had lived in retirement for many years with the mother of the Saviour, how the most blessed of all the winds in Jerusalem—the wind that came upon the parched country in the evening—was called "the wind of God." They listened, fixing such luminous and wondering eyes upon her that she saw at last that they thought her on the verge of the ecstasy. "But you mustn't think me more blessed than I am," she told them, and could tell them no more, since the Master of the Games was ordering them to move on again, since they were moving ahead numbly, like sheep, down a black hallway toward a pillar of light.

"What's that? What's that?" said the novice Constanta, drawing back catching with clammy fingers at her teacher's hand, and staring into square pit that lay under the pillar of light.

"Nothing, nothing." She detached her hand, she had told herself that i would be better not to touch either her son or her daughter in Jesus: thei control over themselves was too likely to be shattered by touch. "It's onl the place where the platform comes down—the platform they're about t take us up on. It'll be down in a little while, it works on four big chains you'll see, darling, you'll see." But she could speak no more, she could no even turn to the boy to show him that she was equally concerned for wha ever thoughts of unclaimed bones and charnel pits had come into *his* head. Her heart had gone utterly wild within her, not at the sight of the hole in the ground, only at the realization that in a very little span of time that platform would come down again, would carry them up into the arena, where it would be necessary for her to look toward the middle rows in the upper tier. And how can I look for them both? she asked herself. Which one shall I look for, miserable sinner that I am—my lover or my helpmeet in the Lord?

Those who were already borne up on the wings of the ecstasy were speaking behind her. One voice said over and over, "Jesus, Jesus, beautiful Jesus." A woman—a modest, quiet farmer's wife—was confessing her sins aloud: berries stolen in her childhood, yearnings after the harvesters who had helped her father in her youth, a passion for raisin wine. The consumptive scribe was no longer plaintive. With his arms upraised and his veined eyelids quivering, he told them all in the words of Saint John how he saw a new heaven and a new earth, for the first heaven and earth had passed away; how there was no more sea; how the New Jerusalem was descending out of heaven, prepared as a bride adorned for her husband; how there would be no more death, neither sorrow, nor crying, neither should there be any more pain: for the former things were passed away. . . .

"Step back, step back!" said the Master of the Games in consternation, as if their lives were precious, as if it would be dreadful if any one of them were bruised by the descending platform. "Watch the platform! Watch the pit!"

And even while she smiled at his solicitude, she was solicitous—in spite of her determination not to touch the novice or the lad, she was drawing them back, she was holding their hands until the creaking block had settled into place and the clanking chains were still. "Come," she said, "it's firm, it's perfectly firm, you see," and she stepped onto the heavy planks and drew the two of them after. There was room for the thirty, there would have been room for a hundred, and it seemed to her that the crowd of them would look shabby and pitiful, coming up into the light in a huddled mass, all clinging together in the middle of the square. "Wait a moment, let us arrange ourselves," she said to the Master of the Games in a voice that was courteous and self-possessed in spite of the breathlessness and the sighs. And she turned, as she had often turned in the classroom to establish order for a visiting undershepherd: she turned and set her fellow Confessors in even rows, and asked them to lift up their faces. "We'll look more steadfast to our brothers and sisters who have come to share this hour with us," she said, "if we stand apart like soldiers and hold up our heads."

Yet it was not easy for her to carry out her own instructions. The brilliance of the light through which they moved so dazzled her that she had to shut her eyes; the crazy fluttering within her and the jerking of the platform on its upward journey so unnerved her that she could barely refrain from reaching for Constanta's hand. But it's too late for all that now, she kept telling herself. Your fingers are cold, and life and love are finished, and all of us will make a better crimson confession if we resign each other, if each of us goes to what awaits him at the top of the vent alone . . . "How is it with my teacher?" said her son in Jesus in a whisper. "Well, well, perfectly well," she told him, blinking against the unbearable brightness and trying to smile. But surely, she thought, he can see that I am dying of fear—I'll never live to see the lions and the middle rows—my fright will burst my heart before I set foot on the sand.

And yet she stepped onto that sand—white and unruffled and newly spread for their blood. She saw it, stretching out in one vast, glittering oval under the sun, and was strangely conscious of the miracle of sight. A little altar, myrtle-wreathed and smoking, stood at the edge of the vent: Roman humanity had set it there for those who wished to recant—and that was foolish, foolish—but the green of the myrtle and the smell of the incense were wonderfully sweet. The Master of the Games told them to walk straight forward; and she was able to walk, though it seemed to her that she was standing still—the palms and the purple and the garlands and the roses and the stern, just, melancholy face came floating toward her on a tide of sun-drenched marble and shattered light. Once and once only she glanced to her left—the cages were there as she had guessed they would be, small and far away, at the very end of the arena. They looked strangely unimpressive, like the wooden packing cases which the sculptor used to put together in his yard near her house on the Aventine, only there were gratings on the front, and behind them tawny mass and nervous movement—flick of a tail, glint of an eye in the dark. "Look up, look up at the yellow Cross in the middle rows," said somebody behind her. But how can I look? she thought. How can I look when I do not know which one of them to look for, when I cannot tell which one of them in my gone life I truly loved?

"Turn to the left now and walk forward about twenty paces."

And so they did, like obedient children, until the novice Constanta, moving a little ahead of Paulina, caught sight of the lions. Under the avid eyes of fifty thousand, she stopped and turned. She raised her skinny fist and thrust it into her mouth and flung herself against her teacher's breast.

"No, no, no," said Paulina. But it was good, it was blessed, and why she had sought to avoid it, why she had renounced the nourishing sweetness of human touch in the hour of death, she did not know. Let us touch each other, she thought, let us love each other. Your need begets my strength, your fear begets my courage—I have no talent except a capacity for love. And now that the bony little body had flung itself against her, she knew that the crazy fluttering within her would soon subside and cease. Passing her hands over the poor thin back, feeling the warm and mortal breath coming and going against her neck, breathing the sweetness of the new-washed hair, she knew that the wine of the New Testament was flooding into her heart, laving it of every trace of terror, filling it utterly, even to bursting, with love.

"Be of good heart, dear sister in Jesus," said the lad whom the Lord had delivered from the elephants.

But there was no need for that—the novice had already straightened and turned toward the cages. Clutching her teacher tightly by the hand, she lifted her head and walked forward, and nothing, not even the roar that issued from one of the dark boxes and the other earth-shaking roar that answered it from the tiers of seats, could halt her steady progress across the unruffled sand.

But let it flow gently, let it flow quietly, dear Jesus, Paulina prayed, let it not bear the heart out of my body utterly, as long as I can be of use—this tide of love. Stop, stand, wait a little—we have come our twenty paces and the Master of the Games would have us stop and stand; and that is well, and I should look about me—I will be the stronger, I will serve the better if I know how it will be. Six cages, six lions. Two at a time they will let them out, since there are only two keepers in blinding-bright corselets to open the cages—and it will be long, and blessed are those who will be the first to go. The ones of us who stay until the end—our spirits will be sorely tried and our bodies will be unfathomably tired. White sand—a veritable desert of white sand between us and the cages, and halfway across it a bluish shadow —first, indefinable coming on of the ecstasy?—a bluish shadow in the shape of the Cross. And all around the vast curve of the marble barrier, a row of Aethiopian archers. When we are mauled and bleeding, will they dispatch us with merciful arrows? No, no, a childish thought, as childish as taking the hole at the bottom of the shaft for a charnel pit. The arrows are for the lions—no bow will bend, no arrow will cut through the air until the last of us is gone. And here, beside me and around me, my brothers and sisters, whose spirits I have seen in their nakedness, whose faces I will behold in death. Beautiful upon the mountains are the feet of them that preach . . . Beautiful upon the sand are the bruised feet of them that wait for death . . . But gently, let it flow gently, my Saviour, so long as their eyes are upon me and their hands are clutching at my fingers. There will be time enough in the long last hour for the mind to reel and the heart to burst with the wine of the New Testament, the wine of love. . . .

The barred fronts of two cages were opened and fell forward with a clang. Sinewy, ponderous, and kingly even in their half-starved state, the lions issued out of the dark and shook themselves and merely stood, perplexed by the shouting, dazzled by the sun. But how are they to know we are intended for them? she asked herself, passing her arm around the back of her son in Jesus. Somebody should have smeared us with blood.

"Saviour, my Saviour, my beautiful Saviour!"

Brave voice, brave human voice lifted up shrill and high to goad the bewildered lions, to make the shaggy power bestir itself and come. But it begot nothing but the swish of a tail and the twitch of muscles in the tawny back and side, and one of the Confessors fetched up out of the uttermost depths of his spirit an audible and shaking sigh.

"Come quickly!"

"Amen. Even so come, Lord Jesus!"

"I am the Resurrection and the Life. Whosoever believeth in Me shall not perish. . . ."

"Verily I say unto you, today you shall be with Me in paradise. . . ."

"My teacher," said Constanta, "when will they come?"

"In a moment—as soon as—" But she could not finish, because the lad had come round from beside her and was standing before her, had quite unaccountably taken her face between his two cold hands and was staring gravely and sweetly into her eyes. She thought with wonder that she had never known how beautiful he was—wide-eyed, open-mouthed, his dark curls falling loose around the whiteness of his cheeks and brow.

"Give it to me now, my mother in the Lord," he said, smiling. "Give me the kiss of peace, but not on the forehead, on the lips."

Holy, holy, holy! Almost as holy as the sanctified and delectable wafer passed between the parted lips in the sunny basilica of an Easter morning— mortal mouth, mortal kiss, kiss of peace, kiss of farewell. But gently, let it flow gently, my Redeemer, even though he departs from me as I knew he must, even though he is racing headlong toward the leaner of the lions, on and on—twenty paces, thirty paces over the sand. And now, as he traversed the faint blue shadow of the Cross, the lion crouched—crouched and quivered and waited with his ears laid back, unbelievably still. One prodigious bound, and a roar drowned out by the shouting from the seats. His prey was under him when he came down—dead?—mercifully dead? Perhaps, perhaps, she told herself, clinging to Constanta. For all the snarling and the pawing and the licking, her son in Jesus did not move. There was an instant when the sight of the bulky head reared up with a severed arm between the teeth made her turn aside. But almost at once she turned back again, thinking: Lord, let me look with steadfastness upon the ruin of his flesh, some life may stir in his poor body yet, he yet may turn and look at me . . . Then the shouting subsided and the lion walked away, dragging the mangled arm before him, dribbling a line of blood along the sand. And what remained was bearable—bloody and distorted, the arm gone and the flesh of the face partly licked away—but dead, blessedly dead.

And now they were going, a little group of six or seven of them led by the consumptive scribe was going, each of them known to her in the last fellowship—one she had held in her arms during a paroxysm of fright, another had told her in his homesickness about his cottage and his barn, for another she

422

had bound up an ulcerated ankle—and each of them stopped to embrace her, to set on her lips the kiss of peace.

"We know, dear sister in Jesus, why it is that you wait."

"Blessed are they to whom the Lord has given strength to abide steadfastly unto the last."

"Sit beside me at the table of our Father in heaven tonight."

"Cover me if you can if the lions so deal with me that I am unseemly."

"Thanks, thanks."

"The brightness of the Lord has already fallen upon your face. Surely He is about to manifest Himself."

No, no, I will never see my Saviour. All through my life, I never turned to see my Saviour. My back was set against the entrance into heaven, and the light of heaven fell only faintly from behind me over my shoulder, and the flowering thorns of my mortality held fast to my feet. I never knew the Lord—I only knew His children, whom I could see and kiss and touch: sweet, transitory shadows passing before me through His muted radiance, moving across my narrow band of time and space. But they were beautiful beyond all saying, these His children · tender and giving in their lives, strong in the final fellowship, and splendid in their deaths. . . .

Splendid in their deaths, and hastening to meet them. If she saw the ultimate agonies of the first seven who had gone forth—emaciated body hurled down under the unbelievable leap, torn side, dissevered foot—she saw it all between the crowded heads and shoulders of those who were the next to go and could not go without farewells. If there were screams, snarlings, avid shouts, they came to her through the words of her brothers and sisters:

"Kiss me, Paulina."

"Kiss me also, dearly beloved in Christ, and bless me."

"We will die quickly, let not your heart be greatly troubled for us."

"Christ is among us, He will sustain us, He will fold us securely in His peace."

She kissed them—all of their cheeks were cold and some were salt with weeping. She kissed their brows and their cheeks and their lips, and now the wine of the New Testament had so wrought with her reeling heart that she could not clearly see their faces or remember their names. Each of them was all of them. In every mouth, she kissed the mouths of all the children of Jesus, yes, and the mouth also of the embarrassed gladiator who had come this morning with the loaves and figs, and the sad, shamed mouth of the patrician woman who sat appalled behind the marble barrier, and every mouth that she had ever kissed or yearned to kiss. The veil of time was rent for her then by this sweetness, so that her kisses went out to those who already lay beneath the earth and those as yet sealed up within the womb of time, waiting to receive the kiss of life and know the kiss of death. "Bless me, my sister," said each of them, floating toward her out of the mist and the brightness. "Yes, surely, surely," she whispered, and made the sign of the Cross, and wondered of a sudden why it was that she had been making it with her left hand.

Because of Constanta, of course, she told herself. Because my novice has the fingers of my right hand imprisoned in her icy little fist and thinks out of mortal love to endure with me until the last—but she is frail and young and gently bred, and I will not have it so. Four lions are ranging now among the dying and the dead, and others of us are going forth, and more will go when these are gone, and if she waits with me until the end of this she will have to pick her way through mangled trunks and strewn entrails and puddles of blood. . . .

"Have you forgotten me, my teacher? Have you been carried away from me by the ecstasy?"

"No, my daughter in Jesus, I have not forgotten you. I will never forget you," she said. "You were born to me out of my empty womb in the last days of my life, and I nursed you in darkness with the milk of my spirit, and you must believe without question that I will love you until my death and beyond my death. Only, it is clear to me now that I must wean you. Kiss me and go with those of us who will be setting forth in a moment—"

"But why must I go now, my teacher?"

"Because my heart is weighed down with my care for you. Because I cannot turn to the Lord, troubled as I am with mortal tenderness. Because I am your mother in Jesus, and you are my child, and the child obeys the mother. I never had a child to obey me in the world. Obey me now, and show me that the Lord has truly given me a child."

Wide eyes, obedient, assenting. Thin arms, stranglingly tight around my neck. Sweet breath, breath of a child, smelling of figs and sleep. Sweet breath, last kiss. Farewell, Constanta, daughter in Jesus. Farewell, Flavia Corbia, old grandmother—so, so, take my little one by the hand and lead her from me. Draper's son, weaver's daughter, carpenter from Dyrrachium, vintner from Salmantica—having taken leave of you each, I can now possess you all. Farewell, farewell. Yet let it flow gently, gracious and beneficent Father. The wine You have poured out for me has swollen my heart to bursting, and I must linger while they hasten, I must remain until the last of these is dead. . . .

Watch, watch, never take your eyes from that which comes to pass on the clotted sand beyond the faint blue shadow. Watch, watch—Could ye not watch with Me one hour? Six lions now—dear Jesus, grant my little one the newest and the swiftest. No, no—he is for the farmer's wife—in one wild plunge, he crushes out all dreams of harvesters forever. My little one must take the sated one, the sullen one, his eyes sick and sleepy, his yellow beard all stiff with blood. So, darling; stand, darling; wait, he is coming. Not to plunge—oh, Jesus, Jesus!—to snarl and strike—heavy paw clawing at the cheek—and she gone down, she thin and whimpering on the sand.

424

Yet turn, turn, since these last seven also are departing, and they are worn with waiting. Farewell, my fellow-watchers, strong and steadfast unto the end. Courage—good courage and an easy death.

Yet even now I cannot go forth from this little hollow I have made with my feet. Even now, while the last of these are dying, my feet are caught in the flowering thorns of the world. One earthly fulfillment, one consummation yet remains—there are the middle rows in the upper tier, and one face and another face—look for them soon, look for them now before the ecstasy outshines all sight. Husband, is that your rough red beard still showing through the unfolding veils of brightness? Beloved, can I see them still beyond these shimmering mists—your loving and tormented eyes? Together, standing together? The bounty of God passes all comprehension that the two of you should stand together. Fade then, and merge into the all-annihilating radiance. Be lost to me forever—and forever repossessed. I cease to love you, and I love you both. In all good conscience and sweet peace at last, I love you both, dear children of God.

She turned then and walked steadily out as far as the bluish shadow. She would have passed it without looking up, if it had not been that the corpse of Constanta lay slantwise across it, the head thrown back, one skinny arm flung up, one rigid finger pointing to the sky. How strange, she thought, it is as if she wanted to show me something. It is as if she saw the messengers of God descending in a cloud of glory out of heaven, and wanted to make sure that I would see them too . . . Sated and sullen, the beasts circled around her, but she did not look—her eyes were fixed upon the dear, dead flesh, the body and the blood. "Cover me if you can," one of the Confessors had said, "if I am unseemly." But nothing that was human was unseemly to her now, and when she bent it was not to cover the crushed and bleeding chest, it was only to press her mouth against the cold, unbreathing lips.

She started back from the foul, warm blast of a lion's breath. Look up before he comes again, she told herself, seeing him padding off to nuzzle at a mangled corpse. Look up, she wanted you to see . . . And there, against the blinding blueness of the sky, was the substance that had cast the shadow—a massive wooden cross set high above the carnage, and on that cross the dying quarry-slave. They had hung him up because he could not walk to the lions. They had cast a length of purple over his naked shoulders and set a thorny crown upon his head. And she knew with a kind of holy wonder why it was that she had yearned over him in prison: her earth-bound sight had found in his face the face of her crucified Lord. He smiled upon her and spoke, but she could not hear him for the shouting. The noise from the tiers was loud and hateful now—they were tired of the chase, they were sick with the blood, they wanted it finished, and she was the last. He spoke again, the same words over and over, and she strove to read them on his dying lips. She did not have much time—the tawny beast was crouching and quivering—but she made out enough to know that he had

425

said, "Inasmuch as ye do it unto one of these least my little ones, ye do it unto Me."

The crowd fell silent for the last magnificent leap, and when her body went down under the weight of the lion, there was no more shouting, there was only a universal sigh. He left her seemly enough—her garments still about her and only a little blood on her thighs and chest. Her face was in the shadow, darkened by the overhanging body of him who had watched with her until the last, and he and he only knew how it was with her, whether she had gone forth in peace, assured that her sins, which were many, were forgiven, since she loved much.

Chapter 34

SIXTY-ONE CHRISTIANS died that day in the first spectacle provided for the Roman populace under the persecution launched by the Emperor Decius— thirty by the teeth of the lions, thirty under the feet of the elephants, and one on a cross. The two consuls who had served as donors of the games, paying alike for the gladiators, the acrobatic interludes, and the beasts, were men of culture, with strong propensities toward Stoicism. They had seen to it that there was no tawdry glitter to obscure the stark awesomeness of the sacrifice; they had sat through the carnage, erect and expressionless in the donors' box, like statues of themselves; and, if they left their places early, it was not to hurry to a banquet, since neither of them could eat—it was only to talk with the Master of the Games, to reassure themselves that he meant to conduct himself as he had promised he would, staying at the edge of the charnel pit until dusk, behaving with sober courtesy toward those who came for the bodies, doing what he could to find such as were asked for, and under no circumstances accepting from the mourners any gift or fee.

It was a surprising fact, remarked on by all the public slaves responsible for the condition of the Flavian Amphitheater after the games, that every one of the bodies of those who had died for the Name had been claimed before dusk. The bearing of those who came to ask for them—"I am looking for a man of about fifty, with two moles on the nape of his neck . . ." "A woman, young, with reddish hair, three months pregnant . . ." "A boy, fourteen, very thin, the right arm gone" —the bearing of the mourners was quiet, controlled and impressive, so much so that, though the times were hard and gratuities were scarce, nobody remembered until afterward that notes should have been taken, that descriptions of important members of the congregation could be turned in at the Urban Prefect's office for a good price. There was a hushed air of exaltation about them all, though most of their eyes were red with weeping. They sought their corpses among the other dead as one might seek for a dear face in a living multitude; and when the mangled flesh was yielded up to them, they received it without horror, they took it to themselves with love. It was noted, too, that some of them stopped to concern themselves in their searching with that which was certainly no affair of theirs—to cover the indecently exposed body of a female acrobat who had fallen from a rope, to close the glaring eyes of a dead secutor, to open the clenched hands of a Thracian retiarius and lay them crosswise on his chest. And the claiming of the bodies was executed with so much order and dispatch that afterward, when the pit was closed, the slaves attached to the Flavian Amphitheater began to say among themselves that the brotherhood of Jesus was plainly organized as well as any Roman camp: there was no telling what they might be able to do if they could clear sixty-one bodies out of a crowded charnel pit without the slightest confusion in a matter of a couple of hours.

But actually the members of the congregation had no sense of orderliness. They had never been more heavy-hearted, more baffled, more desperate than they were in this business of claiming and burying their dead. Since the martyrdom of the blessed Fabian, there had been no real shepherd among them: the elder Novatian, at odds with the others over the question of the lapsed, had retired to a cell and given himself up to recurrent ecstasies; the elder Moyses lay in prison; and the elder Cornelius, though he was fearless and swift in the execution of every task that came to his hand, shrank from assuming authority. Before he could make up his mind what the proper procedure was, twenty members of the congregation had gone to the charnel pit where ten would have served. If a man could claim three bodies, as he told himself afterward, pressing his fist against his splitting brow, he could just as well claim six—six could be laid decently, one against the other, in the same cart. Nor did the sense of wild crisis subside once the bodies were taken from the pit. The most urgent problem was the problem of the graves—where they were to bury their Crimson Confessors they did not know. Three weeks since, an edict had gone out from the imperial council to the effect that any man, woman, or child found henceforth in the Christian catacombs, or in any of the Christian cemeteries that lay on the outskirts of the City, would immediately be arrested and taken to the Urban Prefect for questioning. No graves—sixty-one bodies and not a grave—so they had said on their slow progress down the ramps, once the spectacle was over, once the scarlet testimony of faith had been written on the sand. And if the graves were eventually found—if one member of the congregation had a garden where he could bury ten, if another could take six, if the cousin of another could provide for twenty behind a villa on the Appian Way—it did not seem to them that they were dealing effectively with the crisis, but that miraculous solutions were being given to them in the hour of their utmost weakness by the merciful hand of the Lord.

The elder Cornelius had a garden within the City—so he said in private to the deacon Alypius—a garden surrounded by a wall of myrtle hedge grown so tall and thick during this time of troubles that nothing could be seen from any side of it, not even funeral torches by night. There was room for six graves under the poplars and the cypresses, and if he could have two or three able-bodied brothers in Christ to help him—no, not Marcianus, Marcianus had already arranged to accompany those bodies to be sent to the Appian Way—if there were any others that anybody could think of at the moment—no, never mind, he could find the proper people himself. Whom they should bury there he would not presume to say; that the land which was his should be sweetened with the flesh of those who had died this afternoon was enough and more than enough. And yet, if the deacon Probus should care to lay the body of his yoke-fellow in Jesus there, he would have every right, since he had always labored hard and unflaggingly and more or less without honor, and was just such a man as would never raise his voice to ask that a grave be made nearby, where he could visit it in his loneliness. And that poor, pitiful cousin of hers, so shattered that he could scarcely stand on his feet and yet insisting that he should see the burial as he had seen the crimson confession—who would think of dragging *him* to some distant clump of sepulchres ten miles out on the Appian Way? Who would think of exposing him, marked man that he was, to the troops of Guardsmen that would certainly be patrolling the highways tonight?

It was duly arranged then that the body of Paulina, wife of the deacon Probus, should be among the six that were brought to the house of the elder Cornelius; and the Lord was gracious, the Lord was kind, there was no confusion—by the hour when the inhabitants of the City were rising from the evening table, every body was where the members of the brotherhood had meant it to be. The atrium of the elder Cornelius, long neglected, was scrupulously cleaned. Six dining couches were brought into it and made ready with white linen to receive the dead; and a tall iron candelabrum, filled with new wax lights and garlanded with the palms that signified martyrdom, was set up, behind the row of couches prepared for the dead. Women—within half an hour the house was crowded with women—washed and anointed the bodies and strewed them with spices and dressed them in white cloth. Men—artisans, patricians, scribes from the government offices— bore the burdens from the bath to the atrium and hurried back to the bath again to cleanse the marble of the blood. And when these tasks were done, there was no silence—in all the rooms, the voices were lifted up as one voice, singing the Kyrie: "O Christ, Lamb of God, that takest away the sins of the world, have mercy upon us. Have mercy upon us and grant us Your peace."

During the larger part of the waning evening, Favorinus had remained on the second floor of the house. The deacon Probus and the young deacon named Alypius had brought him back with them from the Flavian Amphitheater and had found him a place to stand in a corner of the crowded banquet chamber; but he had wandered out, he had stood in the middle of the room with visitors milling about him; and somebody else—he did not remember who—had taken him by the hand and led him out of the room and up a flight of stairs into the empty library of the Cornelii. Why they had chosen to lead him away—whether it was because some rite too sacred for the eyes of the uninitiate was about to be performed, or out of mercy, because it was plain that he suffered and should be given the right to suffer alone—why they had taken him up the stairway like a tired child, he did not know. They had seated him in a chair, before a massive table; and as they had left him so he had remained, with his arms laid out in front of him and his forehead on the wood, through sunset, through dusk, and into dark. He had not risen when the rumble of the cart that bore the bodies had sounded in the street. When the bearers had come with their burdens through the hallway beyond the open door of the library, he had heard them pant and sob, but he had not lifted his head to see.

"O Christ, Lamb of God, that takest away the sins of the world . . ." Some twenty times now they had sung it, and he waited for the second "Have mercy upon us," always louder than the first, always torn out of them in urgency on a kind of wail. He waited, breathing the dark and ancient smell of the wood under his face, and in the span of silence between the final "peace" and the new beginning, he let out his suspended breath on a long and audible sigh. And it was unfitting that he should have done so, that he should be sitting as he was, with his arms flung out across the table and one side of his face exposed, since an ageing virgin of the congregation had stopped on the threshold with a lamp, her withered countenance blurred in a cloud of light. "O Christ, Lamb of God . . ." He tried to move, but he could not really move, he could only make a futile gesture with the fingers of his numbed right hand. "I have brought you a lamp," she said, and set it well away from him on the corner of the table, and made the sign of the Cross above him and was gone. "Have mercy upon us . . ." A yellow reflection of the flame wavered in the depths of the polished brightness, came as far as his mouth, so that he kept breathing upon it, beclouding it with mist. "Have mercy upon us, and grant us Your peace."

The flame of the lamp moved sidewise intermittently in a recurrent draught. That was because the door downstairs was being opened to let in the visitors, the ones who were coming to take their leave of the six who lay in the atrium on dining couches draped in white cloth; and for an instant it seemed to him in his dreamlike state that *she* was in the vestibule to greet the guests, was offering consolation to one of the mourners, had taken somebody by the hand and was leading him through knots of solemn whisperers to the feet of the dead. But no, no, no, he thought, pressing his forehead against the wood. They had carried her body up the stairway, they had laid it on the floor of the bathroom down the hall and washed away the blood. She lay in the atrium with her hands put crosswise on her chest over a palm leaf—she was one of those six whom the visitors had come to see. And, if she was to be seen at all, she must be looked at quickly. A grave had been made for her, a grave was being hallowed for her by chanting voices rising from the back of the house, and in an hour or so she would be shut up beyond all seeing in that closed grave. But he could more easily believe that he could go to the house on the Aventine and find her under the hanging lamp, smiling and picking the lint out of her loosened hair—he could more easily believe that he could journey back to the villa in the Campagna and find her sitting at the window with a dusty cloth between her hands than that he would find her lifeless body on a couch in the atrium, with wax lights burning at the head.

Somebody stopped in the doorway, indistinguishable in the shadow. Somebody with a plate. A plate, with bread and a brown slice of meat upon it, came into the area of light in a workman's leathery hand. "No—no—I couldn't possibly eat," he said. Who could swallow food, having seen what he had seen this afternoon? Yet that seeing had been strange—he pondered it while the footfalls of the retreating workman sounded down the hall— that seeing had taken place always and only at the very front of his head. Not once, not even when the quicksands of unconsciousness had trembled beneath him and Probus had dragged him back from them with a hard, admonishing hand—not once had he received into the inner chambers of his mind the stark enormity. Scraps of it, yes—she embracing and sustaining the others, she wandering alone and dazed among the circling lions, she looking toward the upper tier with exaltation blazing white in her face, she turning unsurprised to see the crouching beast and steadying herself with one thin hand against the Cross. Scraps and patches, but never the whole of it, never that she had been given to the beasts in a public spectacle, never that she had died for the Name in the Flavian Amphitheater, never the imponderable total of the unendurable truth.

Grasp it, master it, hold it. Say to yourself: She is gone from the earth, like a light put out, like a dragonfly trampled on. Say she is dead and go downstairs to the atrium and see and accept her dead . . . He strove with it, panting, until he could strive no more, until there was nothing in his consciousness but the wavering, misted bar of light reflected in the wood, until he found himself thinking vaguely that they were not singing anymore, that, for all he knew, they might be bearing the bodies out to the graves . . .

Then suddenly there was a brightness falling across the polished top of the table from above, and he saw that it was Prisca carrying a lamp, standing between the table and the open door. She was flushed and breathless, incongruously alive in her rumpled white tunic, with small beads of sweat on her round white brow.

"I was bringing you a light."

She had said it in a whisper. Now that the singing had ceased, he knew that the house was filled with whispers. None of them could take upon himself the blank finality—all of them were whispering as if their voices could awaken the unhearing dead.

"I was bringing you a light, but somebody else must have thought of that." Her eyes, strangely veiled—could they possess some childish insight into his guilt?—her eyes made no claim upon him, stared fixedly down at her own feet. "I suppose I ought to go—they need me downstairs. Anyway, I know you'd rather be alone."

"No, wait." Surely she would offer to lead him—uncertain that he was, confused and ignorant of their proceedings—through the little crowds of whispering visitors to the dead. Unless they knew, unless he wore his secret in his ravaged eyes. But when he brought himself to look at her again, he saw nothing equivocal, nothing evasive in her candid, milky face. "Tell me, is there anything going on downstairs? Any sort of holy service, I mean," he said.

"Oh, no, nothing. The first prayers are over." Her pride in her knowledge rang through her whisper. "There won't be anything now except the service at the grave."

"When will they be buried?"

"Soon now, the elder Cornelius says. I imagine it'll be in less than an hour."

Oh, God, then I had better go at once, he thought, straightening and grasping the edge of the table. I must look at her this one last time and touch her hand—if they have not guessed what there was between her and me, if I am permitted to look and touch. For how can I know how it will be with me if I do not see her now, and waken afterward in the black nights that are to come, and think: If I had seen her face, if only I had seen her face. . . .

"Did you want to come downstairs, my master?"

"Yes, yes, that's what I was thinking of." But suddenly fear was upon him, unstringing his knees, and he could not rise.

"I can take you to the atrium if you want to see the Confessors."

"Prisca—have you seen her?"

"Oh, yes, I saw her. I helped them make all the Crimson Confessors ready for the mourners. They let me comb her hair because I'd know exactly how she wore it."

"Is she—"

432

For the first time her big clear eyes shone full upon him. She smiled—she actually smiled and shook her head. "No, my master, the lion hardly did anything to her at all. There was only one bad mark, and that's covered with the palm leaf. You'd never know a lion touched her—she looks exactly as if she were asleep."

She went a pace before him, holding the lamp in her left hand and leading him along with her right, drawing him on by a fold of his dalmatica —a bitter recollection of the lost white face haggard with jealousy because he and this little one had stayed so long in the springtime woods kept him from taking the blunt and childish hand. From the stairs he looked down on a multitude of heads in the hallway outside the atrium—women's heads, decently veiled, men's heads, solemnly bowed; they were moving and the movement made him dizzy; he closed his eyes and felt as if he were standing in a small boat on a pitching sea. "It's sad that you're so alone," she said, waiting on the step below him. "If only my lady were here to comfort you . . ." To take my rain-drenched body in her arms, he thought, to take my hands and hold them warm between her breasts . . . Then he knew with a start that the child was speaking not of his beloved but of his sister, so utterly forgotten, so lost to him that he would feel no surprise if he were to find her lying among the six downstairs with a palm across her chest.

"Open your eyes. You mustn't fall, my master."

To fall, to faint, to give voice to any of the vague and equivocal phrases that kept floating to the margins of his consciousness and forming on his lips—that would be to betray her, to confess to these grave whisperers: With me and my cousin Paulina it was as you must have guessed . . . But there was no curiosity in any of the turning faces. If some of them who stood in the hallway started back, if a wide path was made for him and Prisca, it was only because the visitors were startled by the lamp in the hand of the little slave.

Open entrance to the atrium, stark, flanked by ungarlanded columns of yellowish marble. Somebody—the elder Cornelius, Olympian, bearded—standing in the doorway and raising his hand. In interdiction? In public condemnation? To bar the unforgiven pagan seducer from the forgiven dead? But he only said, "Your cousin Paulina lies on the third couch from the right, Favorinus Herennius," and, making the sign of the Cross with his lifted hand, he moved aside from the doorway.

Black candelabrum festooned with palms at the far end of the atrium, and in front of the candelabrum, on either side of it, the line of six white couches, utterly still, appallingly still. Three from the right—white face, oh, shut, white face! You lied to me when you said she looked as if she were asleep. Dead, dead, unreachable, dead!

"Did you want me to come with you, my master?"

"No! I'll go alone!" he said in a voice that must have made the whisperers in the hallway turn and start. And now he could not think about them

433

anymore. If he staggered, if he made some audible sound of grief, he could not care. Quickly, quickly he went in unreasoning hope toward that unstirring thing in front of the dark and wind-stirred palms, as if distance alone had taken it out of his reach, as if, by standing close to it, bending over it, addressing it, he could make it rise. "Paulina," he said, coming so close that the frozen rigidity of the soles of the feet pressed against his knees. But the hands were so still that they erased even the recollection of touch; the mouth was so pale and stern that it blotted out even the remembrance of her smile.

"Behold," said one of the other mourners, crouching over the knees of one of the other dead, "behold the fruits of the Lord's first reaping."

Behold, he thought, staring down upon her veined and untrembling eyelids, behold the fruit of my living heart! There was a time when she smiled and spread her skirt and walked with her mortal hands held out in welcome before her, but then I came, and now she is still. Sweet words and hurrying breath poured inexhaustibly from her parted lips, and now there is nothing there, not so much as could mist the surface of a mirror or stir a mote of dust. She thought, she dreamed, a million subtle and various images succeeded each other in the high, bright chambers of her brain, and in my yearning I destroyed them all. There is nothing but dreamless darkness now behind that cold, unstirring brow. . . .

Unable to bear the blankness and looking up from it, he knew with a shock that he had come to the atrium at a time reserved for those who were chief among the mourners. It was plainly a mother who crouched sobbing over the knees of the boy whose right arm was gone; it was a wife who rocked and chanted above the body of the death-sallowed workman; it was a sister whose withered fingers tried futilely to interlace themselves with the unresponsive fingers of a martyred virgin of the congregation; the girl who sat staring into the face of the consumptive scribe had plainly been his beloved; the lad who knelt at the feet of the broad-bosomed woman of the Campagna was surely her child. Ah, God, what am I doing here? he asked himself. Why am I not with the other lesser ones in the hallway? Why am I here among these few who have been given time to make the bitterest of the farewells? What will be said of her and me, since I am standing like a chief mourner at her feet? And where is *he*? Where is *he*?

"I am the Resurrection and the Life," said the wan and sorrowful sister, looking up at him shyly.

"In my Father's house are many mansions," said the boy from the Campagna, patting the soles of his dead mother's feet.

The wife stopped rocking for an instant and nodded gravely. The girl who sat beside the scribe fetched up a heavy sigh. And then there was some movement behind the candelabrum that stood guttering near *her* head; the palms shivered and the flames wavered and *he* issued forth, his left hand

434

dragging at his beard, his eyes red with much weeping but prepared to look again upon his dead.

He walks as in a dream—he does not see me. What shall I do? Flee him? Turn and flee? But before he could turn he felt the bloodshot eyes upon his face, and could not look, could not sustain the awful, naked question in the eyes. The hand that grasped the beard was tightly clenched; the muscles in the hairy arm were tense; the reddish hair along that arm began to move of itself, each separate hair bristling like a living thing.

"Favorinus Herennius—" said the deacon Probus in a hoarse whisper.

He could not answer.

"Favorinus Herennius, believe me, if I had known you were here I would not have come out from the colonnade—"

"Yes, my cousin—"

"I'll go back to the window. Take your leave—take your leave of my wife—say farewell to her as you see fit, alone and in peace."

The other mourners also vouchsafed him his final moment. One of them covered her face, one of them turned aside her head, one of them closed his eyes. In silence shaken only by the loud throbbing of his stricken heart, he moved up until he stood above the palm leaf that lay across her chest, he closed his eyes, he bent and laid his lips upon her hand. "Forgive me," he said in a whisper; and suddenly the knowledge that if man had not been created mortal she could have forgiven him, could have held out her hand to him kindly, kindly, from some trailing constellation, some inexpressibly beautiful cloud of light—suddenly that knowledge so worked within him that he wept aloud in the wet and gasping sobs of a child, and reeled blindly back toward the decorous murmurings in the hall beyond the door.

"Think of the risen Christ! Think of the opened sepulchre!" said somebody in a whisper, touching his elbow.

"God will comfort you, the Saviour will be with you," said the little Prisca, and led him toward the stairway, this time by the hand.

The room was intolerably oppressive to him now, dark except for the meager light in the corner of the table, smelling of musty scrolls and death. He stopped at the edge of the table and wrenched his hand out of her soft, warm grasp. "Pull back the curtains!" he said in a peremptory and hateful voice. "Let in some air!"

"But it's turned chilly outside, my master."

"Do what I tell you! Pull back the curtains!"

"But you will be sick tomorrow morning—"

"Do what I tell you!" Let me be dead tomorrow morning, let there never be another morning for me! "Pull back the curtains and leave me to myself!"

And yet when she was gone and the draught was blowing at his back, heavy with the smell of the new-turned earth of the graves, he experienced such disintegrating horror as he could never have known if she had remained. Sitting again in the chair still warm from his body, resting his forehead against the wood and closing his head away from the world in his folded arms, he kept seeing the reddish hair rising along the bony arm, kept seeing the naked question leaping into the bloodshot eyes. And now his sense of guilt was so heavy and immediate that it was as if he had murdered her, as if he had torn the life out of her body with his own hands . . . Sickness and shuddering and the smell of his own sweat, the sweat of his horror. Darkness and his forehead aching violently against the wood and a purplish wheel of light spinning against the blackness of his brain. Time passing, and the darkness nibbled at by the faint yellowishness seeping between his arms and the wood, and the silence encroached upon by rustlings and murmurings and whispers . . . And he knew without lifting his head that the multitude assembled on the floor below had roused itself, was going out with the bodies to the graves.

Sighing, he pulled himself up and went to look out of the window, standing to the side of it, against the wall, because the light behind him fell through the window and cast a wan square of yellow on the grass; and he felt now that it would be a desecration even for his shadow to lie across the hallowed earth below. Lights were borne first into the black and leafy vista that lay before him—twelve streaming torches, reddening the poplars and the cypresses and the six narrow trenches with their uneven edges, lighting also the uplifted faces of those who bore them, some white with exaltation, some shining and raw with tears. Thereafter came the dead, carried on stretchers and covered to the chin with linen. Twice he started and stepped in spite of himself directly in front of the window, thinking that this was she—but he could not be certain. Most of the corpses looked alike in the wavering light at this distance; upon all of them had been stamped the pale, dull anonymity of death. And, since he could not tell which grave it was into which she was being lowered, he looked distractedly from grave to grave. "Dearly beloved, we are gathered together . . ." said the resonant voice of the elder Cornelius, rising above the wind in the leaves and the sound of the sobbing. But he did not listen. The stone rolled away from the door of the sepulchre, the solemn Traveler met at twilight on the road to Emmaus, the many mansions, the sea of crystal, the palm-strewn streets of paradise—let them comfort themselves with such matters if they could He did not believe in them, he could never believe in them. He could only rest his back against the wall and take the stroke of her death full, full upon his living heart.

And, having done so, he saw little reason to stand at the window and watch the tender and holy magic which they were weaving out there in the garden. It was more fitting that he should find some symbol of his own, some stern and pitiless ritual to mark the moment when they covered her with earth. He turned and walked back to the table and stood above the lamp and, when he conjectured that the moment had come, he put out the flame between his thumb and finger and stood unbreathing in the total dark. Stood so until all sense and thought were drained away, until the purple wheel of light spun wild again before his eyes, until a roaring sounded in his ears—and then sank down into the chair again, telling himself that there had been at least one instant when he had merged himself with his beloved, had known her nothingness, had shared a portion of her death.

He fell asleep to the surge and fall of voices: now that the dead were put away they felt no need to whisper anymore. Low voices rose in solemn converse in the atrium below him; a few uncertain voices still broken with weeping were borne up from the garden; other voices, strong with reassurance, said Christian farewells in the vestibule and trailed away down the midnight street. In his dreams, he did not completely detach himself from the place and the hour. In his dreams, he knew that she was dead and that her brothers and sisters in Jesus Christ had seen her buried and were departing from the house of the elder Cornelius, in whose garden they had made a grave for her and would raise a stone engraved with the legend: "At everlasting rest in the Lord." But his dream multiplied those who had come to look upon the martyrs a hundredfold. He saw them issuing from the house by the thousands; he saw them streaming out of the vestibule in an orderly, unbroken procession through the deserted City, across the outlying fields, into the distant woods, to the very edges of the vast expanse of the sea. They walked in darkness, but they bore their radiance with them. Each of them carried a little lamp, and the accumulated brightness of all those lamps made an arc that swept the sides of the overhanging mountains and stained the edges of the sky with gold. Their voices were low and seemly, but the multitudinous aggregation of their voices was loud enough to drown the roar of waters breaking on the shore . . . They are lingering late, they are speaking still downstairs, he told himself in his dream. But when he wakened the place was utterly quiet—so quiet that he would have thought himself forgotten, would have believed that they had gone away and left him in a deserted house if it had not been that the corridor outside the doorway was drenched with yellow light. Somebody had kindled all the wax lights, all the lamps, even the smaller ones in the niches in the halls.

After a little while there were footfalls. They came sturdily up the hallway and then grew slower, less confident as they approached. It was Prisca—he knew that it was Prisca before she appeared on the threshold with her head down and her hands behind her back. Her tunic was neat, and her hair was glossy and orderly. Now that the dead are buried, he thought in his bitterness, she has taken the occasion to press out the wrinkles and brush her hair.

"If the elder Cornelius hadn't sent me I wouldn't have come," she said, less in apology than out of wounded sensibility—she turned her head in his direction but would not fix her eyes upon his face. "I told him you were sick, I told him you wanted to be alone, but he wouldn't listen. He says it isn't good for you to sit up here by yourself. He says he wishes you'd come down and sit with the rest."

"Are there many left?"

"Nobody but the elder Cornelius and the deacon Probus and two of the women and myself. Everything's in order now, and we're having a cup of broth. The elder Cornelius thinks you ought to have some too."

Everything in order—he was wounded by the satisfaction in her voice. Everything in order—he knew that satisfaction, he had felt it himself, returning from the Forum after the final, fiery rites for Celestus Falconius. Everything in order—the table set and the wicks trimmed and the floor swept of every last vestige of funeral greens, yes, and the air itself sweetened with the crisp fragrance of burnt applewood and thyme, lest any hidden corner might still harbor some influence of the banished dead. "Did you scrub out the atrium?" he asked in his anguish.

"Oh, no, they'll probably scrub it tomorrow," she told him in complete candor. "Tonight we only swept it. We were terribly tired."

"And they want me to shove food into my stomach?"

"They only thought you'd better have a cup of broth. The rest of us are eating. And everybody, even the deacon Probus in all his trouble, is anxious about you and wants you to eat."

"Very well, I will eat then," he said, "for the sake of Jesus Christ and the elder Cornelius and the deacon Probus and any of the virgins of the congregation who may still be sweeping the contagion of reality out of the atrium, I will eat. Go down and I will follow. And I can walk by myself, there's no necessity to take me around by the hand."

It was to the banquet hall that she led him, going a good distance before him; and everything there was as he had imagined it would be. A candelabrum crowned with four wax lights had been set in the middle of the table. At one end of the long board, a fresh white linen cloth with the folds still showing upon it had been spread. Six orderly places had been laid out on the cloth, with silver spoons and cups and unwrinkled napkins; and a large silver bowl, filled with water and crowded with the first green herbs of the season, gave off the scents of thyme and marjoram. He did not dare to look at the figures seated around the end of the table: he hated them too much. He loathed them for their hunger, for their decorous quietness—how could they sigh and settle themselves within this closed and glowing room—and she in the dark, she lying in the vast, raw, open dark?

"Here is the place set out for you, Favorinus Herennius," said the voice of the elder Cornelius.

He seated himself and knew that *he* was there, directly opposite, on the other side of the board, with nothing but the bowl of herbs between. I will not be shielded from my avenger by mounds of marjoram and thyme, he thought, and took the bowl and set it aside and forced his eyes to focus on the hairy arm, the chapped red hand.

"You also, little sister," the elder said, plainly trying to distract the attention of the others from the strange behavior of the guest. "Sit down, sit down, we have no need of service. Everything's on the table, we can serve ourselves."

Broth ladled out of another silver bowl into his cup. A plate of bread—his hands were numb, he almost dropped the plate of bread. Butter, cheese, a sprig of water-cress—oh, veined and mortal hand that carried the sprig and the rusk from the plate to the lips, how is it with you now? And, glancing from the hairy arm to the hateful food, hearing their voices speaking all around him of the lapsed, and the strange comportment of the elder Novatian in this crisis, and the wreath of myrtle that somebody had laid day before yesterday on the tomb of the blessed Fabian—hearing their voices and the jangling of their voices like a cythera wildly out of tune, he knew that he could not live out more than an hour of this without going raving mad, that the world was intolerable to him, that somehow, somehow he must tear himself out of the world. . . .

"Eat a little broth, Favorinus Herennius," said the wan virgin of the congregation who sat at his right.

He looked up and saw her face, faded like old parchment and netted over with delicate wrinkles. But what is *she* doing here? he asked himself. I thought I saw her lying in the atrium with the dead. But even as he stared in utter amazement, he knew that it was only that she bore a marked resemblance to her martyred sister. Yes, yes, he told himself, taking a rusk of bread and tearing it to shreds, and flattening the shreds into white masses on the tablecloth, she was the one who tried to interlace her fingers with her sister's fingers. How can she eat? How can she sip the broth?

"Late as it is," said the elder Cornelius from the head of the table, bending forward and looking past the plump, round-eyed face of the second virgin of the congregation in order to catch the attention of the deacon Probus, "late as it is, and much as I hate to trouble you with it in your sorrow, there's still this matter of the money in the catacomb. . . ."

He did not hear the rest of it. At the mention of the sorrows of the deacon Probus he had summoned up all the depleted powers within him, had forced his glance to move along the hairy forearm, over the stooped shoulder, over the open and shaking mouth to the bloodshot eyes. Red—fiery red with weeping—and the pupils black, like coals burnt out. And suddenly, as he looked, those eyes grew conscious of his gaze and did not turn aside. Somewhere in the depth of that expiring fire something stirred, like the fabled phoenix rising again in the ashes; the parted mouth breathed out a sigh. And it was as if the deacon Probus had given him a signal, had said to him: Brother, our anguish is the same, we know the grave.

"The money in the catacomb . . ." the elder Cornelius said again, as if the look that had passed between the two of them had been a palpable force, had torn his sentence apart.

"But I told you twenty times that I was going to look after that," said the voice of the deacon Probus, rough with exasperation and weeping. "I have the key, I know the way, I'm staying at your house tonight. It's a settled matter. Before you're out of bed tomorrow, I'll be gone."

"But I've been thinking, my brother in Jesus—" the elder's words fell mildly, slowly, like separate drops of balm poured out for the relief of pain— "I've been thinking, considering everything—the danger involved, and what you've seen and suffered today—I'd rather you'd stay home and sleep, I'd rather go myself."

"You?" It was bitter, it was almost derisive. "Yes, you, by all means—you can easily be spared, seeing how it is these days with all the shepherds— Fabian in his grave and Moyses in prison and the saintly Novatian so shocked with the behavior of the lapsed that he has to renew himself in solitary meditation—it's three weeks and more since anybody but an angel has been permitted to intrude himself into his cell. Yes, you, of course—no other! The only elder we have left—you're naturally the one who should expose yourself."

"Then wait until tomorrow. We'll call a council and settle on another." The plaintive voice of the faded virgin broke tentatively in. "But I must have some money. Forty-two more came in tonight from the outlying towns to try to hide themselves in the City—forty-two, and all of them hungry, and in the confusion of the crimson confession I doubt that more than ten of them have been fed. Tomorrow at noon they will be sitting on my doorstep, since they are assigned to me. And I have nothing to give them—believe me, my father, nothing, not even a loaf of bread."

"Not only that," said the plump, white virgin. "What about the widows and orphans of those who confessed the Name this afternoon—can they be expected to wait? And the oil and the spices for the dead—they were bought in secret and on credit. Eunice has only until tomorrow to bring the payment to the Greek who let her have them. Otherwise, she'll be informed upon."

But that's ridiculous, thought Favorinus, pressing his forehead against his knuckles. Why should anybody go for money into an interdicted catacomb at such a time as this? I have money, I'll go now and wrest some money out of the old woman up on the hill, I've done it before . . . And he opened his mouth to tell them to name their sum when he was stricken dumb by the unbelievable actuality: he had no money, no money at all. The house of the Herennii would be interdicted, too. Whether it was even inhabited now, he did not know. If his mother was still in the palace, she must be living behind drawn curtains—unvisited, alone, hounded by spies who lay in wait for his return, driven into a panic by every rustle in the garden, every knock at the door. Her iron boxes and her money-bags—her gold, her silver, the titles to her tenements and her splendid properties would all have been confiscated by the State. The mother of a traitor, the wife of Celestus

Falconius, the proud rejector of the matrimonial pretensions of the Decii —she would scarcely have been treated with imperial consideration. She could call herself fortunate if she had been permitted to remain in her palace on the Palatine with some of her furniture and a few of her slaves . . . He closed his eyes and saw her now as he had seen her last—her silvery veils thrown back, the pinkness of her scalp showing between her sparse, disordered curls. And this lesser sorrow worked strangely upon him; this lesser sorrow so wrought with him that two meager tears were driven out of his eyes and fell among the flattened bits of bread on the cloth.

Pity, disintegrating Christian pity—and all of it misplaced: the elder Cornelius was looking solicitously at him from beyond the candelabrum and the bowl of fragrant herbs; the withered virgin at his right was offering him a fresh napkin for his eyes. Fools, fools, do you imagine for an instant that I would weep for *her* like this? he thought, covering his face with his hands and shaking his head. These niggling tears are for my mother and my empty house. I would howl, I would rip your decorous silence into bits, I would drive you in terror from your rusks and your cheese and your broth if I allowed myself to think with pity of my dead. . . .

In the closed darkness that he had made for himself, he heard them stirring and sighing. They were pushing their silver cups and spoons away; they were rising, as she would never rise; they were thinking of their beds and their herb-sweetened linens—and she pillowed on the crumbling earth, and she closed up forever with corruption in the dark . . . "My brother in Jesus," said the voice of the elder Cornelius, coming from behind him now, addressing the deacon Probus over his head, "if you see anybody standing about near the gate of the catacomb tomorrow—anybody, even a child—don't go to the gate. Turn back at once, I charge you as your father in Christ, I charge you solemnly, in the name of God."

"Yes, my father." But there was no conviction in it. The voice was as dull, as weary as the burnt-out eyes.

"May the Lord Jesus walk with you, and cause His countenance to shine upon you—"

"You also. Leave me a little bread and wine set out for breakfast. Tomorrow I may eat—I couldn't eat tonight."

And then, when there was no longer whispering or rustling or the sound of footsteps on the marble floor, he knew that all the others, save only the deacon Probus, had departed from the room, that he and the deacon Probus were sitting face to face in an empty chamber, together and alone at last. And, though his heart knocked furiously in his chest, he did not rise to follow the others. Terrible as it was that the two of them should confront each other, it was fitting that this was so, seeing that their anguish was the same, seeing that they knew the grave.

Yet silence was more intimate, more perilous than speech. And, taking his hands away from his face and encountering only lowered eyelids and a thin, set mouth, he knew that they must talk of such casual matters as two could discuss without ever looking into each other's eyes. He sighed and shifted a little in his seat. "Will you try to sleep?" he said.

"No, scarcely." The voice implied that the question had been foolish. The chapped red fingers beat impatiently upon the cloth.

Shall I stay with you then, my brother in sorrow? he thought. Shall I sit with you here while the others lie folded in scented linens? Shall I keep watch with you while the first night wanes and the whiteness of morning breaks for the first time across the unsodded surface of her grave? But he knew that his presence in the silent banquet room was worse than useless. Only one bond could make a fellow-watcher endurable at such a time as this: the bond of love. Whosoever did not love—they had known it in their hearts, all these good Christians who had risen and said their blessings and taken themselves upstairs—whosoever did not love the deacon Probus, remaining with him at such an hour, could only give him pain. And who loved him? Who had ever loved him? Not Cornelius, not his fellow-deacons, not the virgins of the congregation. Only Paulina, only the dead . . . And, staring down at the hairy hands, raw and ungainly in the light from the candelabrum, it seemed to him that the Christian fellowship, or destiny, or blind chaos moving purposeless through time and space had done so monstrous an injustice here that any decent heart must cry out against it, yes, even the heart of him who had robbed this pitiable being of his only love. That the deacon Probus should bear the burdens and never receive the rewards thereof—who would kiss him when he came back from his wretched journey, who would look fervently into his shifting eyes or take his stiff and unresponsive hand?—that he should suffer and be given no balm—it was an injustice not to be borne.

"My cousin Probus," he said haltingly, since it had always been difficult for him to utter the name, "about that errand you're to do tomorrow—I wish you'd let me go instead."

The reddish hair along the lean forearm stirred again, moved in the brightness like a living thing. "That's out of the question," said the flat voice after long silence. "The cemeteries are all guarded now. Guards have been known to wait inside the catacombs. Whoever goes tomorrow has scarcely an even chance of coming back free."

"Scarcely an even chance?" So little, so blessedly little? Wild exultation tore like lightning through the oppressive blackness around his heart, and he could scarcely keep the crazy smile from breaking on his face. A Guard in the catacomb? Death waiting in the darkness? Why, take a knife then, take a long, well-polished knife and brandish it—invite the thrust and cancel out all guilt and anguish in an instant—

"An even chance is a generous estimate."

"Let me go, my cousin." The thrill of his hope for deliverance trembled under his words. "Let me go nevertheless."

"Why?"

He felt—he did not dare to see—the bloodshot eyes opened and fixed upon him. "Because I stand in need of it," he said.

"To atone for something?" The question was so completely bled of passion that it wakened neither shame nor fear. And yet he could not answer—he could only sit staring down at his own locked hands, waiting for the dull voice to fill up the gaping silence. "I have been thinking, my cousin Favorinus," said the deacon Probus at last, "that you should not burden yourself with more than your just share of these things that have come about. If I had a lamb and I pastured it in a barren meadow, and it strayed away into another man's meadow and ate there certain poisonous leaves from a vine, then he that grew the leaves—I suppose in some measure he also is culpable. But I who kept the lamb in the barren meadow—I am the one who is to blame!"

"No, no, never think it, my cousin!" Never bow your head to the rank injustice of blind chaos that made you barren. "She would never have wandered without urging. Never think it, and let me go in your place tomorrow, and never ask me why. Only know that I must, only know that I must."

"And I—suppose I also feel that I must go, my cousin?"

"Then say to yourself: His need is more urgent than mine is, since he has nothing and I have my Lord. If you were guilty—and let whatever God exists bear witness that you are guiltless, wholly guiltless in my eyes—if you were guilty, you have works and prayers and penances with which to cleanse yourself. It's otherwise with me—I have no way to rid myself of this inward sickness, this monstrous burden. What I have seen this afternoon and known tonight will weigh upon me as long as I live. I have no way to cleanse myself except the way of death."

"For all men—and for you also—there is the way of Jesus."

"No, never, not for me. Never deceive yourself with that—it was enough that she should have deceived herself. What I am, I am—and what I am is incongruous, out of tune with everything. For you there are a hundred places in the world, but I have no place left, no place at all—not in my mother's house, not in the houses of the Stoics and the Greeks, not in the Emperor's court, not in the cellar where you sleep—I tried them all, and I know. So, for all these reasons, you must let me go in your place tomorrow. And believe that there is still this much virtue left in me: I will bring you the money if I can. But if I should die in the catacomb, the world and I will lose nothing, and I will have preserved a very good and worthy servant for your Lord."

The hairy hand extended itself, moved toward him across the table, came as far as the outermost of the flattened bits of bread. For an instant he thought that it was about to touch him, and he turned sick with the fear that he would not be able to receive it in love. But it only left a key lying in the midst of the litter, and withdrew again to bring out other things: a piece of parchment—doubtless the map to show him the way to the catacomb—and a little wooden Cross. "Take them with you," the deacon Probus said, rising and stepping back from the table. "The key's for the money-box in the closed niche in the little room. The Cross belonged to Paulina—I have other things of hers, you can keep it if you like—only you'd better wear it under your tunic so nobody'll see. The map—I thought you might want to look at it now to make certain that you understand. I'm going out, but I'll be coming back again, in case there's anything you want to ask me about. If not, don't wait for me, go up and sleep—provided you can sleep. The Lord Jesus walk with you—I'll see that you're wakened—I'm going out—I want to look at the grave."

Chapter 35

THERE WERE two ways of penetrating into the recesses of the Catacomb of Calixtus, both of them clearly drawn on the parchment map in the workman's pouch that dangled over his thigh. There was no need to unveil the wool-muffled lantern to look at the drawings again: all through the sleepless night he had traced them with the tip of his finger, over and over; all through the three-mile walk the two possible routes—one of them neat and angular, the other devious and winding—had hung, together with the image of her lifeless face, before his eyes.

By landmarks on either side of the Appian Way—the ones he could see when utter silence gave him courage to unwrap the lantern for a moment—he knew that he was almost at the end of his journey if he meant to take the more direct and simple way. Not more than a hundred paces from the square Mithraic monument that he had identified in a hasty bar of light, at the end of this grove of ilex trees, less seen than scented in the total blackness that comes just before dawn, there would be an embankment, a sudden thrust of rock, and somewhere in the side of it an oven-shaped opening, not to be seen even in daylight, to be found only by groping fingers, since the members of the congregation had draped it weeks ago with a hanging vine. If he entered by that opening, the rest of his task would be easy. He need only walk down a steep flight of stairs, pass along a narrow gallery, and enter a square cubicle at the end of it, where the money could be found in a closed niche in the wall. And he was sorely tempted to take that easier way, since his stomach had rejected the food he had eaten, since the beating of his heart was erratic with the long walk from the City, since the blackness had become so oppressive to him that he yearned for the instant when he could safely snatch the square of woolen from the light.

But the second way was the one that the maker of the map had recommended "for use in times of trouble." If you continued to walk until the outcroppings of rock along the highway slanted off and fell away, if you passed another grove of ilex and cut at a sharp angle across a barren stretch of stubble field adjoining this second grove, you would come to a sand-strewn wasteland that seemed to have no connection whatever with the catacomb. In fact, there was nothing there but a series of old excavations, deep yellowish excoriations on the face of complete desolation, warrens and burrows and passages that had once led down into a group of sand pits exhausted half a century ago. An enterprising Christian had discovered in some other time of trouble that there was very little distance between the highest of the burrows and the deepest of the galleries in the catacomb, and had connected sand pit and burial place by means of a rough and perilously curving stair. And—as he kept telling himself to argue down his nagging desire to have done with the matter—it would be far safer for him to enter the Catacomb of the Bishop Calixtus by this longer, deeper, more devious journey through the underlayers of the earth. In fact, since a rattling hay-wain approached and came up with him just as he caught sight of the embankment, he did not dare to grope along the rock in search of the oven-shaped opening; and he found himself beyond the stony ledge, with streaks of setting constellations at his shoulder, before he realized that he had missed the place.

Those stars were hidden soon in the black leafage of the second ilex grove. When they appeared again, they seemed to be floating on the edge of a blurred, flat stretch of dark. The stubble field, he thought, and stepped away from the road into the yielding, crackling stuff, holding his covered light aloft, lest the brittle stalks take fire. Twenty paces, fifty paces, eighty paces, and the small dry rods were cutting less frequently into his shins, and the soles of his sandals were filling up—his feet could feel the familiar grate of sand. And now, even if twenty plumed Guardsmen were to rise and spring at him out of the treeless expanse around him, he must unwrap the lantern: there were many entrances into the sand pits, and he must find the one directly in line with a sandstone boulder into which had been scratched three Christian symbols—a dove, an anchor, and a Cross.

He dropped the square of woolen and groped wildly about to find it in the sand at his feet. The ancient female slave who had wakened him and served him his morning meal at the house of the elder Cornelius had warned him to keep his lantern muffled until he reached the upper levels of the catacomb. The air in the deepest galleries, she had said, was so moist that even the strongest flame could not survive it unless it was shielded. He found the cloth and draped the lantern again, allowing only a thin ray to fall across the desolation—greyish sand and scrub and boulders shaped like monstrous tortoises. He stumbled from one boulder to another, bruising his shins, cutting his feet on bits of splintered stone. And quite by chance he found it promptly—he might have looked for an hour if he had not rested his hand on it to steady himself: a piece of sandstone on whose level top were scrawled the three childish scratchings: a Cross, a lop-sided anchor, and a ridiculous dove.

Dark as the open night had seemed to him, it was much darker in the narrow tunnel of the sand pit. The shrouded lantern, scarcely visible outside, shone here like a rising moon, and yet the glow it cast was very weak: he could see nothing in his groping progress but the little patch of sandy ground directly in front of him and the knuckles of the hand that held the light. It was cold, bitterly cold, and always colder. Stretching out his fingers, he felt an icy moisture on the wall; draughts blew at him from intersecting passageways; and a hollow, deep-voiced sound of wind kept reverberating in other corridors above and below. Once, staring into the blackness with heightened concentration, trying to evoke a clearer recollection of the drawing on the map, he thought he saw a light, another crazy subterranean moon reeling about some fifty paces down the hall. But it was lost to him again in an instant, before either terror or mad exultation could take hold on his heart; and, moving his own lantern about, he sighted stretches of drenched wall and standing puddles—what he had seen must have been only the reflection of the light he carried in his hand.

There was a moment when he stopped dead still in a penetrating cross-current of draught, robbed by darkness and his creeping advance of all sense of time and space. According to the map, the stairway rose out of this passageway at a point about half a mile into the sand pit, and it seemed to him that he had already walked for an hour and covered miles. He uncovered the lantern for an instant—the old woman had known whereof she spoke, the light began to fade almost at once—and saw that the flight of steps still lay some thirty feet ahead. But at the foot he stopped again, profoundly disquieted by the realization that he was about to enter the catacomb itself, to grope along a narrow gallery whose walls were hollowed out and crowded with the dead.

How many have they buried here? he asked himself, draping the cloth more securely around the lantern and picking his way up the stairs. Hundreds of them, thousands of them, shoved in their shrouds or their linen bands into the cells of the honey-combed wall—he started down the corridor and felt them at his feet, at his knees, at his arms, beside his face: tier upon tier of the sealed-in dead. All sealed? Securely sealed? He could see in the meager glowing of the muffled light the slabs that stood between him and the things within the crypts: thin sheets of marble, little blocks of tile, scratched with an anchor, painted with a dove. And he realized of a sudden that he was breathing through his mouth with small and shallow breaths, that he did not dare to take this air into his nostrils, heavy as it must surely be with the foetid smell of death.

Turn left, take fifty good, long steps, he told himself. Find the first intersecting corridor that opens on your right, and turn again, and walk without another turn until you come upon a second flight of stairs. You are not stifled, you are not confined. There is nothing to the right or left of you but sealed-up crypts—put out your hand, put out your hand and feel. Putting out his hand and touching softness—it was nothing, it was only crumbling earth—he started and snatched the cloth away and set the lantern at his feet. But that which he saw in the slowly waning light was decorous and beautiful and calm—the crypts all neatly sealed and set in even rows, the corridor clean-swept except for faded petals here and there, the earth-colored arch of the ceiling reaching up, pointing through darkness toward the heavens.

And even when the light went out he felt no fear. He rested his back against the wall, against the crypts, and took a long, slow breath through his nostrils. The smell of the catacomb was blameless and sweet—smell of dark earth, smell of cool subterranean springs, smell of clean, hidden roots and sprouting bulbs and moss. He breathed it, and as he breathed it he thought with wonderment and a sense of blessedness how everything, even the corruption which dwelt with her now, must be finished at the last, how whatever came to pass in that closed grave in the garden of the elder Cornelius must some day come to this: dark, consoling breath of earth, and nothing left but the clean decency of bones. This knowledge was sweet to him beyond any knowledge that he had ever come upon, so sweet that he wept and turned his head and pressed his mouth against the earthy wall. And it was as if she had held the tender sods up to him in her dead hands; it was as if a promise of ultimate peace were growing now, green as a vine, out of her lifeless heart.

A resurrection of remembrance was granted to him also then. Her living image, obliterated for him by the stern, pale corpse in the atrium last night, arose to him again. Groping along the gallery, counting his steps and making his turns in the total dark, he did not even miss his light, he found himself so blessed in the recollection of her changing face, suffused with life, made beautiful by love. He ascended the second flight of steps swiftly, careless of the slippery moss that covered them, and when he saw a light again—misty and far off, probably close to the end of this upper corridor—he told himself: It is nothing, it is only another reflection, before he realised that the flame of his lamp had gone out in the lower gallery some time ago

If that is my death bearing the light, then I must follow it, he thought Seeing her still, seeing her smiling subtly through her blown, brown strands of hair, he quickened his pace. Twice in his going he lost sight of the other lantern and found it again, once around the corner of another passageway, once flickering beyond what seemed to be the angle of a half-closed door. And suddenly the prospect directly before him was lighted with a wan yellow radiance, and was a room—a cubicle, the very room to which the map had directed him: he knew it by the paintings on the whitewashed walls: a lamb, a broken loaf, an amphora tipped and pouring blood-red wine. My death is in this room, he told himself, stopping on the threshold to steady himself, and to reach into his girdle for the knife. Where is the crimson plume? Where is the sword? But the figure that raised the lantern and flashed the light into his face was only Prisca, only his little slave.

If he did not shatter the silence with curses, it was only because he could not permit himself, even in his rage and bafflement, to desecrate the quiet of the burial chamber. He hated her milky face, merry and self-congratulatory above the lantern. She had broken in upon his solemn tryst with the dead beloved; she stood where his merciful executioner should have stood; and—since he could not let this child witness violence—she had robbed him of the one quick blow that could set him free.

"Here it is. This is the room you're looking for, my master," she said, and set her lantern on the floor, and smiled.

He did not answer—he could not trust himself to answer. He stepped into the cubicle and shut the creaking door behind him and tried to hide his fury by staring at the solemn things—the iron candelabra, the moist and faded frescoes, the rough-hewn coffin set in a shadowy niche in the wall.

"I got here only a little while before you," she told him in an excited whisper. "The minute I heard the deacon Probus go to bed, I knew that you were the one who would be going. But I couldn't start at once, I had to wait till I'd made perfectly sure he'd gone to sleep. I didn't have to walk, I was very lucky—I stopped a farmer at the gate, and he let me ride in the back of his hay-wain—he brought me all the way. I passed you a little way down the road, but I thought I'd come in first and surprise you."

He could not bear the conspiratorial look, the breathless whisper, "Have you lost your mind? How do you think I'm to get you out of here?" he said.

"Oh, you needn't worry about me. If it hadn't been for me, you'd be in serious trouble now yourself. Look—you don't even have a light in your lantern. You'd never be able to find the niche in the dark. Besides, I brought a leather bag with me—a traveler's bag to carry the money in. I'll walk along behind you and carry it. Nobody'll stop me."

"What I had to do here," he said in a cold and bitter voice, "I would much rather have done alone."

He had hurt her as he had meant to hurt her. She stared at him with stricken eyes, and chewed the corner of her trembling underlip. "I'm sorry, but since I'm here I might as well help you," she said, looking behind her at the traveler's sack that lay beside the coffin on the floor. To keep the coins from jingling, she had stuffed the bag with odds and ends of clothing. "Get me the money now and scold me tomorrow. If you scold me now, I'll cry and make a nuisance of myself."

No, he thought, walking past her to the covered niche—two little wooden doors opening into the wall between an ill-drawn dolphin and a scarcely identifiable lamb—no, give me until tomorrow and I will teach myself such gentle words to say to you as *she* would have me say. Tomorrow, since I must live until tomorrow, I will have learned to stroke your cheek and smooth your hair . . . He opened the door and found the small iron box and unlocked it. There were some thirty of the clinking golden coins, and he poured them onto the floor beside the light. "There," he said, straightening and replacing the empty box and closing the little doors. "There's the money—suppose you put it in the sack. I'm too tired to do anything more."

And indeed he could not bring himself to kneel beside her and help her stuff the jingling coins into the bag among the girdles and the tunics and the handkerchiefs. He could only stand with his back against the wall and watch the apt and hasty movements of her blunt little hands. There was nothing in him now but heartsickness and unfathomable weariness. I will never be able to walk back to the City, he thought, and closed his eyes, and let his chin sink down upon his chest, and felt his hands grow heavy and numb with sleep. . . .

"My master!"

She thinks I am about to fall, he told himself, and opened his eyes and saw the fear in her face before he heard the footsteps in the hall.

"God save us, my master—it's the Guardsmen—they're coming."

"Why did you come here?"

"Because I love my master. Because I want to be with him wherever he is," she said.

Still gazing at him with her shining eyes, she rose and hoisted the bag over her shoulder. The footfalls were loud now, echoing, multiplying themselves in the hollow corridor. He came and stood beside her and faced the door. There was only an instant of waiting before it swung open. A single Guard—a brawny Italian with grizzled hair and bulging muscles—stood on the threshold with a lantern in one hand and a drawn blade in the other.

Bright blade, he thought, sweet steel, foregone deliverance. . . .

"What are you doing here?" the Guardsman said.

"Visiting a crypt. Visiting the coffin of this holy martyr, who was my teacher." He made a wide, dramatic gesture in the direction of the shadowy coffin. Why he had said these things, he did not know, but for some strange reason they moved him, so that his eyes filled up with tears.

"You know this catacomb is interdicted?"

"Yes, I know it." He nodded and fetched up a heavy sigh.

"You know you will be taken to the Urban Prefect?"

"Yes, I'm aware of that also. I only regret that I was foolish enough to bring this little slave."

The guard set down his lantern, stepped forward, and snatched the knife from his prisoner's girdle. "And this—what's this for?" he asked, breathing out a cloud of garlic and raw red wine.

"Nothing. If I had intended it for resistance, I would have resisted. You see, I'm peaceable. I'll go wherever you like. Only, as I said—" his eyes, wet and blurred, sought the soft black eyes of the Guardsman, "it's a pity—isn't it?—to involve an innocent slave."

"What's your name?"

"Favorinus Herennius—an important name—one that ought to bring you a promotion. But this child here—"

She flung herself between them, she clasped her master's knees, she pressed her face against his thigh. "Let me go with you. I want to go with you wherever you are—anywhere, anywhere," she said.

It was the Guardsman who put an end to her pleading. He took her by the shoulder and plucked her off and set her rudely on her feet. "Go—take your lantern and get out of here," he said. "Go the way you came. There's nobody watching on the other side, out by the sand pits. Go and stay out of this stinking hole—if I ever find you here again I'll throw you into prison like anybody else."

"Put me in prison now. Take me along with my master."

"Get out. I've arrested one miserable brat already, and I want no more of them chalked up to my name. Go home and tell your father to beat you black and blue and see that you keep alive until such time as a man can make proper use of you. After that you'll have less taste for creeping around in a pile of bones."

"Listen, my master—"

"No," he said, trying to force tenderness into his flat and tired voice. "Be a good slave to me and go back to the house where I saw you last night—for many reasons, it'll be better so. Tell our friend, the one who suffered the terrible loss yesterday afternoon, how things went with me here. Tell him not to worry, say it's exactly as it ought to be—"

Her eyes widened and she started. He knew that she had suddenly remembered that there was desperately-needed money in the bag on her shoulder. Her blunt fingers closed more tightly on the leather strings. "I'll be a good slave, then. I'll do what you tell me, my dear master," she said, and came and kissed him full on the mouth and was gone.

"Tell me your name again," said the Guardsman, taking him by the shoulder and pushing him through the doorway.

"Favorinus Herennius."

"Herennius, did you say? Not the Emperor's nephew—"

"Yes. My mother is the sister of the Empress Etruscilla."

The hand grew gentler, more respectful, slipped from this shoulder to his elbow. "Then *you're* the nephew of the Emperor," said the wondering voice, echoing down the black gallery through which they moved.

"That needn't trouble you—I'm fallen out of favor."

"I know, my lord, but I'll find you a litter. I'll take you back to the City in a litter, nevertheless."

Chapter 36

THREE TIMES in the course of the short reign of the Emperor Decius large crowds had assembled without invitation outside the imperial palace, trampling the grass, encroaching upon the beds of herbs and exotic flowers, scrawling their protests and exhortations in chalk and charcoal on the stairways and the columns and the walls. The first unasked-for visitation had come on the day he had let it be known among his closest confidants that he intended to establish a censorship; and who it was that had borne the word into the streets, how so vast an assembly of disquieted equestrians could have found their way to his door in less than an hour he had never been able to tell. The second visitation had been equally mysterious. The Urban Prefect, issuing from the Emperor's private chambers with the outline of the edict against the Christians which he was ordered to compose in the absence of Favorinus Herennius, had been stopped at the head of the flight of marble stairs by the sight of an unexpected multitude, inexplicably informed about the content of the papers in his hand. Were there to be spectacles? they had asked. What prices would be paid for revealing the hiding-places of Christians? Whom would a person see if he wanted to offer the Government a bargain in incense for the projected general sacrifice?

And now on this third occasion—the Emperor was a little disturbed that this should be the third occasion, there was for him a troubling finality in the mystical number three—on this third occasion the arrival of the populace in the imperial gardens was even more puzzling than it had been in the past. For months they had known that no truce was possible with the chieftain Kniva, and yet they had gone quietly about their own affairs. For weeks they had been hearing and repeating the wild rumors of two hundred thousand Goths in arms and ready to penetrate the weak defenses on the Danubian frontier, and yet they had not been curious enough to come. For ten days they had seen couriers leaving the imperial palace and riding east and west and north and south with warnings for the legions to make ready to march out of Little Asia and Hispania and Gaul, and yet they had shown no signs of stirring out of their usual apathy. It was strange, then—strange and inexplicably ominous to the Emperor Decius—that they should have gathered in his garden by the hundreds on the day he had decided, during a conversation with the Dean of the Senate at the levee, that the northern crisis was one which his son Herennius could not face alone, that he would leave the City within three or four days and lead the northward march of the legions himself.

During the usual breakfast with his intimates in the little dining room he had watched the waiting crowd outside—watched it through a narrow space between two crimson curtains while the Secretary of the Privy Purse told him that the taxes on luxuries had yielded far less than expected, while the Secretary of Petitions had urged him to save a little time for a delegation of citizens from Nicopolis, while the Urban Prefect remarked to him that yesterday's spectacle in the Flavian Amphitheater could be considered a credit to the two consuls who had given it, conducted as it had been with old Republican simplicity and dignity. What do they want of me this time? he asked himself, thinking not of the weary and diminished company who stood about making careful and savorless conversation, thinking of those other numberless and nameless ones who had come as special pleaders in the hour of the State's dire exigency. Somebody out there, he thought, has hides for bucklers that he wants to unload on the Tribune of Supplies. Somebody else has a cousin he would like to see transferred from Dacia to a safer camp on the Persian frontier. Makers of wagons, growers of pigs, breeders of horses, owners of shipping barges—all of them are there. I can never take a step without the vultures. I have only to formulate a thought and the vultures scent it out and congregate around my head.

One of his Aethiopians—all these months, and still, for the life of him, he could not remember the fellow's name—came winding in and out like a cat among the little groups of chatterers, carrying across his outstretched arm a splendid length of crimson cloth. A general's cloak, he explained in his blurred Latin. A present from the Pontifex Maximus, who was confined to his bed this morning with another attack of jaundice. Months ago, at

454

the priest's request, the Vestal Virgins had begun to weave the woolen; and this morning—shortly after the news of the Emperor's heroic intentions had reached the Temple of Vesta—the eldest of the ladies had finished the stitching with her own hand . . . He took it from the slave and showed it with pride to those who happened to be standing near him—the Urban Prefect, the Overseer of the Wardrobe, the somber strategist with whom he had been planning the northern campaign. He held it up and flashed it across the heads of the others so that Valerian might see it—the Dean of the Senate was on the opposite side of the table, forcing himself to drink the sour wine.

For an instant he saw an image of himself in his martial trappings—unassailable, unapproachable, consecrated to the military safety of the State—forging his way through the company assembled in the little dining room, cutting across the crowd of special pleaders gathered outside. To be a general now, he thought, to vault triumphant over three or four days of complicated questions and equivocal solutions that stand between me and my going, to have nothing before me but walls to be defended, watchtowers to be held, clusters of barbarians to be met on such-and-such a bank or in such-and-such a wood—a soldier's unquestionable duties, simple and sharply defined. . . .

"Shall I take it upstairs, my lord and my master?" said the Overseer of the Wardrobe.

"No, not for the moment. I want to show it to the Secretary of the Privy Purse. It's a flawless piece of weaving, a beautiful piece of cloth." But all the time he was thinking that he would like it better when the collar had been worn away with chafing against his helmet, when the hem was thoroughly bespattered with mud. And, drawing the somber strategist a little apart from the others, he began to hold forth not too coherently on the morality a man finds among the members of a hard-pressed legion. On the long marches, in the sieges, on the eve of battle, every legionary was virtuous, devoted to his Standard, tender with his fellows, reduced to his basic decency by the imminence of death. . . .

In the midst of that discourse he noticed that the eye of the strategist had wandered from him. A tribune of the City Guard, his head bent down, his face intent, his helmet with its scarlet plume held against his shining breastplate, had thrust himself unannounced into the little dining room. The guests watched him make his way to the Urban Prefect; they watched the Urban Prefect send him over to Valerian; they saw the broad, pink, attentive face of the Dean of the Senate quiver with surprise and then compose itself in a fatuous and self-satisfied smile. "A report about the Christians, no doubt," the strategist ventured, turning his head in the direction of the departing officer. But the Emperor vouchsafed him no answer—the Emperor blotted out the sickening recollection of the sacrifice to the State which he had witnessed from the imperial box yesterday afternoon, and continued to discourse on military virtue, to point out how few deserters and malingerers had been recorded in the annals of the Republic, to prove that camps and battlefields could completely cure men of those diseases of the spirit contracted in the courts and the cities, could make the meanest centurion a peer of those invincible legionaries who had carried the Standards from the seven hills to the edges of the civilized world. . . .

He stopped only because Valerian had quite abandoned his role of Olympian serenity and was urgently beckoning. He handed the crimson cloak to the Overseer of the Wardrobe and walked around the table and followed the ponderously moving Dean of the Senate out of the dining room and into the hall. His annoyance at the interruption was such that he made Valerian wait, plainly close to bursting with whatever news there was to tell, while he bent over the bronze dolphin on the fountain and drank a long draught of water that he did not want. He straightened then and wiped his mouth slowly with the sleeve of his toga, rejecting the eagerness in the rosy face, refusing to look into the insistent eyes. "Well, what's the matter now?" he said.

"There was a fellow in here from the Urban Prefect's office—"

"I saw him."

"Somebody was arrested in one of the catacombs before sunrise this morning, with incriminating possessions on his person—"

He could not bring himself to ask who. Closing his hand on the wet, metallic tail of the dolphin, he could not determine whether it was loathing for this pink mound of aristocratic flesh or incomprehensible fright that made him ask, "What incriminating possessions?" instead.

"Very incriminating, my lord and my master. A map of one of the catacombs, with secret passages coming in from abandoned sand pits. Also a little wooden Cross."

"Anybody of any consequence?" Because he had forced it, afraid that it might come out of him in a whisper, it was louder than it needed to be.

"Yes, my lord and my master. Favorinus Herennius." The Dean of the Senate lowered his eyes, stared fixedly at his own feet.

My pain is such, the Emperor thought, that it is obvious even to this imperturbable idiot. *He* with a Cross!

"If you'd care to have him brought up here for questioning—"

"Why? Hasn't he been questioned? Picked up at sunrise and still not questioned? Are you managing this business the way you managed the censorship—never do today what can be put off until later—wait, wait until all parties concerned have had time to take themselves out of reach?"

"He has been questioned, my lord and my master. I only thought you would want to talk to him yourself."

Talk to him myself? Face him out across the battered table where we used to eat the morning meal together? Shout, rage, while he stands as he stood on another occasion, untouchable in his insolence—Cross-kisser, blood-drinker, haunter of Christian graves? "What in the name of all the gods do you imagine I would have to talk to him about?" he said.

"I only thought, inasmuch as he is your nephew—"

"My nephew? Have I given anybody reason to believe I act on grounds of family feeling? If I left my son in Dacia at the mercy of two hundred thousand barbarians—"

"I was not implying what my lord and my master chooses to think. The case of Favorinus Herennius is very peculiar. His answers to the usual questions—the ones they put to him in the Urban Prefect's office—cast very little light on his status under the present law. The tribune was puzzled—the Urban Prefect was puzzled—I brought the matter to your attention because, quite frankly, I was puzzled myself."

If you are puzzled, he thought, sneering into the shining and impervious face, then the world is about to fall apart. "Are you indeed?" he said.

"Yes, distinctly puzzled. In the matter of the sacrifice, for instance—"

Wild hope unmasked him, made him look up with bare and vulnerable eyes. "Did he sacrifice?"

"No, my lord and my master, he did not. But not on the grounds that he confessed the Name. He told the tribune he was out of the habit of burning incense—had given it up months ago."

"Why? I assume he gave his reasons—he was always full of reasons—"

The eyes shifted again, stared foolishly at the dolphin on the fountain. "It's hard to tell—they were distinctly puzzled down there, as I said. So far as I could gather, his reasoning ran something like this: He knew no human being who was worthy of an act of worship, and he saw no evidence of the existence of God."

He said it to wound me, he said it to remind me that I am no demi-god or hero, in spite of all the public burning of incense. And that was unjust of him, that was bitterly unjust. He knows me—I dealt with him man to man in the house on the Esquiline and in the imperial palace. I told him my doubts, I showed him my weaknesses. He knows I never thought myself a god!

"So you can see, my lord and my master, that we're dealing here with a kind of legal dilemma. To set up a separate category for atheists when our real purpose is to single out Christians would lead to all sorts of confusion, all sorts of unpleasantness. And we can't arbitrarily count him a Confessor either—that was one thing he made clear—he stated outright that he was not a Christian—"

"Then what was he doing with a Cross on his person?"

"I asked that myself, my lord and my master. It seems the Cross was important to him not as a religious object, but as a memento of somebody who is dead."

Some deacon, some elder, some Christ-ridden scholar who took him from me. Dead now, wiped out now, and I am glad of it, I rejoice in it with all my heart!

"Of course, there's still the matter of the map. It's particularly bad for him because he refuses to say what he was doing with it. He being who he is—a patrician from one of our best families, a trusted member of your council, and your nephew—they've been treating him with respect and consideration; they've kept him in one of the upper chambers. But five or six of them have been at him with questions ever since he came in, and nothing's to be gotten out of him, even though he can scarcely keep his eyes open for want of sleep."

A patrician, inheritor of all the ancient honors bestowed in the days of the Republic . . . Son of a senatorial family, with all the casual and subtle charm of those who trace their ancestry to kingly skeletons in Etruscan tombs . . . A trusted member of my council, inventive, eloquent, swift in understanding . . . My nephew, beautiful, elusive, restless, always seeking —my nephew whom I loved . . . And suddenly, with violent clarity, he saw him sitting in the Urban Prefect's office, with five or six ruthless officers of the City Guard hurling questions at him, and he half dead for sleep. The restless seeking—that it should end like this, among Guardsmen and sordid documents in a fly-specked bureau—"Tell the Urban Prefect to get him out of there," he said.

It was scarcely a smile, it was only the faintest motion at the corners of the smooth, benevolent lips. But it was enough, it was more than enough. It implied that the Lord of the World—like the Roman Censor and the Urban Prefect and the tax collectors and the provincial buyers of supplies for the City and the legions—the Lord of the World also was corruptible at a certain price. "Surely, my lord and my master. And where would you like us to send him?" the Dean of the Senate said.

"Where would I like you to send him?" His voice, raw with fury and the accents of Pannonia, bellowed through the hallway into the atrium. "Where do you think I would like you to send him? To Africa, to live in a villa behind his orchards? I've confiscated his villas, I've sold his orchards, I've put the money into the treasury of the State. I'd like you to send him—as you know very well—exactly where you send all the rest of the besotted fools—"

"But if he's not a Christian—"

"What do you want? Did you expect him to come to you with a surplice on his shoulders? He had a map. He had a Cross. He belongs in the prison where you keep the rest of them—" he turned on his heel and started back into the little dining room, shouting over his shoulder—"put him in prison and deal with him as you see fit—I have other matters to think about."

He stopped on the threshold, disproportionately disturbed to see that the dining room was empty. They had heard him shouting and had fled by another entrance; they were as swift these days to take themselves out of the range of his righteous anger as other generations of courtiers had been to flee the madness of a Caligula or the cold cruelty of a Tiberius . . . Then let them leave me, he thought, banging the door behind him. I will sit at this table and make up my own mind whether it would be better to march across the wilds of Moesia or cut through Macedonia and Thrace to the shores of the Euxine Sea . . . But the vultures still hovered on the lawn, visible through the rift in the curtain, and whenever he glanced across the board it seemed to him that he could see it smiling at him arrogantly there—the ravaged, mocking face. Go from me, he thought, glaring at it in fury. Go rot in prison, go die at the block or in the arena—I cannot be concerned with you, I am consecrated now to the survival of the State. . . .

And strangely—since he had, as he knew, a feeble memory for details—he heard himself answered out of the past. "Then let me ask my uncle one more question," said the voice of the ruined glory of the high house of the Herennii. "What are we to survive for? Three hundred years of tyrants? Fear in the City, fear in the provinces? No place on earth for a man to hide his head? More and more victims, because there will always be a certain number of fools who would rather die on their feet than crawl about on their knees in such a world?"

Chapter 37

HERENNIUS DECIUS had known how self-indulgent, how unsoldierly it was to take himself off to Epidaurus at such a time—had known it even before he broached the matter to his father in the midnight stillness of the imperial tent. He had come prepared for bitter answers, and perhaps if there had been an outburst he would have gone his way with a disburdened mind, punished beforehand and left to enjoy the fruits of his dereliction in peace. But there had been nothing; there had been only long silence and the old hand trembling on the outspread map. "Go if you like." The tired whisper sounded in his ears, more unforgettable than the harshest rebuke. "I thought you would ask, and I made up my mind to tell you to go if you liked. But I know what you think when you ask me a thing like that. You're the same as the rest of them, here and in Rome. You have no hope. You're on the side of death."

On the side of death? Down the coast of the Euxine, into the Hellespont, and across the Aegean he had pondered that, standing on the deck and staring down into the dark monotony of the heaving waters. And on the last day of the journey, sailing between islands that had once supported fabled and splendid cities, sailing past vine-swathed ruins and deserted colonnades and temples inhabited only by wild doves, he knew that it was so. You are right, my father, he said in his heart. If I had thought of an "expected battle" instead of a "final stand," I would never have come to your tent in the middle of the night to ask for permission to visit Epidaurus. It is because I think I will die on a certain patch of earth as yet unchosen, it is because I look on my life as finished and see that there was less than nothing in it that I say, "Before the battle, I must go to Epidaurus to see my beloved."

The ship came to port in the City of the Healer in the early afternoon, and there would have been plenty of time for him and the twelve tribunes and centurions and orderlies who had attended him on his journey to go up to the Temple before the hour of the evening meal, to bathe in one of the sacred pools and eat their bread and meat and wine at the hospitality of the god. But some strange and sorrowful instinct bade him not to hasten; it was as if he knew that any dream harbored for years was certain to be better than its fulfillment; he dismissed his men and bathed in the public baths and ate at a cookshop and ordered rooms for the night in a hostel instead. His thoughts of her—visions of how it would be to see her and greet her and kiss her—were shadowed over by certain considerations regarding the city, a far more beautiful and prosperous city than any he had visited since he had left Rome. Wandering about alone and unrecognized in the crowded avenues, stopping at the bazaars where courteous tradesmen offered ointments and potions, charms for health and doves for sacrifice, votive tablets and little images of the Healer, he thought how Epidaurus had grown opulent on human wretchedness, how the state and splendor of Epidaurus—these gleaming statues, these silken awnings, these beds of crocus and hyacinth—increased in proportion to the amount of sickness and madness and weary incapacity in the world.

It occurred to him then that she was sick, and that he did not know how sick she was, and that some dark, perverse necessity of his spirit had so worked with him that he could almost wish her sick unto death. But why, why? he asked himself, trying to erase the ravaged and yearning image of her face that he had conjured up, trying to see her again as a child with a bewitching mouth and vital eyes and a braid of luxuriant hair. And he knew that she also could accuse him of being on the side of death. To be among the dying is to be committed to nothing, not to a husband, not to a spoken vow, not to a promise sealed between the gods and oneself. To be among the dying is to be justified in taking whatever is at hand. . . .

He dreamed of her that night in the high, clean room in the sumptuous hostel. It seemed to him that she came into the room in saffron silk, so urgent as to be wanton, her hair disheveled, her dalmatica torn open to offer him a vision of her body. And the knowing of her was so actual to him that in the midst of it he uttered a shout of exultation, and brought one of his orderlies in upon him from the hall, and could not explain. And the bitterness that came upon him when he lay down again to drowse out the rest of the hours before morning was not due alone to his shame at the wretched incident; it rose also from a heavy conviction that his dream had outstripped

461

his life: he would not know her tomorrow or any other day; all that he would ever have of her was what he had had tonight.

He came to the Temple of Aesculapius in the mid-morning, dressed in his purple trappings and followed by a retinue of twelve men. Almost at once he saw that it had been a mistake to come in such ostentation. They knew him immediately and greeted him with ceremony and led him about with pomp and pride. He sacrificed at the main altar, he was ushered into the private apartment of the high priest, he was told a dozen stories about miraculous recoveries, he completed a tour of the corridors and sleeping chambers and solaria and baths before he dared to be so petty and discourteous as to state that, though the Temple was certainly wonderful beyond all imagining, he had a private errand to attend to, he wished to be brought to Drusilla Herennia, a close relative, a childhood friend. Her name, when he uttered it to the shaven priests who had been excitedly exhibiting one marvel after another, brought down a strange, charged silence. They stared, they pursed their lips, they exchanged swift glances. If they had not assured him, with obsequious alacrity, that they would summon in a moment a certain reverend son of the Healer who had her in his special charge, he would have been certain she was dead.

They left him alone to wait for her counselor and spiritual father in a sunny little room where everything had been presented by somebody. The iron bench on which he seated himself, trying to hide his agitation, bore a votive tablet proclaiming that Lavinia of Toletum was grateful for her deliverance from stones in the kidney, and he was reading it when the reverend son of the Healer came soundlessly into the chamber and closed the door. Some blind, instinctive anger stirred within him at the sight of the saffron hem and the lean, bare feet, so that he could not bring himself to raise his head.

"I stand in readiness to serve the son of the Lord of the World in whatsoever manner he may require," said the remote voice after a silence.

He lifted his eyes and took exception to everything he saw—the long, loose body, the face bled of everything but the inhuman sweetness of continued austerity, the solemn mouth, the shapely and shaven head. "I came to inquire about one of those who dwell here at the Temple—"

"I know. Drusilla Herennia. Ever since I met her on the ship coming over from Rome, she's been a special charge of mine—my daughter in the god."

And suddenly, looking at the subtle body, he saw the source of his hate and felt the flush suffusing his cheeks. This priest who stood so self-contained and remote between him and the cedarwood table—he knew that she had desired this priest, knew it as surely as he knew that he had been born of his mother, knew it in his blood.

"They tell me she's a relative of yours."

It was said gently, patiently, to prompt him out of his untoward and awkward silence. The flush deepened, and he tightened his grip on the edge of the bench. What do you take me for—a five-year-old child? he thought, glad that he had not risen, glad that he had stubbornly clung to his imperial prerogatives by sitting stolidly in the middle of the bench. It is true that you are smooth and exquisite with wanting nothing and I am unripe and tormented with desperately needing everything. But I have set the seal of Rome on the frozen wilderness in the shape of a camp, and you must speak to me as to one who comes to you in purple shoes. "She's my cousin," he said.

"So she's really your cousin?"

"Certainly she's my cousin. Her mother is the sister of the Empress Etruscilla. Hasn't she ever told you so?"

"Oh, yes, she told us that many times." The grave and courteous face remained undisturbed by his rudeness, and this cultivated serenity reduced him to nothing, reduced him as effectively as Gallus's brash vulgarity. "Only, we always find it better to reserve our judgment in such matters. There are a good many with us who claim to be related to all sorts of notable people. Some go further—some believe they are descended from the gods."

He could not look at the priest—staring straight in front of him he saw a vision of a horrible, witless face. Ask then and know, he thought. But he could not ask directly, not with these cool, self-possessed eyes fixed upon him. "Do you mean to imply that you thought she was lying?" he said.

"Lying? Oh, no, we would never think of calling it 'lying'. Those who are disquieted in their spirits, obsessed with an illusion, estranged from the world as it is—however you may wish to put it"—it was plain that he was trying, in detached and inhuman mercy, to put it as delicately as he could— "those who have reached the point to which Drusilla Herennia has come cannot possibly be accused of deliberate deception. In fact, they believe they are the sole possessors of an ultimate truth."

"I'm to take it that she's mad then?"

"Not raving mad, my son. The god was unusually merciful to Drusilla Herennia: her time of violence was short. And, except for four or five days of discomfort when the wound was almost healed, she was spared any pain."

"The wound? How could she wound herself in a place like this?" he said, knowing that he was venting his horror in reasonless fury. "Aren't there any guards here? Surely you can keep a sick woman from stabbing herself."

"She didn't stab herself, my son. She beat the back of her head, just here"—he turned a little and raised his beautiful, supple fingers to the place where his shaven head curved out of the nape of his neck—"just here, against a stone. But I beg you not to distress yourself too much at the thought of that. I've spent twenty years and more in this Temple, and my experience here has taught me that the capacity for suffering declines along with and in proportion to the capacity to understand. You, for example— you, in full possession of your senses—you feel that blow, or imagine you

463

feel it, as she never felt it. It was light to her; she had lost much of her capacity for suffering; and this dispensation, that we feel less as we have more to endure, this seems to me the most convincing proof of the mercy and justice of the god. . . ."

There was more, but he did not listen. He was seeing her dashing her head against a stone; he was seeing her with the blood running from that spot which he had always yearned to kiss, the gentle curve just above the nape of the neck.

"For nine days after she sustained the injury," the priest was saying, "she lay in a stupor, and we had no hopes, we counted her among the dead. I sat with her day and night and dropped honey mixed with milk between her lips. I knew she had not utterly broken off her connection with the world because there were times when she would close her fingers on my hand. . . ."

Daemon, he thought, evil daemon, dealer in matters of shame and darkness—she groped for you, she clung to you, her sick spirit rose up to take hold upon you even when her mind and her body were given over to death. And you did not love her, you did not want her—you are beyond all loving and all wanting. And I that desired her past all enduring—me she forgot.

"On the tenth day she sat up like a child wakening out of a refreshing sleep, and asked for bread and milk. We gave her bread and milk, and she laughed and made much of us. She remembered nothing. When we asked her how it was with her, she said she had never felt so well, so light in the spirit, so close to the god. We had to ask her to put up her hand and feel the bandage before she would even confess to a little pain in the head. And since that day she has been utterly happy. She sings, she teases us, she tries to weave a little, she makes us garlands out of flowers and shells. The god in his infinite mercy has taken all the years in which she suffered out of her remembrance. The god has transformed her into a happy child."

"Direct me to the lady Drusilla Herennia," he said, rejecting the cool pity in the level grey eyes, staring down at his purple shoes and speaking in the tone of one who issues a command.

"She is much changed, you know. Before my lord and my master, the son of the Restorer and Preserver of the World, goes to see his cousin, it might be well for him to ask himself whether he would not rather remember her as she was in more auspicious days. Besides, if he should be overcome, if he should lose hold on himself, it might be unfortunate for her also. Here at the Temple we have one simple rule to guide us in our dealings with her: we say to ourselves, 'Drusilla Herennia is a child, a little one, seven or eight years old at best. Let us expose her to nothing—no word, no sign, no expression of the face—that would not be completely suitable in the presence of a child.' Is my lord and my master sure that he wishes—"

"Perfectly sure. Take me to her, however she is and wherever she is," he said.

They left the room; they passed down a corridor which imperceptibly became an open portico; they stepped out onto a vast stretch of lawn, enclosed in an ancient wall which was covered with vines and had been mellowed to the color of honey by centuries and the sun. He had not meant to look about him—his heart was closed against the place; and yet the even greenness, clean and radiant in the direct shafts of noontide light, closed away from the world, open only to the wide and vacant blue of heaven, broken here and there by tables draped in spotless linen, canopied now and again by clumps of venerable trees, was lovely enough to call up out of his rigid body a long and shaking sigh. It was the hour of the noonday meal, and of a sudden they were no longer walking alone. Hundreds of others, bright as flowers against the grass in their varicolored dalmaticas and tunics, moved without haste in the direction of the tables. Decorous laughter and courteous conversation mingled with the sound of rustling leaves and the monotonous surge and fall of the sea. The talk that flowed around them blossomed with tender names: they called each other "my little one", "my soul's sister", "my crocus", "my doe", "my darling". And, through a mist of sudden and uncontrollable tears, he saw that the young ones were tempering their paces to the feebleness of the old, that the lame were leading the blind.

"They are happy in each other. By far the greater number of them are happy, in the god and in each other," the reverend son of the Healer said.

They passed between pillars through an opening in the wall. The sense of height and the vision of azure, sun-slashed waters broke upon him.

"This is the lichen rock—they sit here in the mornings and read and sun themselves," said the voice of the priest, quiet at his shoulder. "She tried to leap from this lichen rock in the hour when the daemon seized her. We caught her, we held her—it was then that she struck her head against the stone. And I can assure my lord and my master, and call the god himself to witness, that she will not be alone henceforth for an instant. Her brothers and sisters in misfortune are constantly with her, and I am with her much myself."

Be with her then, he thought, standing at the edge of the lichen rock where she had stood in her agony. Be with her and teach her not to leap from perilous rocks and eat poison berries and blister her skin in the sun. Comfort her body with such potions as I cannot make; ease her spirit with skills that I will never understand. Besides, I cannot tarry. There is a patch of earth, as yet unnamed, to which I go. Watch her when I have no sight to watch her, when death and the ravens have taken my eyes . . . And for the first time, it was possible for him to think that, the world being what it was, he must teach himself to be thankful for this passionless compassion, this inhuman mercy, this serene detachment from all that is, this solemn resignation before all that cannot be. The path down from the lichen rock was narrow and treacherous, and when the priest offered him his arm to cling to, he took it. "I am grateful for the skill and patience that the son of Aesculapius has used in dealing with my cousin," he said.

She was not at the foot of the slope—nothing was there but ruffled sand and shining wet rock and painfully brilliant water. They followed a line of footprints, with the dazzling brightness in their eyes and the noise of waves in their ears, and walked without haste for about a quarter of a mile before they saw the two figures kneeling on the beach, some four feet apart—the boy facing them, the woman with her back to them—both utterly absorbed in what lay between them: a domed and intricate structure molded out of the damp white sand.

The boy saw them first, and rose and brushed the sand from his knees, and took himself off, laughing and shouting something at her over his shoulder —his words were lost in the thunder of the sea. "Remain where you are for a little, my lord and my master," said the priest advancing a little. "Let her come to us—I think she will come."

There was an instant when he thought he could not bear to watch it—the crazy headlong running, the hair loose and wild and streaked with white, the face upturned and twisted by witless laughter, the body, thin and old with sickness, executing the hoydenish motions of a little girl. But it did not seem hideous, once she had flung herself into the loveless embrace of her father in Aesculapius and started to speak. Her voice, unchanged, still musical, was babbling on about incongruous but happy things: a boat with yellow sails that had come out of the east, the grapes they had given her for breakfast, the cheek of her father in Aesculapius, newly shaven—she stroked it, she touched it with her parted lips. The priest inclined his rigid body toward her; and every now and then he nodded his shaven head. But after a little, as if out of consideration for the outlander who stood behind him, miserably waiting, he took her by the shoulders and held her off. "You have a visitor, my daughter," he said.

"A visitor?" The pale, loose face was drained of laughter and filled with trouble. "No visitors, no visitors—I'll get it again, the pain in the back of my head. Come and see the basilica, come and see my starfish—I found him in the sand."

"But the son of the Lord of the World has done you the honor of coming all the way down from Dacia to see you."

"The son of the Lord of the World?" She sighed in her bewilderment— she raised her clenched fist and rubbed it into her furrowed brow. "But Alexander Severus"—he had reigned in her childhood, he had lain these twenty years and more under a lonely barrow in the Arabian desert—"he was so young when they murdered him, he never had a child."

"True, true. But you have a visitor come all the way from Dacia nevertheless. There he stands—no, there—"

The poor brown eyes, emptied of all their luminousness and crossed by streaks of red, squinted against the sun.

"You know him, my daughter. He was a friend of yours when you were little. I'm sure you can remember him if you try."

"But what about my starfish? Come and see him before he dries up in the sun."

He led her closer—head down, eyes lowered and unwilling. He brought her so close that every line was visible on her ravaged cheeks and brow. "Be good now, my daughter. Take his hand and give him the kiss of greeting. You remember your cousin Herennius Decius."

"If you say so, my father . . ." Brief and ghostly kiss, offered up by a good child who has learned to pride herself on her obedience. Cold, sand-clotted fingers laid in his and pulled away.

"She will remember you, my son. Only it will take her a little time to collect herself."

"I remember him," she said, plainly wounded because her effort at courtesy had not been good enough. "I'll tell you how I know him: he gave me a pigeon, a little tame pigeon with a chain on its feet. It choked on a chick-pea, its feathers got sick. All of a sudden it turned over on its side. I was the one who did it, I fed it the chick-pea, but it's not my fault, nobody ever told me how it would be. I never wanted anything to die, not even my father, though he looked so kind in his toga when the flames went up. I never wanted anything to be dead. Kiss me, my cousin, and tell me I'm forgiven. I wrapped it in a handkerchief—I did what I could—I planted a crocus on its grave."

He took her in his arms, striving against his weeping. The reverend son of the Healer walked a few paces toward the edge of the beach and stood gazing out at the waters, so that anything might be said. But what was there to say, except that she was forgiven? And in an instant she was out of his grasp, out of his reach, making pitiful attempts to smooth her dress, to rearrange her streaked and disheveled hair. "You must not rumple me like that," she told him. "I must keep myself decent and seemly for the god."

"Is there anything I could send my cousin on my way up to Dacia?" he asked, when he had wrung the weeping out of his throat and made his voice something suitable for the ears of a disquieted child.

"Yes, a bale of hay for the sacred herd," she said. "But you're poor, you have no money, and everything is so splendid here. It'd be a pity if you sent us anything shabby. Everybody'd laugh at it, and there's been enough of that, let's have no more of that—" She started back, she raised her fingers to her lips, she looked at him so intently that he was impelled to look down at himself, at the crimson cloak and the purple shoes brilliant against the whiteness of the sand. There was an instant when he saw understanding come surging up behind her eyes; it surged like a billow, and broke into laughter, cold, like a spatter of foam. "Look how he has dressed himself up!" she said, flinging out her emaciated arms, inviting a host of invisible

467

and malignant witnesses to enjoy the sight. "Look at him! In a crimson cloak! In purple shoes!"

"My daughter, you are forgetting yourself," said the priest without moving, his eyes still fixed on the swirling waters.

"I'm sorry, I'm sorry." She came forward again, so close that the air was tainted by the mingled smell of sweat and salt that rose from her hair. "You must try to be patient with me. I'm still wicked. Come, I'll kiss you kindly, I won't forget myself."

He held her close, he forced himself to press his mouth against the damp and acrid curls. He took her face in his hands and gave her three kisses, on the chin, on the forehead, on the lips. But they were nothing, those kisses, since he did not know what they were—whether he kissed a sick child in pity or the ruin of what had once been a beautiful woman in disgust.

"And that's all there is, I'll have to go now and look after my starfish," she said, stepping back and smoothing her dalmatica with her trembling hands. "Where is my reverend father in the Healer? Oh, there you are, looking at the water, always looking at the water. Come now, hurry, if we go at once there may still be a little of the starfish left in the shell."

He came and stood beside her, with his beautiful, passionless hand cupped around her elbow. "But thank your cousin first for all his kindnesses," he said.

"Thank you, thank you. Thank you for coming all the way from Dacia. Thank you for dressing yourself up in a crimson cloak and purple shoes. It was kind of you to think of that, but I can't pretend to be the Empress. And, now that I think of it, it would be better if you sent us nothing, nothing at all. The sacred herd is fat enough, God knows, and we're well enough off as we are."

The priest pursed his lips and whistled—a long, shrill whistle that sounded above the noises of the sea. The lad who had been with her in the beginning emerged from behind a great black rock some fifty paces off, and came running toward them, leaping over boulders, clapping his hands and calling her name. And now her thoughts were all for her playfellow; she had forgotten both her cousin and her reverend father; she had spread her skirt and pushed back her hair and was kneeling down again beside the domed basilica. He could hear her voice, childish and querulous, raised behind him as he turned to follow the priest along the beach: she wanted no colonnades, it was better to leave things as they were . . . They climbed up the slope of the lichen rock and walked in silence across the sunny lawn. The children of Aesculapius were still sitting over the linen cloths and the shining silver dishes. So little time, he thought—all that I dreamed about all my life come and gone in just so much time as it takes to eat a little bread and meat and drink a goblet of milk. . . .

"May I speak with you, reverend father?" said an old woman, stopping them under a magnificent elm tree. Her body was heavy and dropsical, but her face was sweetened by a vague smile.

"In a moment, in a moment, my daughter. Go along ahead of us and wait for me on the bench by the herb-bed. I have yet a few words to say to the son of the Lord of the World, and then I will come."

He was sorry to see her dismissed; he wanted no private talk, no serene detached consolations. But the son of Aesculapius did not have the air of one who is about to deliver himself of pious pronouncements; he fumbled in his saffron-colored girdle and brought out a square of papyrus and looked at it in perplexity. "My son," he said, "although I can easily imagine how eager you are to be alone, there's a matter here which I must ask you to consider before you depart. This is a letter from the lady Sabina to Drusilla Herennia. I had it in my chamber, I picked it up and brought it with me when they told me you were waiting. It came to the Temple two or three days after your cousin was seized by the daemon. We could not read it to her then, of course, and it seemed useless to trouble her with it afterwards. But the contents seem urgent, and if there were anything you could do in regard to it you would lift a heavy burden from my mind."

He took it and opened it and read it in the dancing coins of light that came through the elm leaves. It was strange to see again the tight and elegant handwriting that he remembered from invitation scrolls sent in delicate ivory boxes from the Herennii to the Decii long ago. But the words themselves were enough to dispel all memories—he had not read the salutation before he found himself knitting his brows and setting his teeth into his curling lip.

"My daughter (if indeed what I keep in my bitter poverty at the rate of three hundred denarii a month in idleness and self-indulgence in a Temple can be called my daughter): I do not expect you to answer this. I only wish you to know that your brother is in dire trouble with his uncle. It was not enough that he should leave me desolate in this house, and rob me of my properties, and besmirch the honorable name of the Herennii. He has done more—he has been found in an interdicted catacomb with a shameful symbol on his person. He is now in the Urban Prefect's prison, and, so far as I or any of the few friends who still condescend to visit me can determine, he is in imminent danger of death. I cannot help him. Perhaps nobody can help him. Yet there is one with whom a word from you might bear weight, since he was foolish enough to love you in better days. If your criminal indolence will permit it, in the name of all the gods, trouble yourself to pick up a pen and write a few words to the only one left who might help us. To me, I know you will not write, though I am old and sick and without comfort. Well, perhaps you will see fit to come in time to see me buried. Sabina Herennia."

He read the letter twice and folded it again. Appalled as my father was at my departure from the camp, he thought, he was merciful enough to spare me the knowledge of this. . . .

"Is there anything you can do in regard to that, my lord and my master?" said the priest.

"Yes, provided there's any need. The old woman—the lady Sabina Herennia—may very well be exaggerating for purposes of her own."

"Do you think so? You know the lady, of course—but it seemed to me there was real distress there—"

"May I keep the letter? I'll speak of it to my father," he said.

"Certainly. Keep it. I'm deeply grateful to have the worry lifted from my shoulders."

He saw, with wonder, that this was so. In the world, the reader of such a letter would have itched to ask a dozen questions. But here, where the honey-colored walls shut out the rest of the earth, where there was no concern except with suffering, curiosity was blessedly dead.

"Thank you, my father. You have been a source of comfort to my cousin, and she was very dear to me—" He stopped, noting with quiet grief that he had put it in the past.

"Yes, I could see that. Heavy as they are, they pass—these sorrows. I commend you to the god, my son, and wish you a serene life and a quiet grave." His eyes were already moving toward the dropsical old woman on the bench; and the young man was relieved that no more passed between them—that there was only the ritual "farewell".

Chapter 38

EVERY DAY at that hour in the afternoon when the slants of light from the barred upper windows began to redden and weaken a little, every day at the time when those who still lived in the world outside began to bathe themselves in warm water and anoint themselves with cinnamon and cassia so that they might come without any odor of their mortality upon them to the banquet table to discourse and to love, every day at the same time, more or less—because after the day of the going forth there was no exactitude in the reckoning of the hours—a tribune or a centurion of the City Guard walked into the common room of the prison and called his name. "Favorinus Herennius," the Guardsman would say, always with the same note of weariness sounding under the grandiloquent syllables; and whether he was weary of the century, or the persecution, or this monotonous process repeated over and over without the slightest results, it was impossible to tell. Every day the murmurous conversation, no more disturbing to the continuity of thought than the rushing of a distant waterfall, would come to a stop. The eyes—incurious, only considerate—would turn in his direction while he rose and reminded himself that there were fetters on his feet, and made his way across the floor. Whatever thought had occupied him before the Guardsman came, he carried with him through the doorway and up the narrow stairs.

He never turned his mind upon what was to come: it was cheap and futile and always the same.

Always the same, whether it was the Urban Prefect or the Dean of the Senate who was waiting for him behind the big, document-strewn table in the fly-specked office. The same still when the two of them were otherwise occupied and a tribune of the City Guard had been entrusted with the honorable duty of trying to transform him into a hypocrite or a liar. The same courtesy—"Sit down, your Illustriousness, there's no need for you to stand." The same arguments—"Even the strictest of the Stoic disciplines doesn't forbid a man to burn a little incense; Zeno himself would advise you to conform." The same reassurances—"No torture, naturally; no orders yet from the Lord of the World. He's doubtless very busy in Dacia; your case will be held suspended until such time as we have received directives from the Emperor himself." And always, toward the end of it, when their faces had sagged and their voices had grown weary of the monotony of it, the same question: "Suppose there *are* no directives, suppose there never is an order for your release or your execution—do you want to stay in prison indefinitely?"

He always pretended to be weighing that question. "Do you want to stay in prison indefinitely?"—it was an excellent line to leave hanging in the air; and if he seemed to be pondering it, they were willing to let well enough alone—he could make his ironically ceremonious bow on the threshold of the Urban Prefect's office and depart. Thinking on the way back down the corridors and the stairways how earnest the tribune had been, how ponderously the Dean of the Senate had worked himself up to the delivery of the climactic line, how much conspiratorial intimacy the exquisite Urban Prefect had managed to drape over it—"You know as well as I do that the normal instincts of a civilized man are bound eventually to reassert themselves"—thinking how all their hopes were balanced on that and only that, he smiled a sour smile. There were moments when he was tempted to turn back and tell them how it was with him: the spirit so worn and vulnerable that the thought of crowded streets and lighted rooms was like a blow upon an open wound, the spirit so stricken that it could sustain its suffering only in the isolation and the dark.

From morning until night he sat on a three-legged stool against the brick curve of a beehive arch, leaving it only when he was summoned away by the voice of a Guardsman or forced to go to one of the darker corners to tend to his bodily necessities. The others would lie down in their piles of rags about an hour after night had settled in; but he would often sit through four or five hours of total blackness, staring at the opposite side of the archway, staring as if he could still see the water dripping or the roaches scurrying there—too intent to lie down, too alert for sleep. Sometimes he would fall into a numbness, a kind of semi-dream, and then it would seem to him that he was standing at twilight above a pool in a place of utter desolation, waiting for the dark and troubled waters to grow quiet enough to yield him up an image of his face.

No, if the fetters had fallen from his feet and the heavy portal had been opened by a mysterious hand, he would never have looked up, he would never have moved. Since the hour when the Emperor Decius had ed him away from his father's memorial feast, his life, like a stallion gone out of control, had been bearing him furiously and inexorably on. And now that it had thrown him off, no place on earth could have been more congenial to him than the dark and hidden ditch in which he lay. Here he could stop, here he could rest, and that was blessed. How else could he draw his naked spirit up out of the depths and ask of it: "What have you done? How is it that I, who could not crush a spider or beat a hound, have so dealt with my frail and exquisite fellows, the sons and daughters of men, that wherever I passed I left a broken or insensate heart?"

To answer those questions, to summon up and know the past, to see why and how it was that he had brought down death and black chaos—this was his only concern, his only occupation. Somewhere outside the circle of his bitter brooding another life went on: the child Prisca came and brought him bread and apples, the old Jew whom he had seen and talked with on the rubble pile went to be tortured evening after evening; somebody saw a vision of Saint John the Divine walking back and forth in the foetid darkness; somebody was released, and somebody died. But in all these matters he had no part and wanted no part. If the old Jew bade him good morning, he answered briefly, his eyes fixed on the ground. If the little slave sat down beside him and asked him how it was with him, he drove her off by telling her that he was well enough so long as he was let alone. Nor was it only that he needed the isolation, the utter silence. It was also as if he had written a leper's warning around himself on the damp earthen floor: "Here is contagion, flee and save yourselves."

Charis . . . Always in the wan light of the morning, when the faces round him were still pasty with sleep, he started with Charis. She and the little company and the precious clutter they had gathered around them: the scrolls, the cythera, the monkey, the ancient statues, the mirror and the flute. Her house—they had always known it, they had often said as much—was a lighted vessel bearing a muffled glow across a black, uncharted sea. They had held out their hands to him and drawn him in; they had shut him away with them from the yearning and the loneliness and the icy indifference that he had known in the palace of the Herennii; and all that they had ever asked of him was that he be resigned and wise and kind. Never lift the wind-lashed curtain, never contemplate the chaos outside. Love the old things, draw the lost and beautiful things that nobody cares for anymore tenderly out of their graves. Write your little discourse on Musonius, and I will find the scrolls for you—I will labor for you as diligently as if you were Plato himself. Give me two hours, and I will make myself

beautiful for the evening—not one wrinkle on my face will eve[r]
force you to know that I am mortal and have suffered much. Look
with forbearance upon our corruption. All of us—you and I and and
she—are children of corruption. Call his incapacity "weariness", and say o[f]
her perversity that it is "thwarted love". So, reading elegies and cleaning
ancient paintings and hearing the echoes of notes that were dropped from
the flute and the lyre in happier Achaea, we will make our bitter journey
and never know its bitterness. So, when the hull is split and the water
surges in, we will have only one terrible moment—and even that may be
sweetened by the graciousness of our farewells. . . .

So it had been at the house of Charis, and she content—he knew it now
staring at the apple which the little slave had left on the floor before him—
she utterly content until that hour he had taken her by the shoulder and
pulled aside the curtain and made her see impending chaos and the night
"How can you hide yourselves from the truth?"—he had shouted it above
the gentle talk and the music and the elegies. "Look at the world as it really
is—corrupted, falling apart—and you as rotten as the rest, more rotten still
shot through with a more exquisite and disintegrating corruption. . . ."

And then one day when he had been pondering these matters, he lifted
his eyes from a trampled crust of bread on the floor and saw, without
wonder or pleasure or distress, that she was there. She—Charis—was standing between him and the other side of the brick arch, with a dark brown
cloak flung over her sky-blue dalmatica; and he could not even take it for a
vision; there was too much of the mortal and the ravaged in the prominence
of her collar bones and the roughened skin of her cheeks and the coarseness
of her dry, dyed hair. He asked her how she had found him, not out of
curiosity, only because the question, uttered in spurious amazement, made it
possible for them to avoid the miseries of meaningless greetings; and she
told him that she had found him in the usual way—somebody in the imperial
palace had told somebody else who had told one of Orbiana Festina's Britons—through slaves, by bribing slaves . . . He did not listen, he was distracted by the realization that he had changed as much as she: there was
shock and grief and burdensome pity in her faded grey eyes. She went on
to other matters then: the philosopher Cleander was drinking himself to
death; Berosus had taken his Syrian away to Mytilene: Memphius was
dead, stabbed by a jealous charioteer in a tavern in the Suburra; Antisthenes
half mad with grief, had disappeared. . . .

He heard it all as he might have read a yellowed journal of imperial
events from the time of Antoninus Pius. Nothing was actual, nothing except the impracticable wish to seize her unbeautiful hand and say to her
"Forgive, forgive. Poor wretch that you were, with a brand-mark on your
thigh, you could not bear the world as it was, you had to shut it out with a
tasteful and orderly dream—and I shattered that dream, I went my way and
left you standing alone in the chaos and the dark." Memphius dead . .

He would think of that later, when he had settled other and more crucial things. But now he must listen; she had gone to a great deal of trouble to find him here, and she was telling him in feverish haste the details of some wild plan she had to set him free. . . .

It was insane, it was complicated, it hinged on the frail likelihood that the Governor of Moesia would remember her—rose-colored dalmatica lying on the floor of the bath in the sullen greyness of the Saturnalia dawn. No, it was futile, and he told her so, looking sternly into her worn and painted face: the man was scarcely the sort to be bound by any sense of obligation or gratitude. Yet there was no dissuading her, she was going to Moesia nevertheless; she could get through Greece and Thrace into Moesia on the proceeds of what was in the house—the cythera, the scrolls, the statues, the flute. Trebonianus Gallus was closer to the Emperor's son than anybody else in the Empire was—he had told her so. She would go to Moesia and ask him for a favor and receive it, too: she was not utterly worthless, she still had charms for certain men, let him wait, let him wait and see . . . Somehow he found the strength to gainsay her over and over. He was gainsaying her still when the Guardsman came into the common room and called his name. And on the way up the stairway he knew that she would go before he could see her again, and thought how utterly ridiculous it was: she selling everything she owned and taking ship and traveling over stretches of wilderness to try to do for him what he could do in less than half an hour for himself . . . "Why don't you burn a few grains of incense and have this business over with?" said the Urban Prefect, getting up out of his chair and offering him a piece of fruit. And, for the first time, he knew precisely why it was: because he could not do the thing that *she* had refused to do, could not dishonor the Cross for which *she* had died among the beasts.

The same questions, the same answers. The same tired reassurances: "No word concerning you has come down to us as yet from our master and our lord." And suddenly, as if he were hearing it for the first time, it was borne in upon him that his uncle *was* in Dacia, had gone northward to make a desperate stand on the Gothic frontier and might not live to enter Italy again, to open the Senate and visit the Temple of Vesta and talk with his fellows over a table spread with pottery dishes and apples and sour wine and bread. Oh, God, he thought, clutching at the edge of the Urban Prefect's table, I cannot remember his voice, and I may never hear it again. The veined and spotted hands, the wrinkled neck, the decent fringe of iron-grey hair, the ice-blue eyes may soon lie buried under a barrow in an alien land. And I left him in fury, I did not even offer my thanks for the honor he did me in these latter days, or for the hard and awkward love he gave me when I was a lonely child . . . "Are you ill, your Illustriousness?" said the Urban Prefect, rather shortly. He had been pointing out, in elaborate and polished sentences, how the philosopher Seneca, a nonconforming Stoic if there had ever been one, had thought it only proper to show one's respect for the religion of the State by an occasional sacrifice; and his sensibilities had plainly been wounded by the prisoner's fixed and vacant eyes. No, not ill, said the prisoner; he had merely thought of something . . . Something that might change his attitude in connection with this wretched and interminable affair? No, nothing like that, only a random memory. . . .

And when he sat on the three-legged stool again, when he was immersed again in the murmurous, lulling conversation and the soothing semi-darkness, he strove to see his uncle Decius, and saw him as he had never seen him in actuality, saw him standing on the steps of the Temple of Vesta and gazing into the clean and orderly chamber, at the swept hearth and the iron pot and the sacred fire—all the ancient things, all the glorified and sanctified remnants of the past. Backward, always backward—Vesta and Livy and Horatius and Cato . . . The raw wine that was good enough for our forefathers, the merciless justice that served the necessities of an austere Republic, the bloody sacrifice of the beast at the altar, and on the battlefield and—in the arena and on the hilltop appointed for execution—the bloody, necessary sacrifice of the human heart. Withered arms, still sinewy with the terrible effort of turning back the wheel of time. Blue eyes, cold with staring the old dead glories out of their graves. Old voice, hard as iron—he remembered it now—raised always above the drivel and the obscenities and the joyless laughter, exhorting a nation of degenerates to be what their ancestors had been in the ancient days . . . You also, my lord and my master, he thought, sighing aloud; and a mild and motherly woman, passing him on her way to the dark corner where all of them went to relieve themselves, laid her hand briefly and inoffensively on his head. You also, my uncle, could not endure the rotting world and the sick century, and turned your back and gazed steadfastly into a dream. And I—I turned from you in bitterness and disgust, because you would not see what I was forced to see: that the Roman Censor was a suckling pig; that the death of Philip was a bloody murder, not a sacrifice; that the plebes wanted rolls in the shape of butterflies; that the roofs of the tenements were falling in; that the Christians were deluded innocents, not enemies of the State. And if you closed your door and your heart against me, you could do no less in your exigency. What else could you do, with no light shed upon you but the light of your dream, and all the rest blind chaos and the dark?

Looking up from his meditation, he saw that his evening meal—a piece of sausage and a rusk of bread on a big moist cabbage leaf—was lying in his lap. Somebody had placed it there, but who or when he did not know. There was an unusual volume of cheerful noise all about him. Some thirty visitors had come into the prison, all of them noisy because all of them were children; and he recalled with surprise that nobody but Guardsmen and children had entered the common room for ten or twelve days. Sitting on the three-legged stool, chewing on the hard sausage and easing his dried lips with the moisture on the leaf of cabbage, he vaguely watched them as they moved about among the little crowds of the wretched—girls and boys, none of them younger than ten and none of them older than fifteen, all as fresh as if they were visiting their grandmothers on the morning of a feast-day, They were conspicuously busy, proudly busy. Some of them had bread and wine to distribute; some of them were delivering messages and letters; some of them were quoting directives from "our dear undershepherd whom the congregation has recently forbidden to expose himself to any further danger." Five or six of them were serving as barbers—it was the click of the shears that had conjured up for him a nostalgic blend of odors: soap and steam and oil of balsam. Others—mostly the older girls—had taken upon themselves the tasks of surgeons, were binding up the running sores left by the fetters and measuring out the drops of ointment in the pink palms of their hands.

"How is it," he said, without meaning to say it aloud, "that only children ever come here any more?"

And he was startled that he should receive an answer, that the mild and quizzical old son of Abraham who had come to his defense on the rubble heap should be sitting against the opposite wall, should hear and reply. "I'll tell you how that happens, your Illustriousness," he said. "The elder Cornelius says that everybody except the little ones should stay at home and save his skin—at least for a month or so. You see, the persecution's been very rigorous these days. A good many have been taken on their way back to the street, and some have been followed and arrested in the tenements, and just about a week before you came a couple of centurions walked in here and took them all. But the children are safe. So long as they don't declare themselves to the Guardsmen, they can come and go as they please. And there's nothing they won't set their hands to, either. They'll do anything, anything at all, from bringing a person a bowl of ink to making arrangements for the burial of the dead."

His first impulse was to leave the old man unanswered. He thought, in a kind of panic, how his priceless silence might never be rendered back to him again, how all his searching might henceforth be broken in upon by sallies of good-natured Semitic volubility. Yet the rueful eyes were so gentle, peering at him from beneath the mobile and shaggy brows, the clay-colored face was so friendly, crossed by its innumerable wrinkles and constantly changing under an incongruous series of frowns and smiles, that he could not in human decency offer less than a routine reply. "So none of the older ones visit here now?" he said.

"Was there anybody in particular you wanted to communicate with, your Illustriousness? It's easy enough to take messages back and forth, you know. The children carry letters, dozens of them every day. That little Prisca—she brought you the stuff in the cabbage leaf—she'd be able to carry a message for you, I'm sure. Where is she? Oh, yes, over there under the window, combing old Lucinius's hair."

477

He saw her standing in the path of one of the red slants of sunlight. It was a euphemism to say that she was combing the hair of the venerable grandfather who sat on a stool before her, receiving her ministrations with the dignity of an honored consular. She was looking for lice, she was solemnly, deliberately pursuing the lice through the flowing white locks, with the comb in one hand and tweezers in the other; and the look of intense concentration on her face was so winsome and childish that, for the first time in an uncountable succession of days of grief and isolation, he smiled.

"Why don't you call her over here, your Illustriousness? She should be finished with that by now. She's been at it long enough."

"No, no, let her alone." He realized of a sudden that she had not been spending much time of late sitting silently on the floor beside him. The brooding, the staring, all the manifestations of the interdiction that he had drawn around himself had wounded her and sent her away at last; and he could not regret it, he knew that it was better so.

"Is there somebody else who might serve as well as she?"

"No, nobody. I don't want to see anybody. I'm better off by myself."

He had uttered it with a conscious implication; but the old man only shrugged and sighed. "Yes, so we think, so all of us think in the beginning," he said. "But afterward, when the turmoil we brought with us boils itself away and we know what we think and what we are, then it's different, then we stand in need of friends. Didn't your Illustriousness have any friends among the members of the Lord's congregation?"

"I had a cousin among the Christians. Her name was Paulina. She died in the arena," he said.

And somehow it was infinitely good to have said it. It was as if he had redeemed his tongue from the desecration of holding converse on any theme except his sorrow. It was as if, by pronouncing her name and uttering the manner of her death above the cheerful noise, he had sent to her, dead and buried though she was, an earnest of his unfaltering devotion.

"Your cousin?" There was an astounded look in the little beady eyes. "Paulina—the wife of the deacon Probus—she was your cousin?"

"Yes," he said, suddenly appalled by a conviction that he had said too much. "Excuse me, I'm ill at the moment, I never could digest sausage—"

"Certainly, certainly, my son." He pulled himself up to his knees; he started on his knees around the side of the beehive arch, saying over his shoulder, "Whatever it is that you have to bear, bear it in peace."

The grave behind the house of the elder Cornelius yielded her up in his dreams that night—not as a presence, only as a sound. He walked in a forest, under the aromatic, interlocking boughs of balsam and yew, and the earth on which he walked gave voice to a subterranean music—sound of the rippling of invisible waters, secretive music of an underground spring. Wherever that music was, the earth was moist and sweet; no blade or shoot of silvery fern-frond withered; no violet or anemone drooped its head. Ah, God, he thought, waking on his bed of rags with the pungent fragrance of the forest still in his nostrils—that was her love, that hidden spring, moving out from its source through limitless stretches of darkness. That was the issue of her living heart before I brought her to her death. Closed off, forbidden to flow into its appointed human outlets—never to the lover, never to the child at the breast—it wandered off and trickled gently in and out among the roots of things, feeding the secret plant, laving the thirsty stone. And what dark wonders it encountered there, what chaste and quiet consummations were granted to it in its hidden journeyings, I in the urgency of my desire refused to ask myself. . . .

He thought of her, lonely and loving and vulnerable in her shy and diffident youth. He thought of her breathing the scent of pines in the rented villa at Tibur; he thought of the separate hollows in the bolster on her bed, and bowed his head on his knees and wept. How blessed for her that the New Testament of love unbounded and triumphant had shattered the stone of shame that sealed the spring! How blessed that the issue of her living heart had not soured into rancor within her, had flowed outward, always outward, in unfailing freshness and abundance, to her crucified Lord and to the children of men. . . .

Her faith—he knew it now—had been no cold and rigorous exercise of virtue, no shutting out of life, but life itself. All the quickening impulses that might have gone to the lover in her arms or the helpless seed sprouting beneath her girdle—the passion, the ecstasy, the tenderness—had flowed out to Christ and to her mortal brothers and sisters—growing, multiplying, opening out in a hundred directions. That love of hers had been deeper in its penetrations than worldly love could ever be—more chaste, more joyous, content in its unceasing motion, content in its limitless giving, beyond disappointment, beyond bereavement, inasmuch as it wanted nothing for itself. . . .

And suddenly his grief and his remorse were so swollen within him that tears were not enough. He flung himself face down among the filthy rags; he ground his fists into the earthen floor; he spoke in whispers into earth itself, as if those channels through which her living love had moved were open to him still, as if her ears, unsealed in that dark house of silence and corruption by the exigency of his love, might listen yet, might hear. Poor child, he said in his heart, poor loving daughter of a grieving God, poor giving sister of confused and miserable men, forgive me also, love and forgive. Forgive me that I said the hoarded love within you spent itself upon a dream. Forgive me that I called it self-deception—that love which brought Him to a felon's cross. Forgive me that I thought all those who broke the bread with you in the sweet and bitter fellowship of These Last Times were cowards too weak to look at truth. I say it now—and you must hear me even in your grave—I had no truth to bring to you that could have served you better than your dream. That I should think the love in my transitory

479

body and my unanchored soul could have been more to you than you already owned—that I should imagine I could requite you in the fraction of a night—that I should presume to satisfy a love so vast that it could never be satisfied with less than the love of all the children of men—this was the wildest of delusions. What fruit it is that He and you and they will bear, I do not know as yet; I only dimly understand. But the fruit of my arrogant truth is bitter, the fruit of my truth is destruction.

He pondered these things until the hour of dawning, hearing around him such sounds as she must have heard in the last nights of her sojourn on the earth: the rustlings, the turnings, the isolated phrases rising from the mouths of dreamers, the long, impatient sighs of those who could not sleep. Then, much earlier than usual, when the sky was only beginning to pale beyond the bars of the high windows, he heard the Guardsmen coming down the corridor with the old son of Abraham, and he started to his feet. It was as he had feared it would be: those who always waited to receive their tortured elder at the top of the stairs had not yet awakened; and, before he could cross the room, weighed down as he was by fetters and fearful of stepping on the crowded bodies of the prisoners, the door had clanged shut again and the elder Moyses, like a bundle of rags in the uncertain light, was rolling down the stairs. Hurrying as much as he could to the spot where the old man lay, he was seized by a shivering: a strange, creeping sensation ran up and down his spine, and there was a tingling at the roots of his hair. He knows, he told himself, stepping over the sprawling legs and the vacant faces. He knows how it was between her and me—that was why he told me so solemnly that I should bear whatever I have to bear in peace. There was a time in her isolation and her terror when she could endure it no longer, when she crept to his side and whispered in his ear: "I had a cousin who took me in love and murdered my faith and left me in the chaos and the dark."

He stopped at the foot of the steps and stood staring down at the little Jew, at the bruised and swollen face, at the tips of the clay-colored fingers, all blistered and festering from the application of fire. He stared unseen; the eyes were closed; the words that came on a sigh out of the cracked and battered lips were addressed to nobody, were released merely for the easing of the heart. "Ah, well, so it goes," said the elder Moyses in a whisper. "One of these days they will make an end of me, and then there will be no more of it, which is just as well, just as well. . . ."

And if he knows that it was I who thrust her into this place, then he knows other things also, he told himself. Knows what torments were visited upon her naked spirit here. Knows whether it was in horror or in numb weariness that she went to her death. Knows how she moved and spoke and where she lay by night and against what part of the dripping wall she used to rest her tired head. Knows and may die—since any day now they will make an end of him—knows and may die with all that terrible and essential knowledge unrevealed, snuffed out forever like the other flames that flicker always more faintly in his brain. Knows and must be asked . . . He knelt and lifted the old louse-ridden head and pillowed it on his knee. "Is there anything I can do to lessen your pain? I came as soon as I could," he said.

The rueful face—more plainly visible to him now because the light was growing and pulsing beyond the upper windows—was cracked into innumerable amiable wrinkles by an incongruous, an almost merry smile. "Is that you, your Illustriousness?" he said in a whisper. "Have you left your stool? Are you finished with the solitary searching? It's soon enough, considering. Yes, you've done very well indeed."

"How is it with you, my father?" The epithet, which he had never addressed to anybody but Celestus Falconius—he wondered how it had come to fall from his lips. Doubtless, during the "solitary searching" he had heard it a thousand times, from the prisoners and from the children; and he asked himself vaguely how many other Christian phrases had impinged upon his consciousness, whether in a moment of distraction he might call Valerian or the elegant Urban Prefect "my brother", or say to the centurion who brought the order for his release or execution, "Depart in peace."

"A little worse than yesterday and a little better than tomorrow. I've been thinking, I'd better settle whatever remains to be settled, and quickly. One of these mornings, very soon now, I'll save them the trouble of pitching me downstairs."

He kept his silence, partly because there was nothing to be said and partly because the battered face that looked up at him from the pillow of his knee was unquestionably regarding him with good-humored mockery. One bruised eye winked at him—it was hard to believe, but it was so. The brow was crossed by quizzical wrinkles, and the cracked lips were twisted in a conspiratorial smile. "Yes, in a week at the most—I can tell it in my bones—it'll be over, I'll be dead."

"Are there many matters for you to settle, my father?" He held his elbows hard against his sides to control another assault of the creeping and the shuddering.

"Oh, yes, a great many. Some of them you probably know about. Matters of policy, public matters, Christian matters—" The mild Semitic tongue hurried on, as if to reassure him, as if to ease the shuddering. "That business of the scroll, for instance—the one that all of us signed here a week or so ago—you know what that was about?"

"Not very clearly, my father." It seemed to him that his impatience must be evident in his voice.

But the elder Moyses continued in a breathless, cheerful whisper, broken now and again by little gasps of pain, to tell him the history of that scroll. "We set great store by it, you know. We've talked of nothing else for days. I myself did the writing—I could have used your help, but you were busy with your solitary searching. I hear you were an expert with the pen yourself, the Emperor's scribe or something like that."

This is a tortured man, he told himself. This is a broken man, old and dying. It will cost you nothing to be kind. "I'm sorry I was too distracted to serve your purpose. What was it about?" he said.

"I can give it to you word for word—I went over it often enough . . ." He closed his eyes and repeated in a whisper, "To the elder Cornelius and the elder Novatian, our two undershepherds, whom the blessed Fabian left in charge of the fold, greetings from those of us who are in bonds and who expect hourly to be called to our crimson confession. Also, this request: Be gracious and forgiving, according to the spirit and the letter of our Redeemer, who died to save sinners. Let the lost sheep, who in their fright and in their childishness burned incense before the daemons, be freely forgiven. Appoint for them a proper period of penance, and let them return thereafter to free-hearted fellowship with their brothers and sisters in Christ. Also to alms and prayers and the breaking of the bread."

"I think you put it very well. I see no way in which you could have put it better, my father. It's about the lapsed, isn't it?" He was glad he had a Christian term which might serve for a show of interest.

"Yes, the lapsed. That little Prisca who used to sit beside you on the floor before you drove her away—her father was one of the lapsed, you know. I was talking to her late last evening—you didn't notice, you were in one of your dreams—and she tells me that everybody who might have looked after her has been taken away: her father interdicted because he burned the incense, the deacon Probus going to Carthage to carry our Roman tithes to the persecuted there, you here in prison, and the blessed Paulina gone. There are many like her—many children of the lapsed—they've lost their mothers and fathers, they have no homes. It's for them, as well as for the poor wretches who gave way to fear and worshipped the daemons—it's for them, too, that we wrote the petition to the elder Cornelius and the elder Novatian."

"And have you had an answer?" He asked it automatically, thinking only that it had been sweet to hear her name. "The blessed Paulina. . . ." He formed it soundlessly with his lips, "Paulina. . . . the blessed Paulina gone. . . ."

"If your Illustriousness would care to call it an answer. Whatever we ask of those two, it's always the same. The elder Cornelius says 'yes' and the elder Novatian says 'no', and we try to satisfy ourselves with a compromise. It seems that there won't be any general forgiveness—that's out of the question. However, each of us who makes his crimson confession is to receive in return for it the forgiveness of one of those poor wretches—that's the way it finally turned out. But it's a niggling bargain, a very ungenerous and coldhearted bargain."

"And the blessed Paulina—what stand did *she* take?" he said, more because he was impelled to speak the name than because he believed such matters as the fate of the lapsed could have concerned her in those last days, desperate as she was—afraid and ashamed and bereft of her Lord.

The elder Moyses wrinkled his forehead and contracted his stubbly brows. "Don't you know what stand she would have taken, my son?" he said at last. "I thought you knew her very well."

"I knew her—that is, I thought I knew her." It was the easier to say because the battered eyelids sealed up the eyes. "Somehow I thought you understood how it was between her and me—that I loved her and gave her cause to hate herself and sent her to her death—that I robbed her of everything she owned—her loyalty to Probus, her place among her fellows, her faith in her God—"

"I understood you loved each other, you and she," said the old, cracked lips, scarcely stirring. "I understood you had each other after the manner of the flesh—in the last days she told me so. But all the rest—that she hated herself and died because you made her hate herself, that she died bereft of her faith in Jesus Christ and estranged from Probus, that she was an exile here among her brothers and sisters in the Lord—this is simply not so, and you have only invented it to punish your unhappy soul, my son. I tell you, and may God bear witness to it, that the blessed Paulina spent her latter days on earth in a holy state of Christian grace. She made her peace with Probus—with my own eyes I saw them embrace, and I saw her face thereafter, and, as I hope to rest my head upon the knees of my Redeemer, I know that she was utterly at peace. To those of us who shared the darkness with her here she gave of herself with a generosity beyond anything I have ever known. Out of all that have come here, I have never seen another that gathered to her spirit so much love. Nor do I think that our Lord and our Saviour, who pitied the publican and the sinner, is so obsessed with perfection that he would throw away a spirit such as hers, even if it was darkened a little by mortal dust."

The last sentence had been uttered in a hoarse whisper. The clay-colored flesh of the face had gone pale, and the bruises on it showed purplish in the growing light. "Rest a little, my father. You'll wear yourself out," he said.

"In a moment. But wearing yourself out isn't as bad as your Illustriousness seems to think. To wear yourself out—to let the life flow out of you in labors in the Lord's vineyard, to whisper out the breath of life in comforting your mortal fellows—that's the best way, the easiest way to make an end. That's how it was with her—with the blessed Paulina, I mean. Anybody who tells you, my son, that a lion took her life in the arena can't see God's truth. It was here that she rendered up her life, day by day but always more and more, very willingly and of her own accord. To the little ones of Jesus she freely gave it. To the weak ones and the sick ones and the ones who couldn't sleep because they were frightened. To all that had need of her—yes, and through all that had need of her, to God also, to God Himself.

I remember how she sat in that corner"—he pulled himself up on his elbows and pointed his grey finger at the place—"over there, never moving, scarcely aware of her mortal body, already freed of all her human necessities—she sat over there in that corner for hours, holding the head of a dying man on her knees. I can still hear her voice lifted up from that end of the table in the responses of our Eucharist—so thin, so weary with loving and giving that I remember at the time I thought it was not a human voice anymore, it was more like a cry of liberation thrown back by a naked spirit already on its way to heaven. Oh, no, she was gone before they called her, the blessed Paulina. What could they do with her, they and their lions? All that was mortal in her had been given away to the children of men—and One and One only can touch the rest."

That corner over there . . . that end of the table . . . As soon as the others were awake and he was free to go, he went to those places, back and forth, over and over again, the clink of his fetters lost in the growing conversation, the strangeness of his movements unmarked by the kind, incurious eyes. Why such a pilgrimage should ease him, his reason could not tell him; and yet it was consoling and sweet, it was almost as consoling as her living embrace to kneel on the floor where she had knelt, to sit on the bench where she had sat, to touch the wood where she had laid her veined and mortal hand. The clarity with which the images conjured up by the elder Moyses revealed themselves to him was enough to establish their actuality. While he had thought of her as one in terror, he had never been able to summon up her face. Kind now, almost blithe now, it rose to him out of the impenetrable shadows in the corners and under the beehive arches: it turned upon him from a group of chattering women to offer him a wise and innocent glance. And when he sat on the ground beside the three-legged stool, when he told himself again that she was dead and under this ground, his bitter grieving was sweetened by a strange conceit: he could not rid himself of the thought that it was a healing herb, healing for him and for all the children of men, that was growing from the shell of her spent heart.

Chapter 39

THE ENDLESS haggling with sharp-witted antiquarians in the shops of the Via Sacra, the dusting and wadding and carting away of statues and cedarwood tables and musical instruments that had once been dear, the bleakness of suddenly revealed patches of wall and drapeless windows—these things were depressing to such chance visitors as the philosopher Cleander and the poet Statilius. But on the mistress of the ravaged house they made no impression at all. Once she had succeeded in eradicating from her memory his alien and inattentive face, so remote and unknowable as to be utterly lost to her, she had been capable of no lesser griefs. Had the cythera brought less than half of what they had paid for it? That was nothing. Had the hand of the marble Apollo been shattered in the jolting cart on the way to the buyer's house? That was nothing, too. Everything was nothing, including the information that the lady Paulina was no longer among the living. Pack the clothes, see the slave who has come from the shipping office with news of a vessel leaving for Greece, go into the court and empty the bag of birdgrain for the pigeons. Burn the letters, strip the bed. . . .

Since all significance is gone from life—stricken out in an instant by the cold mouth in its stubble of prisoner's beard—see no significance in anything. Reject all offers of financial help from friends, not because it is unfair and a blot on the final page of friendship to accept a loan that may never be returned, but because the present sum of money would seem to be enough. Keep the fat and stupid Levantine, take him on the trip—not as a tie with the sweet and wounding past, only because it is too late to sell him now and try to buy a better slave. The wretched little monkey, take him, too—not as a mute witness of all that was and may or may not be again, but simply because there is nobody to hand him over to—who wants a monkey afflicted with eczema along the spine? And if there comes a moment in a denuded room or later on the deck of a ship when the heart must ask itself: "Why do I go at all? What good is there in any of this for him or for me?" then say that, as the bird stricken by an arrow in mid-air continues in the same direction for a few more yards before it falls, so the stunned spirit, having a way, will follow it yet a while. I do what I have said I would. I go where I have committed myself to go.

And, once she had accepted the meaninglessness of the whole procedure, it was easy for her to break the total of the journey down into certain segments, each with its circumscribed obligation. For instance, on the first and dullest part of the voyage, between the Port of Rome and the Straits of Sicily, she charged herself with only a negative duty: not to get seasick; and when the chalky curve of the Sicilian coast lay before her and she could say to herself that she had not vomited over the side of the ship nor taken to her bed to whine and chew on and sniff at cinnamon bark like one of her fellow-travelers, a spoiled sixteen-year-old patrician bride, she felt that progress was being made, that a sane and dependable program was working out successfully.

The second lap of the journey, that blue and balmy stretch of the Mediterranean between Sicily and the legendary island of Crete, called for closer social intercourse with the others on board if she was to collect the sort of information that she was looking for. There was more chatter now about ports and hostels and final destinations. All the scenic distractions had fallen away—no fishing-craft and few sailing vessels, no distant peaks to be discerned or conjured into being out of a cloud of mist, nothing now but the opalescent monotony of a warm spring sea. Besides, with six days of quiet watching behind her, she knew which of the aimless pacers of the deck would be easiest to approach. Not the banker from Narbo, who plainly took her for a courtesan; not the doting equestrian mother, who fancied that every woman on board was enamoured of her pig-faced son; not the lively little old lady from Carthage, who used bright henna on her hair and nails and was careful to appear only in the company of people of unquestionable status. Before she could approach anybody at all, even with so innocuous an object as to ask where it would be best to disembark and what conditions a traveler might expect in the northward reaches of Thessaly or Thrace, she had to make certain that she would be given a courteous reception; poised and efficient as she considered herself, she knew that an offhand answer or a cool look would bring her to the point of tears. And even when she had done her best for herself—she spent hours anointing the wrinkled flesh of her neck and pulling bits of sun-dried skin from the bridge of her nose and flattening her hair after the sallies of the wind—even when every flaw was seen to and every fold of her dalmatica was in place, she found it difficult to approach the meanest of them—the diffident medical student on his way to Alexandria or the plebeian matron who was going to her brother in Cyprus because, as she made plain to everybody on board, her husband had died without leaving her a denarius to her name.

And yet, sometimes asking and always listening, she learned much, she learned more than she could have wished. Learned that it made no difference where one left the ship—at Antron, Methone, or Rhizus; the chances of getting a guide or a wagon or even a decent meal at a hostel in any of them were equally slim. Learned that Thessaly and Thrace—there was nothing but a hopeless flinging up of hands at the mention of Moesia—had been so beaten down and cleaned out by the legions which had marched through them that most of the shops were barred and most of the fields were bare. Learned that priests of Mithras, formerly untouchable in their sanctity, had been clubbed and robbed by bandits and left dying in the forest, that virgins dedicated to Artemis and Apollo and carrying the holy torches that had always kept them inviolable had been raped by deserters. No, nobody in his senses would entrust himself to the wilderness above Perinthus, or, for that matter, venture out of the comparative safety of the fringe of cities along the Euxine Sea.

But that was the fourth and last stage of the journey, that plunge into the wilderness. To contemplate it now would serve no purpose—one obligation at a time, and every obligation in its proper place. And the third segment, the voyage on the Aegean, in and out among the fabled islands of Greece—that she had reserved for pure pleasure, for a temple emerging from the wine-dark sea, for the fragrance of cleft cedarwood blazing in the dusk, for owls and falcons and chattering sea-crows whose sires had inhabited Calypso's isle.

And, if the ship had not taken on a load of honey at Cos, this stage of the voyage might also have furnished the expected yield. It was the smell of that honey—thick and overpowering with an unbearable memory—which cancelled out all dreams of the fatherland that she had nurtured in the house of the patrician Marcellinus and shared with such other dreamers as Cleander and Antisthenes. It was the clinging smell of the honey which made every island a place to be fled: Carian marble steps cracked and tufted with grass, faces of gods and goddesses bespattered with bird-lime, starved goats nibbling at the scant furze on the cliffs, a family of peasants shamefully seeking the eyes of those who had come to the prow to see the sights—the mother in the midst of the brood, a ragged and debased Andromache, holding up to Romans, to crass and cruel Romans, a beautiful, antique, begging hand . . . It was the inescapable, gagging sweetness of the honey that brought the murdered past, alive and bleeding still, into her dreams. One night she woke with a cry out of a tormented sleep, thinking that she was lying, not among the other passengers on the deck, but on the earthen floor of her father's miserable hut, seeing above her, not the lively face of the old woman from Carthage, but her mother's face, yearning over her sleeping children, pondering some desperate solution. One afternoon, when she stood in casual conversation with a group of the others, she became aware that an advocate from Corinth was looking at her appraisingly from head to foot, and it was as if she were standing again on the stone block at Delos—involuntarily she looked for the crosses drawn in chalk on her feet. And on another occasion, when the woman bound for Cyprus was complaining of a swollen vein at the back of her leg, she suddenly became conscious that the mark of the brand had been smarting for several days; she laid her hand in her lap and felt it covertly through the fold of the silk. Is it bigger, could it be growing, can it be cancerous? she asked herself, and knew no peace until she could withdraw into a sheltered place and see.

No, she was not well. Her legs ached, her hair was lifeless, her tongue was sore with ulcers caused either by the salt air or the unaccustomed food. On the way from the island of Scyros to Rhizus—she had decided quite arbitrarily that she would stay on the boat as long as possible, disembarking at the northernmost coastal town—the sickness of women came upon her, unseasonably and violently, and manifested itself not only in a debilitating loss of blood but in erratic heartbeats and a continuous humming in her head. She was so dull that she could not trust herself to look to the simplest matters. Once, when she was dressing after a futile attempt to wash the impression of disgust from her body, she remembered with a shock that she had not kept her eye on the bag of money which she had taken off along with her girdle: anybody could have stolen it; it was lying behind her, between the bucket and the dalmatica. Once, eating with three of the other passengers in the captain's cabin, she was embarrassed to find herself unable to recall their names. Yet there were moments when the dullness gave way to an even more distressing symptom: the smallest infraction, the most trivial inconvenience could fling her into a rage. Once, when the monkey Cyrillus tugged at her arm while she was trying to thread a needle, she struck him from her lap with the flat of her hand; and three times—once over a pert snicker, once over a bowl of soup spilled because of the lurching of the ship, once because of a lost book—she clenched her bony fists and pummeled the head and shoulders of her Levantine slave.

The so-called city of Rhizus was nothing. The Corinthian advocate had forewarned her, but she had refused to believe him. "Nothing," had meant to her no public baths, no theater, no statues, no street of shops. It had never occurred to her that anything which called itself an urban settlement could be a shallow crescent of mud and matted willows and dilapidated huts lying between a wilderness and the sea. There was nobody here but sailors and fisherfolk with their filthy children and their suspicious, snarling dogs. An odor of dead creatures of the water and rancid oil and frying fish hung over everything. The lights in the windows—already kindled for the evening when she came up from the shore—looked strangely dim, perhaps because the oil was bad, perhaps because the brightness of the sea had affected her eyes. For close to an hour she wandered about, with the monkey on her shoulder and the Levantine dragging the heavy bags up behind her, trying to find either a hostel or a townsman who looked friendly enough to answer a traveler with courtesy. But those whom she passed in the muddy, darkling streets appeared to her, in her bewildered state, to be less than human. She had a wild notion that the outpost of Rhizus was peopled with such beings as had been put off ships or driven out of other cities; the advancing light of the dimly burning lanterns revealed to her faces unshaven and unwashed, dour and cruel mouths, angry or vacant eyes. And, when she summoned up the courage to ask—of a prostitute who sat on the stoop of a house from which she had plainly been ejected—where a person could find a hostel, she was told that there was no hostel, that there was only a cookshop some ten doors down, and that she must hurry if she wanted to eat.

The cookshop was ill-lighted and dirty and dank with steam. One entered, through a slit in a greasy leather curtain, a low square room with five or six tables. Some lamps burned on some of the tables, and at three or four of these tables the uncouth diners sat, one pair of them quarrelsome, being far gone in wine. In the middle of the earthen floor, on top of a pit filled with hissing red coals, was a battered bronze cauldron, and the fat Syrian proprietress stood over it while she tossed in clams and mussels and crayfish, stopping now and again to thrust out her pale plump nether lip and blow a string of oily hair out of her eyes.

She did not look up until she and the visitor stood face to face, with only the cauldron and the fishy steam of the cauldron between. Her eyes, light and evil in her sallow face, could not manage a steady glance. "What would you like to eat? Clams? Mussels? A lobster? I can give you a lobster and bread with red wine for a denarius," she said.

But to eat anything out of that loathsome kettle was impossible. Her stomach heaved within her; she felt as if the earthen floor beneath her were pitching, like the sea. "No, I would rather have an egg."

"Certainly, certainly. Boiled or fried in fat?"

"Boiled," she said, remembering from her lost childhood a hideous story of a Thessalian hag who murdered children and saved the fat for rendering and frying. "A boiled egg and half a loaf of bread."

"As you say, my lady." She reached into a pouch of rags hanging over her voluminous skirt, pulled out an egg and held it up with pride, as if she had produced it by magic. "Yours, boiled, in a moment. Sit down and wait," she said, and popped it into the filthy, fishy water.

At the table in the corner, she told herself that she would have to get out of here at once—sit on the beach and wait for another ship, walk the streets until she found someone to take her north. But any such plans were preposterous, of course: she might be robbed and murdered on the beach, and if she walked the streets she would be taken for a prostitute. The egg was brought to her on a dusty plate, and she ate it, and it tasted like any other egg. The Syrian woman offered her a room—right here behind the cookshop, my lady, with a cot and pillows, and cheap as dirt at two denarii—and she took it and paid another denarius to have a matting brought in for her slave. And, unbelievably, in a room visited by bold rats and entered again and again by drunken and apologetic diners, in a bed so grimy that her skin crept at the thought of lying in it, she eventually fell into a stunned, unbroken sleep.

On the first day she did not waken until the middle of the afternoon. It took her more than an hour to drag herself out of bed: the time of day, the strangeness and filth of her surroundings begot in her a nightmare immobility. And even after she had managed to comb some of the snarls out of her hair and to wash herself in a basin of tepid water brought in from the cookshop by her Levantine, she was too exhausted to reassume the blithe efficiency, to step into the outer room and inquire how a person could find a carriage or a wagoner or a horseman bound for one of the northern cities of Thrace. For the better part of another hour she sat on the edge of a rickety chair, and it was past dusk when she forced herself to part the curtain and walk into the noise and squalor of the adjoining chamber.

She had told herself, in justification of her delay, that there would be more likelihood of getting information after the crowd had gathered; but when she saw their faces, lean and brutal or fat and sly, and heard their talk, an unbelievable mixture of violence and obscenity, she could not bring herself to ask them anything. She had made up her mind to order fish—fish, even cooked in a homogeneous mass in a dirty cauldron, was bound to be dependable in a seaport town. But when she sat at the table, with the greasy Syrian bending above her, exuding fish, she could not help herself, she had to ask for meat—and did not inquire what kind of meat was to be had, since it was plainly better not to know. Her request was relayed in Greek and Syrian and some strange northern dialect from one table to another, and begot ill will. An old hag in the opposite corner did an imitation of a fine lady putting on airs, and two sailors, standing near the cauldron and talking with the proprietress, looked at her over their shoulders and shook with such mirthless, scornful laughter as she had never heard before.

The meat came, unrecognizable in a slimy stew. The Levantine would have none of it—he sat on the floor at her feet, swallowing oysters by the dozen; and, since the others were watching her and she had made so much trouble by asking for meat at all, she felt herself obliged to eat at least half of it. Much to her surprise, once she had begun to eat she could not stop. Her stomach, empty and imperious, proved itself stronger than her delicacy;

she ate greasy gravy and unidentifiable vegetables and chunks of gristle and fat; if the meat was tainted, and she strongly suspected that it was, she did not care. Two pieces, utterly unchewable, she gave to the monkey who sat shuddering on her knees. He consumed them, but slowly, looking at her over the recalcitrant fat with bright, reproachful eyes. And when the last of the stew was gone and she had wiped her mouth and her fingertips clean with a piece of bread dipped in wine, she found that she had courage enough to wander over to the cauldron where the Syrian and a crowd of sailors stood, howling with laughter over some obscene remark.

Were any of the gentlemen going to Marcianopolis or Philippopolis or Serdica? she asked in the clear, shy voice that Favorinus Herennius had called the voice of a bird and the patrician Marcellinus had compared to the notes of the flute. They all burst into laughter—at the pure Attic dialect, at the gracious and indirect form of address. She flushed, but the flush seemed to have more to do with some secret and violent thing that was going on in her stomach than with her embarrassment. Raising her head a little and offering them a self-depreciatory smile, she told them that she must somehow get to Moesia, her case was urgent, she had crucial business there. If there was anybody here, or any acquaintance of anybody here who could take her a little way into Thrace, she would pay him well . . . Moesia? they said. Who was crazy enough to go into Mocsia at a time like this? Nobody here, certainly, though on a second mention of good pay, one of the younger sailors recalled that his cousin knew a wagoner who sometimes went to Thrace. Tomorrow or day after tomorrow, if the gracious lady would care to wait—he mimicked her pronunciation, he thrust out his chin in a way that made her hate herself—he would stop by and let her know whether he'd take a passenger and what he'd consider a decent price . . . She turned then and walked back to the table, partly because of an overwhelming sense of futility and partly because she had suddenly become aware of a pair of eyes staring at her from the other side of the cauldron through a cloud of steam. Stranger's eyes, eyes of the male, stripping away every ornament that her life had veiled her in, reducing her to a white and paltry thing, seeing and sneering at her nakedness.

She stayed in the cookshop a little longer, held there by a feverish necessity to see the possessor of those eyes, held there in spite of the fact that the skin of her face was behaving very strangely, was alternately burning hot and icy cold. Half an hour went by in noise and filthy talk before he came round to the other side of the cauldron. He was a powerful man, strong and bullish, in spite of the fact that he must have been close to fifty. His hair was short and grizzled, and his face was clay-colored and surly, with hanging jowls and a short, blunt chin. He did not look at her again; in fact, he passed her with deliberate inattention. Some of the others called their farewells to him as he strode toward the entrance, but he did not condescend to turn. He took up his cloak, black and lined with bearskin, threw it over his shoulders, and walked through the slit in the leather curtain into the night.

"*He'll* be going to Marcianopolis," the Syrian said, bending to take away the dishes. "He and eight others like him go up there every month or so to spend what they get on the road. And a high time they have of it, too, I can tell you, with their thieves' money—everything they want—women and roast lamb and Syrian wine."

Strangely enough, the mention of the roast lamb had a more powerful effect upon her than the news that the staring stranger was a bandit and went more or less regularly through the wilds of northern Thrace. At the very mention of roast lamb she had to rise and pick up Cyrillus and excuse herself.

"Shall I come with you, my lady?" said the Levantine.

His face, pale and moon-round in the shadow under the table, looked inexplicably malicious; the blubbery lips were curved in an idiotic smile. "No, no," she said, entertaining for an instant the ridiculous notion that her slave had poisoned her. He hated her—of that much she was certain; and she did not want him watching her if she had to vomit. "Stay here and enjoy yourself, I'd rather be alone."

She was sick, so sick that four times she had to go out through a rear door into the muddy, moonlit court to vomit. She was cold, so cold that she had to go back into the cookshop, with her teeth clicking and her whole body jerking, to ask that a brazier of coals be brought into the room—a service which was rendered at the exorbitant price of six denarii. Somebody in the disorderly crowd out there had found it amusing to ply the Levantine with wine, and he returned to her wildly drunken and intolerably arrogant. He let out an audible snicker when she lurched for the door, and would not lift a hand to help her into bed. Once in her delirium she woke and looked at a rat and saw it growing to the size of a hound and was on the point of throwing the bag of money at it. "But that's a crazy thing to do," she said aloud, and the enormous rat scampered away, if he had ever been there. Something—either the sea or her sickness—was roaring in her ears, and she sat up and listened and fell back and slept.

She woke in the whiteness of the sunrise. There had been the voice of a monkey whining and chattering in her dreams. "Cyrillus," she said in a whisper, knowing suddenly that for the first night since the beginning of the voyage the little creature had not slept curled against her side. She had a dim recollection that she had seen him last on a stool near the brazier; and, sick as she was—her throat burning with bile, and such a pain in her stomach that it seemed about to burst—she got up and went to look for him, reeling as she walked, feeling the rickety furniture give way under her weight. He was lying on the stool, with the wan warmth of the burnt-out fire still shed around him, his knees drawn up, his paws over his eyes. Through the spread grey fingers, she could see those eyes, glazed and open. She touched him once, twice, three times, prodding the scarcely-fleshed ribs with the tip of her finger, before she could accept the fact that he was dead.

And then, as if she had been a murderer driven by the threat of punishment to conceal her victim, she was obsessed with the need to bury him, to put him under the earth at once, before the Syrian could return to the cookshop, before her slave could waken out of his drunken sleep. Shaking and gasping and trying to keep her teeth from chattering, she found a scarf of Egyptian linen and bundled the stiff and springy little body up in it. She had made it look like an Egyptian mummy; and wildly, reasonlessly, she laughed at it and then snatched it up and covered it with kisses and rocked it against her breast. Still kissing it, she carried it through the rear door and into the court where she had vomited during the night, where stunted willows and heaps of fish-bones and scaly skins and discarded mussel shells were revealed in the pitiless whiteness of the dawn. With the sharp point of a broken spoon that she found in the garbage, she made a shallow grave. When it was dug and the bundle was squeezed into its narrowness, she scarcely had the strength to ladle the earth back into place; and yet she knelt for a long time above the mound, shuddering and trying to shake off the delirium, exposing her body to the damp and chastening winds borne in from the sea. Why am I here? she asked herself in all sanity. What good is there in any of this for him or for me? But before she could give herself an answer purplish darkness began to close in upon her, and it was through purplish darkness, hissing with whispering voices, that she found her way back to bed.

For that day and the following three it seemed to her, when she was aware of anything but fever-dreams, that she was on the point of death. Whatever she could do for herself, she did: she dragged herself across the room to vomit in the court, she pulled the money with slippery fingers out of the money-bag and laid it in the Syrian's dirty palm, she held the bowl of milk to her own mouth in spite of the shaking of her hands. Never, except in the direst necessity, did she ask for any help from her slave; for, whether she was sane or raving, her belief that the Levantine was her mortal enemy was the same, and there were times when he seemed so menacing that she thought of asking for the services of an advocate to set him free.

The sign of his enmity was slight, very slight: all he did was chew at his thumbnail, pressing it against his teeth and making a hideous clicking sound. In the past, she had needed only to glance sidewise at him for his slobbered thumb to fly out of his mouth and his plump arm to wipe his dribbled chin. But now he chewed constantly, methodically, maliciously. He chewed and made it obvious that he was chewing away her authority over him bit by bit, that he had no fear of her, that there was nothing to keep him from putting poison in her milk or smothering her with a pillow in the middle of the night. The most terrifying part of it all was that she could not bring herself to reprove him. When she heard the sickening sound, she had to turn away and pretend to be occupied with something else, and her effort to control herself so exhausted her that she would break into an icy sweat.

On the third evening of her sickness and the fourth of her stay in the room behind the cookshop, it seemed to her that she was growing better. Her fever abated—the flesh of her cheeks felt moist and cool and there were no new cracks in her peeling lips. A kind of tremulous quiet settled around her with the dusk; the Levantine had taken himself off to drink, and there were no sounds except the blurred sound of conversation and the far off roar and grating of the sea. It seemed to her that the hideous room had taken on a crazy, rickety beauty in the purple evening light; she looked at the cobwebs waving softly against the wall, she looked at the matted willows through the door into the court, and a strange excitement stirred her mind and moved along her listless limbs, so that she had some difficulty settling down to sleep. She slept very lightly so long as the noise outside went on, troubled, now that the excruciating pain had passed, by minor things—the stiff edge of the dirty coverlet rubbing against her chin, the pressure of the money-bag at the back of her head. But suddenly, toward morning, it seemed to her that all discomforts had been miraculously taken away; and she slept profoundly, in perfect comfort, as if the softest of goosefeather pillows lay under her head.

The delicious sense of well-being was still with her when she wakened at mid-morning with the sun in her eyes. The coverlet was flung far back. It must have grown warm, she thought, I must have done that in my sleep. She waited for her peace to be broken by the clicking sound, but it was blessedly absent—the Levantine had probably gone out to order her morning milk. In order to pay for the milk, she slipped her hand under the pillow—and started up with a cry. The bag was gone. Her rings, too—she looked at her fingers, still bearing the marks of them, and knew how utterly she was undone.

"Have you seen my Levantine?" she called to the Syrian who was bustling about in the adjoining room.

"Not for three or four hours," said the cheerful voice. "I thought you sent him to see somebody about a wagon for Marcianopolis."

"I sent him?"

"That's what he said."

"The liar! The pig! The filthy beast," she said, weeping. "He took every denarius I had, and all my jewels. He's run away, he's robbed me, he's gone."

The Syrian came to the doorway, wiping her spread hands on her greasy skirt and blowing the strand of hair out of her eyes. Her face showed neither distress nor surprise; in a stream of good-humored volubility she made it known that anybody could have expected as much. Slaves were always stealing and running away, especially here where the townsmen dealt in such questionable business that nobody wanted to call the officials

494

in. But the gracious lady mustn't let herself go to pieces like that. She certainly wasn't going to be pitched into the street; she could stay exactly where she was until she found something good for herself in the way of a protector. She would go so far as to say—she pursed her lips and nodded and assumed the same air of magical incantation that she had worn when she produced the egg—there was a protector in the net, so to speak. That Roggio, the one who went to Marcianopolis every now and again—he'd been asking about the gracious lady, and she had a feeling he'd be back again tonight.

Strange day, languorous, equivocal . . . The Syrian was much more fond of her than she had been when the money bag still lay under the pillow. The Syrian took to calling her "darling", and lugged in a great tub of heated water for her to bathe in, and borrowed some cassia ointment from a woman next door. The Syrian stewed her a small pot of oysters swimming in butter and milk, and sat on the floor beside her, urging her to eat, saying that a full stomach sweetens the breath. In fact, though there was no further mention of the somber Roggio, the Syrian took toward the gracious lady precisely the manner that a skilled procuress would take toward a hypocritical and skittish whore. And she—the gracious lady—clean again, delivered from her sickness, hearing for the first time in days a kindly voice, accepted the warm, wan, soothing afternoon and left the night to take care of itself.

The night, too, was warm, so warm that the leather curtain was drawn back, leaving the cookshop open at the front on a vista of matted willows and muddy slopes leading down to the flat nothingness that was the sea. At the last moment she had suffered an assault of terror; but now that she was here, sitting in a corner over another bowl of stewed oysters, with the blank and quiet view before her and the stench of the cauldron mitigated by the fresh air that kept streaming in, she was convinced that the whole thing was something invented to give color to the drab and empty life of Rhizus, a fabrication of the Syrian's idle brain. If he appeared in the cookshop at all tonight, it would not be to ask her to lie with him in return for a journey into the north. It was unthinkable that she should be faced with a decision between remaining here destitute and rendering herself up into his clay-colored hands.

Others came, ten or twelve others, sailors and prostitutes and fisherfolk. Some change—what sort of wild nonsense had the Syrian been whispering into their ears?—some change had taken place in their bearing toward her: one of the women gave her a knowing smile, and one of the sailors, celebrating a safe return from an unsavory venture on the water, sent her a goblet of red wine. The wine lay warm in her stomach and begot in her the same strange stirrings that had possessed her when the hateful room had grown beautiful to her in the purplish evening light. Her breasts, draped in fresh linen, felt soft and alive; her cheeks were moist and pliant, and she breathed the smell of cassia on her hands and sighed. A body, she thought, has a life of its own, quite apart from the spirit that dwells within it. A body may very well continue to hunger and thirst and stir, even after the spirit is dead.

Darkness had entirely blotted out the matted branches of the willows and the muddy gloss of the slope when he entered the room. The sea seemed closer in the blackness; the roar of the waves and the rough grate of the tide on the pebbles was almost as loud as the talk; he seemed to be stepping into the red light of the coal-pit straight out of the sea. He was brusque and surly, and his presence and the force of his mood subdued the boisterousness. A prostitute stifled her squealing laughter, and two of the sailors got up and looked about them for their cloaks, seeing an end to the revelry. For the first time she heard his voice, higher than she had expected and with a note of querulousness in it, asking for mussels—without sand this time, they were rotten enough as they were without the sand.

And now that he was staring at her again, now that he had actually started for her table, there was still no reason for the creeping sensation that was running up and down her spine. She could continue to sit with her eyelids down and her chin on her curled fist; she was free to say whatever she wished.

"I hear you want to go to Marcianopolis," he said, easing his bulky body onto the stool on the other side of the table, laying his big hands palms down on the wine-soaked wood.

She looked at those hands, the split nails, the black tufts of hair growing below the knuckles. She looked and caught her breath, knowing with consternation that she was thinking how heavy and hard and cruel they would be in love. "Yes. Anywhere in northern Thrace. I have to get to Moesia eventually."

"What do you want in Moesia?"

"To get to the headquarters of the northern legions."

He laughed—his laughter came out of him in a snort, like the breath of a bull. "Oh, a camp-follower!" he said.

She looked at him in fury and looked away at once, stared out of all countenance by the contemptuous eyes. "I have something to discuss with the Governor of Moesia." Her voice did not betray her, her voice was firm and cool. "It's very important. It's a matter of life and death."

"With the Governor of Moesia? And of course he'll see you, that's all he's got to do with himself. Listen, my girl—do yourself a service, will you? If you want to go to Marcianopolis, pull in your chin and talk like anybody else. I won't have any woman around me who talks like a schoolmaster."

But what have I done that he should have the effrontery to speak to me like that? she asked herself, trying in vain to keep her eyes on his grey and sullen face. "I think you misunderstand me—" She strove to smile, she pressed her shaking chin against her hand. "When I asked the proprietress whether she knew of anybody who was going up there, I meant to pay for the service, I was in a position to offer a good price—"

"Listen," he said, bending forward again so that it was impossible to avoid his stare or his breath. "Whatever you had in that bag you were lugging around—and remember, it's gone, you haven't got it anymore—whatever you had was a lot less than anything I would call a good price. I serve nobody, I was born free, which is more than certain people can say for themselves."

She could not answer. She kept watching his searching, conjecturing eyes. They moved from her neck to her shoulder, from her shoulder to the half-revealed curve of her breast. He was looking for the mark of the brand— only on the comeliest of slaves did they trouble themselves to put it in a place that would be hidden. The red welt on her thigh—it also had a life of its own: it seemed to be stirring under the folds of silk.

"Well, what's the use of asking you questions? You would only lie," he said.

"Why should I lie?" And why—why in the name of all the gods should I take that ingratiating tone with you, when there is only one way for me to answer: to rise like a gracious lady and leave you sitting here alone?

"Because runaway slaves are always liars."

"I'm not a slave."

"No? A freedwoman? Let out after fifteen years for good service in bed?"

"I was born free," she said, wondering why she should provoke him when her creeping flesh kept warning her against it. "I was born free, and I don't know why you should take this tone with me. All I did was ask for somebody to take me north—"

"And since then you lost your money." His hand, thick and hairy, moved across the table. He prodded the flesh of her arm with one blunt fingertip. "Lost your money, and still want to go to Marcianopolis—don't you? Have to get to Marcianopolis—it's a matter of life or death. Well, I'll tell you what, my girl, I've half a mind to take you. Nine of us are going up there tomorrow, but you don't have to worry about the others—they'll keep their hands off you as long as I tell them to. And I'll tell them to as long as you behave like the well-used slut that you are. There it is, laid on the table, and you can take it or leave it. It makes no difference to me."

He turned round, heavily and slowly—not to get up and walk away, as she had thought, only to show that he was enraged at the silence which had settled on the room. The others were watching. For an instant, glancing wildly around her, she saw nothing but avid, knowing eyes. They have coupled us, she thought, they are seeing us like beasts, naked and together . . . But one of them after the other, feeling his glance, lowered his eyelids and turned back to his bowl of stinking fish.

"But you're not a fool, you know a good thing when you see it," he said, rising and coming round to her side of the table and standing bulky as a bull between her and the others. "You know our little Mama over there will throw you out unless you grease her palm with three or four denarii a day.

You know you've only got one thing to sell, and that's pretty well worn. And what's the use of selling it to sailors in this garbage dump when you can get up north by selling it to me?" He took her by the back of her hair and turned her head and pulled it toward him slowly, until her face was pressed against the leather belt that spanned his girth.

"Let go of me," she said in a whisper.

"No, not yet, there's something I mean to find out—"

"Let go of me!"

"Keep your mouth shut, my girl. This isn't the first time for you." His free hand moved around her neck, passed over her shoulders, felt around her breasts. "Where do you keep it—the brand mark? Don't wriggle," he said, bending down and searching under her dalmatica. "You don't really mind this too much, do you? Yes, here, all the way up, to keep you pretty—"

Now that he had taken his hands from her, she could only lean back, panting, against the filthy wall, her head among the cobwebs.

"Tomorrow?" he said.

And if she said nothing, he had his answer nevertheless. This was not the first time for her, as he had said. And, even though the spirit within her was as dead as the little beast she had buried in the court, the body had a life of its own.

Chapter 40

THE ELDER Moyses—he had been saying so for days, but now the time seemed really at hand—the elder Moyses was on the point of death. The authorities in these matters knew it and made their certainty known without a word: The tribunes and centurions who had assailed his flesh no longer came to drag him to the upper chamber; in fact, when they had returned him last to the common room of the prison they had not pushed him down the stairs but had given him carefully into the hands of those who waited instead. The children also knew it, and the Confessors were accustomed to look for confirmation from the children: in these Last Times the children had become very knowing in things which were customarily hidden from them behind doors and curtains, from the pains of birth to the solemn omens of death. Day and night now—for the discipline of the prison had become very lax, it was as if those in charge had more pressing business to distract them these days—day and night there were always two of the children to sit with the elder Moyses, one to chafe his icy feet and legs and one to wipe the sweat from his forehead and the little line of foam from his lips.

It was Prisca and the boy Timotheus, a dyer's son, that he had chosen to be his watchers; and they had been staying in the corner where he lay—eating there, washing themselves there, resting their heads against that piece of the dripping wall—for three whole days. Others, of course, were with him too, but in the capacity of visitors. The elder Cornelius, so patrician in his ineffectual disguise that only the direct intervention of the Lord Himself could have kept him safe, came regularly and knelt on the earthen floor, his brown, short-sighted eyes swimming in tears that would never quite fall. The deacon Probus came to say farewell—not the eternal farewell, there was no word of that, there was only talk of a voyage that the deacon must make very soon to the hard-pressed congregation in Carthage. And others came also, both Christians and pagans: virgins of the congregation and the old Egyptian woman who kept the shop where the elder Moyses had bought his bread and sausage, young catechumens who desired to be blessed by the hands of a living martyr and rough Italian workmen who had lived on the same floor with him in a tenement in the Suburra—these and many more came out of the fresh spring air into the stench of the common room to take his hand or kiss his cheek—both the unbaptized children of men and his brothers and sisters in the Lord.

Also, less constantly than the children but more frequently than any of the others, Favorinus Herennius was with him. He had carried his three-legged stool from the spot by the beehive arch and set it between the dying body that lay on the heap of rags in the corner and the surging life that kept moving about, in spite of everything, in the rest of the room.

For the most part he kept his silence, merely watching. Never before had he followed the whole process of a slow and expected death. Celestus Falconius had died violently and within a few moments. He had opened his mouth at the end of a riotous feast to add some witty flourish to the conversation, had stammered, and turned black in the face, and fallen forward onto a crystal goblet, filling the sudden, awed silence with the ring of shattered glass. The patrician Marcellinus had until the last hour shown undue concern for the sensibilities of his youthful friend, inventing all sorts of justifications for sending him away: somebody must deliver a paper to the advocate, the hounds were unhappy and needed a familiar voice to pacify them, too many people in the room used up the air he needed for himself. But here nobody raised any objections to his watching. Actually, his having stationed himself at the side of the elder seemed to give the Confessors a melancholy satisfaction; they nodded to him gravely, they touched him reassuringly as they passed.

Death, he thought, can be a gentle and considerate wooer; can come and depart and come again, quiet in his complete self-assurance; can hover for hours at the door of the house of the spirit, knowing that what is his own will come out to him at last. There were times when death and the elder Moyses seemed to have nothing to do with each other, when he raised himself on one elbow and told the elder Cornelius with the voice of authority that the flock could not long remain without a leader, and that there was one and one only—he tapped his blunt, earth-colored forefinger hard, hard on the white Olympian knee—one and one only who could take the shepherd's crook in his hands with full confidence that the Saviour had fashioned him aptly for the hour, for the forgiveness of sins and the binding up of wounds and the healing of contrite hearts. There were times when he saw fit to quiz the slave-child Prisca and Timotheus the dyer's son on their knowledge in matters of the faith, to trouble himself because they could not remember some point that seemed important to him, to console himself afterward with the realization that, all things considered and the times being what they were, they had been taught very well indeed. And then there were other times when it was as if all the curtains of the house had been drawn and the spirit sat behind them in secret converse with the wooer, when phrases borne from his lips on long sighs and carried to those who waited without gave only the vaguest suggestion of the mysteries that were coming to pass within.

He named—beyond all pain now and smiling—those parts of his body which had been afflicted by the torture. It was the child Prisca who gathered from the mumbling and the chanting that he was naming the tormented parts of his body; and it was the dyer's son Timotheus who conjectured that he was offering them, one after the other, as gifts before the throne of God. Whatever Timotheus said, he said softly and with diffidence, after long consideration. He was a tall, lean, big-boned lad, with small dark eyes and skin the color of a peeled almond, beautifully clear and pale. His hands were huge and powerful—he could lift his elder as easily as he could lift a piece of firewood; but he always held them curled and ineffectual on his knees, as if he were afraid of the force that was in them, as if he tenderly loved the world and was afraid that he might do over-loving violence to something precious in the world. With the slave-child Prisca he was plainly in love; and she was very considerate with him, trying always to spare him any pain and going to great lengths to give him his due in praise. So when he said that the elder Moyses was offering up the separate parts of his body, she slapped her knee and said, yes, that was certainly so, and repeatedly nodded her head.

But other matters were not so easily interpreted. There was no saying, for instance, what made the elder Moyses talk of tents—miles of tents made of black goatshair cloth, stretching out in a monotony that seemed to distress him, stopping only at the margins of the sea. There was one named Mariamne whom he called upon often, and her they did not know. There was another named Jeremiah, and whether it was the prophet, as it usually seemed, or a seller of pottery dishes in the Suburra, as he sometimes led them to believe, they could not tell. His spirit would wear itself out with wanting it knew not what—that they should remove the tarnish from the holy dish in which the Body of the Lord was served, the names of his mother and father should be recorded on his gravestone, that the rags under his head should be smoothed out or taken away entirely; and then, utterly exhausted, it would turn back to death for comforting, would weep out his weariness and sleep in peace on the shoulder of death. There were times, too, when he would see fit to lapse from Latin into some strange language; and they were disquieted in their hearts at that, as though it might be the language of some daemon speaking through him, confusing him and them, marring the holiness of his final hours. But this, too, was explained and set to rights: the elder Cornelius said that it was Hebrew, and told them gently how God in His goodness often makes us as little children when we come to our deaths, so that we can go to Him in all innocence and simplicity. They must not trouble themselves, he said. The elder Moyses was only dreaming sweetly of the Sabbath lights and clean meats and unleavened bread he had known in the house of his father as a child.

The third watcher seldom spoke to the other two or to any of the rest who came and knelt a while and departed. Nor did he occupy himself, like the children, with interpretations. It seemed to him that whatever was passing before the dying eyes was strange and weighty and beautiful beyond interpretation, beyond all speech and any language, beyond any conscious thought. It was like the harmonious chorus of the stars, which no man ever hears. And, when he was too worn with stern contemplation to be a fit vessel for it, he pondered the outward signs: the eyes, sunken now and clouded with a kind of webby dark, the hands, held in a strange position, the fingers extended but curled a little at the ends, constantly moving over the filthy cloak that covered the outworn body, as if they were gathering something in. These signs of the ultimate and willing submission to the gentle wooer who stood at the door so absorbed him that he forgot to eat, forgot to sleep. And when he heard his name, "Favorinus Herennius", shouted across the common room in an official voice at an unusual hour, when he looked up and saw that the centurion who called him was carrying a scroll bound in imperial purple, he was still too absorbed to rise at once, but waited, staring, until he was roused to terror by the fright in the eyes of the little slave.

But it was not from Decius—it was from Herennius. The purple which bound the scroll he took from the centurion was not the Emperor's broad ribbon with the golden fringe; it was the purple cord with the tassel reserved for the heir to the rayed crown. He carried the scroll away, unable in his fright to bear the Guardsman's respectful but curious gaze. He stopped with it in a ray of early afternoon light and unrolled the papyrus, thinking that nothing but knowledge of the imminence of his own death could have brought his cousin to write to him after all these years. His own death—he could not find it, skimming the page from top to bottom. *That* news was not there, though what news he could grasp in the first wild reading was tragic enough.

Tragic enough, his sister lost to him and to Herennius and to the world. His sister living in a madwoman's dream at Epidaurus—the clumps of words that told him so began to stand out from the rest. Other phrases, too, of immediate import, asserted themselves: his cousin Herennius—pale, timid sharer of his childish secrets—had taken it upon himself to intercede with the Emperor in his behalf, for old times' sake. The answer—he skipped several lines and lighted upon the answer—had not been negative, only evasive, only a little strange. After the battle—what vast battle preparing itself in the desolate reaches of the northern wilderness?—after the battle, the question would be settled one way or another, so the Lord of the World had said. And his son, plainly embarrassed, went on to explain in an uneasy paragraph the cause for the delay: the Emperor Decius, given more and more to superstition as the hour of decision drew on, had some mystical notion that to set one's affairs in order on the eve of battle was to range oneself on the side of death . . . The rest of the letter was less news than philosophy. In the bleakness of a camp near Apulum, his cousin Herennius had tried to take up the unfinished conversations that had passed between the two of them beside the fish-pond in the house on the Esquiline. What corroding process had been at work through Drusilla's life? The life of his cousin Favorinus also, begun in splendor and limitless promise and confined now to the Urban Prefect's prison . . . And he—he himself born for retirement and set down in the forefront of an army . . . No, he would never understand. . . .

He rolled up the scroll and thought to tie it again with the purple cord. But if he kept the letter—and he meant to keep it for old times' sake—he would have to wear it between his belt and the filthy cobbler's tunic; and he could not imagine himself moving, with a purple tassel dangling at his waist, through all that pain and wretchedness. On the way back to the corner where the elder Moyses lay, he gave the bright silken thing to a six-year-old girl, a little Briton with a tousled yellow mop, who had come to visit her mother. "Here, tie up your hair with this. This'll look pretty on your hair," he said.

He resumed his place on the three-legged stool and bent over the sleeper, resting his elbows on his knees. The face had changed somewhat during his absence; the elder Moyses was resting now from his weary hankerings after he knew not what, had laid his tired head upon the shoulder of death. The lines around his sunken eyes were deep and serene, as if they had been carved there with finality; and only the faintest twitching of the upper lip indicated now and again some persistant residue of the fretfulness. He glanced from the elder to the dyer's son Timotheus, who did not see him: the small, kind eyes were absorbed and remote. But the slave-child Prisca was waiting, breathless and open-mouthed, to hear what he had read. The instant she caught his eye she asked him in a whisper, "What was it? Is the Emperor going to set you free?"

"No," he told her, whispering also lest these earthly matters intrude upon the unearthly serenity of the sleeper. "It was from Herennius Decius. I used to know him. We played together long ago." He stopped himself on the point of mentioning the misfortunes of his sister: he had forgotten that the girl had been her body-slave and had loved her—it was as if all that had happened centuries ago and in another world.

"Will he help you? Will he try to get you out of prison?"

There was an urgency in that which jangled against the quiet of the corner. These last three days of constant proximity to her, the little gestures of affection that he had given her, touching her cheek or her shoulder with the back of his hand as he passed—he wondered now whether they could have been enough to revive a stifled dream. Although she had whispered, he frowned and laid his finger on his lips. "Who knows what'll come of such dealings?" he said, trying to avoid her seeking eyes. "All we can do is wait and see."

And yet no word from him could put down in her the unwarranted belief that the letter held good news. "All we can do is wait and see" she had taken only as a warning against premature rejoicing over something promised but not yet quite brought to pass. The world had broken in upon the four of them. She thought of him, and Timotheus thought of her thinking of him, and he thought of Drusilla, and the elder Moyses was left with no one to stand in solemn attention on the threshold of the house of his spirit. And perhaps, he thought, if we do not await him he will not return. Perhaps he has returned so many times only because he has always sensed that he was waited for . . . Nevertheless, his mind kept moving back to Drusilla, not aching for her, not mourning for her, but pondering, trying to wrest from her some ultimate meaning, as if her life had been some obscure and equivocal passage from one of the ancient philosophers.

Love was the key to the mystery of her destruction: love had grown like a tumor in her spirit and her flesh, love had made her mad—diseased, obsessive love. Since the world as it was had refused to yield up to her the fulfillment of her desire, she had departed from the world, first into her house and then into her locked chamber and finally to the chalky cliffs of Epidaurus, where the windows looked out on nothing—on the blue blankness of the sky and the grey blankness of the sea. And there, she had fashioned a world for herself: a madwoman's world, where every present hour is transmuted by daemoniac magic into a piece of the irretrievable past, where every fellow-sufferer and priest of the Healer takes on the likeness of the irreclaimable beloved.

A bitter gift for love, he thought, staring down at the fetters on his bleeding ankles. We have a bitter gift for love, we have a gift for bitter love—he laughed dryly, soundlessly at the transposition and felt the big, clear eyes of the child fixed upon him in bewilderment—we have a bitter gift for love, we last inheritors of the high house of the Herennii. With us, love is a fatal poison. She drank of it herself and was self-devoured, and I—I was too strong for suicide: I gave my poison to that gentle being who came eagerly out to take it, leaving her novices at their happy stitching and picking the lint from her clothes and her hair. I killed, with love, the only blameless and unasking creature I have known in all my restless wanderings through the world. . . .

And suddenly some familiar echo in the repetition of the word "love" plunged him back into that world's-end Saturnalia feast which the multiplying exigencies of his life had blessedly helped him to forget. He remembered the painter Antisthenes assailing the blond Memphius, holding him by the throat with his lean fingers until the eyes stood glassy in their sockets and the tongue protruded from the painted lips. What had he spoken of, the subtle Greek, before he had turned with murder in his face and laid violent hands upon his minion? Love—love as it was when hope and high purpose and valor and all the rest were gone, love for another diseased and dead-hearted creature wandering about like a ghost in the ruins, rank love grown succulent on the decay of everything else.

"Oh, God," he said in a whisper, bowing his head on his open hands, covering his face. Not only the last inheritors of the high house of the Herennii but all who are born in these Last Times into this shameful and dying world—Antisthenes and Charis and Berosus and the Syrian and every woman who anoints herself for the feast tonight and every man who walks the avenues looking for he knows not what—all of us are tainted with the same desire, all of us have a bitter gift for bitter love . . . One and one only in all that varied company that I have known on earth could make a balm of poison, could take the vial of destruction from me with her veined and mortal hands and transform it into an elixir for the healing of the children of God. . . .

It was with him then as if some of that elixir had fallen upon his own bowed head—no more than the just portion of it which he could claim as a child of God, but enough to ease his parched heart a little, enough to release from his eyes a few assuaging tears. And when he took his hands from his face and looked again at the elder Moyses, it seemed to him that some inexplicable force had communicated his thoughts to the mind of the dying: the cracked lips moved slightly, not in the fretful spasm but in the slow upward curve of a smile.

"He is about to waken," said Timotheus.

"Why, yes, so he is. You always notice that long before I do," said Prisca. There was a slight falseness, a faint overemphasis in her manner and her voice. It was as if she were consciously atoning for a desertion.

Opening his eyes, the elder Moyses told them that he felt no more pain at all, only a marvelous keenness and lightness. Certain of the crimson Confessors had visited him in his sleep and said such loving and happy words to him that he wept a little to remember. He had been so consoled and nourished by their discourse that, if he had not known the Lord had provided otherwise for him, he would have thought he was healed of his sickness and would live to be as old as Father Abraham. He had a longing for light and blameless food, for cool milk and a little honey and a rusk of fresh bread. Let the children go and bring him what he wanted. The bread could be found in the house of the widow Eurycleia about half a mile from the prison. And let nobody say it was a miracle, his asking for the fresh bread and their finding it where he said it would be: it was only that he knew the widow Eurycleia put loaves into the oven at this hour of a Friday morning—Friday, a holy day to take one's leave of the world. Timotheus helped Prisca up by the hand—she was stiff with long kneeling. She kissed her elder on the brow, but casually; her mind was plainly on something else. And in spite of the stiffness she went her way in sturdy, swinging strides, walking with the high-hearted freedom of one who is glad of a chance to carry a new happiness out into a street.

When they were gone, the eyes of the elder Moyses, small and beady and shining through the webby mist focused themselves upon the remaining watcher with concern and tenderness. "You're disquieted in your heart again, my son. I felt it when I wakened. What have you there in your belt—provided it's any affair of mine?" he said.

"A letter from the Emperor's son Herennius. We used to know each other when we were children."

"Concerning your release?" The voice, raised in excitement, was thin, as if the grizzled chest it issued from had room for only a little breath.

"No, nothing's been decided one way or another. He visited my sister at the Temple at Epidaurus. She went there months ago, to be cured of some unexplainable illness, and he tells me in this letter that he found her completely mad."

"Mad?" Folds of distress appeared in the sweat-drenched forehead. "And yet you mustn't despair of her, my son. Sometimes when the illness passes the madness also will pass."

"No, my father, I'm afraid it's otherwise. I mean, I'm afraid it was the madness that brought on the illness in my sister's case. The poison was elsewhere—in her mind, in her heart. For her, love was the only thing that had any significance, and love was a disease with her, a kind of tumor in her spirit. It was as if she was driven to destroy herself with it—" Then, before he could stop himself, he was breaking in upon the dying man's serenity with a bitter discourse on bitter love; he was saying that in these Last Times love must be a morbid, self-consuming thing. Dwell apart, close your eyes, bind up your heart in bands of iron—never love, never love. . . .

And the elder Moyses heard him out, did not once presume upon his prerogatives as a dying man to stop the flood of words. "But many," he said after the last violent sentence had poured itself out, "many have loved each other after the manner of the flesh, male and female, according to God's intention, and not all of them have called it poison. Surely you yourself, my son, can think of some who went to their graves in the belief that it was nourishing and sweet."

"Only one, only the blessed Paulina." He had not thought that the mere voicing of her name would so undo him; he had to wait and steady himself before he could speak again. "For her, too, it was poison, and the end of it was death. But my father has told me—and I believe him, I truly believe him—how before she went down into the everlasting dark she distilled my poison into sweetness and dispensed it like a balm for healing among the children of the Lord."

"Oh, *she*," said the elder Moyses, looking up through the mists and smiling at the vacant vaulting of the ceiling. "We can lay down no universal precepts from what we know of the blessed Paulina. The spirit within her was a very rare spirit. Such transmutations as she wrought with earthly longings, such love as she poured out for us down here in the darkness, I can assure you, my son in Jesus—I beg your pardon, I know perfectly well that you are *not* my son in Jesus—but, as I was saying, all that was very rare indeed."

"And these others, my father—what about these others?" He turned for an instant and looked over his shoulder into the swarming shadow, at the mothers kissing their children and sending them home, at the little knot of men piecing out another petition concerning the lapsed, at the catechumens and novices laboring to erase the filth and mitigate the pain. "Are the rest of these failures, then, insofar as it has plainly not been granted to them to attain to such love?"

"Yes and no. How can I answer such a question?" he said, sighing. "You lean too heavily on my authority—a thing which you've learned from the virgins of the congregation, who make too much of everything. Who am I— or for that matter who are any of us—to say that one kind of Christian love is to be preferred above another? A man should love his neighbor as he loves himself—only so much is written. Such a precept may mean many things to many men, and until the Last Great Day when the shadows are driven from the face of the earth and all the mysteries are made plain, which of us can tell what the one ultimate meaning is—if indeed there *is* one ultimate meaning? Love your neighbor as yourself—to the blessed Paulina that meant the ecstasy of utter identification with whatever child of God seemed to need her, of merging with each of us and all of us, and, through each and all of us, with Him, with Jesus Christ our Lord. You are right, my son—those whom you regarded with concern a moment ago will never know that ecstasy, that selfless merging. They love their neighbors as themselves after another fashion, living not for themselves but for the congregation. If they lay aside their plenty that their neighbor may not starve, if they pray for their neighbor to be delivered up from hell, if they hold their tongues under the torture that their neighbor may not be betrayed, then they have done well according to their lights. And who will say that they are in any wise lacking in neighborliness?"

To that there was no answer. But he was thinking of *her* again, was remembering how she had told him that many had come to the feet of

Jesus as she had come in her hungry and timid youth, out of restlessness, out of unsatisfied love. "And those who come to Christ out of their unfulfilled earthly yearnings, those who wish to lose themselves in Him and yet do not have her gift for utterly escaping out of the self—how is it with them, my father? I should think their hearts would never be eased of their yearning. The need that is in them—how could it be appeased by the stitching of shifts and shrouds and the saying of services in the basilica and the laying aside of bread for the poor? Even here, even while they are waiting to make their crimson confessions, they must feel the old unsatisfied longing," he said.

"Surely they feel it, and often. Most of them are never completely delivered from that restlessness. The older ones among us, those who came late to their Saviour—if we live the life that He marked out for us, we live it only imperfectly at best. But these yearnings that torment us—believe me, my son—in another generation, they will be forgotten. Our children and our children's children will read of them and wonder what strange daemons possessed us, why we so needlessly devoured our own hearts. No, the little ones who are born in Christ—they will need neither the iron discipline of the will nor the ecstasy. The Christian life will be to them a daily, customary thing. Remember, my son, how it was with us in the time of our youth: our highest moments, those moments which cast their glory over all the rest, were the times when we knew ourselves to be in love. That sweet pursuit of a shadow—the Lord has not seen fit to deliver me of it even yet—even now, here on my deathbed, I find myself brooding over a departed face. But to the children these private ecstasies, these obsessions nourished in the secret places of the heart will seem as questionable—yes, as shameful—as a hankering after wine or a longing for fine clothes or a passion for pagan poetry. They will live by twos, male and female, according to God's intention, yes. But the crowning moment of their lives will not be the moment when the door is barred and the light is put out. Their hearts will be lifted up by the thousands, publicly, in the midst of the congregation of the Lord."

The end of his speech had been uttered in a hoarse whisper, and now he was showing signs of the returning fretfulness, was seeking to settle his shaking head more comfortably against the rags that served as his pillow. The peace and kindliness had suddenly been drained from his face; the beady eyes stared out of a mask of severity. "I see that you're frowning, my son, and I assume that you don't like it—this world that is to be."

"Not at all, my father—I mean, I was thinking you'll exhaust yourself with all this talk—"

"You were thinking nothing of the kind." The hands came out over the cover, reached down as if to gather something in, and stopped as though the will had reprimanded them, stopped and came up and folded themselves on the grizzled chest. "You were thinking it will be a drab place—this world of ours—with little likelihood of such ecstasies as *she* experienced in the darkness here, and no room at all for your equivocal and self-consuming love. Well, think what you will, it makes no difference. The foundation stones are laid and the Temple will rise. This is the world that is to come."

"I thought nothing whatever, my father, except that you are—"

"Except that I am dying and still groping after shadows, still saying 'Mariamne'. But I can assure you my Father in Heaven has not dealt so shabbily with me. Even though my head is shaking, He has taken it in His hands and turned it toward the hills. He has lifted up mine eyes unto the hills from whence cometh my help. He has shown me in this darkness the children, strong as the angels of God, carrying on their shoulders the mighty slabs for the building of the New Jerusalem. In the sweat of their bodies they will build it, laboring so long as the light lasts. To the unstringing of their sinews and the pouring out of their hearts' blood they will build it, raising the vaulted arches and the colonnades, joyous in their common strivings and blessed in their shared travail. And when the night is come and they lie down together, two and two, they will know each other after God's intention, in a new innocence. They will not seek in vain and in torment to satisfy the spirit with the nourishment of the flesh. They will take the solace that the Lord has granted them for what it is—sweet release and dreamless sleep and joy over the quickened womb. And, having taken it, they will be delivered again unto the Lord and His congregation, not brooding apart, but dwelling with their neighbors in the world."

But that world in which he was so eager that the children, the builders of the New Jerusalem, should dwell—it was plain that he himself had little concern with it now. He turned his face from the watcher, so that the grey and motionless profile looked like that of a limestone bust laid for wrapping on a heap of rags; and the watcher, knowing that henceforth he could not bring his three-legged stool and sit by the elder Moyses, was overcome by the realization of his own loneliness. With him and with him alone, he thought, I have broken my inner silence and spoken from the heart. To the others I have said only, "Allow me to give you a little of this bacon" or "How is it with your sister—did she sleep last night?" When he is gone forth—and he is going, he has begun to rake again with his curled hands—how it will be with me I do not know.

In a little while Prisca and Timotheus came back with the bread and milk and honey. The almond-colored skin of the boy's face went white and mottled at the sight of his elder; and Favorinus, seeing anew with the eyes of the dyer's son, detected a change: the lips and nose were swollen and the cheeks were stretched and lineless now. He glanced up at the face of the girl—she stood a little apart from them with her head bent down. But she was not distressed: she was still lost in her own high-hearted musings and had not even seen the transformation; her freckled cheeks were bright as apricots from the warmth of the sun, and now and again she glanced covertly at her master out of the corner of her eye, as though there were some happy secret between them.

"I think," said Timotheus, quietly and with diffidence, "that the time of the going-forth is at hand."

She started a little and looked, but did not make an answer.

"I'm afraid," said the boy, plainly aggrieved, "that you might as well have stayed here watching with your master. Our elder is beyond honey and bread."

But at that, as if the pained voice of one of his little ones had come to him through the curtained windows and drawn him from the arms of the wooer and back to the threshold, the elder Moyses opened his eyes and stopped the raking and tried to lift his hands. "On the contrary," he said. "Take the bread, my daughter in Jesus, and dip it first in the honey and then in the milk, and give it to your brother in the Lord so that he can feed it to me."

She flushed and went about her task so awkwardly that some of the milk was spilled from the shallow bowl, but there was no sign of remorse in her averted face. The kind, dark eyes of her brother in Jesus looked beseechingly at her as she gave him the bread, but she did not follow his powerful and gentle hand as it held the rusk between the swollen lips.

"Say to the widow Eurycleia," said the elder Moyses, "that I will see her husband in heaven tonight and tell him that she makes good bread."

Thereafter he said nothing. Or it would be closer to the truth to say that he said everything in a single syllable, endlessly repeated. With his arms flung out at his sides and his head tilted far backward on the mound of rags, he voiced one loud, long "Ah!" after another, sometimes harsh as though in bitter anger, sometimes deep and long-drawn as though in wonder, sometimes tender as though in compassion, sometimes with mild regret, fetched up on a sigh. And at the sound of that reiterated "Ah!" silence came upon the common room of the prison. They turned—Favorinus had a startling glimpse of a hundred white faces turning all at once. They rose—and he rose with them, and took up his three-legged stool and stepped back with it, looking at them over his shoulder. They came, drawn by the "Ah!", with fixed eyes and parted lips, making no sound but the clinking of chains; and as they came he turned and hurried toward them, until he—the uninitiate, the intruder—could no longer be accused of standing in the forefront of those who were gathering to witness the death of the martyr, until many of them had advanced beyond him and had come down on their knees on the earthen floor.

He also knelt and looked over the heads of snarled hair and the emaciated shoulders at what was being consummated in the corner. Something was amiss there—not with the dying, the syllable was coming to utterance easily now, was purling from his mouth like hastening water—but with the ritual procedure that had been set for such high moments as this. Those kneeling

510

in the front turned and looked uneasily about them. There were whispers, beckonings, significant glances, until somebody—a plump twelve-year-old novice, awkward and red in the face—detached herself from the crowd and knelt opposite the boy Timotheus at the elder's feet. But where is Prisca? he asked himself. That was Prisca's place . . . And suddenly he knew with a spasm of his heart that the one who knelt at his left here at the rear of the assembly had followed him from the hallowed corner: the head that his eyes lighted upon was the silky head of his slave.

"Ah-ah-ah . . ." The crowded shoulders swayed to the rhythm of it. Somebody in the back row began to chant in a strong voice that a new heaven and a new earth were come, since the old had passed away; but somebody toward the front shook his head and gave passionate utterance to something else:

> "The eyes of the Lord are upon the righteous,
> And His ears are open to their cry . . .
> The righteous cry, and the Lord heareth,
> And delivereth them out of all their troubles.
> The Lord is nigh unto them that are of broken heart;
> And saveth such as be of contrite spirit.
> Many are the afflictions of the righteous;
> But the Lord delivereth him out of them all.
> He keepeth all his bones:
> Not one of them is broken . . .
> The Lord redeemeth the soul of His servants:
> And none of them that trust in Him shall be desolate."

"These words are more suitable," said a young government worker to Favorinus in a whisper. "The others came from the New Testament, and these are from the Old, which is only right, since our elder came through the Law of Moses to us and to the Lord."

It was this whispered communication that set the first of them weeping. One after another of them wept, freely and loudly, like children, until there was no silence after the "Ah!" had ceased, but only communal weeping and words of mutual consolation: "Now he is with them both, the Father and the Son, in paradise." Nor in the ardor of their compassion did they forget the uninitiate, the strange and silent one who had so often carried his three-legged stool to the side of their elder. Him also they lifted up from his knees; him also they embraced and comforted. Many came and held him briefly to their breasts and touched his forehead with the kiss of peace. And it was long before the two of them were left standing alone and face to face—he and his slave.

"Let us embrace and comfort each other, and thank God together for the deliverance of the elder Moyses into heaven and the hope of your deliverance into the world." She said it looking downward. Her lashes lay against her freckled, milky cheeks, and her foot moved slowly, making a groove with the tip of the sandal in the earthen floor.

"Why did you leave your rightful place?"

"Oh, it wasn't particularly my place. Lydia has worked very hard among the sick, and she deserved it just as much as I."

There was duplicity in that, and the child was something less than an accomplished liar. She reddened again, and the foot that was drawing the groove stopped in its progress. "Tell me the truth. Why did you do it?" he said.

"To be with you." The big clear eyes were fixed upon him in complete candor for an instant, and then turned back to the floor.

"That's very wrong of you, Prisca, and you know it. Go back to the corner now and tell your brother in Jesus you're sorry for what you've done."

"Oh, I'll have to go back anyway to help with the body. But you don't have to be so severe with me. You might at least give me as much as you gave all the others. All I want of you is the kiss of peace."

She did not wait for him to give it; she came and claimed it, locking her cool, clean arms around his neck, turning her head against his cheek, brushing his cheek with her silky hair. And in spite of himself, as he laid his lips against her brow, the clinging of her ripening body so wrought with his abstinence and his long loneliness that there was a vague stirring within him. Outside this filth, this darkness, and this death, he thought, there is the freshness of a leafy world: there are baths from which the flesh emerges supple and rosy and warm, there are voices talking casually in cheerful lamplit rooms, there are green vineyards and new-turned fields, fragrant in the warm rains. . . .

"Let me kiss you also, my master."

"No." He put her from him, holding her by the shoulders.

"Why not?"

"You're young, and you don't know what you're doing. The kiss you want to give me is not the kiss of peace."

"No, my master?" She stepped back and smoothed her tunic and disciplined her smiling face. When she looked at him again, she was as grave and self-contained as any little daughter of the Lord. "Well, then, I must go back to the corner, or they'll begin to wonder what I'm about."

"They have reason to wonder," he said.

Chapter 41

AT ANY other time in the history of the Empire, the citizens of the outpost town of Abrittus, lying in the dank and open plain almost within sight of the western shore of the Euxine, would have murmured bitterly at any suggestion that they should play host to the Emperor and the heir to the purple and the Governor of Moesia all at once, that their houses and inns should be crowded with centurions and bodyguards come in with their lords to attend a military council, that their year's store of fruit and grain— not to be renewed until harvest time—should be commandeered to feed two hundred grim, unasked-for guests. But there was no murmuring. The keepers of the wine shops and the cookshops did not raise their prices, and the two-wheeled carts rumbled steadily in from the outlying farms, bearing the turnips and the bacon and the slaughtered hens and geese and sheep. Whoever was appointed to receive a guest received him well, was generous with basins and oil and coverlets, sent him forth well fed to the business of the day and stationed a slave on the threshold with a lamp to light him home at night.

"For, look," they said among themselves, "however destitute they leave us when they go, we will be more fortunate than the men of Philippopolis. The men of Philippopolis—yes, and the women and children, too—are most of them dead. And those that are alive are even worse off—without their tongues, without their eyes—prisoners in the Gothic camp or wandering about in the woods with bloody stumps where their hands used to be." The accounts of the siege and rape of that Thracian city had lost nothing in their eastward journey. The cats, the rats, the infants that had been devoured in the weeks of starvation, the mysterious fires that had sprung up night after night inside the walls, the wholesale massacre that had taken place when the gates were opened—everybody in Moesia and Dacia and Thrace was telling about them now. And the walls and streets of Abrittus, like the walls and streets of most northern cities, were scrawled in chalk with vilifications of one T. Julius Priscus, former Governor of Thrace, who had betrayed the city, selling it to the enemy in return for safe-conduct for him and his garrison, and accepting afterward a rayed crown and a purple cloak at the hands of the Goths.

No, by comparison it was a small thing to put up with—a military council. They were even capable of feeling a strong surge of emotion at the sight of the dignitaries who had come to attend it. They leaned from their windows to catch a glimpse of the *real* Lord of the World, his bald forehead still stirringly scarred by the bite of an arrow: he had caught part of Kniva's host off their guard and had given them a shameful beating, sated as they were with the luxuries that had fallen to them, weighted down with spoil and prisoners, and suffering more than they admitted to themselves from the siege—the Roman war-engines within the city had killed hundreds of them with huge stones, and hundreds more had been hideously burned by arrows tipped with inextinguishable Persian fire. The cookshops of Abrittus sounded with applause for the swart little Governor of Moesia who had brought every able-bodied legionary out of his province into the field, though to do so was to leave his own scattered cities exposed to the barbarians. They drank toasts in the wine shops to the successor to the purple, and remarked with almost womanish tenderness on the paleness of his skin and the blondness of his hair; he had the northern look, he might have been a son of theirs, they said.

The room in which these three had been meeting for the last four days was an upper room in the best hostel in town. But the view from the one wide window was blank and unlovely: nothing but the mean houses and narrow streets of Abrittus, softened by very little leafage, since summer came late in the neighborhood of the Euxine Sea. The innkeeper had obligingly removed the bedroom furniture and had sent up the largest of his tables from below. But now that the maps and charts and pens and bowls of ink and essential correspondence had been set out, there was scarcely room for a man to put his elbows down. If the curtains were pulled open, a dank wind kept shifting the sheets of papyrus about; if the curtains were drawn and the lamps were lighted, a nightmare atmosphere of evening settled on the chamber in the middle of the day, and the air became so heavy that, desperate as the business before the three of them was, one or another of them was always on the point of falling asleep. The Emperor sat on a curile chair with his back to the window. To his right, well around the corner of the table, sat the Governor of Moesia on a precarious antique, inlaid along the arms with cedarwood. Opposite the Governor, very weary and trying still to find a place for his elbows, sat the heir to the rayed crown. Courtesy had prompted him to assign the elaborate cedarwood atrocity to the visiting dignitary and to keep the sturdy, armless chair for himself, but he had begun to wonder about the wisdom of that. The antique groaned repeatedly under the twistings and fidgetings of Trebonianus Gallus, and the possible fate of the chair kept rousing undue concern in him, kept distracting him from the matters at hand.

In the last four days they had been taking stock of their situation with the help of their spies and several Gothic prisoners. Their position—the young man's father had admitted it only grudgingly, had allowed himself to accept only the most unquestionable of the encouraging reports—their position was much more favorable than they had dared to think. It was true that the city of Philippopolis was a heap of charred ruins. It was true that half a dozen villages were level with the earth and that hundreds of Roman citizens, tied to each other with ropes, were stumbling along in the van of the Gothic host. But it was also true that the one sound beating which his father had administered in the plain south of Nicopolis had shaken the wild and volatile Gothic self-confidence. One of the nephews of old Berig had died in that encounter, and Kniva had been disturbed enough to call the wandering detachments of his army in. It was an established fact that the host was marching northward now in a single body, with only one aim in mind: to disappear into the forests on the other side of the river. And there were indications—indications so frequently repeated as to be almost indisputable—that Kniva would be willing to leave his prisoners behind if he were permitted to march north without any further encounters with Moorish cavalry and arrows tipped with miraculous fire and war engines that hurled gigantic stones. . . .

But here at Abrittus they were of another mind. Decius and Trebonianus Gallus were of another mind, at any rate. They held that to let the host pass unopposed into its northern fastnesses was only to invite another invasion in the rich weeks of the harvest. And he—the heir to the purple—was forced to agree. Their plan was to pass the Gothic host, intercept them on their northward route, and force them to fight somewhere close to the shore of the Euxine. Today they were discussing the terrain, and his own part in that discussion had dwindled to a series of nods and shrugs. All that he knew about this section of the wilderness was what he had seen through the blur of the marsh-fever during his march across it a week ago: no farms, no houses, vast stretches of tall, thick, yellowish grass, here and there a clump of alders, no rise in the ground that deserved to be called more than a knoll, little lakes bordered with willows, a few muddy streams. And if he was justified in his ignorance—after all, he could not help his sickness—he was discredited nevertheless with his father and with Gallus. He had returned from Epidaurus only *after* the Gothic horde had broken down the weak Thracian defences. It was a miracle that, in the general panic, he had been able to rejoin the Roman forces at all.

"Here, then," said the Governor of Moesia, picking up a pen and drawing a spattered circle around a spot on the map just above Abrittus and a little shore of the Euxine. "If you want to meet them in an open plain, with nothing to impede the archers and the cavalry, this would be the place."

He tossed the pen onto a list of supplies requested by the tribune Acinus Brabarius, and a trickle of ink oozed from the tip of it. Herennius watched the trickle apprehensively and sighed: it had not shaped itself into anything that could, by the remotest imagining, be interpreted as a "P". What the Emperor was saying to the Governor of Moesia was lost upon him. He was thinking again of the visit which he and his father had made yesterday at sunrise to the Temple of Jupiter, the only temple in Abrittus—smelling of stale incense and tainted somehow by the priest who kept it, a sallow, unhealthy fellow with very bad teeth which he kept exposing in an obsequious smile. Unfortunately, there had been only geese available for the sacrifice. Unfortunately, the imperial hand had been over-zealous with the sacrificial knife: the blood had spurted on everybody around the altar and had marked out, on the breast of the Emperor's toga, a rough facsimile of a "P". Peace—the "P" stood for peace, the priest had said. The barbarians would be so decisively defeated in the next battle that there would be years of peace. Yet the ice-blue eyes had remained disturbed and preoccupied: plainly, in the Emperor's mind, the "P" stood for something else. "Perish?" "Panic?" Herennius could scarcely ask, and during the remainder of the service he had pondered a dozen possibilities. But on the way back from the temple to their quarters at the inn, he had had a kind of revelation, had chanced to see the letter "P" on the back of a coin that he was turning over in his hand in his nervousness; and on the reverse side of it was the long-jowled, sloe-eyed likeness of Philip the Arabian. He had slipped the coin back into his money-pouch and talked with forced liveliness of trivial things; but all the while he had known with a strange certainty that his father's gloomy silence could be attributed to one thing only: the ghost of his murdered predecessor had intruded itself upon the council.

Yet the ghost was not with them now; there was no trace of his workings in the cold, clear eyes that scanned the map, no unsteadiness whatever in the hand that seized the pen and sketched the plan of battle on the back of Acinus Brabarius's request for twenty sides of bacon, fifty measures of dried peas, and two hundred loaves of bread. It was a complicated battle plan, involving more than a hundred thousand men—legionaries, auxiliaries, cavalry. The young man, bending forward to look at it, felt for the first time some superiority over the Governor of Moesia: he understood the symbols and the lines, he had seen them drawn a hundred times, he had played with discarded sheets of papyrus very much like this one in the house on the Esquiline. He could tell at a glance that the line which the imperial army would present to the Goths would be something under half a mile long, and that three solid rows of archers and slingers would be at the front of it, advancing before both the main body of the infantry and the two spread wings of the cavalry.

"Osrhoenians with bows and slings—they know them now, they're frightened to death of them by this time," the Emperor said.

"Persian fire arrows?" asked the Governor of Moesia.

"A few—only a few at the start. Just enough to make them remember what they got at Philippopolis. Here, look at this center block—" he covered the wings of the cavalry on either side of it with his two veined and weathered hands. "Right behind the archers and the slingers, my eight legions and their auxiliaries, a hundred and thirty lines of them—and the war-engines bringing up the rear, to remind them of the stones."

The heir to the purple envisioned that solid central block in the field—a vast, shining rectangle, presenting a halfmile front to the Gothic host and extending back in orderly ranks to the depth of four hundred feet. The leathery hands were taken away, and he saw the cavalry also—on each side of the infantry, three thousand Moors and Spaniards drawn up in twelve rows—swift, mobile, tested in other engagements, ready to wheel at a blast of the imperial trumpet, ready to close in from the sides as soon as the legionaries and auxiliaries had initiated the direct attack.

"Will it do?" said the Lord of the World—not to Herennius, only to Gallus.

"Admirably, admirably. The fact is, my lord and my master, it's pretty much what I was thinking of myself."

"Your twenty-five thousand Moesians—I haven't accounted for them here. You understand, of course, that you can put them where you please." The stern face, turned directly upon the Governor now, was somewhat softened by lines of gratefulness. "In the van, in the rear, wherever you want. It's up to you," he said, lifting the pen again, ready to draw the Moesians in.

Trebonianus Gallus got up from his creaking chair and wandered to the one wide window. "I only want to be sure you'll make the best possible use of me," he said, staring out at the mass of grey cloud that was congealing over the damp and ugly roofs of the town. "It's only a suggestion"— he did not turn, he threw it casually over his shoulder, still staring at the melancholy sky—"but it seems you have as many as you need, and maybe more. Suppose the Moesians were to act as a mobile unit. Suppose we kept ourselves out of sight until the battle was really joined, and then came in. Not that you'll need it, but I always think it's safer to keep a reserve—fresh men who can come in at the most opportune time—"

"Yes . . ." said the Emperor, but in a voice that was distinctly negative. It was unorthodox, and it did not fall in with what he had been thinking of; "Yes, but . . ." He laid the pen and the plan aside and looked at the map. "Where could you be out of sight? So far as I can see, there's nowhere here for you to hide—nothing but a little scrub at best—"

Maybe it looked like scrub on the map, the Governor said, but actually —he turned from the window and hovered over Decius's shoulder and outlined a spot on the map with his dark and stubby finger—actually there was a good stretch of alders and willows there, more than a mile of them. He and his Moesians could move into them in the middle of the night and stay there until such time as they were summoned into action by the trumpet. It was half a mile at most to the scene of the fight.

Yes, said the Emperor, it would certainly be an additional safeguard for the main forces—his mind was kindling to it now, there was a kind of glitter in his icy eyes—but to leave two legions detached and exposed to the enemy, with nothing to hide them but a little screen of trees. . . .

But the Governor of Moesia, though he did not minimize the danger, made it quite clear that he was not the sort of person who would shrink from taking risks at a time like this. In an oratorical tone that made Herennius cringe, he assured the Lord of the World that every man in the Moesian legions, steeped as they were in the ancient discipline, devoted as they were to the common cause, would do as much as he. In fact, when he was finished, it was plain that something more than another expression of everlasting gratitude was called for; and the Emperor cleared his throat and said that when all this business was over Trebonianus Gallus could count upon a solid indication of his gratefulness.

The Governor shrugged and rubbed his knobby cheeks to a darker shade of red. The gods knew, he said meditatively, easing himself back into the creaking cedarwood antique, the gods knew that he could use a little consideration. He was getting on—for twenty-five years he had served the Empire, and the last fifteen of them in holes like Sarmizegetusa where there wasn't so much as a steam bath to take the aches out of an old provincial administrator's bones . . . For a fat post in Egypt, thought Herennius, he leaves his cities exposed, with nobody but Guardsmen on the walls. For an appointment in Syria he will station his legions within reach of the Gothic lines, with nothing to hide them but a few scrubby trees . . . And he set his elbow down among the pens and pressed his mouth against his hand to hide the scornful smile.

Yet for all his contempt he had to grant the man his consummate skill in the vulgar game of politics. If the Governor of Moesia saw himself eating ox-heart stuffed with mussels at a table in Heliopolis or sitting in state in a palmy court in Damascus, he permitted the vision to bring no light into his goggling eyes. His Emperor was stern and hard-pressed, and he conducted himself precisely as a soldier should in the presence of his stern and hard-pressed Emperor, hunching over the corner of the table and looking very grave, saying that there would be plenty of time to settle his little affair after the victory. But there was another matter—he said so haltingly, diffidently—there was another matter that he felt impelled to mention now, a piece of information that had come to his attention almost by chance, when, on his way down here to Abrittus, he had stopped at Marcianopolis. It had disturbed him, it had made him wonder whether those his lord and his master had left behind him were really serving the imperial interests. Not that he meant to suggest that the Dean of the Senate or any other member of the administration would consciously move counter to the Emperor's wishes; the whole matter was probably the result of some oversight, some bit of blundering stupidity. But did the Emperor know—he did not ask the question until the veined hand resting on the corner of the map had twitched with nervousness—did the Emperor know—it was so preposterous that he could scarcely bring himself to quote it, though he had it on irreproachable authority, from the man's own mistress—that his nephew Favorinus Herennius was shut up in the Urban Prefect's prison, wasting away there, poor wretch, with a pack of filthy Christians?

The heir to the purple got up and walked to the window, unable to control his face. Wretched as he felt at the sudden recalling of his cousin's miserable state, he could scarcely stifle his laughter at the thought of what was bound to come of all the Governor's maneuvering. All that fine waiving of his own concerns, all that deft and subtle use of everything at hand to curry favor with—all thrown away! Were you drunk, he thought, glancing over his shoulder at the ruddy face, were you so drunk in Marcianopolis that you forgot to ask the lady how things stood between her lover and the Lord of the World?

The eager expressions of sympathy for the unfortunate scion of the Herennii had come to a sudden stop, had doubtless been halted by a cold glance from the ice-blue eyes. From his place at the window, Herennius could see the Emperor take up the map and make a screen of it between his face and the face of his guest. "I'm in full possession of the details in the case of Favorinus Herennius," said the iron voice. The corner of the map trembled, but whether because his father's hand was shaking or because of the damp wind that swept in through the window, it was impossible for him to tell. "He is in prison at my order for consorting with Christians. He was found in a catacomb where they bury their dead, with an incriminating document and a Cross. The woman who asked you to use her influence might have saved herself the trouble. No appeal will affect his case one way or another—his case rests with me—and it ought to be obvious to anybody that at the moment I have other things to think about."

For an instant the Governor of Moesia was gratifyingly at a loss, but only for an instant, only long enough for a few big desultory drops of rain to splash onto the window sill. Then he settled back in his chair and rested his cheek against his hand and looked up at the Emperor with an air of candor and wonderment. "So that's the way it is with Favorinus Herennius!" he said. "The fact is, my lord and my master, if it hadn't been that you seemed to trust him so completely, I might have had some doubts myself. His father was a slippery sort, wasn't he? I always think that kind of thing runs in the blood. No, now that I stop to consider it, the fellow never was what I would call a Roman—not a trace of piety in his body—the whole time I was with him, he never sacrificed. His friends, too—I always wondered whether my lord and my master could have known what sort of friends he had. Drunkards, perverts, atheists, every one of them. And the woman— to tell the truth, I was ashamed to be seen with the woman in Marcianopolis. A very questionable sort—a Greek, a freed slave."

Dog! thought Herennius, seeing the knobby face through a blur of fury and turning from it. Don't look at *me* for confirmation, *I* want no part it! He stared at the somber clouds above the black roofs of Abrittus and thought of the poor woman, how she had made the expensive and perilous journey by sea and by land, how she had crossed the wilderness as far as Marcianopolis —which the Goths had failed to set upon only by chance—how she had staked her ultimate hope on this shameless liar. And suddenly he was struck by a thought that made his heart stand still, as if a cold fist had closed upon it: We, too, he told himself, are putting our trust in this dissembler. And why should he keep his word with us any more than he kept it with that deluded woman? Why should he come to save us from defeat when the only loyalty he knows is loyalty to success?

"Enough of Favorinus Herennius," the Emperor said, lowering the map with a steady hand. "I think we understand each other—about the battle line, I mean. We'll talk again. I'll see you at the table tonight."

It was a dismissal and a curt one, but the Governor of Moesia chose to take it as the natural course of things. He rose and pushed the cedarwood atrocity back against the wall and gathered up his documents without an undue show of haste before he started for the door. Long after the door was shut behind him, the young man at the window could not bring himself to voice his disturbing thought; it seemed a mad thing to hurl at the tired back, the bald and ageing head with its fringe of iron-grey hair.

"What are you doing at the window?"

"Nothing. Thinking—"

"What's there to think about? Everything's settled and in good order now."

"Yes, so it is. Only I was wondering—" it was preposterous, he could not say it.

"If you were wondering about your cousin, I'll tell you what I just told Gallus: let it rest. After the battle, I'll settle it one way or another."

"I know. It wasn't that. I don't know why it occurred to me, but all of a sudden I wondered if he'd really come—Trebonianus Gallus, I mean—"

"What are you talking about?"

"When we give him the signal. Are you so sure of him? Do you really think he'll come?"

He expected the head to turn; he expected to be fixed by the cold blue glance. But there was no movement except a stiffening of the shoulders and an almost imperceptible stirring of the hand on the arm of the curile chair. "Why shouldn't he come?" said the irritable voice at last. "What do you imagine he'd do if he didn't come?"

"Wait. Wait in that little forest to see how it turns out." There was no use stopping now; he had already shown himself for what he was—a weakling who in an hour of promise still raised the prospect of defeat, a morbid brooder, ranged forever on the side of death. "If we lost the battle—if both of us were out of the way—he knows that he's next in command. He'd come to terms with Kniva, too I know him better than you do—he'd sell his own mother if he thought it would serve his purpose—"

It seemed to him for a moment then that his father was about to divest himself of the mask of ancient Roman virtue, was about to turn and show for once a troubled, utterly human face. But if there was an instant of indecision, it passed in silence; and what broke the silence was the stern and soldierly voice, pitched to the rostrum and the bivouac. "That thought never entered my head, and you may be certain it never entered his, either. You're the only one who tortures himself with such notions. Nobody else, including the Governor of Moesia, has the slightest expectation that this engagement will go against us. What do you think his Moesians would do to him if we won the day and he had been insane enough to gamble on our defeat?"

"I don't know, I didn't think of that, my father." It was a fool's answer, said in the nervous, halting voice of a fool.

"Think of it then. Think of something else besides your woman at Epidaurus. I wouldn't have to lift a finger to punish him. To prove it was none of their doing, his own tribunes would see to him. An hour after the battle, they'd be here with his head."

Wrapped in a bloody towel, he thought, remembering the other delegation that had come up to imperial headquarters after the battle of Verona. Wrapped in a bloody towel and cloven through the middle with a butcher's ax . . . He turned his face toward the window, as if the recollection might manifest itself in the shape of a bloody "P" in the middle of his brow. "My father is right, he'd never dare to do it. The risk is too great. All he wants is a post in Syria or Egypt—"

Some legionaries in the square had sighted him at the window. They clanged their swords against their shields and honored him with three long "hails", and such citizens of Abrittus as were still walking the streets in the spattering rain joined in. The Emperor rose, but did not come to the window. Stooped a little after long sitting, he gathered up his documents and rolled up the map. "What are you looking at out there?" he said.

"Nothing. I was wondering if it's ever going to stop raining."

"What difference does it make?"

"No difference at all—except that sometimes it brings on the fever."

But that was not the reason. He had really been thinking how hard graves would be to dig in such a mass of mud—a thought as groundless as his father's obsession with the bloody "P", the shameful thought of one who had taken his place long since on the side of death.

Chapter 42

IT WAS harder for Favorinus Herennius to resign himself to the decline in the moral temper of the common room than for any of the decimated group of Christians still waiting there to make their crimson confessions. They could say that the Lord had withdrawn himself from the prison because their faith had faltered; they could fill up the empty hours with prayers for His return—the vacant spaces under the beehive arches and the high windows resounded day and night now with their invocations. And, when they were weary of self-recrimination, they could take comfort in the words of the elder Cornelius, could remind themselves that it was not only they who suffered from this savourlessness: the leaven of life, the promise and the hope, seemed also to have departed from the City, perhaps from the whole world.

But he could not profit by these vague consolations. For him, the reasons for their heavy-heartedness were plain and bald enough. And, when they spoke of His face shrouded in clouds or of the latter-day weariness of the spirit, he was hard put to it not to tell them that they were suffering because their elder Moyses had died and left them, because they had not been called with the seventy of their brothers and sisters who had confessed the Name in the arena two weeks ago, because this last assault of terror had left them so weak that they doubted their strength to withstand another like it and had begun to ask themselves in the secret places of their hearts: How much is a man expected to endure, even for Jesus's sake?

What was left in the prison was a sorry band at best. Whether or not the Lord had found them unworthy of martyrdom, he thought in his new cynicism that the Urban Prefect must certainly have considered them poor material for a public spectacle. All that were comely or confident in their bearing, all that were lovely in their youth or impressive in their vigorous old age had been given to the beasts; the ugly, the weak and hesitant, the ones who had neither the charm of innocence nor the serenity of resignation —these had remained. And, though they expressed their mistrust of their own worthiness by bursts of self-accusation and harsh exercises of penitence, they were just as likely to manifest their misery in sulkiness and pettiness. They were capricious and tyrannical with the children, sending them on unnecessary errands and expecting major remedies for minor ills. They felt themselves neglected by the elder Cornelius if he let a single day go by without visiting the prison. They quarreled with each other bitterly over questions of fact and questions of doctrine: the Anti-Christ had *not* been born in Dalmatia, he had been born in Pannonia; the virgins of the congregation *were* as suitable vessels for the Holy Spirit as any deacon or acolyte. And their abject confessions of weakness only gave rise to new differences, since there was always somebody among the listeners to seize and magnify whatever shortcomings the confessor might admit.

Since it had been over the matter of the lapsed that he and the elder Moyses had first fallen into conversation about the blessed Paulina—time and change were taking her further and further away from him now, even the memory of a memory was transitory and dear—he saw with sorrow that the attitude toward the lapsed had changed completely in the two weeks since the second harvest of the Lord's reaping: those who were left in the field had ceased to circulate petitions, and when they said their customary prayers for lost souls they said them with considerably less than the former grace. The elder Cornelius had urged them three times to additional action. The elder Novatian and certain of the more stringent deacons had swayed a good part of the congregation to their point of view, possibly since the violence of the persecution seemed to be spent and those who still remained untouched had less to fear for themselves in a procedure based on stringency. He himself—he said it diffidently and wearily, as if he foresaw the answer —had never wavered from his belief in the necessity for forgiveness. But his was a poor voice, compared to the eloquent and prophetic voice of the elder Novatian, and he could not hope to bring the lost sheep back into the fold without the unflagging support of those who suffered for the Name. Twice when he appealed to them he was answered by silence. The third time a sharp-tongued draper's wife gave utterance to what most of them had been thinking for days. "Let *me* sacrifice and be one of the lapsed," she said. "Let one of them buy *my* way into the Kingdom of Heaven by making a crimson confession."

No, as things were now in the Urban Prefect's prison, he could find the blessed Paulina here no longer. That love which she and the elder Moyses and the best of those who had followed her to the bloody sand had shared in common, that love which had mingled a fervent yearning for the divine with an ardent acceptance of the human was the only thing in all of this which he could understand—and it was gone. To seek for her in what was left was to lose her altogether. His pilgrimages to the place under the window or the bench at the table where she had sat had become empty rituals—useless, repeated wringings of the arid heart. "The spirit in *her* was a very rare spirit"—elusive, hard to grasp, impossible to hold—so he told himself from the hour when the elder Moyses had departed from him, first in an effort to prod himself in his flagging search, then in desperation, and finally in bitterness. If *this* was humanity, these self-indulgent wretches with their childishness and their meaningless dissensions, then the spirit in her had been a very rare spirit indeed.

Nor was he gifted with the mellow Christian patience that sustained the elder Cornelius or with the wry Semitic resignation that had kept the elder Moyses even-tempered to the last. When they indulged, out of sheer boredom, in furious arguments over their dogma, he would tell himself that it was cruel and mean-spirited of him to listen with contempt, and he would try to throw in an unprovocative question to indicate his own attentiveness, but the contempt was in him nevertheless. Before the death of Moyses, in the days when there had been more lovable creatures than these to gather around the big table, he had made it his custom to show his respect by standing apart from them, but plainly at attention, while they celebrated the sacrament of the Eucharist; and an unwillingness to work an open affront upon their vulnerable spirits prompted him to do so still. But it was useless and worse than useless; the words, repeatedly assailing his dulled and irritable brain, had lost the power they had had for him when they came to him first, passing through the lighted curtain into the little vestibule of her house on the Aventine. In an attempt to be gracious, he had done himself inestimable harm, had robbed himself of the magic of that evening when her voice had floated into a silence still ringing with the words of the breaking of the bread.

She was gone from here. Everything that could stir his insensate heart, that evening when heaven and earth had mingled in his dream was gone from here. If now and again some faint motion took place within him, it did not rise from anything that came to pass among the Confessors: it was begotten by tidings from the world. Not that he dreamed again of the lighted rooms and the new-turned fields. He had drawn back from that consuming beauty as a frozen wolf draws back from fire; he had renounced the touch which had kindled it; he would not permit the little slave even to put ointment on the sores under his fetters or to lay the healing pads of saturated linen on his ailing eyes. Yet she had not left him. If he would not have her close to the three-legged stool, laying her stubby fingers on his knee, she was with him nevertheless, sitting crosslegged on the floor some four or five paces off from him and gazing at him with her big clear eyes. And all that was suppressed in touch came flowing out of her in chatter. Breathless from the haste with which she had finished off her other duties, prodded by the knowledge that dusk was coming on and she would soon be expected in the house of the virgin of the congregation with whom she was staying, she poured out such a stream of chatter as he had never heard from her before.

Most of the time he scarcely listened. The hour she spent with him was a dismal hour: worn out with the petty exasperations of the day, heavy-hearted at the prospect of the soulless Eucharist, and acutely aware in his exhaustion of the afflictions of his body—the sores, the lice, the burning in his eyes—he sat with his elbows on his knees and his chin in his hands, staring into space. But one evening he heard her say "my lady and my mistress", and knew that she was speaking of his mother, and remembered with a vague inward stirring the grey head bowed and unveiled, the pale scalp showing through the scanty curls.

"What were you saying about the lady Sabina?"

She sighed the heavy sigh of children trying to imitate the resigned patience of their elders. "I suppose I'd better go back to the beginning. I was saying she's sold my father to a friend of hers named Flavius Labeo."

"Oh, God," he said without fervor, "now *that* is on my shoulders, too. Because of me, something's been done in my house that Celestus Falconius would have been ashamed to do—separate the father from the child."

"Don't worry over that," she said, smiling at him. "I could take care of that in no time at all. All I'd have to do is go up to the palace and get myself properly sold to the same master. My father told me so."

"Your father? When did you see your father?"

"Yesterday. In the street. But don't let the others hear you say so." Her eyes were bright with the conspiratorial look. "My father's interdicted. I'm not allowed to speak to him. But I did it anyhow, I don't care."

"Why didn't you go up to the palace and give yourself over to your mistress?" he said, rejecting the look, staring instead, with ill-concealed disgust, at a young man who was atoning for the general unworthiness by standing every night between dusk and midnight in the position of the crucifixion, his skinny arms spread out against the dripping wall. "Flavius Labeo would be a good master. He's rich, he's easy-going, he's considerate with his slaves. If you want to do me a service, go and get yourself sold to him. If it should so happen that I never come out of here, then I could say to myself that you've been well provided for, and that would give me some measure of peace."

"But how can I do that?" she said, smiling and playing with the hem of the skirt that fell in folds around her rosy knees. "I'd really be in serious trouble with the congregation if I did that. And my master—" she looked at him obliquely, tilting her head and putting on a mask of mock-solemnity— "my master is so concerned about what sort of impression I make on the congregation. Nobody except people like elders and deacons are even supposed to speak to my father, much less live with him, you know. And what would they think if I decided all by myself to go to him after he got himself a yellow certificate for the price of his share in the Kingdom of Heaven? I can imagine how they'd talk behind my back—they're not so perfect anymore. They'd say I went to live in a fine house because I was sick of eating bread and bacon and sleeping in a crowded hall. That Lydia, too—she'd be certain as life to say I gave myself up so I could make wreathes and polish goblets instead of catching lice and washing sores."

"From what I know of Flavius Labeo, he wouldn't object if you wanted to come here."

"No, I suppose he wouldn't. My father says he's very loose about such things. But no matter how easy-going he is, I'd have my duties. I couldn't come here whenever I wanted anymore—I wouldn't have the time. Anyway, it's out of the question. I can't live with my father—I can't even speak to him—nobody, especially children and novices and catechumens, can have anything to do with the lapsed. The elder Novatian says that faintheartedness is like a plague—it spreads by contagion, especially among the young."

"But isn't there any chance of getting your father forgiven? It seems to me you haven't been giving much thought to that," he said.

"Oh, but I have!" She flushed and blinked against a sudden accession of easy, pitying tears. "You don't know how it is around here, you don't pay the slightest attention, otherwise you'd know how hard it is to get anybody forgiven. My father wants to be forgiven, especially now, since things are quieter and he's at Flavius Labeo's. He's lonely for the members of the congregation, he wants to come back to the breaking of the bread, he can't sleep right—he's afraid he'll die in his sleep and be horribly punished in the afterworld. But who's to forgive him? The ones who went two weeks ago—all of them had people of their own to speak for among the lapsed, more serious cases than his—after all, he's not sick, and compared to some of the others he's still very young. And these, here"—she tossed her head in the direction of the young man who stood in the position of crucifixion against the wall—"none of us would dare say a word about the lapsed to any of them—you see what sort of state they're in. They're so furious with the lapsed that some of them have even been saying they won't speak for anybody when the time of their crimson confession comes. Every one of the lapsed can burn in hell, for all they care."

"You're much too hard on them," he said without conviction.

"Am I? I'm sorry. I didn't mean to be." She bent forward and forced him to stare for an instant into the wet brightness of her eyes. "I only wanted you to know that I have no home and nobody I can turn to now. Nobody except my master. Nobody else in the world."

He rejected that look, he closed his mind against her. After all, he told himself, it was not such a sorry fate to sleep in a hall crowded with other orphans of the persecution, to eat the bread and bacon of Christian charity, to come and go through the streets of the City on such errands as were called for in the building of the New Jerusalem. And if his sleep was broken that night, it was not the thought of her helplessness and loneliness that intruded upon his rest. It was the vision of his mother, sitting unveiled and disheveled among her empty money-bags—unpitied and unvisited—in the vast emptiness of the palace on the Palatine. *Her* helplessness was without remedy, *her* loneliness was forever; if anybody stood in need of him, it was she. And the same fierce impulse that had driven him to berate the Nubian who had stared curiously down upon her shamed and vulnerable head stirred in him again in the foetid darkness, and set him to dreaming that he had climbed to the window and was wrenching at the bars, trying to go to her, to stand between that pitiable head and the just sneers of the world. . . .

Pity nagged at him, pity unnerved him. It was probably the ravages of pity that left him so raw and defenseless when he stood in the painful brightness of the Urban Prefect's office before the clean and benevolent Valerian. It was bad enough that he should suddenly find himself acutely aware of his own filthiness—the stench of his body, the unshaven beard, the louse that kept biting at his armpit because he could not bring himself to catch and crush it in the presence of the great pink mound of fat, scrubbed to a glow and anointed with balsam and cinnamon. There was no need for the Dean of the Senate to undo him further by asking in a rich, elegiac voice for more pity still: Had he taken any time of late to think how things stood with his uncle up there on the northern frontier? Didn't he ever reproach himself for the additional worry, the unnecessary pain that he was putting on the shoulders of his already overburdened Emperor?

And, although he kept throughout the first half of the interview the usual remote and impenetrable look, there was an urge in him, curiously and disgustingly confused with the temptation to go after the louse, to abandon himself, to shout at his benign inquisitor, even to weep. Through the flourishes of conscious rhetoric he could see the ice-blue eyes staring in frozen attractiveness toward the unseen host. He could hear the iron voice, cracked with exasperation, shouting from the rostrum at the disheartened legionaries. He could see the ageing feet dragging through the everlasting mud. . . .

Furthermore, said the Dean of the Senate, looking down at his own reflection in the polished table—he could not bring himself to look at the prisoner, possibly because he also felt the shameful stirring of pity and possibly because what stood before him, tattered and hairy and bony and streaked with dirt, was an offense to his eyes—furthermore, he wished to inform Favorinus Herennius that his present situation was cause for continual distress among all his friends: they had been pursuing the matter of his release without rest. The Secretary of the Privy Purse had pleaded for him—vainly, but with the best intentions—to the distracted Empress Etruscilla. The Urban Prefect had pointed out in a long letter to the Emperor—though there had been no reply as yet—that he felt a persistent uneasiness about incarcerating a man who was plainly a Stoic in a prison where everybody else was a Christian. And Ummidius Pessinus, when he had last sent dispatches to Trebonianus Gallus, had asked the Governor of Moesia to do whatever he could in behalf of his former host—

That speech was never finished. All his shame and loathing for his own filth, all his furious irritation at the secret doings of the louse, all the unbearable pity in him was transmuted into rage and broke on Ummidius Pessinus's unoffending head. He called the man a busybody, an ass, a blundering fool. He shouted that now *two* idiots had carried the affair to the Governor of Moesia, who was the one man on earth most likely to slander him before the Emperor. He hated Gallus and Gallus hated him—he shouted it, banging on the edge of the table until he brought in the Guardsman who had conducted him up to the Urban Prefect's office. Let it be understood—he continued to beat on the table with his left fist, for the Guardsman had taken hold of his right elbow—let it be understood that he wanted no help from anybody—

And needed none, needed none at all, the flustered but still reassuring Dean of the Senate said, walking round the table and putting a plump pink hand on his arm, escorting him toward the threshold with the air of one who draws a guest to the banquet table for a sliver of partridge and a glass of wine. Needed nobody, needed nothing. Could settle the entire affair within half an hour by burning a little incense. Should only bear in mind the fact that he, Valerian, or the Urban Prefect, or anybody who happened to be on duty in the Urban Prefect's office would be at his service at any time, morning or night, if he should happen to decide he wanted to sacrifice.

She was waiting for him when he came back into the common room, sitting idly on the floor beside his three-legged stool, though there was much that she might have been doing in his absence: a workman was binding up his own sores with shaking fingers, two children were pulling each other's hair in the middle of the chamber, and an emaciated Syrian had brought on a coughing fit by trying to drag a heavy bench into a strip of sun. On his way down the stairs he heard somebody murmur against her—probably a certain widow whom he could never look at because of the hideous red rash on her face. "She'll look after *you*, never worry about *that*," she said in a spiteful whisper behind his retreating shoulders. "The rest of us could bleed to death under her nose, and she'd never care." Other eyes followed him as he crossed the vast vacant stretch of the common room, emptied now of all but the wretches and a few of the children—the small inquiring eyes of Timotheus the dyer's son, the round and excited eyes of the plump novice who had knelt instead of Prisca at the deathbed of the elder Moyses, the self-consciously forbearing eyes of the young man who would atone for all delinquencies, including this one, by assuming in an hour or so the position of his Saviour on the Cross. Plainly the little slave was expecting that all these glances would eventually converge upon her. She prepared herself as he came on, squaring her shoulders and thrusting out her chin and freezing her face into an unconvincing smile. Her eyes were moist and red and over-bright; they were often so these days. You, too, he thought—by burning a few grains of incense I could be of service to you, too: I could keep you at the palace until you were of an age to marry, and then I could buy you a little shop or a kitchen garden and set you free . . . Her nose was dripping, but she was too proud to wipe it in the sight of all the watchers; and for the first time in days he was sorry for her, so sorry that he forgot the leper's warning and laid his hand briefly on her silky head.

"What did they say to you up there, my master?"

"Nothing." He regretted that he had to tell her so—he earnestly wished that he might have paid her better for her disgraceful waiting. Besides, she was disproportionately wrought up; it was as though she had been saying to herself in his absence: If there is no good news today, good news will never come. "A routine business, the same question over and over—why don't I sacrifice."

"That's what I keep wondering—why *don't* you sacrifice?"

It was a long time before he could find voice to answer. A strange and startling reversal had taken place in his brain. That question which had seemed so preposterous to him that he had never given it a moment's thought —he was considering it attentively now. "Why don't you sacrifice?" The Urban Prefect and the Dean of the Senate, the tribune in charge of the prison and the centurion who sometimes took the place of the tribune, the Emperor, his cousin Herennius, Charis, his mother—all of them seemed to be asking it together. "Why don't I sacrifice?" He shook himself and stared at the dripping wall, sorry that he had echoed her, trying to obliterate the annihilating conviction that, if he still refused to burn his few grains of incense, it was no longer because of any high resolve; it was only because, now that he had gone his stubborn way so long, he could not retract without exposing himself for a weakling and a fool.

"Yes, why don't you?" she said in a whisper.

He shifted his glance to a heap of dirty rags in a dusky corner, the rags on which the elder Moyses had taken leave of the world, not crying "Mariamne" as the uninitiate might think, but seeing the children of the congregation at their labors among the ruins of the Empire, building the New Jerusalem. "That's a strange thing for you to ask," he said at last, drawing back from her a little. The hem of her skirt had fallen lightly over his feet, and the air around him was fragrant with the scent of her—a fresh, clean smell, like the smell of warm rain.

"I don't see why you should think it's strange." Her eyes accused him of being in league with the rest of the world against her. "*They* talk about it enough, I can tell you. Maybe you haven't heard about it, but two of them sacrificed at the last crimson confession—walked straight up to the altar and burned their incense in front of fifty thousand people. Most of these won't even get as far as that—you wait and see. And if baptized Christians can do it—people who know they're selling their chance to get into heaven—why shouldn't you, when you don't even have a chance to get into heaven?"

If she had fallen silent, it was only in embarrassment. The flush on her speckled cheeks was not for the incongruous cynicism in her voice and her face; it was there merely because she had ungraciously reminded him that they were not for him—the glassy lakes and golden streets of Paradise. He held his tongue, still staring at the familiar heap of faded rags, remembering how the young and the comely and the strong had gone forth in the Lord's second reaping, and measuring how much, since that hour, had been lost. . . .

"Well, why don't you?" she said again in a belligerent whisper.

"It's hard to say. I'd tell you if I could. A moment ago I thought it was because I couldn't turn back, now that I've come as far as this, without making a fool of myself. But mostly I think it's something else, something about the blessed Paulina. It's as if I'd made a kind of unspoken promise to the blessed Paulina—" No promise, no promise, he thought, rubbing his aching eyes and trying uselessly to conjure her up, to see her standing in her tucked white dalmatica between him and the blank and glistering wall. Living, she would never have permitted me to make such a promise, but since she is dead I cannot go to the Urban Prefect or the Dean of the Senate and hold out my hand for my little mound of incense. To burn it would be to consume the last of her, to turn away, forgetting and ungrieving, from her grave. . . .

There was the sound of weeping beside him. She had drawn up her knees and bowed her new-washed head upon them. Her round, clean arms were clasped to hide her face. Her whole body was shaking with the violence of her stifled weeping, and he could not even lay a soothing hand upon her—so many eyes were watching the two of them from the dark.

"What's come over you? What's the matter?"

"Oh," she said in a shaken whisper, "I feel so sad—I feel so sad when I think of the blessed Paulina, even though I know she's with her Redeemer in Heaven—"

Poor liar, poor innocent little liar, he thought, and did not touch her, only looked down at her and sighed. How many years will have to pass over this head before you can tell yourself the truth: that you loved me and hated the love I had for her, that you felt the world turn sweet when she was gone, that you weep in bitter bafflement now because we have shut you out again, because I remain committed in spite of death?

"I don't know why it is—I keep thinking of her grave."

That grave—that raw trench in the garden of the elder Cornelius—in some secret place within you, you know that I am buried there, that the earth that covers up her flesh lies also on my living heart. We are together in death, and death has shut you out from us—you and all others—so long as I walk upon the earth and behold the light of the sun. . . .

"Don't cry anymore. There's no use in crying," he said.

"I think if you were free I'd never cry again—"

He pondered it: the shop, the kitchen garden, the manumission on the day before the Christian marriage: "I, Prisca, take thee, Timotheus, to be my wedded husband, my yoke-fellow in the building of the New Jerusalem, my one chaste chalice given to me by the bleeding hand of my Crucified God." It was strange, he thought, how many stray bits of their Gospels and their rituals had come to lodge in his brain. For he was thinking also how you cannot put the new wine into the old wineskins, nor mend the old garment with the new cloth. . . .

"Never again. I mean it." Her voice came sweet and muffled out of the moist shadow of her arms and knees.

Oh, but you would. Morning and night you would be forever weeping, he told himself. If I took you—and who am I, obsessed and tainted as I am, to swear that I would not take you if you came to me with the smell of youth and warmth and warm rain about you—if I took you I would leave you because my heart is dead, and then you would have real cause for weeping. And if I did not take you, it would be worse for you still, with bitter watchings of my goings out and comings in, and opulence gone sick on its own fruitlessness, and cold, dry, solitary age that knows the worthlessness of dreams. . . .

"If you lived with me, you would have more reason for weeping than you have now," he said.

She must have sensed the finality in that. She stilled her crying and wiped her face and went her way without another word; and for the better part of an hour after she was gone, he experienced something not altogether removed from peace. But before dusk had descended on the common room, before the virgins of the congregation had come with the sanctified bread or the pale young man had stretched himself against the wall in the shape of the Cross, he saw with annihilating clarity that his sense of peace was an illusion. He heard them whispering her name and reporting her delinquencies to the virgins of the congregation and the other visitors; he remembered the hard ring of cynicism in her voice and the glint of shrewdness in her eyes. No, he told himself, he could do nothing now to save her from the taint that was in him: in spite of the charmed circle, in spite of the leper's warning, in spite of his stern discipline of his own hands and face, he had marked her with his own contagion. To stay, to go—he would leave it to blind chance, it made no difference. She, too—the lamb that chance and the beloved had given into his keeping—she, too, was lost.

Chapter 43

THE GODS are with us, the Emperor Decius thought—not with high-heartedness, high-heartedness was as far behind him as the clear springs and mossy
farm-sheds of his Pannonian childhood—only with the quiet assurance
which had been for four decades his sole kind of happiness. The gods were
with them, with the legionaries and the auxiliaries, with the Spanish and
Moorish horsemen and the Osrhoenian archers and slingers who were
acting out, under the faintly warm sun of a spring morning, those maneuvers that he had sketched for them in the upper room of the hostel at Abrittus. He had invoked the immortals quietly, and they had quietly come:
Vesta had spread her ample robe to cover the perilous advance on one hundred thousand horse and foot northward, past the Gothic flank in the thick
of the night; Jupiter had stopped the everlasting rains and given them sun,
to kindle comfort in their hearts; Mars, with a drawn sword in one hand
and a sheaf of burning fire-arrows in the other, was pointing the foremost
ranks toward the Gothic host.

That host—he viewed it from the back of his dappled Spanish horse,
which stood pawing at the earth on the one knoll in all the blessedly even
plain—that host, like most of the tragic factors in a man's existence, was far
less formidable than it had been in conjectures and dreams. He and the six
mounted tribunes around him had been estimating its size for the last quar-

ter of an hour, shading their eyes against the light and peering at it over the serried heads and drawn javelins of half their own infantry. It was smaller than they had thought—two hundred thousand had dwindled to seventy-five thousand. It was—in spite of the fact that it had arranged itself hastily into three roughly demarcated lines, each of them about twenty men deep—miserably disorganized. Panic—the bloody "P" on the front of his sacrificial tunic had probably stood for panic, Gothic panic—had stricken it as soon as it sighted the Roman lines falling into order across its northward route of retreat. Their hearts had been smitten and their eyes had been dazzled by all the standards and swords and javelins and helmets and bossed shields flashing in perfect alignment under the sun. To be stopped in flight, to be cut off from the sheltering forests by such a deadly, gleaming, impenetrable block as this—it had undone them, they had voiced their consternation in a hollow cry. Before they could take possession of themselves enough to raise their shields, the Osrhoenians in the forefront of the Roman ranks had poured two rounds of arrows and flinty stones into their defenceless lines. And now their first reply to the onslaught was coming in, desultory and light. Few of them had as yet committed themselves to the inevitable encounter. many stood amazed, watching the archers draw their bows; and others sent up a shrill and childish shriek at the sight of the first of the fiery Persian darts.

"Advance," he said, quietly, since he had learned long since that there was no profit in shouting orders. Orders, during the remaining stages of the battle, should be more or less unnecessary. The tribune Acinus Brabarius at his right turned in his saddle and bellowed the Emperor's word at the trumpeters. The trumpeters, in turn, raised their trumpets, streaming with ribbons of scarlet and purple, and sounded the awaited blare. Just as the brazen blast shattered the air, the Osrhoenians discharged another volley and stepped backward—beautifully, with the precision of dancers—to let the first line of the legionaries move past them, their javelins held at a uniform slant above their erect and helmeted heads. A splendid, faultless advance: ten paces forward at a run, the javelins hurled almost all at once, the swords drawn, then ten more paces at another run to catch them off their guard, to come closing in . . . No, henceforth, if the gods remained in the field, there would be no need for orders. Like the birth of a child, like the consuming of a dry forest by a fire, once this thing had been given its first impulse, it would inexorably fulfill itself.

"They're wild, they're fighting wild," said the tribune Claudius Reggio, stationed at the left of the Emperor. For weeks now, he had been imitating every characteristic of his lord and his master, and his voice was so controlled as to be scarcely audible above the crash of the first impact—Roman swords thudding on Gothic shields and clanging against Gothic swords.

And "wild", thought Decius, was the only word for it. Those of the barbarians whom he could make out beyond the slowly moving ranks of his own infantry were either frozen by fright or made ineffectual by the violence of their rage. Many had not even hurled their javelins. Others, striking wide with their heavy swords or flinging up their arms to bring down the full weight of their battle maces, were caught in their unprotected sides and chests by the close, apt, calculated thrusts of the short Roman swords. They could never recover from this first swift assault; they would certainly waver and break. He watched, through the lines of his moving legionaries, this one and that one and another one—small scenes like those cut in intaglio on onyx rings, little representations of death like the ones that had intruded themselves for weeks after Verona on his dreams. An Osrhoenian archer, trusting his aim enough to shoot through his own advancing lines, sent a shaft straight into the eye of a young Goth, who flung up his arms and struck off his helmet and seized his blond head between his hands. Another barbarian, ageing and with the marks of many battles upon him, took with amazement the push of the blade into the soft and unprotected spot below his ribs and covered his scarred face with his bearskin cloak as he fell. Still another, in the very act of receiving his fatal wound, brought down his mace and avenged it: the Spaniard who had thrust at him died first, his head a mass of brains and blood.

And over it all was the sky, blue and dappled with trails of feathery clouds. He had learned that it was well to look up at it in the midst of the battle; he had learned that, by looking at it now and again, he could gather unto himself some of its remoteness and uninvolved serenity. And, having looked his fill, he did not turn again at once to the minutiae of combat. He raised himself on his horse and looked to right and left, across the breadth of the field, at the two spread wings of the cavalry. The wing on the right was commanded by Herennius—he could see the smaller of the two imperial standards towering above the standards of the legions, the crimson pinions streaming out from it, the gilded eagle almost painfully bright in the sun. Beyond that wing, vague and clouded by the distance, was the little forest of alders and willows in which the Moesian legions stood. And can stand all day, he thought, we do not need them . . . The tribune Claudius Reggio had followed his eye and guessed his thought; he thrust out his lower lip and nodded and smiled. The wing on his left—he looked at it also, wanting to show no partiality—had been put under the command of a certain tribune of the first rank, whose name he was never able to remember. The man was efficient and deserved the responsibility that he had asked for; his wife and children had died in the siege of Philippopolis. Beyond that wing, there was nothing—drenched, lush, moss-green plain, unbroken by anything but clumps of tall grass, stretching down to the very margin of the sea. Then, having seen it all, and somehow able to endure the parts of it the better for having seen the whole of it, he settled himself in his saddle and turned back to the clashing lines. Flawless, magnificent—the gods were in the field, the gods were with him still—the first dense Gothic battalion was giving way, was literally falling apart. . . .

"Cavalry advance," he said, knowing that it was needless. Herennius and the nameless avenger of the dead at Philippopolis had already seized the moment, were rushing down, were fanning out, were thundering and spattering in even lines across the muddy plain: the blast of the trumpet was drowned out by the thud of the horses' feet. And, since his heart yearned after the purple standard on his right, he turned deliberately away from it and watched the green and yellow on his left, watched it until it was carried straight into the second line of the Gothic host.

"My lord and my master," said the tribune Acinus Brabarius, and for once he was not shouting. "Look over there"—he pointed to the right—"over there—do you see?"

He saw—any idiot could see it—that the mass of cavalry maneuvering on the right side had wavered, had come to a halt, had actually broken. The purple standard was still aloft, but it, too, was static. And why had they stopped—Herennius, that blundering fool, why had *he* stopped? The Gothic archers had, to be sure, got enough hold on themselves to send a paltry smattering of arrows into the charging cavalry, but certainly the volley was not strong enough to call for a halt or a break in the line. There were cries, Roman cries, so hollow and harrowing as to make him forget himself. He had to say to himself that nobody in his senses would think of dashing off through packed ranks to ride to the scene; and his first impulse had communicated itself to the horse—he had to talk to the horse and soothe him with the flat of his hand.

Yet somebody was doing it: a centurion was galloping in from the right wing of the cavalry, destroying, at least for the moment, the order of the files that were beginning to advance on the second Gothic line. He drew rein at the foot of the knoll among staring legionaries and beckoned the tribune Claudius Reggio to come down to him; he whispered, leaning far across his horse's sweating neck, and his face was a putty-colored tragic mask between his flashing helmet and his gleaming corselet. Claudius Reggio nodded and wheeled his nervous beast around and rode back up the muddy slope, looking straight before him with fixed and curiously empty eyes. "My lord and my master," he said, bearing himself with such control as his Emperor would require of a soldier reporting a calamity, "your son Herennius is dead."

"Herennius?"

"Yes, my lord and my master." A sob broke his voice, and all around the knoll there was a sound of weeping. "An arrow caught him in the throat."

He saw a vision of Vesta—a hooded, mourning Vesta made of grey and ancient stone—her finger laid across her lips. Only the beast beneath him knew the spasm that shook him, a stiffening of his muscles, a sudden clamping of the knees. The rent in his heart—he bore it in silence; and the silence went out from him, was spread about him until all asking and exclaiming ceased and even the noise of weeping was stilled.

"What is one soldier more or less to the Republic?" he said, gazing into the grieving eyes of the goddess who had succored the City for a thousand years. "The maneuver on the right is not completed. Go tell them I said they should re-group and advance. Let them carry the purple standard into the second line of the Gothic host and plant it there—this is the way to commemorate the dead."

"One soldier more or less to the Republic . . ." The phrase was caught up and carried away, was passed from legionary to auxiliary, was flung up to the mounted Moors and Spaniards in the wings, was flung down to the dying who lay beneath the still advancing files, their faces hidden in the grass and mud. It was only a matter of moments until the cavalry on the right re-aligned and charged again, bearing the golden eagle with its knots of streaming purple into the second battalion of the Gothic host. Sitting on his quieted horse, he watched the perfect execution of that delayed operation, watched it until the first of his tears came stinging into his eyes. The tribunes on either side of him were also silently, copiously weeping, and it seemed to him then that the torn heart within him was the source of a hastening and inexhaustible stream of love. Love for the City and the sacred fire and the dear and holy hearth. Love for the son laid down on the altar of the City like a sacrificial lamb. Love for the defenders of the City who were flinging themselves headlong into combat now, with his name and the name of his son on their lips.

Then I am cleansed and purified at last, he thought in solemn exaltation. When they bring forth the son of Philip with the noose about his neck in the halls of Hades, my son will plead for me. One slain for the State will cancel out the other slain for the State, and justify me when I stand before the tribunals of men and gods . . . Yet he could not utterly put down his weeping, thinking as he was of the slight and comely body growing cold, thinking of the naked soul, still yearning, unfulfilled until the last, tearing itself out of the shelter of the flesh and borne on the wind over clashing armies into the everlasting dark. Forgive me, he said in a whisper, as though it had paused in the press around him and were waiting there, still hesitant, still diffident—forgive me that I did not let you go to Epidaurus with an easy heart, forgive me that I taunted you with your premonitions of death. Whatever you asked of me—and it was little, it was almost nothing—I will perform to do you honor and to give the baffled tide of love within me some release. I will retire your old rheumatic orderly before his time and try to ransom your tortured tribune from Kniva. I will write the Urban Prefect and tell him he can set your foolish cousin free. . . .

"That, too, is crumbling now," said Acinus Brabarius.

He looked up and saw that the view was almost cleared of javelins and helmets. That half of the army which had been drawn up before him at the beginning of the battle had already entered the fight. On both the left and the right, the cavalry had completed its maneuver; the standards were moving inward now against the pale summer sky—there was a moment when he thought the purple one was about to meet the green and yellow one in the midst of the milling mass that was all that was left of the Gothic line. On the wide strip of mud and trampled grass that lay between the confusion and those who waited to be ordered into it lay thousands of dead and dying. He saw them one at a time again: a German auxiliary beating the earth with his great white fists in the fury of his pain, a young Italian trying to hold back his spilling guts with his hands, a severed Gothic head, its long yellow hair matted with blood.

"Let us go into it then," he said. But neither Reggio nor Brabarius could hear him. The noise—the shrieks of the wounded, the war-cries of the Romans, the whinnying of the horses, the shouts of the barbarians—drowned out his voice. He beckoned them and goaded his horse and rode forward over the empty strip, over the staring eyes and the trailing feet and the begging or insensate hands. He had meant to look up at the sky as he crossed the openings, but he did not do it; his horse slipped and stumbled twice in the course of the brief passage, and he set himself instead to staring at the ground and wondering why there should be so much mud.

It was a blessed thing, he told himself, that a man never knew exactly when he entered a battle. A battle, seen from a quarter of a mile off, seemed to have a margin, a definite beginning; but, coming on to it, one knew that there was no clearly demarcated line. First the dead and the wounded were scattered and far apart. One saw them singly, one noted where the sword or javelin had gone in, one was aware of a familiar face. Then, almost imperceptibly, there were more of them lying closer together, and these prone and solid rows in turn gave way to mounds and heaps of dead. Among these barrows a few of the living stood, still wielding and hacking at each other; and then the upright forms grew denser, more confused, so that it was impossible to see the dead. One rode round a Roman legionary in a deadly duel with a Gothic maceman; one trampled down a barbarian ready to hurl a javelin; one jerked aside from an arrow that went whining past one's face. Only then, after having ridden through the midst of it, already sighting the green break beyond the chaos and the howling, one knew that here, now, was the battle—smelling of the raw hides of the Gothic bearskins, smelling of the sweat and the blood. One looked behind and saw that many were falling and had fallen—among them Claudius Reggio whose horse reared riderless in the midst of the crush. Peace to your spirit, may they find your body in this mud and wash it and bury it in a military tunic to the blast of trumpets, brave Reggio!

In one of the open places—this stage of the battle, coming to its conclusion as it was, had many areas of openness, gave much the same impression of light and space as a grove of saplings—in one of the open places he caught sight of an evil and familiar face. Kniva was there, urging the decimated Gothic ranks to further efforts. He stood not thirty feet beyond the Emperor, with only the fallen between—his shield in one hand, his sword in the other, his face white and fanatical in the pale sun, his tunic spattered with blood, his legs encased in curious boots that had the color and texture of bark. But in an instant he was out of sight, hurried away by a group of his companions, and where he had stood there was an unobstructed view. Five hundred feet of meadow, very flat and green, showed through the breaks in the Gothic columns. On the other side of it, strangely immobile, merely waiting, was the third and last of the barbarian lines.

Half an hour went by before he saw that vista again. He had used the interim well, for Vesta and the City: he had sent his javelin with a young man's force and precision through the ribs of one of the chieftain's horned and bejewelled companions; four had gone down under his sword and one under his mace before he gained the rear again and stopped to stare across the field and rest. Out there it was gaudily and variously green, with yellowish patches and silvery-grey patches broken here and there by clumps of minute and close-crowded flowers—watery blue, the same pale and innocent blue as that of the sky. The Goths had not been sending any arrows across this varicolored strip of meadow. So far as he could make out, only macemen and swordsmen and pikemen were ranged on the other side of it—they had probably stationed what archers they had in the forefront of their host. He was wondering why they had been drawn up so far from the others and kept from coming to the aid of their fellows when Brabarius rode up to tell him that the second line had been cut to pieces—all of them taken prisoner or mortally wounded or dead.

"What about our losses? Are they very extensive?"

"No, on the contrary, my lord and my master," several voices said together.

He was suddenly aware that he was surrounded by a little military council—several tribunes, half a dozen centurions, a Spaniard in charge of a squadron of Moorish cavalry, the nameless avenger of the dead at Philippopolis—stunned, grimy, sweating, offering him wan but reassuring smiles. He found himself looking among those known heads for the blond head of Herennius—almighty gods, he thought, how many times will I forget and then remember?

Of the cavalry on the left flank, not more than three hundred had been put out of action—so the Spaniard was telling him. A centurion in charge of a cohort of German auxiliaries set his own losses at one in five. Three Roman tribunes estimated that the total Roman casualties could not exceed one-fourth of the forces in the field, and three centurions disagreed: a sixth or less than a sixth, they said: they knew what they were talking about, they had sent back their wounded, they had counted their dead . . . Those around him were conversing in normal voices now, almost as though they stood together in a room. The clang of battle had died down behind them; there were only intermittent sounds—the cries of the wounded and the screams and whinnyings of the dying beasts. "Look, my lord and my master," said Acinus Brabarius, "our lines are almost formed again, we'll be ready to attack in no time at all."

They were falling into formation, all the survivors. He forgave them that they were still among the living; he forgave them that they stood upright on the earth and raised their faces to their standards and the sun. Good lines, very decent lines, though they were somewhat shorter now and wavered here and there to make way for the hillocks of the fallen. Five-sixths or three-fourths of the force that had vanquished two-thirds of the Goths was enough, even though it was exhausted, to take care of the rest. And yet he hesitated, turning away from the standards, in place and upright now against the pale blue sky; he scanned the varicolored meadow and pondered the inscrutable immobility of the forces on the other side.

"What do you think they're up to?" He addressed the question to Brabarius, since the avenger of Philippopolis had been wounded below the armpit and was very pale, and it seemed ungracious and uncomradely to ask him anything without rounding off the question with his name.

"Maybe they've seen enough to discourage them," Brabarius said. "Maybe they mean to run for it. Kniva must be over there—nobody got anywhere near Kniva. Maybe he's ordered them to make a break for the west."

He considered that and found it sane enough. Southward they certainly would not move again; their northward path to their forests was blocked by a victorious army; and eastward they could not move—there was nothing to the east but the sea.

"Let them run," said the Spaniard. "Let's wait until they start. Then we can trumpet Trebonianus Gallus in. His Moesians will take care of them head-on if they move west. And we can swing around and take them at the rear—and that'll be the end of Kniva and his host."

If they had moved or shown the slightest intention of moving, he might have followed that advice. But they were enigmatically, exasperatingly still. He stared at them, the pikemen and the macemen and the ones with the drawn swords, and wondered if some dim, barbaric sense of honor held them there, willing to make part of the general holocaust, now that the best of their host was dead. Far in the rear of that isolated battalion, shielded by the pikes and blurred by the distance, was the bulky black mass of their baggage train. The prisoners would be there, tied with ropes to one another. The spoils would be there—cattle and silver plate and oil and wine and cloth . . . "We've seen the worst of it—let's finish it alone," he said. For why should the Moesians, who had loitered out the morning in a peaceful little grove, become with small effort and negligible losses the deliverers of Thrace? "Find me a trumpeter—oh, are you here? Well, then, stay by me. The rest of you take your stations. We'll use the same tactics—they served us well and they'll serve us again."

He rode back to his earlier position in the middle of the central block of infantry, guiding his horse as well as he could around the prone bodies of the dead and the dying. The drenched earth, thrown up in clods by the battle, was soft and slippery. Some of the hands and tunics beneath him, crossed and re-crossed by the contending armies, were scarcely distinguishable from the yellow-brown mud. His thoughts were with another body, wondering where they had laid it and what they had covered it with, wondering whether in the stress of the advance they had found time to straighten the limbs and close the diffident grey eyes. A shout rose around him and he started in his saddle, thinking that those enigmatic ones on the other side of the meadow were charging on his forming ranks. But it was nothing: the Goths were still motionless, still waiting. It was only a solemn "Hail!" lifted up by his own to assure him of their devotion—low because they were tired, hollow because they remembered his loss.

Jupiter, Mars, Vesta—the prayer he offered them as he wheeled his slipping beast around and faced the lush and varied greenness was fervorless, automatic. Others in the Roman lines, he hoped, would see the gods advancing before the archers and the slingers over the untrodden grass and the sky-colored flowers. He was earthbound, without exaltation now, and must be forgiven: a father bereaved and yearning for the hour when he could mourn and bury his dead, a veteran too old for the exigencies of long battle— his purple tunic drenched with sweat, his torn heart leaping like a caught fish in his chest. A tribune of the cavalry named Lucius Maesius—as old as he and bleeding from the wound in the shoulder—had taken the place of Claudius Reggio. "Why are we waiting, Maesius?" he said, and wondered at the hoarseness and breathiness of his own voice. "Have they decided to stand and be slaughtered?"

"Who knows, my lord and my master? With barbarians, how can you know?"

He looked once more at the blue sky, pale and cool in these northerly regions even though the sun was mounting toward the meridian. He looked and turned quickly away: bright spots swam in front of his eyes, and he reeled in his saddle with dizziness. "Sound the advance," he said, and heard it sounded, and saw through the files of helmets and the gleaming, lifted javelins an almost imperceptible movement, a kind of eager stirring in the far-off mass of Kniva's host.

Slingers and archers first—not shooting, they were out of range as yet. The first line of the legionaries followed close behind them, but slowly, infuriatingly slowly. He rose in his saddle and shouted to them to hasten, as if his rasping voice could reach them across the thousands of heads. The age-old safeguard of Roman armies—the wide-open ranks and files—was being ruined by their lagging; from his vantage point it seemed that they were treading on each other's heels. And how could an arrow be discharged, how could a javelin be hurled in such a press? Move, hurry, lift your accursed feet, move in the name of Jupiter, you fools—

"What has come over them?" Brabarius said.

A vast, dull murmuring rolled in from the forefront of the mass of infantry. The archers, the slingers, and nine lines of the legionaries—the flower of the northern forces—were out on the meadow, crowding one another there. The cavalry had moved forward at a gallop, trying to cover their confusion, trying to shield the almost static and vulnerable flanks before the word came back to him that the ground was giving way beneath their feet. The varicolored green with its patches of innocent blue flowers was only a veil of mossy stuff thrown over a morass. With every step they took, they were sinking knee-deep into mud.

And suddenly, before his consternation had utterly obliterated his judgment, it came to him—it was given to him in a whisper from some departing deity: the marsh was not impassable, there must be firm footing under the ooze that they were wading in. Those bark-colored boots that he had seen on the legs of Kniva—they were not boots at all, they were caked layers of this ooze. Kniva had crossed, once at least, and doubtless numbers of his companions had crossed with him. If Kniva could cross, they, too, could cross.

He gave that word to Maesius and Brabarius. He shouted it down to the ranks that stood around him. He goaded his horse and rode toward the front of the infantry, telling what he knew to such officers as he encountered in his desperate going: it would be difficult, it might be costly, many would be picked off by the Gothic javelins before they reached firm footing on the other side; but if they kept their ranks open and reached the barbarian line in large numbers and in good order, they could crush the miserable remnant of the host. Kniva had crossed, and they, too, could cross. It was only when he gained the front of the press, when his horse was shuddering and neighing at the first feel of the earth giving way that he remembered Gallus and the Moesians. "Sound for the Moesians!" he shouted to the trumpeter, who had kept by him through all the surging confusion. "We'll get the Moesians," he said, leaning over the neck of his rearing horse and addressing himself to the legionaries and auxiliaries who stumbled around him, knee-deep in the ooze. "They'll miss the marsh, they'll draw them off until we get across."

He did not dismount, though it was plain that he could make better and safer speed on foot. He was a figurehead, a rallying point for all of them, raised up above the plunging, striving masses of the infantry. The fact that some underlayer in the oozing morass could bear the weight of him and his horse—that and the sound of the trumpet shattering the air with its shrill assurance of relief—gave them the courage to wade farther and farther out into the bright, deceptive green. The backs of the archers and slingers who went before him were straighter now; the ranks behind him were stepping slowly but steadily into the cold and yielding stuff; the legionaries beside him looked up at him and tried to smile. The air around him was all bespeckled with bright and giddy spots; his heart, more regular but much more violent in its beating now, was pounding out the moments until Gallus and

543

his Moesian cavalry would thunder in over the plain. He could see that the first line of Osrhoenians had passed the halfway mark, were a little beyond the middle of the morass; but their tribunes had not yet given them the order to draw their bows, and with good reason, too: their ranks were still crowded and uneven, they were encumbering each other, and the first rain of arrows must be terrible and accurate enough to bring red panic down upon this remnant of the host.

"How far away is that forest?" shouted Lucius Maesius, coming up behind him.

"Half a mile."

"We should be seeing them by now. Tell him to sound again, my lord and my master."

"They heard. The wind is right."

"I would sound again, nevertheless."

"Wait—wait—give them a little time in the name of all the gods." A trumpet call for help—a repeated, pleading trumpet call—could drive a hard-pressed army to wild desperation.

And yet he was forced to it, how soon after his brief and panting exchange with Maesius he did not know, since time was distorted by the heavy, perilous going. He was forced to it because the cavalry on the wings could ride no further—their beasts were sinking in chest-deep; they were dismounting and killing their beasts with their swords, and the whinnying and animal shrieking were terrible to hear, and were being answered by the first noise from the other side: a barbarian chant, high and rhythmic and malicious, punctuated now and again by daemoniac squeals of delight. "Sound it again, sound louder, sound with the wind, to the west," he shouted at the trumpeter behind him; and the man, up to his thighs in the hateful ooze, gave him a reproachful look: as if *he*, who had spent his life on the art of trumpeting, did not know to sound with the wind to the west.

He sounded once, and just as the blast went up the archers in the forefront released their arrows: a badly-aimed volley—not more than one in twenty reached the other side. He sounded again, and as he did so there was a change in the Gothic formation—the close-packed rows of macemen and pikemen and swordsmen suddenly fell apart. Fleeing? Fleeing after one miserable round of ill-shot arrows? No, they were not such fools. In the spaces left between the bearskin cloaks and the flying blond locks and the horned helmets, other shapes were stepping in: archers—they had hidden their archers, their archers were pouring a terrible, punishing volley straight into the faces of the advancing Osrhoenians.

And they—the Osrhoenians? Some died and others fell wounded into the mud, and the rest saw what a death it would be to sink, to be sucked down, to disappear in a bubbling mass of slime. And, seeing it, they halted and looked to their centurions, who looked to their tribunes, who shouted wildly, all at odds with each other, "Halt! Advance! Retreat!"

544

Halt—advance—retreat—the confusion had spread to the unhorsed cavalry. Some of them were trying to make their way back between the kicking legs and plunging bodies of their dying beasts. Some of them stood stricken, staring at their bloody hands. Some of them snatched the standards from their fellows and beat their panic-stricken comrades down with fist or sword or battle mace and made for the open stretch of luxuriant grass and pale-blue flowers. Somewhere far behind the Emperor the trumpeter still blew his desperate blast. Useless, useless—in this, too, as in his premonitions of his own death, Herennius had been right: the Governor of Moesia was waiting for the purple in the little grove of feathery trees, the Governor of Moesia was a traitor and would never come.

Another round of Gothic arrows whined through the air, and panic spread before him and behind him in the infantry. He saw from his horse—his horse was static now, was straining and whinnying and could not move another step—he saw from his horse that the marsh was black with thousands now, stumbling at cross-purposes, up to their waists in the slime: the front ranks furiously trying to retreat, the pressure from the rear pushing them inexorably on. "Brabarius," he said, "Brabarius—" But only the dappled beast of Brabarius was there—an arrow had sent the rider down into the mud. "Maesius—" And Maesius was dismounting and fiercely trying to indicate to him above the calamitous noise that he also should dismount. Yes, he thought, that's all there's left to do—get to the front and lessen the press by leading some of them on. . . .

He scarcely felt his own descent into the slime. Just as he let himself down, a flock of Gothic arrows went twanging past his head, and in his watchfulness he did not feel the yielding of the thin green crust, or the going in; he only knew that he was up to his thighs in the oozing cold. To kill the horse—that was simple, he had killed other horses in the midst of other battles. He dragged himself around to the front of the beast through the slime, avoiding the rolling, white-rimmed eyes. "To Mars!" he said, drawing the blade of the sword across the neck. It was a neat and instantaneous sacrifice; but the blood, warm and disintegrating, spurted over his arms and hands, and the windpipe dangled white like a worm, and he could not conjure up one flame of martial fervor in his heart.

And, now that he was down among the infantry, now that he was flailing toward the front line in the midst of the press, he saw such things as he had never dreamed that he would see. Unhorsed, he was one of them and subject to their violence—for who could see in this screaming, shoving, piling chaos that the bald and spattered old man who stumbled and threshed about like the rest wore the purple tunic and crimson cloak of the Lord of the World? Those who were trying to push on kept colliding with those who were striving to go back. They cursed each other, livid face pressed close to livid face; they fell upon each other with fist and mace and sword. The trumpet sounded again—desperately, hopelessly—and they jeered at the futile blast;

they were no longer an army, with honor, with loyalties: the treachery of Gallus had undone them; each man was trying, at no matter what cost to the others, to save himself. Tribunes, pushing toward the rear, thrust their javelins into the bodies of their advancing legionaries. Centurions, laboring toward the front, shoved whatever stood in their way into the mud. A battle mace, heaving at him from behind, came down with a terrible, cracking weight upon his shoulders. Past the flash of swords, past the rearing, foaming head of a dying horse, between fists, under javelins he made his way, seeing a hundred fall, seeing the living and the dead sinking side by side into the black and all-engulfing mud.

I also, he thought, I also . . . And yet he could not die this ignominious death at the hands of his own whom he had served and loved; for their sake and for his own he could not bring the report of such a death to Scipio and Horatius in the netherworld. Panting and protecting his eyes with his uplifted arms—he wished to see his destiny, he would not stumble blind into the dark—he waded through the thick of it, until the upright living grew sparse again like wide-set trees, until the green shone bright before him in the noonday sun, broken only here and there by the uplifted hands and sinking weapons of the valiant slain.

The mud was shallower here: he could feel it rolling away from his belly and his thighs. He was alone—no man in all the Roman ranks had waded out as far as he. But then, he thought, I have always been alone . . . The Gothic line was very close, was coming steadily forward. He could see the white barbarian faces and the jewelled necklaces; he could see the feet, wrapped in their linen swathings, stepping in, sinking down, coming on.

The one who met him was observant enough to know the value of his prize: the crimson cloak had been torn from his shoulders in the press behind him, but the purple of his tunic showed still above his corselet through the spattering of mud. The one who met him came on with a triumphal shout, his javelin poised and flashing in the sun above his head. So death came clean to the Emperor Decius at the hands of the enemy, Roman death, martial death, strong iron crashing through the ribs and silencing the heart. And though no man could find his body thereafter in the watery plain above Abrittus, it was said that he, and his son Herennius like him, died after the fashion of the antique heroes—a shield to the Republic and a sacrifice to the gods.

Chapter 44

For THREE weeks after the battle the skies over the plain above Abrittus were red with the reflections of the bonfires of the Goths. Some thirty thousand of the host were left to dance and chant and clash their swords against their shields over the Roman army lost in the morass. Ten prisoners of war and ten captive horses were slaughtered every night as a token of gratefulness to the gods of the forest; the casks and the amphorae in the baggage train were broken open, and every man, reeling with Roman wine, boasted of his accomplishments; nor was there a single warrior among them, from Kniva to the meanest, who was eager to end the roaring carnival with a parley and a formal peace. Now and again detachments of them issued forth at dawn to burn a village or harry a town, singularly contemptuous of the two full Moesian legions encamped on the plain behind the little forest of feathery trees. The camp they left in peace—there were war-engines and fire-arrows behind its twelve-foot rampart. But such tribunes as came from Gallus to deprecate their lawless doings they dismissed with sneers. The real Emperor and one hundred thousand of his legionaries were buried in the mud, they said; and who was fool enough to think they would take orders from the squat little pretender—the leader of two cowardly legions—who had taken unto himself the purple and the rayed crown?

If another legion had not marched out of Macedonia, after murdering its commander, to share in the promise of rich donatives and special privileges and liberal pensions that Trebonianus Gallus was offering to all who came to the support of his and the Empire's cause, the harrying and the burning might have gone on until the middle of summer. But as matters stood—even the wildest festival grows wearisome, and wives and children were waiting in the forest for trophies and reports—as matters stood, as soon as the new forces had shown themselves on the plain, there was a kind of parley, a kind of peace. Kniva bore himself in the course of these last conversations with some control; the swart little Governor was a clever one, had even managed to wangle a guarantee of his imperial status out of the terrified Senators. And nothing was to be lost by veiling one's contempt: one could always come again, in harvest time when the fields were fat, when the cellars of the cities of Dacia and Moesia and Thrace were rich again with the new bacon and the new wine.

Among the towns that fell during the three red weeks of chaos was the Thracian town of Marcianopolis, notable for the size of its cabbages and for its factory, which supplied the poor of the Empire with a cheap variety of copper bowls and trays. Its walls were sound enough, and there was a new war-engine within the gates—a sturdy catapult which the garrison had affectionately named "the little wild ass"—in good condition and capable of hurling unbelievably enormous stones. The public stores were well stocked with grain and with the ubiquitous cabbages. There were arrows, there were shields and javelins, there were good Spanish blades. Yet on the third dawn after the barbarians made their appearance in the fields around the city, the gates were thrown open. The tribune in charge of the garrison—curiously indifferent to the mysterious disappearance of one T. Julius Priscus who had done a like service for the Goths at Philippopolis—marched untouched with his men through the shrieking, chanting mass of besiegers and left the factory and the houses to the torch and the citizens to the sword. Not all the buildings in Marcianopolis were consumed in the conflagration. Parts of the factory, some forty or fifty of the houses, a row of shops, and a temple still stood when the invaders took themselves back to their camp with their captives and their loot. The largest of the two hostels survived—a three-story limestone building close to the center of town. To that hostel Charis had come the night when the bandit Roggio had left her at the gate with thirty denarii. In the broad eating hall on the first floor of that hostel she had eaten, at the courtesy of Trebonianus Gallus, the one decent meal she had had in weeks—a mound of black beans, a hot loaf, a goblet of good red wine, and a saddle of roast hare. In the loft-room of the hostel—small and airless and furnished with only a bench and a bed—she had been waiting for some twenty days for the messenger that the Governor had promised in his expansiveness to send down to her from Abrittus, with enough money to carry her back to Rome. And, since Roggio's payment was exhausted and the messenger had never come, she had been forced to entertain three visitors a retired veteran, a cousin of the owner of the factory, and a government officer in charge of the municipal granaries—in order to pay for the room and for bacon and porridge and yesterday's bread.

Like all the others in the town of Marcianopolis, she was aroused out of her sleep that morning by the triumphal shrieks of the barbarians and the cries of the betrayed; she heard the dogs of the city set up an eerie chorus of yelps and bays; she saw the one window of the loft light up with the redness of the first of the fires. But unlike the others—they rushed like stampeding animals toward the door, toward the air—she remained where she was when the noise began; she never moved from the edge of her narrow and dirty bed. Nothing, not even the calamitous uproar in the streets, could tear its way through the numbness that had settled and remained upon her since her first encounter with Roggio. This, too—like the nights in the wilderness and the nights with the veteran and the cousin and the government officer—was powerless to rouse her out of her remote and unresponsive state. She heard the clamor surging up the street and approaching the hostel and breaking in the rooms beneath her: the screams, the clang of weapons, the shattering of glass, the thuds of falling tables and chairs; but before she could bring herself to move, the noise departed, was drawn off from the hostel to some other place. She rose then and went to the threshold of her room and listened, and heard nothing in the chambers below but the persistent whining of the innkeeper's hounds. She knew that the hostel was emptied of everybody but herself and the dead.

As in a dream, she wandered to the window. On the other side of the town, several fires were burning; the smoke was growing denser, was making a pale and tarnished thing of the newly-risen sun. In the street below her, half a dozen immobile forms were sprawled in pools of blood across the cobblestones. Out of a window not twenty feet away from her, a woman hung from the waist, like a discarded doll, her hair caught on the twigs of ivy on the wall. And farther off, down the broad avenue that cut between two rows of shops, past the baths, past the temples, a long procession was plodding in single file—captives, tied to each other with ropes and beaten toward the gate by their horned and bejewelled conquerors.

When the last of them are out of here, she told herself, pushing her oily and disheveled hair out of her eyes, I must go, I must leave the city. The wind is up, and there's no telling how far the fires will spread . . . But she knew by the trembling of her knees that she could not go anywhere, even for a little distance, until she had eaten. And suddenly, far more immediate and compelling than any of the things she was seeing through the window, she remembered a storage room at the back of the hostel, dark and giving off the delicious and unnerving fragrances of meat and dried fruit and wine. She had seen it often through an open door from her place in the corner of the eating-hall: rows of dusty amphorae standing one against the other, sausages and figs and bunches of raisins suspended from the ceiling on strings, great white slabs of fish with the bluish edgings of their scales still upon them, little jars of preserved pears and apricots in syrup, little jars of spicy sauce. For weeks now she had seen such food set down only on other people's tables. And such things as an eel with a dab of fish-sauce on it, a crisp loaf, split and steaming, a crackling brown partridge sprinkled with parsley—delicacies which she had eaten morning, noon, and night as a matter of course in the days of Favorinus Herennius and the patrician Marcellinus—had so wrought with her in her hunger when she sat over her porridge and bacon that a palpable quaking took place in her stomach and her eyes filled with tears. Surely not everything in that storage room could have been carried away by the Goths, she told herself, moving toward the threshold. And, though she knew it would be more prudent to wait for an hour or so, she had to make certain that the fish and the sausage were still there, she had to assure her yearning vitals that they would be stilled.

The smell of the fire thickened as she went down the stairs, doubtless because all the doors on the lower floor had been left standing open; by the time she reached the eating hall, the odor was so acrid that she had to keep wiping the water out of her eyes. The floor of the big chamber was covered with slivers of glass and shards of broken pottery. Benches and tables were overturned, and a dead man, his face flattened against the tile, was lying in the midst of the clutter with a bone-handled dagger protruding from his back. Without pausing, she made her way into the storage room and found it far less ravaged than she had dared to hope, found it, so far as she could see in the smoke-dulled light, almost untouched. Dried fruits and sausages dangled against her face; her fingers came into contact with the flaky meat and delicate scales of fish; her groping hand collided with an amphora, and its curved shape gave off the gurgle of jolted wine. Slowly, eat slowly, she thought, tearing down one of the sausages and sucking on it, skin and all. But she could not stop, she must eat more and more, partly because she was ravenous for meat and partly because the savor could scarcely be gotten through the pervading taste of smoke: fish, raisins, nuts, eel, white slices of partridge, turnips with the taste of the earth still upon them, leaves of cabbage, mussels and oysters ravaged with thumb and fore-finger from their shells—she ate them all.

And now that she had eaten, yes, and drunk a little, too—tipping the tall amphora into a little jar that tasted and smelled of dried garlic—now that she was satisfied, it occurred to her that it was dangerous to remain here on the first floor of the hostel: it would be wiser to go back upstairs to the loft. The city had not been completely abandoned; every now and again, pene-trating even into the recess of this hidden room, came a crash or a cry or a barbaric shout; and yet she could not bring herself to get up from the earthen floor where she sat among the strewings of fish scales and sausage-skins and mussel shells. She rested her head and shoulders against a cool and dusty amphora and watched with indifference a rat that had come out from behind a bucket of eels in brine. He went about his business in a leisurely manner, as if he knew that his human enemies had departed forever, as if he took the tarnished, smoky darkness spread by the conflagrations as the setting in of an everlasting night. But I must go, she thought, I must tie such belongings as I have into a napkin and wash my face and comb my hair. I must put on my cloak and come down again and look about in the rooms on the second floor to see whether anything has been left that I could take and sell. . . . But nothing, neither the thought of the possible loot in the rooms above nor the audacity of the rat, could put the will to rise into her listless body. Even when she heard the thud of something falling, she continued to sit, with her legs stretched straight out before her and her hands lying loose in her lap. She could still have hidden herself: there were dark corners, there were barrels, there was the row of amphorae, and yet she made no move to rise. The hound, she told herself, it's the innkeeper's hound come back into the house . . . But when it became plain to her that it was not the hound, when the beat of heavy human feet sounded across the tile floor of the eating chamber, the only parts of her that stirred were her hands and her lips—her hands in a welcoming gesture, her lips in a curious smile.

He was tall, that barbarian, taller than any man she had ever seen. His helmet, adorned on either side with the branching antlers of a stag, grazed the narrow entrance of the storage room. Through the stinging mist that the smoke had brought into her eyes, she could see the cleanness and the power. Well, now, she told herself, all my life I have never seen a Goth, and here is a Goth, now I have seen a Goth. . . .

For an instant, the courage of her total defeat deserted her. Like a starving child, a rejected mistress, an abandoned prostitute, she got to her knees at last and made a begging gesture with her right hand. But that, too, was useless—she saw as much in the fingers that gripped the dagger and in the blue and pitiless eyes.

Some guttural, barbaric utterance broke the silence between them. What had he said, she wondered. Looter? Whore? Slave? It made no difference. She was, as she had always been, nothing—a being who crept on the margins of the lives that other men lived. The blade was at her neck, and the blood, unbelievably her own, was pouring over her dalmatica, and she scarcely knew the pain as she gave herself up to the dark.

Chapter 45

INTO THAT darkness which was the only congenial element to him now—his eyes were sore, even the shafts of brightness that slanted down from the high windows were painful to him, and he suffered acutely on those more and more widely spaced occasions when he was summoned into the upper world—into that darkness came rumors and signs. In some vast bog watered by the many mouths of the northern river the armies of the Empire had contended with the hosts of the forest. All of them, it was said, had fallen, including him whom they called Beast and Anti-Christ, the just old man with the hard, uncompromising dream and the leathery hands and the decent fringe of iron-grey hair. All had gone down in the black morass, yes, and the son of the Beast also, whose letter, dropped from his leather belt—a haunt of lice and a gall to his dry and filthy flesh—had been trampled like everything else, like the rags on which the elder Moyses had died, like any petal or napkin or scrap of papyrus that might once have fallen from *her* fingers, into the brown and indistinguishable dirt of the unswept floor, into that accumulated filth which had become for him a visible form of the uselessness of life and the sordidness of death.

Cities had been put to the torch by the avenging conquerors—Marcianopolis, Adrianopolis, Serdica—burnt offerings, the Confessors said, consumed on the altar for the remission of sin. In Gaul, in Abrittus, in Philippopolis one commander after another had set the rayed crown on his head and taken the purple onto his shoulders; but these were phantoms, transitory, powerless to cleanse the charged air. The summer nights were still foetid, even here under the earth, with brooding eventualities; the summer nights reverberated with thunder which became in his sleep the clash of armies or the roar of the mountains of Africa falling into the sea.

They gave him no news in the upper chambers. It seemed to him sometimes that all news was there for the asking, but he could not bring himself to ask, not of the Urban Prefect, not of Valerian, not of the harried tribune who was there so often these days in his superiors' place. But by hints, by nods, by narrowings of the eyes and pursings of the lips, they gave him to understand what he had long known all too well: that his hours were running fast and thin. So many changes, so many complexities, so many possibilities, they said. How could he know, in times like these, that his friends would not be removed from their influential places? Tomorrow, day after tomorrow, some day next week, his case might be laid before somebody who would prefer to see him gone. While matters remained fluid, while judgment was still in the hands of those who wished him well, why couldn't he do what Zeno or Seneca or Epictetus would have done in his place? A word, only a word, only a few grains of incense . . . Let him know that they had his case at heart, let him send for any one of them any hour of the day or night. . . .

He did not listen, he only looked about him; and one afternoon he saw, through the pinkish blur that was always now between him and any image that he set his eyes upon, some change in the dirty niche in the wall. The official bust of his uncle Decius was no longer there against the fly-specked plaster; a wreath of mourning was crammed into the space where it had stood—laurel intertwined with sprigs of yew. Dead then, gone then, he thought; but he had known it for weeks; and, if he wept, he could not be certain that he was weeping, since his burning eyes were forever delivering themselves of tears. He asked no questions, he merely did what he could to shorten the remainder of the interview; and, once he had seated himself again on the three-legged stool under the beehive arch, he felt no surge of cleansing grief, but fell into stunned contemplation of the trampled filth that he had been staring at all these weeks.

That afternoon he made himself gracious to nobody; he turned his back on the lot of them and pressed his knees and his forehead against the beehive arch and managed to shut out everything except one shrill tenor voice that kept repeating—above the arguments over the date of the Feast of the Resurrection, above complaints against the elder Cornelius and vilification of the lapsed—"When shall I be delivered from the body of this death?" He could no longer bring himself to exchange with them the usual formulae of courtesy and consideration. Sorrow for his dead—even such muted sorrow as his dulled mind could entertain—drove him back to the truth; and the truth was that he loathed their bodies and the filth of their bodies, he despised their minds and the pettiness of their minds, he was appalled at their souls and the awful drabness of their souls.

He might have sat there for hours if an old woman whose garrulousness he could not bear had not tip-toed up behind him and laid an offensively familiar hand on his shoulder and told him with affected enthusiasm that he had a visitor from the upper world. Ummidius Pessinus? Charis? His mother? He wanted none of them, he rejected them all. But the form that was standing in the light of the open door at the other end of the common room—a lean form, swathed in white and given a kind of blurred nimbus by his watery eyes—was the form of the painter Antisthenes. And, try as he would, he could not go to him with a lifted head: he walked through the little groups of the Confessors, seeing nobody, addressing nobody, fixing his eyes on his own fettered and filth-encrusted feet. For he sees my dirt and my sores and my rags, he told himself, and he finds me here—he, the defender of reason—among ignorant eaters of the Body and the Blood, among fools who die like flies because there was One in Gallilee who thought He was the Son of God. . . .

Yet once the two of them stood face to face in the light at the entrance to the prison, it was impossible to stare any longer at the earth; he could not take the clean and supple hand without lifting his eyes. And, once he had looked, he could not look away: what he saw bore such small likeness to what was lodged in his remembrance—the painter Antisthenes had changed as much as he. The wise and narrow face had taken on an air of utter remoteness. The brow, immobile and unwrinkled, looked like the forehead of the dead; the eyes, lightless and grave, gazed directly upon him and yet did not seem to see him; and the mouth above the brown and silky beard was awesomely quiet, devoid as it was of its disparaging smile. What has come over him? he asked himself in wonder. And suddenly he remembered how Charis had said that the little dancer Memphius had been murdered in a tavern by a jealous charioteer. Since the Feast of the Saturnalia this one also, he thought, relinquishing the strangely unresponsive hand, has stood at a raw trench in some garden and turned away again, knowing that only a ghost of himself will henceforth walk the earth, that his living heart was buried in that grave. . . .

"I was very sorry to hear about Memphius," he said, aware and ashamed of the insufficiency. "Charis told me."

"Yes. She and Berosus were kind enough to look after the burial. I have no country place, you know, and Berosus gave him a grave and a little chapel behind his villa in Tibur."

The voice, too, had undergone a disquieting transformation. The sentences issued whole and slow from the scarcely moving lips, each one shaped and considered before it was given utterance. If his thoughts were drawn to that grave at all, they hung above it untroubled; and how was it possible for a living being to be delivered of all of that so soon—the violence, the pitiful image of the corpse stamped like the imprint of a seal upon the brain, the sordidness, the jealousy, the stunned realization of the totality of the loss? "I saw him at Charis's house before I went into hiding—it must have been not long before he died," he said, trying to look directly into the solemn and unseeing eyes.

But the visitor made it plain that he wanted neither condolences nor any direct and revealing look. He had folded his arms across his breast, and now it was he that was staring at his own feet. "I came to you with a purpose," he said in the same controlled and deliberate voice. "But concerning that purpose I cannot speak until all other matters are put aside and I am given the ear of your spirit, the unfaltering attention of your heart. I know—I would not have ventured to come here if I did not know—that the months you have spent in this darkness and isolation have done much to detach you from the concerns and confusions of the world. But I know also that the ties which bind the spirit to mortal things are very strong: if the spirit had not loved the world with a passionate and overpowering love, it would never have descended out of the purity of non-existence to clasp and be compounded with the world. Because of this, before I came to you, I took myself away from the only occupation which draws and holds me now; I came from the holy house of meditation which contains my only joy, my only peace, and went about again from place to place, to find the answers to such questions as may still distract and torment the material portion of your soul. I inquired at the house of the Herennii, and learned there that the Senate had restored to your mother, at the request of one Ummidius Pessinus, a certain almond grove and villa that had belonged to her in Sicily. She can stay there unmolested for the rest of her days, left in peace—whatever peace such a soul as hers is able to find. Your sister, it seems, will remain in the Temple at Epidaurus, and will not or can not return to the world. Concerning Charis, I know no more than she told you when she came to you here: she went to the north, and nothing has been heard of her since. But of your uncle and your cousin Herennius I can tell you known facts that should do much to loose your spirit. It is definitely established now that both of them fell in a battle on some northern plain close to a city called Abrittus. They have been declared indubitably dead by the Senate and have been deified in consideration of their virtuous lives and their heroic deaths. How it is and will be with the Empire you may judge for yourself. Trebonianus Gallus is Emperor now, and even if you could have felt any allegiance to him, knowing him as you did, that possibility has been forever wiped out—it is said of him that he betrayed the Decii for the purple and the rayed crown."

So she has gone to Sicily, he thought, without a visit, without a letter, without so much as a spoken message sent by way of a slave . . . And they have been deified, with chanting and incense, and cast in silver as though they had never raised turnips and hay in Pannonia; they have been given a place in the Forum among the ancient heroes and the gods . . . So the rotten little traitor is Lord of the World these days, and that is what they meant in the office upstairs when they told me I had better make haste before my case was brought before my enemies . . . But these were fleeting considerations; none of them held him, absorbed as he was by the enigmatic bearing of his changed and solemn visitor.

"Believe me, Favorinus, these things that I tell you are only a little more than nothing. Those beings whom we love in this world are shadows cast by shadows, twice removed from reality, twice removed from the One and the All. We know them because they are all that is perceptible to the corruption of our senses, because in our blindness we cannot see the soul which casts the shadow of the flesh, or endure the inexpressible and unseeable radiance which shines behind the soul."

The One? The All? Shadows of shadows, twice removed? The terms were unfamiliar and puzzling, but it was so long since he had been concerned with matters of philosophy that he did not trouble to ask for definitions; he merely stared at the austere white robe and wondered what doctrine it signified.

"Yet it was very kind of you to go to so much trouble for me," he said without conviction, since he knew in his heart that there had been more real human affection in the old bitterness, the old barbed and sardonic wit, than in this detached and deliberate consideration. "It was very kind of you, and I am glad you have found some way to be at peace."

A group of the children were coming through the open door behind his visitor, and he waited to reply until his sentences could fall complete and weighty into comparative silence. It was a sacred day, and the prisoners were to partake of the Eucharist. The round arms of the girls were indented by the handles of the baskets of sanctified bread, and the clean, thin hands of the boys were grasping the cruets of blessed wine. Timotheus was in the front rank, but Prisca came in after the others, alone and still in disgrace, carrying nothing, and wearing, like a badge of her revolt, a sprig of apple-blossom in the hollow between her two full breasts. He was on the point of explaining the cruets and the baskets, but he saw that it was needless: the little procession had passed as bodiless as shadows cast by shadows before the eye of Antisthenes.

"Peace," he said when the noise had been carried away into the dank and dreary center of the room, "peace is not the proper word for what I have found in the house of the master. Peace—I tell you so because it is said of you in the world outside that you have had a loss as annihilating as mine—peace is a static thing, and does not have the power to draw the soul away from its obsession with the dead. What I call you to is not peace, but eternal seeking; not stillness, but an ever-quickening upward motion; not resignation, but a fervent yearning after the divine. Peace comes to few of us who are with the master. Even to the master himself it comes seldom and remains only for a little while, though that while seems to him to partake of eternity. But even to those of us who have not yet known the time of ecstasy when the spirit casts off all that is temporal and corporeal—yes, and its body, too, its envelope of flesh—even to those who wait for, rather than experience, the divine instant, the search itself is blessed: the slow relinquishing of shadows, the striving toward the inexpressible sweetness of union with the ultimate and unnamable One, of which nothing can be said but that It is, though Its existence is enough and more than enough."

"And who is he—your master?"

"Plotinus—a philosopher. His name is known only to a few. He grows in silence; he goes to no man; he knows that those whose thirst is strong enough will find the spring. If I said that he sent me to you, I would say too much. Few of his disciples would approach him for another man; his absorption in the One and the All is so intense that even the most advanced among us can scarcely find courage to ask his own questions or plead his own cause. But one morning three days ago I came upon him in his garden, eating honey from the honeycomb; and, seeing that he was already committed to a mortal occupation, I named you to him, and he did not withdraw, but listened as one might listen who has only half roused himself from some inner communion. I told him what strivings and seekings you had experienced, and I added as an afterthought that you have been here for many months, a solitary stranger among those who deceive themselves concerning the crucified Jew. Strangely, it was the afterthought that drew him most. He said, before he left me for the arbor where he contemplates, that much has already been accomplished in your case. You might rise—I repeat his words exactly, I have forgotten nothing that he has ever said in my presence—you might rise very quickly out of the first circle of mortality, seeing that so much has been stripped from your spirit: the ties of your birth and the ties of your worldly business and the ties of your fleshly love."

He did not answer. He stared at the cluttered floor and saw an image of the master, his eyes more remote than the eyes of his disciple, seeing all and seeing nothing, gazing directly through the sons and daughters of men who love their shadowy loves and die their shadowy deaths on an immaterial and transitory world. He saw the fixed white face, dazzled with the effulgence of the One and the All. He heard the dispassionate voice quietly renouncing all who are fools enough to demand anything more of It than that It should be. He saw the poised hand raised in blessing but swift to withdraw, swift to renounce the corruption of human touch. . . .

And then, so clearly, so wholly that for an instant he could have sworn that the grave had no power to imprison or consume, he saw what he had told himself in his bitterness he would never see again—a breathing image of the lost beloved. He saw the wide-set eyes as he had seen them on that night in the little vestibule when they had brooded dark and compassionate over his awakening; he saw the corners of the lips indented by the wise

557

and innocent smile. Oh, you were mortal, mortal, he thought and transitory. Your way was never to renounce the human, but to move always closer to the throbbing core of our mortality. In these shadows, among these fleeting presences, you sought and found and loved whatever was divine. The divine was made flesh to you, and the flesh was made divine, and it was with you as the elder Moyses said it was before he departed from us: dying in love, you died in grace, you died in all that we can know of God. . . .

Far away, less real than the voice of the beloved, less actual even than the voices of the Confessors quarreling over the arrangement of the bread and wine on the Eucharist table, far away and entirely self-possessed, the voice of the painter Antisthenes—who had suffered much and found his blessedness in secession from humanity—was expounding the doctrine of the master who went to no man but waited for the thirsty to seek out the spring. Was summoning the spirit of Favorinus Herennius to rise out of sordidness and confusion, to free itself by the purely ceremonial burning of a little incense, to come to that high and holy house which stood above the ruins of a dying world. Was saying that this spirit might hope in a matter of a few short years to rise triumphant through the second and third circles and spring in its pure form toward its one true intention: utter forgetfulness of its mortality and complete commingling with the One and the All. . . .

"But what about all these?" he said, breaking violently in upon the harmony of the discourse, taking the disciple of Plotinus by the arm and gesturing at the convocation of shadows gathered around the table, toward the core of the filth and the dark. "What good is there in all that for any of these down here?"

"These?" For an instant the grave glance took them in, albeit from a distance—their sores, their dirt, their rags, their fettered feet, their faces grown stupid and resentful for want of the world and the sun. Then the eyelids came down and washed the eyes forever of that shameful vision, and made them pure again to stare at the white and bodiless radiance of the One. "Who knows?" said the painter Antisthenes, gazing at the filthy floor. "Even among these"—he lifted his head in their direction but did not give them his sight—"even among these there might be some rare spirit that could be saved."

"What do you mean by a rare spirit? How many rare spirits would you expect to find in a place like this?"

"If there were one or two, it would be a great wonder. One in ten thousand —so the master has told us repeatedly, lest we grow too certain of the destiny of our own spirits—one in ten thousand will pass through the fervor of the search and issue into that ecstasy which is peace."

"One in ten thousand! But unfortunately there is something in me that would never rest, that would devour itself day and night in paltry mortal concern over the other nine thousand nine hundred and ninety-nine. To

558

save one in ten thousand I would not violate at their altar any foolish loyalty I still may have to my dead!"

If it was possible for one already so remote to detach himself, the disciple of the master withdrew from the field of contention. "I cannot urge you further; I can only point out to you that to be obsessed with all of them is as ruinous to the purification of the spirit as to be obsessed with one of them," he said. "I will come to you again, if the master finds in his wisdom that it would be well for me to come. Nor is there any real reason for haste. Even if the Emperor Gallus should drive your spirit out of the mortal flesh that holds it now, it would find another earthly dwelling place, it would move always to a higher and purer house until such times as, needing no mortal habitation, it went to the One. All is well in eternity. Farewell."

He was gone now, and it was good to walk back toward the usual and the bearable—the wretches who were not pursuing the pure intention of their souls through the second and third circles, but were all too preoccupied with the material aspects of the Eucharist: the unfolding of the soiled napkins, the orderly arrangement of the chipped goblets, the building of a precarious pyramid out of little rucks of bread. The elder Cornelius was already with the flock, had probably passed the two of them while they stood near the threshold talking of the master and the All and the One and the stripping of the spirit. He had taken his place at the head of the table, and was mixing, in a duly sanctified silver bowl which he had brought along with him, the proper proportions of water and wine. The Confessors were taking their seats on the benches, and the children—all except Prisca, who had retired into a corner to stuff her bit of apple-blossom out of sight—were forming a clean and orderly circle, a kind of screen between those who sat at the board and the raw darkness of the dripping walls. "Are we all assembled then, lambs of the flock?" said the elder Cornelius. And perhaps because he was sorry for them—they had been rejected by the one who had been found worthy among ten thousand, they had been consigned to the lowest circle in their confusion and their ignorance—he could not turn his back on their pitiful feast, he had to stop as he had stopped in better days to watch them partake of the Body and the Blood.

One rare spirit in ten thousand worthy of regeneration, and the rest forgotten? She—the breathing presence who had risen from the grave to protest all rejection—would not have it so. Who, for her, had not been a rare spirit? The self-seeking lover, the ungiving husband, the children of the Lord as they come to be when they had lived too long in darkness— quarrelsome and trivial and ailing in their flesh and in their spirits—she had seen the holy and invisible essence that shone at the core of all of these and had come forward to embrace it, unguarded and liberal and joyous, with her own soul's intention shining through her flesh, her voice, her eyes. For nothing mortal, stripped of its outward trappings, was unseemly to her; nothing human was beyond the pale of her love.

And these, he thought, looking at them over the bony shoulder of Timotheus the dyer's son, seeing their faces in the light of the lamp, hearing their hushed breathing rise and fall in the moment of meditation before the breaking of the bread—what are they, if the eye pierces the outward envelope and sees the stripped spirit? What are the pure and ultimate intentions of their souls? If I were not mortal and bounded in time, if I could look back at them from the vantage point of a hundred years, what could I see of them, what could I know of them save that they were Confessors of the Name? When the world has died and been born again, no man will remember—as no man should remember—their pettiness, their vanities, their bickerings, their obscure hungers and insufficiencies. All that will be said of them—and all that should be said of them—is that they offered up their lives for what was, according to their lights, a high purpose. And their purpose, viewed from eternity where all is well, was the same purpose for which she lived and died: to bring love, divine and mortal, into a meaningless and suffering world.

"The Lord be with you," said the voice of the elder Cornelius. But it was weary, it was despondent. It told all too plainly how the sole shepherd left with the starved and harried flock believed no longer that he could save the sheep or that the sheep could save themselves. It was if he had said to them: You are beyond salvation, unless the Son of Man, who suffers everything and pities everything, comes down to you in this ultimate hour from His Cross. . . .

"And with your spirit." The response of the faithful was listless. Most of them had breathed it out on a sigh.

"Lift up your hearts!"

"We have them up unto the Lord."

And the uninitiate, who stood outside the circle, stared at the darkening doorway where the Guardsman had stationed himself for the night, and was grieved that they should have said it without conviction in the presence of the servant of the Beast. Oh, God, he thought, she should not have gone forth with the first of them. She should have been held for the final going-forth, she should be here with them now. She was the leaven that gave savor to the loaf, she was the burning wick that lighted all the dullness of the wax. And it was I, it was I who robbed them in this hour of her voice—that voice so weary with loving and giving that, to the elder Moyses, it was no longer human, but was a cry of liberation thrown back by a naked spirit already on its way to heaven. . . .

"We thank Thee, God, through Thy beloved Servant Jesus Christ, whom in these Last Times Thou hast sent us as Saviour and Redeemer and Messenger of Thy council, the Spirit who comes from Thee. . . ."

In these Last Times . . . The dyer's son Timotheus, startled by the sudden sharp intake of breath behind him, turned his small, kind eyes, but only for an instant, upon the face of the uninitiate who stood behind him, and then looked back, flushing a little, at the hopeless visage of the elder Cornelius, bent over the bowl and the plate and veiled on either side by the brown, incongruous fall of his Olympian curls. In these Last Times . . . Those words had fallen like drops of healing balm upon his heart that evening in the little vestibule when the air had been delectable with the smells of wine and fish and bread; and it had strengthened and sustained him then to know that not he alone, but thousands of the children of the Lord also, had taken the bitter knowledge of finality unto themselves, had seen the crack in the orb of the world and watched the settling in of the dark. And it is come, it is upon us even now, he told himself; and this also was a kind of peace: to rest in acceptance of universal disintegration, to know, and know in common with thousands of the children of men, that this was the end of it, this was the last. All that was dear to me, he thought— and took hard consolation from it—all that I knew and loved is gone. If they were to come to me tomorrow and say to me, "The Emperor Gallus in his infinite mercy has told us to loose you and give you permission to go where you please"—where would I go, whom would I seek? There is no house in all the world where I would care to rest, no face in all the world that I would wish to see. I would stand aimless and lost, a stranger in the streets, with nothing to draw me anywhere, once I had visited her grave. . . .

"To fulfill Thy will and to prepare for Thee a holy people, He stretched forth His hands when He suffered. . . ."

A holy people . . . a people delivered from the obsessions of the dying. And one generation at least must pass before the contagion of death is taken away—so she had said in the villa in the Campagna, gathering up her little heap of paraphernalia: her book, her stole, her crumpled handkerchief, her keys. Her lambs, her novices, stitching behind the grey curtain on a great white length of linen—shroud for a perishing world or swaddling clothes for one as yet unborn?—they did not know, they were too young to know; they laughed, and the divided curtain yielded up the sound of their chatter and the gleam of the sunlight on their new-washed hair . . . One lamb, one lamb of their flock was given also into my keeping, was consigned to me on the evening of eternal leavetaking by the veined and mortal hands of the beloved. "Promise me, my cousin, swear to me that if you should remain longer than I in this world, you will do whatever you can to help the child." The daughter of a holy people, nurtured in the faith to build the New Jerusalem over the crumbling ruin . . . And there she sits, an exile barely tolerated at the table of the Lord, and one glance from me is enough to make the fever of her sickness glow in her face. I have touched her with my contagion, my corruption is upon her. So long as I live, she is committed to decay, she is in bondage to death. . . .

"And when He had delivered Himself up to a voluntary passion, to loose death and to break asunder the bands of the devil, and to trample hell and to enlighten the righteous and to manifest the resurrection. . . ."

He knew perfectly well that these words had nothing whatever to do with him. They concerned the death and the resurrection of one Jesus of Nazareth, who had taught in Syria and been crucified on a certain hill called Golgotha, whose all-pitying and never-resting Spirit, preserved in the memories of men, walked through the ruins of a passing world, summoning the dying and the as yet unborn to a fellowship of decency and love. And yet one phrase after another came like the answers to the alternate questions of his spent heart. A voluntary passion . . . Surely he could take upon himself a voluntary passion, surely he need not wait out the posthumous hours for death to come and find him here, surely all that remained for him was to lift up his head and go to be with her in death. And by so doing he might loose death and break asunder the bands of the devil, might deliver one daughter of a holy people from the ties of his corruption, might free her spirit for the building of the New Jerusalem by day and the one chaste cup by night . . . It might even fall to him to enlighten the righteous, he thought, smiling a little, to do one small thing before he died to add to the power of the world that was to come. For these are the righteous, he told himself, these wretches whose souls' intention is the one hope of the sons and daughters of men. Lift up their hearts in the hour of their desolation, think how it would be with their hearts if the one pagan who has dwelt with them here in the darkness should confess the Name and thereby manifest the resurrection. *Her* resurrection, he thought, weeping and hiding his face from the kind and questioning eyes of the elder Cornelius. For to say now, "I also, insofar as my blindness would permit it, have seen something of the light that streams down from the Cross," would be to manifest *her* resurrection, to make plain that she has come to me, a breathing presence, out of the shut darkness of her grave.

"He took a loaf, gave thanks, and spake: 'Take, eat, this is My body, given for you.' Likewise also the cup, and said, 'This is My blood, poured out for you. So often as you drink this cup, you commemorate Me. . . .'"

It was the moment for going. The elder Cornelius had lifted the silver bowl, and all the faded, disconsolate eyes were fixed upon it. No one would turn, no one would see.

"Remembering therefore His death and resurrection, we offer to Thee the loaf and the cup, and give thanks to Thee that Thou hast counted us worthy. . . ."

He had learned to walk warily in his chains, to make very little noise, and not one of the faithful was aware that he had crossed the common room and was standing near the Guardsman at the door.

"And we beseech Thee that Thou send down Thy Holy Spirit upon this offering of the church. Unite it and grant to all the saints who partake of it their fulfillment with holy Spirit, to the strengthening of faith in truth, that we may praise Thee and glorify Thee through Thy Servant Jesus Christ. . . ."

It seemed a strange thing to be doing, but the Guardsman showed no surprise. He had apparently been informed that the patrician prisoner might come to him with just such a request, and he leaned forward attentively, courteously, so that there was no need for that prisoner to raise his voice against the weary "Now and forever, Amen."

"I should like to see whoever is in charge in the Urban Prefect's office."

"Yes, your Illustriousness. At this hour it is usually the Censor Valerian," the Guardsman said, and bowed, and was gone.

And before the cup, passing from lip to lip, had made the rounds of the Lord's table, before the last emaciated hand had received its rusk of sanctified bread, the monumental shape of the Dean of the Senate had appeared in the dark, not to be disregarded, since it was preceeded by a torchbearer and followed by two centurions, the one holding a granite bust of the Emperor Trebonianus Gallus in a nest of laurel on a silver tray, the other carrying a metal pan alive with fire. "Nobody will ever know," said Valerian in a sententious and resonant voice, "how fortunate it was that you made up your mind to ask for us tonight. Tomorrow morning the Urban Prefect is to send a list of every prisoner under his supervision to the camp of the Emperor at Abrittus—"

"Before you send it, you must change the accusation that is set down against me," he said, raising his voice, because it was his purpose also to enlighten the righteous, and they had turned to hear and see.

"I know. We have the bust. We have the fire and the incense—"

"Take them away," he said. "Their presence here is a desecration, they have no place among us. It was not because I wished to sacrifice that I asked you to come, it was because I wished to be reckoned along with these, my sisters and brothers. I have heard their teachings and seen their spirits. Henceforth count me no different from the others; like them, I confess the Name."

Chapter 46

THE ELDER Cornelius—he was soon to be the Bishop Cornelius, unanimously named by all the members of the Church of Rome in its first open assembly since the beginning of the Decian persecution—the elder Cornelius was, of course, among those who had gone to the hill outside the City to witness the crimson confession of Favorinus Herennius. He had been impelled to watch the beheading of the young patrician both as the one remaining shepherd of the flock and for certain personal reasons. With the blessed Paulina and the deacon Probus he had maintained a long if not too intimate friendship, and with the young man, bound to these two by some obscure bond that was better left unexamined, he had felt a certain sympathy as strong as it was difficult to define. Besides, during his many visits to the Confessors in the Urban Prefect's prison, he had often been drawn to stare at the enigmatic and touching presence: he had taken a fancy to the emaciated person, the traces of high breeding that still remained in the gestures and the tone of the voice, the brooding eyes, the never-answered question in the marred and bearded face. Yes, after his fashion the elder Cornelius had been fond of the Confessor Favorinus Herennius. And, simply because the young man's claims to the honors of martyrdom were irregular and equivocal —he had rejected baptism and had said that he did not consider himself in the proper frame of mind to receive the Eucharist—it had seemed all the more necessary for an unquestionable authority to be on the scene, to see that the last acts of this strange Confessor should be recorded with weight and dignity, and that the body should be borne back to the City and washed and strewn with spices and buried in an appropriate place—in the garden where his cousin Paulina slept, there was yet room for one more grave.

For the Church of Christ in Rome had reason, as the elder Cornelius knew, to feel considerable gratefulness to this anomalous martyr. Because of him, the last of the Confessors had manifested, before the end of the persecution, some of the selflessness and ardor that their predecessors had given to the first high days: from the moment he had concluded their disconsolate Eucharist with his confession of the Name, many of them had been borne up on the wings of ecstasy and all of them had experienced at least the beneficent effects of mortal affection and close human fellowship. And, since those who languished in the prison for the Name's sake were the heart of the congregation, every member thereof had felt the new pulse, the new stirring. Not since the first going forth to the beasts had there been such sweetness in communion, so many visions, so complete a certainty in the love of Christ the Lord. Also, because of him, the thorny problem of the lapsed had been dealt with at last. Miraculously, in a matter of moments, it had become the will of the Confessors that the lapsed should be forgiven. Nothing more had been needed than that which he had said: "Grant to the gardener Sylvanus, in consideration of my confession, forgiveness and the right to return to the breaking of the bread. I ask it in part because he was my slave, and in part because the blessed Paulina charged me with the care of his child." Moved by that, shamed by that—for if the unbaptized could forgive, how could it be otherwise with the children of a merciful Lord?—they had labored over a petition more lengthy and eloquent than any of the others, a petition so persuasive to the entire congregation that even the elder Novatian dared not oppose it.

In fact, on the long, slow walk back to the City with the corpse and the linen napkins sanctified by immersion in the freely-given blood, it seemed to the elder Cornelius—who was not given to facile acceptance of heavenly intervention—that something beyond chance, some stern and holy necessity conceived in heaven had moved the subtle and uncompromising Stoic to bring his death upon himself. That he had brought it upon himself, the elder Cornelius had no reason to doubt: patrician friends of his had pointed out that so tawdry a Lord of the World as the former Governor of Moesia, with so tainted a record and such questionable claims to the purple, would scarcely have dared to order the execution of the nephew of a deified Emperor and the last survivor of an eminent senatorial family if he had not been provided with a solid charge to act upon. And if Favorinus Herennius had waited for the general release and lived out the rest of his life in philosophic retirement, the Church of Christ in Rome would never have known the blessed stirring, the quickening of the beat of its long-tried and much-wearied heart. . . .

The stretch of country that they crossed—he and the children and the two strong laborers who bore the covered bier—was rich with the prodigality of summer. It was early morning still, and the birds had not yet had their fill of singing. The air was sweet with the warm emanations of roses and pulsed with the music of the thrush. They walked without fear of interference, taking the open highway instead of the lanes and even breaking now and again into some sacred song appropriate in the presence of the dead; for, though the persecution was not yet officially over, it was known in every city of the Empire that the new Lord of the World was displeased only with such Christians as were troublesome on other accounts, that he had not made more than the most superficial gestures towards the gods on the occasion of his assumption of the purple, and that the Church of Christ might hope to rest secure in his indifference. And, perhaps because the Emperor of All the Romans could no longer be called the Anti-Christ, perhaps because the burden which they carried was not, in the strictest sense, the mortal remains of a member of their brotherhood, they permitted themselves a certain Roman laxity in regard to the body of Favorinus Herennius: on the spots of blood on the white linen sheet that had been laid over him, they had placed green willow wands and slips of alder and yew, though they had avoided anything quite so pagan as flowers.

The elder Cornelius led the procession. Behind him there was a kind of secondary leader, the novice Prisca, to whom her fellows had assigned the superior place as a matter of course. The dead man had been her master in the upper world; she had sat with him often beside the beehive arch in the Urban Prefect's prison, and her grief at the block on the green hill had been so violent that the elder Cornelius had asked himself whether it was as edifying as it was said to be to expose the young ones of the flock to the sight of even a holy death. But by this time a rapt quietness had settled down upon her. Whenever he glanced solicitously back at her over his shoulder, she lifted a wet face to him, and nodded to show him that he need not trouble himself about her, and tried to smile.

They had come a good way from the hill—they were, in fact, within sight of the City—thrust up like a foam of marble out of the greenness of the newly-flourishing earth—when she came up beside him and spoke. "My father in God," she said, with the diffidence that is good and seemly in a Christian maiden, "I wish to ask a question—"

"Yes, my daughter?"

"How long does it take to enter into heaven?"

"To enter into heaven? There is a difference of opinion concerning that. Some say until Doomsday, some say as long as it took for the Lord to issue from the tomb, and some say, since He has loosed the bonds of death, it happens, in the twinkling of an eye, so fast that the soul is there before the body knows the pain."

"And which do *you* believe, my father?"

Although he inclined toward the second, he told her in pity that he was by no means certain and that many of the most learned in matters of doctrine had offered excellent arguments in support of the last.

"Then," she said, keeping pace with him and staring down at the poppies and bluebells at her feet, "my vision may be true."

"Did you have a vision, my daughter?"

"Oh, yes, a most blessed and immediate vision, while they were taking him up and putting his head and his body on the bier and binding his head to his body with the linen band. I could not look at what they were doing with him, and I looked at the sky instead—"

Her voice had taken on the sweet, shrill note of the ecstasy, and others from the back of the procession came up to listen: a dyer's son named Timotheus, a plump little Briton slave named Lydia, several novices, several catechumens; even the two strong laborers, who bore the bier on which the body lay, bent forward from the shoulders, straining to hear.

"The clouds rolled back and the heavens were opened," she said. "And there in the midst of the sapphire and the gold was the great white throne of God. And all around the throne were little clouds, as light as feathers, and on two of these, apart and yet together, with a space of sky between them, were the blessed Paulina and the blessed Favorinus—he who in his rest is my brother in Jesus, but was in his life my dear and beautiful lord. And the Presence on the throne said, 'My son, what have you brought me?' But my master Favorinus had only a silver goblet, and I was afraid for him, for I asked myself: What would that Presence want with a silver goblet? But it was not an empty goblet, it was filled to overflowing, and my master Favorinus, whom I often saw weeping during his sojourn on this world, told the Lord of Heaven how he had filled it with his tears. And the Lord of Heaven leaned forward and smiled upon him who was once my master, and such sweetness, such radiance was in his smile that I was blind to heaven and earth, and did not see them bind his head to his body, or straighten out his hands, or cover his face. And, as my spirit came back into my body, I heard other voices, perhaps the voices of angels, whispering to one another that tears were enough. Are tears enough, my father in Jesus? What I saw in my ecstasy—was it a true vision, could this be so?"

And what could he say to her, the elder Cornelius, seeing that the Lamb of God Himself had said: "Blessed are they that mourn, for they shall be comforted?" "It would be hard for me to think," he said, "that a false vision could intrude itself into so holy a moment as that in which your master took leave of us. The seal of peace was on his face when they covered it with the linen. Be at peace, also, my daughter, in the certainty that he rests in God."

978   F.W.